Audrey Meeker

colors by **Sarah Davidson**

Feiwel & Friends
New York

THANK YOU TO MY PROFESSORS, FRIENDS, AND PARENTS,
FOR CHEERING ME ON THROUGHOUT THE PRODUCTION OF THIS BOOK.

THANK YOU TO SARAH, WHO WAS A WONDERFUL
COLLABORATOR AND AN EVEN BETTER FRIEND.

AND THANK YOU TO MIRANDA, FOR TAKING ME
SWING DANCING THAT VERY FIRST TIME.

A Feiwel & Friends Book
An imprint of Macmillan Publishing Group, LLC
120 Broadway, New York, NY 10271
mackids.com

Library of Congress Cataloging-in-Publication Data is available.

Our books may be purchased in bulk for promotional, educational,
or business use. Please contact your local bookseller or the Macmillan
Corporate and Premium Sales Department at (800) 221-7945 ext. 5442
or by email at MacmillanSpecialMarkets@macmillan.com.

First edition, 2024
Edited by Rachel Diebel
Cover and interior design by Steve Ponzo
Production editing by Avia Perez
Color by Sarah Davidson

Printed in China by RR Donnelley Asia Printing Solutions Ltd.,
Dongguan City, Guangdong Province

ISBN 978-1-250-86404-8 (paperback)
1 3 5 7 9 10 8 6 4 2

ISBN 978-1-250-86403-1 (hardcover)
1 3 5 7 9 10 8 6 4 2

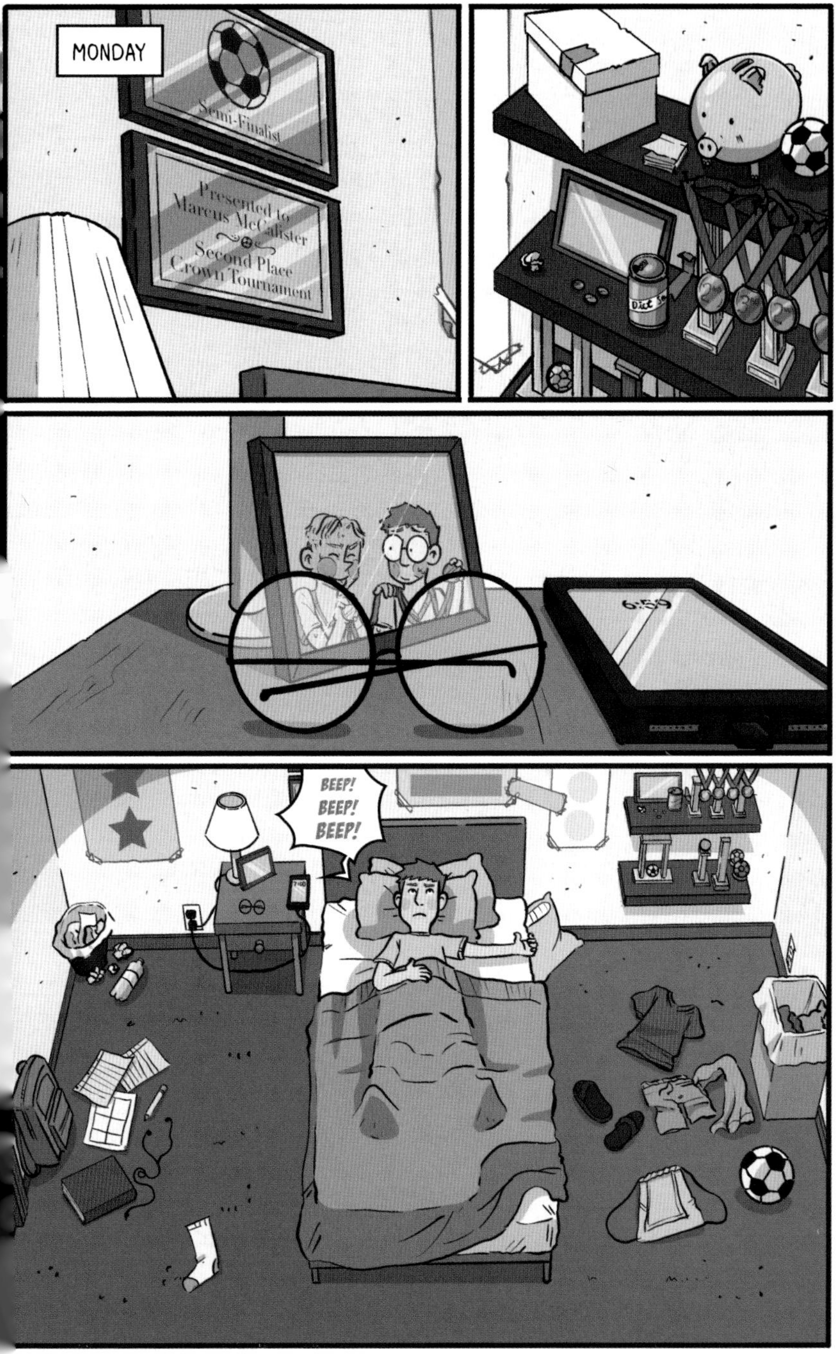
MONDAY
Semi-Finalist
Presented to
Marcus McCalister
Second Place
Crown Tournament
6:59
BEEP!
BEEP!
BEEP!

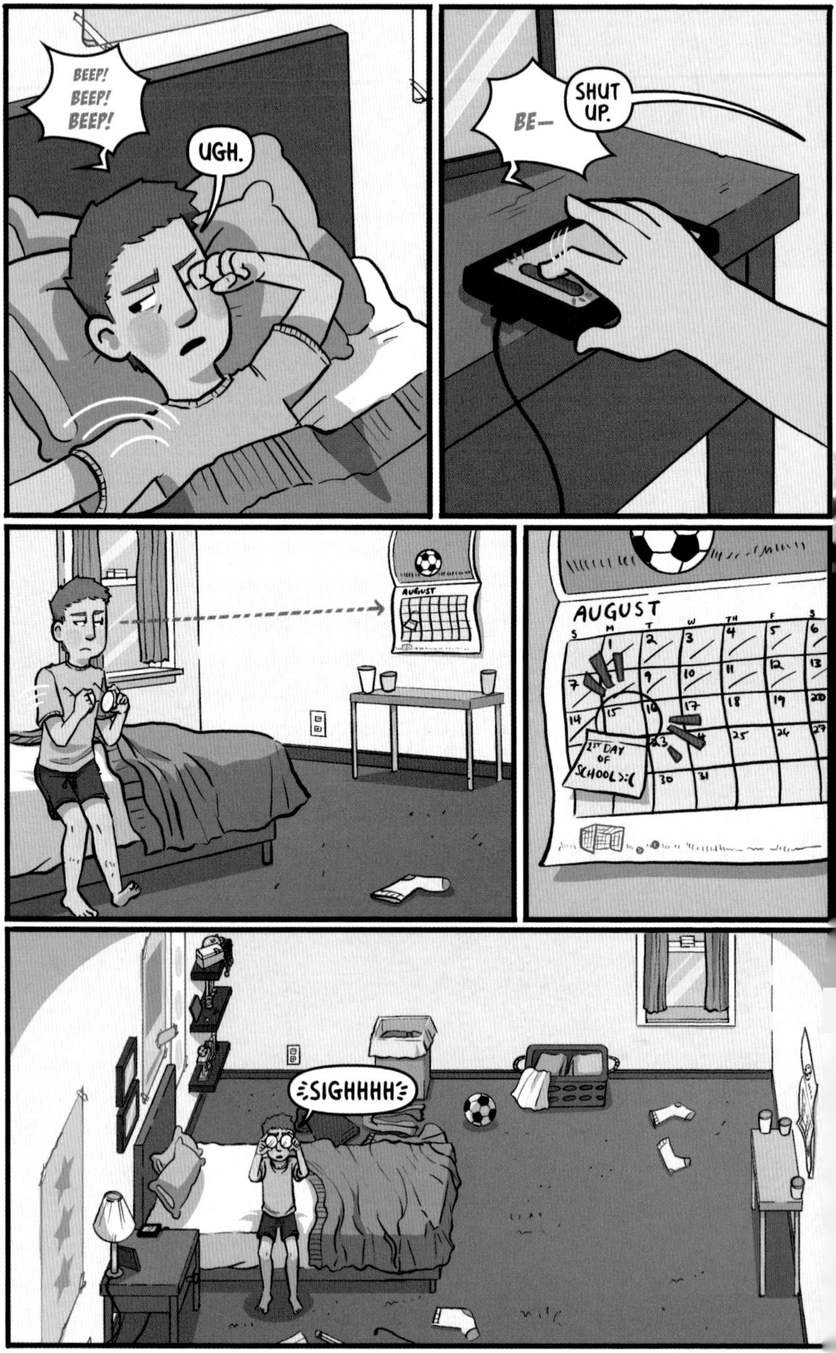
BEEP! BEEP! BEEP!
UGH.
BE—
SHUT UP.
AUGUST
1ST DAY OF SCHOOL >:(
SIGHHHH

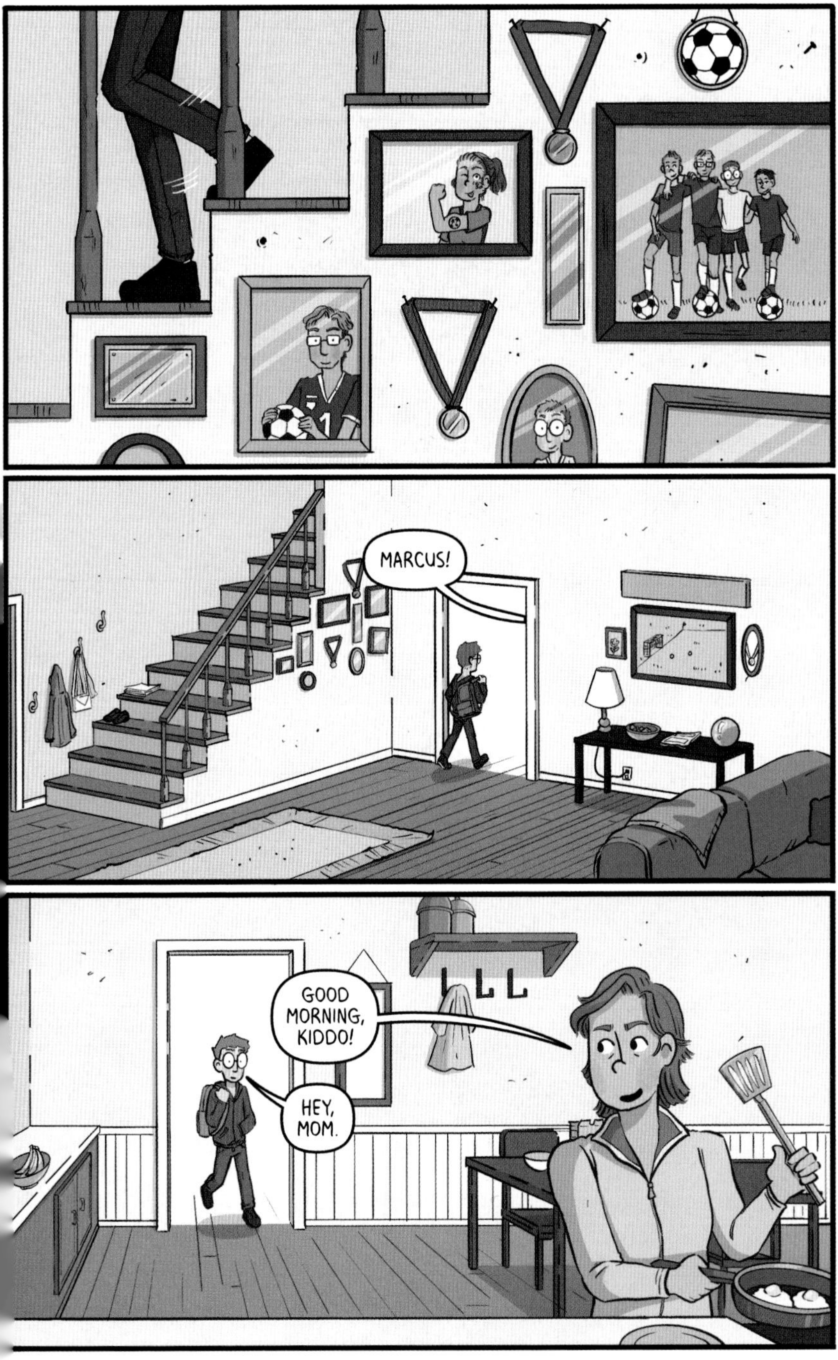
MARCUS!
GOOD MORNING, KIDDO!
HEY, MOM.

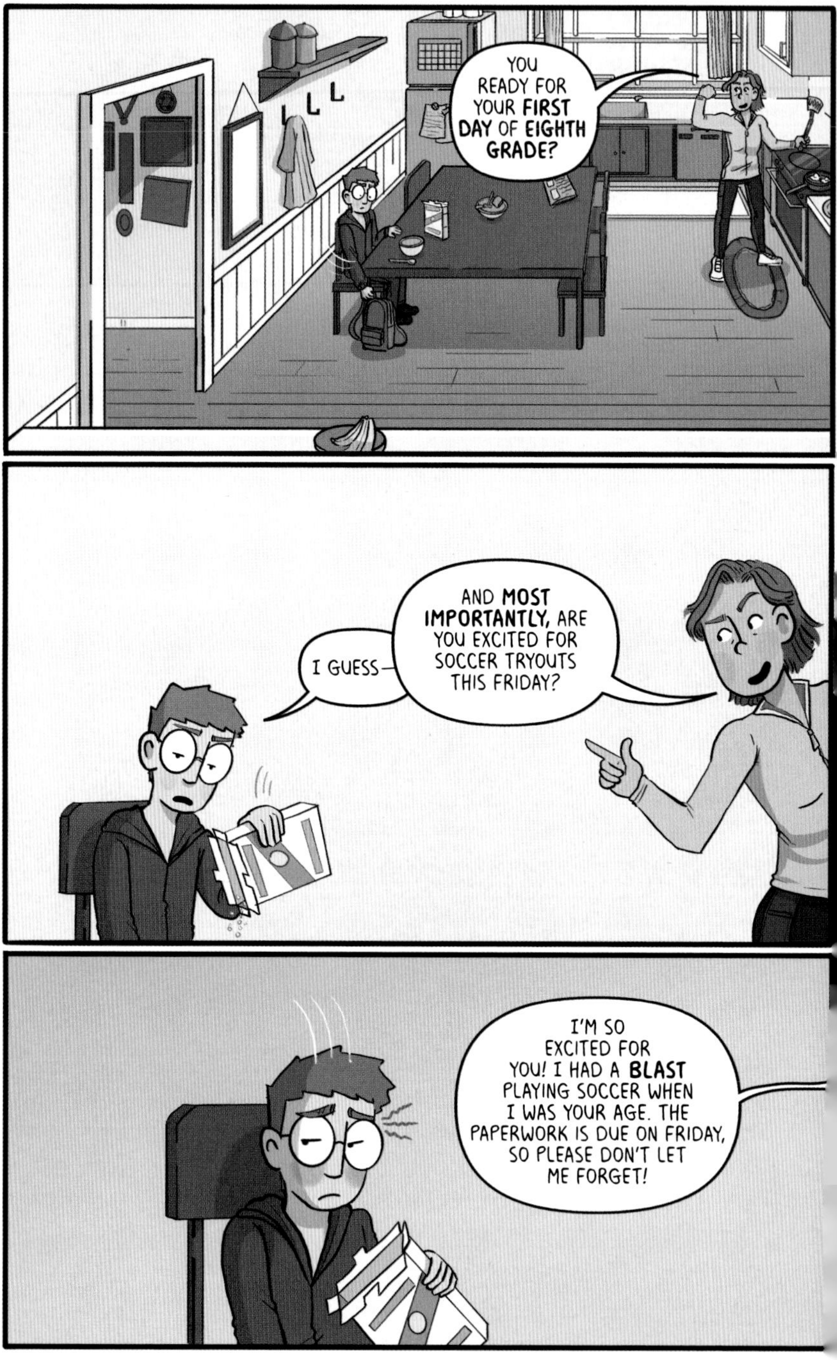

YOU READY FOR YOUR FIRST DAY OF EIGHTH GRADE?
AND MOST IMPORTANTLY, ARE YOU EXCITED FOR SOCCER TRYOUTS THIS FRIDAY?
I GUESS—
I'M SO EXCITED FOR YOU! I HAD A BLAST PLAYING SOCCER WHEN I WAS YOUR AGE. THE PAPERWORK IS DUE ON FRIDAY, SO PLEASE DON'T LET ME FORGET!

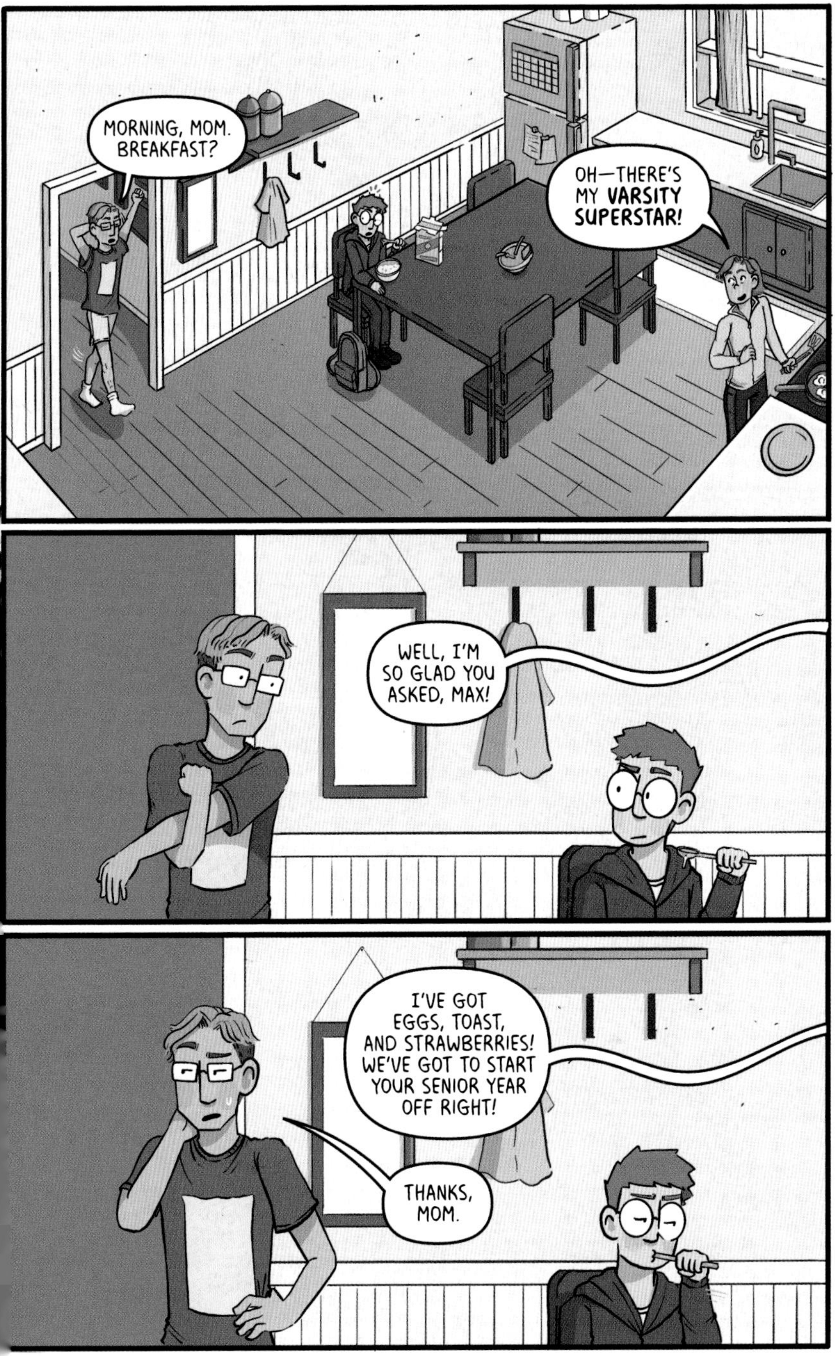
MORNING, MOM. BREAKFAST?
OH—THERE'S MY **VARSITY SUPERSTAR!**
WELL, I'M SO GLAD YOU ASKED, MAX!
I'VE GOT EGGS, TOAST, AND STRAWBERRIES! WE'VE GOT TO START YOUR SENIOR YEAR OFF RIGHT!
THANKS, MOM.

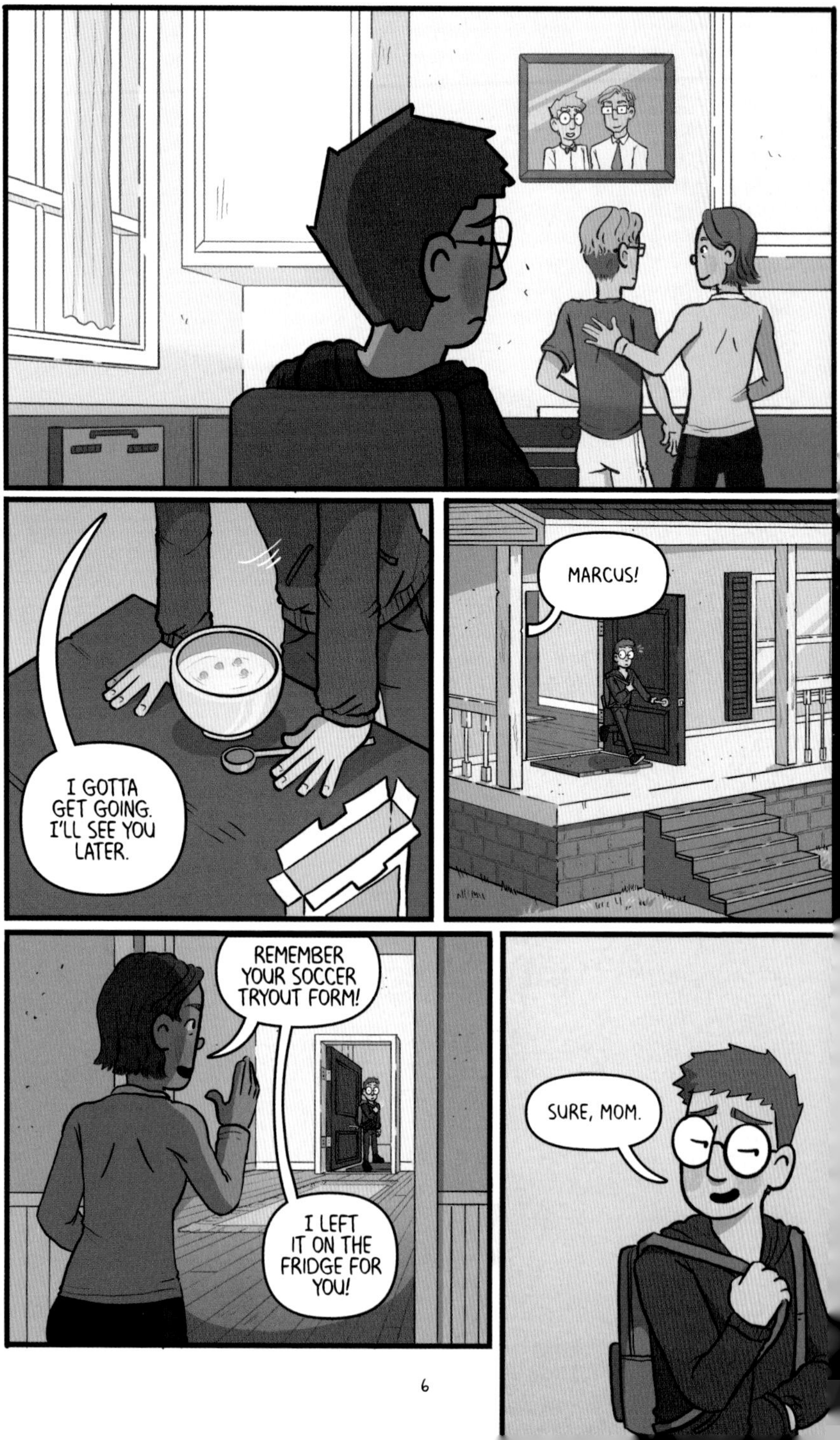
I GOTTA GET GOING. I'LL SEE YOU LATER.
MARCUS!
REMEMBER YOUR SOCCER TRYOUT FORM!
I LEFT IT ON THE FRIDGE FOR YOU!
SURE, MOM.

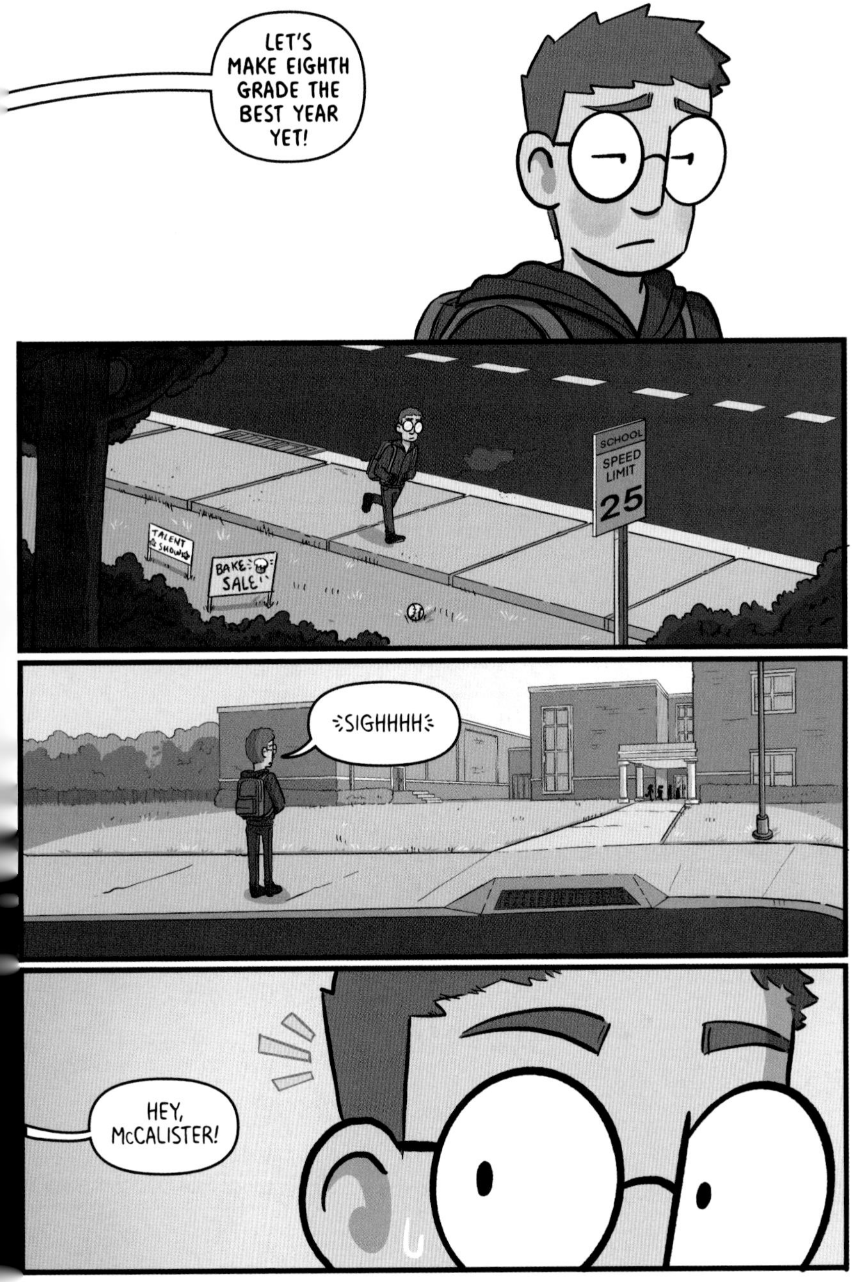
LET'S MAKE EIGHTH GRADE THE BEST YEAR YET!
TALENT SHOW
BAKE SALE
SCHOOL
SPEED LIMIT
25
SIGHHHH
HEY, McCALISTER!

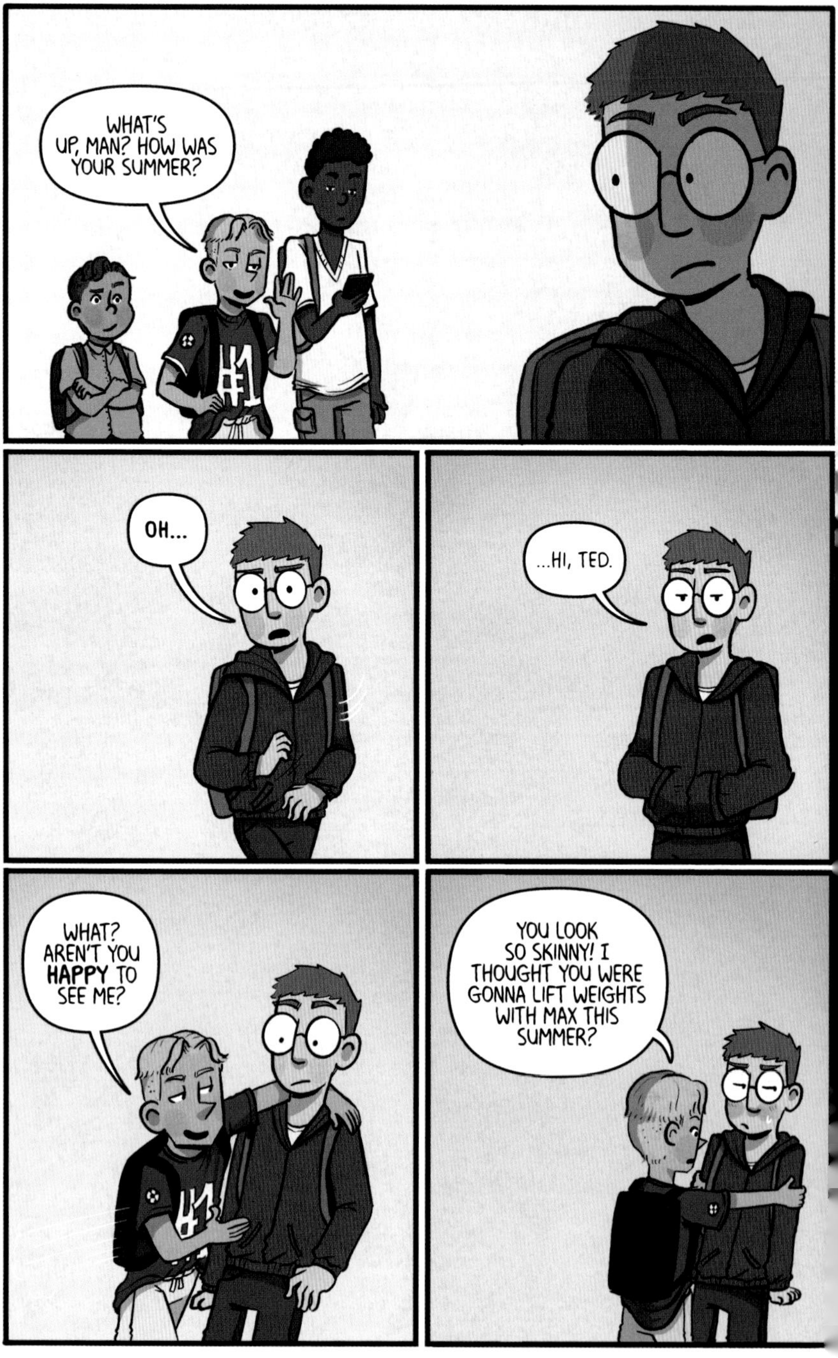
WHAT'S UP, MAN? HOW WAS YOUR SUMMER?
#1
OH...
...HI, TED.
WHAT? AREN'T YOU **HAPPY** TO SEE ME?
#1
YOU LOOK SO SKINNY! I THOUGHT YOU WERE GONNA LIFT WEIGHTS WITH MAX THIS SUMMER?

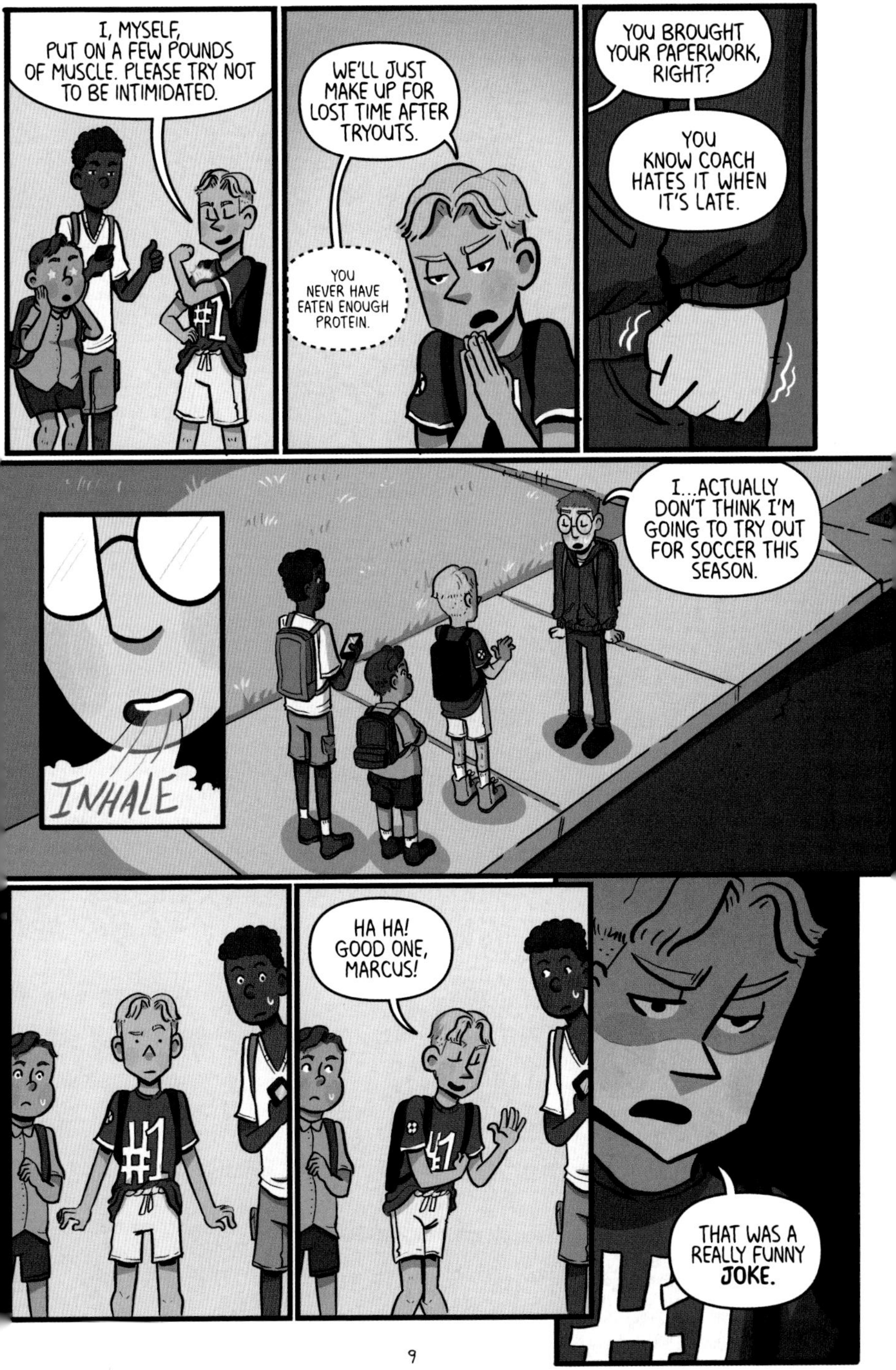
I, MYSELF, PUT ON A FEW POUNDS OF MUSCLE. PLEASE TRY NOT TO BE INTIMIDATED.
WE'LL JUST MAKE UP FOR LOST TIME AFTER TRYOUTS.
YOU NEVER HAVE EATEN ENOUGH PROTEIN.
YOU BROUGHT YOUR PAPERWORK, RIGHT?
YOU KNOW COACH HATES IT WHEN IT'S LATE.
INHALE
I...ACTUALLY DON'T THINK I'M GOING TO TRY OUT FOR SOCCER THIS SEASON.
HA HA! GOOD ONE, MARCUS!
THAT WAS A REALLY FUNNY **JOKE.**

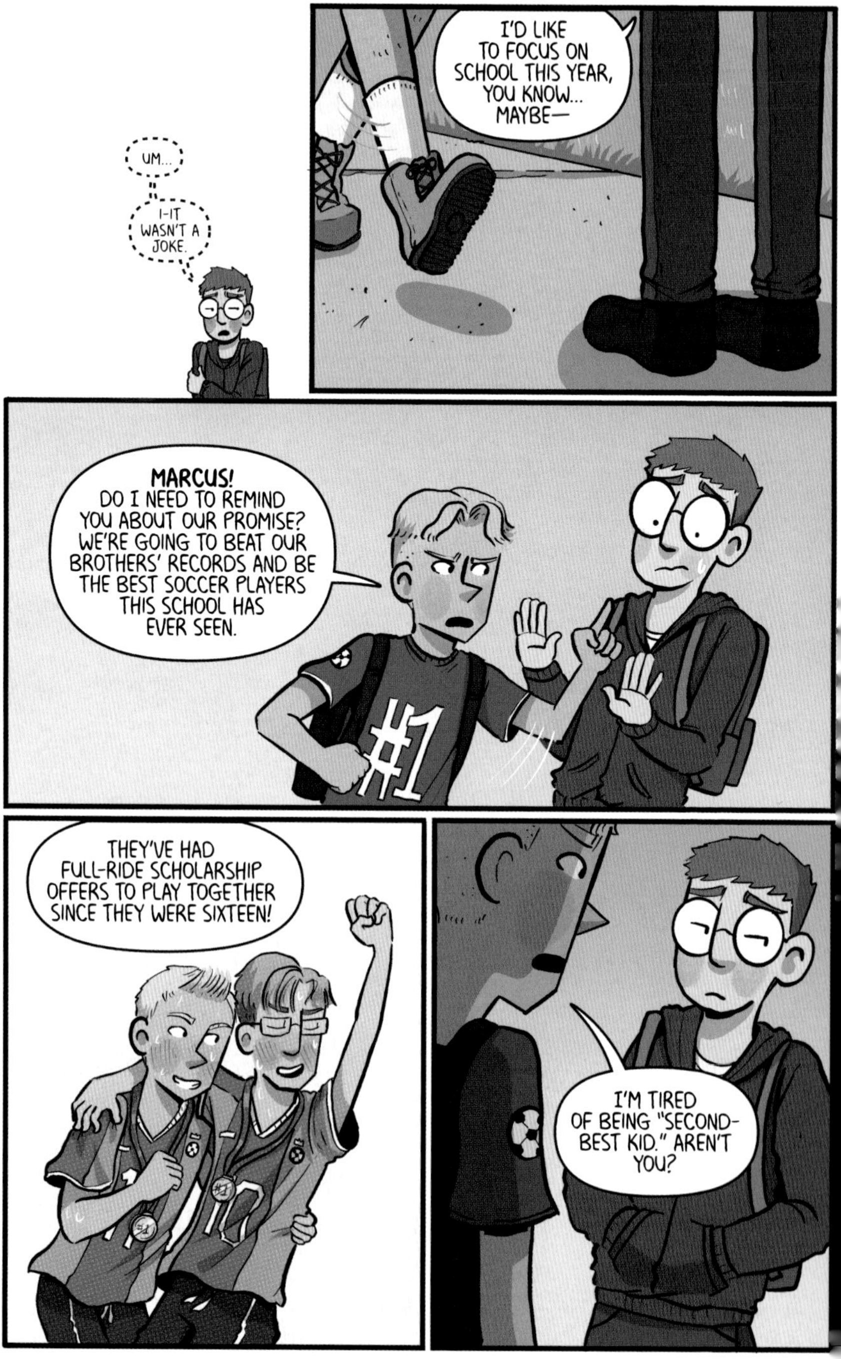
UM...
I-IT WASN'T A JOKE.
I'D LIKE TO FOCUS ON SCHOOL THIS YEAR, YOU KNOW... MAYBE—
MARCUS! DO I NEED TO REMIND YOU ABOUT OUR PROMISE? WE'RE GOING TO BEAT OUR BROTHERS' RECORDS AND BE THE BEST SOCCER PLAYERS THIS SCHOOL HAS EVER SEEN.
#1
THEY'VE HAD FULL-RIDE SCHOLARSHIP OFFERS TO PLAY TOGETHER SINCE THEY WERE SIXTEEN!
I'M TIRED OF BEING "SECOND-BEST KID." AREN'T YOU?

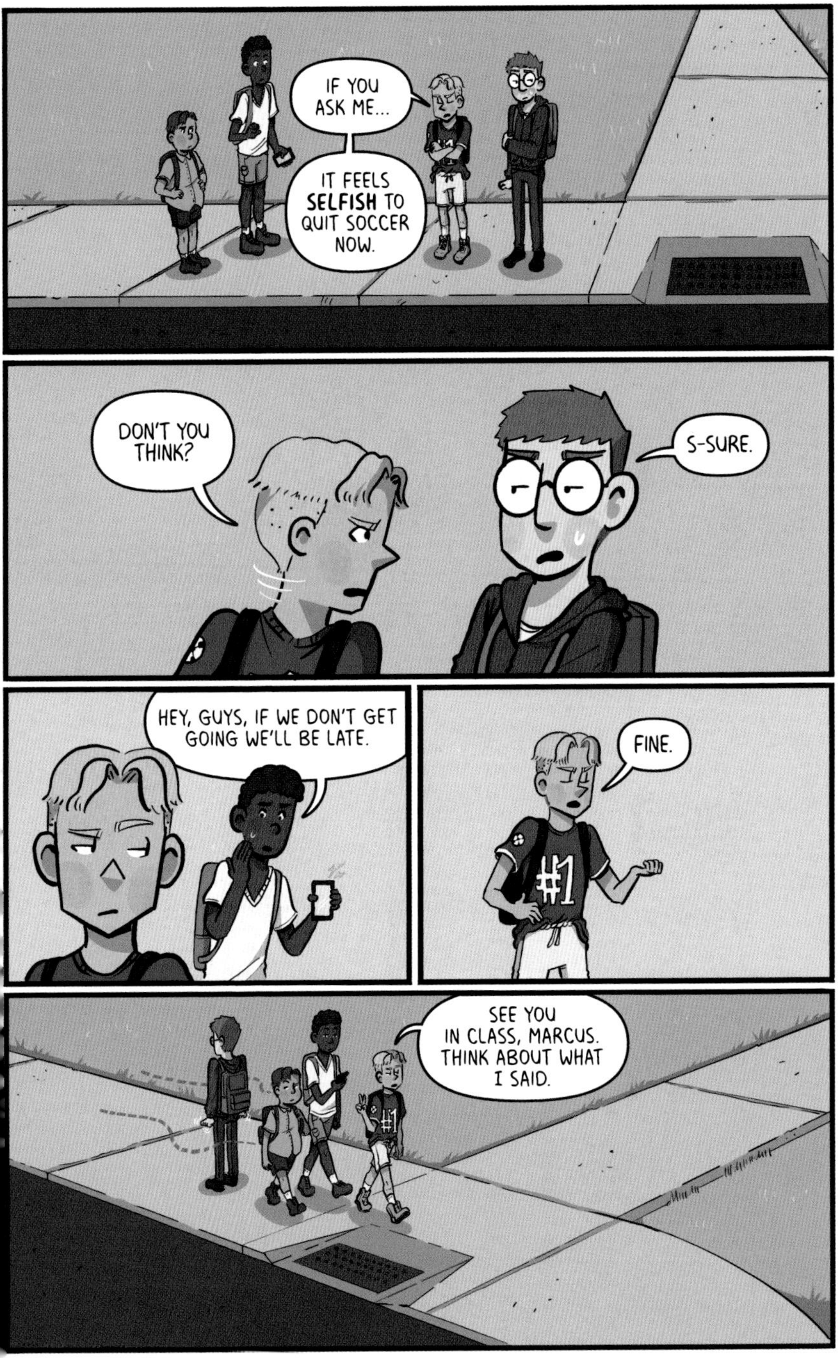
IF YOU ASK ME...
IT FEELS **SELFISH** TO QUIT SOCCER NOW.
DON'T YOU THINK?
S-SURE.
HEY, GUYS, IF WE DON'T GET GOING WE'LL BE LATE.
FINE.
#1
SEE YOU IN CLASS, MARCUS. THINK ABOUT WHAT I SAID.

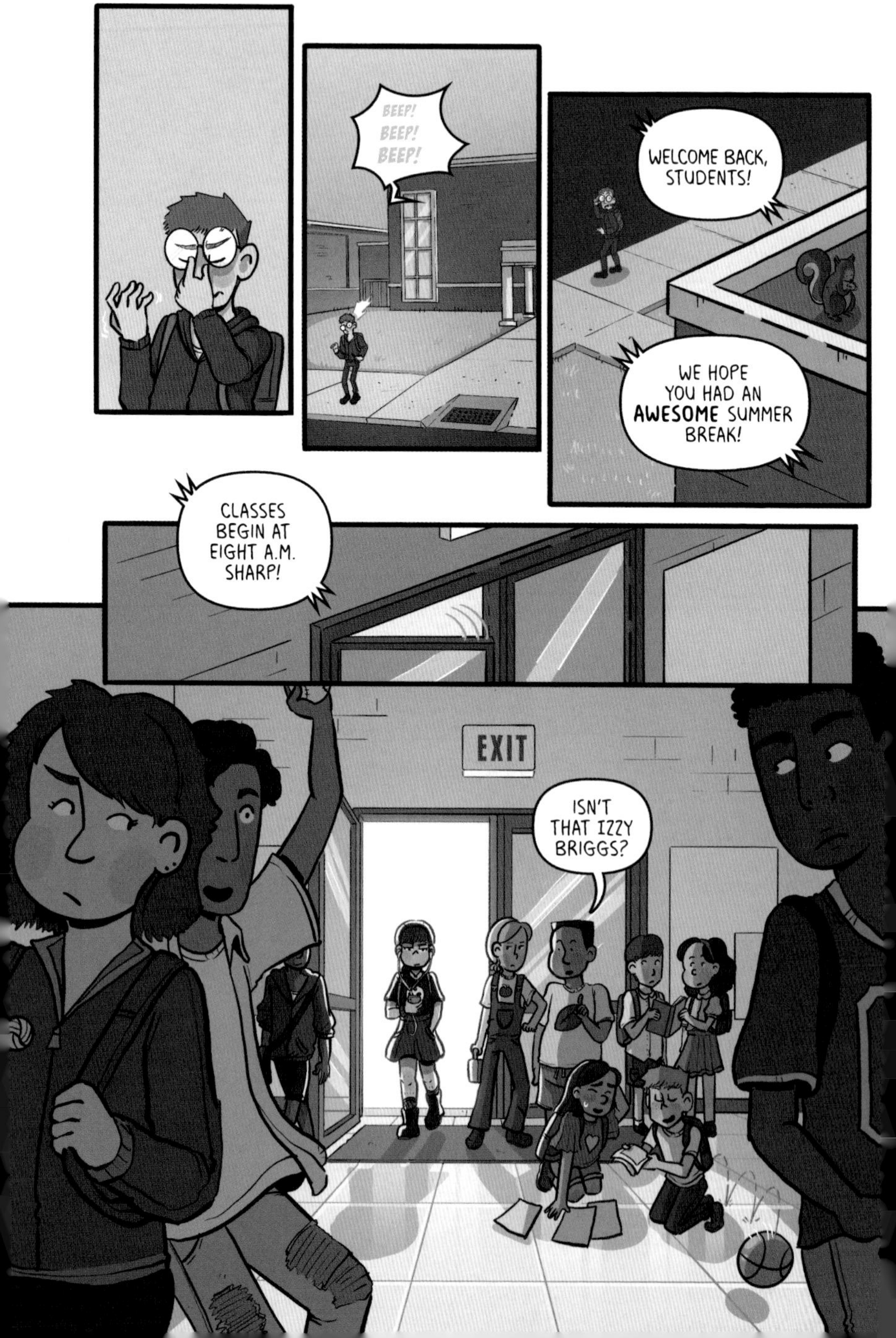
BEEP!
BEEP!
BEEP!
WELCOME BACK, STUDENTS!
WE HOPE YOU HAD AN **AWESOME** SUMMER BREAK!
CLASSES BEGIN AT EIGHT A.M. SHARP!
EXIT
ISN'T THAT IZZY BRIGGS?

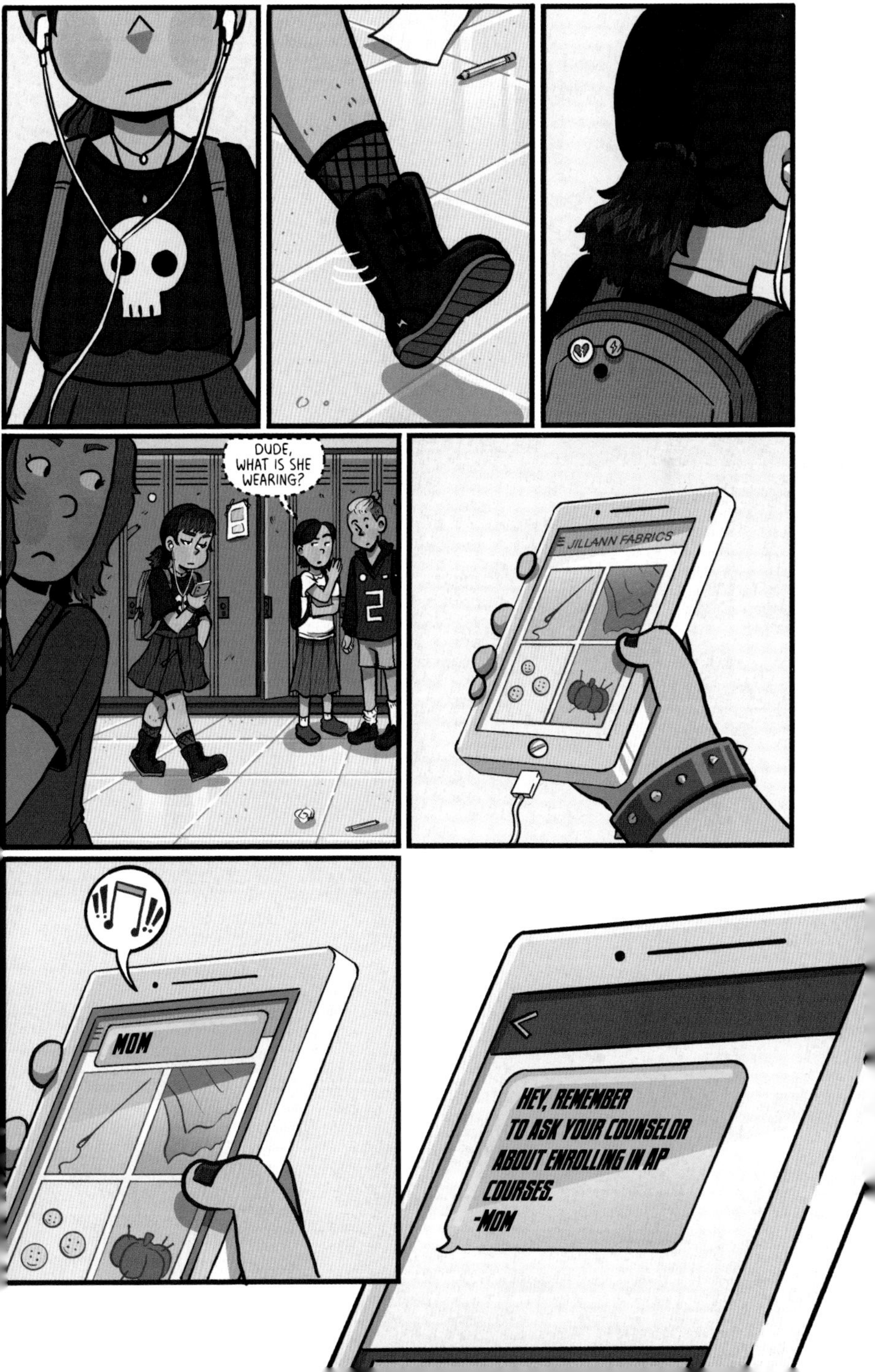
DUDE, WHAT IS SHE WEARING?
JILLANN FABRICS
MOM
HEY, REMEMBER TO ASK YOUR COUNSELOR ABOUT ENROLLING IN AP COURSES.
-MOM

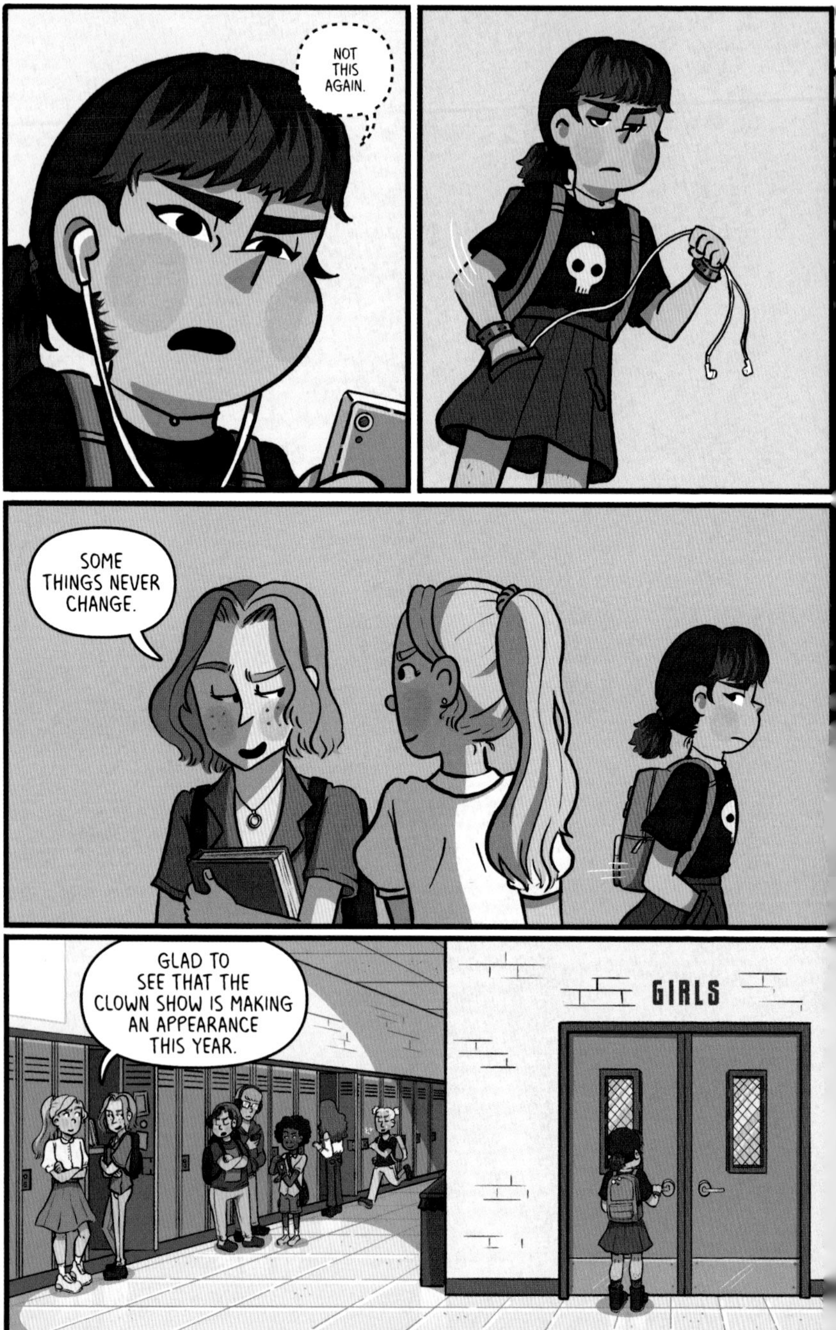
NOT THIS AGAIN.
SOME THINGS NEVER CHANGE.
GLAD TO SEE THAT THE CLOWN SHOW IS MAKING AN APPEARANCE THIS YEAR.
GIRLS

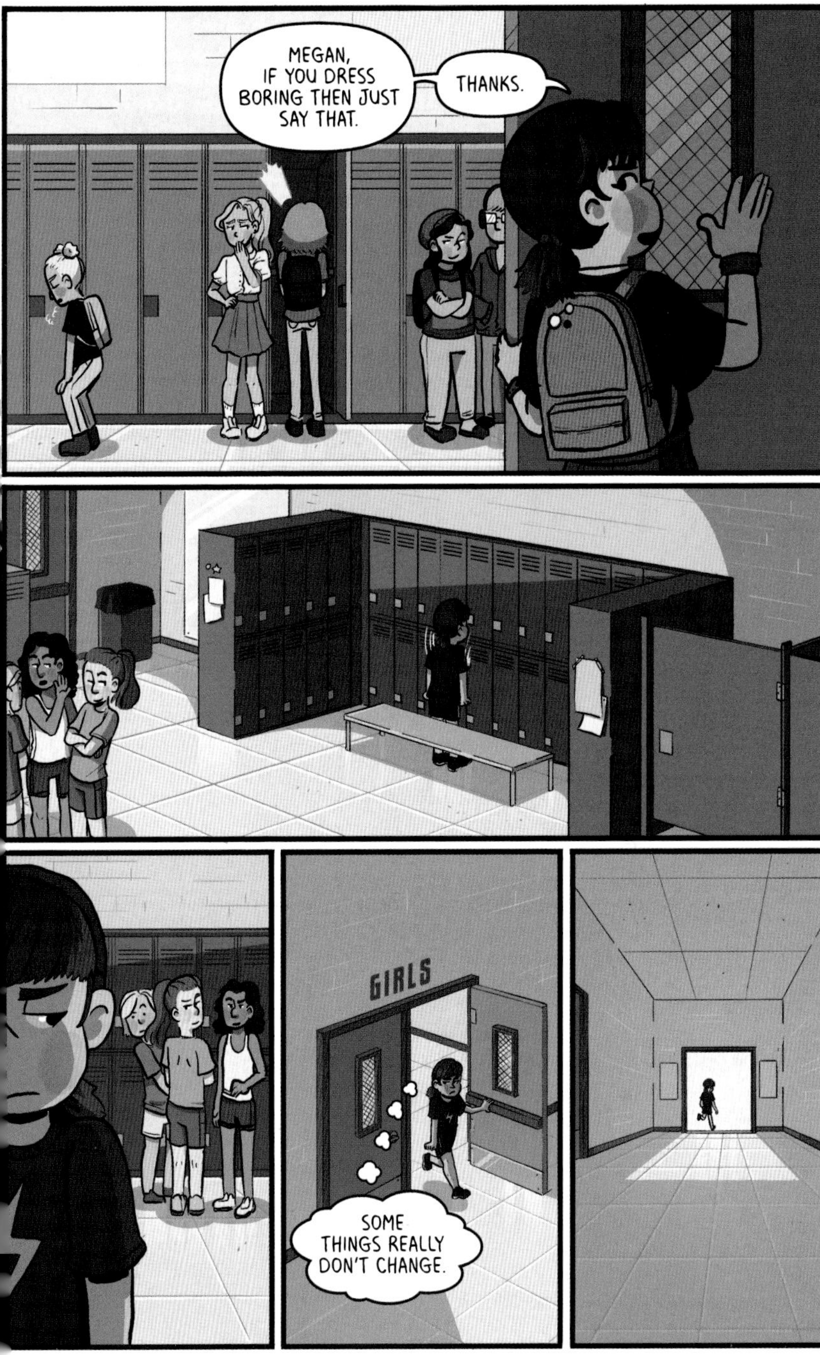
MEGAN, IF YOU DRESS BORING THEN JUST SAY THAT.
THANKS.
GIRLS
SOME THINGS REALLY DON'T CHANGE.

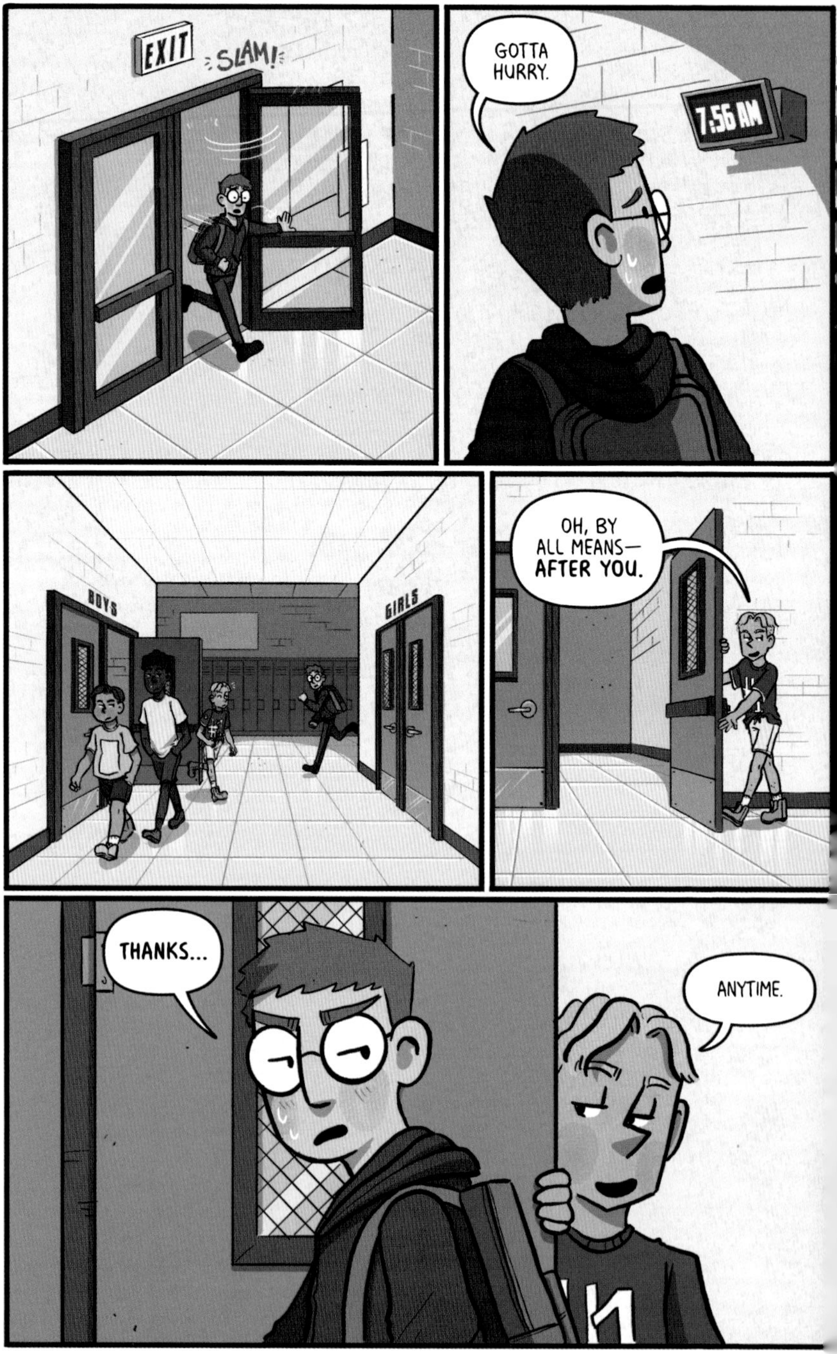
EXIT
SLAM!
GOTTA HURRY.
7:56 AM
BOYS
GIRLS
OH, BY ALL MEANS—AFTER YOU.
THANKS...
ANYTIME.

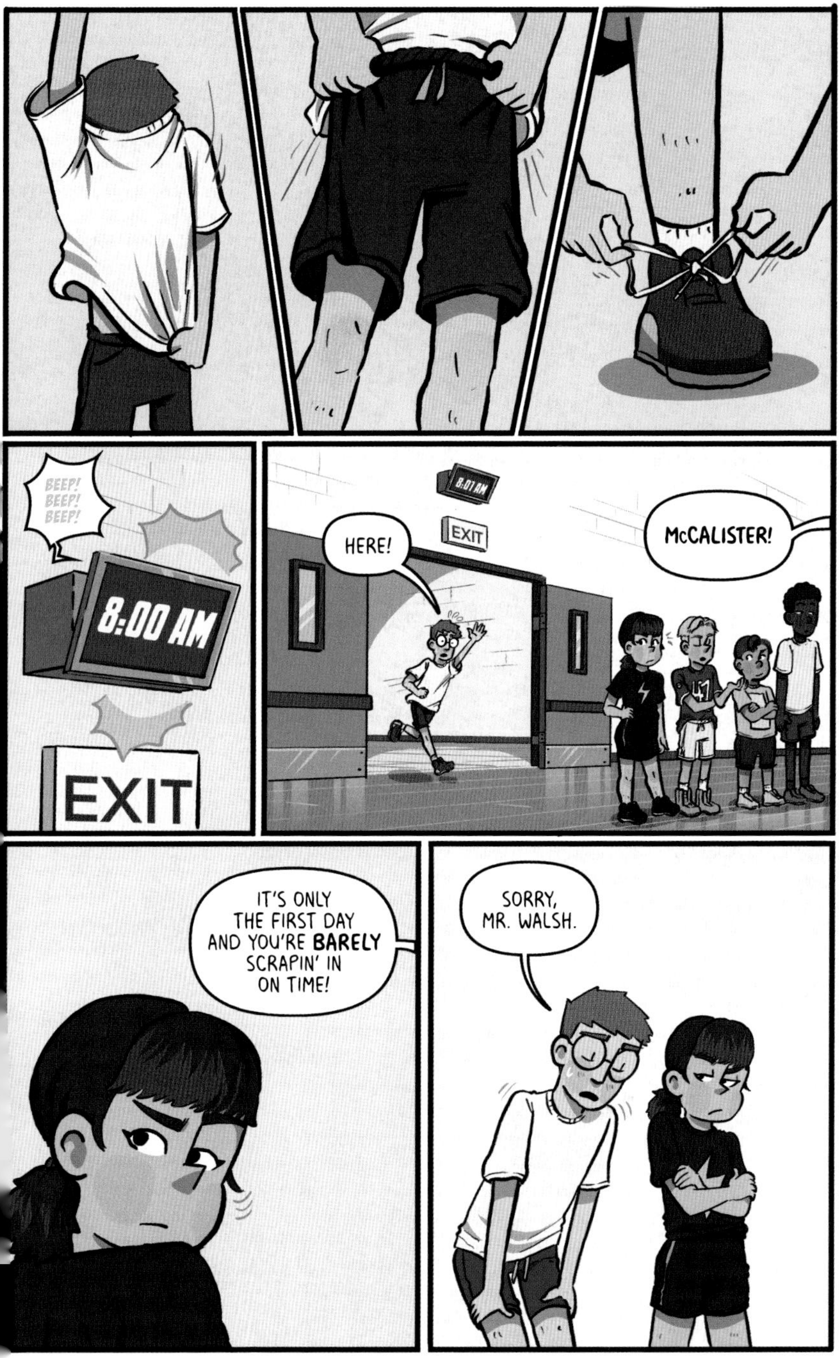
BEEP! BEEP! BEEP!
8:00 AM
EXIT
8:01 AM
EXIT
HERE!
McCALISTER!
IT'S ONLY THE FIRST DAY AND YOU'RE **BARELY** SCRAPIN' IN ON TIME!
SORRY, MR. WALSH.

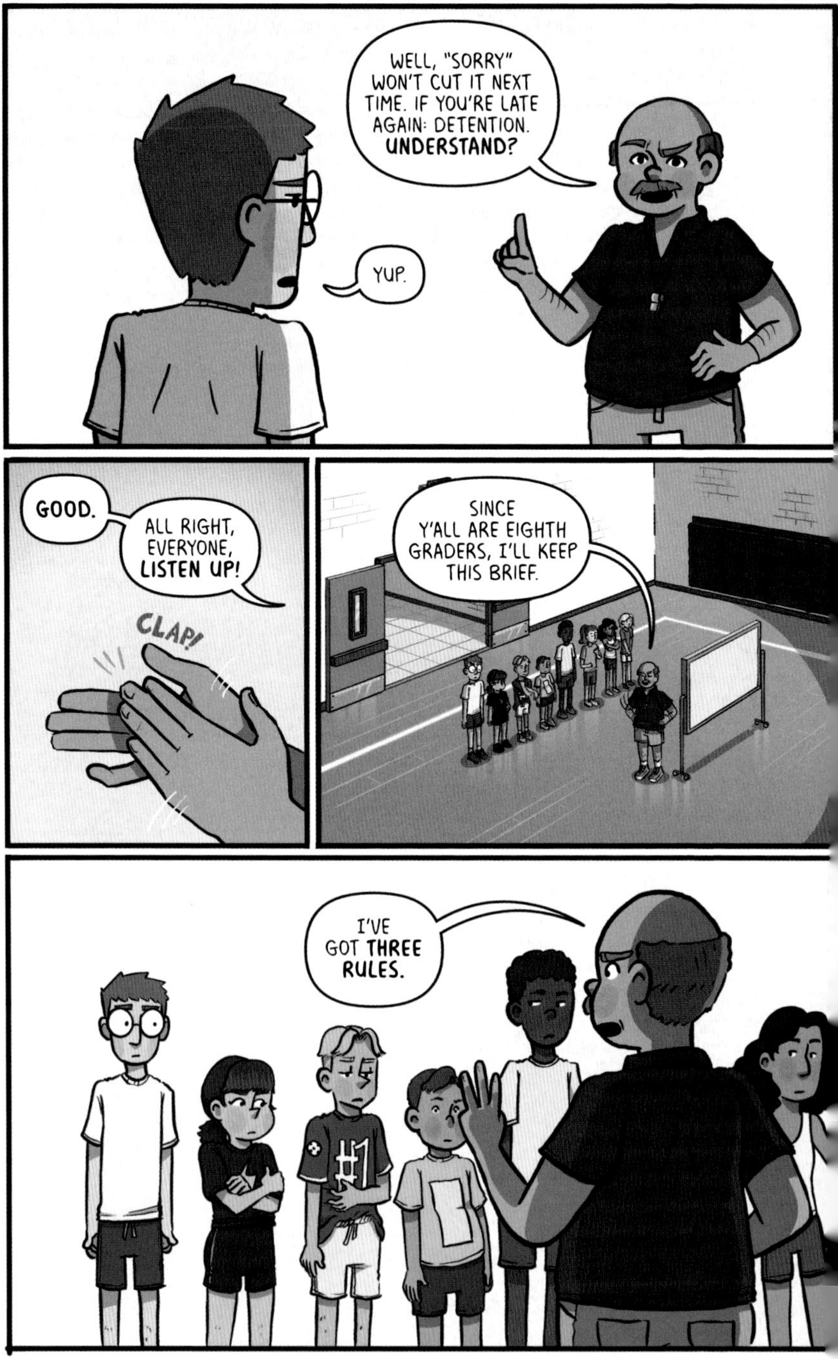
WELL, "SORRY" WON'T CUT IT NEXT TIME. IF YOU'RE LATE AGAIN: DETENTION. **UNDERSTAND?**
YUP.
GOOD.
ALL RIGHT, EVERYONE, **LISTEN UP!**
CLAP!
SINCE Y'ALL ARE EIGHTH GRADERS, I'LL KEEP THIS BRIEF.
I'VE GOT **THREE RULES.**

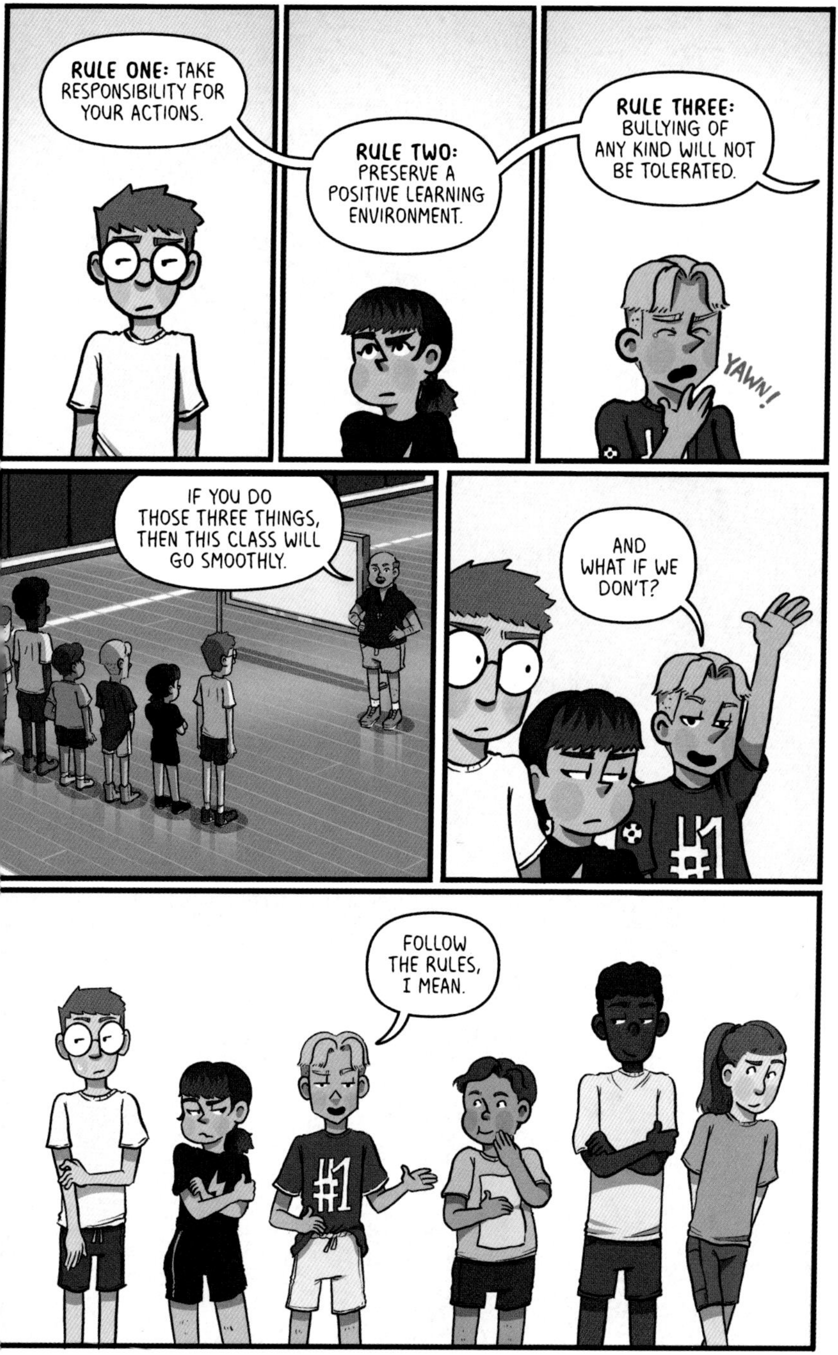
RULE ONE: TAKE RESPONSIBILITY FOR YOUR ACTIONS.
RULE TWO: PRESERVE A POSITIVE LEARNING ENVIRONMENT.
RULE THREE: BULLYING OF ANY KIND WILL NOT BE TOLERATED.
YAWN!
IF YOU DO THOSE THREE THINGS, THEN THIS CLASS WILL GO SMOOTHLY.
AND WHAT IF WE DON'T?
FOLLOW THE RULES, I MEAN.

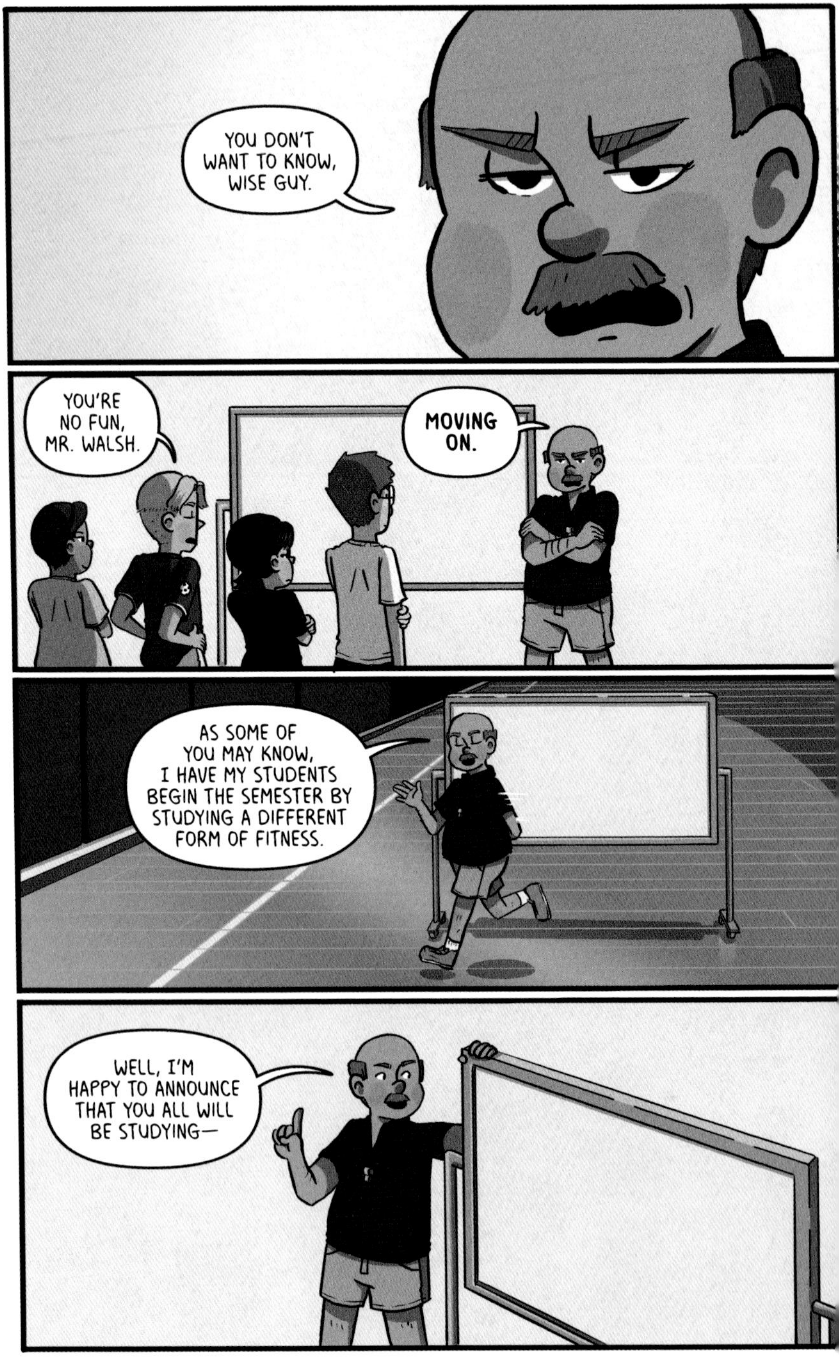
YOU DON'T WANT TO KNOW, WISE GUY.
YOU'RE NO FUN, MR. WALSH.
MOVING ON.
AS SOME OF YOU MAY KNOW, I HAVE MY STUDENTS BEGIN THE SEMESTER BY STUDYING A DIFFERENT FORM OF FITNESS.
WELL, I'M HAPPY TO ANNOUNCE THAT YOU ALL WILL BE STUDYING—

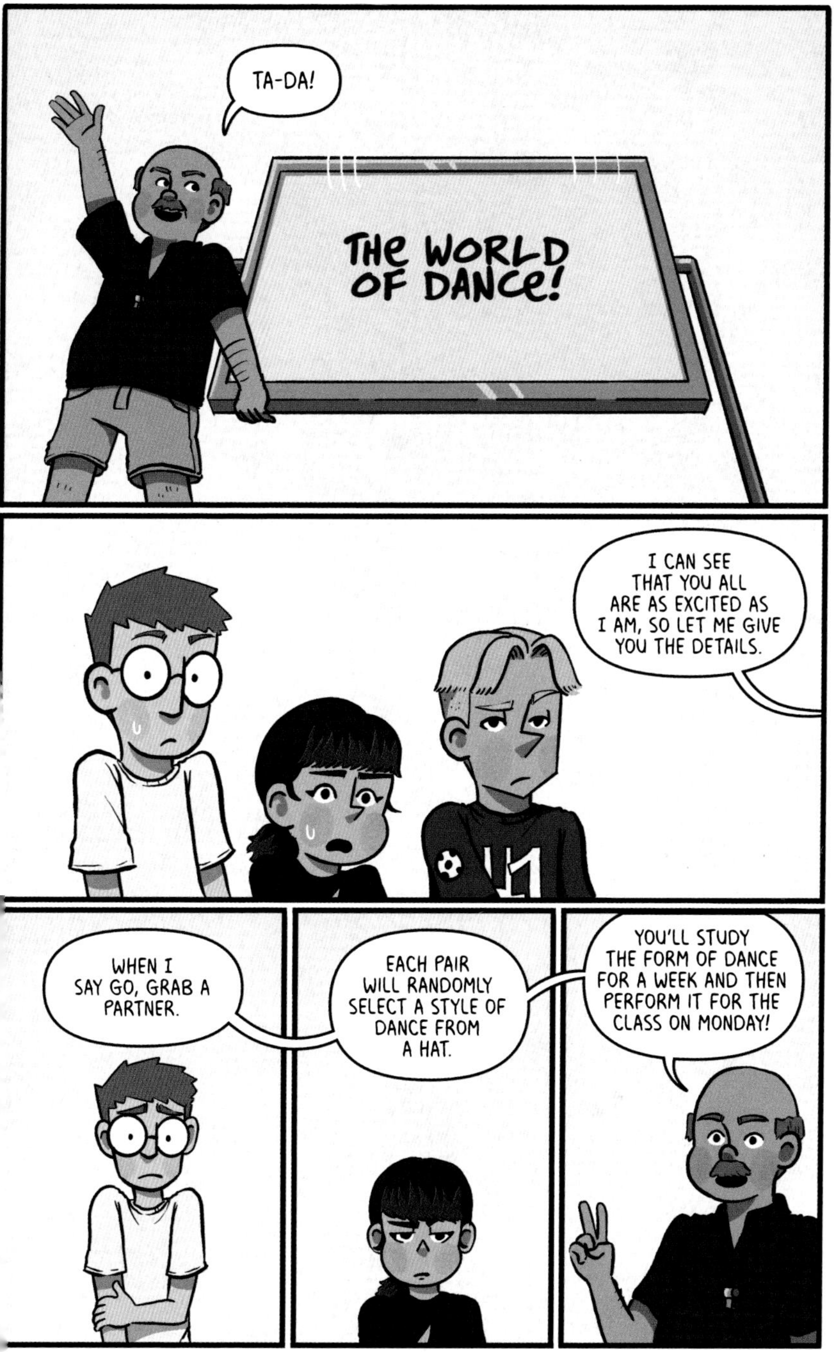
TA-DA!
THE WORLD OF DANCE!
I CAN SEE THAT YOU ALL ARE AS EXCITED AS I AM, SO LET ME GIVE YOU THE DETAILS.
WHEN I SAY GO, GRAB A PARTNER.
EACH PAIR WILL RANDOMLY SELECT A STYLE OF DANCE FROM A HAT.
YOU'LL STUDY THE FORM OF DANCE FOR A WEEK AND THEN PERFORM IT FOR THE CLASS ON MONDAY!

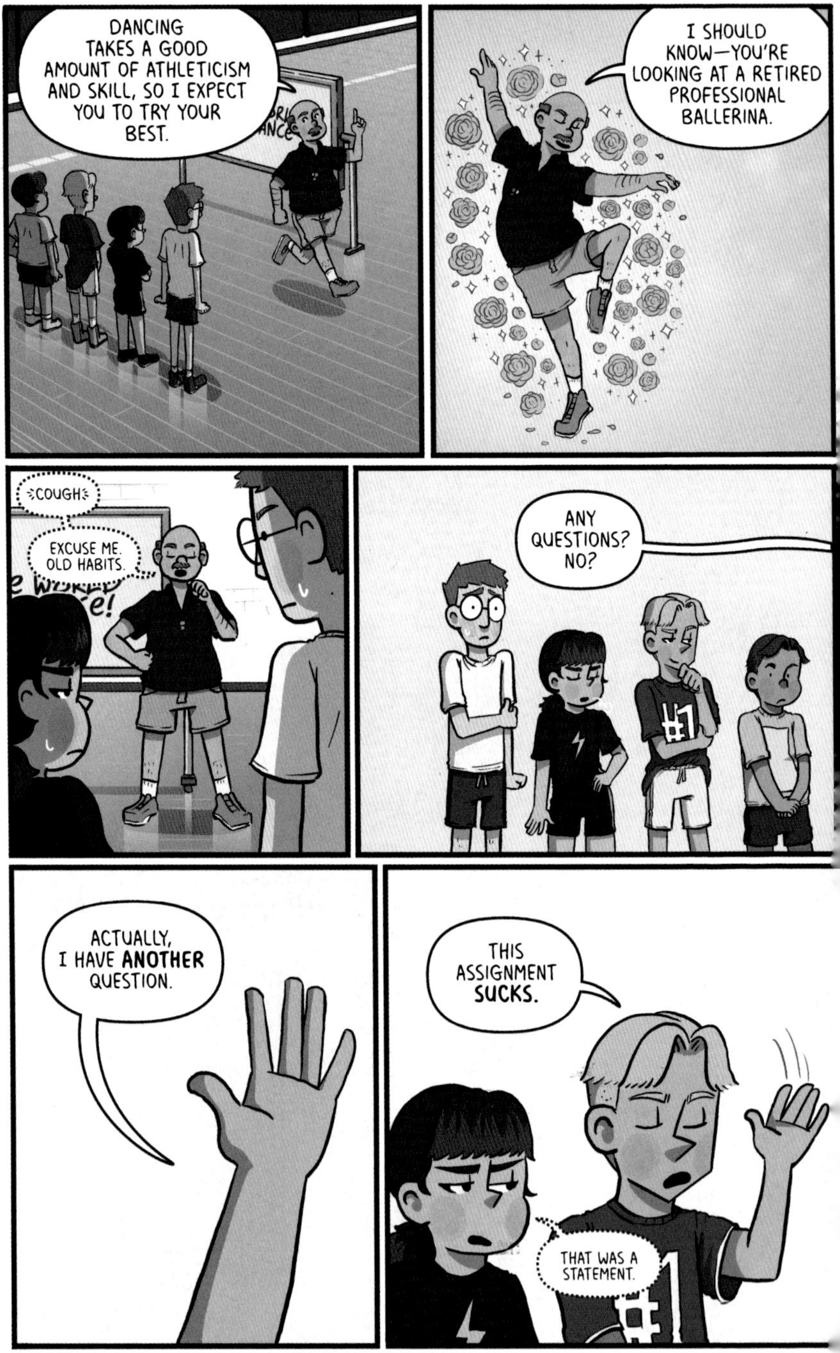
DANCING TAKES A GOOD AMOUNT OF ATHLETICISM AND SKILL, SO I EXPECT YOU TO TRY YOUR BEST.
I SHOULD KNOW—YOU'RE LOOKING AT A RETIRED PROFESSIONAL BALLERINA.
COUGH
EXCUSE ME. OLD HABITS.
ANY QUESTIONS? NO?
ACTUALLY, I HAVE **ANOTHER** QUESTION.
THIS ASSIGNMENT **SUCKS.**
THAT WAS A STATEMENT.

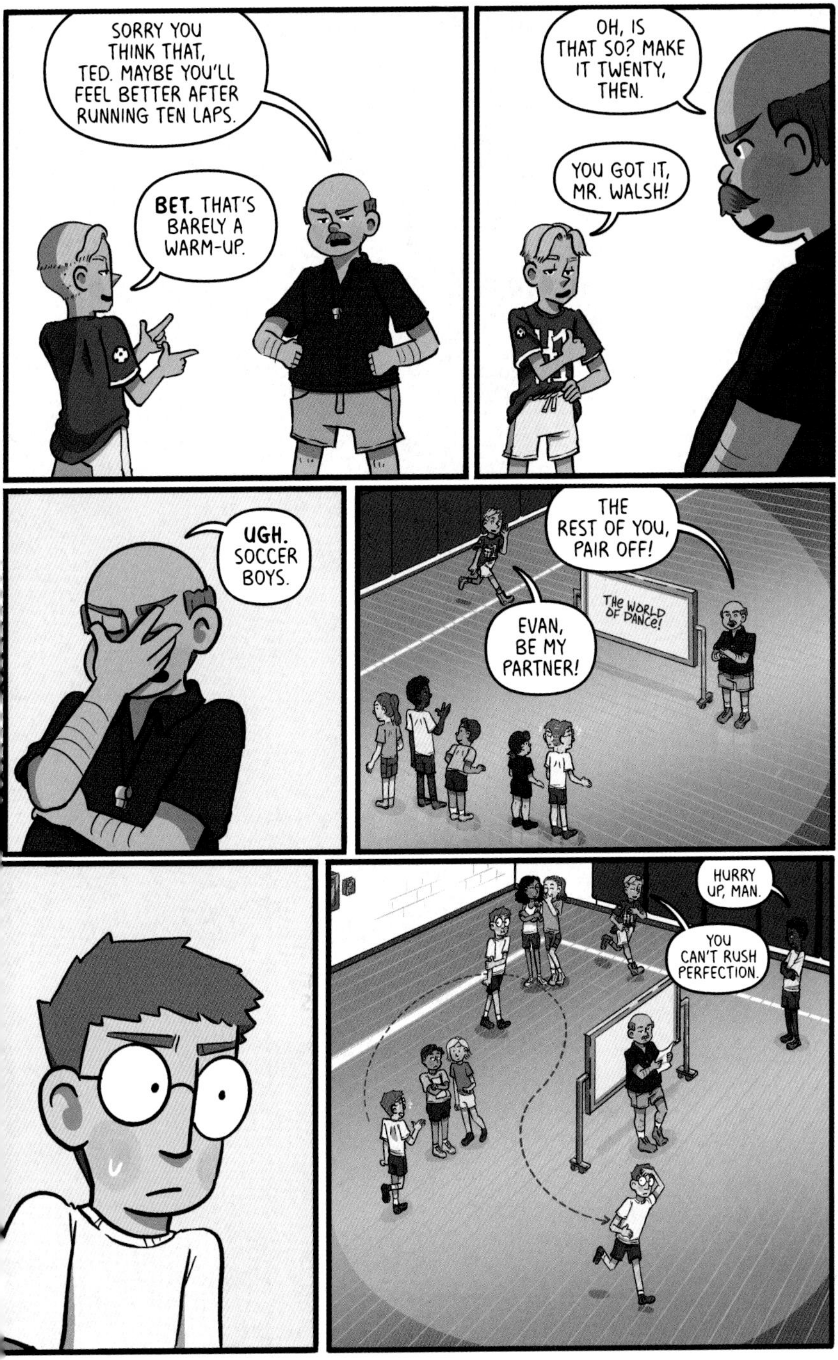
SORRY YOU THINK THAT, TED. MAYBE YOU'LL FEEL BETTER AFTER RUNNING TEN LAPS.
BET. THAT'S BARELY A WARM-UP.
OH, IS THAT SO? MAKE IT TWENTY, THEN.
YOU GOT IT, MR. WALSH!
UGH. SOCCER BOYS.
THE REST OF YOU, PAIR OFF!
THE WORLD OF DANCE!
EVAN, BE MY PARTNER!
HURRY UP, MAN.
YOU CAN'T RUSH PERFECTION.

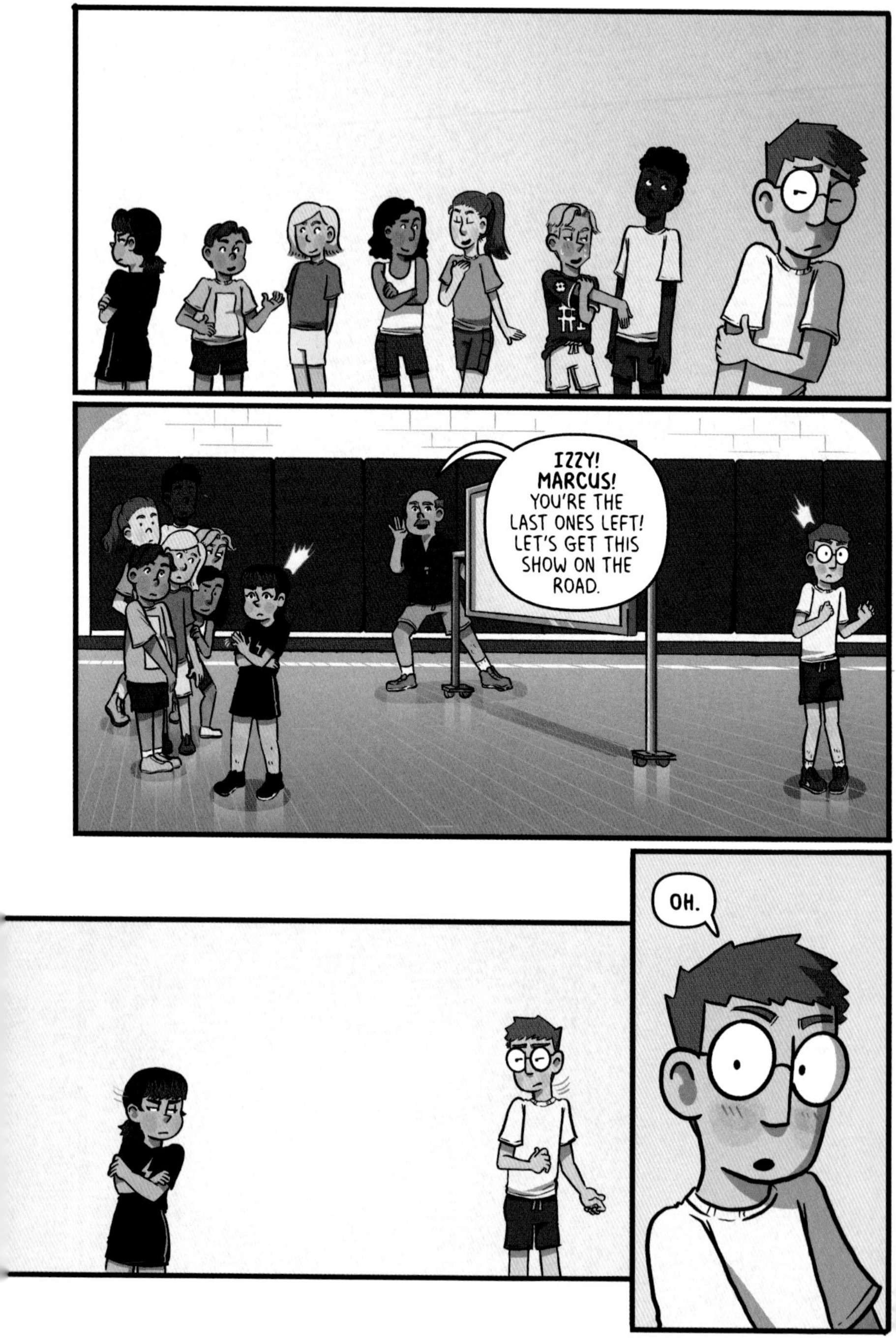
IZZY! MARCUS! YOU'RE THE LAST ONES LEFT! LET'S GET THIS SHOW ON THE ROAD.
OH.

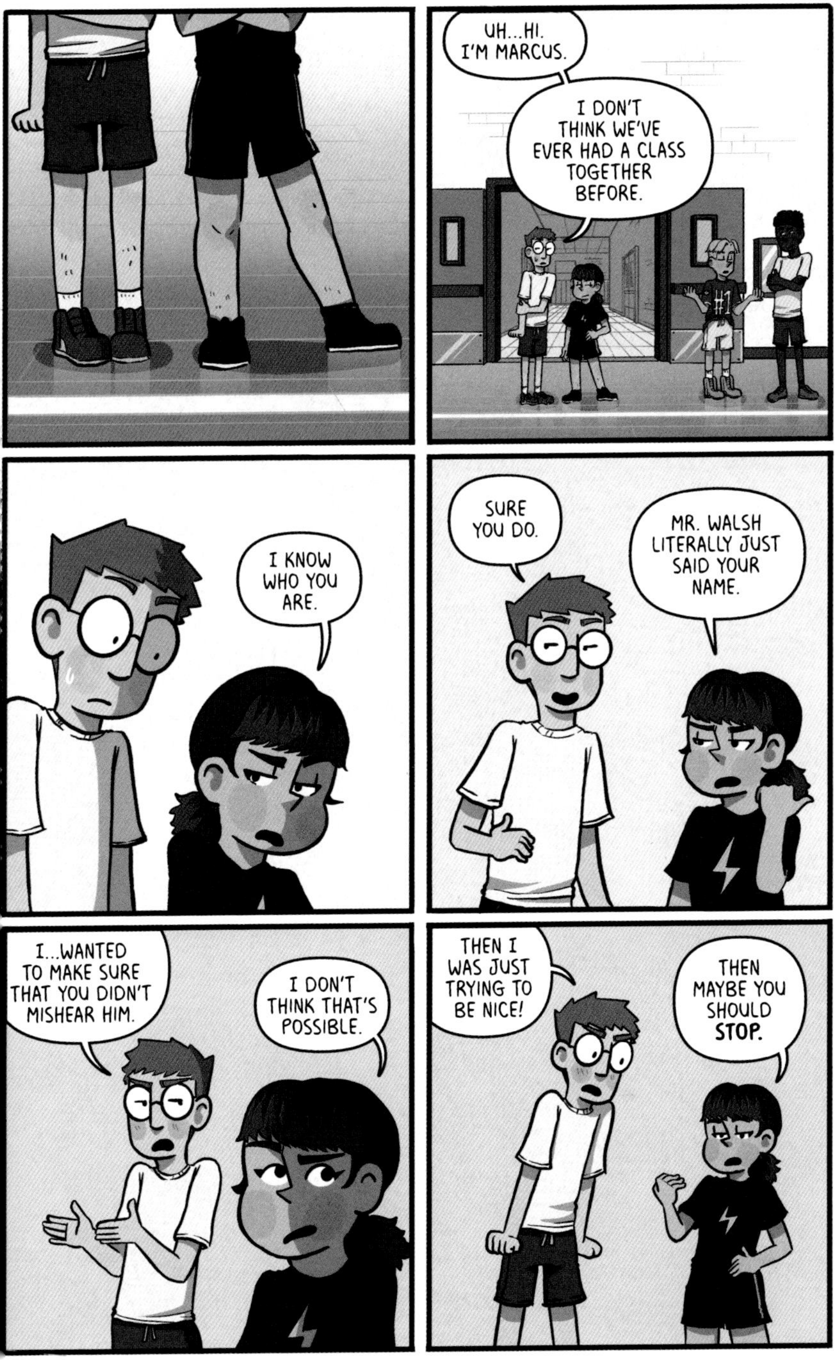
UH...HI. I'M MARCUS.
I DON'T THINK WE'VE EVER HAD A CLASS TOGETHER BEFORE.
I KNOW WHO YOU ARE.
SURE YOU DO.
MR. WALSH LITERALLY JUST SAID YOUR NAME.
I...WANTED TO MAKE SURE THAT YOU DIDN'T MISHEAR HIM.
I DON'T THINK THAT'S POSSIBLE.
THEN I WAS JUST TRYING TO BE NICE!
THEN MAYBE YOU SHOULD **STOP.**

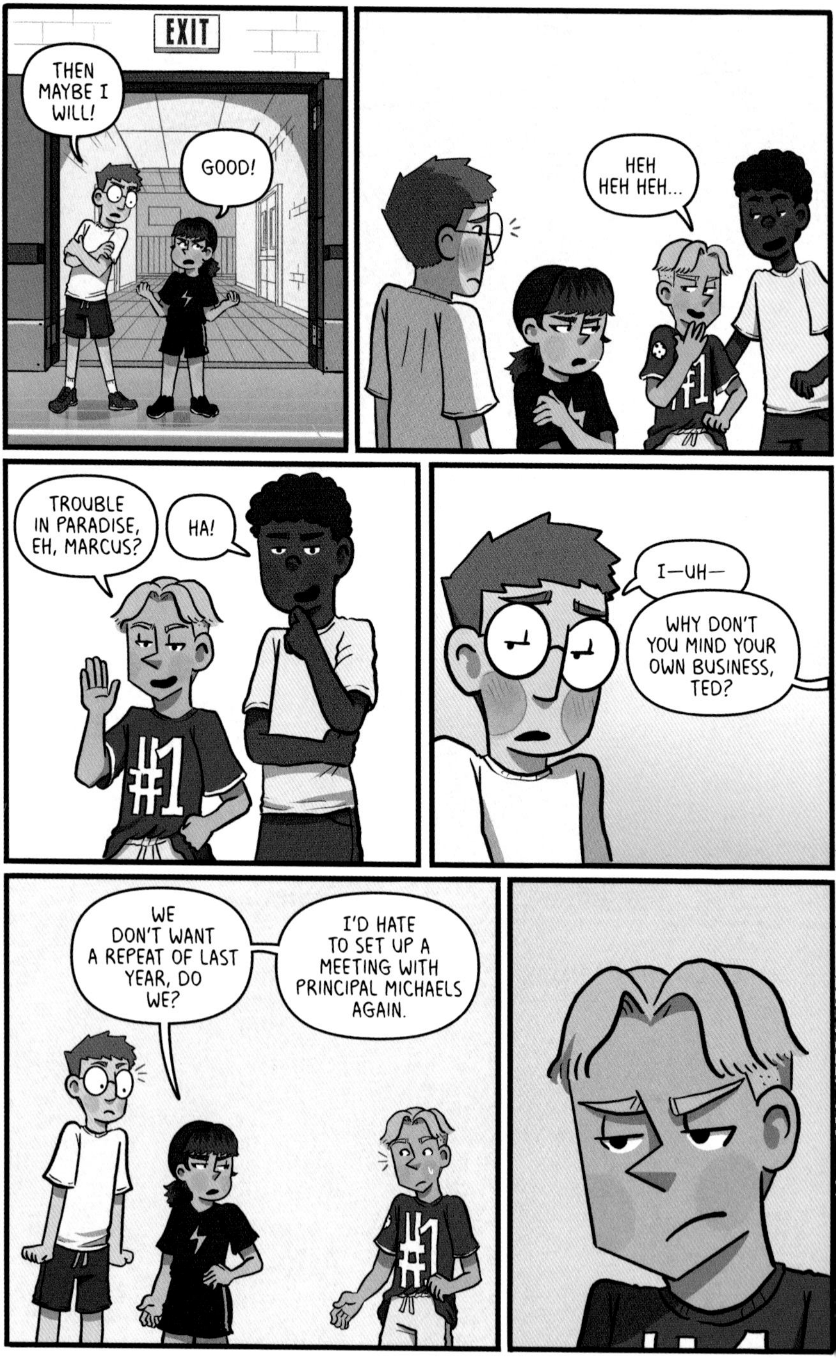
EXIT
THEN MAYBE I WILL!
GOOD!
HEH HEH HEH...
TROUBLE IN PARADISE, EH, MARCUS?
HA!
I—UH—
WHY DON'T YOU MIND YOUR OWN BUSINESS, TED?
WE DON'T WANT A REPEAT OF LAST YEAR, DO WE?
I'D HATE TO SET UP A MEETING WITH PRINCIPAL MICHAELS AGAIN.

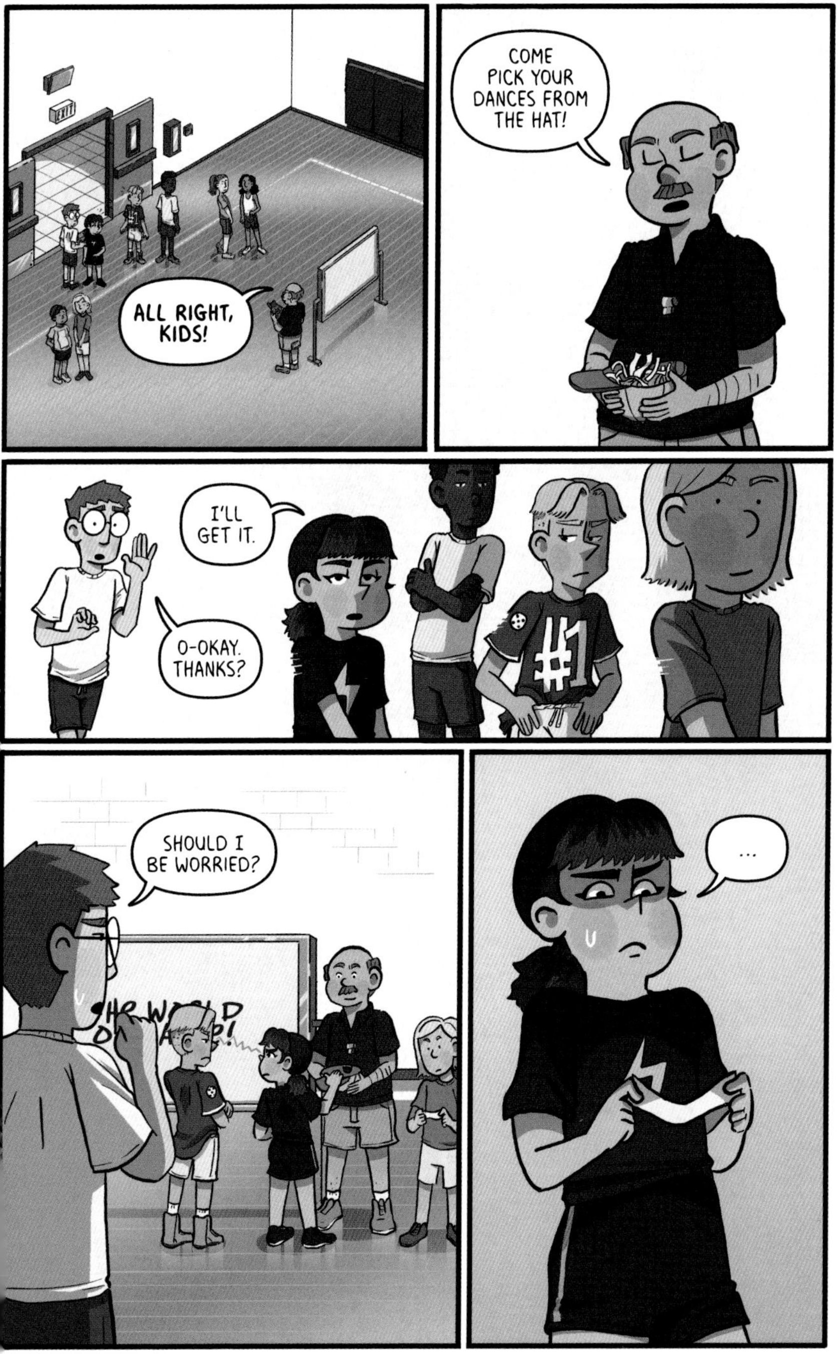

ALL RIGHT, KIDS!
COME PICK YOUR DANCES FROM THE HAT!
I'LL GET IT.
O-OKAY. THANKS?
SHOULD I BE WORRIED?
...

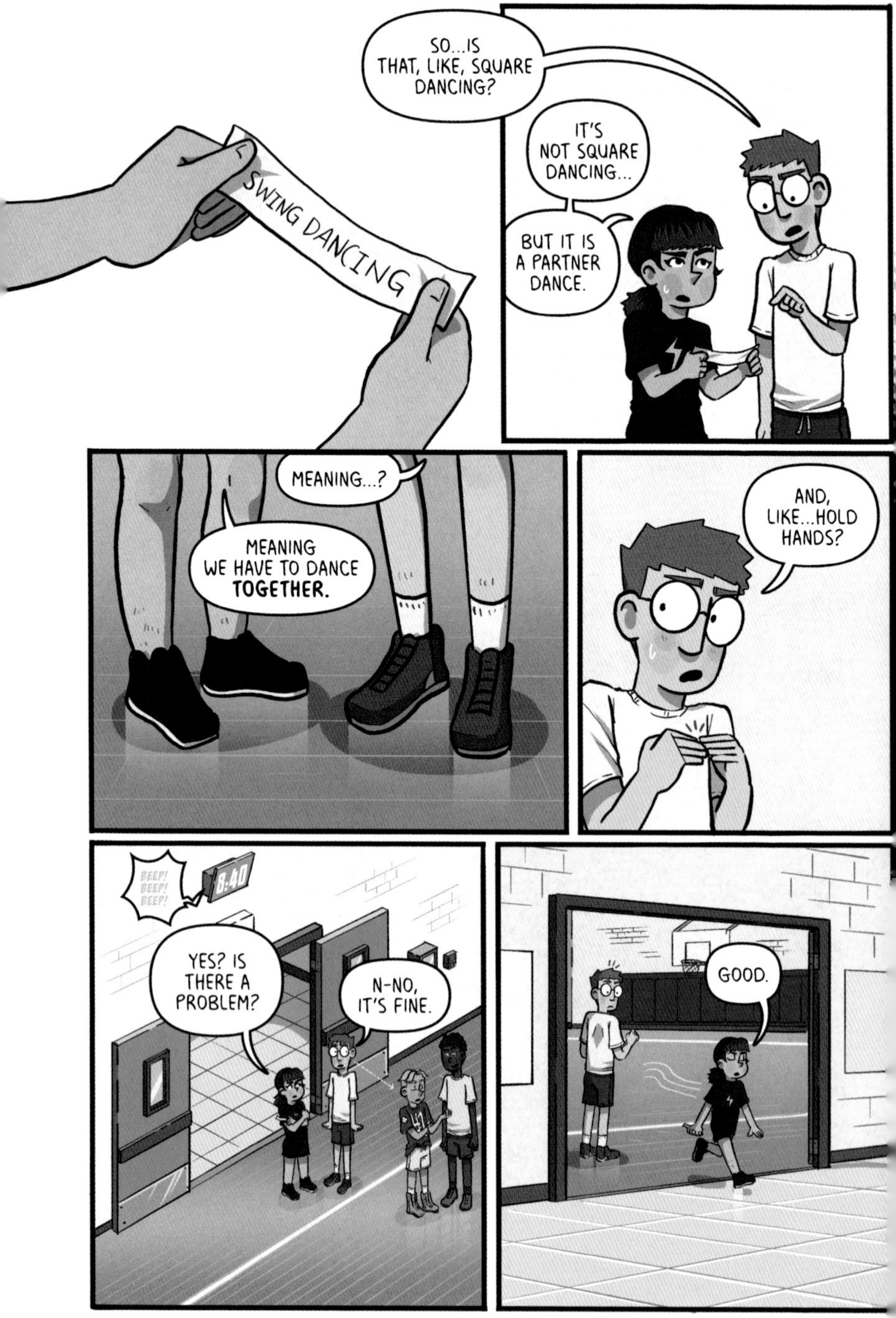
SWING DANCING
SO...IS THAT, LIKE, SQUARE DANCING?
IT'S NOT SQUARE DANCING...
BUT IT IS A PARTNER DANCE.
MEANING...?
MEANING WE HAVE TO DANCE **TOGETHER.**
AND, LIKE...HOLD HANDS?
BEEP! BEEP! BEEP!
8:40
YES? IS THERE A PROBLEM?
N-NO, IT'S FINE.
GOOD.

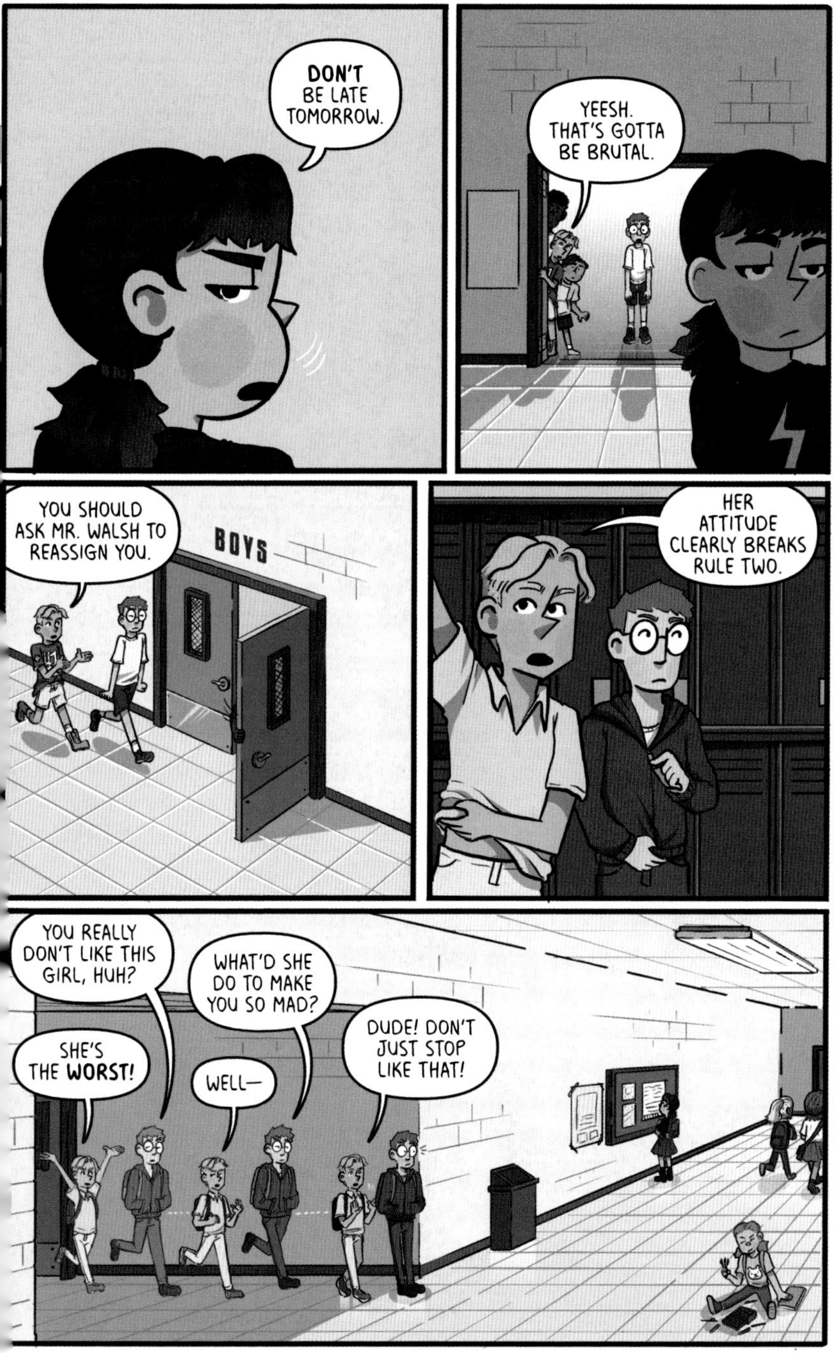
DON'T BE LATE TOMORROW.
YEESH. THAT'S GOTTA BE BRUTAL.
YOU SHOULD ASK MR. WALSH TO REASSIGN YOU.
BOYS
HER ATTITUDE CLEARLY BREAKS RULE TWO.
YOU REALLY DON'T LIKE THIS GIRL, HUH?
SHE'S THE **WORST**!
WHAT'D SHE DO TO MAKE YOU SO MAD?
WELL—
DUDE! DON'T JUST STOP LIKE THAT!

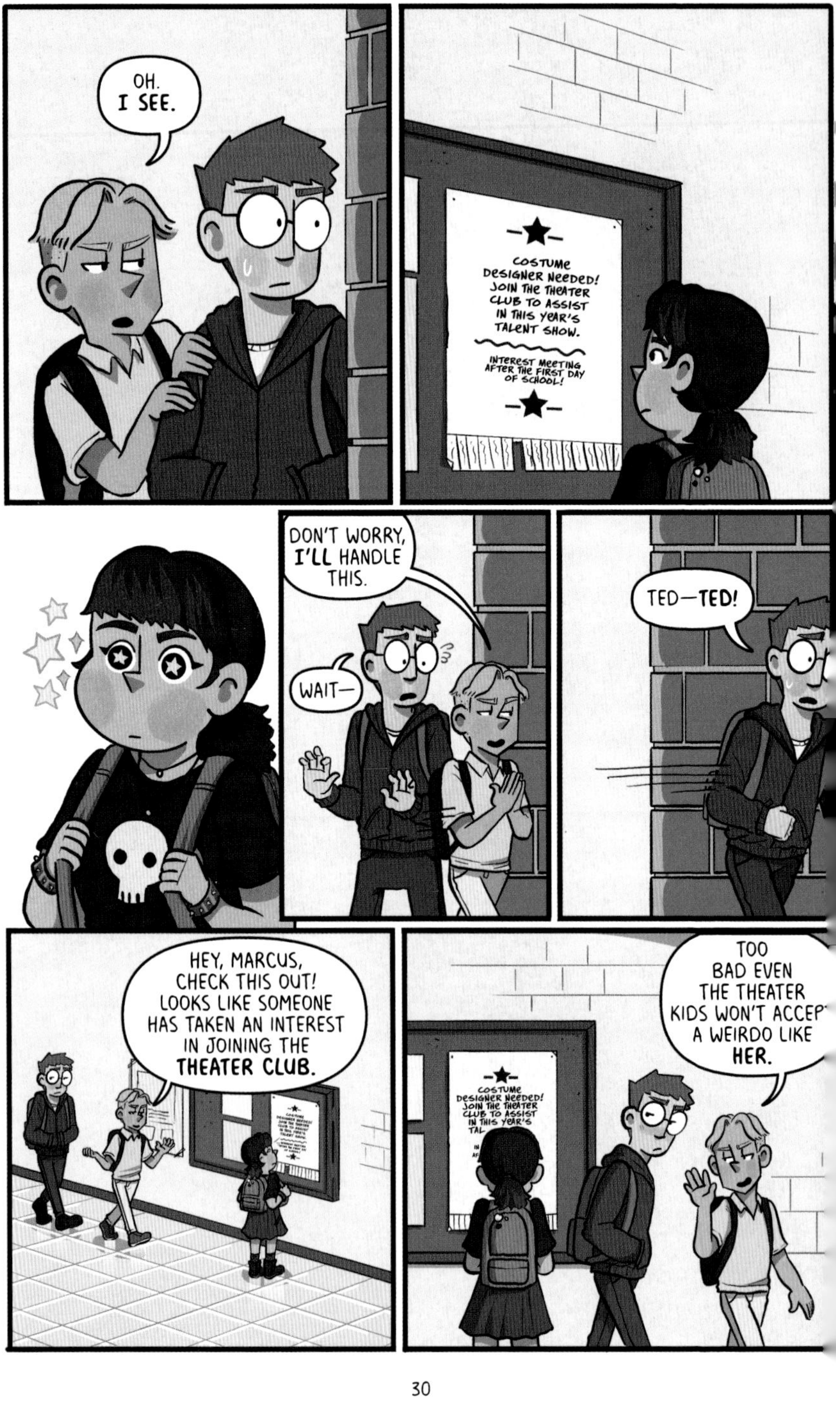
OH. I SEE.
COSTUME DESIGNER NEEDED! JOIN THE THEATER CLUB TO ASSIST IN THIS YEAR'S TALENT SHOW.
INTEREST MEETING AFTER THE FIRST DAY OF SCHOOL!
DON'T WORRY, I'LL HANDLE THIS.
WAIT—
TED—TED!
HEY, MARCUS, CHECK THIS OUT! LOOKS LIKE SOMEONE HAS TAKEN AN INTEREST IN JOINING THE THEATER CLUB.
TOO BAD EVEN THE THEATER KIDS WON'T ACCEPT A WEIRDO LIKE HER.

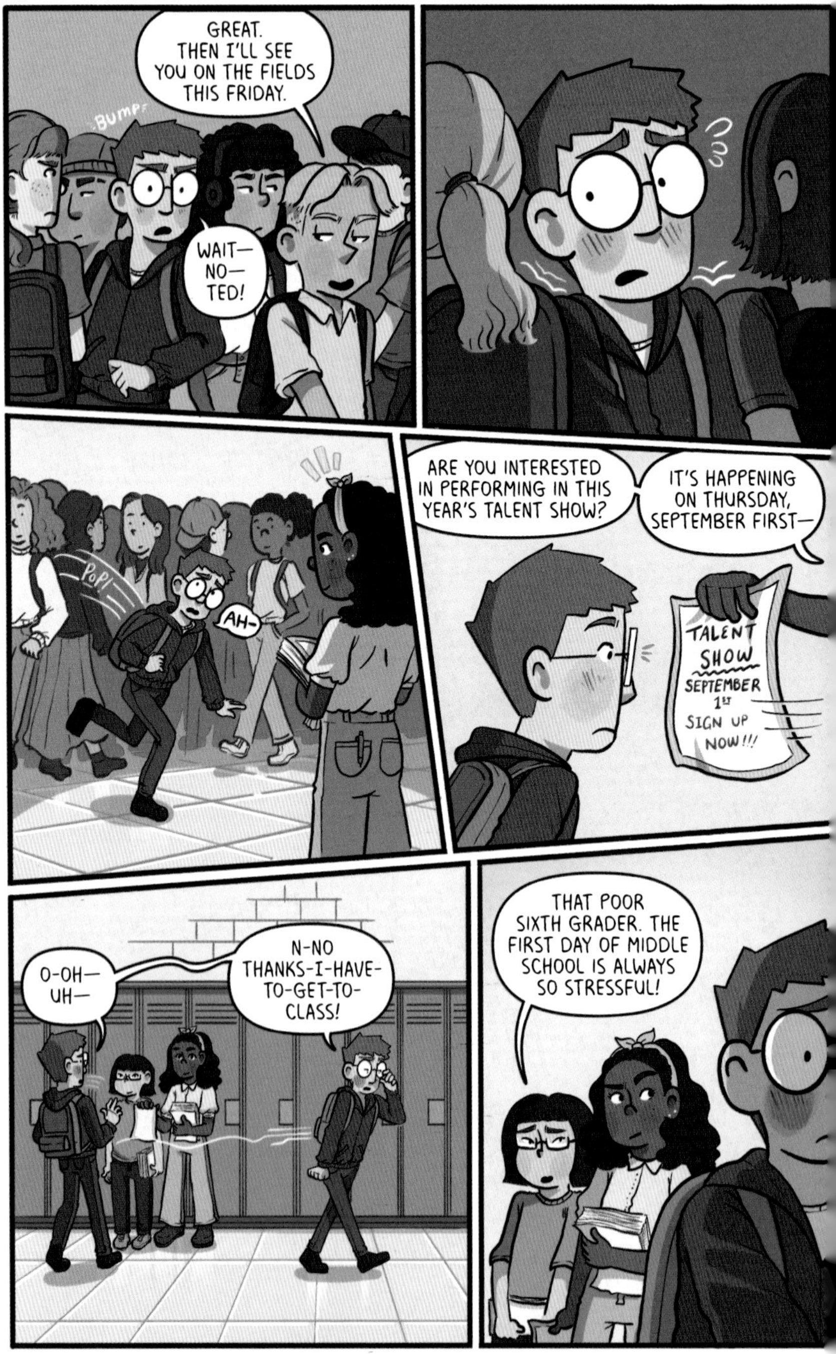

GREAT. THEN I'LL SEE YOU ON THE FIELDS THIS FRIDAY.
BUMPF
WAIT— NO— TED!
POP!
AH-
ARE YOU INTERESTED IN PERFORMING IN THIS YEAR'S TALENT SHOW?
IT'S HAPPENING ON THURSDAY, SEPTEMBER FIRST—
TALENT SHOW
SEPTEMBER 1ST
SIGN UP NOW!!!
O-OH— UH—
N-NO THANKS-I-HAVE-TO-GET-TO-CLASS!
THAT POOR SIXTH GRADER. THE FIRST DAY OF MIDDLE SCHOOL IS ALWAYS SO STRESSFUL!

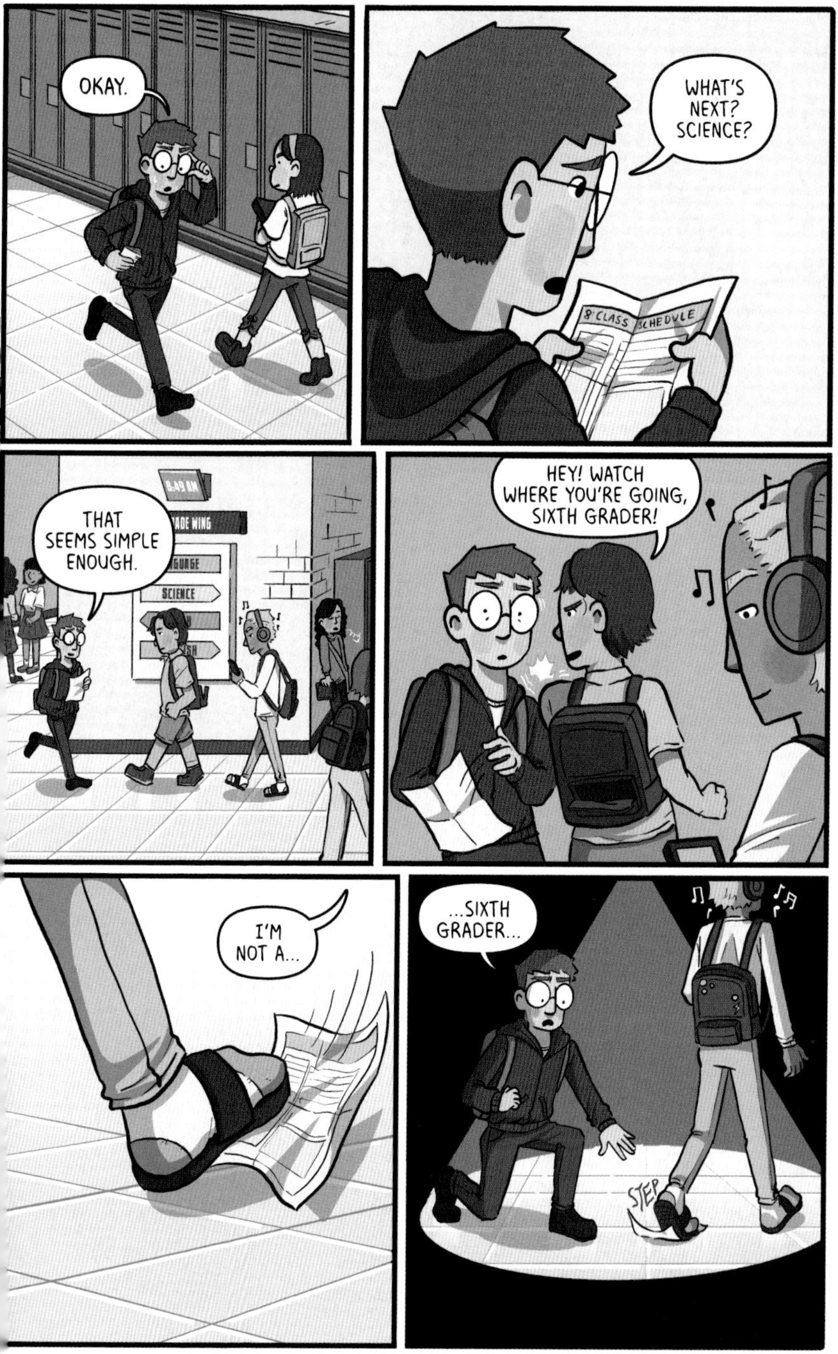
OKAY.
WHAT'S NEXT? SCIENCE?
CLASS SCHEDULE
8:49 AM
SCIENCE
THAT SEEMS SIMPLE ENOUGH.
HEY! WATCH WHERE YOU'RE GOING, SIXTH GRADER!
I'M NOT A...
...SIXTH GRADER...
STEP

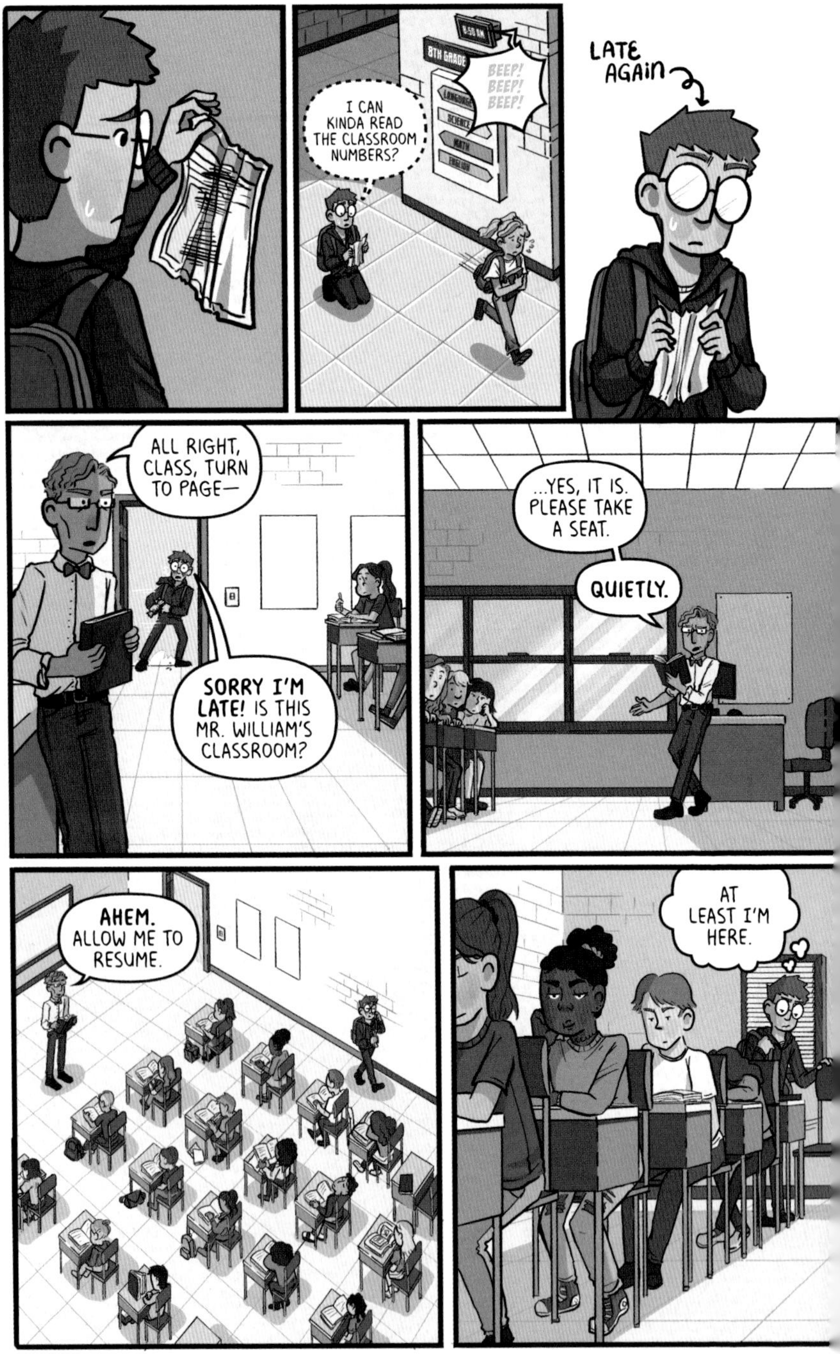
8:50 AM
8TH GRADE
I CAN KINDA READ THE CLASSROOM NUMBERS?
BEEP! BEEP! BEEP!
LATE AGAIN
ALL RIGHT, CLASS, TURN TO PAGE—
SORRY I'M LATE! IS THIS MR. WILLIAM'S CLASSROOM?
...YES, IT IS. PLEASE TAKE A SEAT.
QUIETLY.
AHEM. ALLOW ME TO RESUME.
AT LEAST I'M HERE.

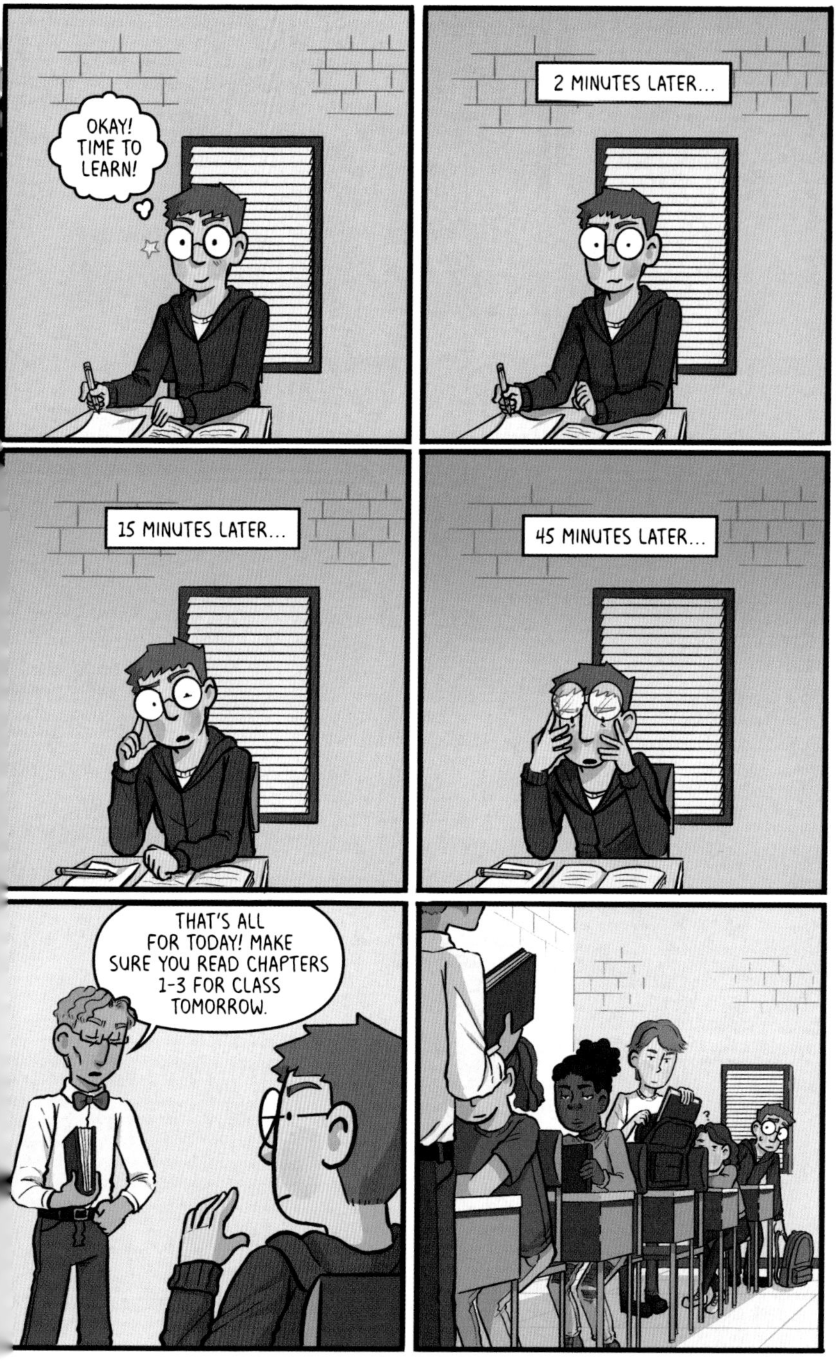
OKAY! TIME TO LEARN!
2 MINUTES LATER...
15 MINUTES LATER...
45 MINUTES LATER...
THAT'S ALL FOR TODAY! MAKE SURE YOU READ CHAPTERS 1-3 FOR CLASS TOMORROW.

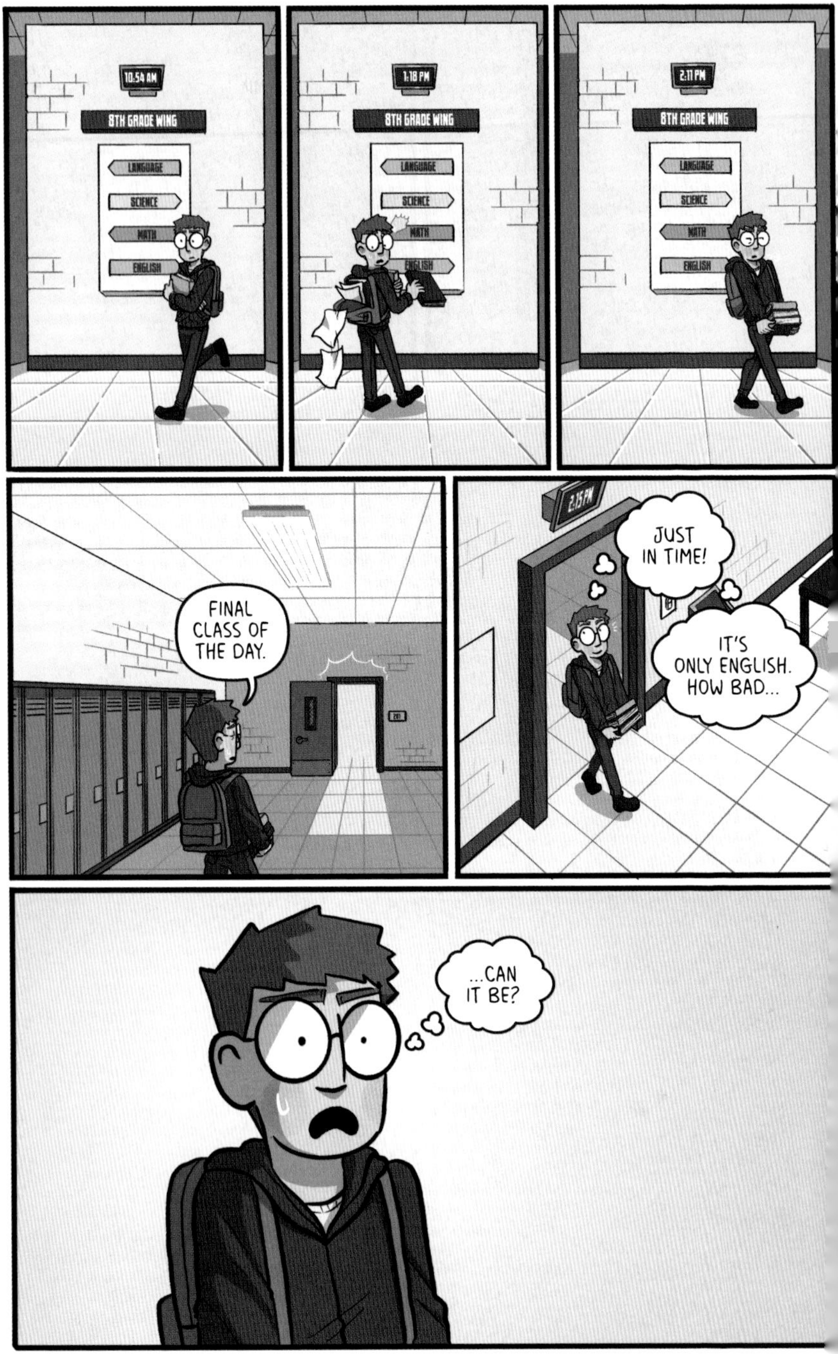
10:54 AM
8TH GRADE WING
LANGUAGE
SCIENCE
MATH
ENGLISH
1:18 PM
8TH GRADE WING
LANGUAGE
SCIENCE
MATH
ENGLISH
2:11 PM
8TH GRADE WING
LANGUAGE
SCIENCE
MATH
ENGLISH
FINAL CLASS OF THE DAY.
2:15 PM
JUST IN TIME!
IT'S ONLY ENGLISH. HOW BAD...
...CAN IT BE?

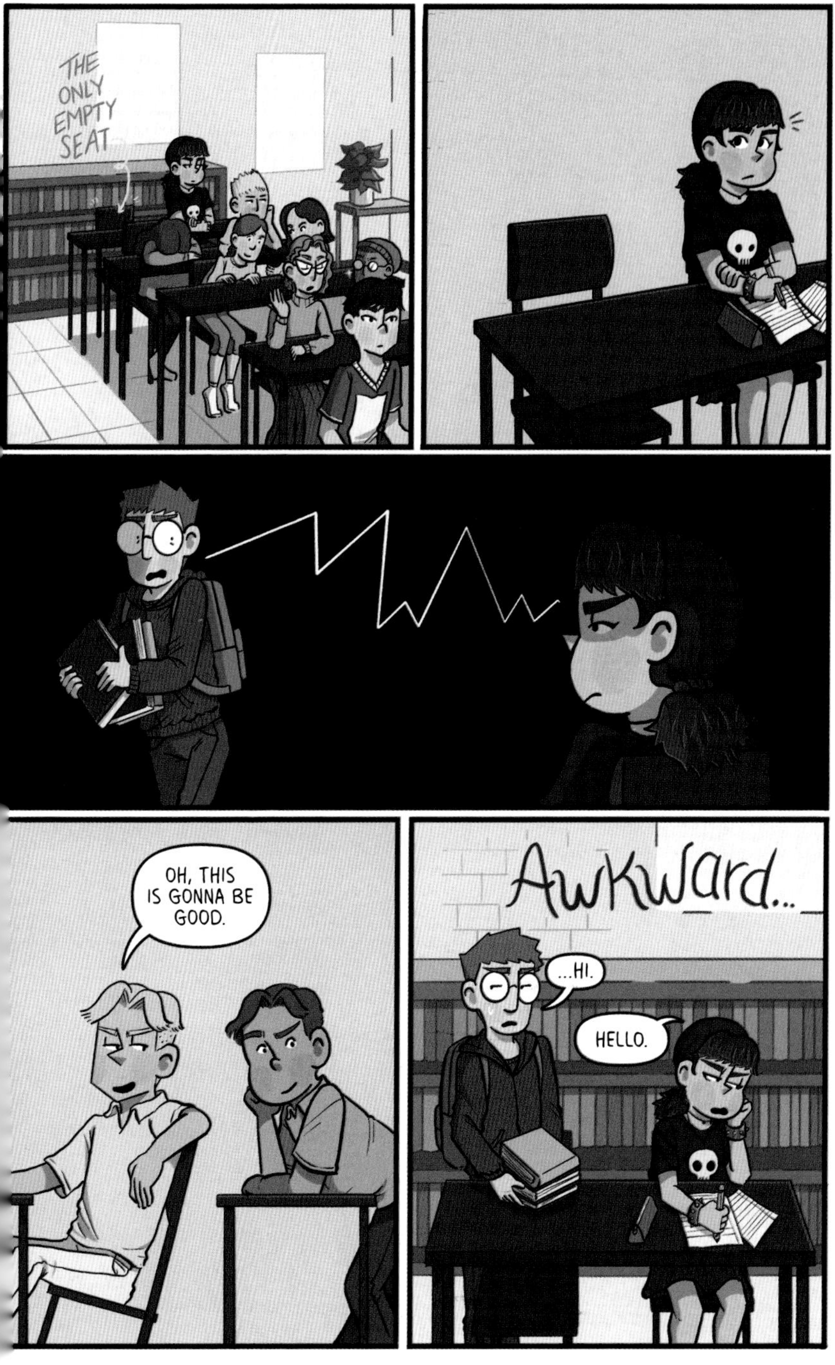
THE ONLY EMPTY SEAT
OH, THIS IS GONNA BE GOOD.
Awkward...
...HI.
HELLO.

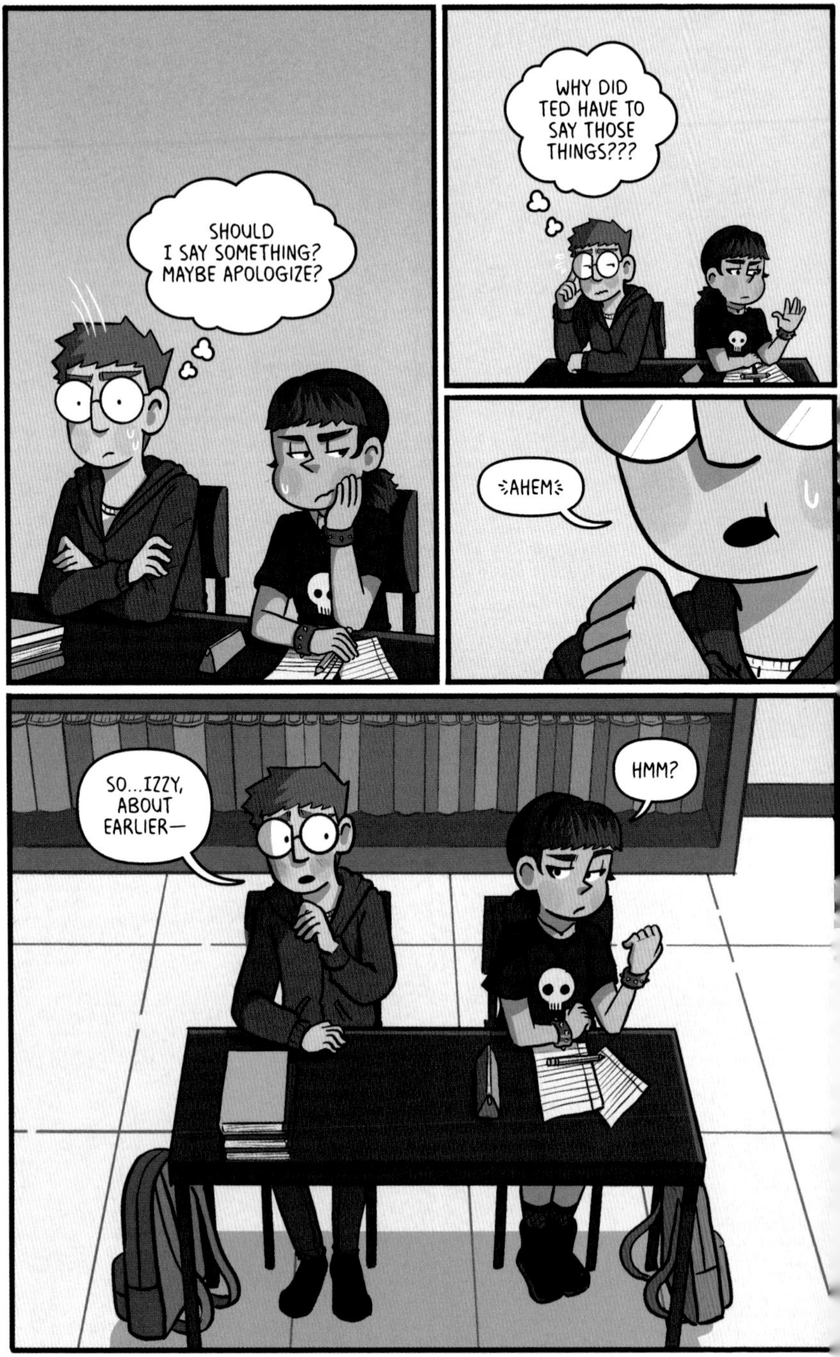
SHOULD I SAY SOMETHING? MAYBE APOLOGIZE?
WHY DID TED HAVE TO SAY THOSE THINGS???
AHEM
SO...IZZY, ABOUT EARLIER—
HMM?

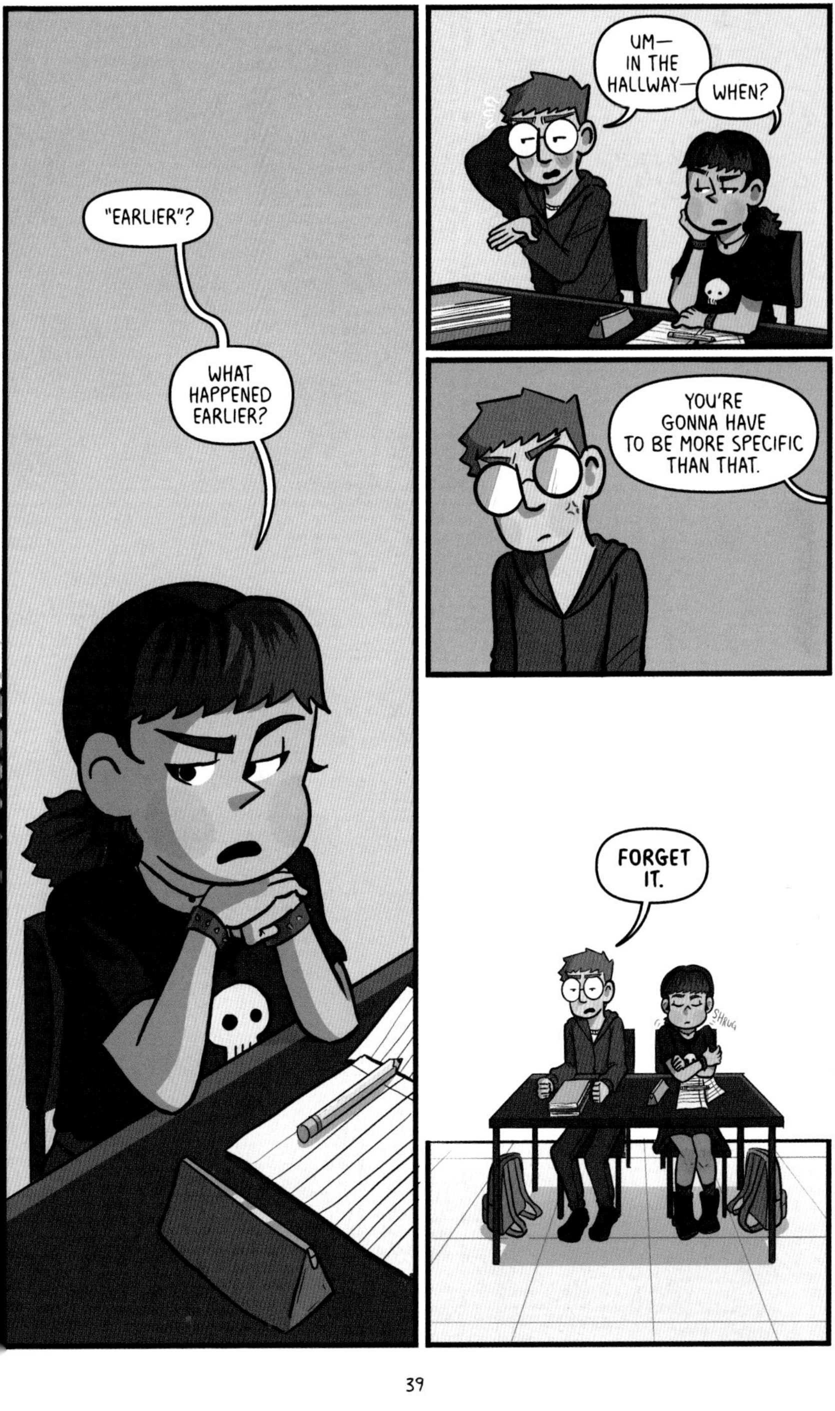
"EARLIER"?
WHAT HAPPENED EARLIER?
UM— IN THE HALLWAY—
WHEN?
YOU'RE GONNA HAVE TO BE MORE SPECIFIC THAN THAT.
FORGET IT.
SHRUG

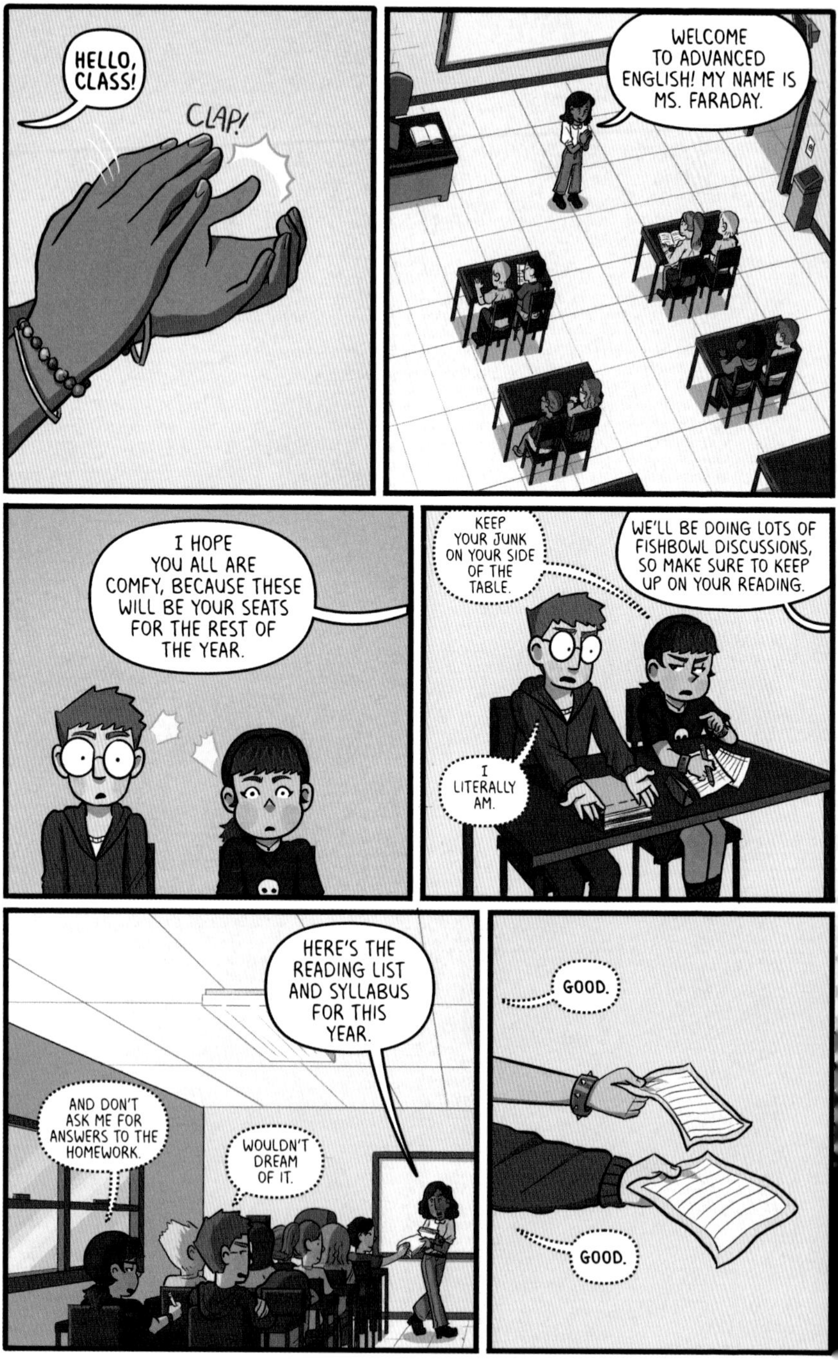
HELLO, CLASS!
CLAP!
WELCOME TO ADVANCED ENGLISH! MY NAME IS MS. FARADAY.
I HOPE YOU ALL ARE COMFY, BECAUSE THESE WILL BE YOUR SEATS FOR THE REST OF THE YEAR.
WE'LL BE DOING LOTS OF FISHBOWL DISCUSSIONS, SO MAKE SURE TO KEEP UP ON YOUR READING.
KEEP YOUR JUNK ON YOUR SIDE OF THE TABLE.
I LITERALLY AM.
HERE'S THE READING LIST AND SYLLABUS FOR THIS YEAR.
AND DON'T ASK ME FOR ANSWERS TO THE HOMEWORK.
WOULDN'T DREAM OF IT.
GOOD.
GOOD.

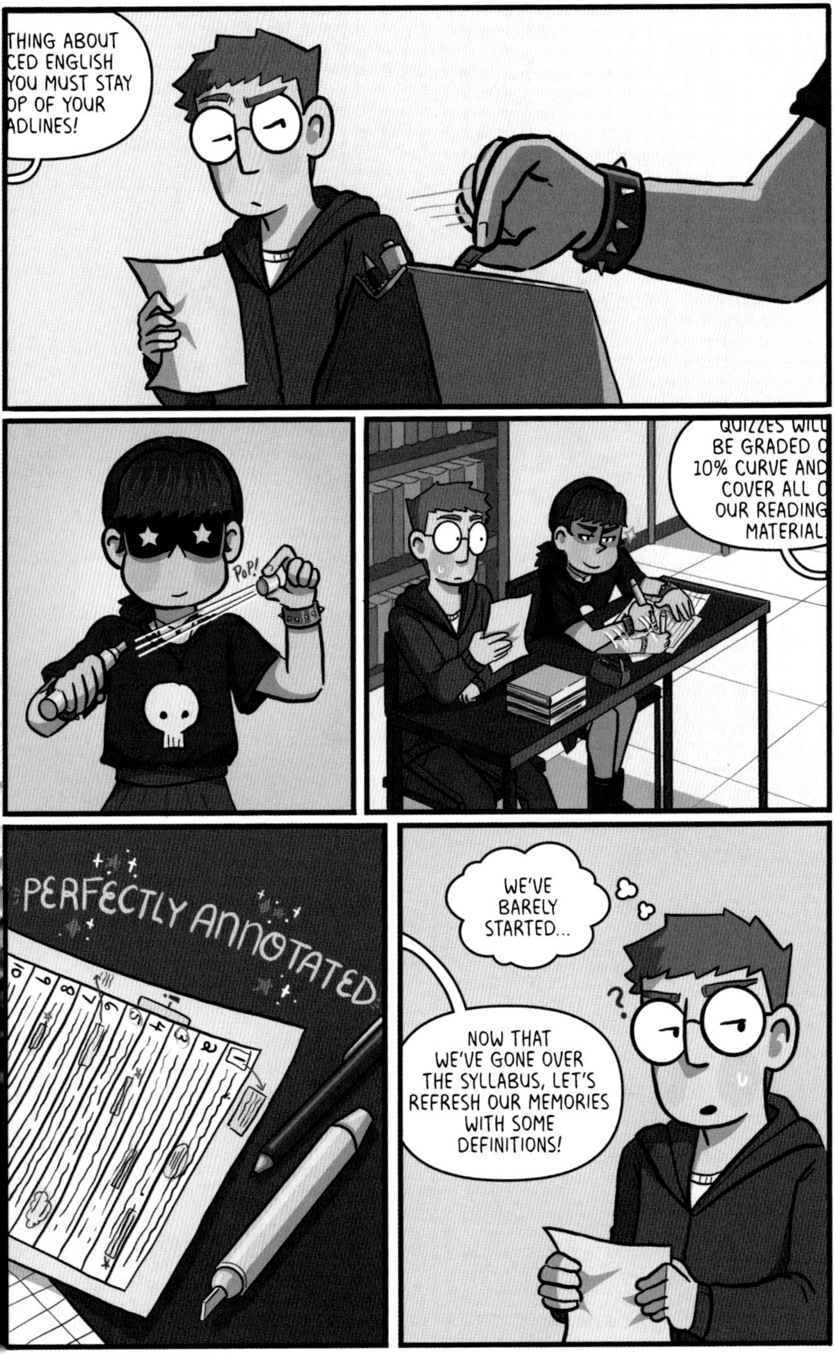
THING ABOUT
CED ENGLISH
YOU MUST STAY
OP OF YOUR
ADLINES!
POP!
QUIZZES WILL
BE GRADED O
10% CURVE AND
COVER ALL O
OUR READING
MATERIAL!
PERFECTLY ANNOTATED
WE'VE BARELY STARTED...
NOW THAT WE'VE GONE OVER THE SYLLABUS, LET'S REFRESH OUR MEMORIES WITH SOME DEFINITIONS!

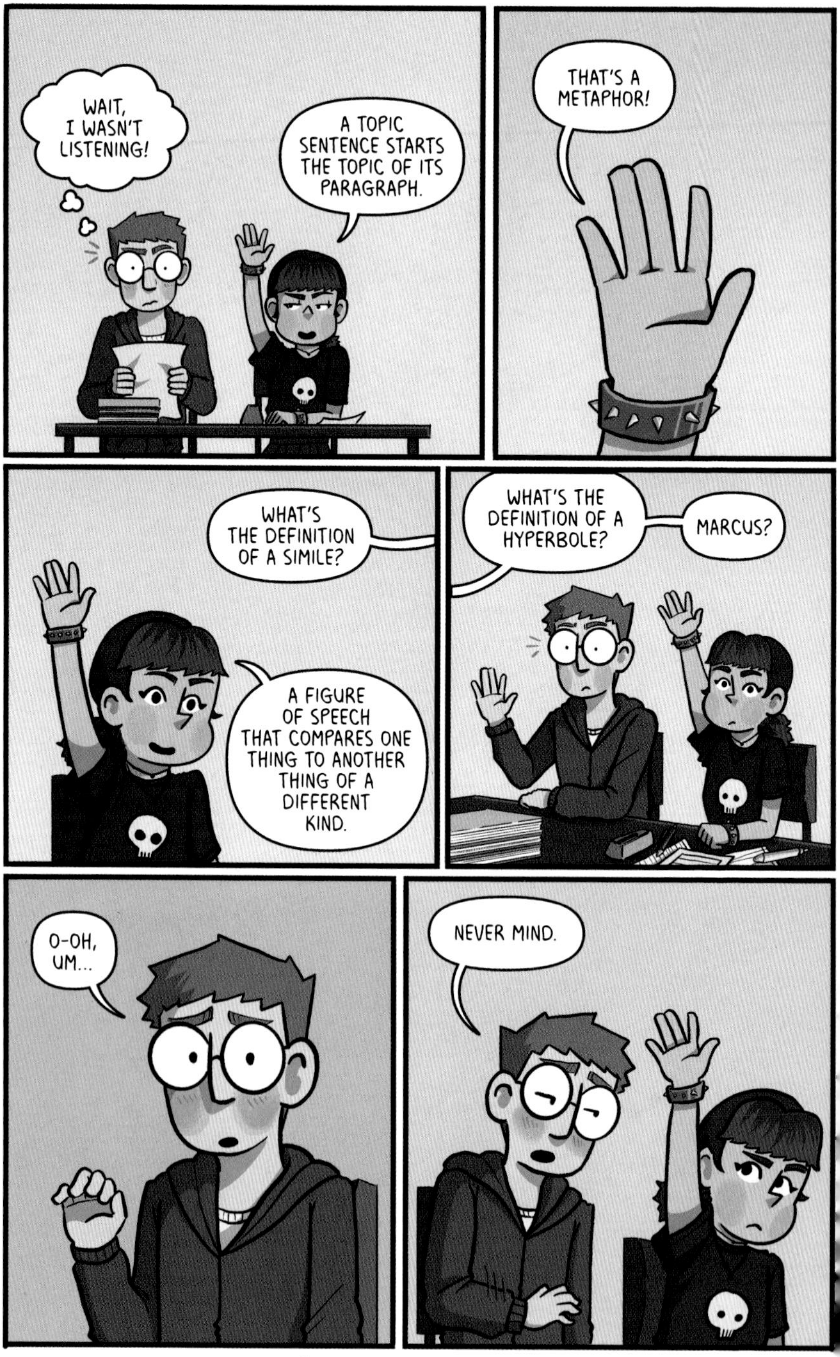
WAIT, I WASN'T LISTENING!
A TOPIC SENTENCE STARTS THE TOPIC OF ITS PARAGRAPH.
THAT'S A METAPHOR!
WHAT'S THE DEFINITION OF A SIMILE?
A FIGURE OF SPEECH THAT COMPARES ONE THING TO ANOTHER THING OF A DIFFERENT KIND.
WHAT'S THE DEFINITION OF A HYPERBOLE?
MARCUS?
O-OH, UM...
NEVER MIND.

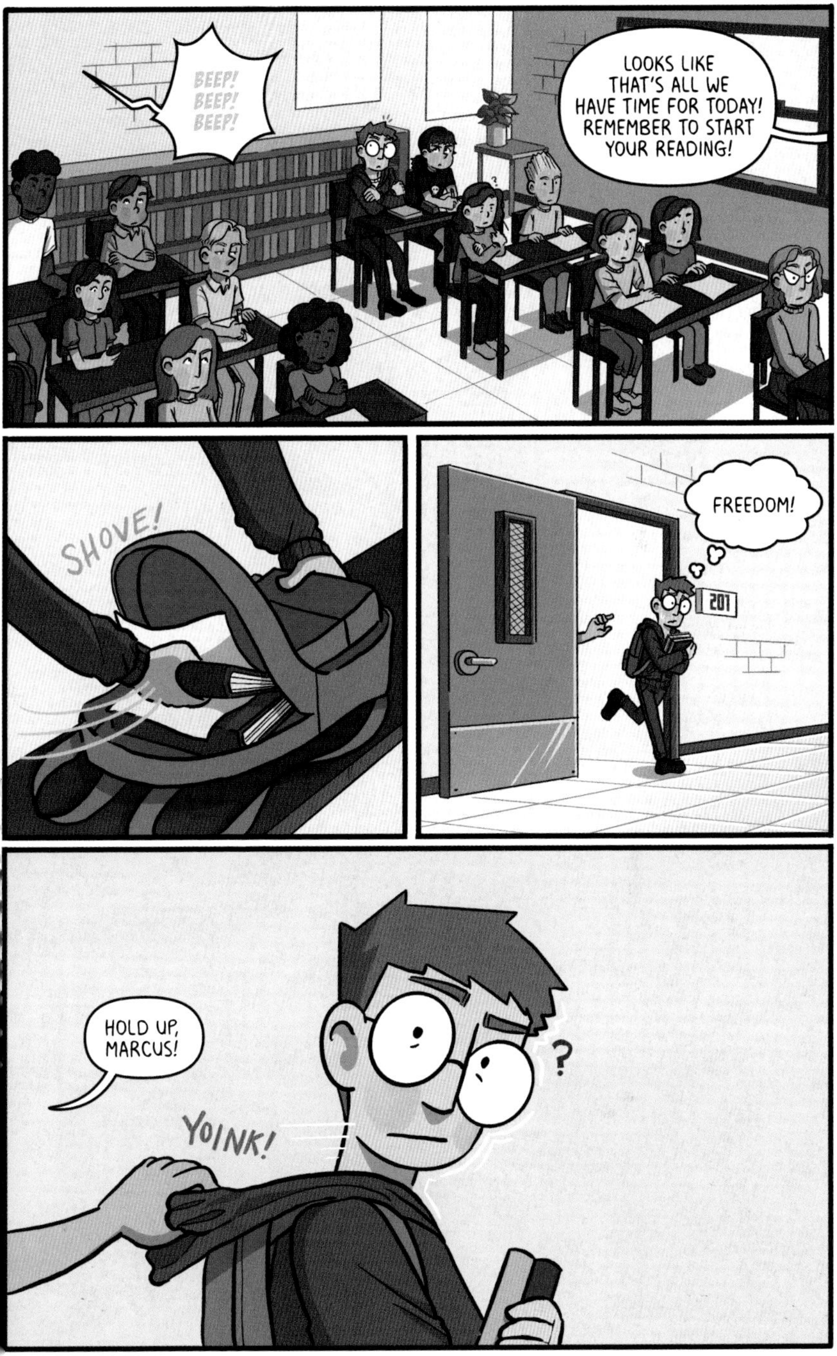
BEEP! BEEP! BEEP!
LOOKS LIKE THAT'S ALL WE HAVE TIME FOR TODAY! REMEMBER TO START YOUR READING!
SHOVE!
FREEDOM!
201
HOLD UP, MARCUS!
YOINK!

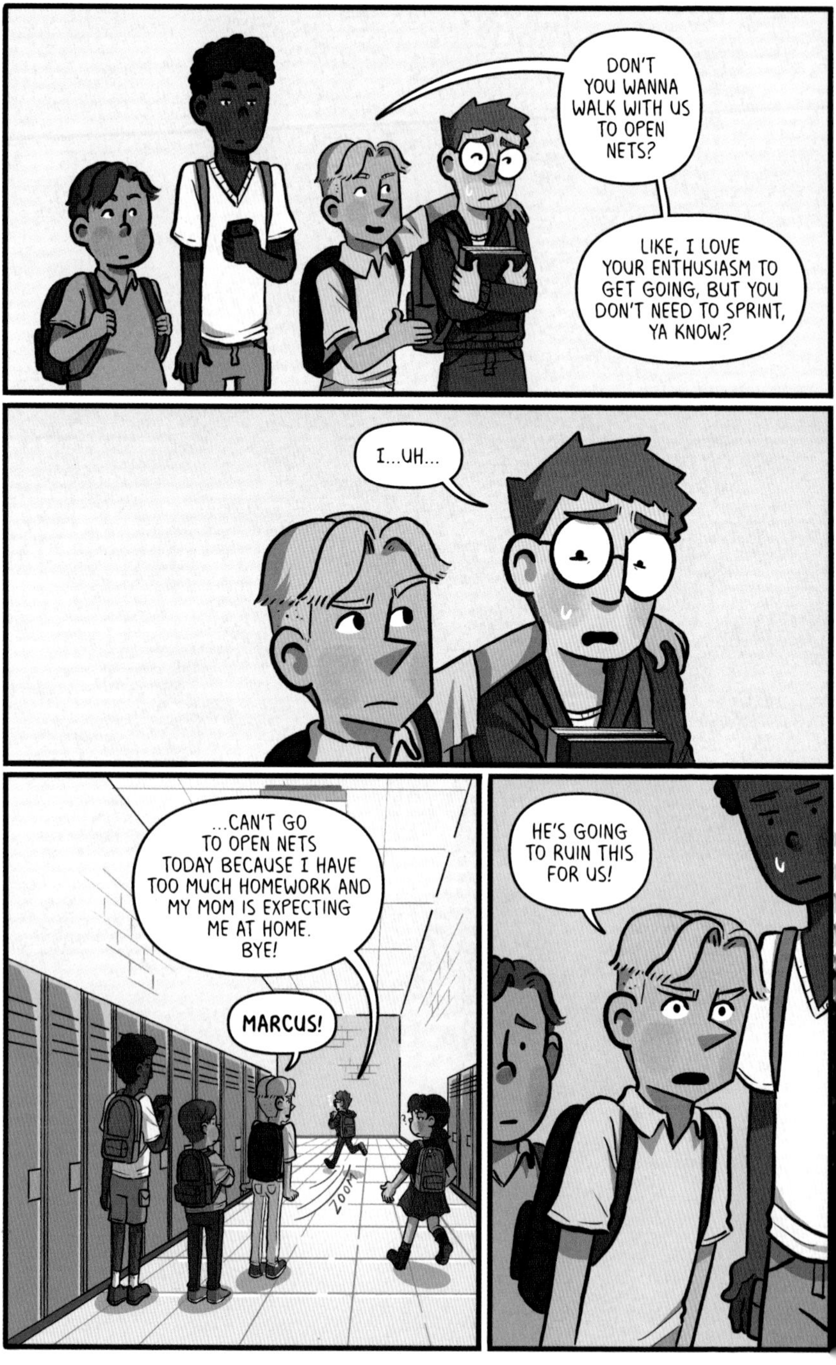
DON'T YOU WANNA WALK WITH US TO OPEN NETS?
LIKE, I LOVE YOUR ENTHUSIASM TO GET GOING, BUT YOU DON'T NEED TO SPRINT, YA KNOW?
I...UH...
...CAN'T GO TO OPEN NETS TODAY BECAUSE I HAVE TOO MUCH HOMEWORK AND MY MOM IS EXPECTING ME AT HOME. BYE!
MARCUS!
ZOOM
HE'S GOING TO RUIN THIS FOR US!

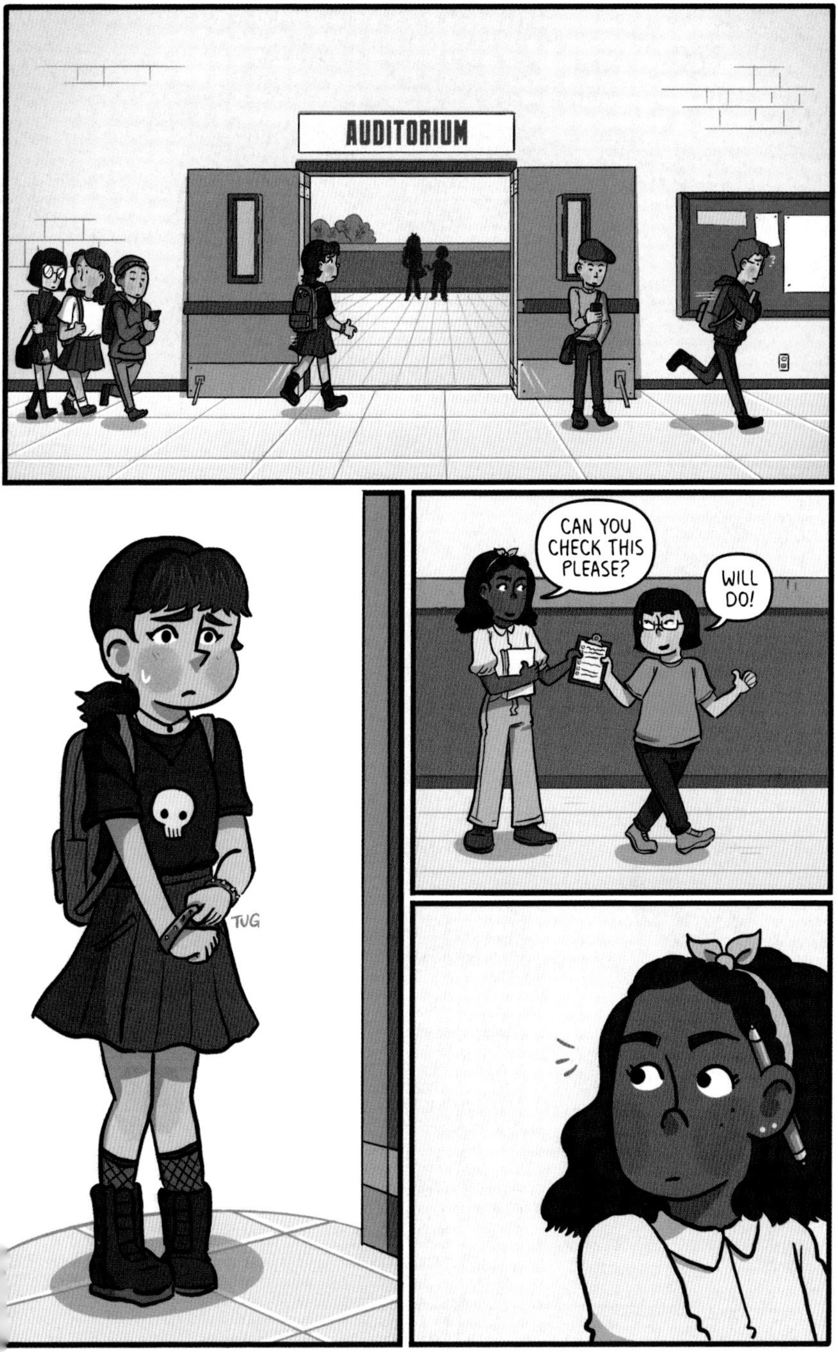
AUDITORIUM
TUG
CAN YOU CHECK THIS PLEASE?
WILL DO!

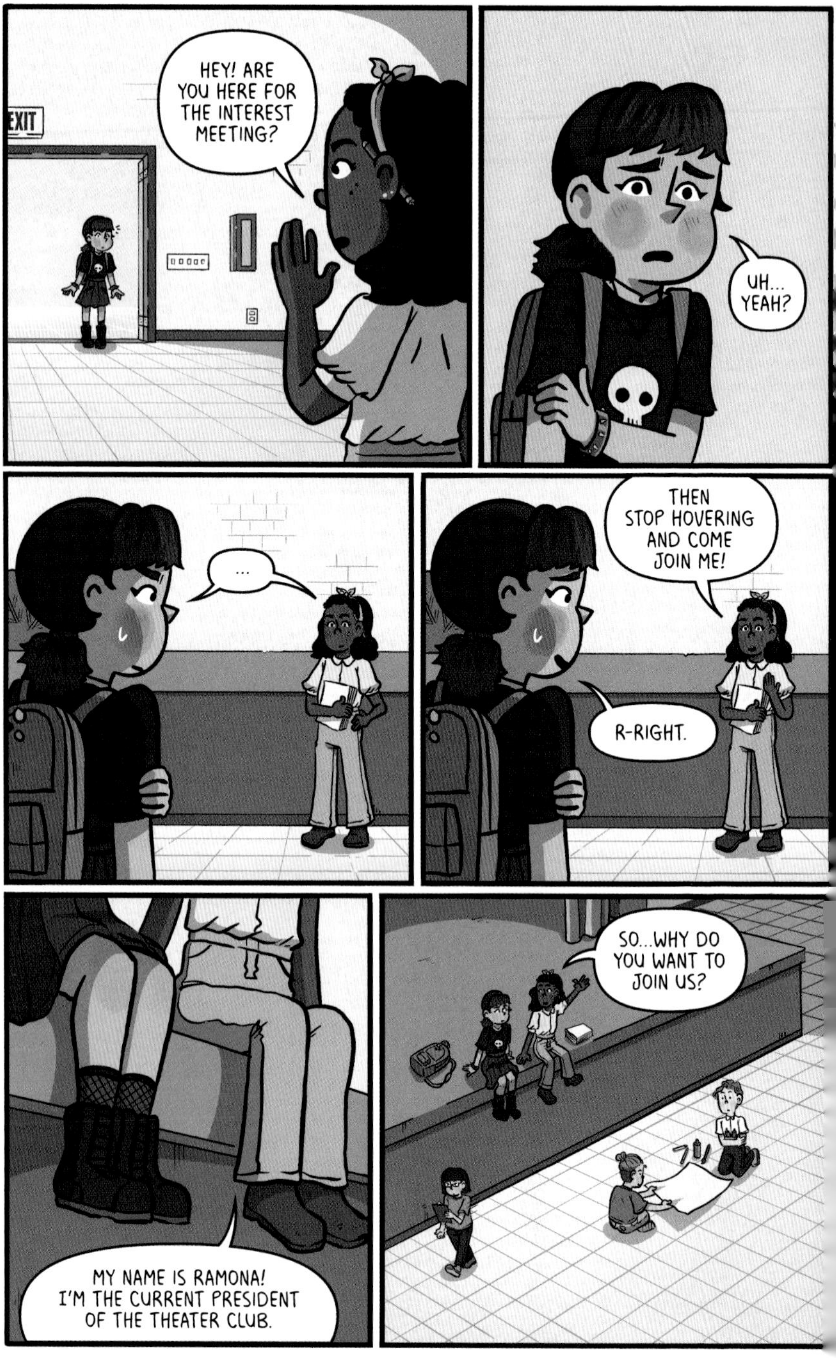
EXIT
HEY! ARE YOU HERE FOR THE INTEREST MEETING?
UH... YEAH?
...
THEN STOP HOVERING AND COME JOIN ME!
R-RIGHT.
MY NAME IS RAMONA! I'M THE CURRENT PRESIDENT OF THE THEATER CLUB.
SO...WHY DO YOU WANT TO JOIN US?

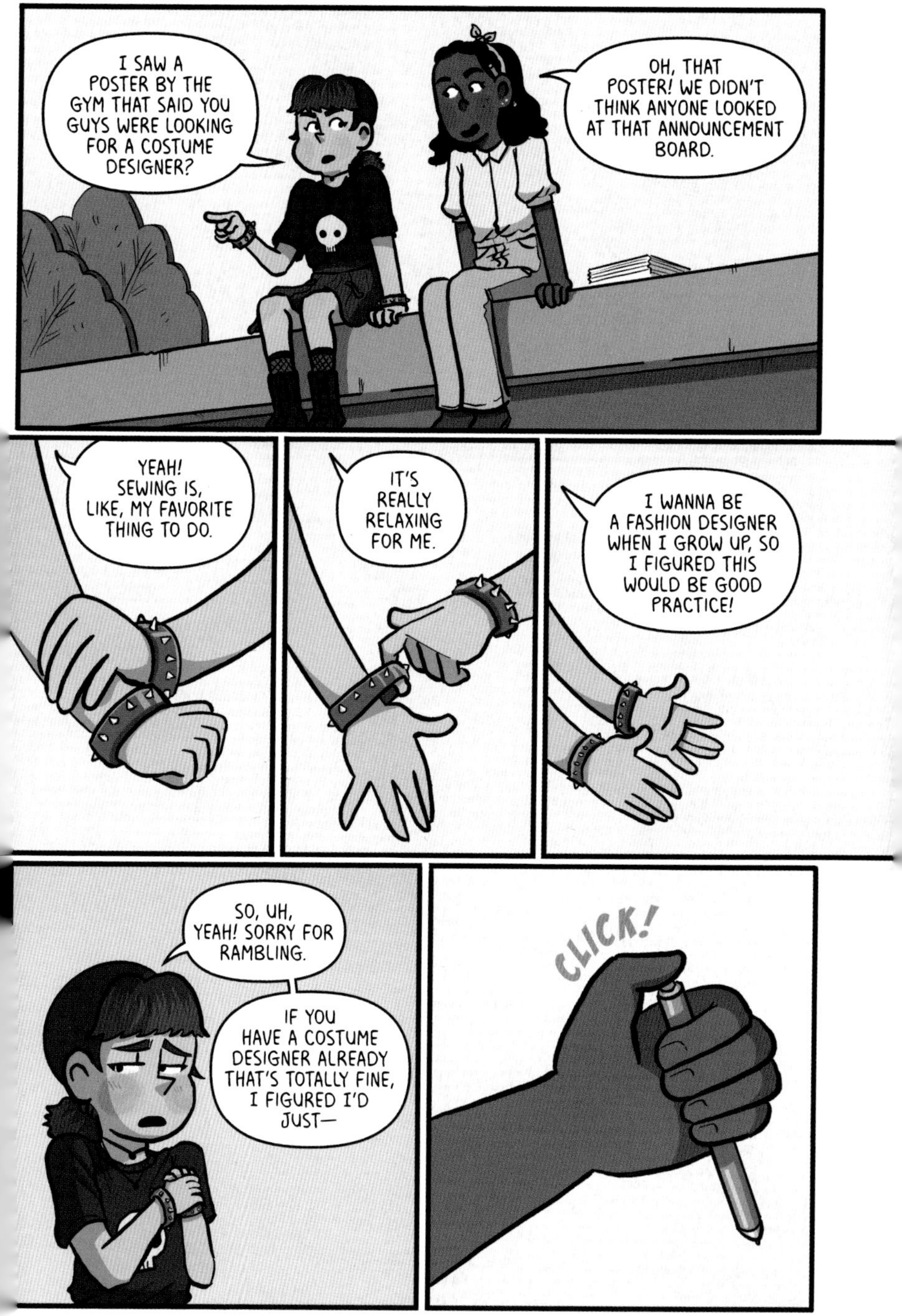
I SAW A POSTER BY THE GYM THAT SAID YOU GUYS WERE LOOKING FOR A COSTUME DESIGNER?
OH, THAT POSTER! WE DIDN'T THINK ANYONE LOOKED AT THAT ANNOUNCEMENT BOARD.
YEAH! SEWING IS, LIKE, MY FAVORITE THING TO DO.
IT'S REALLY RELAXING FOR ME.
I WANNA BE A FASHION DESIGNER WHEN I GROW UP, SO I FIGURED THIS WOULD BE GOOD PRACTICE!
SO, UH, YEAH! SORRY FOR RAMBLING.
IF YOU HAVE A COSTUME DESIGNER ALREADY THAT'S TOTALLY FINE, I FIGURED I'D JUST—
CLICK!

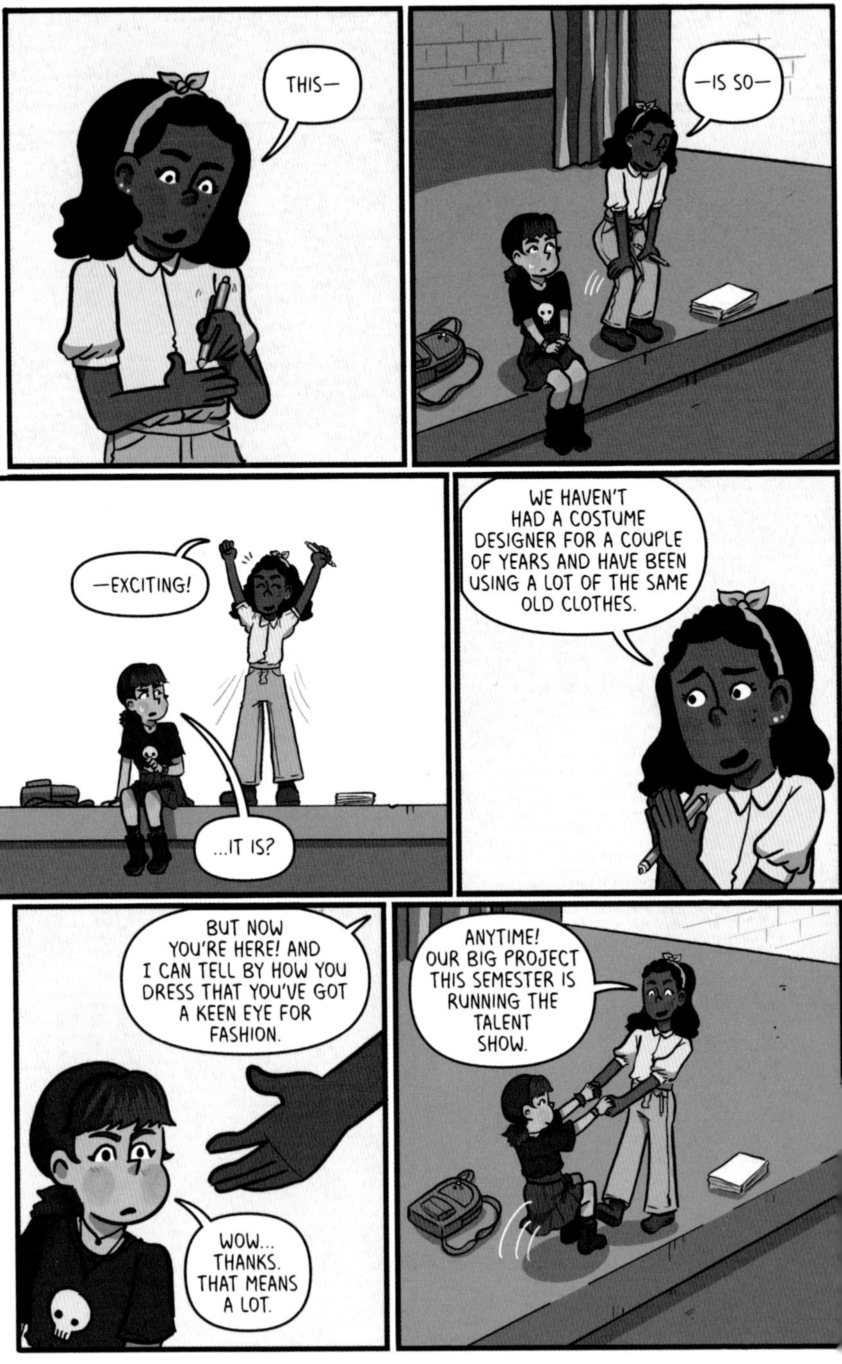
THIS—
—IS SO—
—EXCITING!
...IT IS?
WE HAVEN'T HAD A COSTUME DESIGNER FOR A COUPLE OF YEARS AND HAVE BEEN USING A LOT OF THE SAME OLD CLOTHES.
BUT NOW YOU'RE HERE! AND I CAN TELL BY HOW YOU DRESS THAT YOU'VE GOT A KEEN EYE FOR FASHION.
WOW... THANKS. THAT MEANS A LOT.
ANYTIME! OUR BIG PROJECT THIS SEMESTER IS RUNNING THE TALENT SHOW.

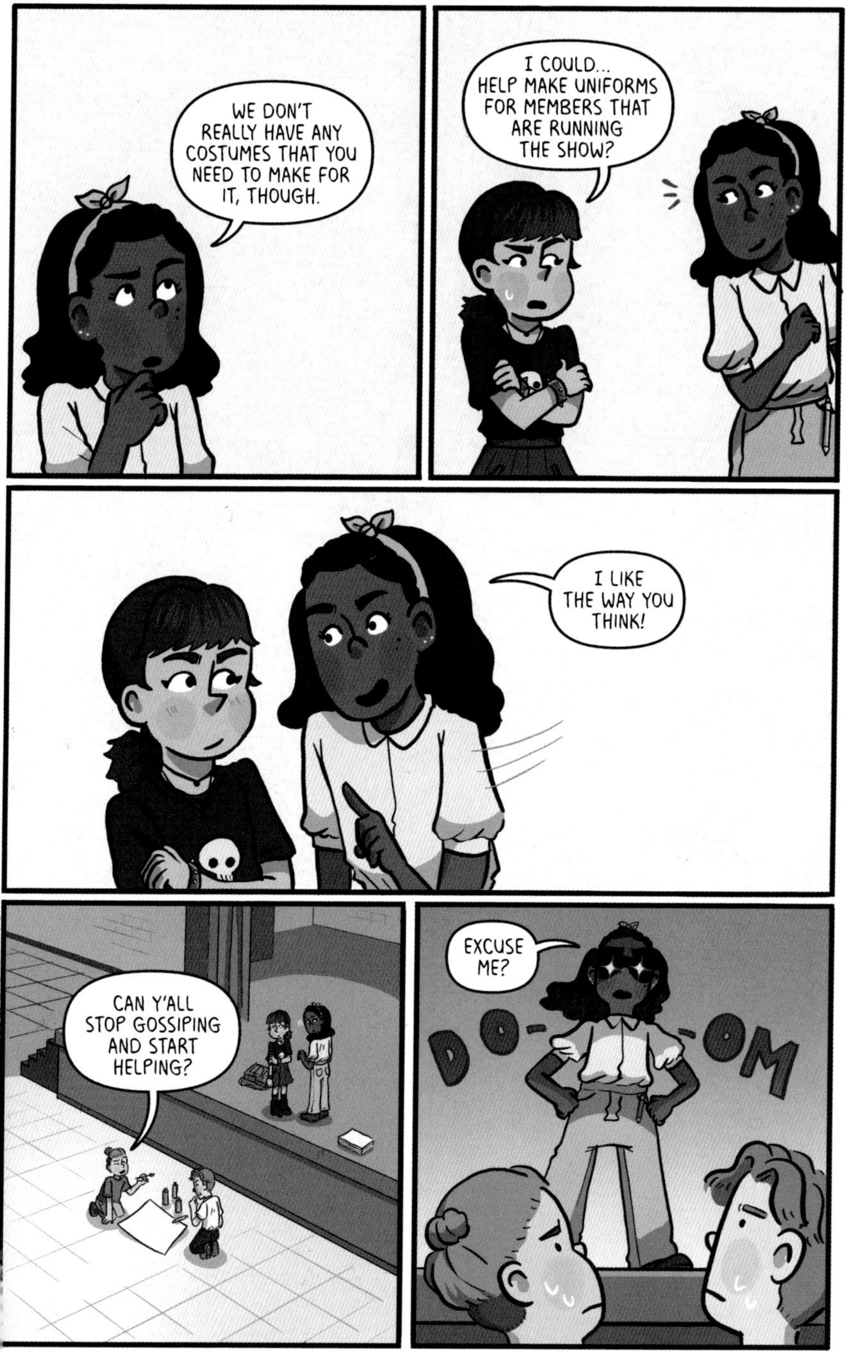
WE DON'T REALLY HAVE ANY COSTUMES THAT YOU NEED TO MAKE FOR IT, THOUGH.
I COULD... HELP MAKE UNIFORMS FOR MEMBERS THAT ARE RUNNING THE SHOW?
I LIKE THE WAY YOU THINK!
CAN Y'ALL STOP GOSSIPING AND START HELPING?
EXCUSE ME?
DO-OM

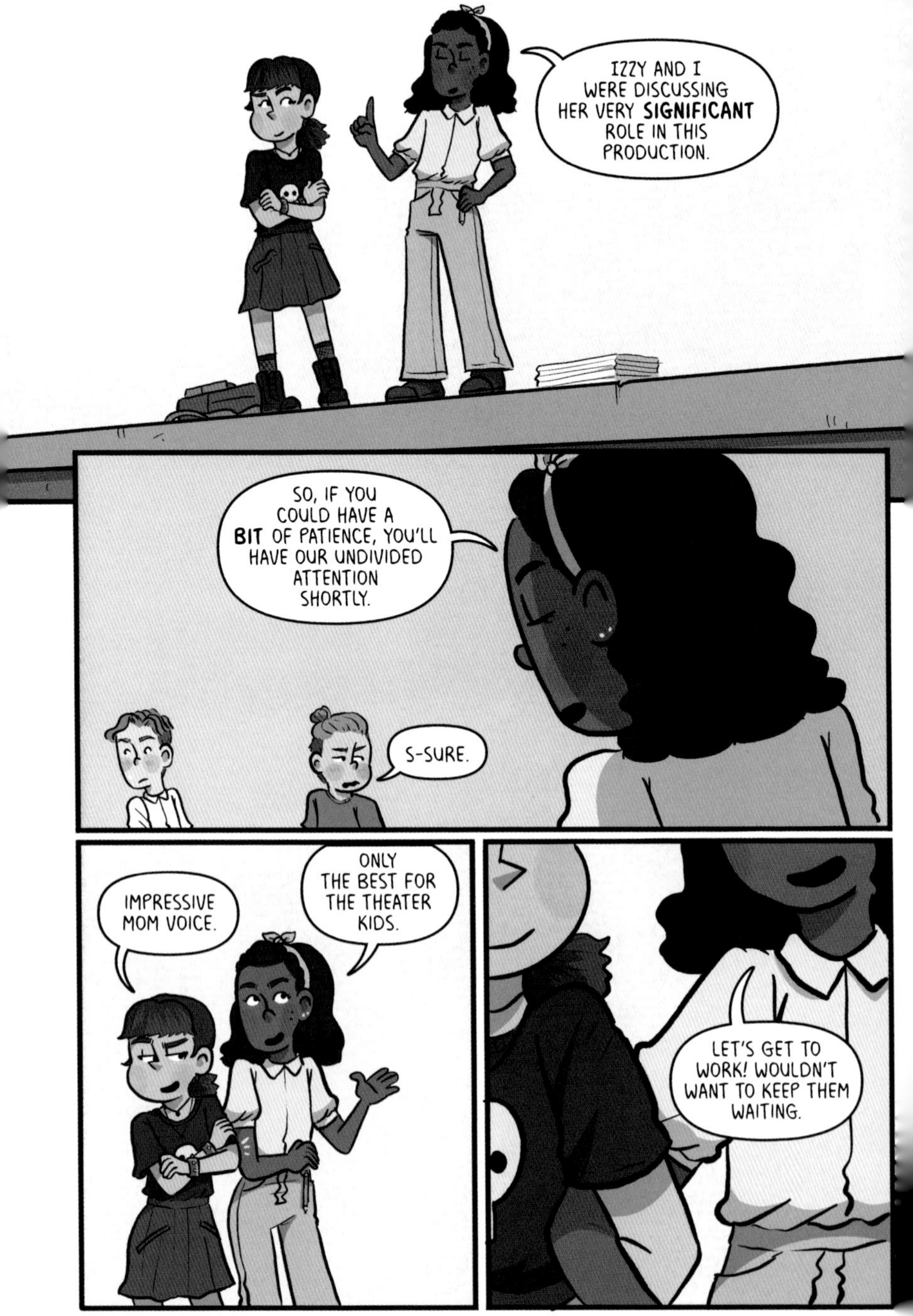
IZZY AND I WERE DISCUSSING HER VERY **SIGNIFICANT** ROLE IN THIS PRODUCTION.
SO, IF YOU COULD HAVE A **BIT** OF PATIENCE, YOU'LL HAVE OUR UNDIVIDED ATTENTION SHORTLY.
S-SURE.
IMPRESSIVE MOM VOICE.
ONLY THE BEST FOR THE THEATER KIDS.
LET'S GET TO WORK! WOULDN'T WANT TO KEEP THEM WAITING.

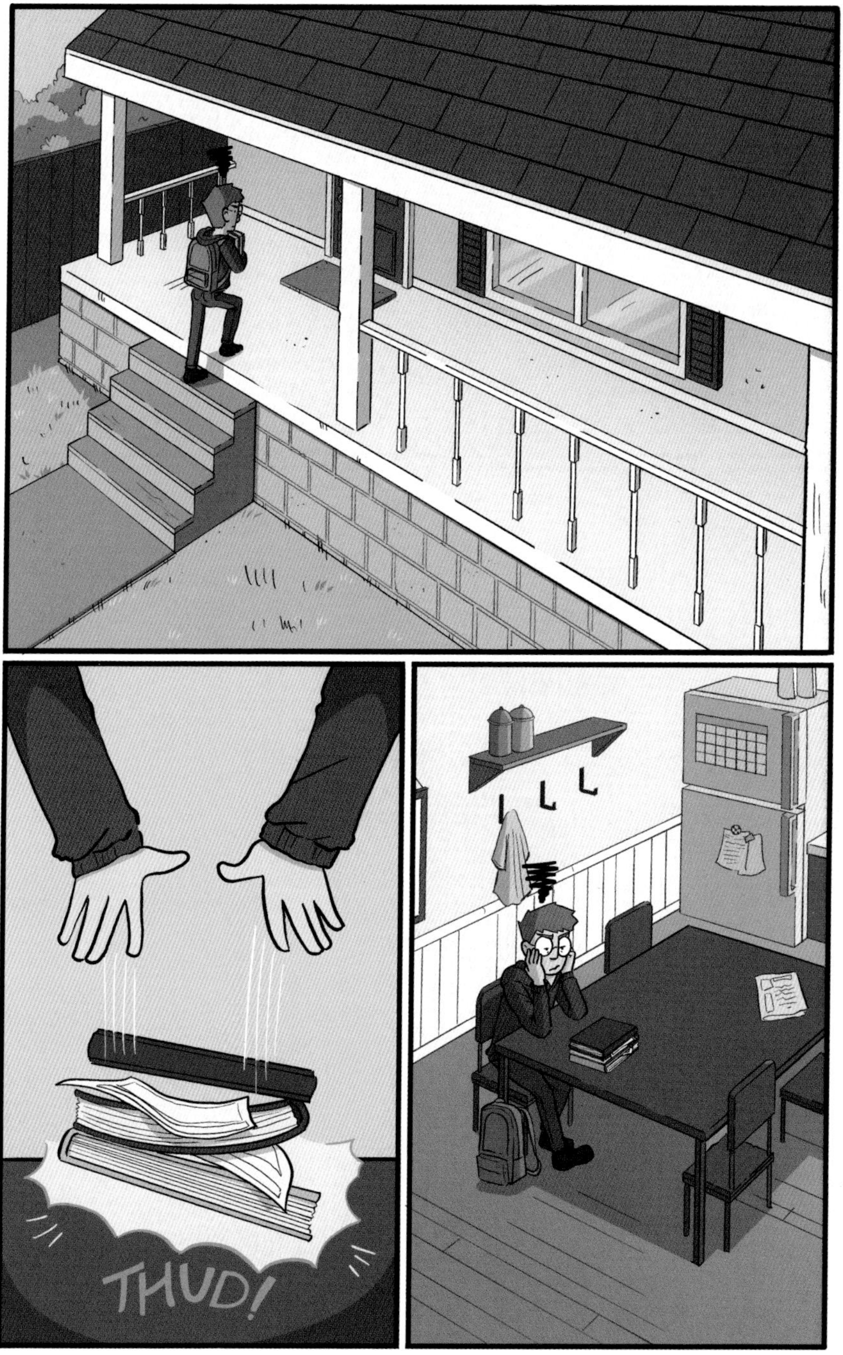
THUD!

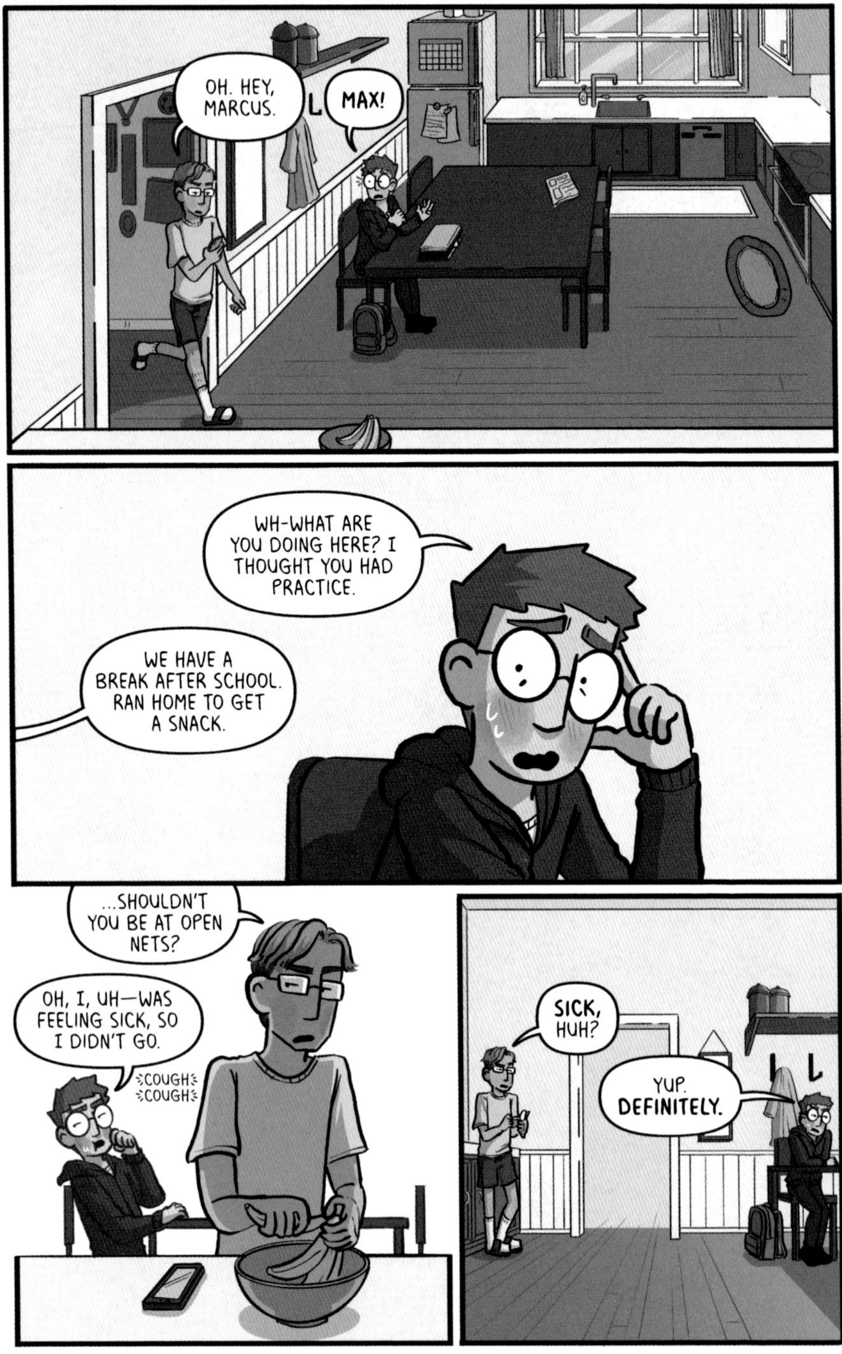
OH. HEY, MARCUS.
MAX!
WH-WHAT ARE YOU DOING HERE? I THOUGHT YOU HAD PRACTICE.
WE HAVE A BREAK AFTER SCHOOL. RAN HOME TO GET A SNACK.
...SHOULDN'T YOU BE AT OPEN NETS?
OH, I, UH—WAS FEELING SICK, SO I DIDN'T GO.
COUGH COUGH
SICK, HUH?
YUP. **DEFINITELY.**

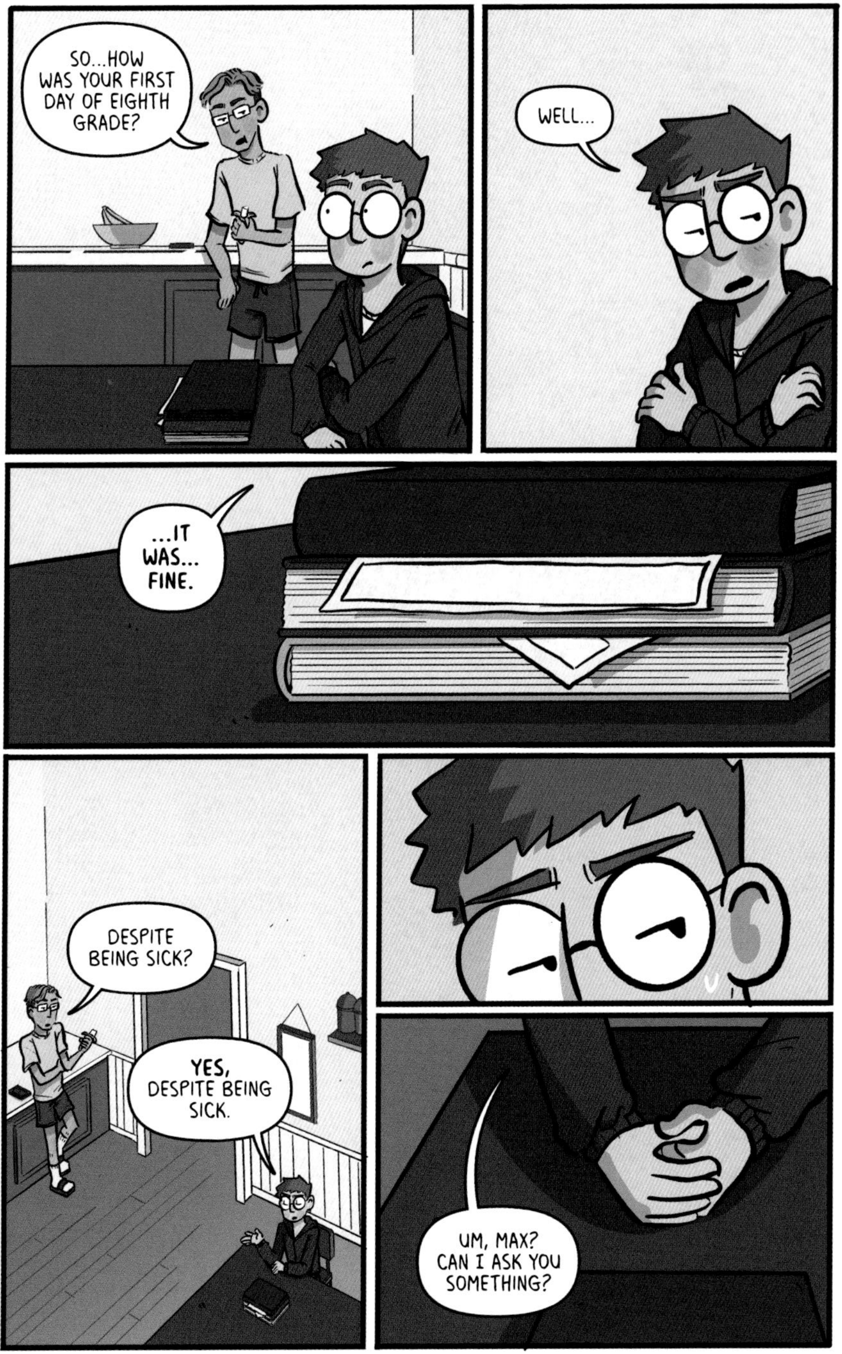
SO...HOW WAS YOUR FIRST DAY OF EIGHTH GRADE?
WELL...
...IT WAS... FINE.
DESPITE BEING SICK?
YES, DESPITE BEING SICK.
UM, MAX? CAN I ASK YOU SOMETHING?

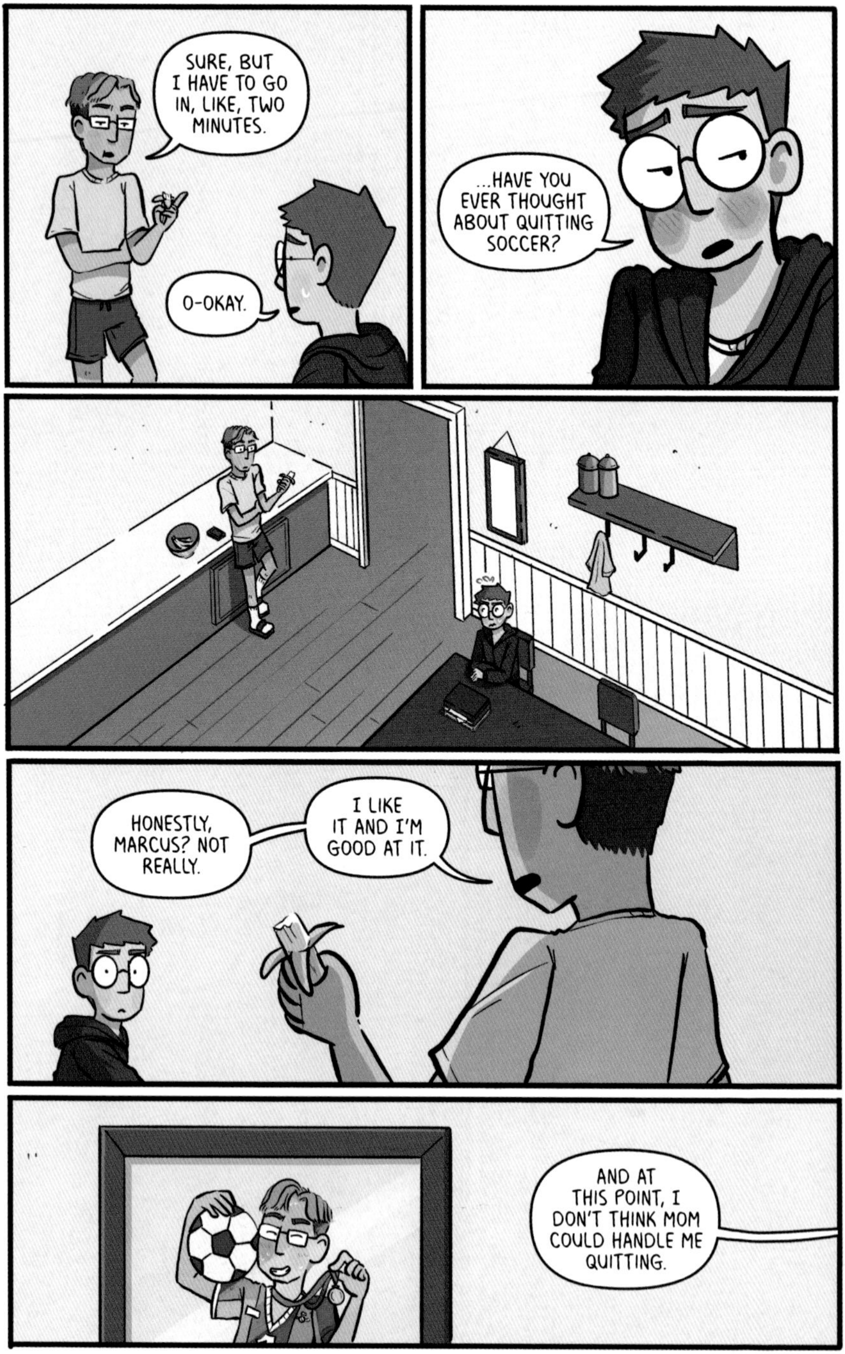
SURE, BUT I HAVE TO GO IN, LIKE, TWO MINUTES.
O-OKAY.
...HAVE YOU EVER THOUGHT ABOUT QUITTING SOCCER?
HONESTLY, MARCUS? NOT REALLY.
I LIKE IT AND I'M GOOD AT IT.
AND AT THIS POINT, I DON'T THINK MOM COULD HANDLE ME QUITTING.

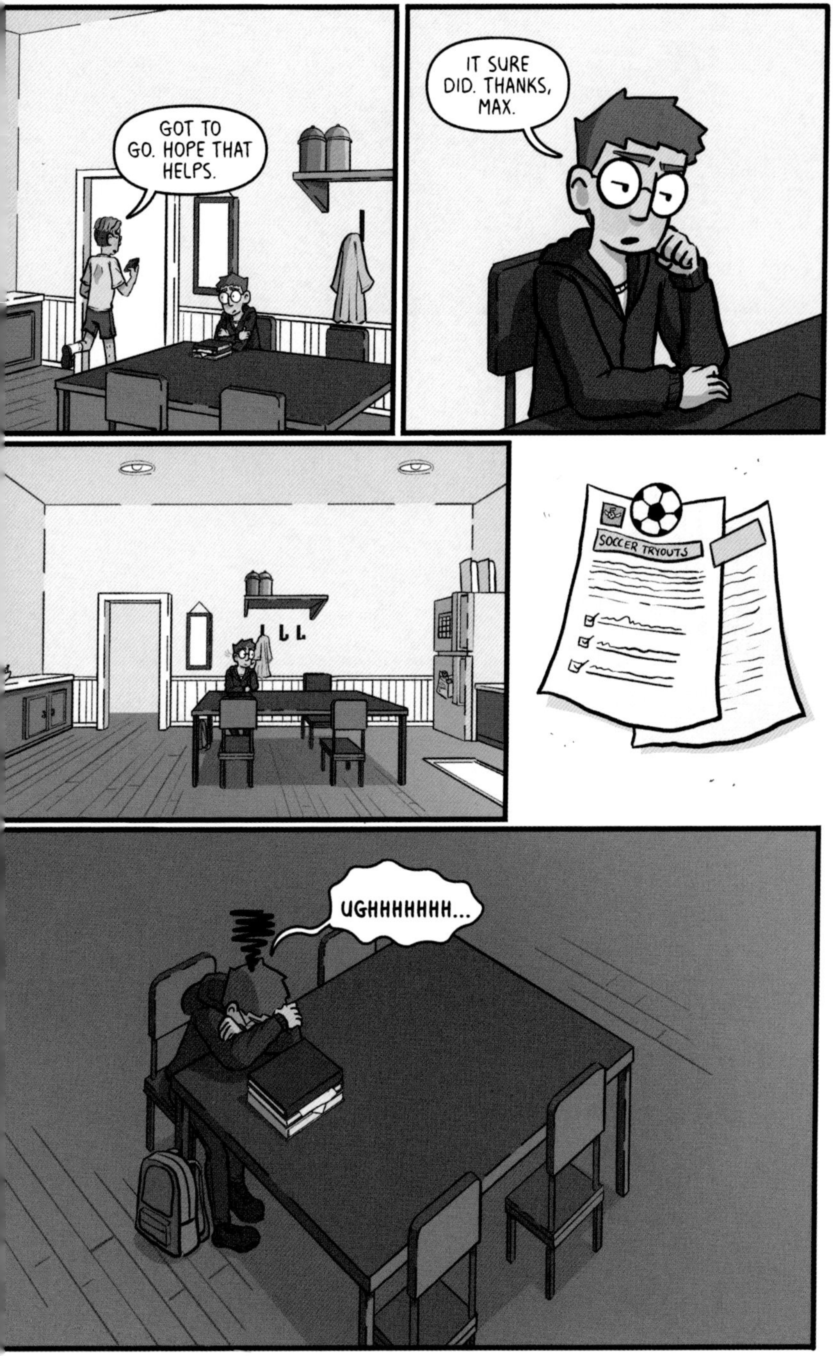
GOT TO GO. HOPE THAT HELPS.
IT SURE DID. THANKS, MAX.
SOCCER TRYOUTS
UGHHHHHHH...

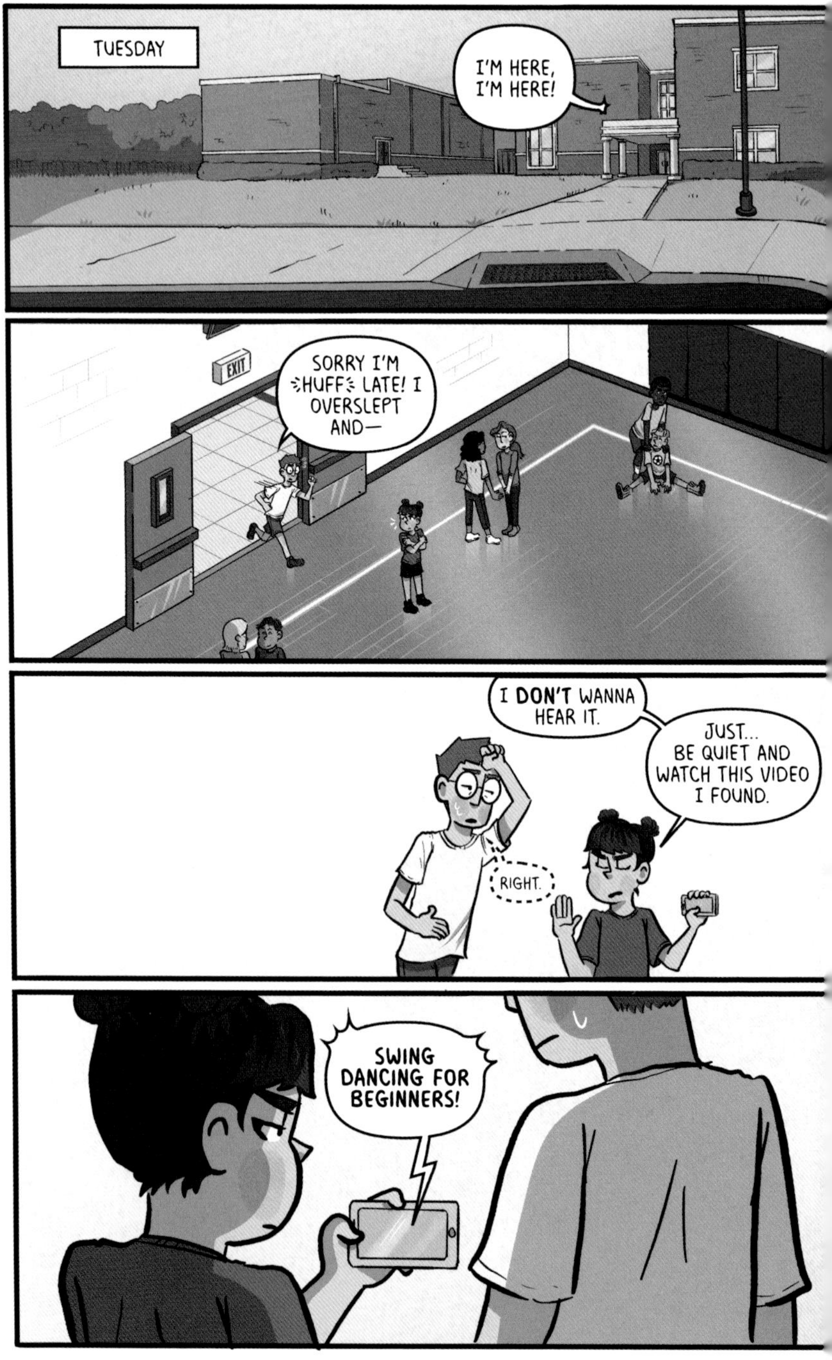
TUESDAY
I'M HERE, I'M HERE!
SORRY I'M HUFF LATE! I OVERSLEPT AND—
EXIT
I DON'T WANNA HEAR IT.
JUST... BE QUIET AND WATCH THIS VIDEO I FOUND.
RIGHT.
SWING DANCING FOR BEGINNERS!

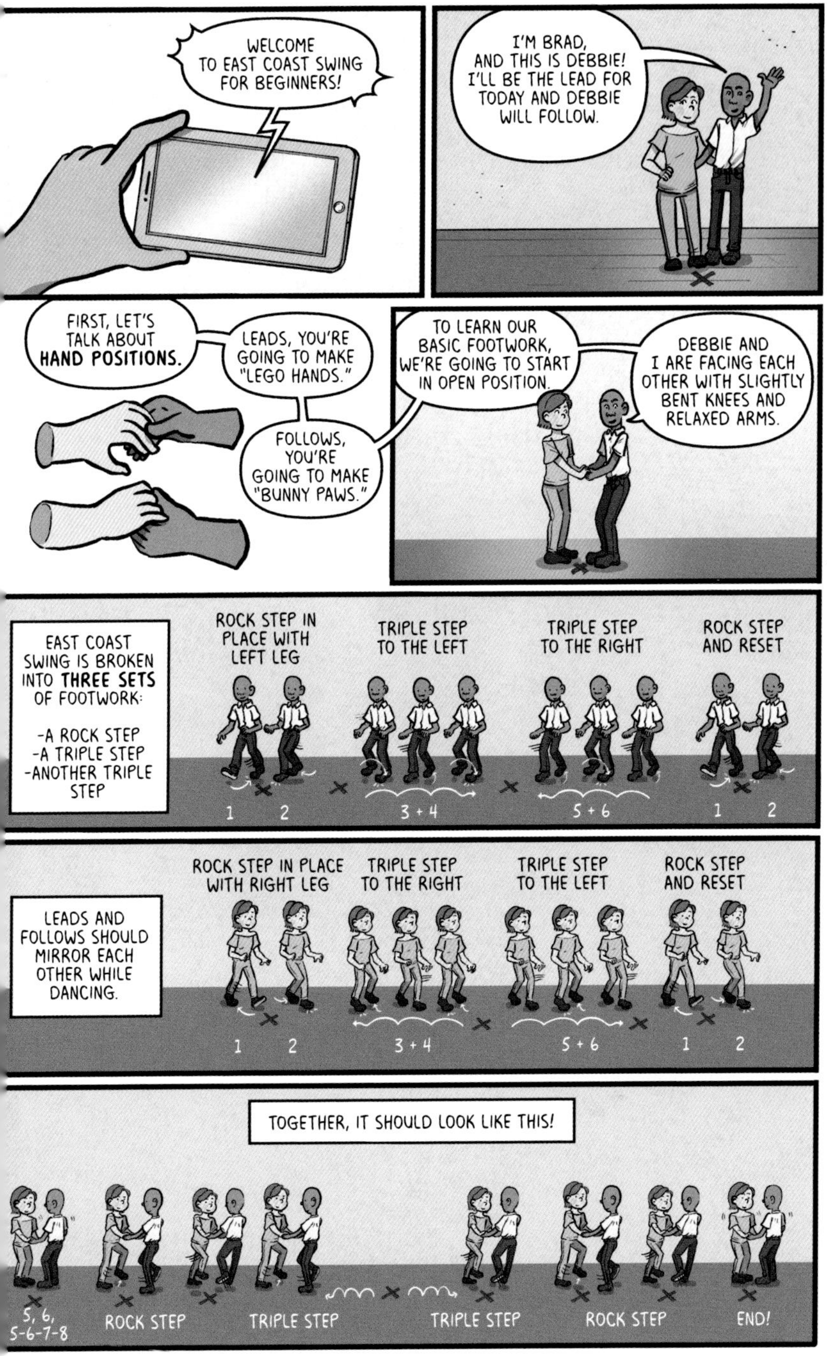
WELCOME TO EAST COAST SWING FOR BEGINNERS!
I'M BRAD, AND THIS IS DEBBIE! I'LL BE THE LEAD FOR TODAY AND DEBBIE WILL FOLLOW.
FIRST, LET'S TALK ABOUT **HAND POSITIONS.**
LEADS, YOU'RE GOING TO MAKE "LEGO HANDS."
FOLLOWS, YOU'RE GOING TO MAKE "BUNNY PAWS."
TO LEARN OUR BASIC FOOTWORK, WE'RE GOING TO START IN OPEN POSITION.
DEBBIE AND I ARE FACING EACH OTHER WITH SLIGHTLY BENT KNEES AND RELAXED ARMS.
EAST COAST SWING IS BROKEN INTO **THREE SETS** OF FOOTWORK:
-A ROCK STEP
-A TRIPLE STEP
-ANOTHER TRIPLE STEP
ROCK STEP IN PLACE WITH LEFT LEG
TRIPLE STEP TO THE LEFT
TRIPLE STEP TO THE RIGHT
ROCK STEP AND RESET
1
2
3 + 4
5 + 6
1
2
LEADS AND FOLLOWS SHOULD MIRROR EACH OTHER WHILE DANCING.
ROCK STEP IN PLACE WITH RIGHT LEG
TRIPLE STEP TO THE RIGHT
TRIPLE STEP TO THE LEFT
ROCK STEP AND RESET
1
2
3 + 4
5 + 6
1
2
TOGETHER, IT SHOULD LOOK LIKE THIS!
5, 6, 5-6-7-8
ROCK STEP
TRIPLE STEP
TRIPLE STEP
ROCK STEP
END!

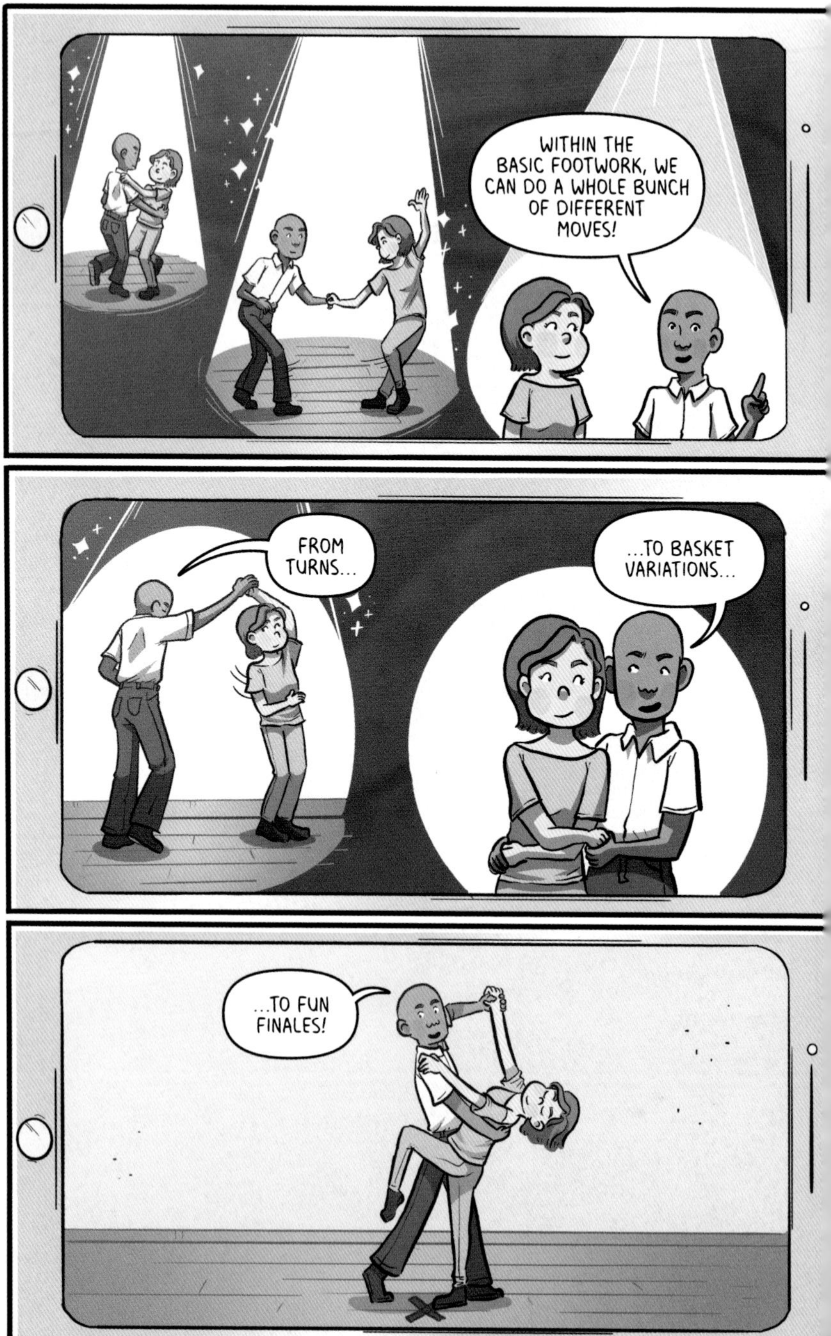
WITHIN THE BASIC FOOTWORK, WE CAN DO A WHOLE BUNCH OF DIFFERENT MOVES!
FROM TURNS...
...TO BASKET VARIATIONS...
...TO FUN FINALES!

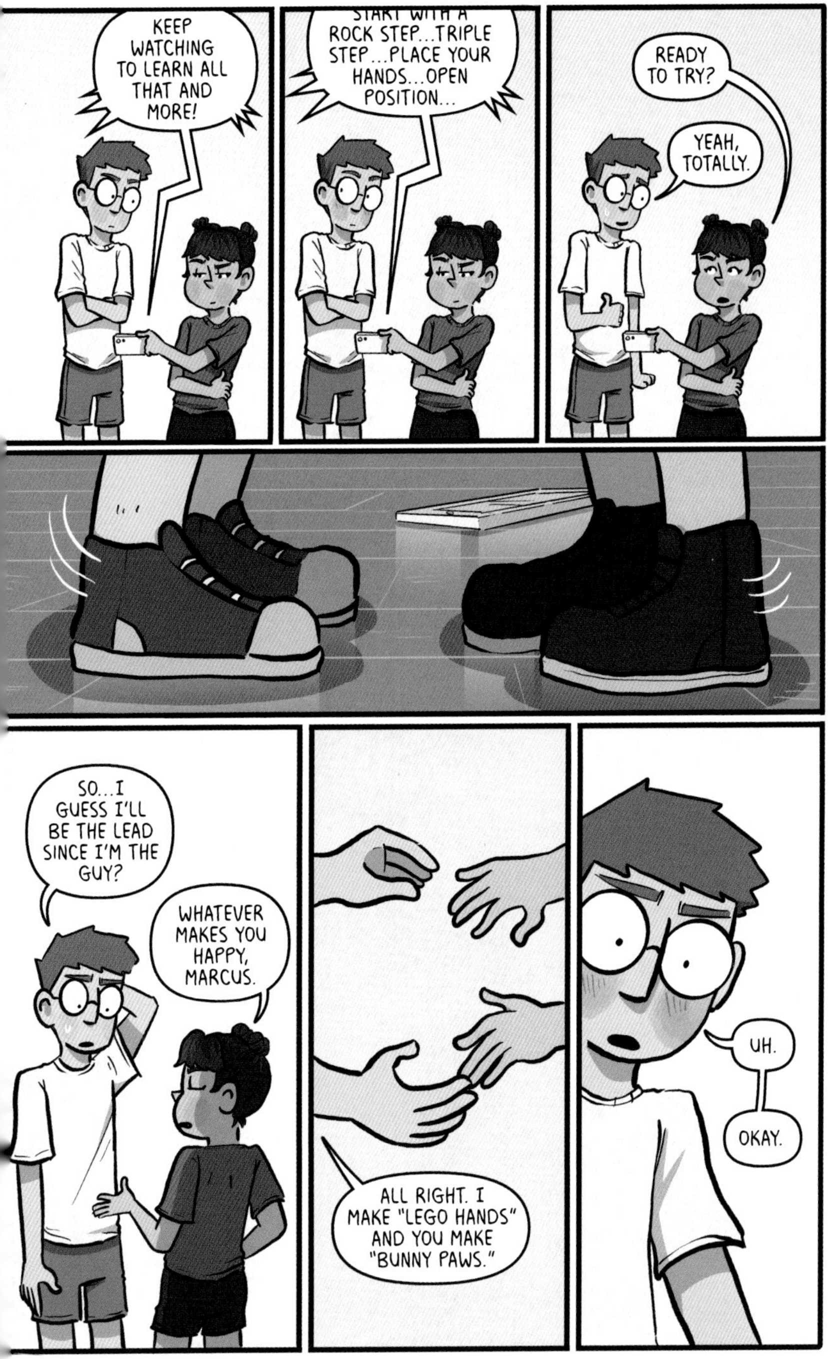
KEEP WATCHING TO LEARN ALL THAT AND MORE!
ROCK STEP...TRIPLE STEP...PLACE YOUR HANDS...OPEN POSITION...
READY TO TRY?
YEAH, TOTALLY.
SO...I GUESS I'LL BE THE LEAD SINCE I'M THE GUY?
WHATEVER MAKES YOU HAPPY, MARCUS.
ALL RIGHT. I MAKE "LEGO HANDS" AND YOU MAKE "BUNNY PAWS."
UH.
OKAY.

HOLDING HANDS

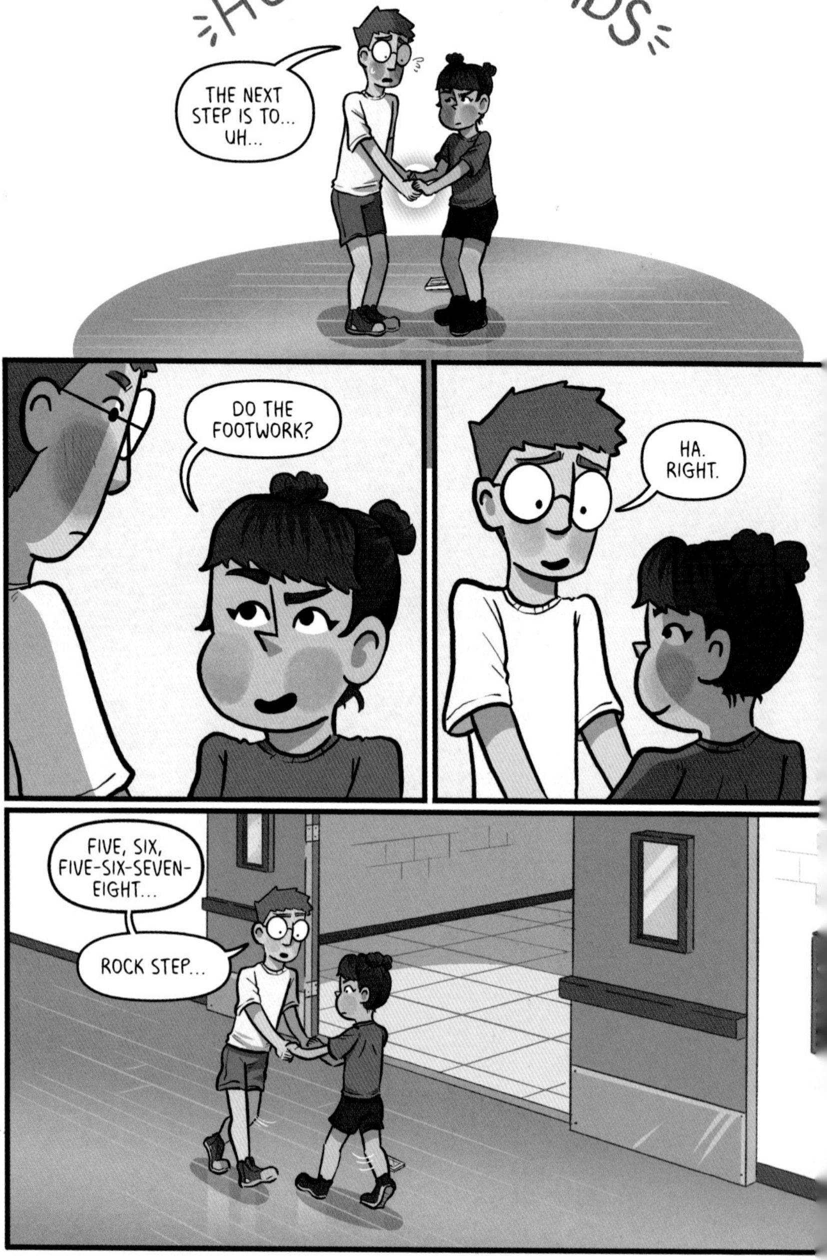
THE NEXT STEP IS TO... UH...
DO THE FOOTWORK?
HA. RIGHT.
FIVE, SIX, FIVE-SIX-SEVEN-EIGHT...
ROCK STEP...

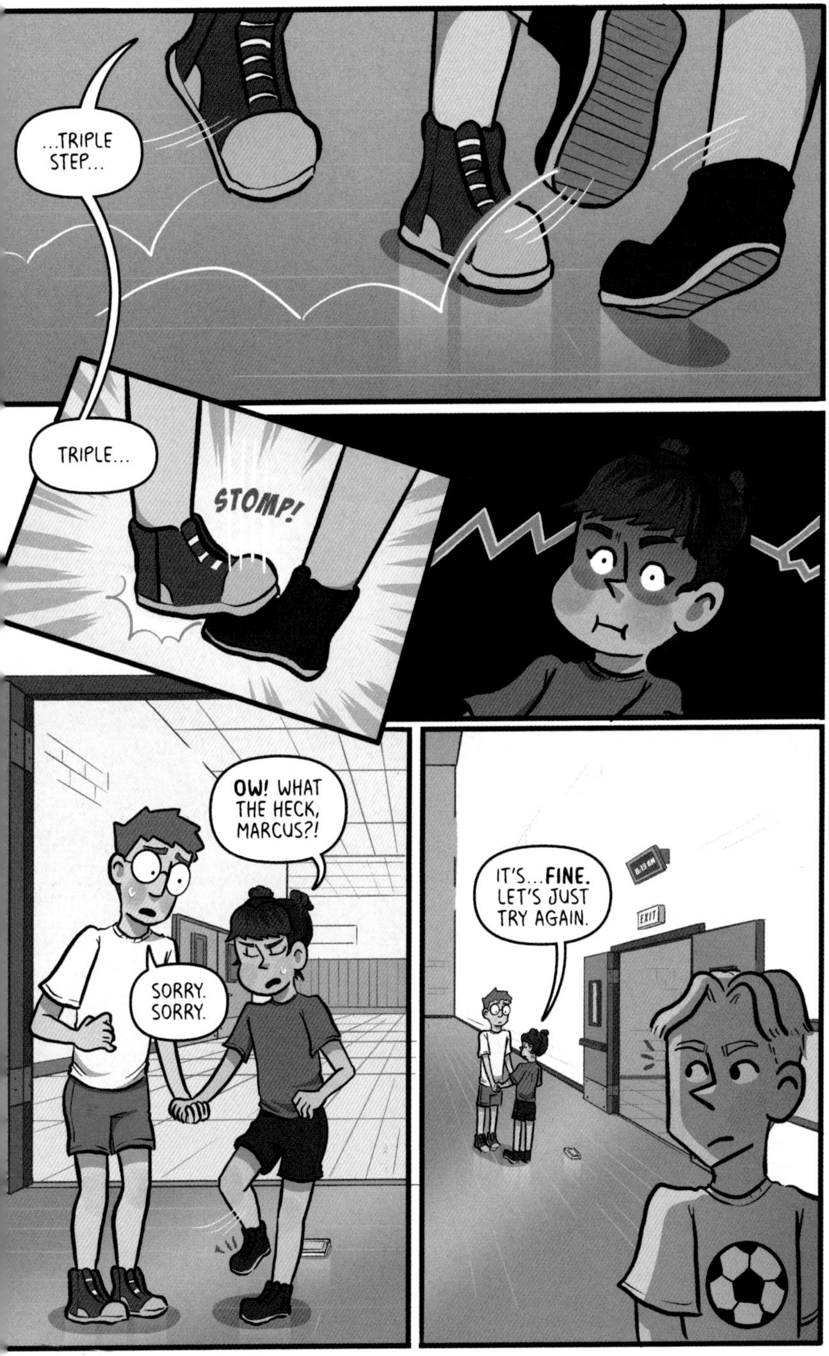
...TRIPLE STEP...
TRIPLE...
STOMP!
OW! WHAT THE HECK, MARCUS?!
SORRY. SORRY.
IT'S... FINE. LET'S JUST TRY AGAIN.
EXIT

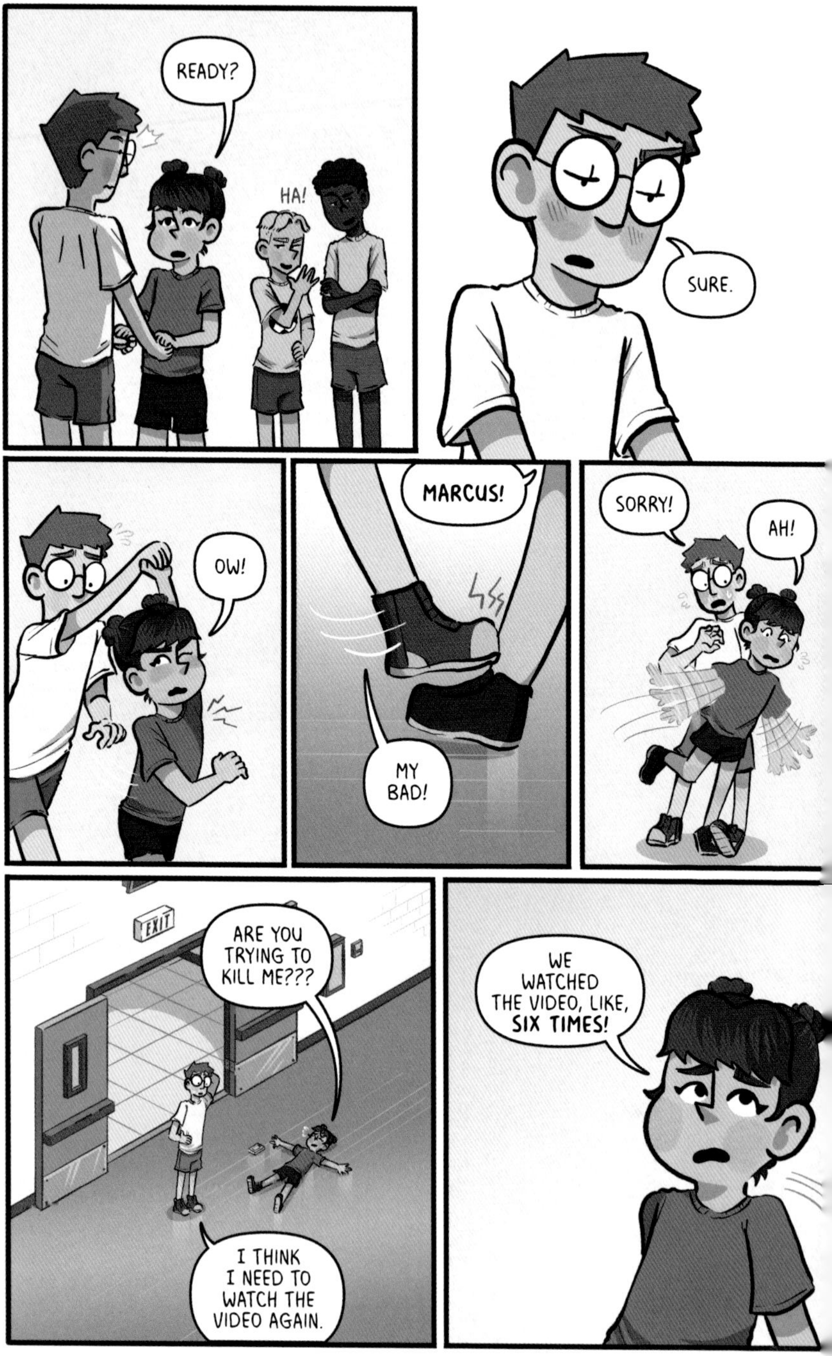
READY?
HA!
SURE.
OW!
MARCUS!
MY BAD!
SORRY!
AH!
ARE YOU TRYING TO KILL ME???
I THINK I NEED TO WATCH THE VIDEO AGAIN.
WE WATCHED THE VIDEO, LIKE, **SIX TIMES!**

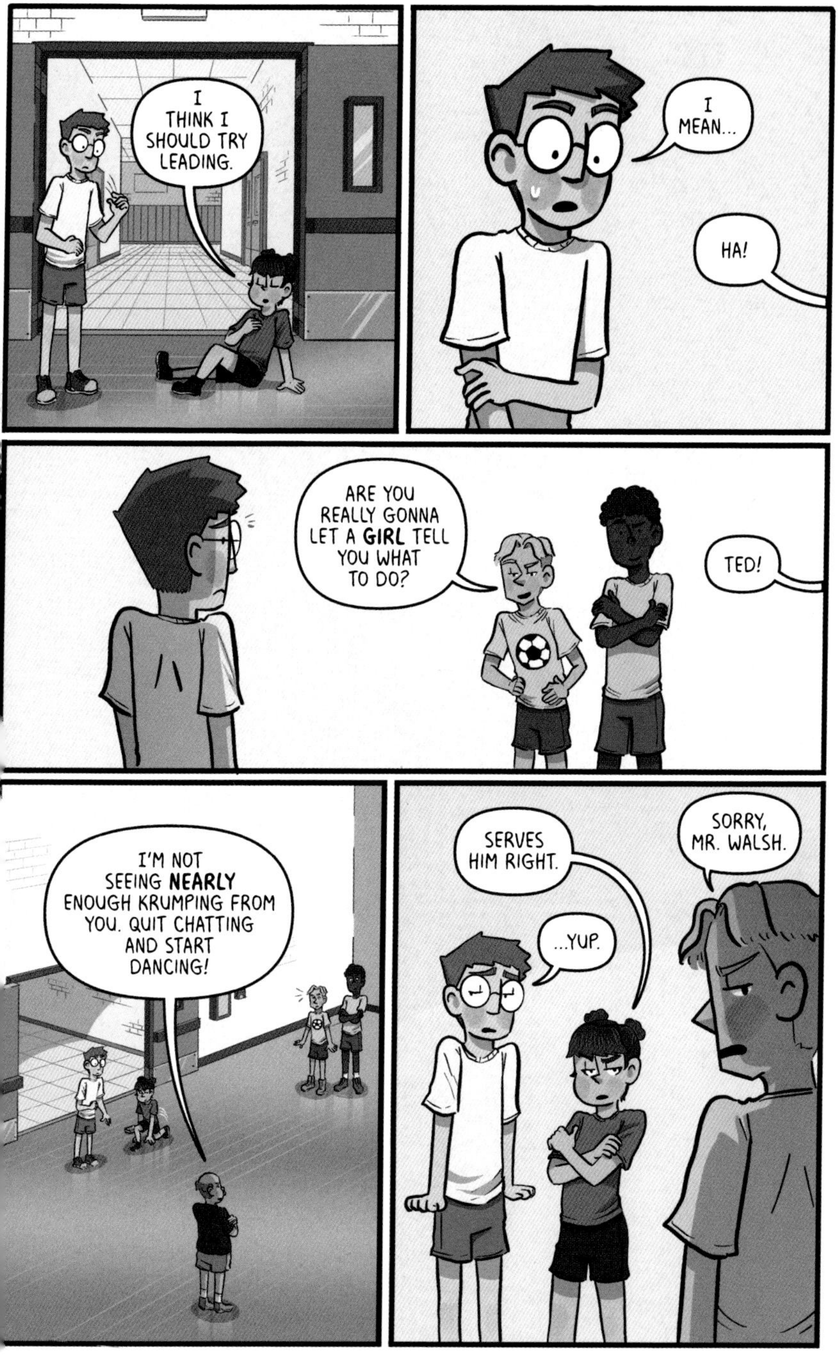
I THINK I SHOULD TRY LEADING.
I MEAN...
HA!
ARE YOU REALLY GONNA LET A **GIRL** TELL YOU WHAT TO DO?
TED!
I'M NOT SEEING **NEARLY** ENOUGH KRUMPING FROM YOU. QUIT CHATTING AND START DANCING!
SORRY, MR. WALSH.
SERVES HIM RIGHT.
...YUP.

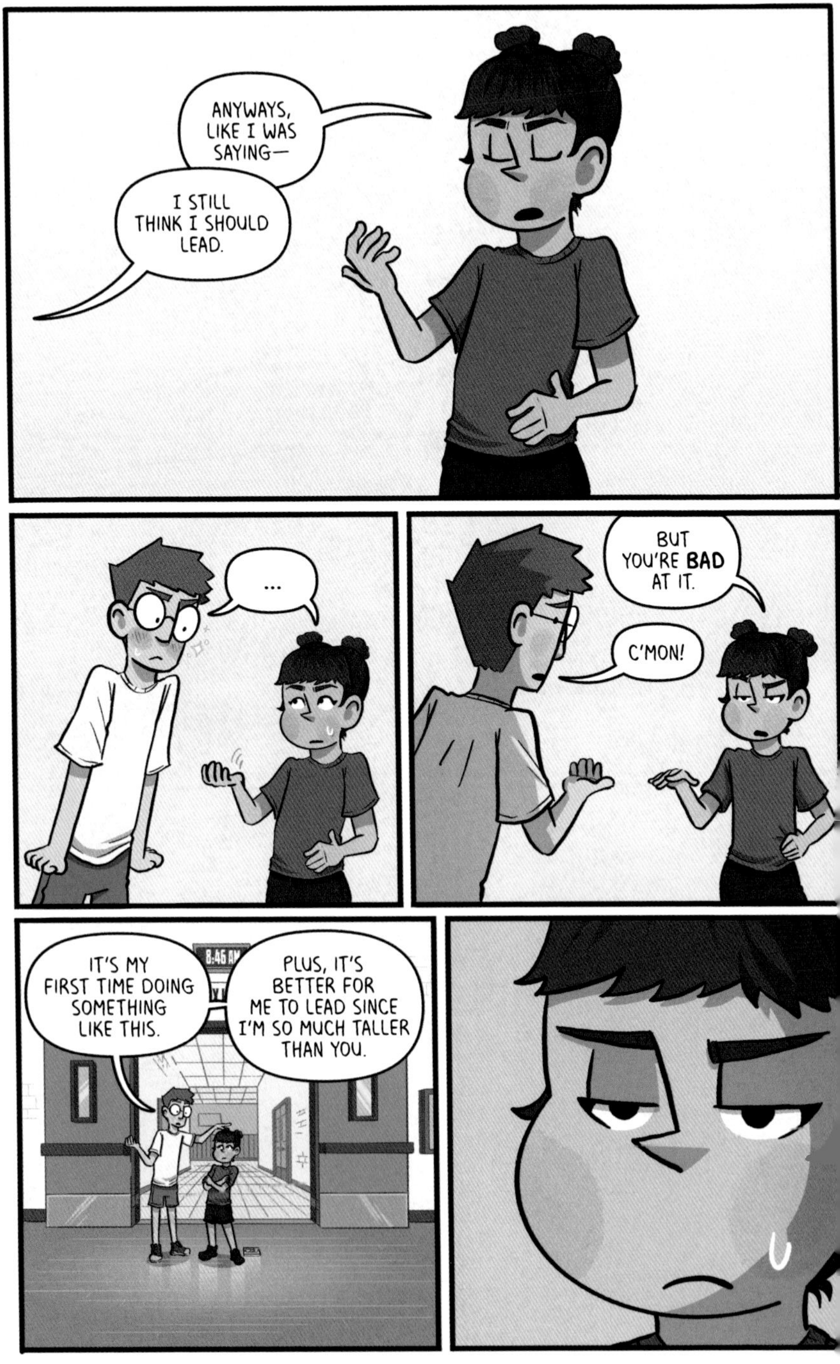
ANYWAYS, LIKE I WAS SAYING—
I STILL THINK I SHOULD LEAD.
...
BUT YOU'RE **BAD** AT IT.
C'MON!
8:46 AM
IT'S MY FIRST TIME DOING SOMETHING LIKE THIS.
PLUS, IT'S BETTER FOR ME TO LEAD SINCE I'M SO MUCH TALLER THAN YOU.

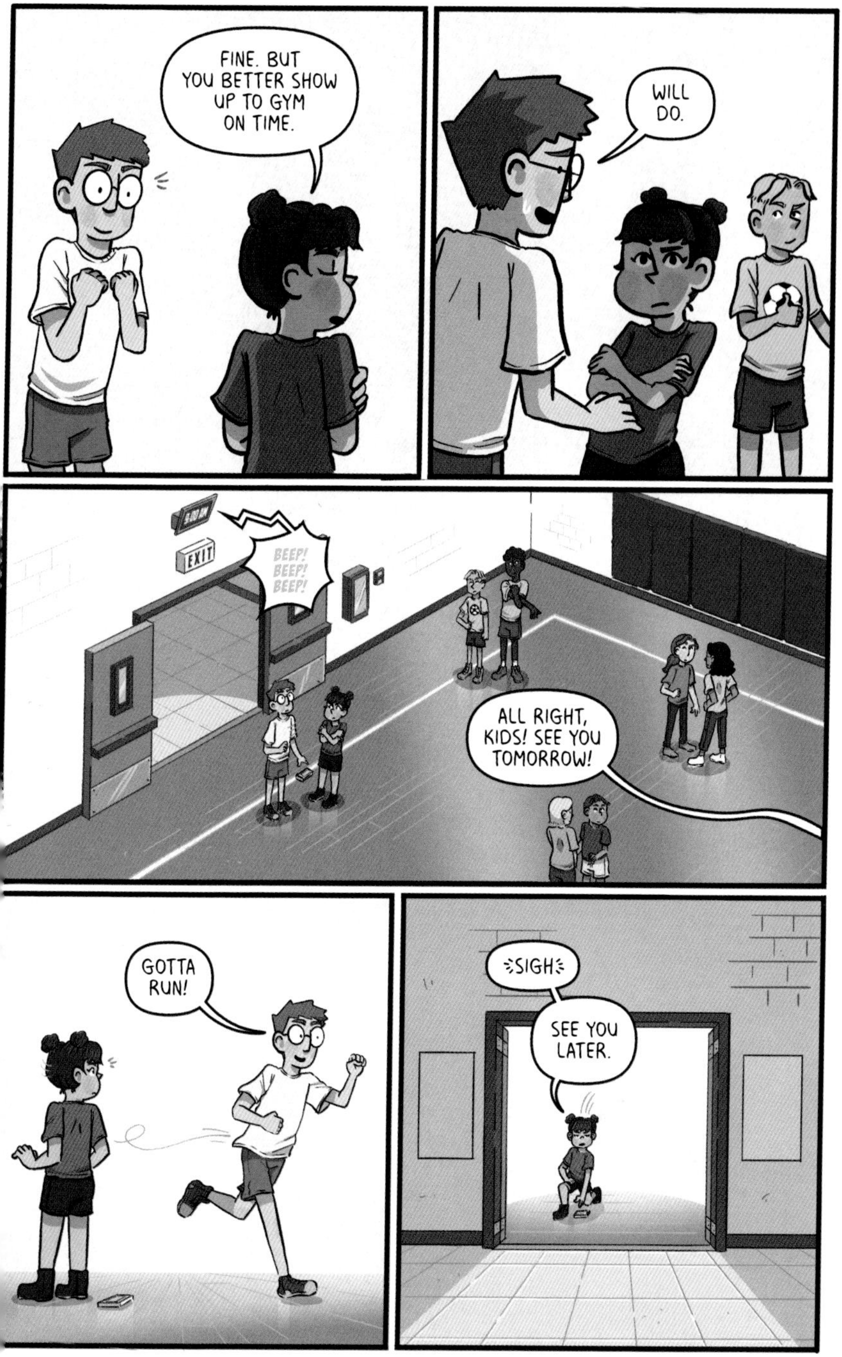
FINE. BUT YOU BETTER SHOW UP TO GYM ON TIME.
WILL DO.
BEEP! BEEP! BEEP!
EXIT
ALL RIGHT, KIDS! SEE YOU TOMORROW!
GOTTA RUN!
SIGH
SEE YOU LATER.

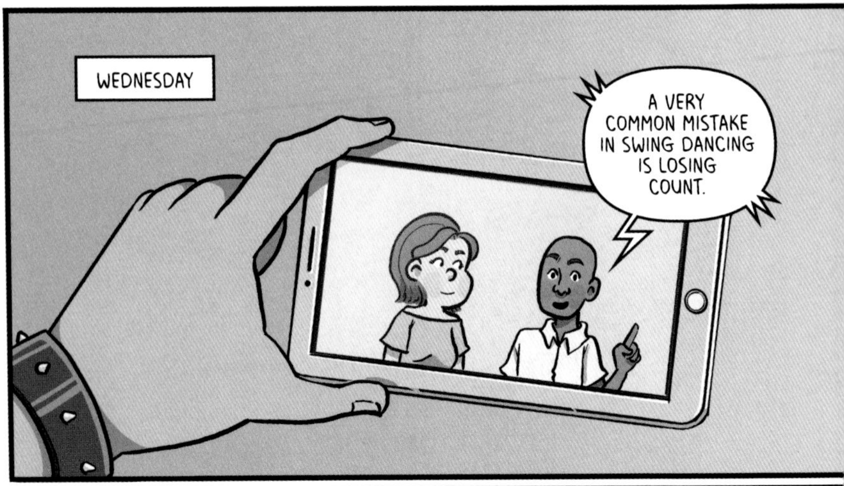
WEDNESDAY
A VERY COMMON MISTAKE IN SWING DANCING IS LOSING COUNT.
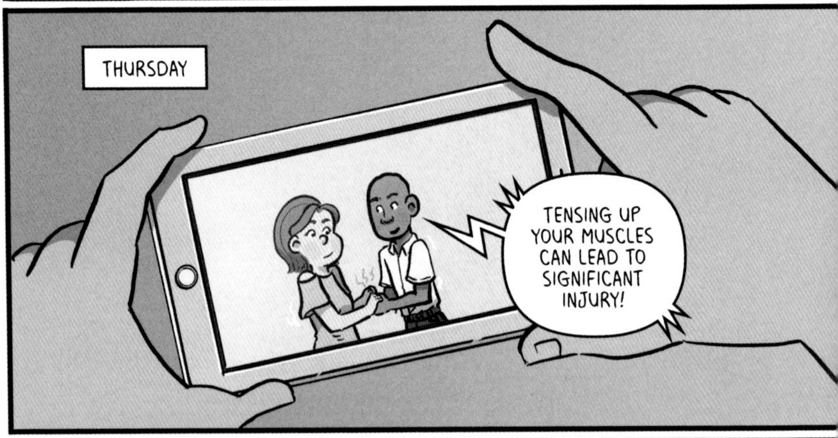
THURSDAY
TENSING UP YOUR MUSCLES CAN LEAD TO SIGNIFICANT INJURY!
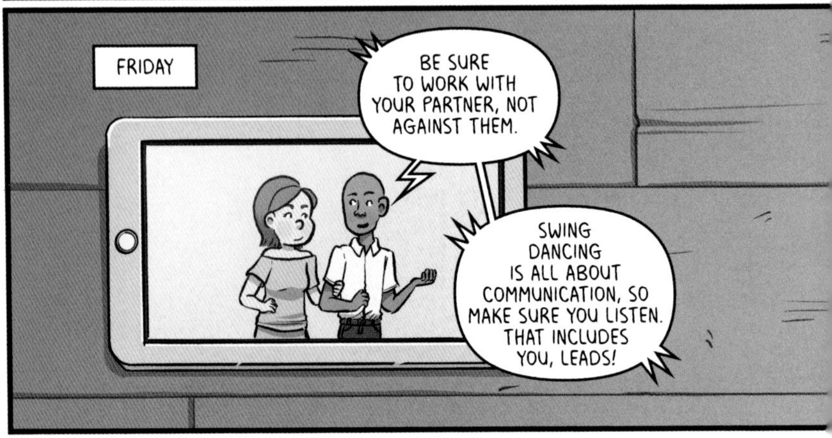
FRIDAY
BE SURE TO WORK WITH YOUR PARTNER, NOT AGAINST THEM.
SWING DANCING IS ALL ABOUT COMMUNICATION, SO MAKE SURE YOU LISTEN. THAT INCLUDES YOU, LEADS!

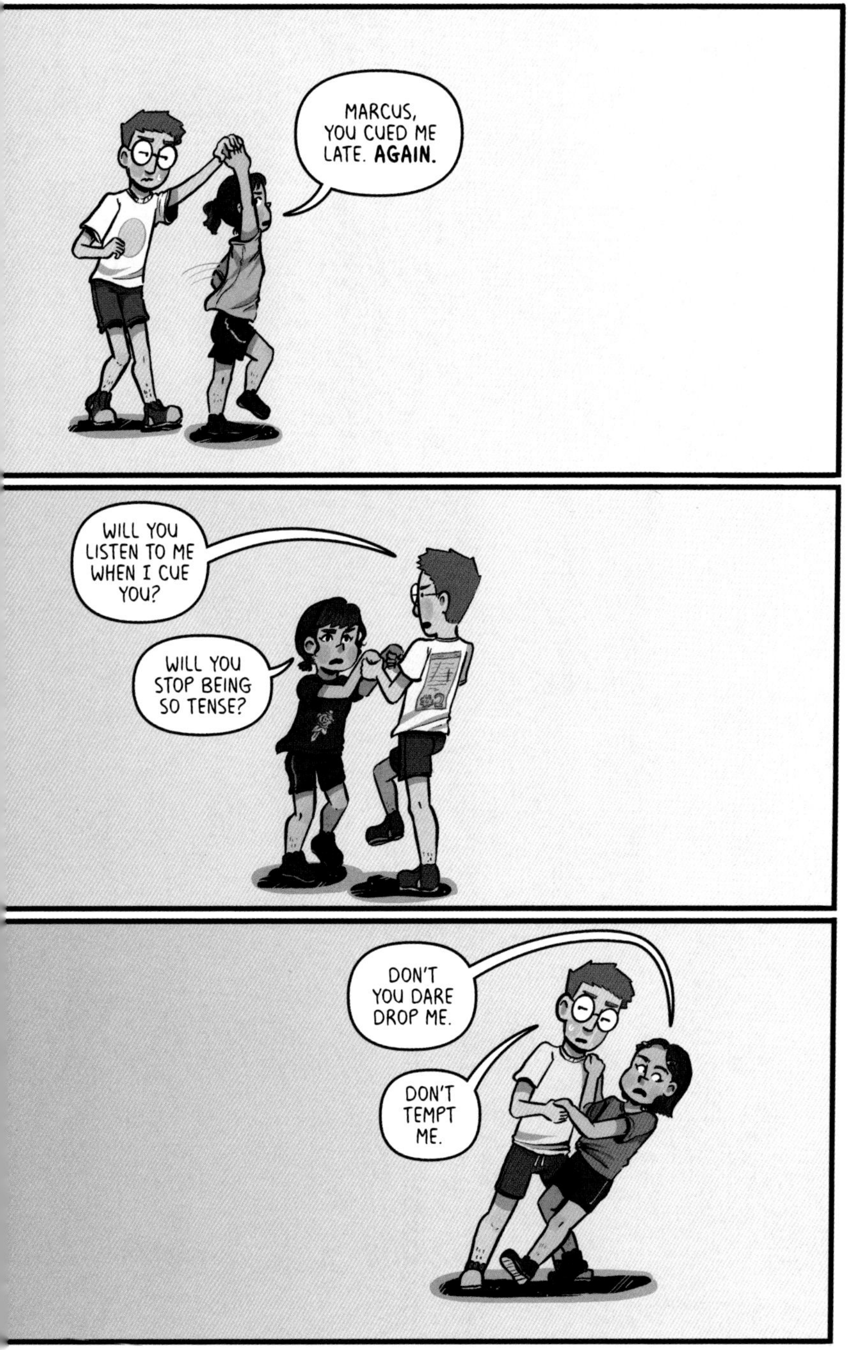
MARCUS, YOU CUED ME LATE. **AGAIN.**
WILL YOU LISTEN TO ME WHEN I CUE YOU?
WILL YOU STOP BEING SO TENSE?
DON'T YOU DARE DROP ME.
DON'T TEMPT ME.

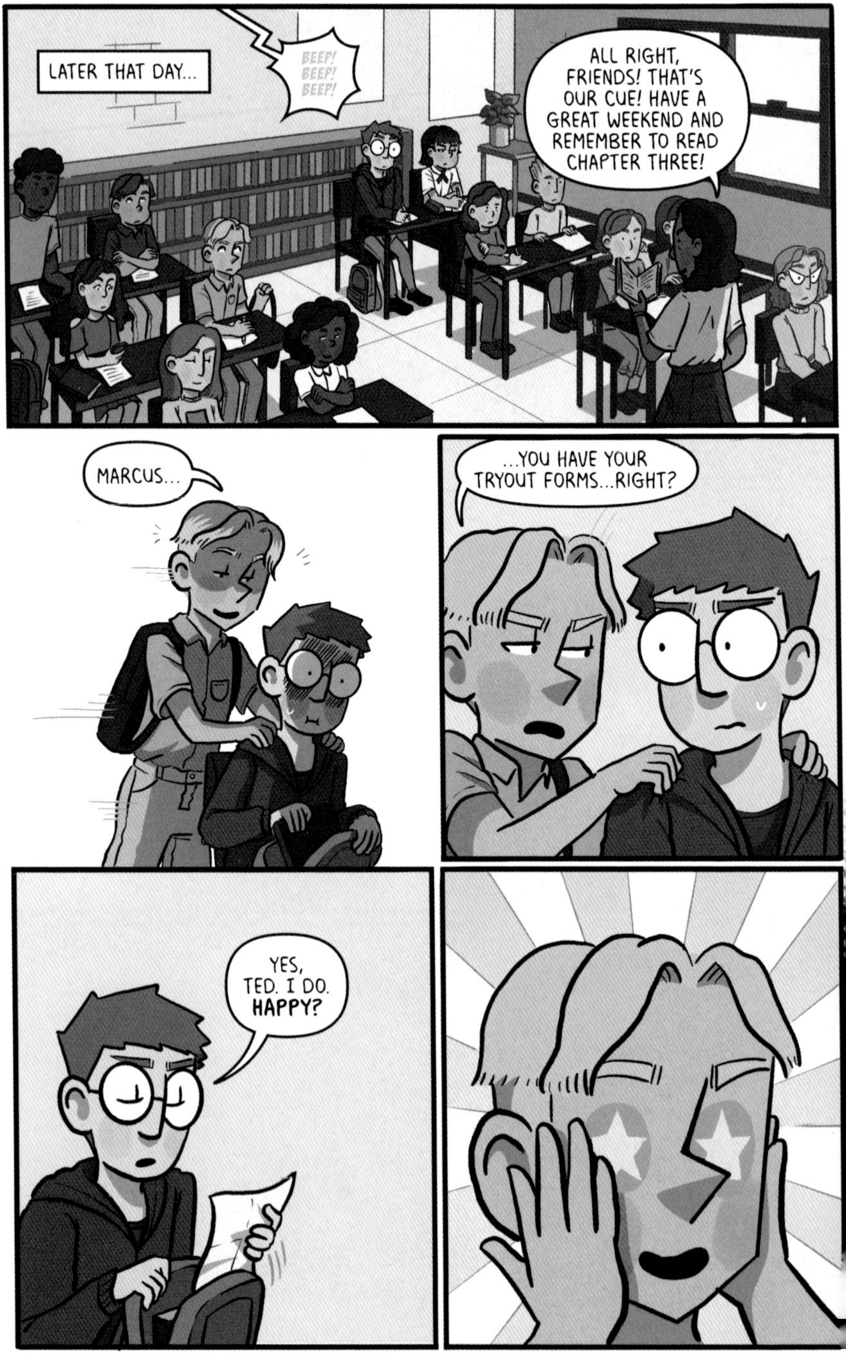

LATER THAT DAY...
BEEP! BEEP! BEEP!
ALL RIGHT, FRIENDS! THAT'S OUR CUE! HAVE A GREAT WEEKEND AND REMEMBER TO READ CHAPTER THREE!
MARCUS...
...YOU HAVE YOUR TRYOUT FORMS...RIGHT?
YES, TED. I DO. HAPPY?

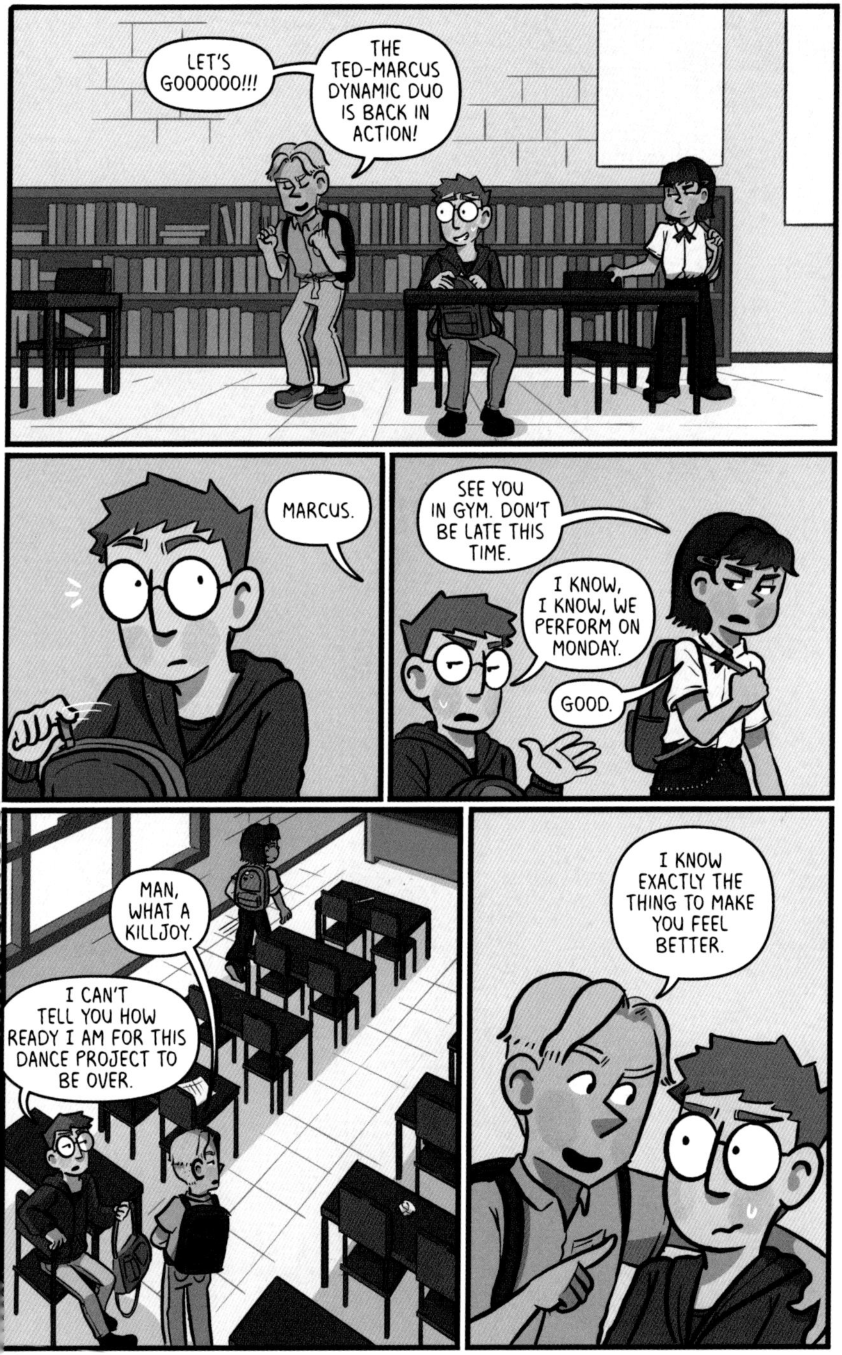
LET'S GOOOOOO!!!
THE TED-MARCUS DYNAMIC DUO IS BACK IN ACTION!
MARCUS.
SEE YOU IN GYM. DON'T BE LATE THIS TIME.
I KNOW, I KNOW, WE PERFORM ON MONDAY.
GOOD.
MAN, WHAT A KILLJOY.
I CAN'T TELL YOU HOW READY I AM FOR THIS DANCE PROJECT TO BE OVER.
I KNOW EXACTLY THE THING TO MAKE YOU FEEL BETTER.

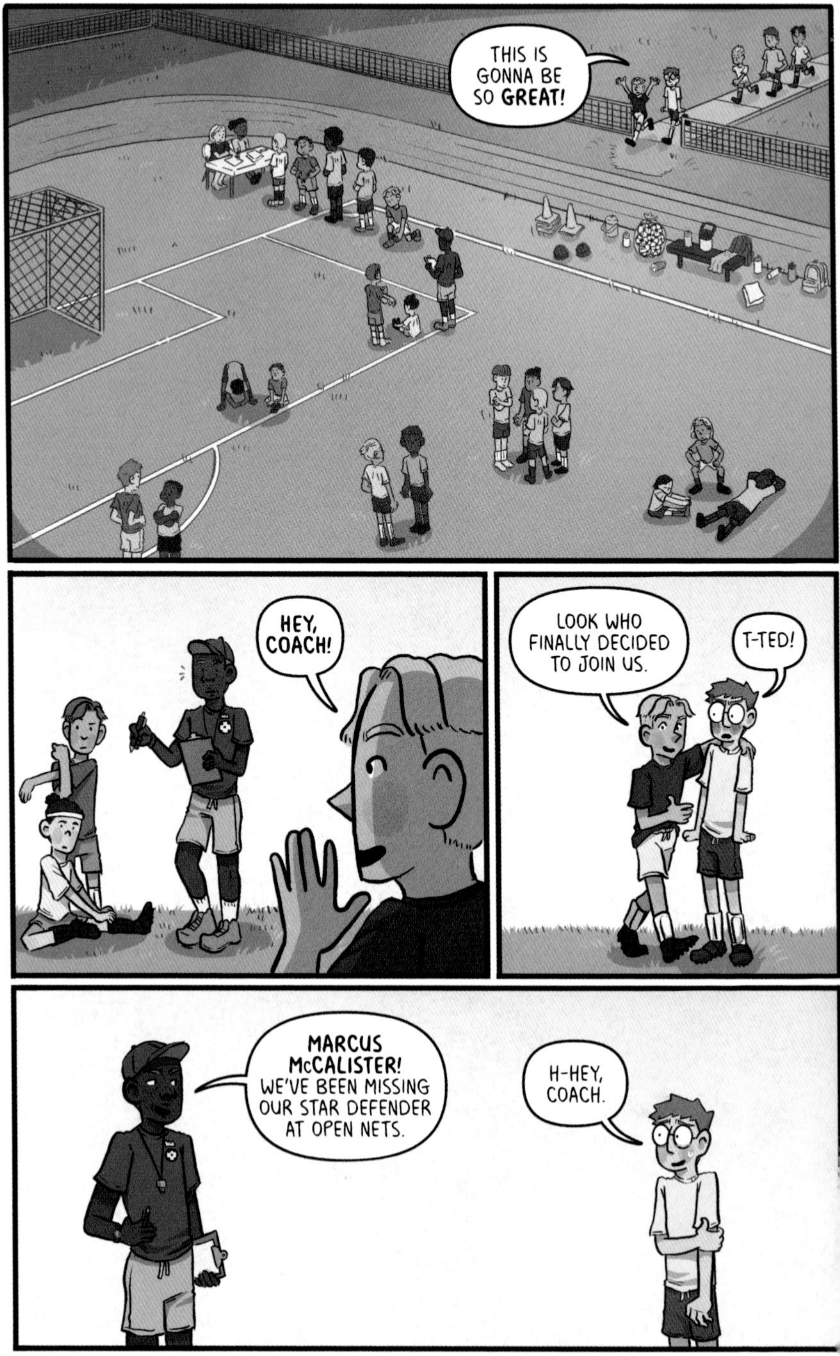
THIS IS GONNA BE SO **GREAT!**
HEY, COACH!
LOOK WHO FINALLY DECIDED TO JOIN US.
T-TED!
MARCUS McCALISTER! WE'VE BEEN MISSING OUR STAR DEFENDER AT OPEN NETS.
H-HEY, COACH.

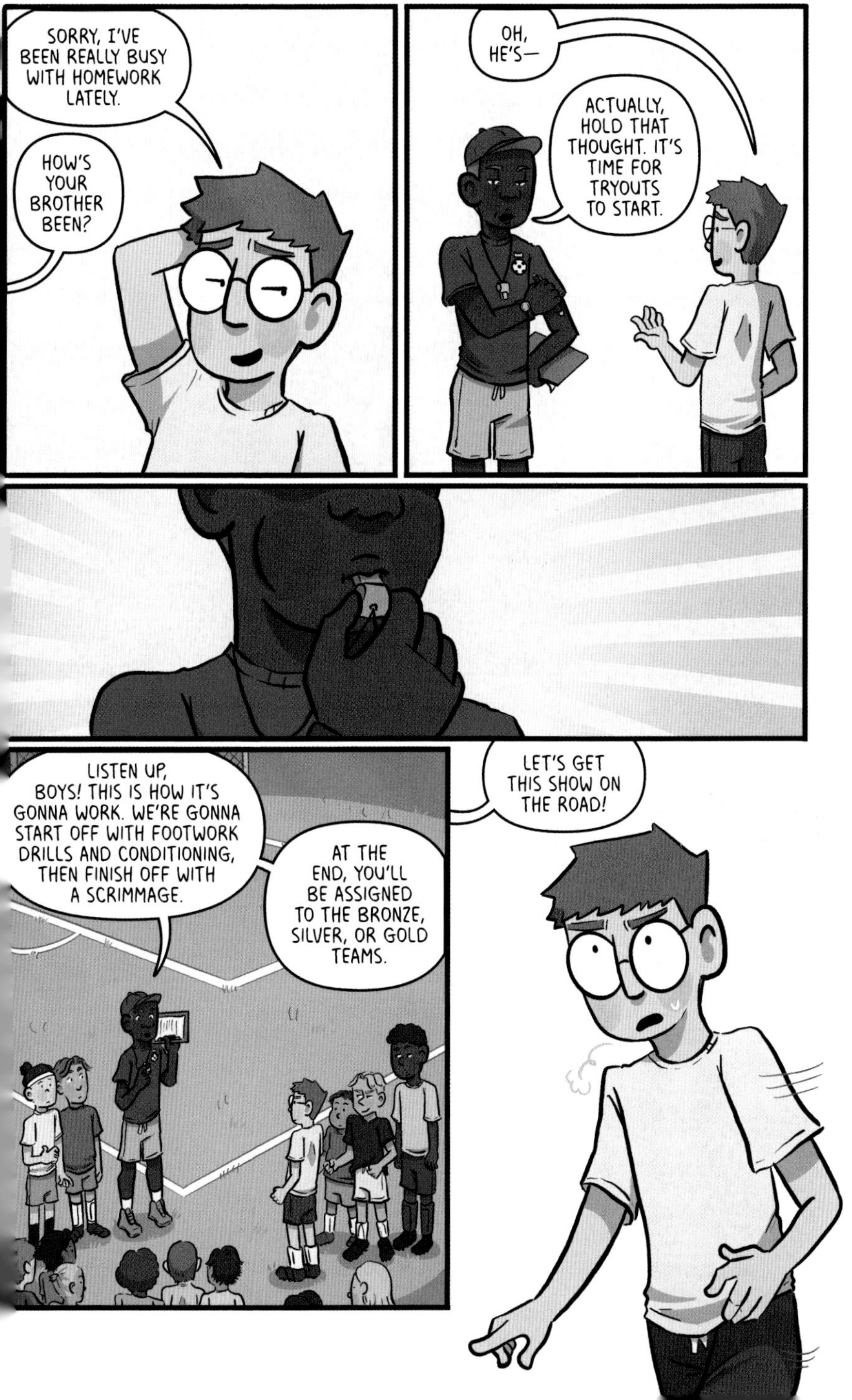
SORRY, I'VE BEEN REALLY BUSY WITH HOMEWORK LATELY.
HOW'S YOUR BROTHER BEEN?
OH, HE'S—
ACTUALLY, HOLD THAT THOUGHT. IT'S TIME FOR TRYOUTS TO START.
LISTEN UP, BOYS! THIS IS HOW IT'S GONNA WORK. WE'RE GONNA START OFF WITH FOOTWORK DRILLS AND CONDITIONING, THEN FINISH OFF WITH A SCRIMMAGE.
AT THE END, YOU'LL BE ASSIGNED TO THE BRONZE, SILVER, OR GOLD TEAMS.
LET'S GET THIS SHOW ON THE ROAD!

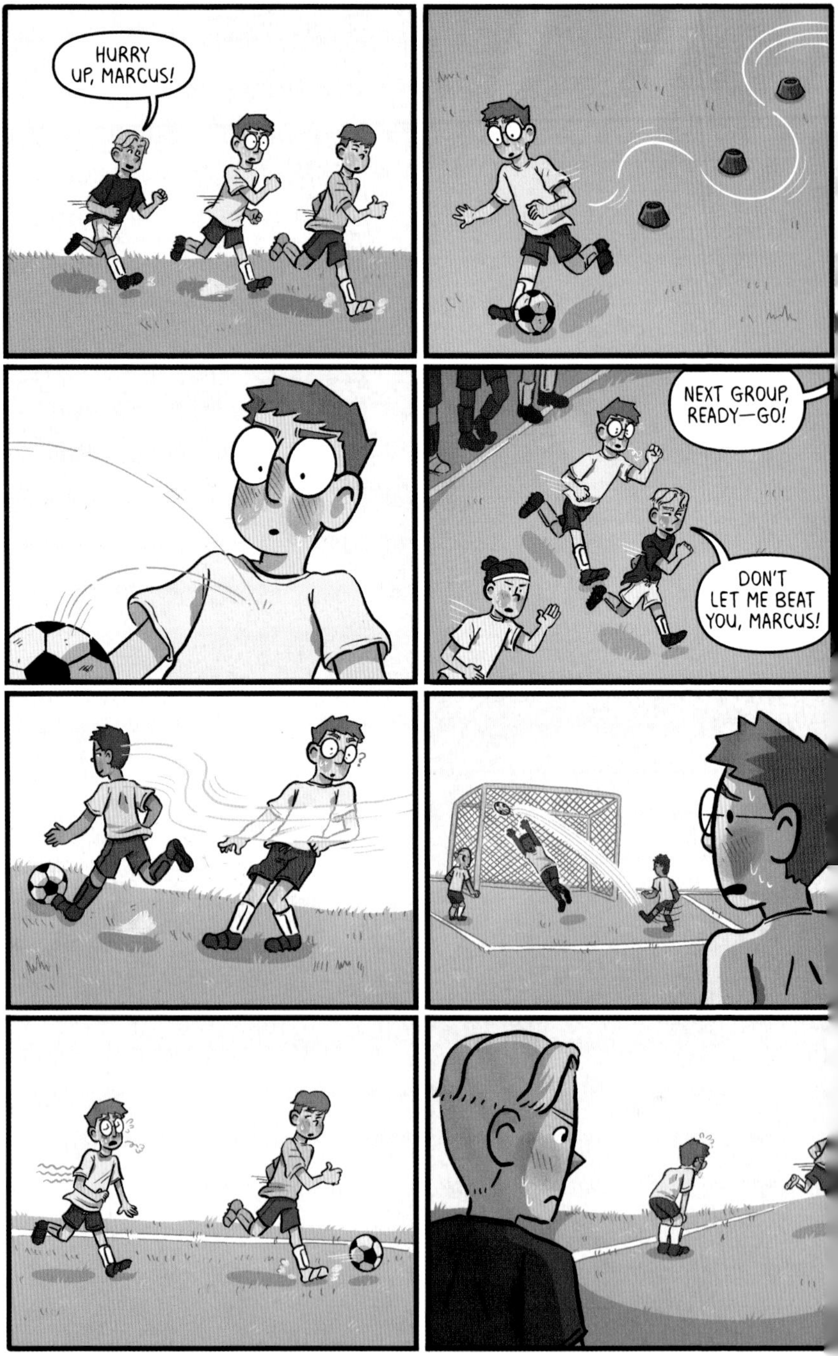
HURRY UP, MARCUS!
NEXT GROUP, READY—GO!
DON'T LET ME BEAT YOU, MARCUS!

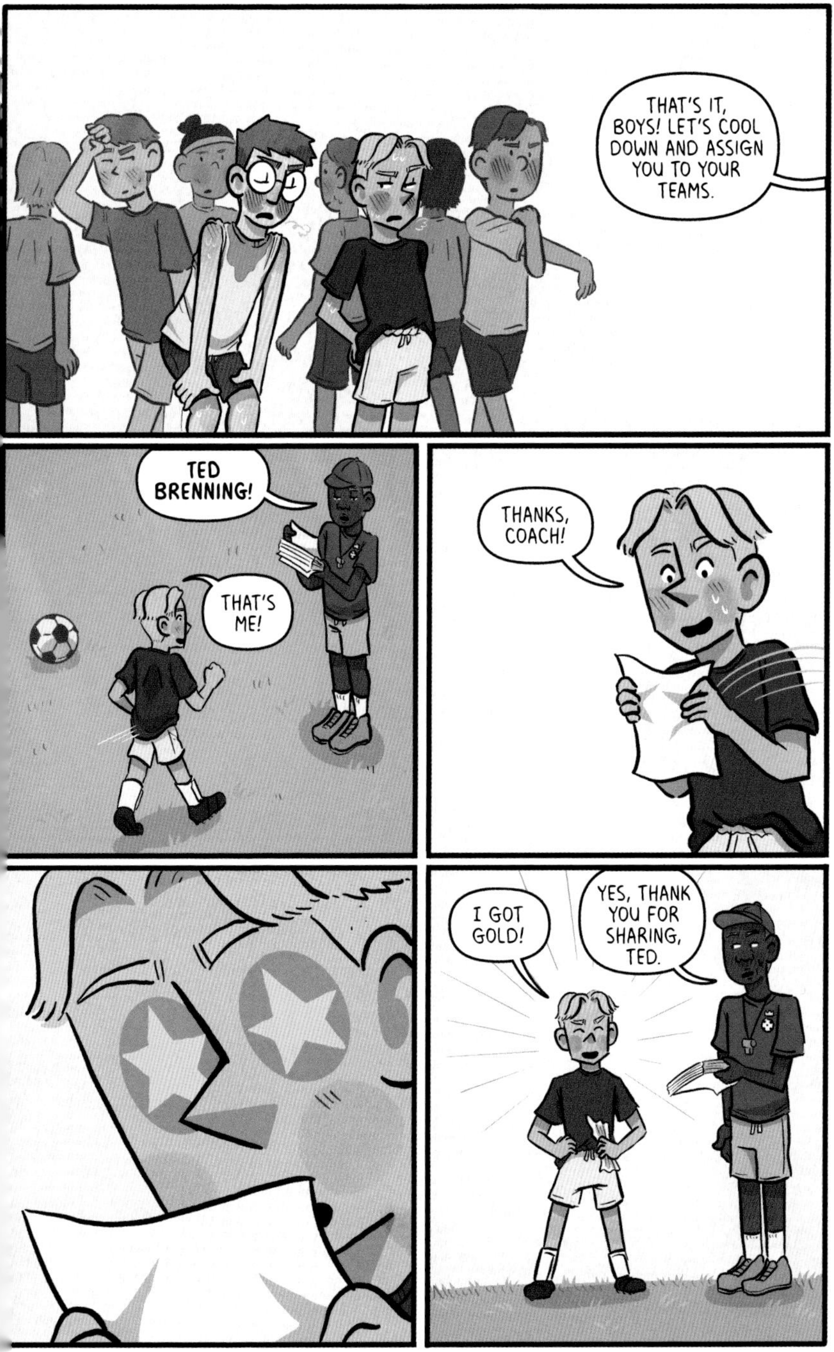
THAT'S IT, BOYS! LET'S COOL DOWN AND ASSIGN YOU TO YOUR TEAMS.
TED BRENNING!
THAT'S ME!
THANKS, COACH!
I GOT GOLD!
YES, THANK YOU FOR SHARING, TED.

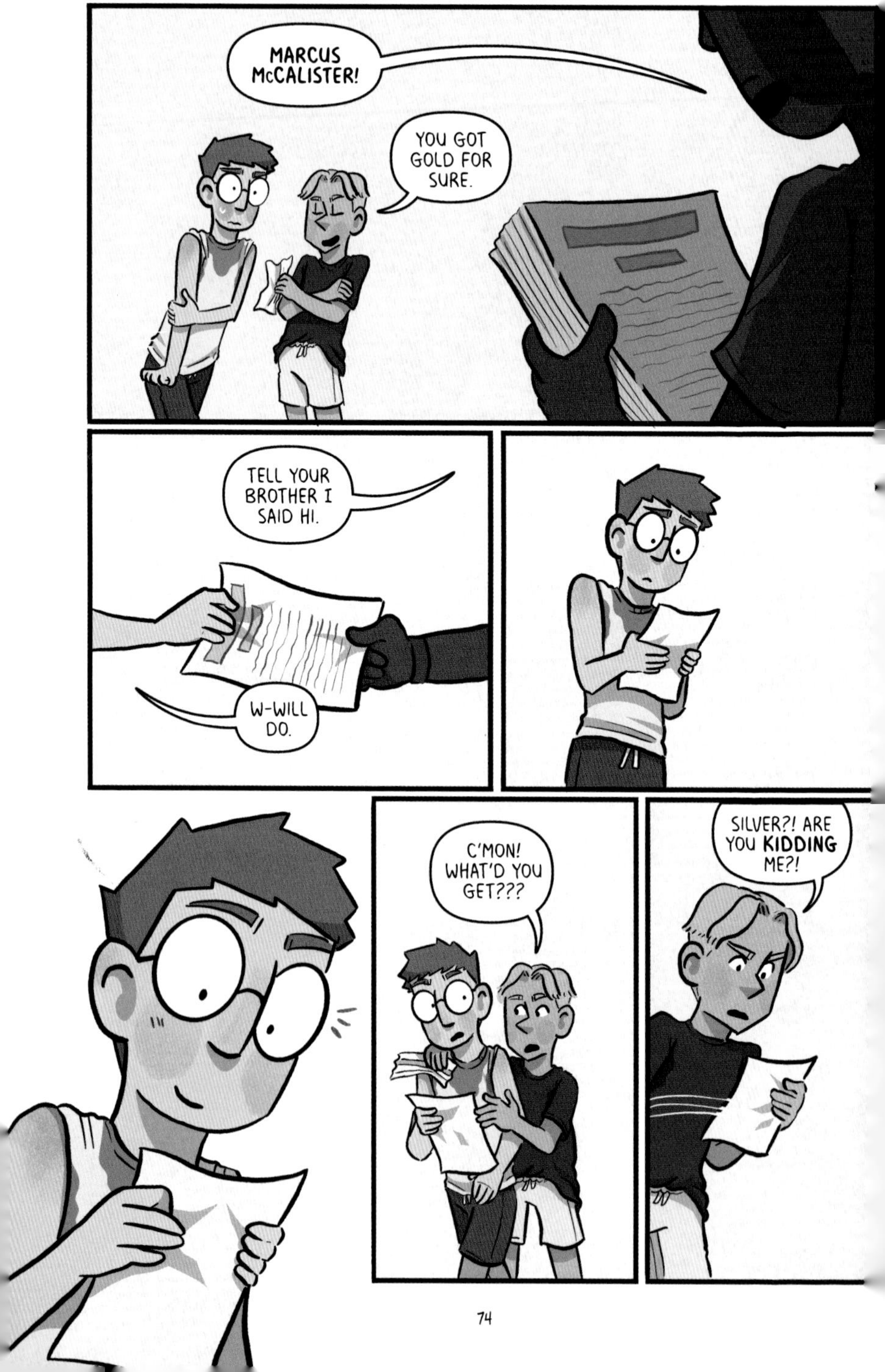
MARCUS McCALISTER!
YOU GOT GOLD FOR SURE.
TELL YOUR BROTHER I SAID HI.
W-WILL DO.
C'MON! WHAT'D YOU GET???
SILVER?! ARE YOU KIDDING ME?!

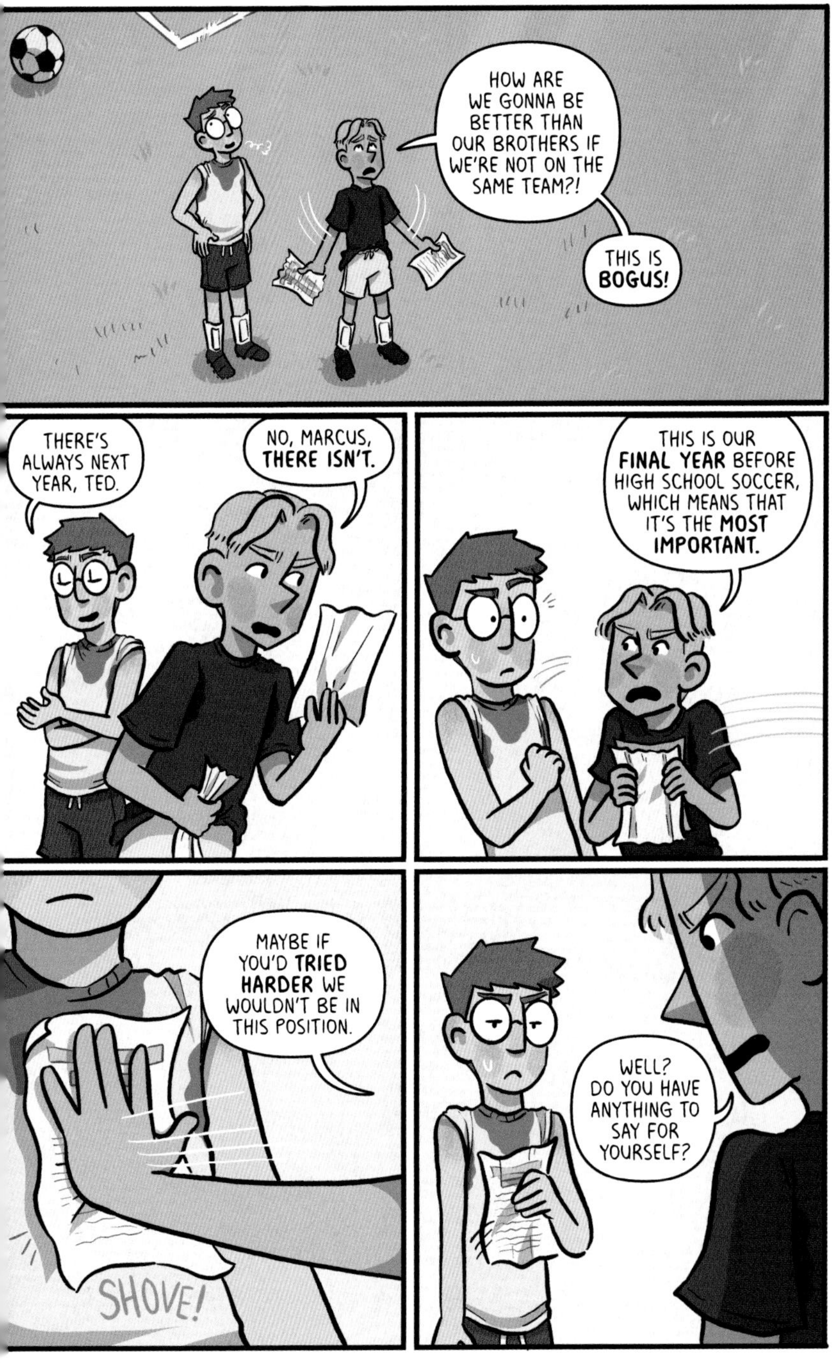
HOW ARE WE GONNA BE BETTER THAN OUR BROTHERS IF WE'RE NOT ON THE SAME TEAM?!
THIS IS **BOGUS!**
THERE'S ALWAYS NEXT YEAR, TED.
NO, MARCUS, **THERE ISN'T.**
THIS IS OUR **FINAL YEAR** BEFORE HIGH SCHOOL SOCCER, WHICH MEANS THAT IT'S THE **MOST IMPORTANT.**
MAYBE IF YOU'D **TRIED HARDER** WE WOULDN'T BE IN THIS POSITION.
SHOVE!
WELL? DO YOU HAVE ANYTHING TO SAY FOR YOURSELF?

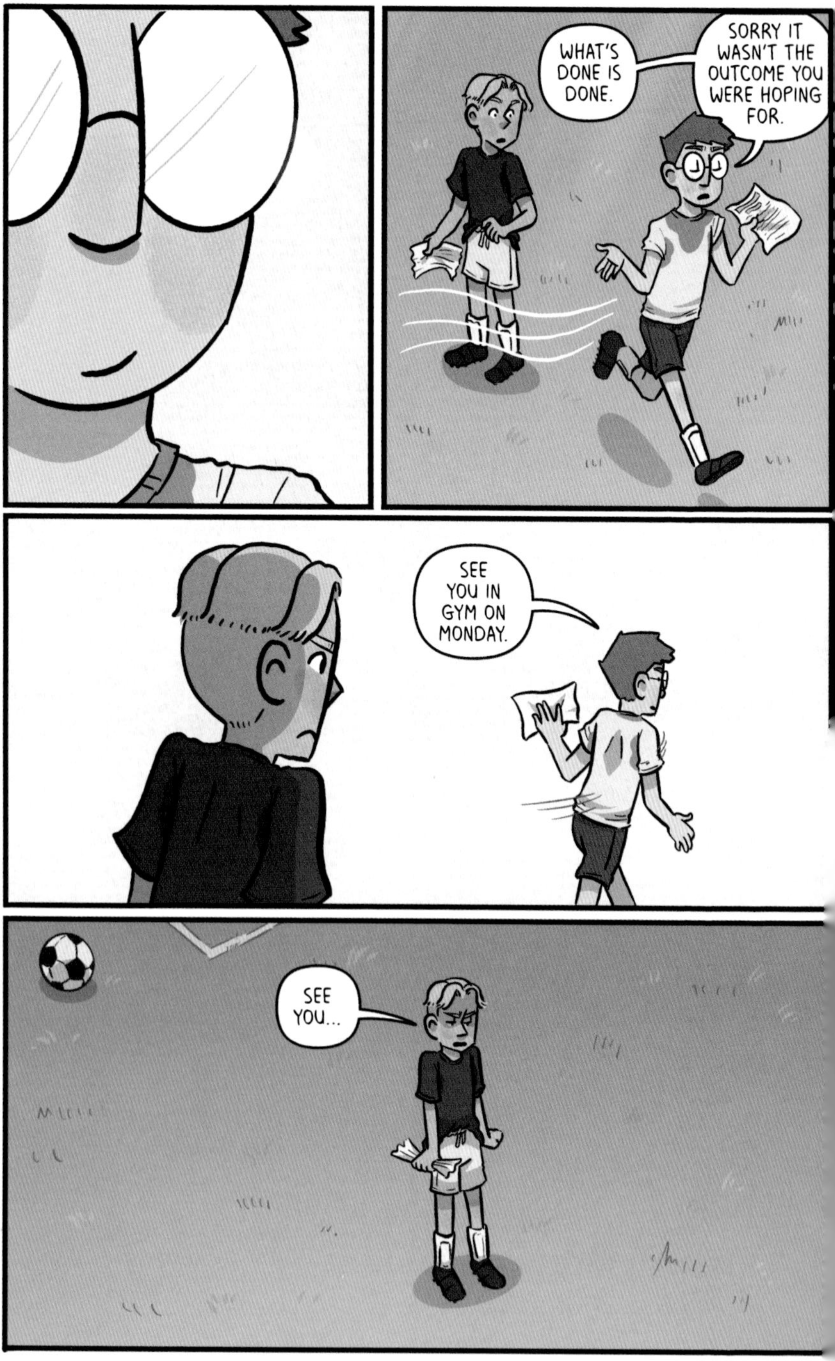
WHAT'S DONE IS DONE.
SORRY IT WASN'T THE OUTCOME YOU WERE HOPING FOR.
SEE YOU IN GYM ON MONDAY.
SEE YOU...

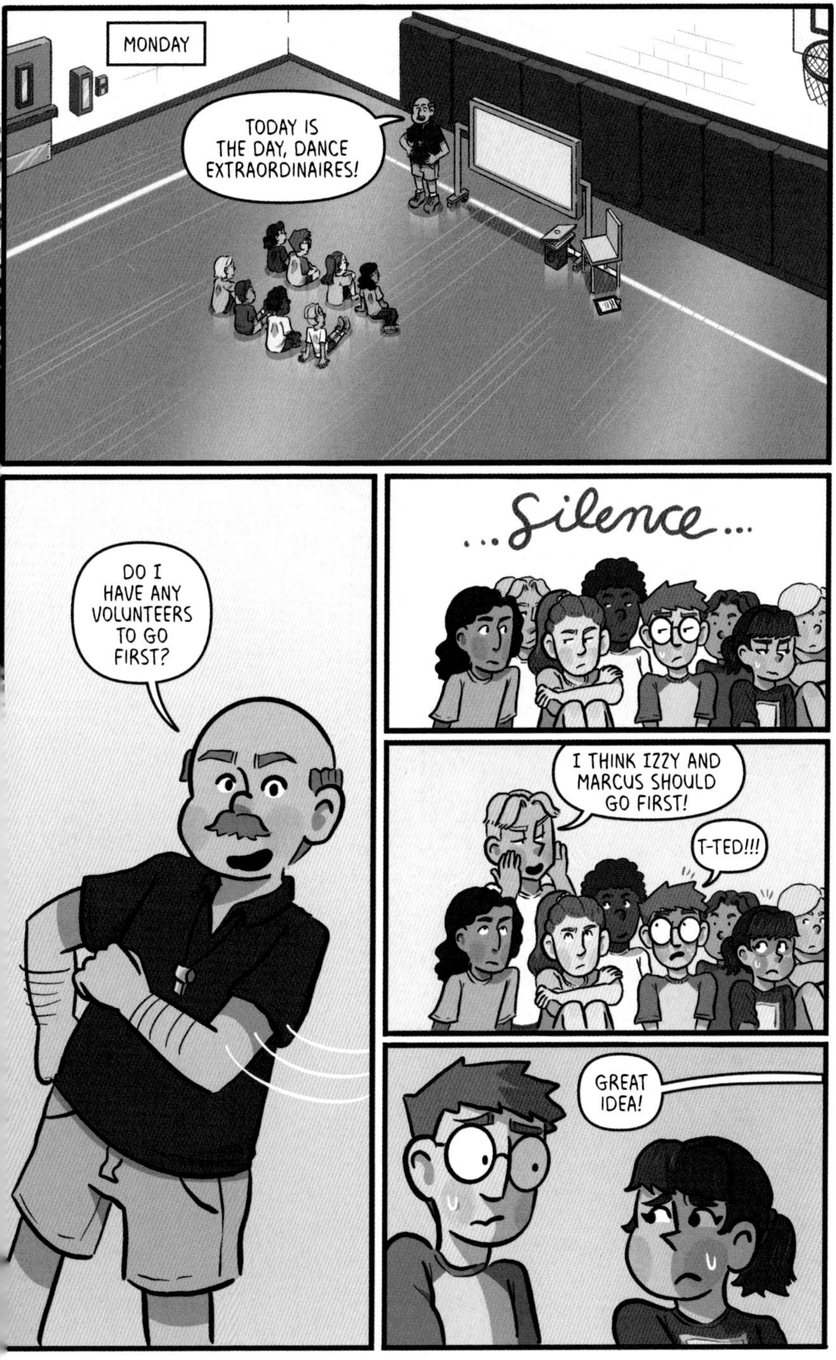
MONDAY
TODAY IS THE DAY, DANCE EXTRAORDINAIRES!
DO I HAVE ANY VOLUNTEERS TO GO FIRST?
...silence...
I THINK IZZY AND MARCUS SHOULD GO FIRST!
T-TED!!!
GREAT IDEA!

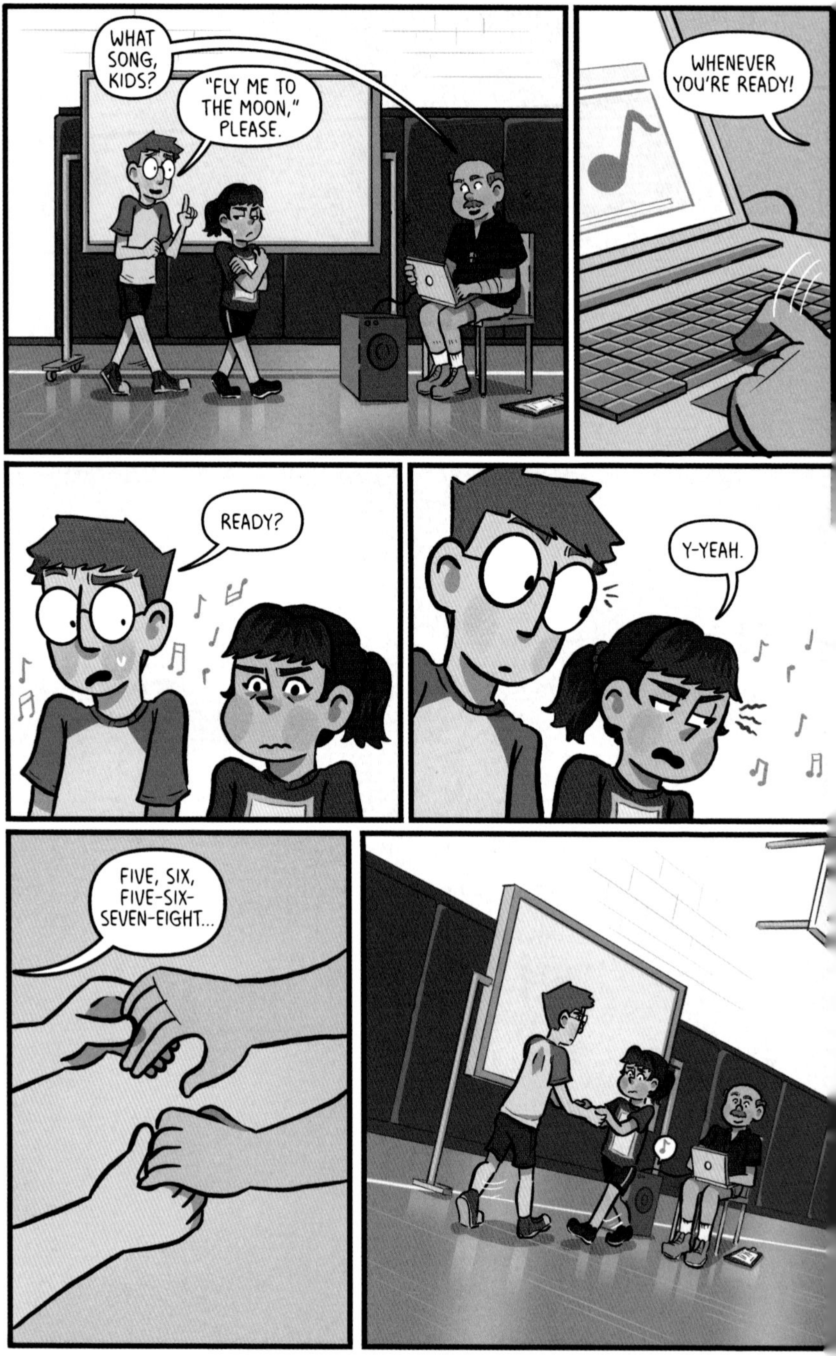
WHAT SONG, KIDS?
"FLY ME TO THE MOON," PLEASE.
WHENEVER YOU'RE READY!
READY?
Y-YEAH.
FIVE, SIX, FIVE-SIX-SEVEN-EIGHT...

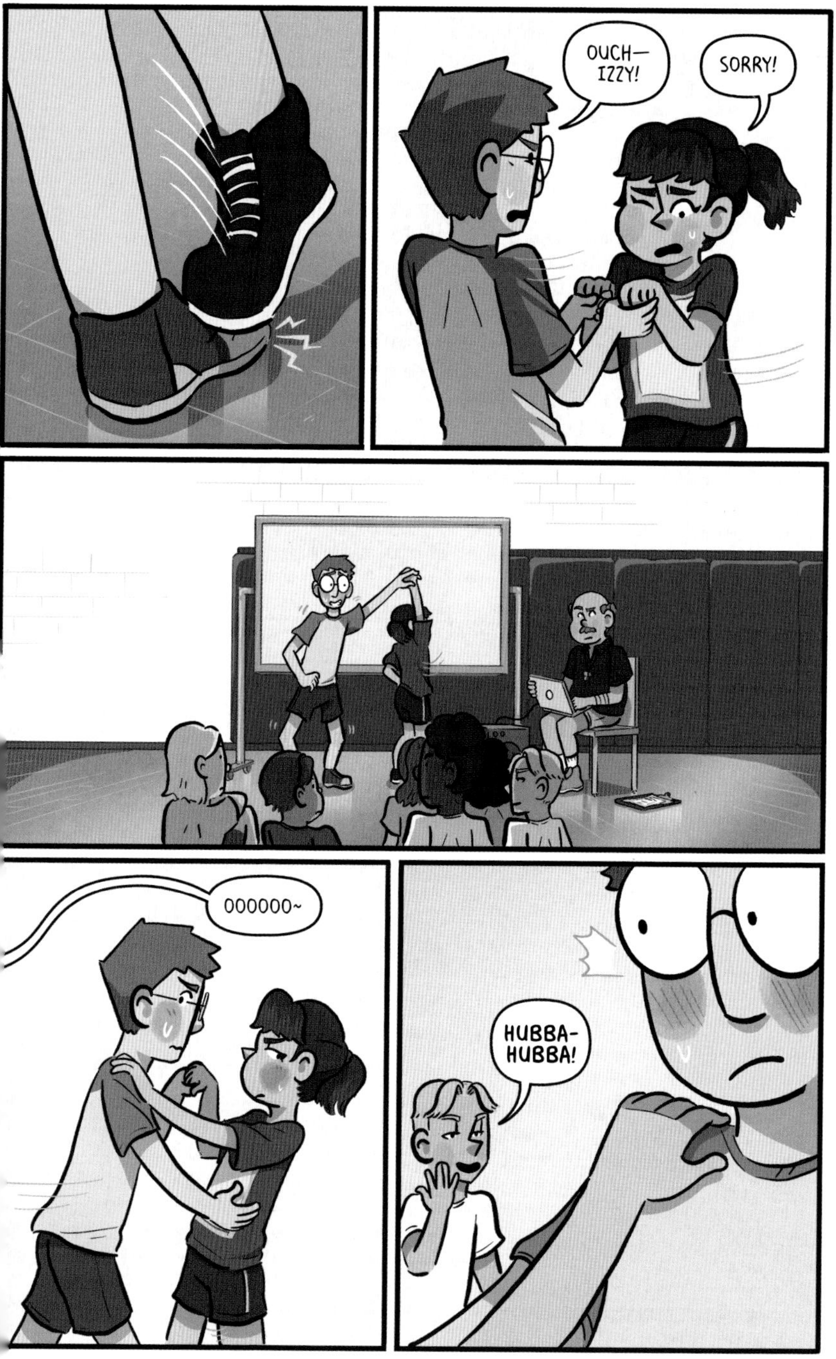
OUCH—
IZZY!
SORRY!
OOOOOO~
HUBBA-
HUBBA!

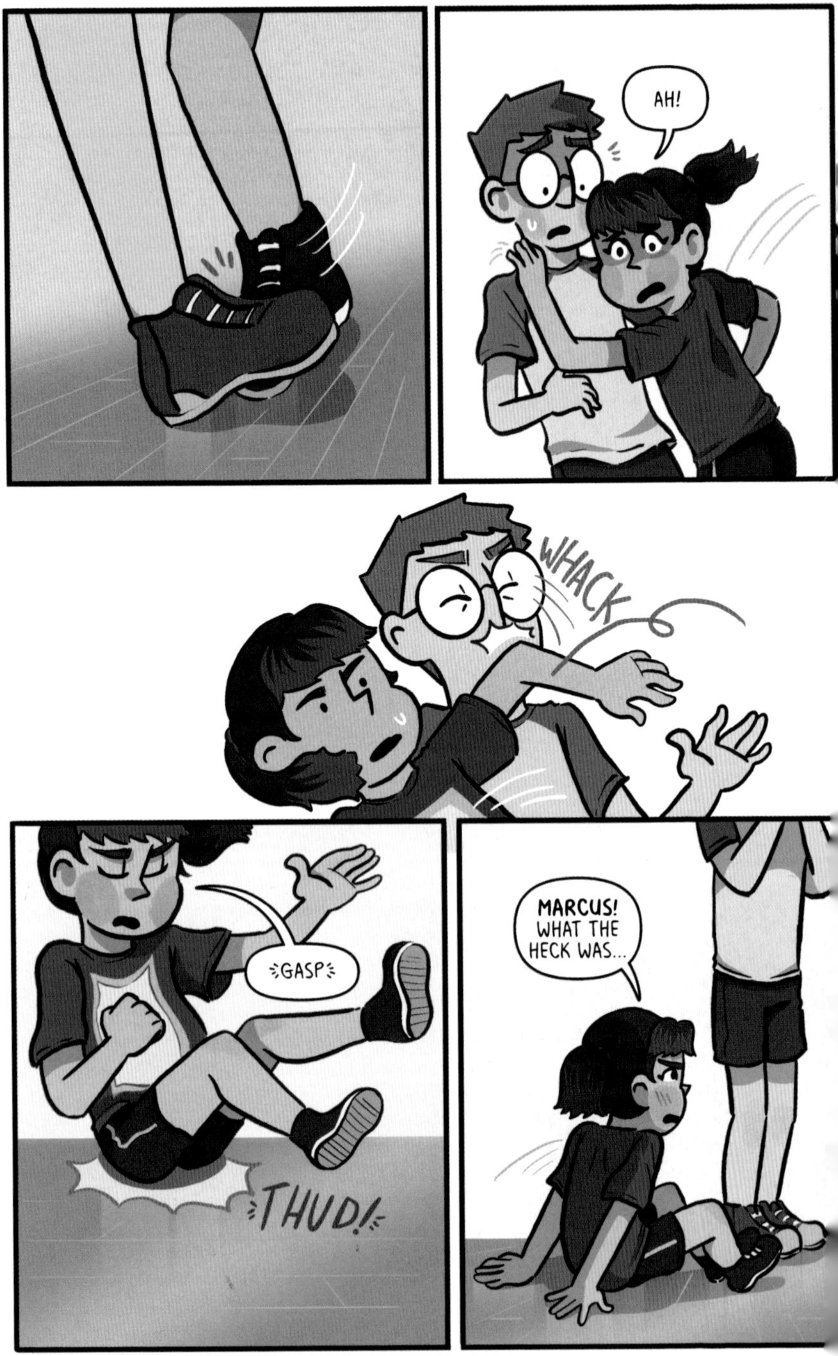
AH!
WHACK
GASP
THUD!
MARCUS! WHAT THE HECK WAS...

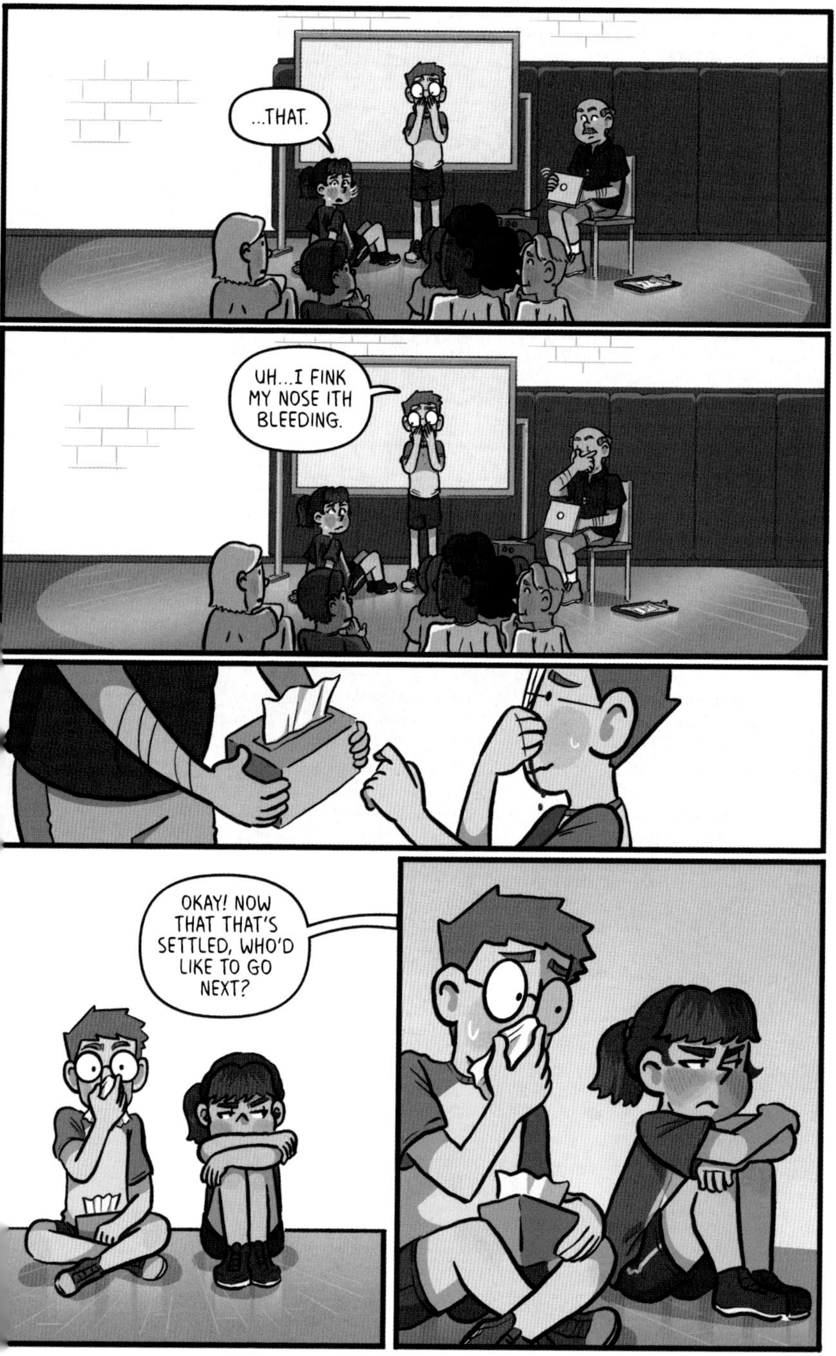
...THAT.
UH...I FINK MY NOSE ITH BLEEDING.
OKAY! NOW THAT THAT'S SETTLED, WHO'D LIKE TO GO NEXT?

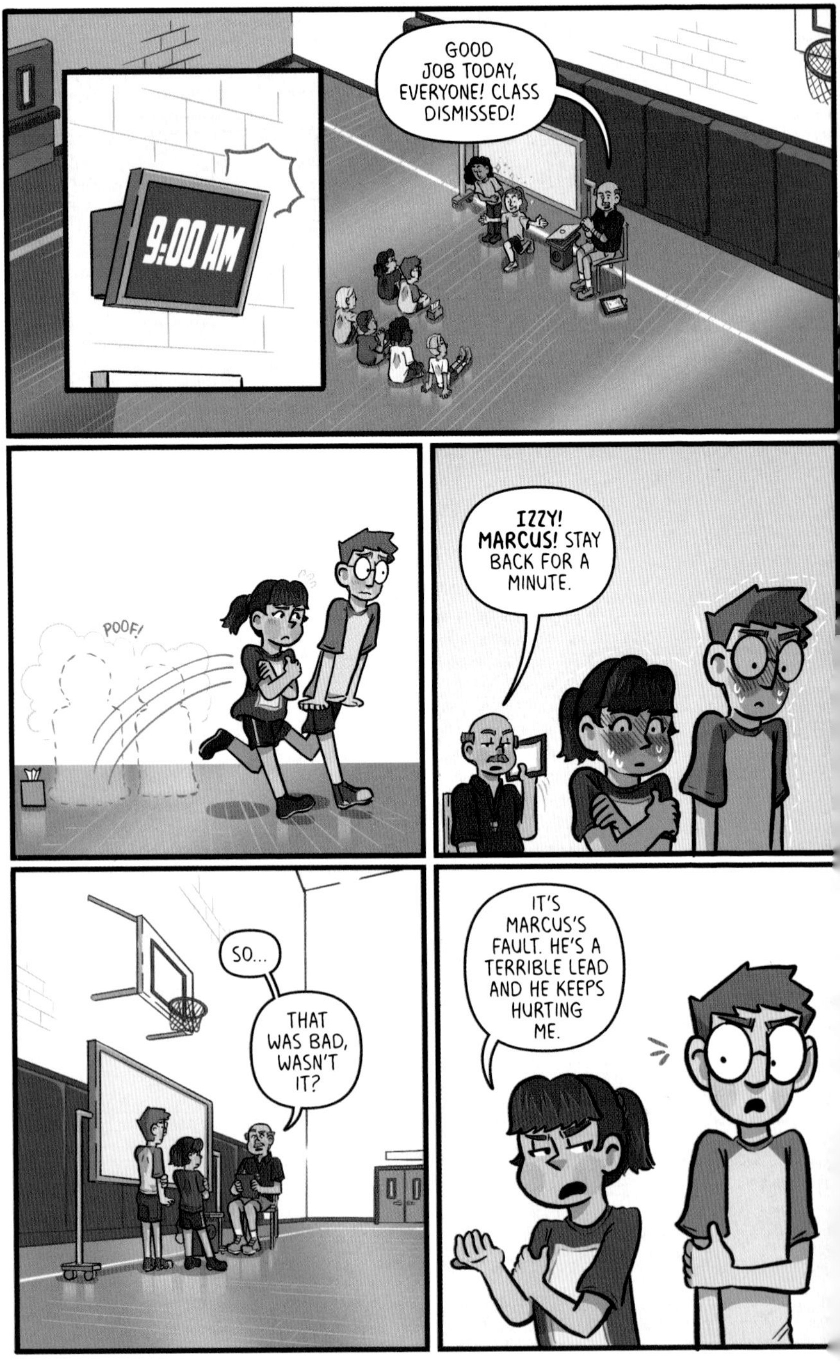
9:00 AM
GOOD JOB TODAY, EVERYONE! CLASS DISMISSED!
POOF!
IZZY! MARCUS! STAY BACK FOR A MINUTE.
SO...
THAT WAS BAD, WASN'T IT?
IT'S MARCUS'S FAULT. HE'S A TERRIBLE LEAD AND HE KEEPS HURTING ME.

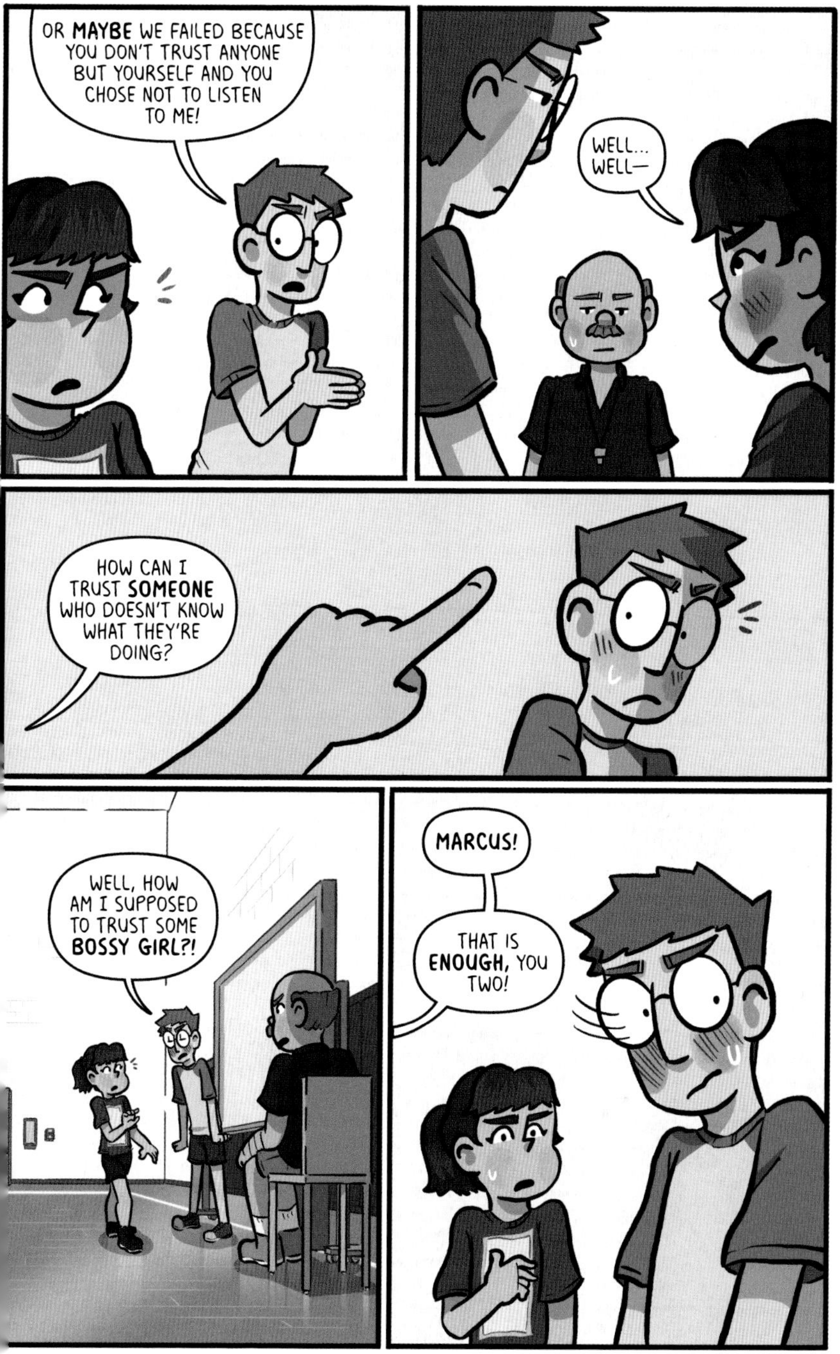
OR MAYBE WE FAILED BECAUSE YOU DON'T TRUST ANYONE BUT YOURSELF AND YOU CHOSE NOT TO LISTEN TO ME!
WELL... WELL—
HOW CAN I TRUST SOMEONE WHO DOESN'T KNOW WHAT THEY'RE DOING?
WELL, HOW AM I SUPPOSED TO TRUST SOME BOSSY GIRL?!
MARCUS!
THAT IS ENOUGH, YOU TWO!

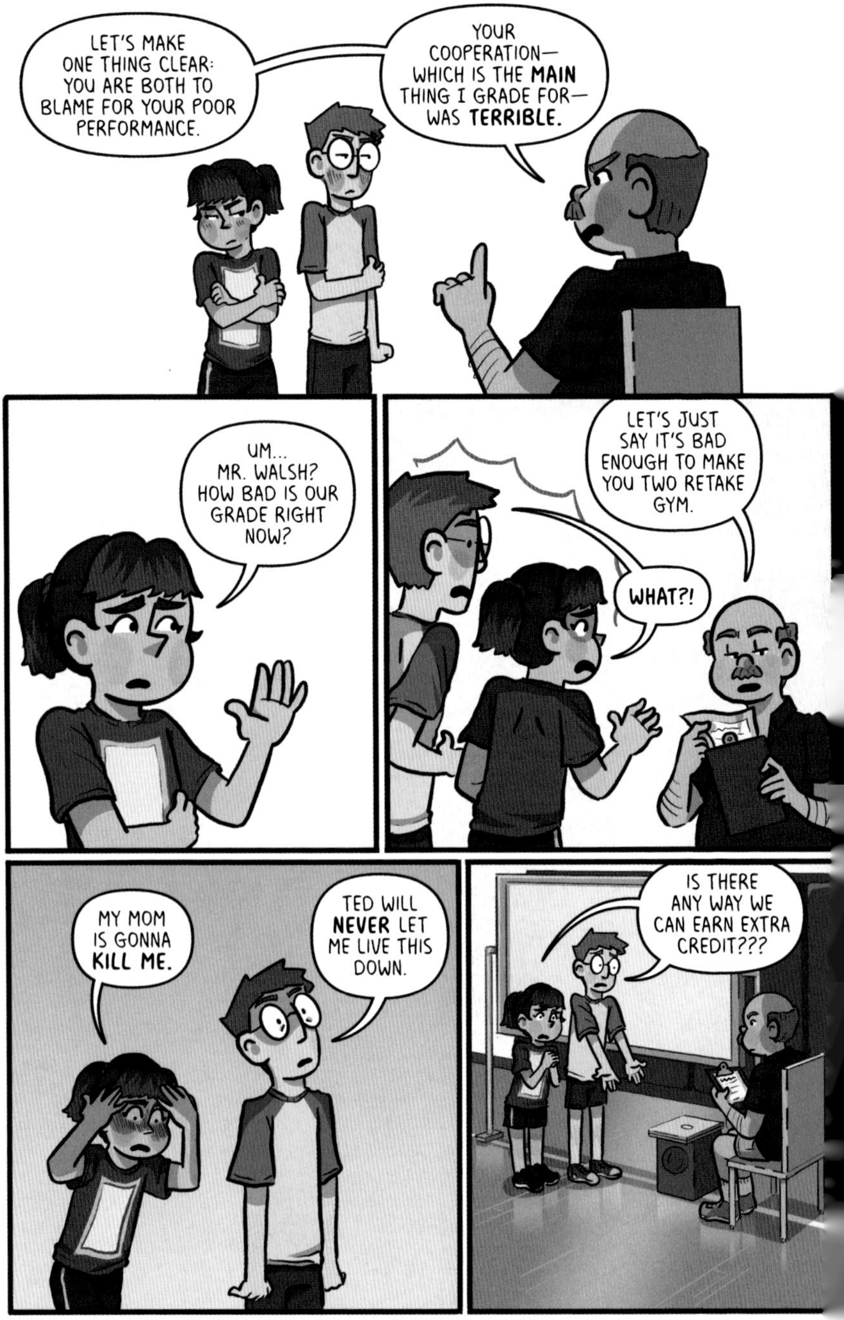
LET'S MAKE ONE THING CLEAR: YOU ARE BOTH TO BLAME FOR YOUR POOR PERFORMANCE.
YOUR COOPERATION—WHICH IS THE **MAIN** THING I GRADE FOR—WAS **TERRIBLE.**
UM... MR. WALSH? HOW BAD IS OUR GRADE RIGHT NOW?
LET'S JUST SAY IT'S BAD ENOUGH TO MAKE YOU TWO RETAKE GYM.
WHAT?!
MY MOM IS GONNA **KILL ME.**
TED WILL **NEVER** LET ME LIVE THIS DOWN.
IS THERE ANY WAY WE CAN EARN EXTRA CREDIT???

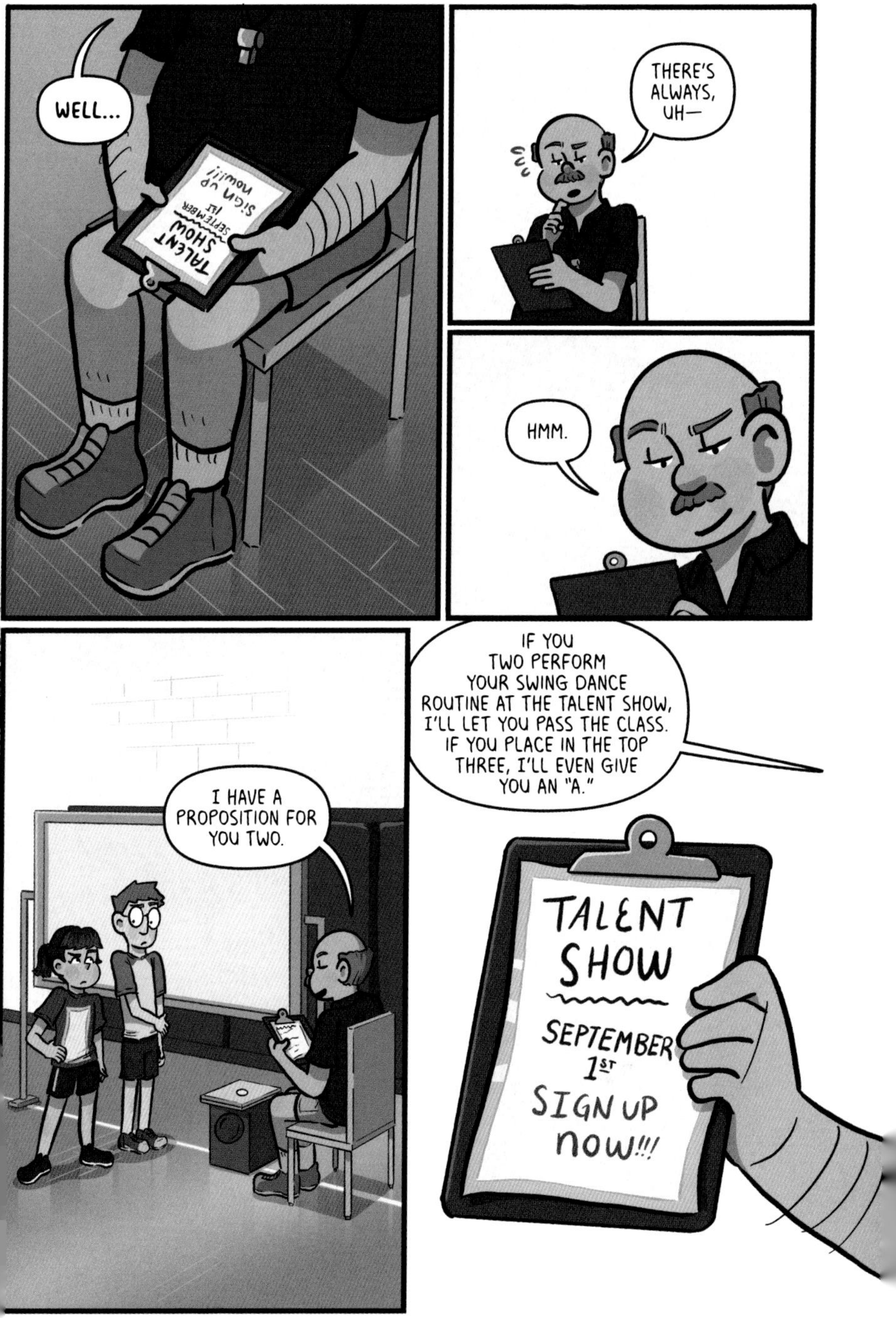
WELL...
TALENT SHOW SEPTEMBER 1ST SIGN UP NOW!!!
THERE'S ALWAYS, UH—
HMM.
I HAVE A PROPOSITION FOR YOU TWO.
IF YOU TWO PERFORM YOUR SWING DANCE ROUTINE AT THE TALENT SHOW, I'LL LET YOU PASS THE CLASS. IF YOU PLACE IN THE TOP THREE, I'LL EVEN GIVE YOU AN "A."
TALENT SHOW
SEPTEMBER 1ST
SIGN UP NOW!!!

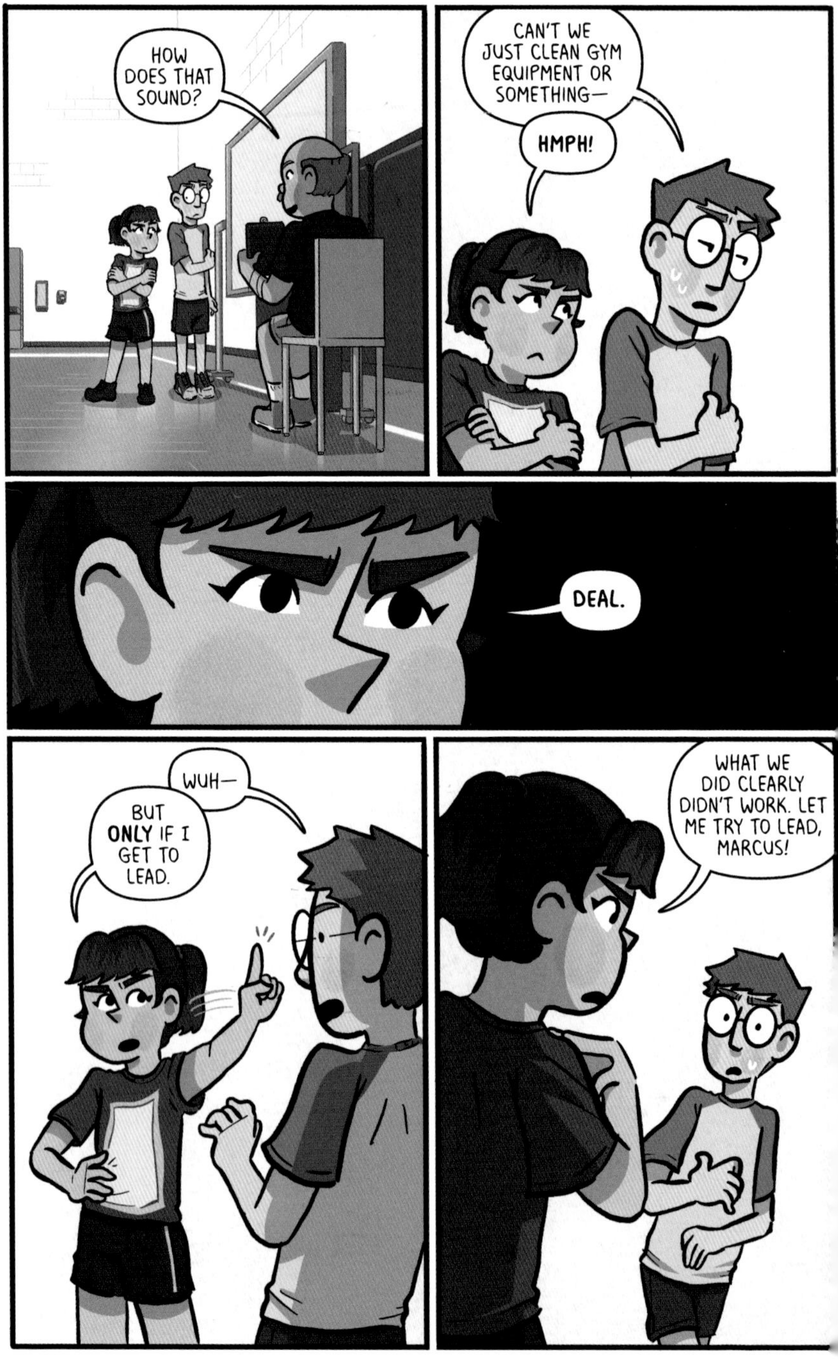
HOW DOES THAT SOUND?
CAN'T WE JUST CLEAN GYM EQUIPMENT OR SOMETHING—
HMPH!
DEAL.
WUH—
BUT **ONLY** IF I GET TO LEAD.
WHAT WE DID CLEARLY DIDN'T WORK. LET ME TRY TO LEAD, MARCUS!

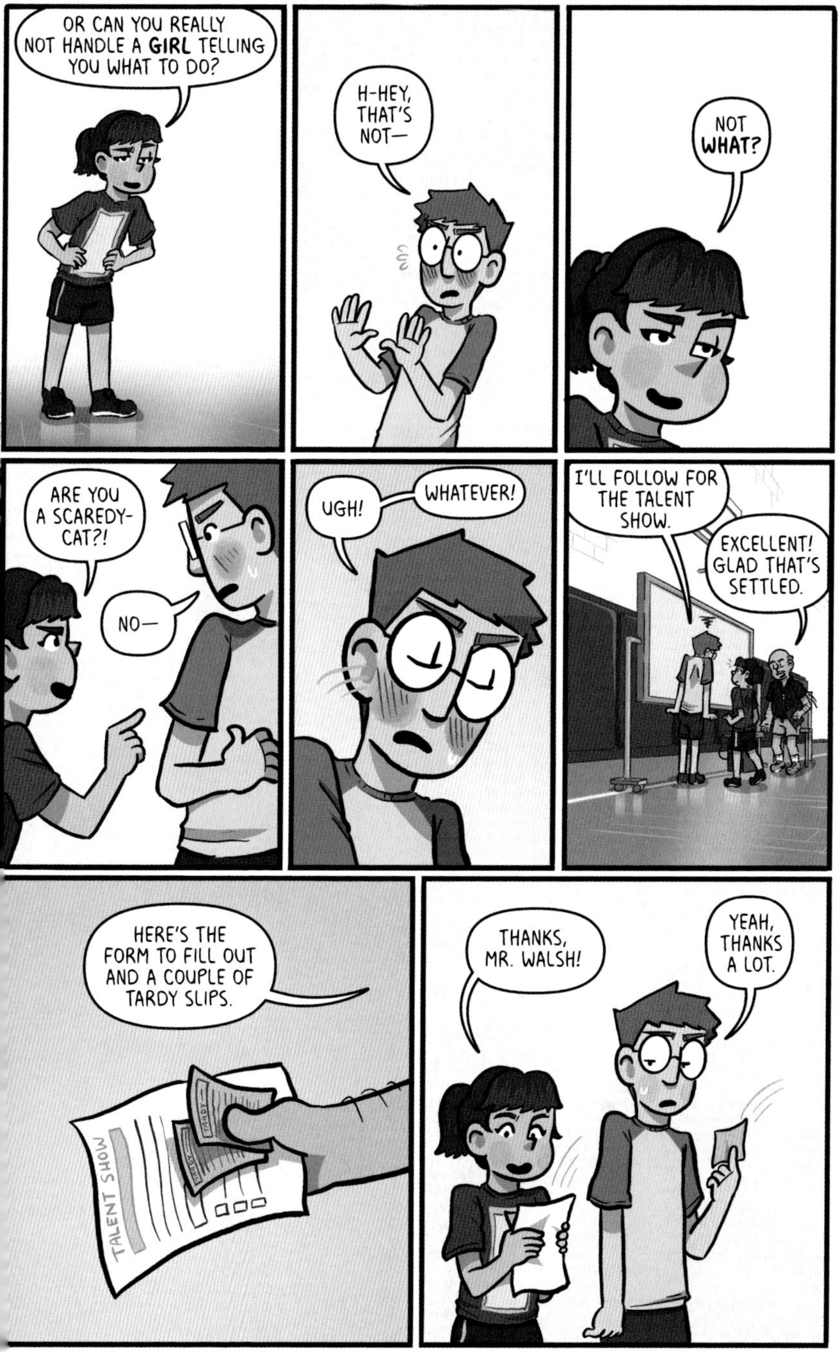
OR CAN YOU REALLY NOT HANDLE A **GIRL** TELLING YOU WHAT TO DO?
H-HEY, THAT'S NOT—
NOT **WHAT?**
ARE YOU A SCAREDY-CAT?!
NO—
UGH!
WHATEVER!
I'LL FOLLOW FOR THE TALENT SHOW.
EXCELLENT! GLAD THAT'S SETTLED.
HERE'S THE FORM TO FILL OUT AND A COUPLE OF TARDY SLIPS.
TALENT SHOW
TARDY
THANKS, MR. WALSH!
YEAH, THANKS A LOT.

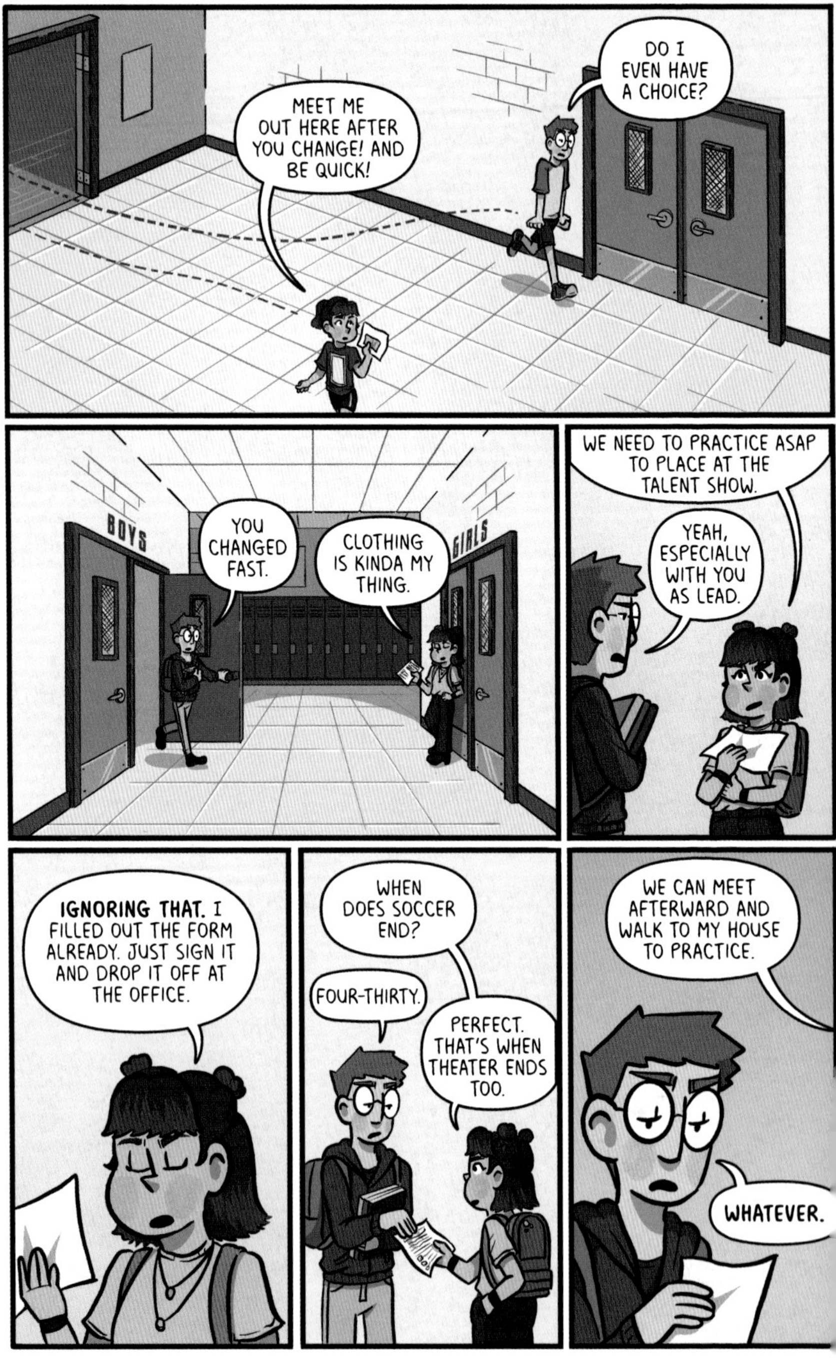
DO I EVEN HAVE A CHOICE?
MEET ME OUT HERE AFTER YOU CHANGE! AND BE QUICK!
BOYS
YOU CHANGED FAST.
CLOTHING IS KINDA MY THING.
GIRLS
WE NEED TO PRACTICE ASAP TO PLACE AT THE TALENT SHOW.
YEAH, ESPECIALLY WITH YOU AS LEAD.
IGNORING THAT. I FILLED OUT THE FORM ALREADY. JUST SIGN IT AND DROP IT OFF AT THE OFFICE.
WHEN DOES SOCCER END?
FOUR-THIRTY.
PERFECT. THAT'S WHEN THEATER ENDS TOO.
WE CAN MEET AFTERWARD AND WALK TO MY HOUSE TO PRACTICE.
WHATEVER.

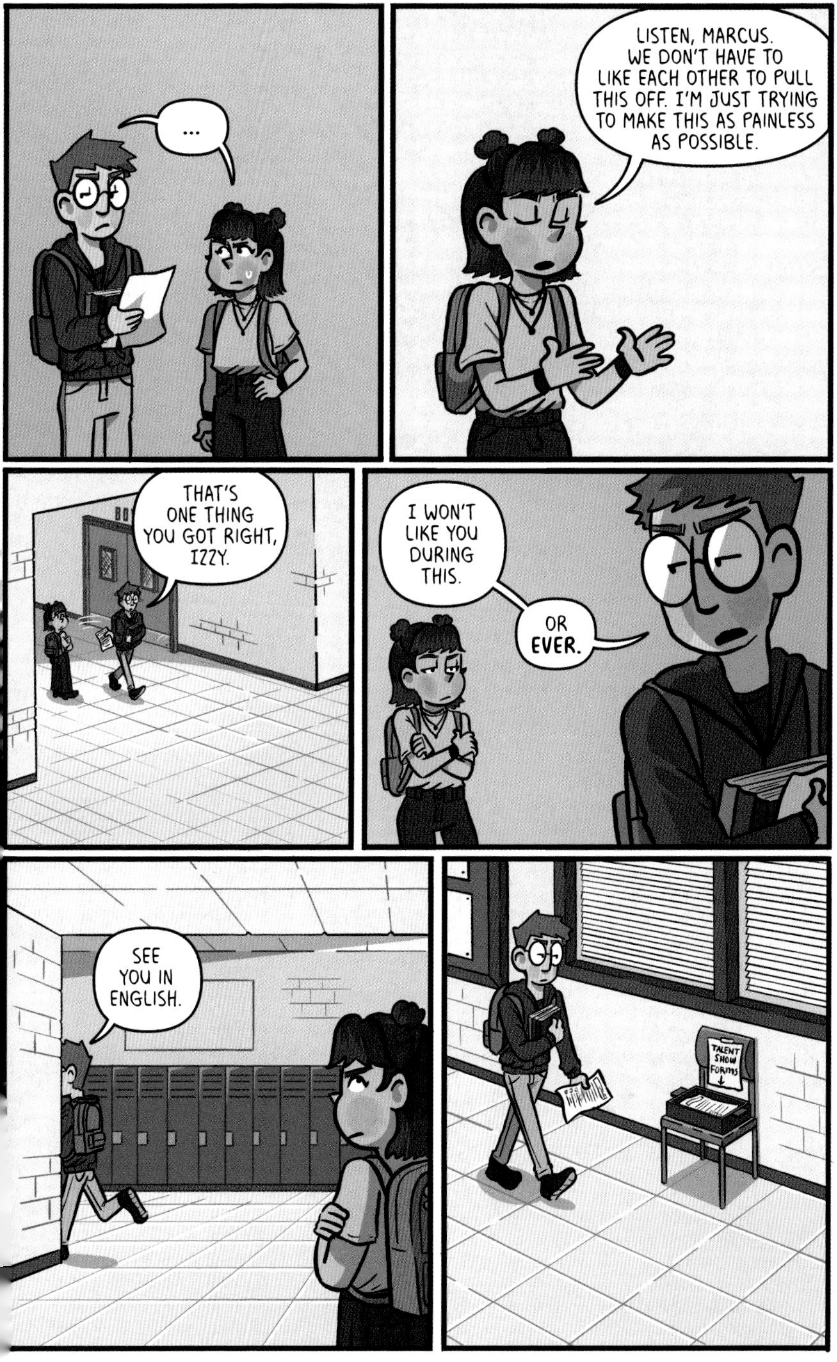
...
LISTEN, MARCUS. WE DON'T HAVE TO LIKE EACH OTHER TO PULL THIS OFF. I'M JUST TRYING TO MAKE THIS AS PAINLESS AS POSSIBLE.
THAT'S ONE THING YOU GOT RIGHT, IZZY.
I WON'T LIKE YOU DURING THIS.
OR EVER.
SEE YOU IN ENGLISH.
TALENT SHOW FORMS

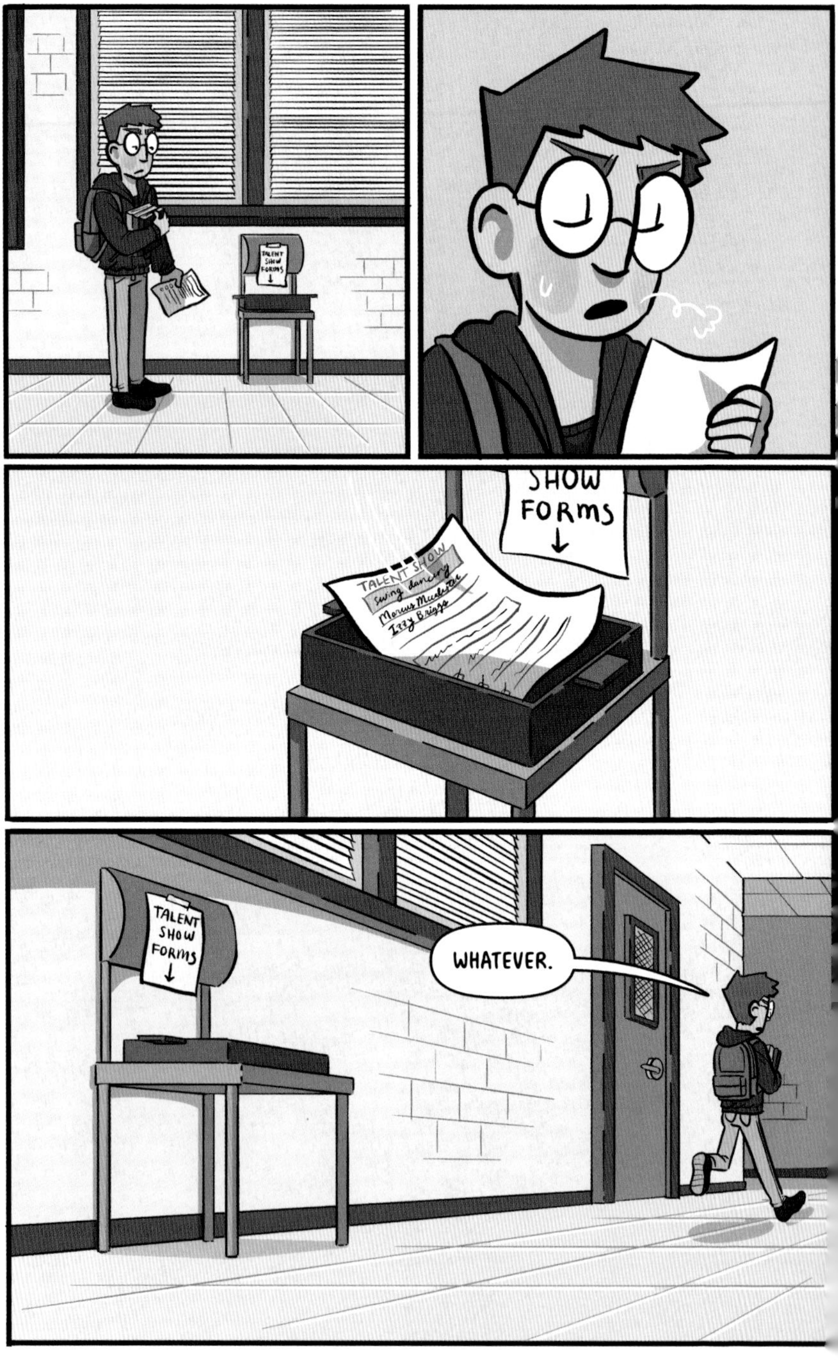
TALENT SHOW FORMS ↓
SHOW FORMS ↓
TALENT SHOW
swing dancing
Marcus Mudafie
Izzy Briggs
TALENT SHOW FORMS ↓
WHATEVER.

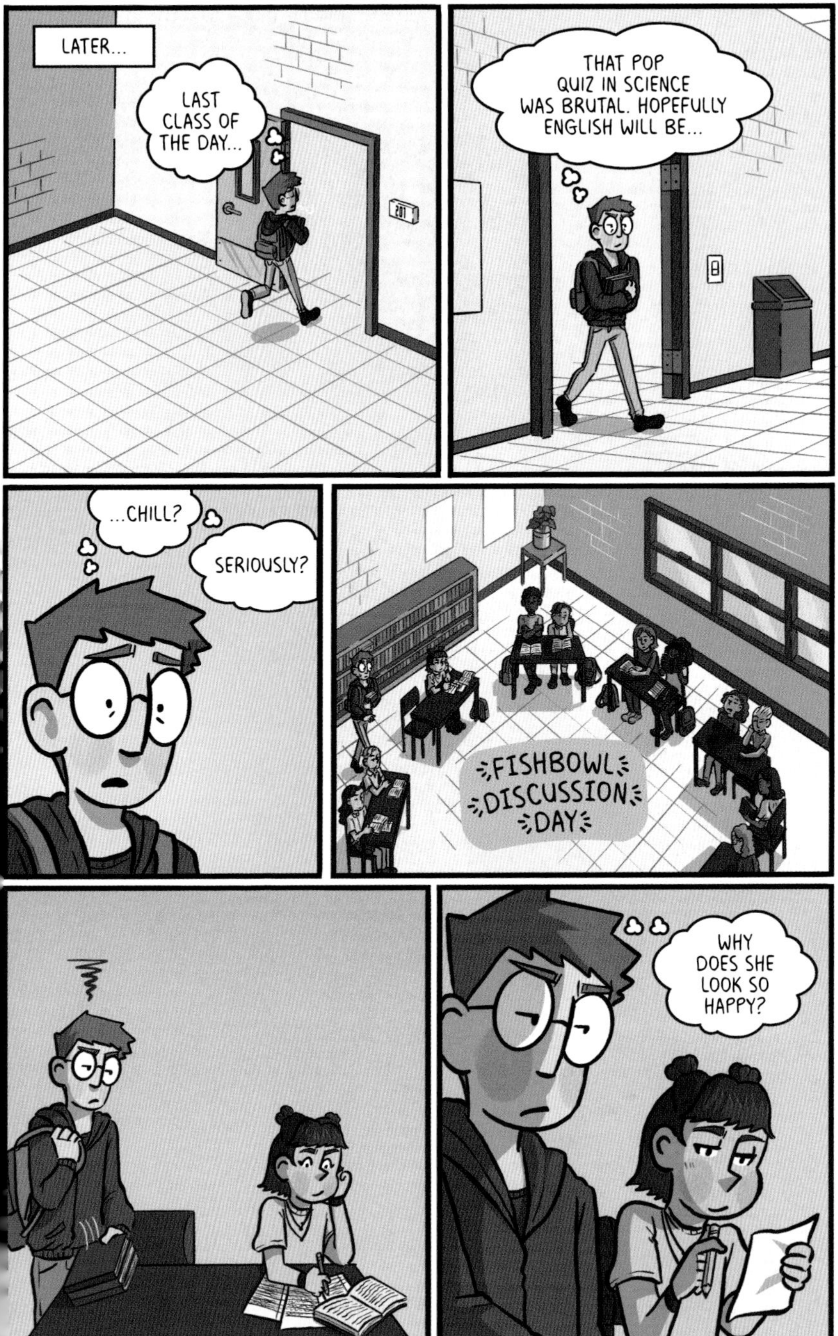
LATER...
LAST CLASS OF THE DAY...
201
THAT POP QUIZ IN SCIENCE WAS BRUTAL. HOPEFULLY ENGLISH WILL BE...
...CHILL?
SERIOUSLY?
FISHBOWL DISCUSSION DAY
WHY DOES SHE LOOK SO HAPPY?

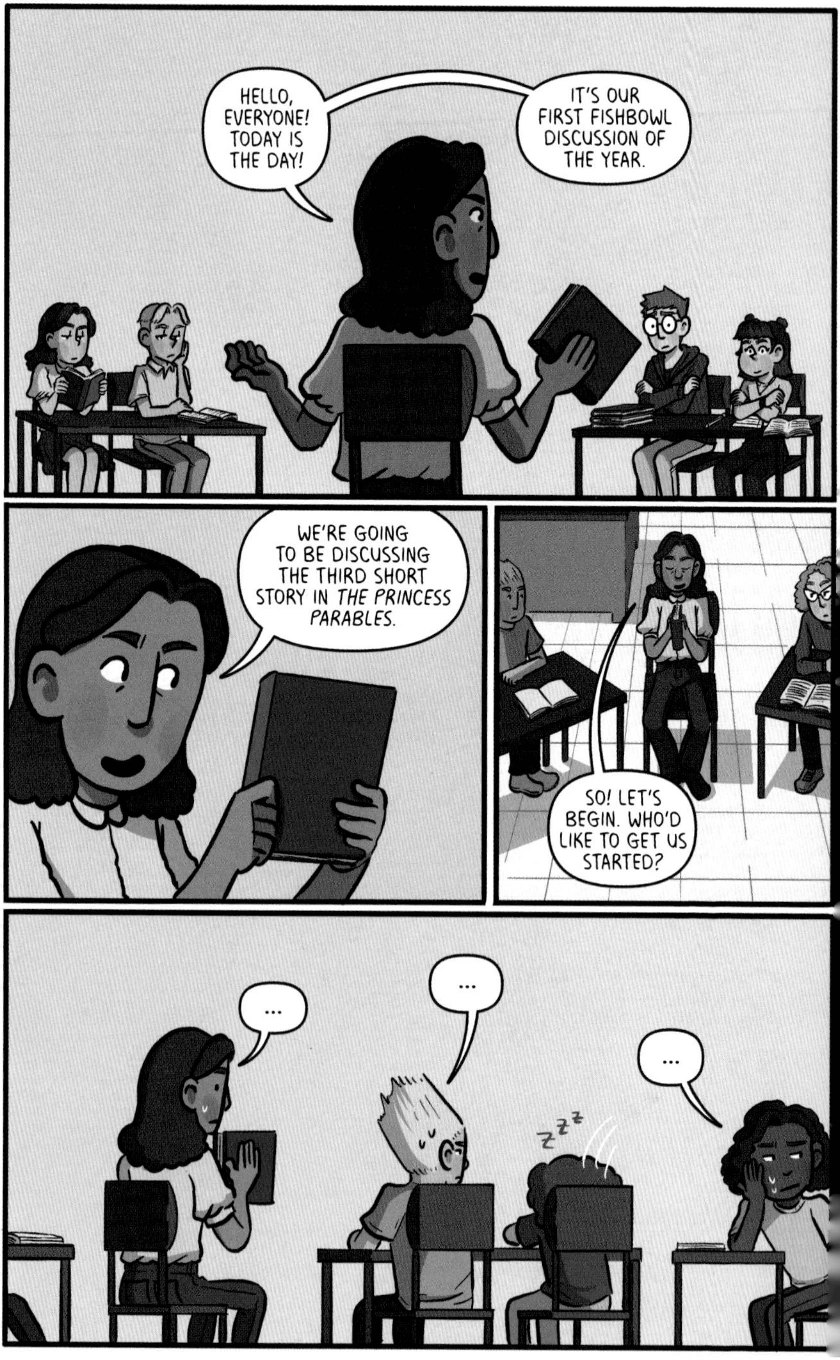
HELLO, EVERYONE! TODAY IS THE DAY!
IT'S OUR FIRST FISHBOWL DISCUSSION OF THE YEAR.
WE'RE GOING TO BE DISCUSSING THE THIRD SHORT STORY IN *THE PRINCESS PARABLES*.
SO! LET'S BEGIN. WHO'D LIKE TO GET US STARTED?
...
...
Z Z Z
...

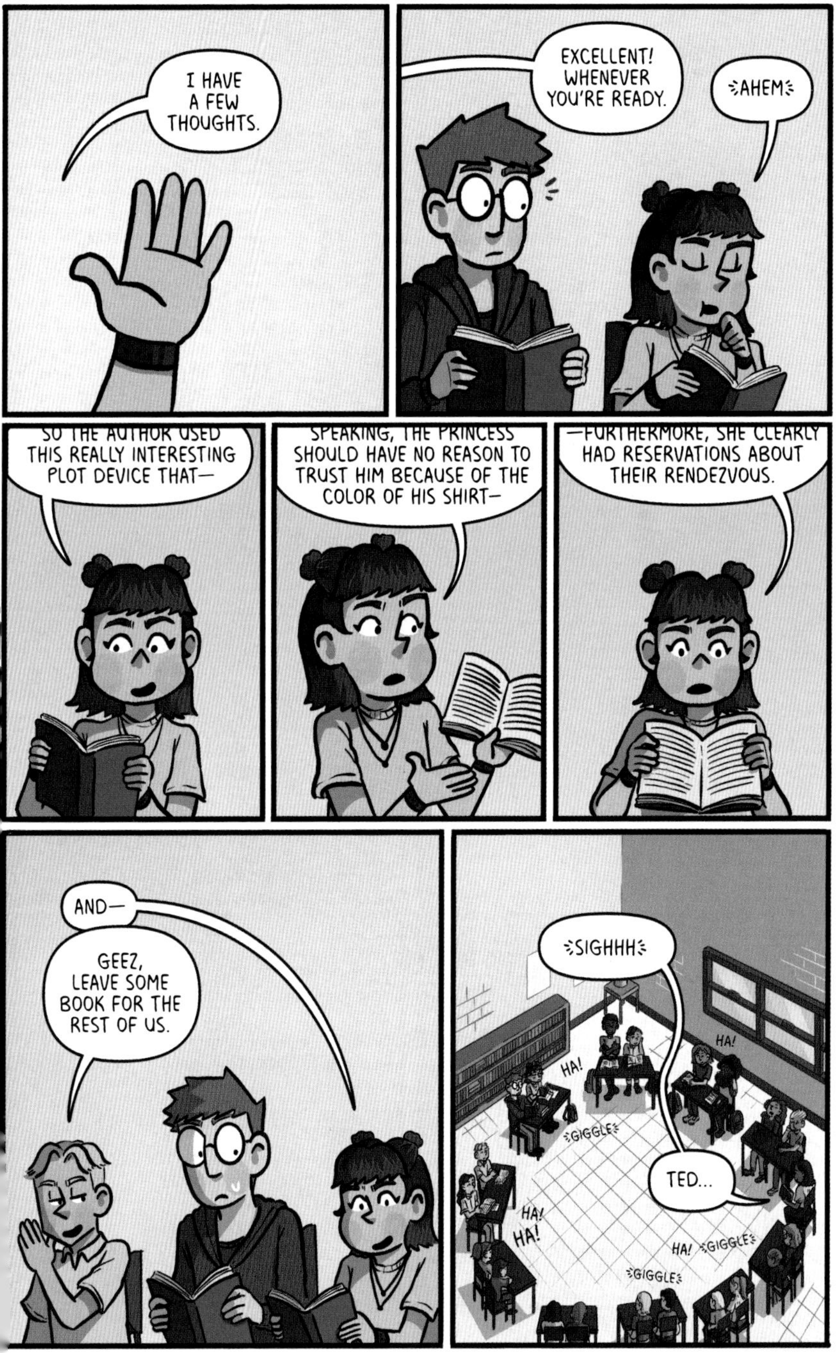
I HAVE A FEW THOUGHTS.
EXCELLENT! WHENEVER YOU'RE READY.
AHEM
SO THE AUTHOR USED THIS REALLY INTERESTING PLOT DEVICE THAT—
SPEAKING, THE PRINCESS SHOULD HAVE NO REASON TO TRUST HIM BECAUSE OF THE COLOR OF HIS SHIRT—
—FURTHERMORE, SHE CLEARLY HAD RESERVATIONS ABOUT THEIR RENDEZVOUS.
AND—
GEEZ, LEAVE SOME BOOK FOR THE REST OF US.
SIGHHH
HA!
HA!
GIGGLE
TED...
HA! HA!
HA!
GIGGLE
GIGGLE

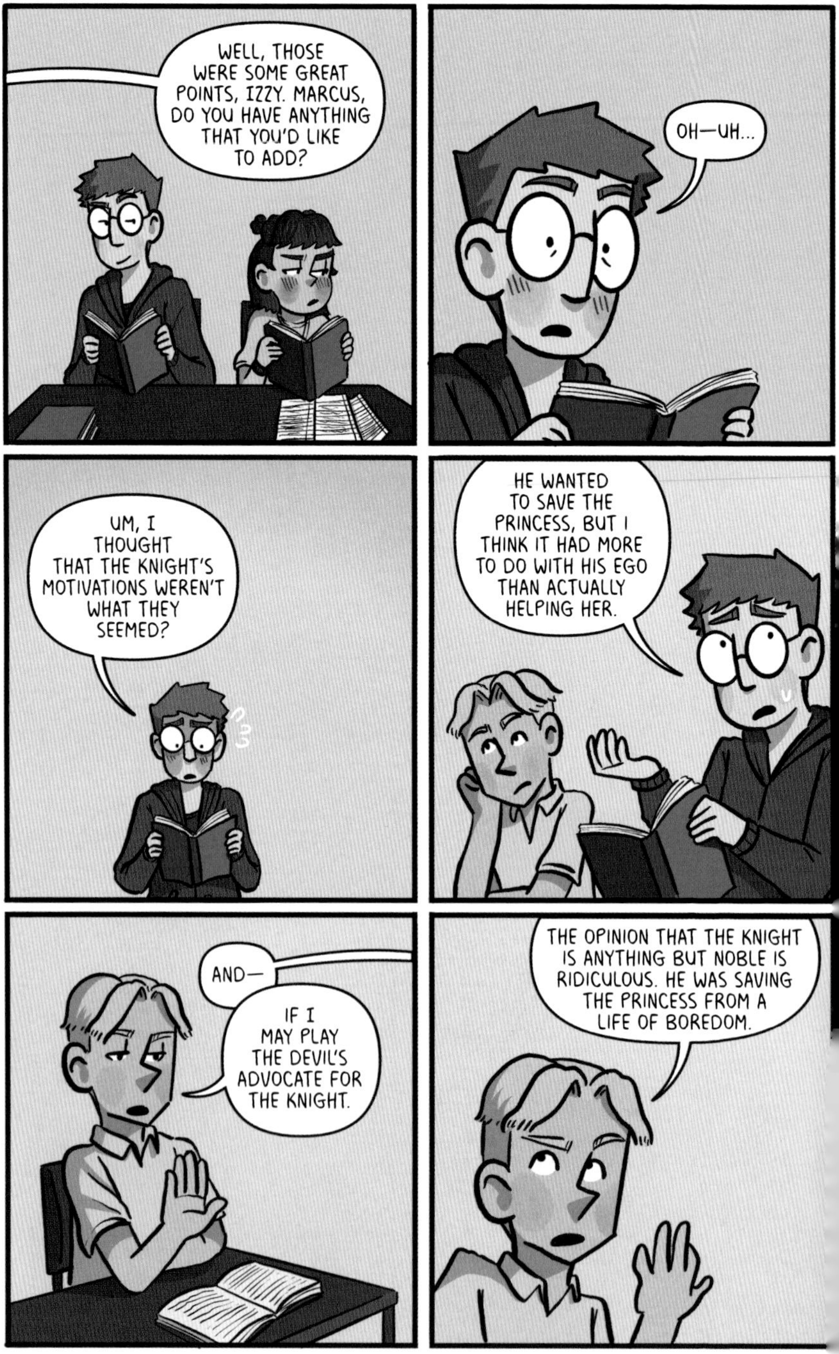
WELL, THOSE WERE SOME GREAT POINTS, IZZY. MARCUS, DO YOU HAVE ANYTHING THAT YOU'D LIKE TO ADD?
OH—UH...
UM, I THOUGHT THAT THE KNIGHT'S MOTIVATIONS WEREN'T WHAT THEY SEEMED?
HE WANTED TO SAVE THE PRINCESS, BUT I THINK IT HAD MORE TO DO WITH HIS EGO THAN ACTUALLY HELPING HER.
AND—
IF I MAY PLAY THE DEVIL'S ADVOCATE FOR THE KNIGHT.
THE OPINION THAT THE KNIGHT IS ANYTHING BUT NOBLE IS RIDICULOUS. HE WAS SAVING THE PRINCESS FROM A LIFE OF BOREDOM.

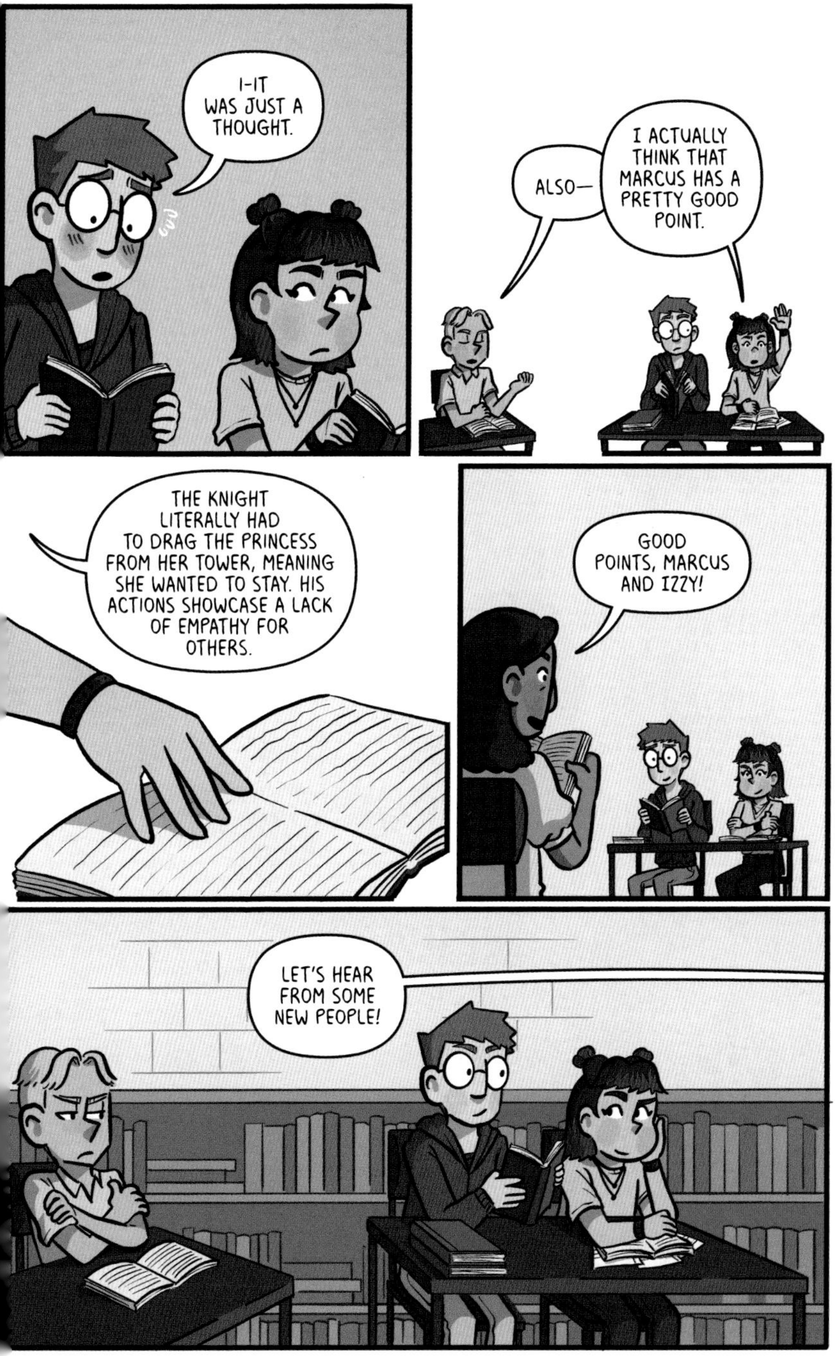
I-IT WAS JUST A THOUGHT.
ALSO—
I ACTUALLY THINK THAT MARCUS HAS A PRETTY GOOD POINT.
THE KNIGHT LITERALLY HAD TO DRAG THE PRINCESS FROM HER TOWER, MEANING SHE WANTED TO STAY. HIS ACTIONS SHOWCASE A LACK OF EMPATHY FOR OTHERS.
GOOD POINTS, MARCUS AND IZZY!
LET'S HEAR FROM SOME NEW PEOPLE!

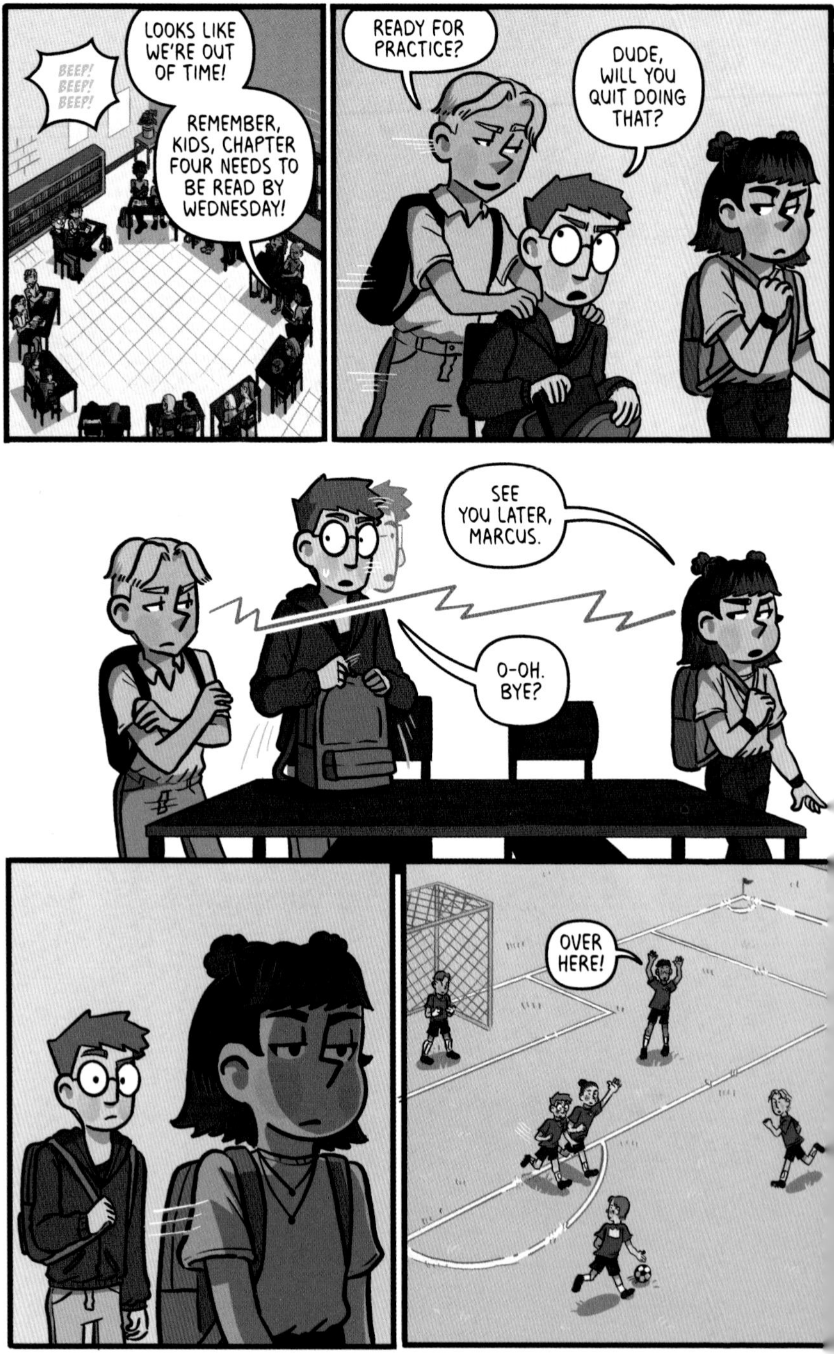
BEEP! BEEP! BEEP!
LOOKS LIKE WE'RE OUT OF TIME!
REMEMBER, KIDS, CHAPTER FOUR NEEDS TO BE READ BY WEDNESDAY!
READY FOR PRACTICE?
DUDE, WILL YOU QUIT DOING THAT?
SEE YOU LATER, MARCUS.
O-OH. BYE?
OVER HERE!

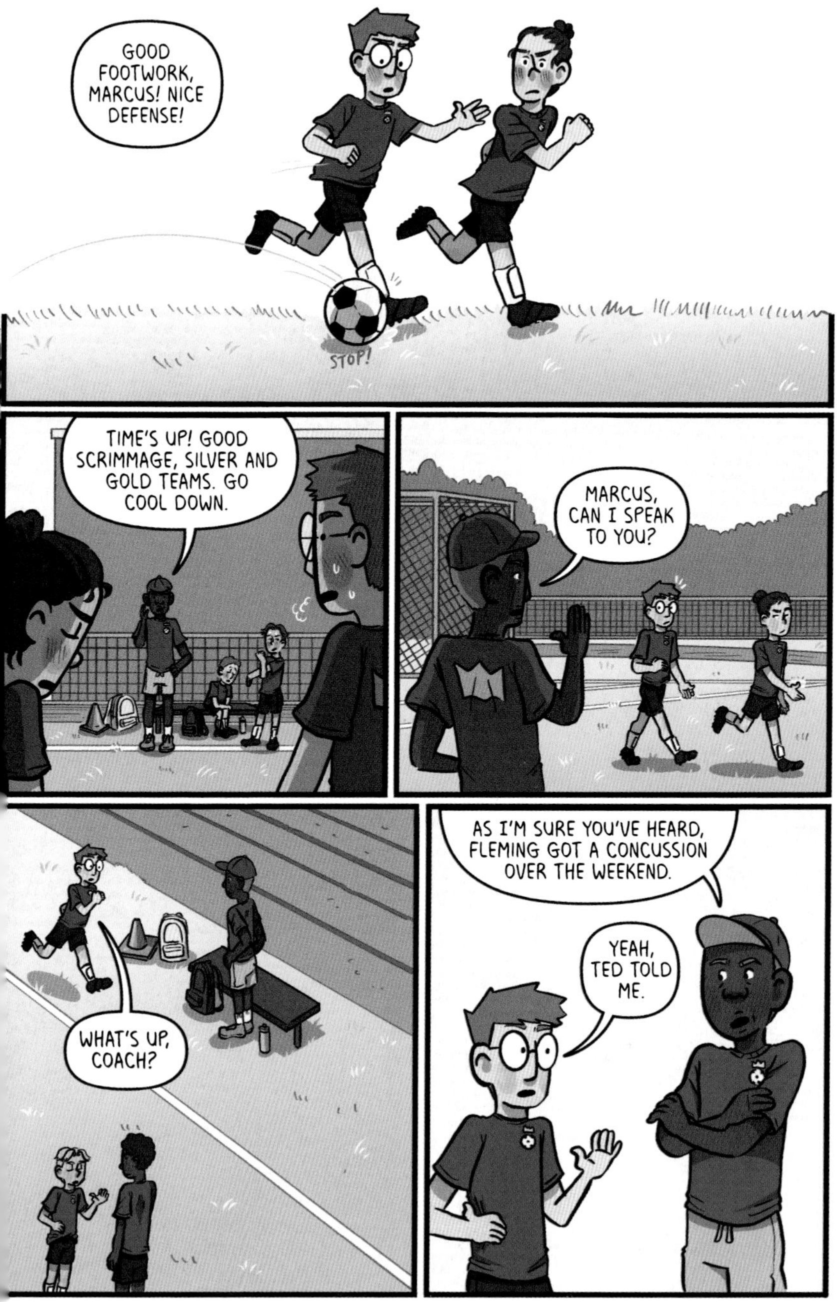
GOOD FOOTWORK, MARCUS! NICE DEFENSE!
STOP!
TIME'S UP! GOOD SCRIMMAGE, SILVER AND GOLD TEAMS. GO COOL DOWN.
MARCUS, CAN I SPEAK TO YOU?
WHAT'S UP, COACH?
AS I'M SURE YOU'VE HEARD, FLEMING GOT A CONCUSSION OVER THE WEEKEND.
YEAH, TED TOLD ME.

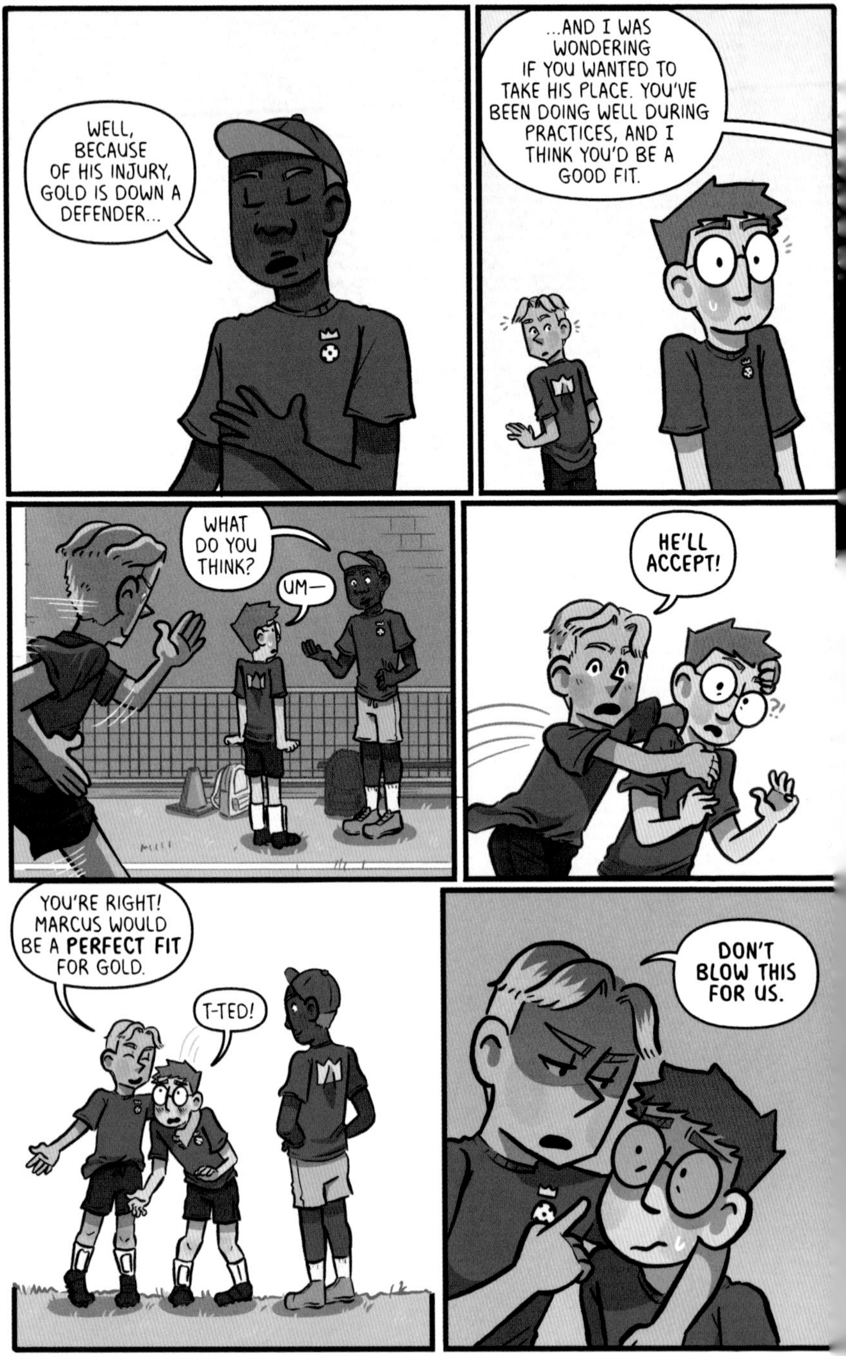
WELL, BECAUSE OF HIS INJURY, GOLD IS DOWN A DEFENDER...
...AND I WAS WONDERING IF YOU WANTED TO TAKE HIS PLACE. YOU'VE BEEN DOING WELL DURING PRACTICES, AND I THINK YOU'D BE A GOOD FIT.
WHAT DO YOU THINK?
UM—
HE'LL ACCEPT!
YOU'RE RIGHT! MARCUS WOULD BE A **PERFECT FIT** FOR GOLD.
T-TED!
DON'T BLOW THIS FOR US.

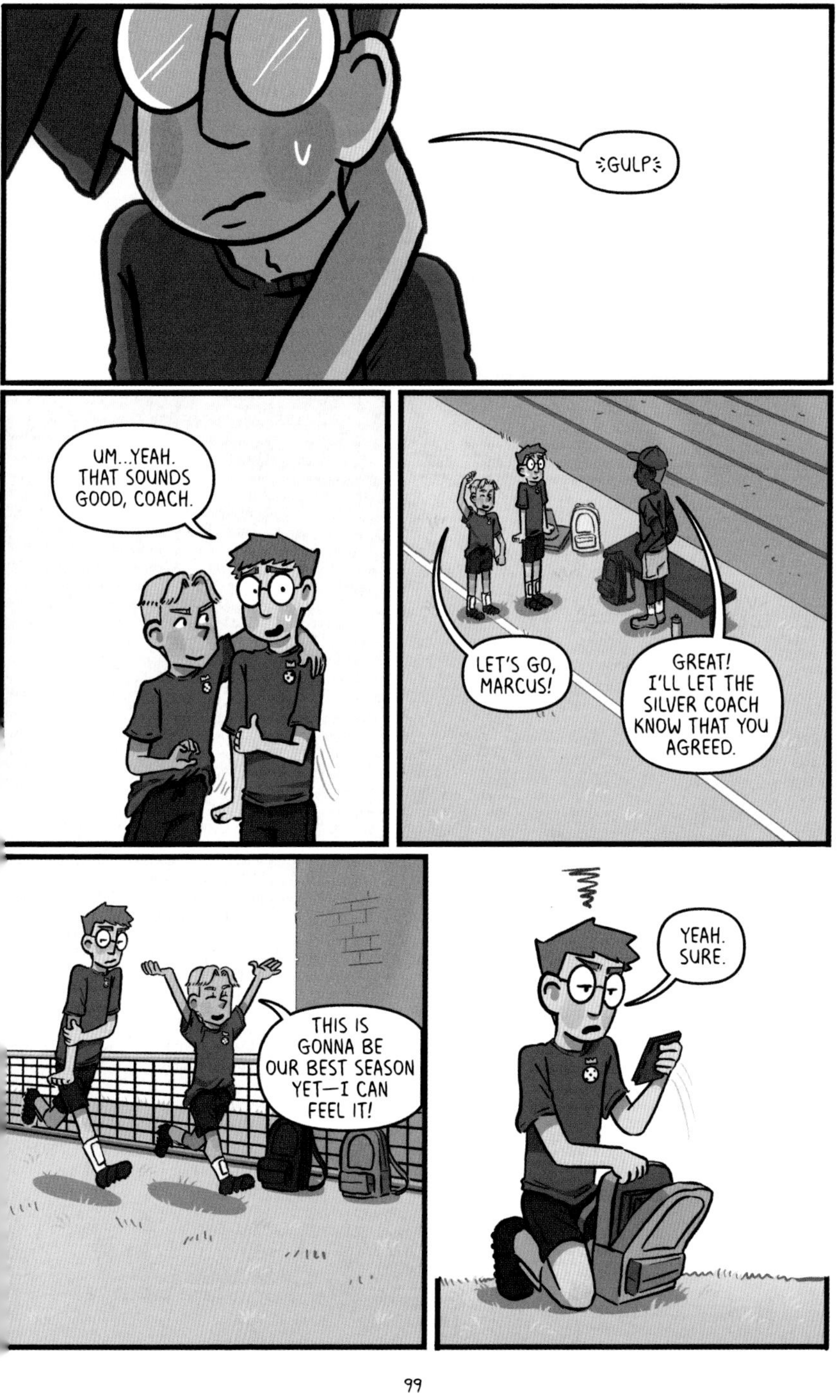
GULP
UM...YEAH. THAT SOUNDS GOOD, COACH.
GREAT! I'LL LET THE SILVER COACH KNOW THAT YOU AGREED.
LET'S GO, MARCUS!
THIS IS GONNA BE OUR BEST SEASON YET—I CAN FEEL IT!
YEAH. SURE.

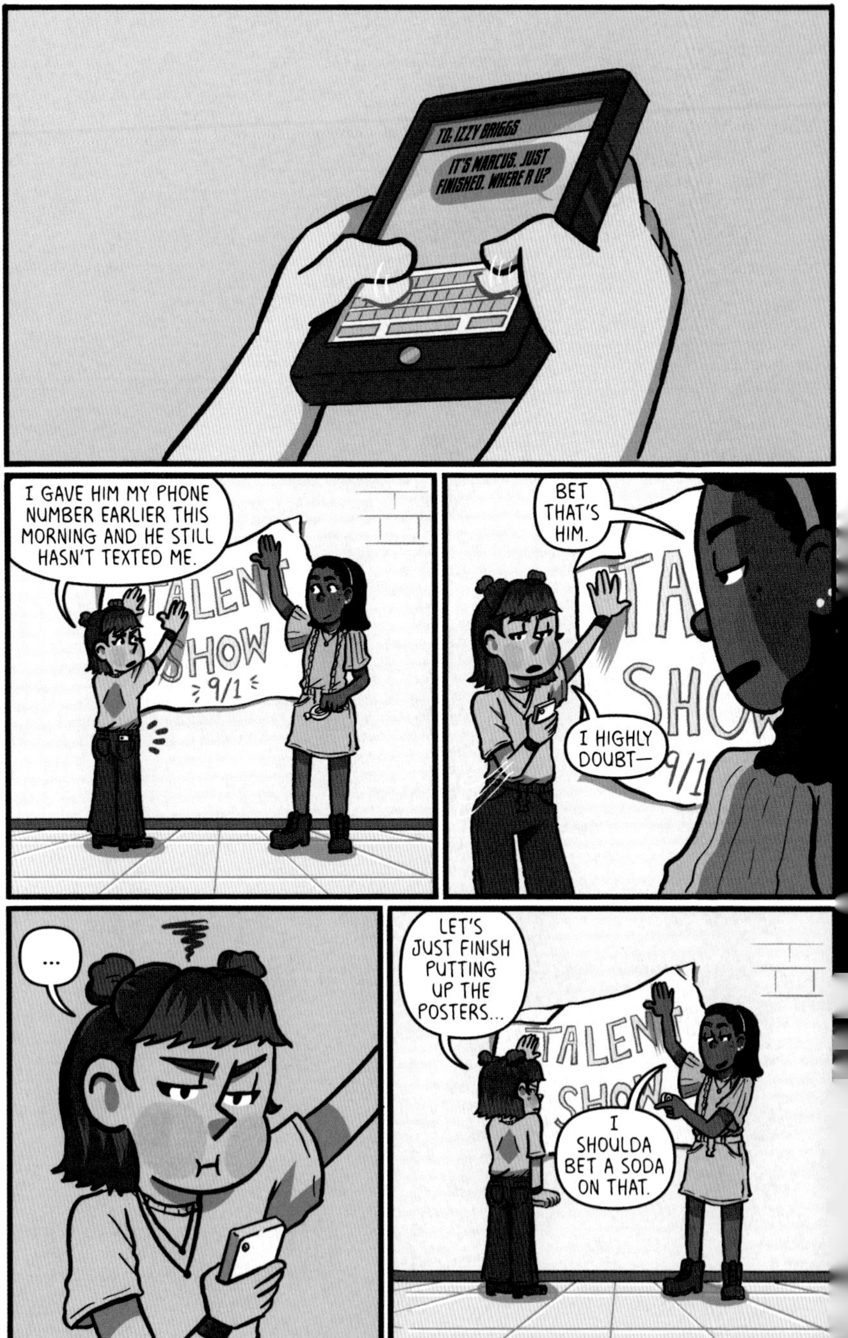
TO: IZZY BRIGGS
IT'S MARCUS. JUST FINISHED. WHERE R U?
I GAVE HIM MY PHONE NUMBER EARLIER THIS MORNING AND HE STILL HASN'T TEXTED ME.
TALENT SHOW 9/1
BET THAT'S HIM.
I HIGHLY DOUBT—
...
LET'S JUST FINISH PUTTING UP THE POSTERS...
I SHOULDA BET A SODA ON THAT.

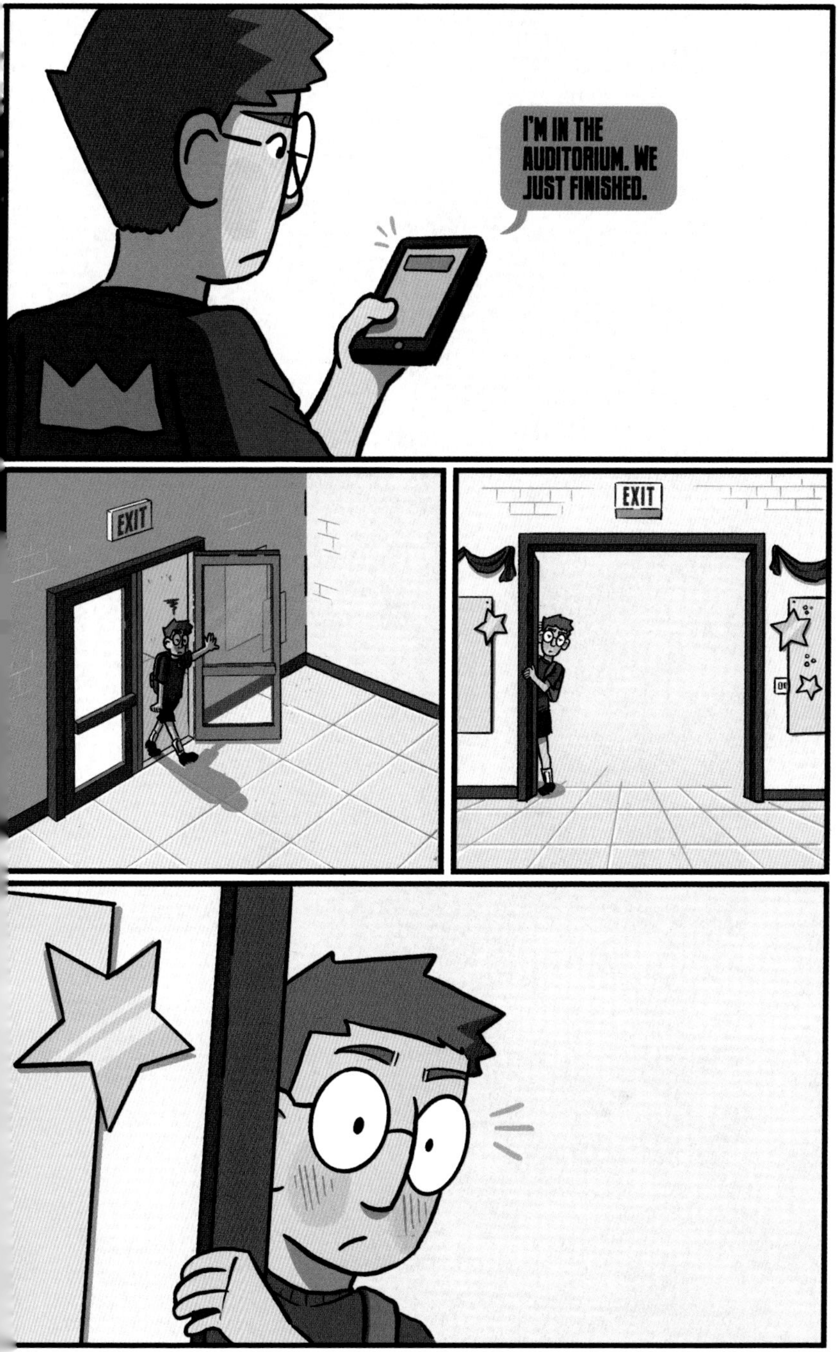
I'M IN THE AUDITORIUM. WE JUST FINISHED.
EXIT
EXIT

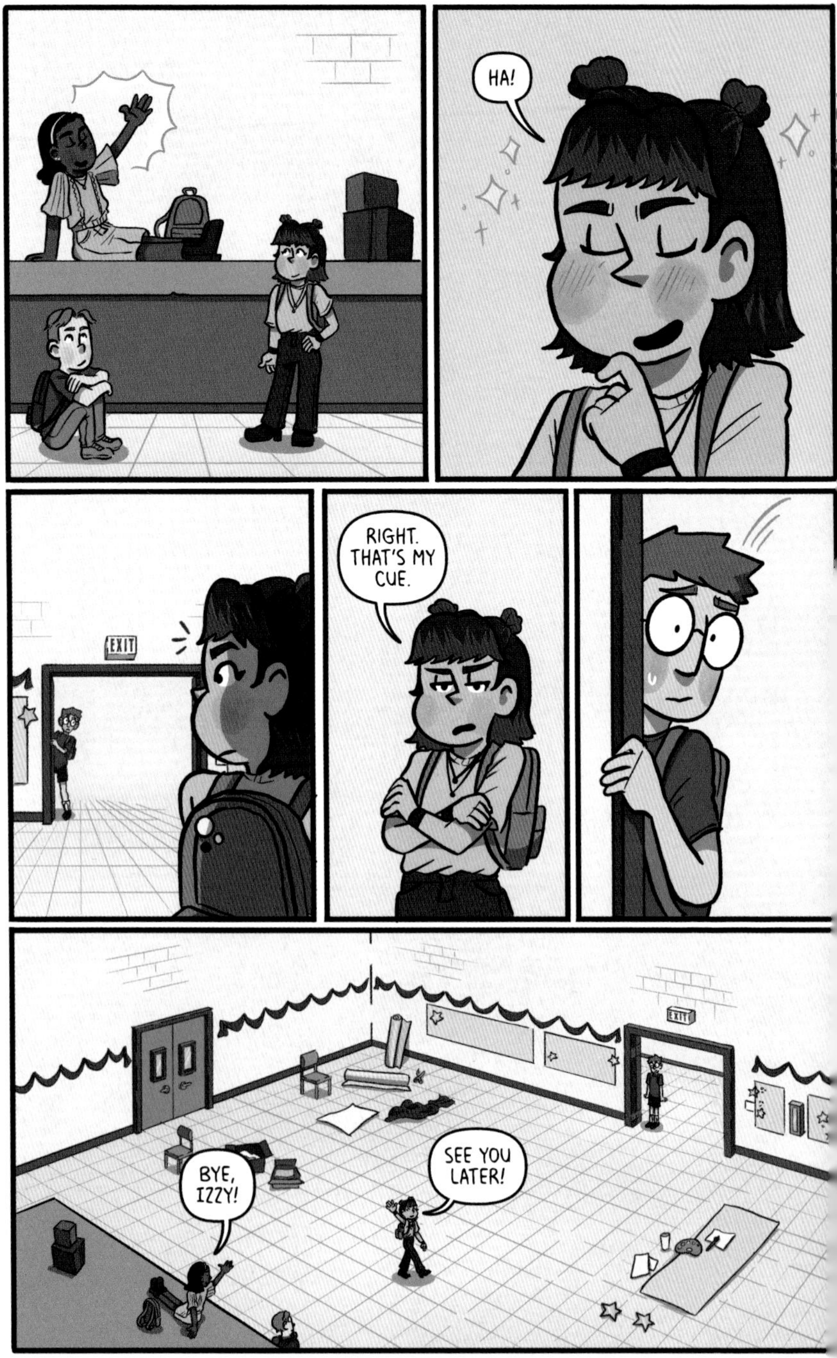
HA!
RIGHT. THAT'S MY CUE.
BYE, IZZY!
SEE YOU LATER!

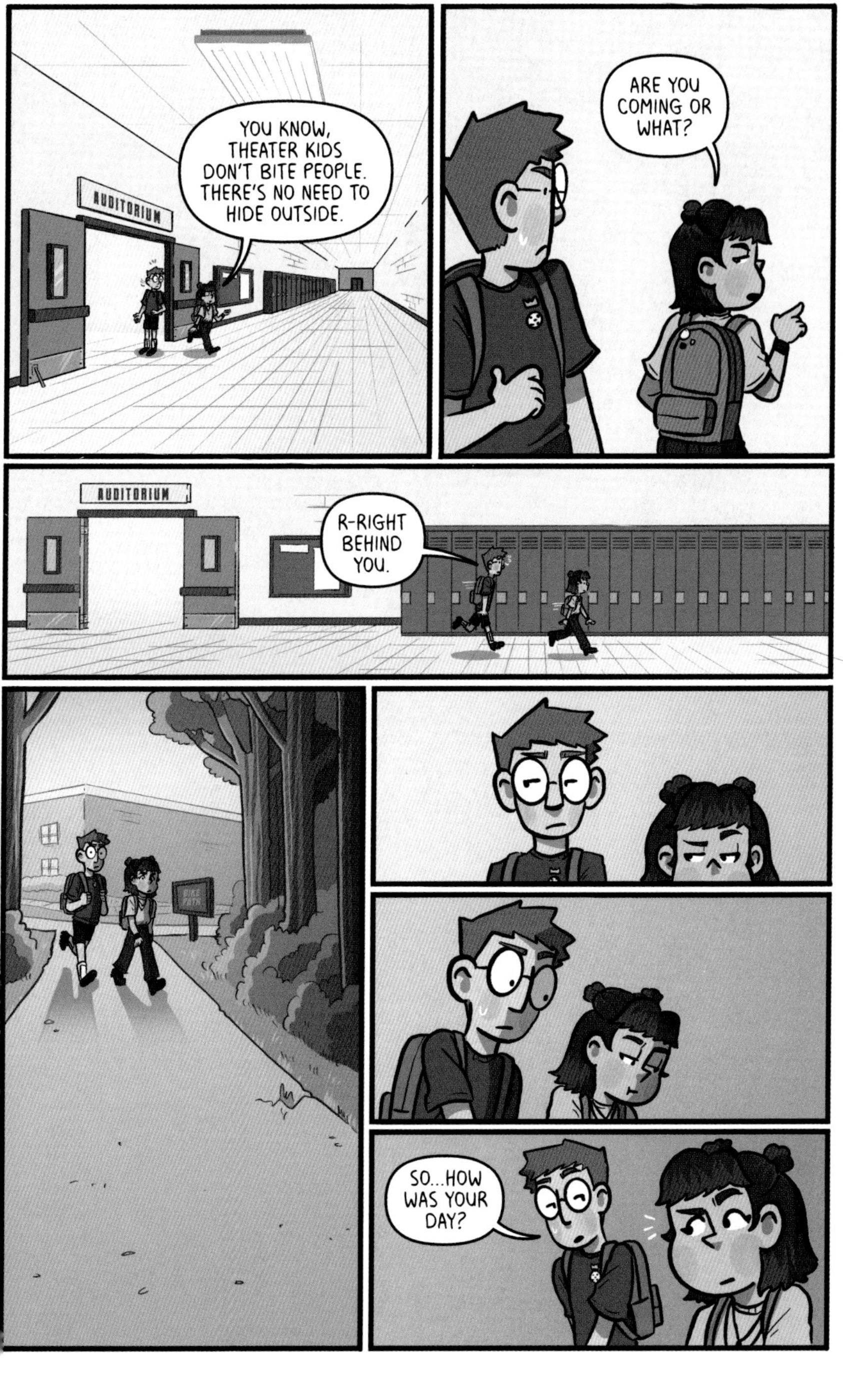
AUDITORIUM
YOU KNOW, THEATER KIDS DON'T BITE PEOPLE. THERE'S NO NEED TO HIDE OUTSIDE.
ARE YOU COMING OR WHAT?
AUDITORIUM
R-RIGHT BEHIND YOU.
SO...HOW WAS YOUR DAY?

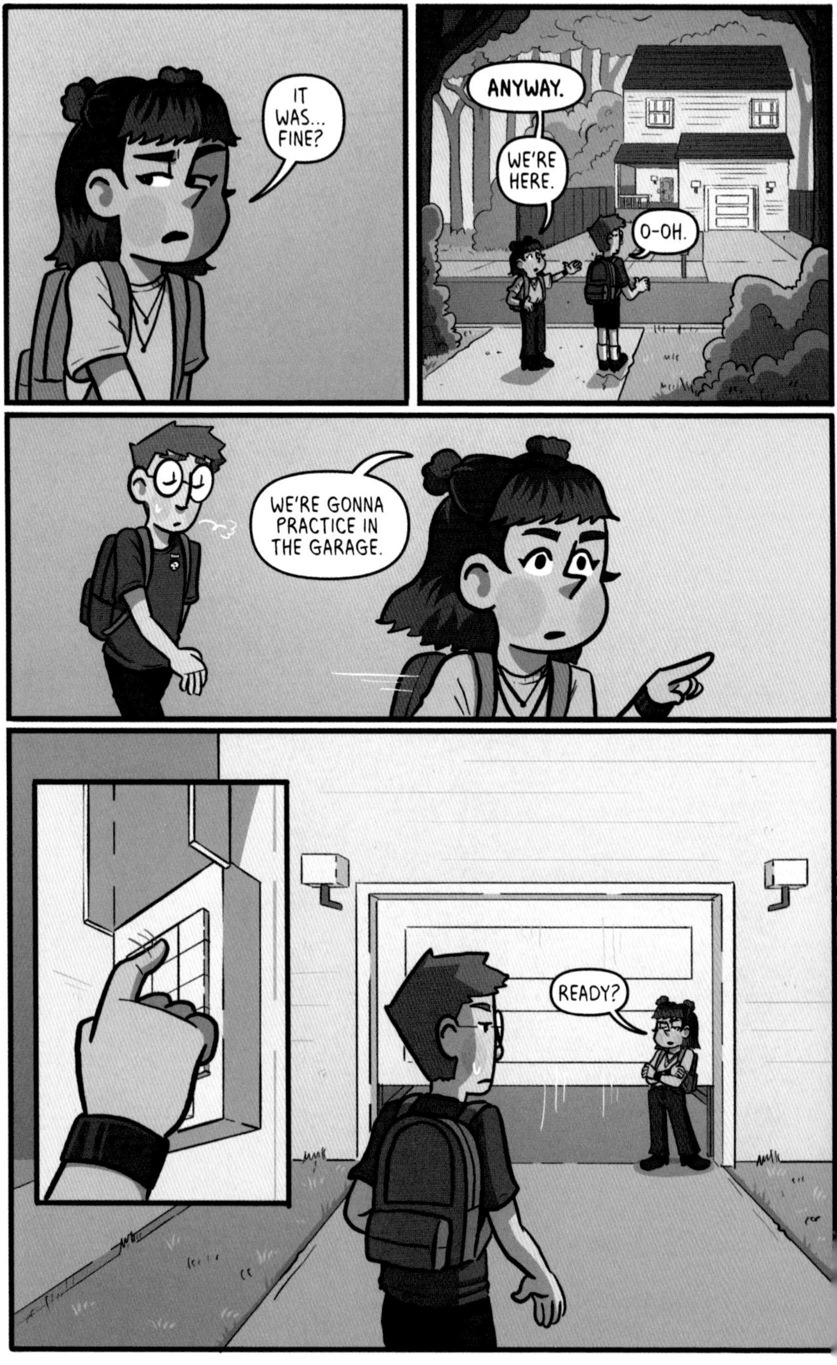
IT WAS... FINE?
ANYWAY.
WE'RE HERE.
O-OH.
WE'RE GONNA PRACTICE IN THE GARAGE.
READY?

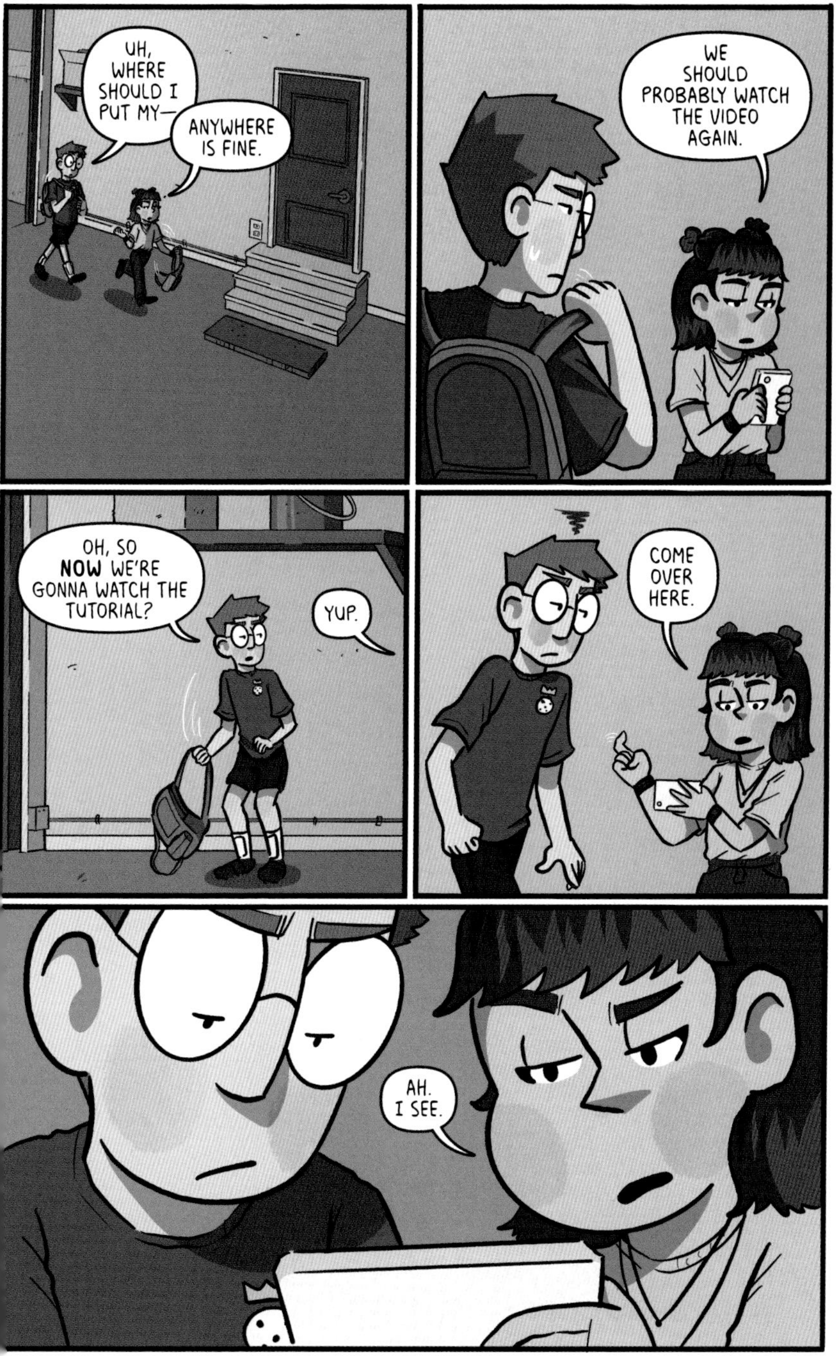
UH, WHERE SHOULD I PUT MY—
ANYWHERE IS FINE.
WE SHOULD PROBABLY WATCH THE VIDEO AGAIN.
OH, SO **NOW** WE'RE GONNA WATCH THE TUTORIAL?
YUP.
COME OVER HERE.
AH. I SEE.

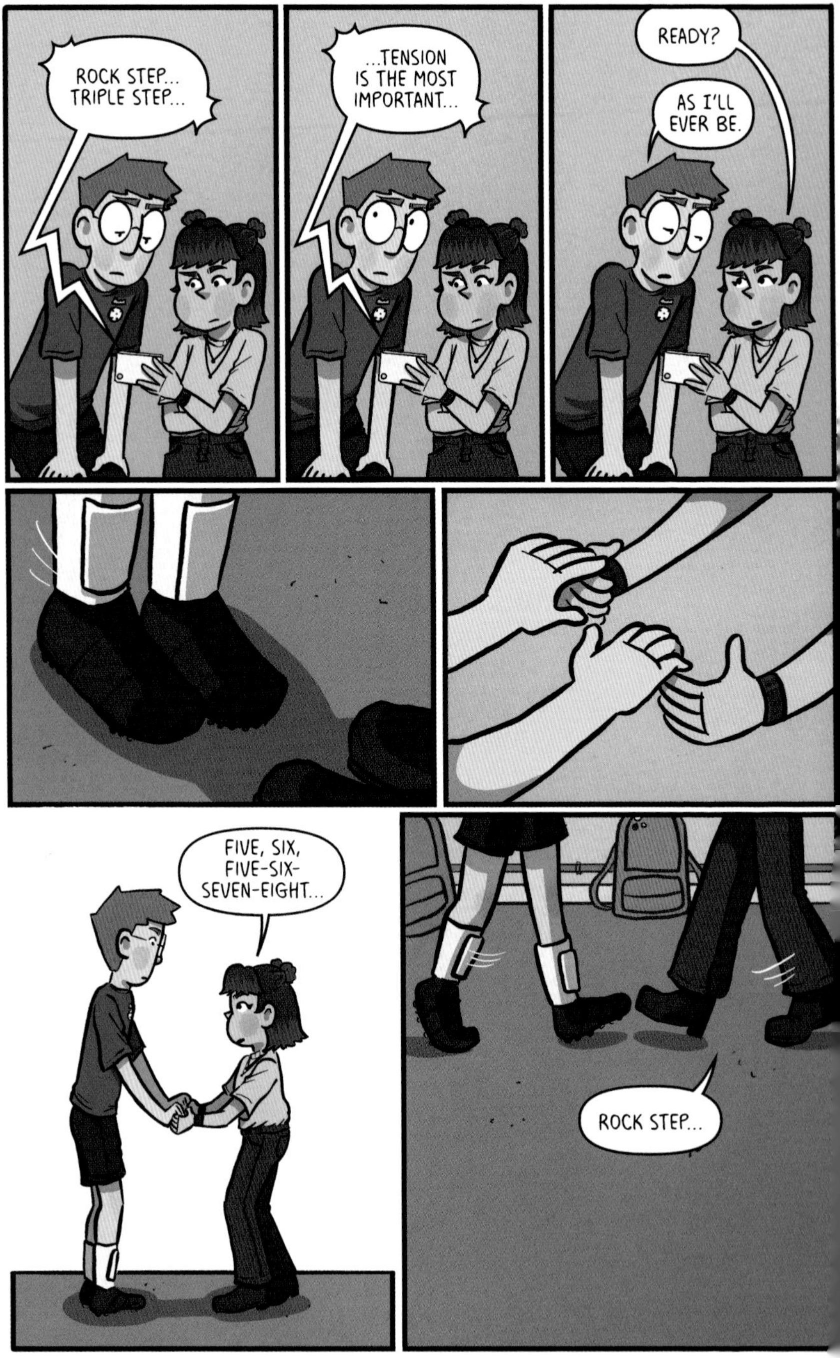
ROCK STEP... TRIPLE STEP...
...TENSION IS THE MOST IMPORTANT...
READY?
AS I'LL EVER BE.
FIVE, SIX, FIVE-SIX-SEVEN-EIGHT...
ROCK STEP...

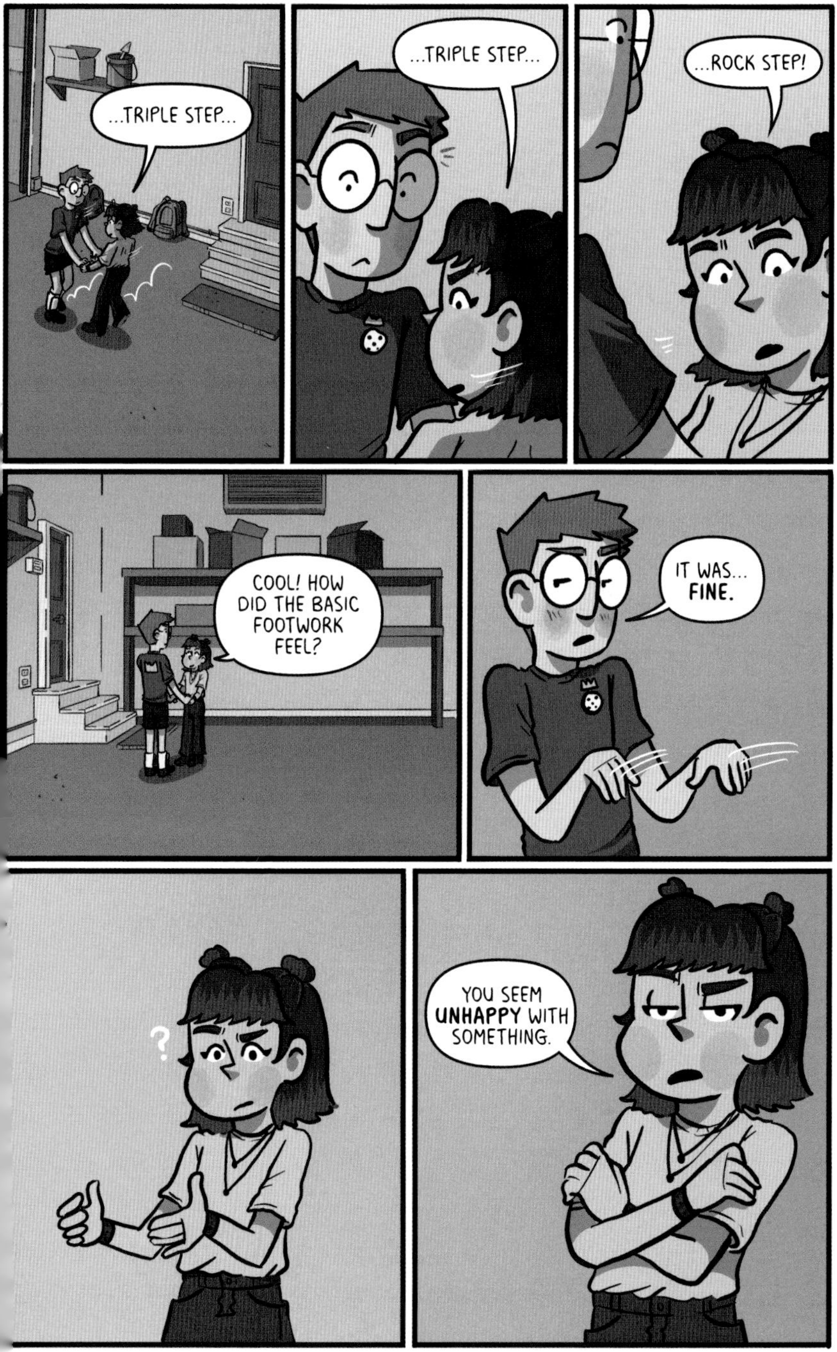
...TRIPLE STEP...
...TRIPLE STEP...
...ROCK STEP!
COOL! HOW DID THE BASIC FOOTWORK FEEL?
IT WAS... **FINE.**
?
YOU SEEM **UNHAPPY** WITH SOMETHING.

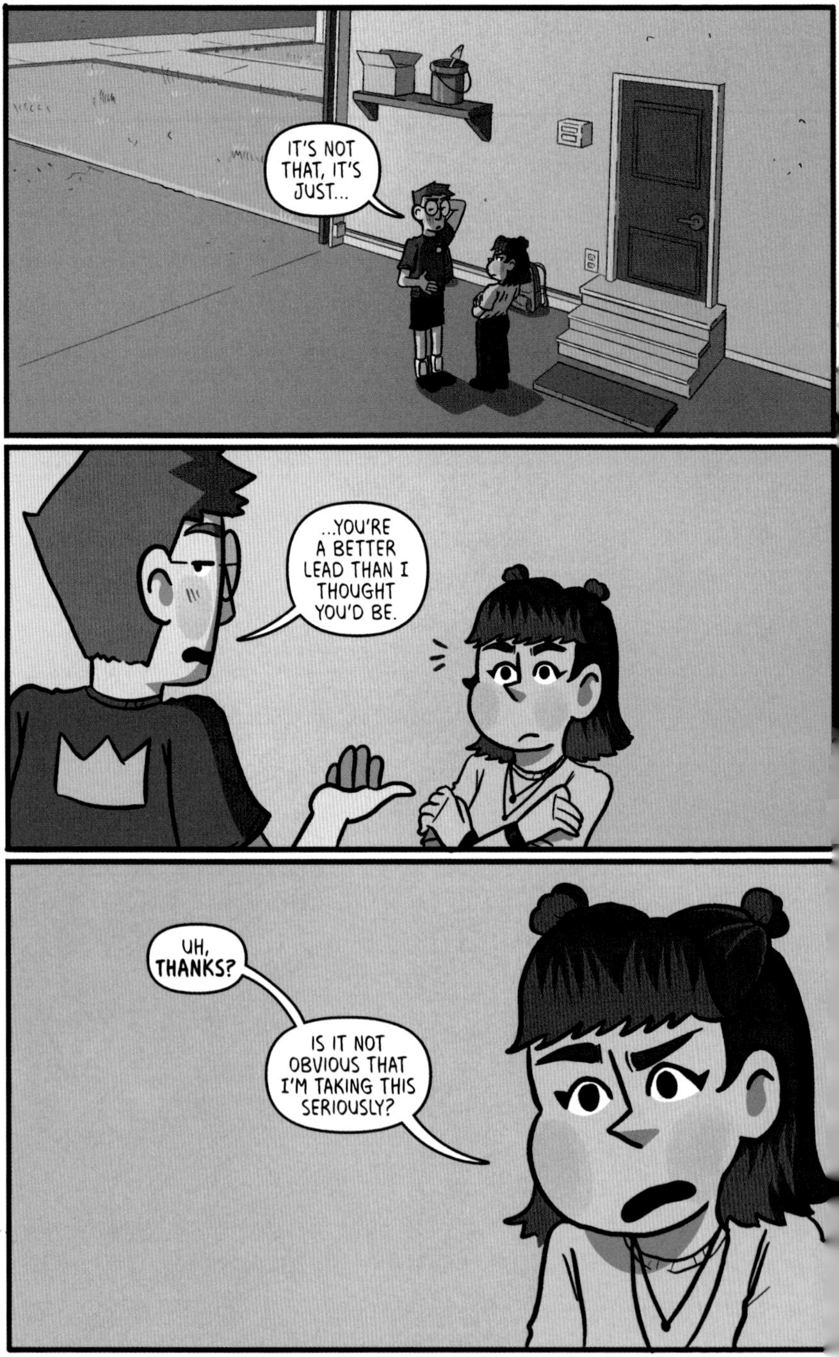
IT'S NOT THAT, IT'S JUST...
...YOU'RE A BETTER LEAD THAN I THOUGHT YOU'D BE.
UH, **THANKS?**
IS IT NOT OBVIOUS THAT I'M TAKING THIS SERIOUSLY?

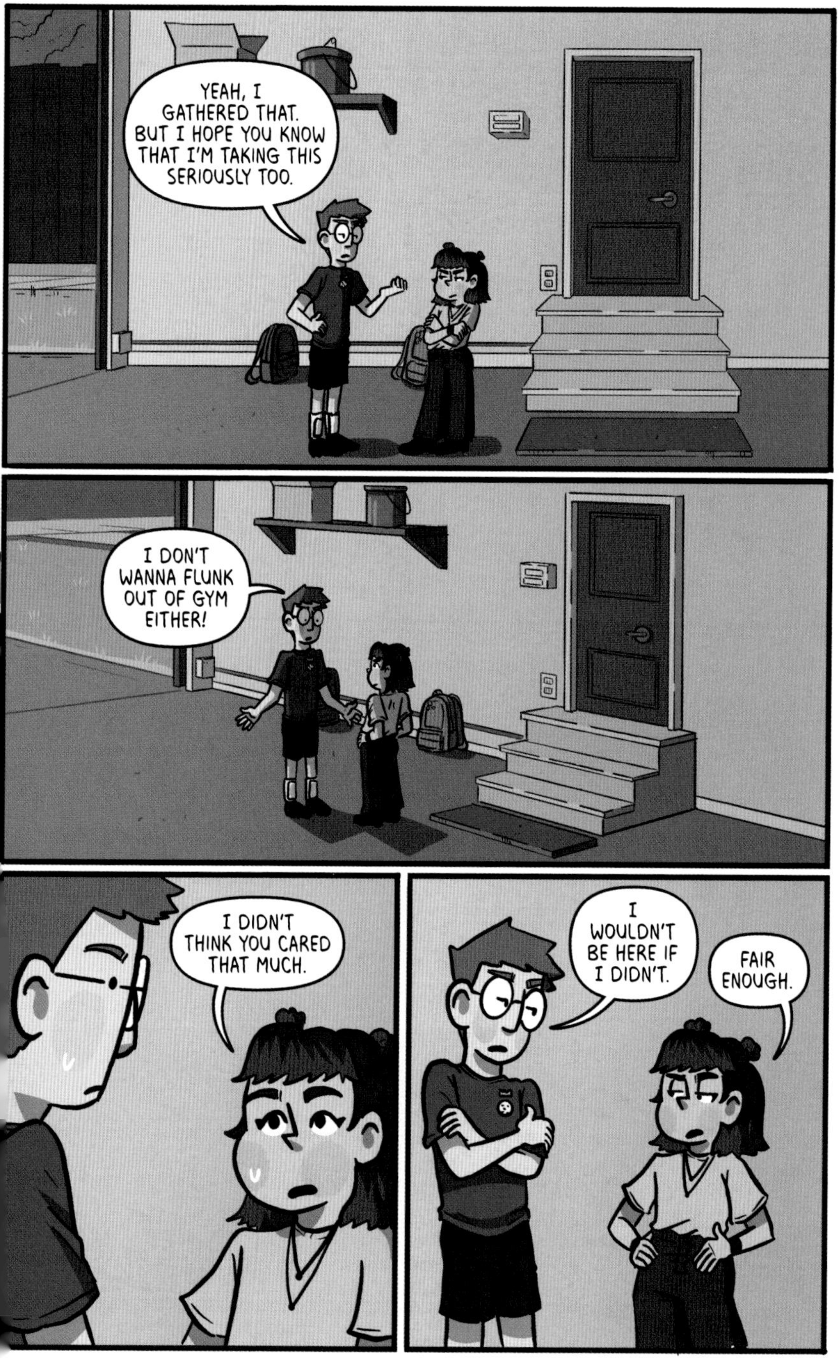
YEAH, I GATHERED THAT. BUT I HOPE YOU KNOW THAT I'M TAKING THIS SERIOUSLY TOO.
I DON'T WANNA FLUNK OUT OF GYM EITHER!
I DIDN'T THINK YOU CARED THAT MUCH.
I WOULDN'T BE HERE IF I DIDN'T.
FAIR ENOUGH.

FOR WHAT IT'S WORTH, YOU'RE WAY BETTER AS A FOLLOW.

THANKS, BUT DON'T LET BEING A LEAD GO TO YOUR HEAD.

NO PROMISES.

READY TO KEEP GOING? WE'VE GOT A LOT OF MOVES TO COVER.

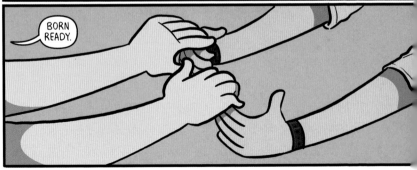

BORN READY.

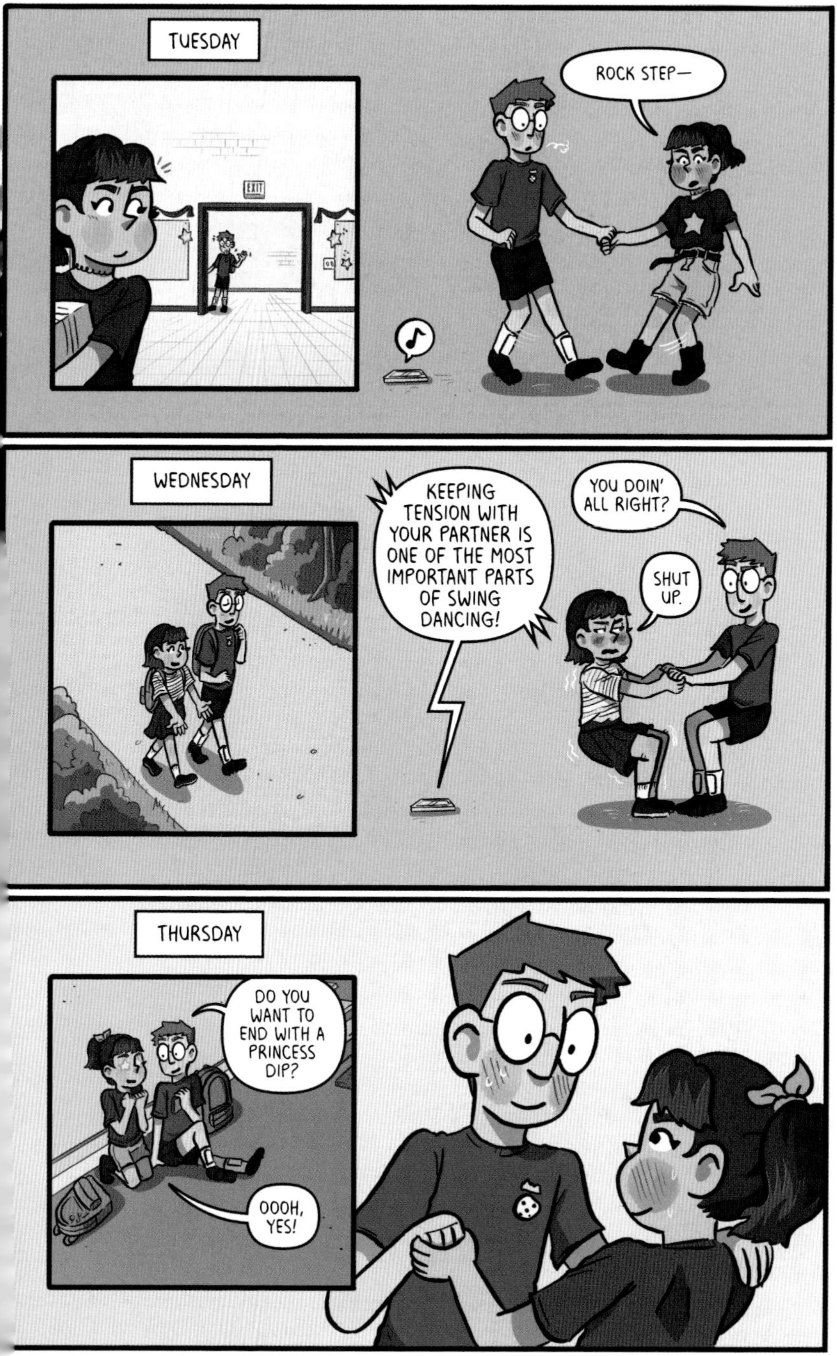
TUESDAY
ROCK STEP—
WEDNESDAY
KEEPING TENSION WITH YOUR PARTNER IS ONE OF THE MOST IMPORTANT PARTS OF SWING DANCING!
YOU DOIN' ALL RIGHT?
SHUT UP.
THURSDAY
DO YOU WANT TO END WITH A PRINCESS DIP?
OOOH, YES!

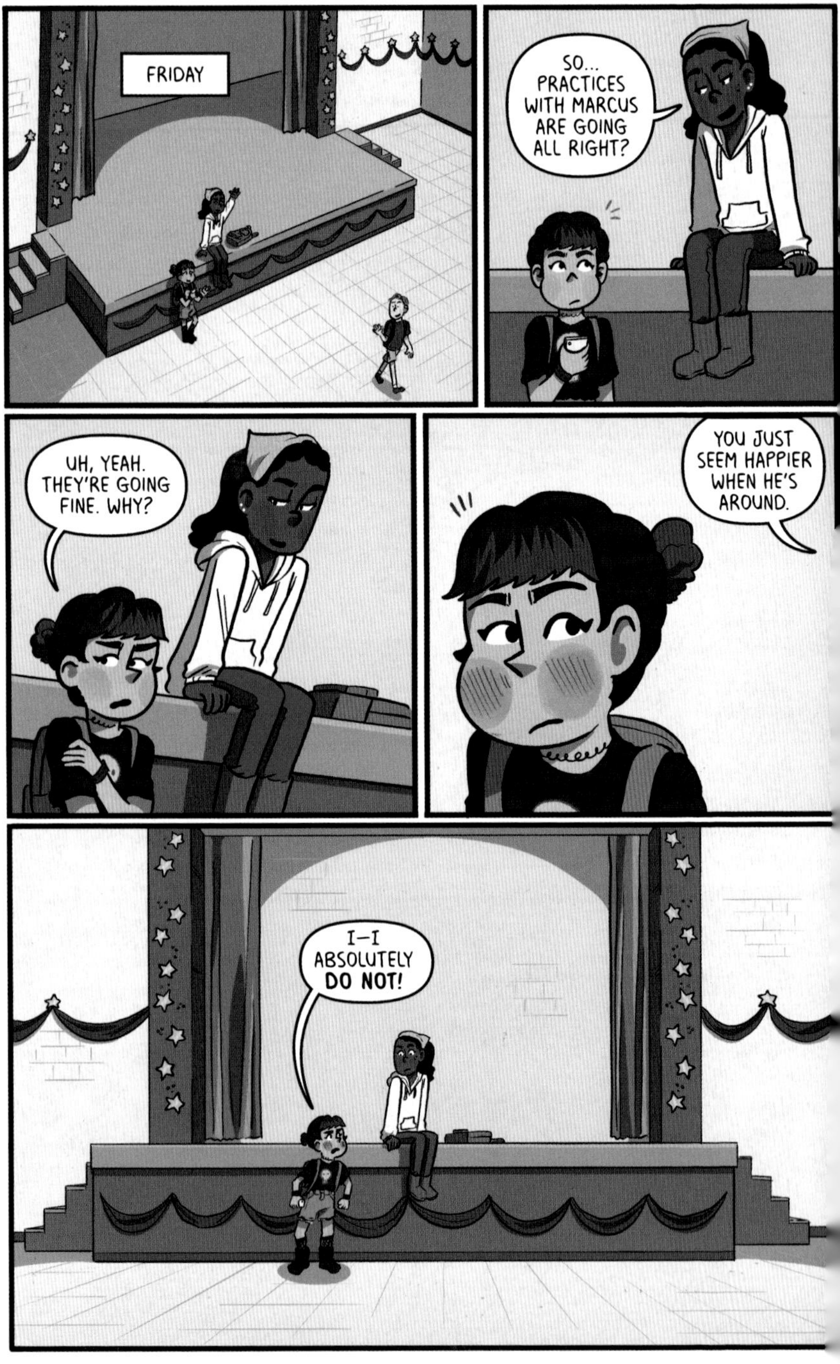

FRIDAY
SO... PRACTICES WITH MARCUS ARE GOING ALL RIGHT?
UH, YEAH. THEY'RE GOING FINE. WHY?
YOU JUST SEEM HAPPIER WHEN HE'S AROUND.
I—I ABSOLUTELY **DO NOT!**

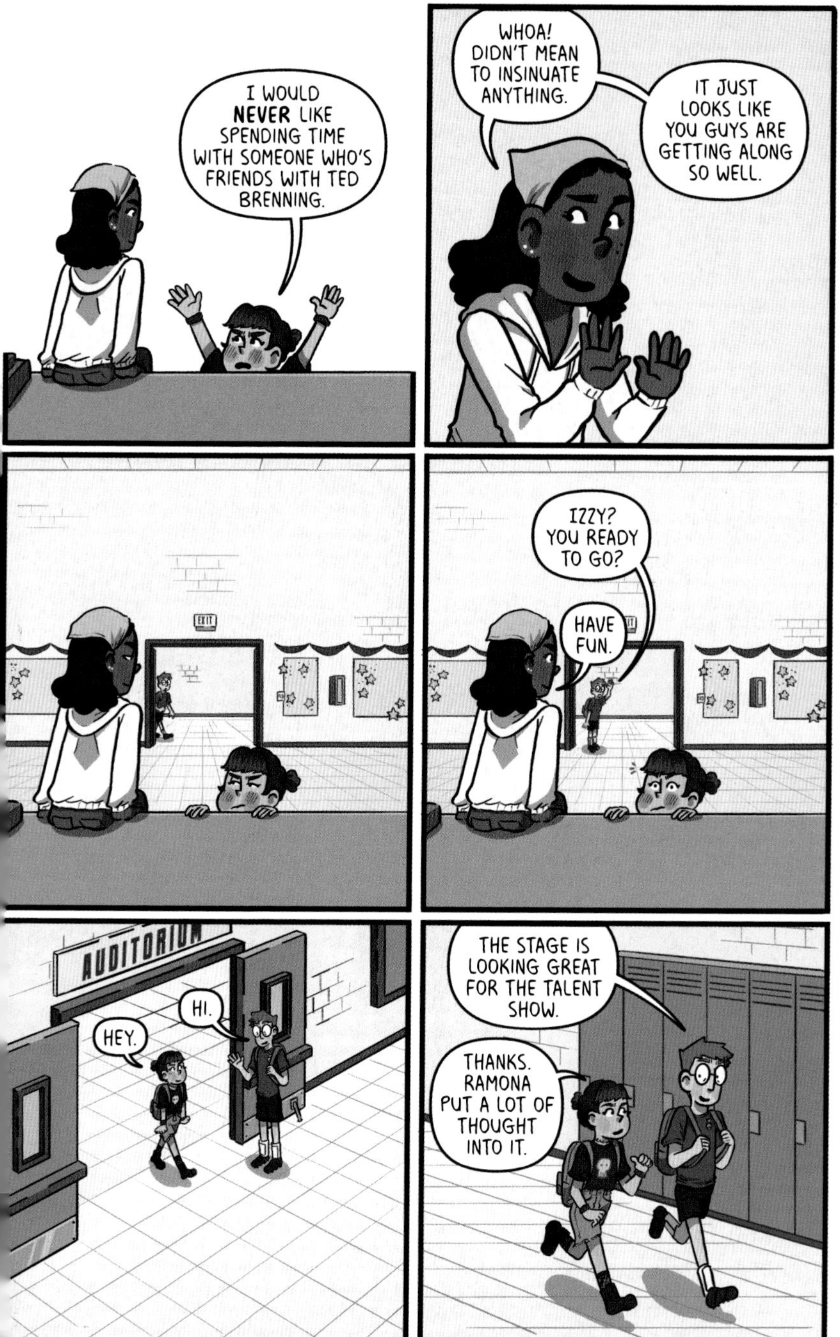
I WOULD **NEVER** LIKE SPENDING TIME WITH SOMEONE WHO'S FRIENDS WITH TED BRENNING.
WHOA! DIDN'T MEAN TO INSINUATE ANYTHING.
IT JUST LOOKS LIKE YOU GUYS ARE GETTING ALONG SO WELL.
EXIT
IZZY? YOU READY TO GO?
HAVE FUN.
AUDITORIUM
HI.
HEY.
THE STAGE IS LOOKING GREAT FOR THE TALENT SHOW.
THANKS. RAMONA PUT A LOT OF THOUGHT INTO IT.

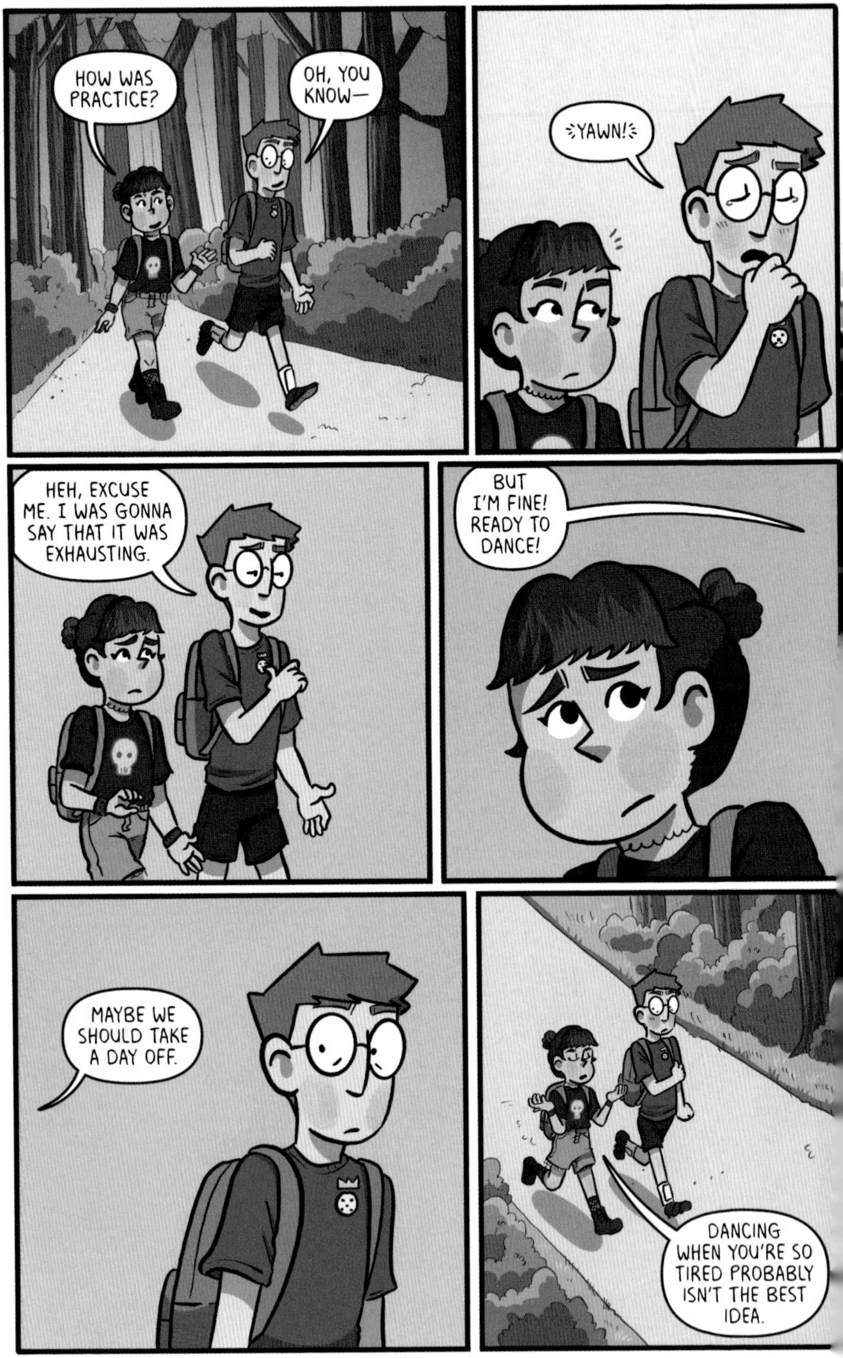
HOW WAS PRACTICE?
OH, YOU KNOW—
YAWN!
HEH, EXCUSE ME. I WAS GONNA SAY THAT IT WAS EXHAUSTING.
BUT I'M FINE! READY TO DANCE!
MAYBE WE SHOULD TAKE A DAY OFF.
DANCING WHEN YOU'RE SO TIRED PROBABLY ISN'T THE BEST IDEA.

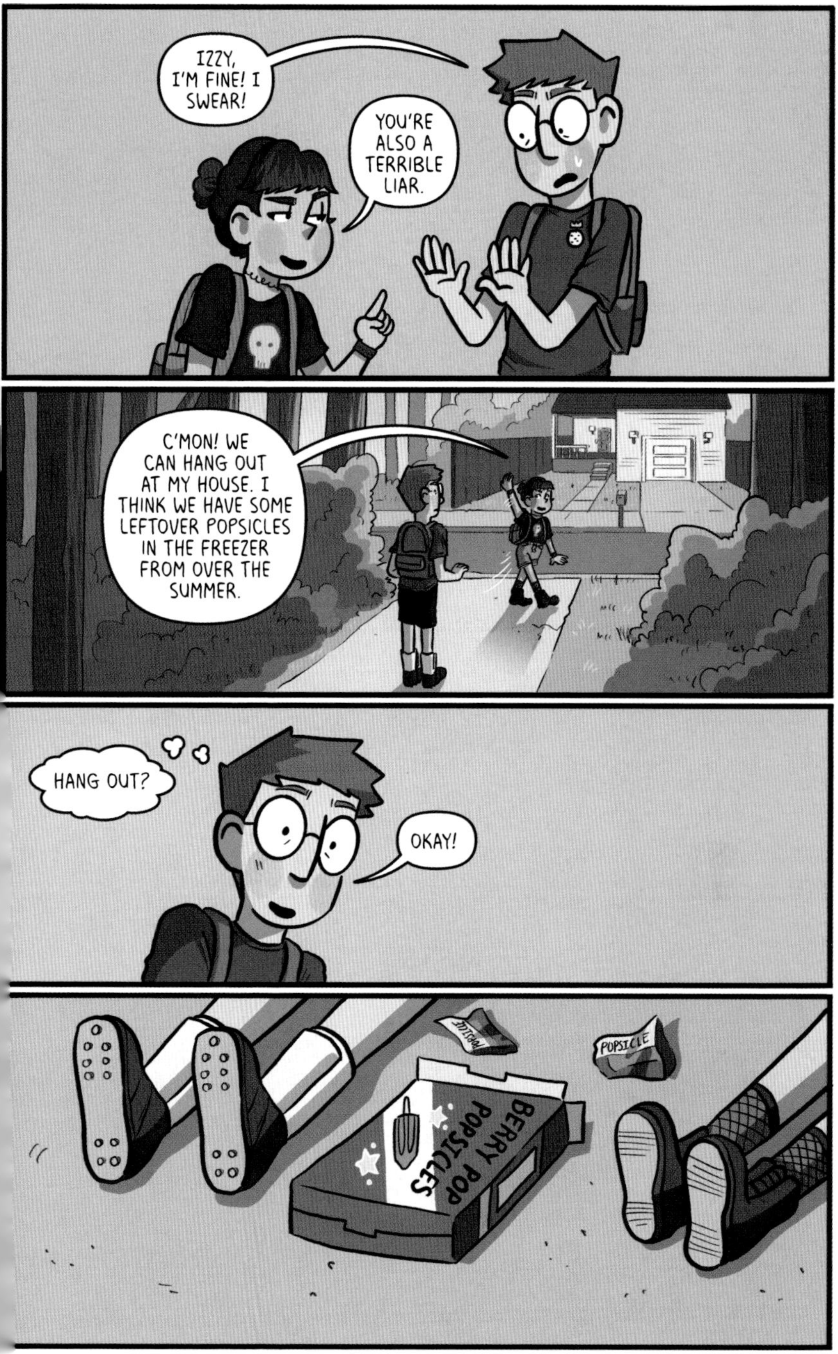
IZZY, I'M FINE! I SWEAR!
YOU'RE ALSO A TERRIBLE LIAR.
C'MON! WE CAN HANG OUT AT MY HOUSE. I THINK WE HAVE SOME LEFTOVER POPSICLES IN THE FREEZER FROM OVER THE SUMMER.
HANG OUT?
OKAY!
POPSICLE
POPSICLE
BERRY POP POPSICLES

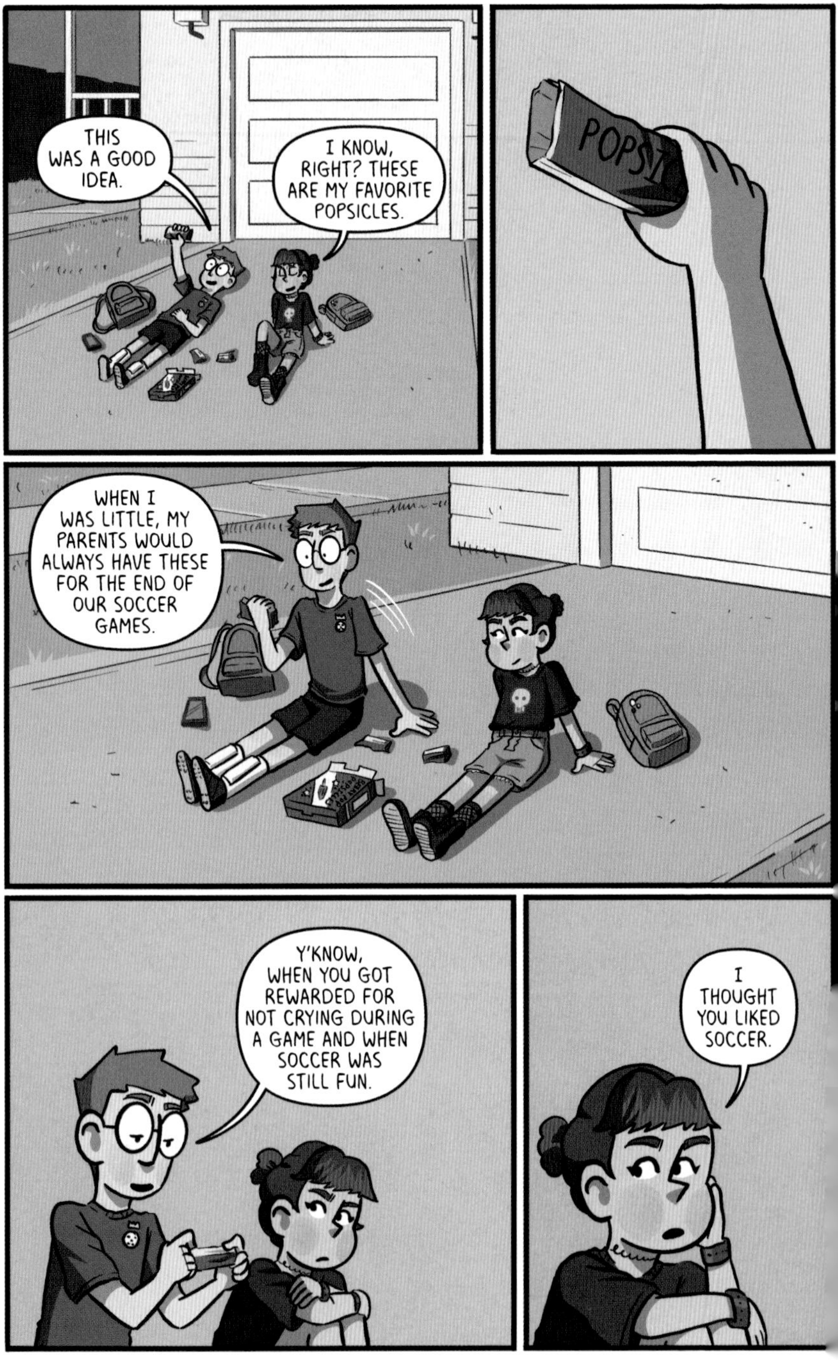
THIS WAS A GOOD IDEA.
I KNOW, RIGHT? THESE ARE MY FAVORITE POPSICLES.
POPSI
WHEN I WAS LITTLE, MY PARENTS WOULD ALWAYS HAVE THESE FOR THE END OF OUR SOCCER GAMES.
Y'KNOW, WHEN YOU GOT REWARDED FOR NOT CRYING DURING A GAME AND WHEN SOCCER WAS STILL FUN.
I THOUGHT YOU LIKED SOCCER.

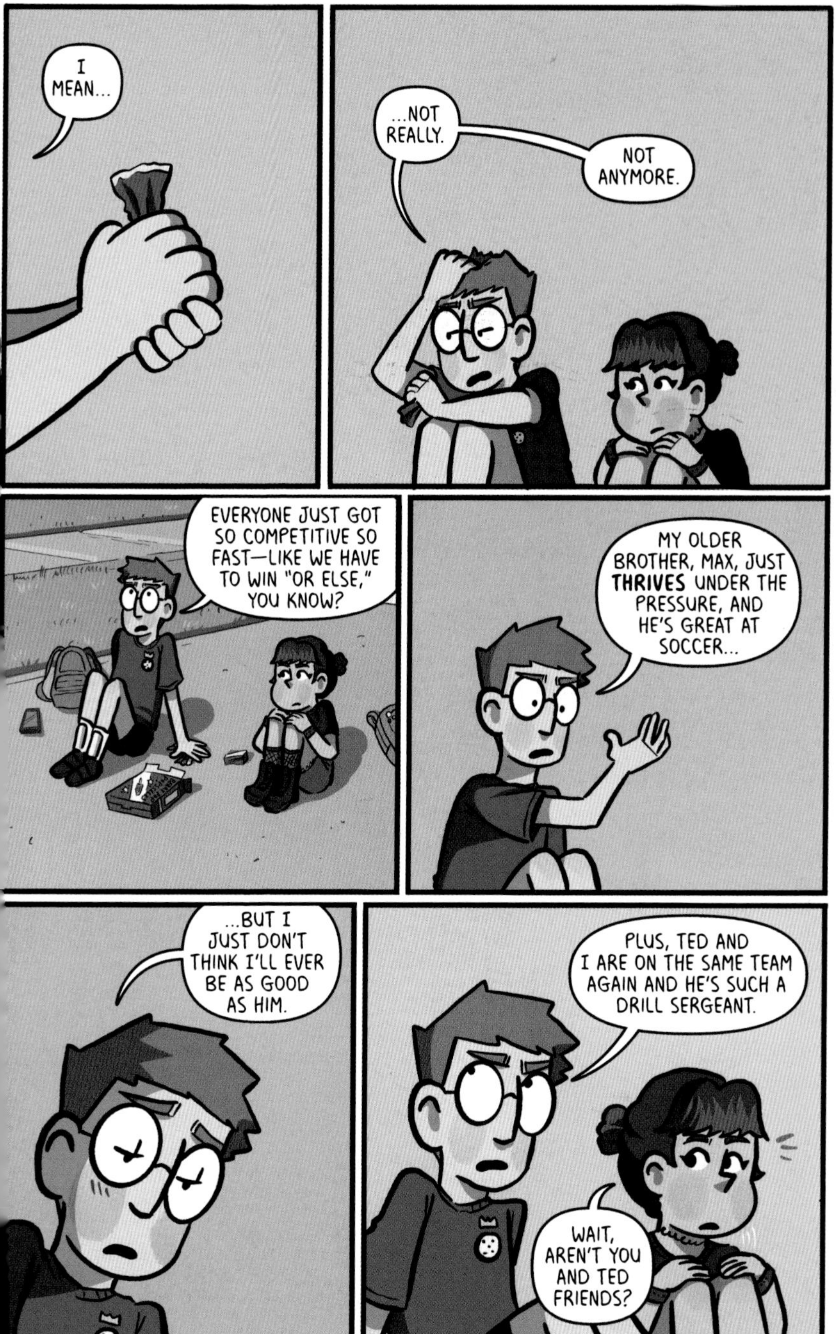
I MEAN...
...NOT REALLY.
NOT ANYMORE.
EVERYONE JUST GOT SO COMPETITIVE SO FAST—LIKE WE HAVE TO WIN "OR ELSE," YOU KNOW?
MY OLDER BROTHER, MAX, JUST **THRIVES** UNDER THE PRESSURE, AND HE'S GREAT AT SOCCER...
...BUT I JUST DON'T THINK I'LL EVER BE AS GOOD AS HIM.
PLUS, TED AND I ARE ON THE SAME TEAM AGAIN AND HE'S SUCH A DRILL SERGEANT.
WAIT, AREN'T YOU AND TED FRIENDS?

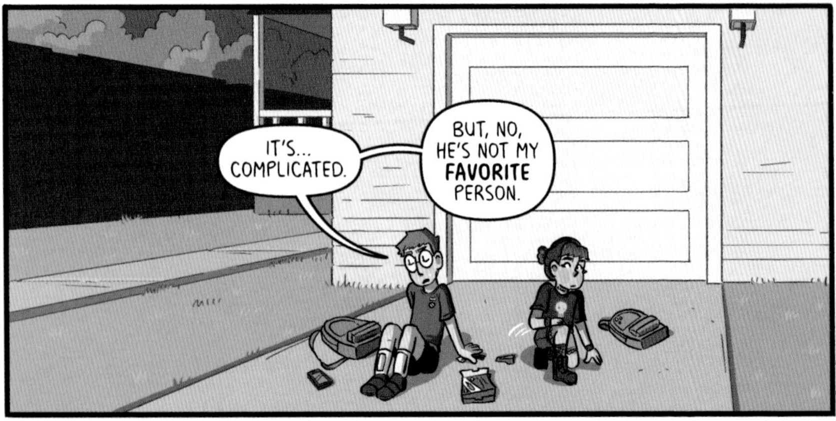
IT'S... COMPLICATED.
BUT, NO, HE'S NOT MY **FAVORITE** PERSON.

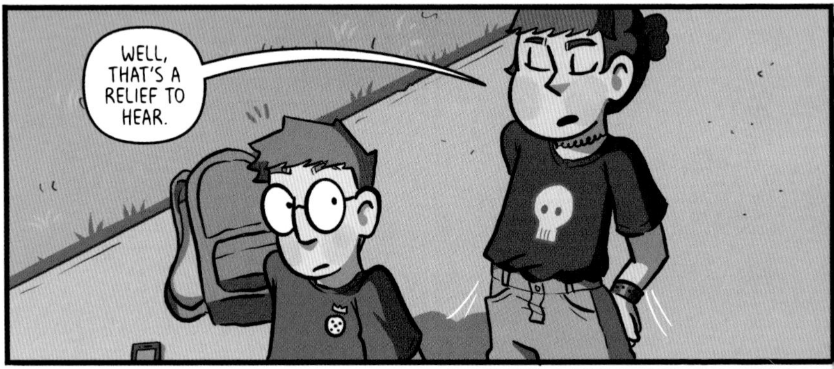
WELL, THAT'S A RELIEF TO HEAR.

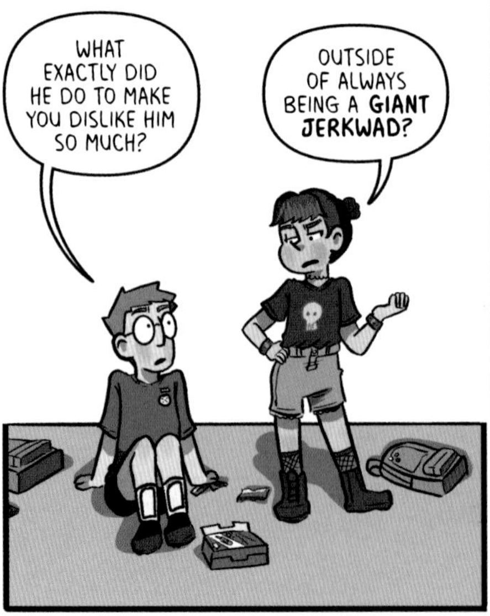
WHAT EXACTLY DID HE DO TO MAKE YOU DISLIKE HIM SO MUCH?
OUTSIDE OF ALWAYS BEING A **GIANT JERKWAD**?

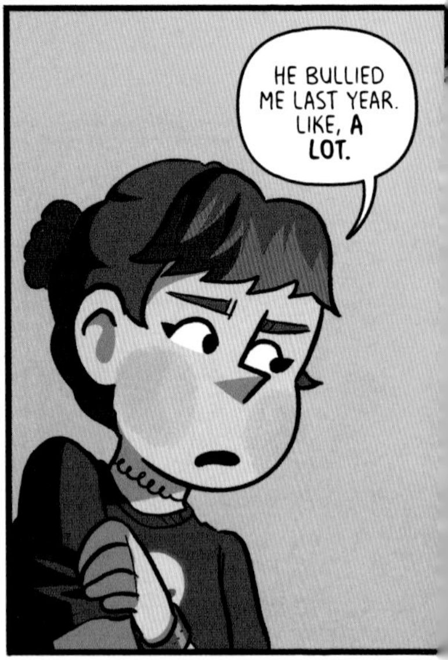
HE BULLIED ME LAST YEAR. LIKE, **A LOT.**

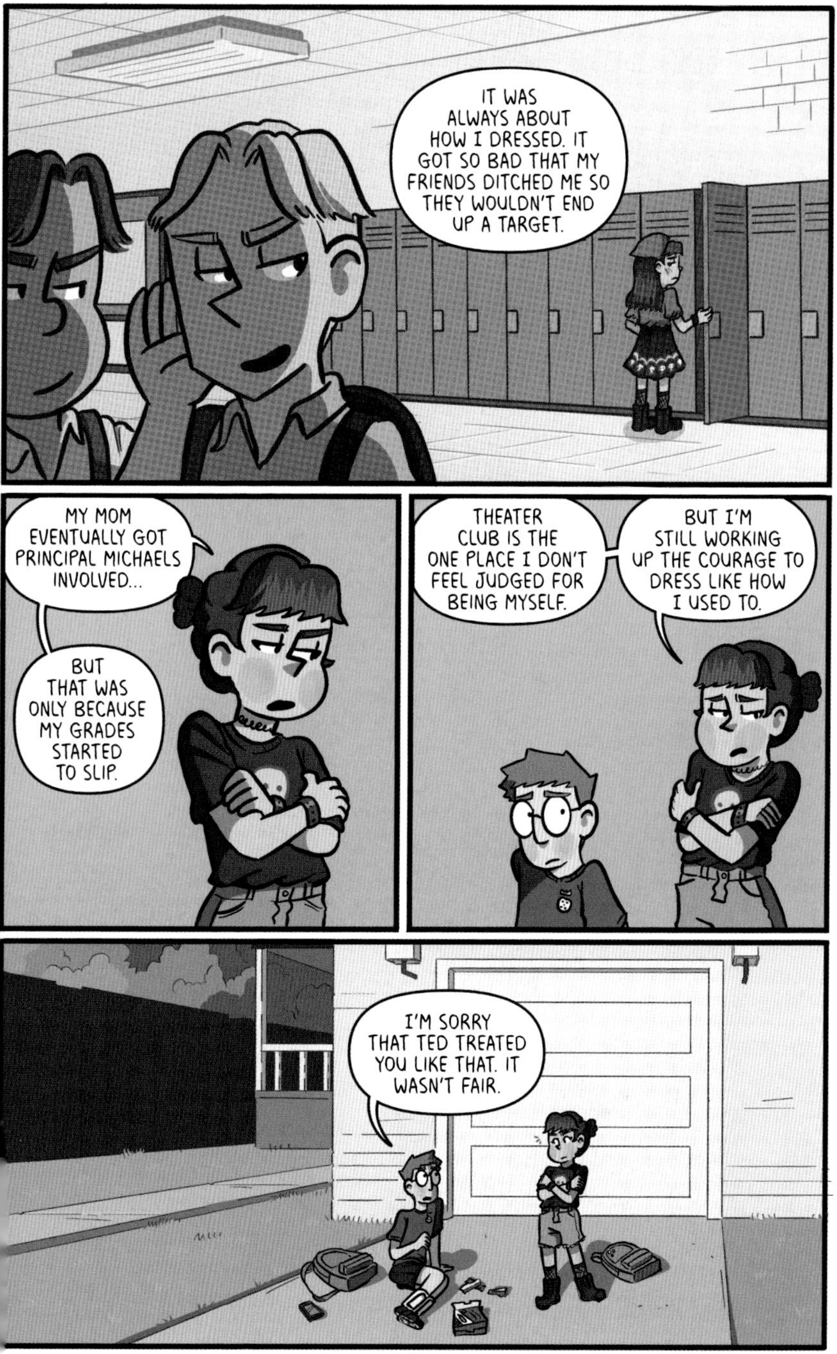
IT WAS ALWAYS ABOUT HOW I DRESSED. IT GOT SO BAD THAT MY FRIENDS DITCHED ME SO THEY WOULDN'T END UP A TARGET.
MY MOM EVENTUALLY GOT PRINCIPAL MICHAELS INVOLVED...
BUT THAT WAS ONLY BECAUSE MY GRADES STARTED TO SLIP.
THEATER CLUB IS THE ONE PLACE I DON'T FEEL JUDGED FOR BEING MYSELF.
BUT I'M STILL WORKING UP THE COURAGE TO DRESS LIKE HOW I USED TO.
I'M SORRY THAT TED TREATED YOU LIKE THAT. IT WASN'T FAIR.

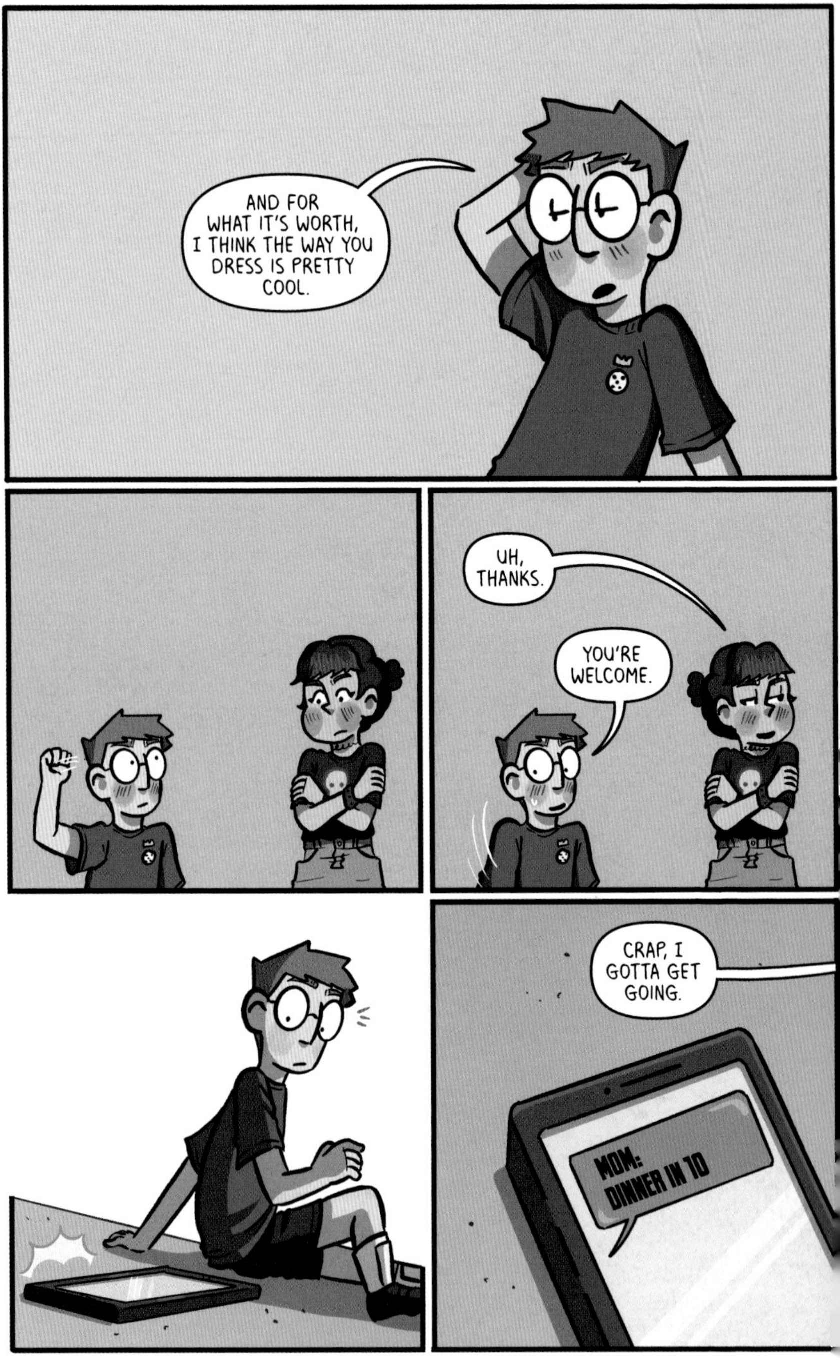
AND FOR WHAT IT'S WORTH, I THINK THE WAY YOU DRESS IS PRETTY COOL.
UH, THANKS.
YOU'RE WELCOME.
CRAP, I GOTTA GET GOING.
MOM:
DINNER IN 10

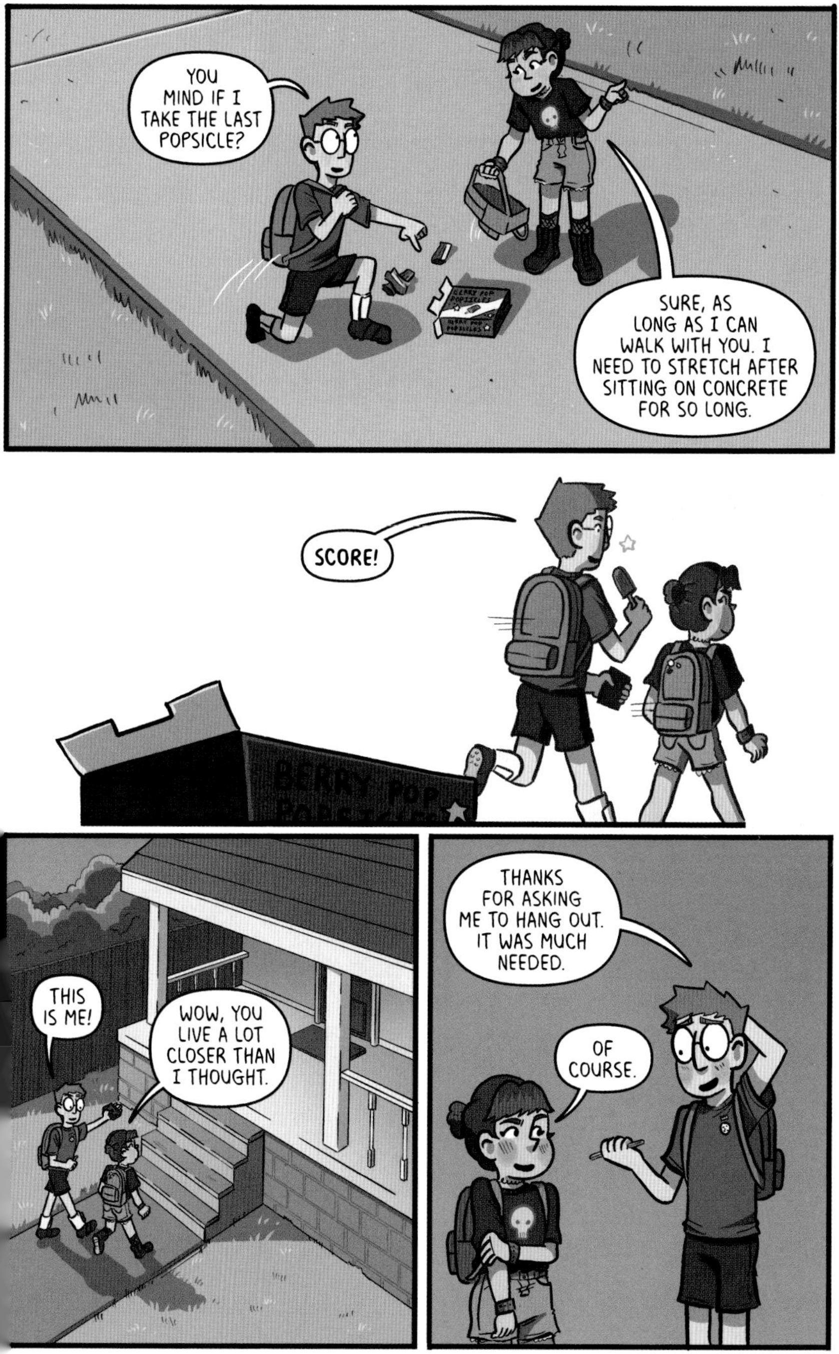

YOU MIND IF I TAKE THE LAST POPSICLE?
SURE, AS LONG AS I CAN WALK WITH YOU. I NEED TO STRETCH AFTER SITTING ON CONCRETE FOR SO LONG.
SCORE!
BERRY POP
THIS IS ME!
WOW, YOU LIVE A LOT CLOSER THAN I THOUGHT.
THANKS FOR ASKING ME TO HANG OUT. IT WAS MUCH NEEDED.
OF COURSE.

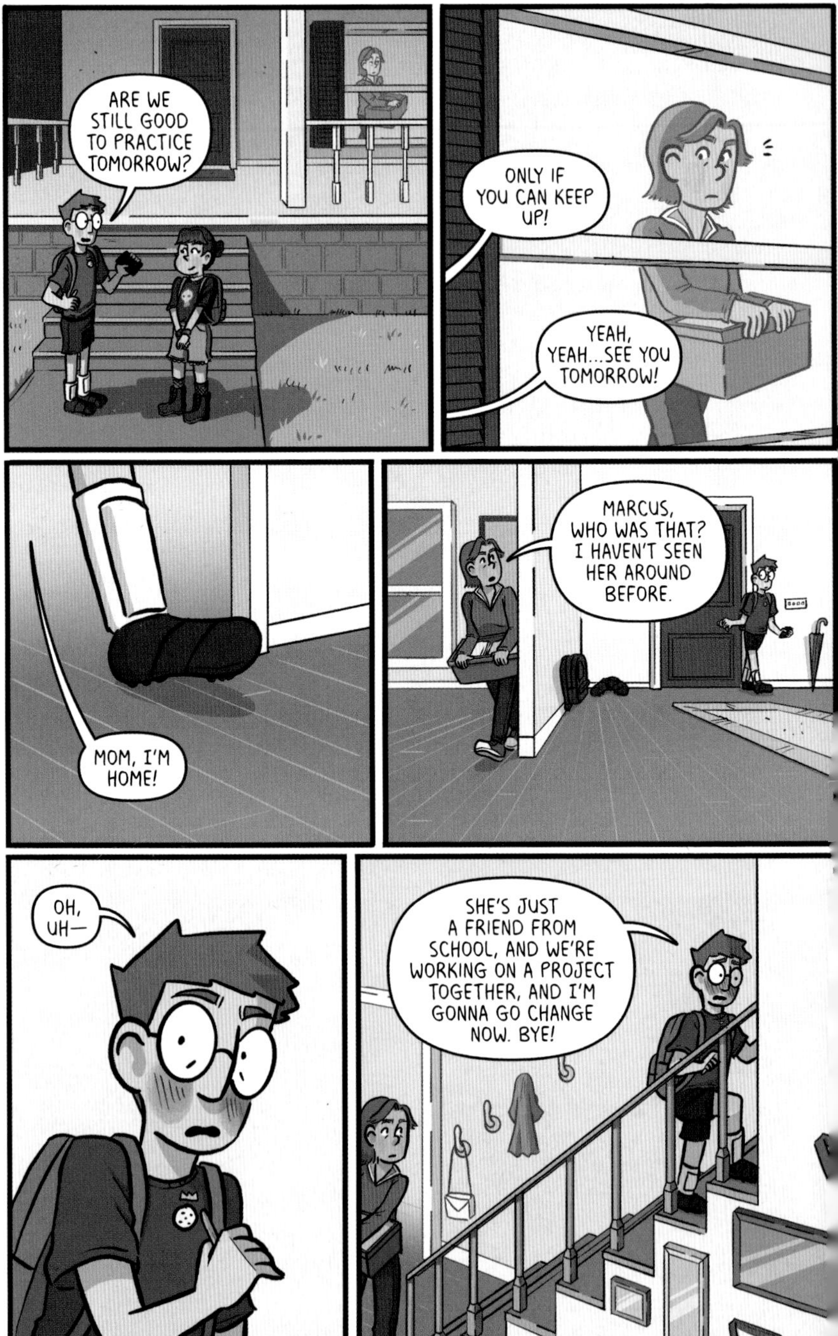
ARE WE STILL GOOD TO PRACTICE TOMORROW?
ONLY IF YOU CAN KEEP UP!
YEAH, YEAH...SEE YOU TOMORROW!
MOM, I'M HOME!
MARCUS, WHO WAS THAT? I HAVEN'T SEEN HER AROUND BEFORE.
OH, UH—
SHE'S JUST A FRIEND FROM SCHOOL, AND WE'RE WORKING ON A PROJECT TOGETHER, AND I'M GONNA GO CHANGE NOW. BYE!

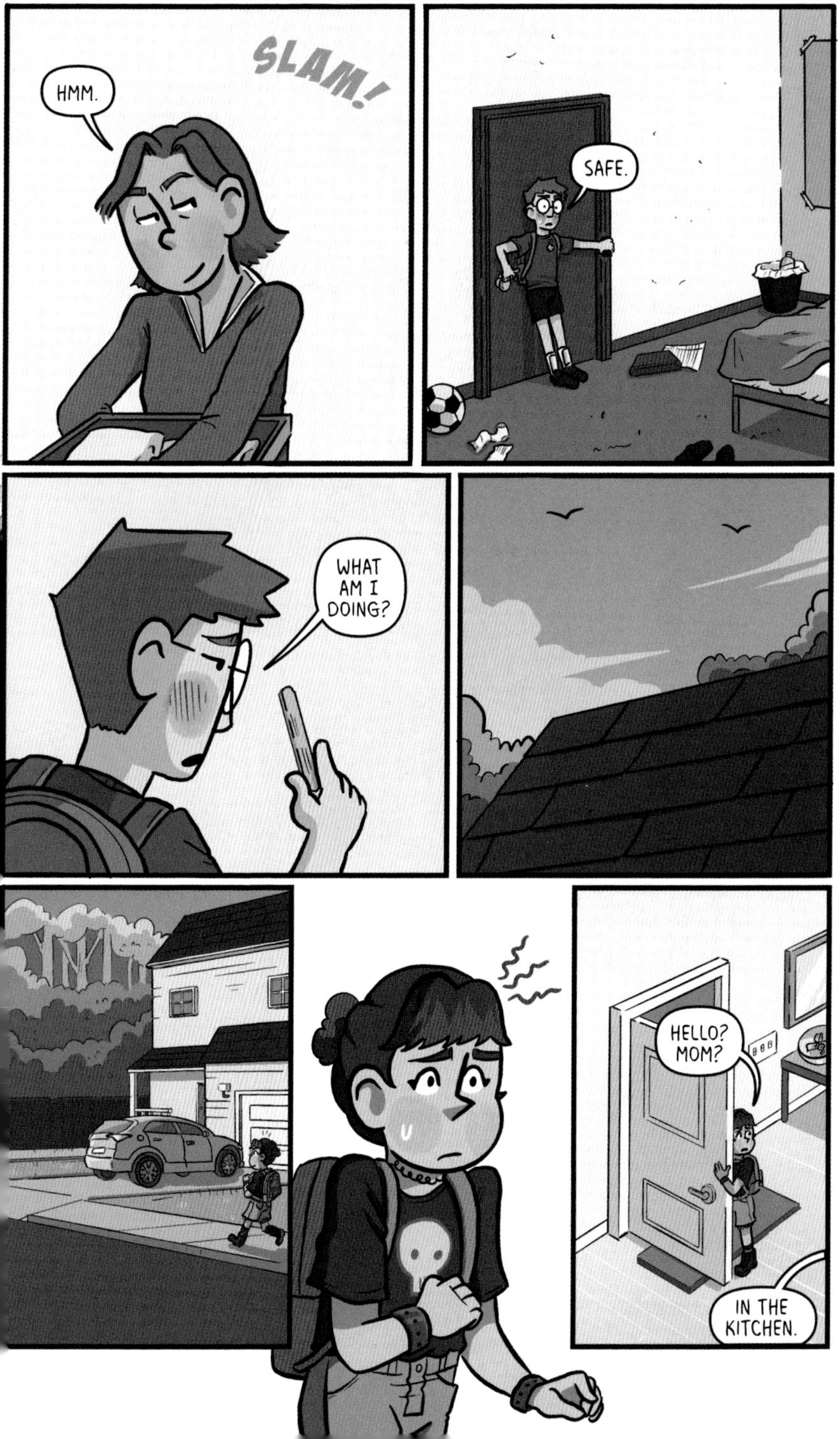
SLAM!
HMM.
SAFE.
WHAT AM I DOING?
HELLO? MOM?
IN THE KITCHEN.

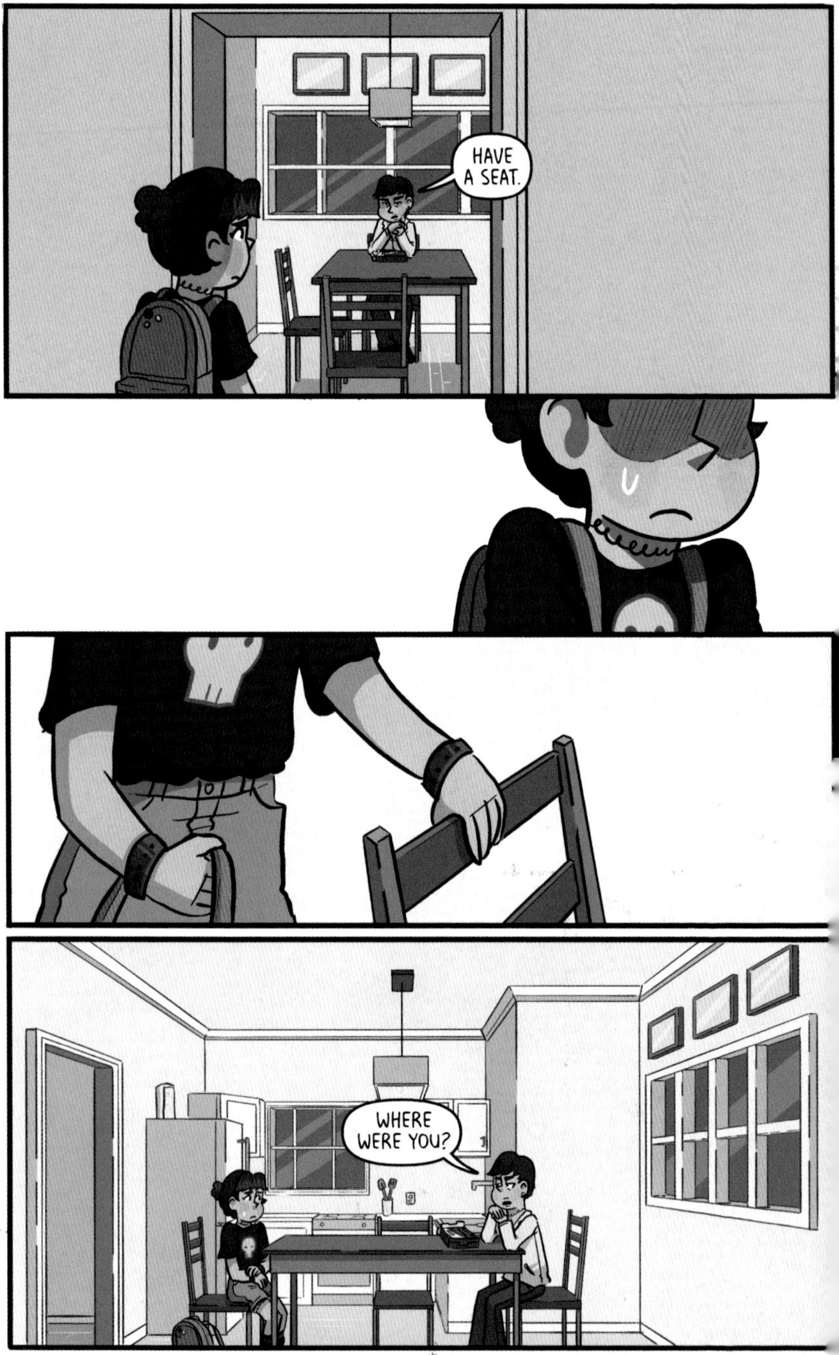
HAVE A SEAT.
WHERE WERE YOU?

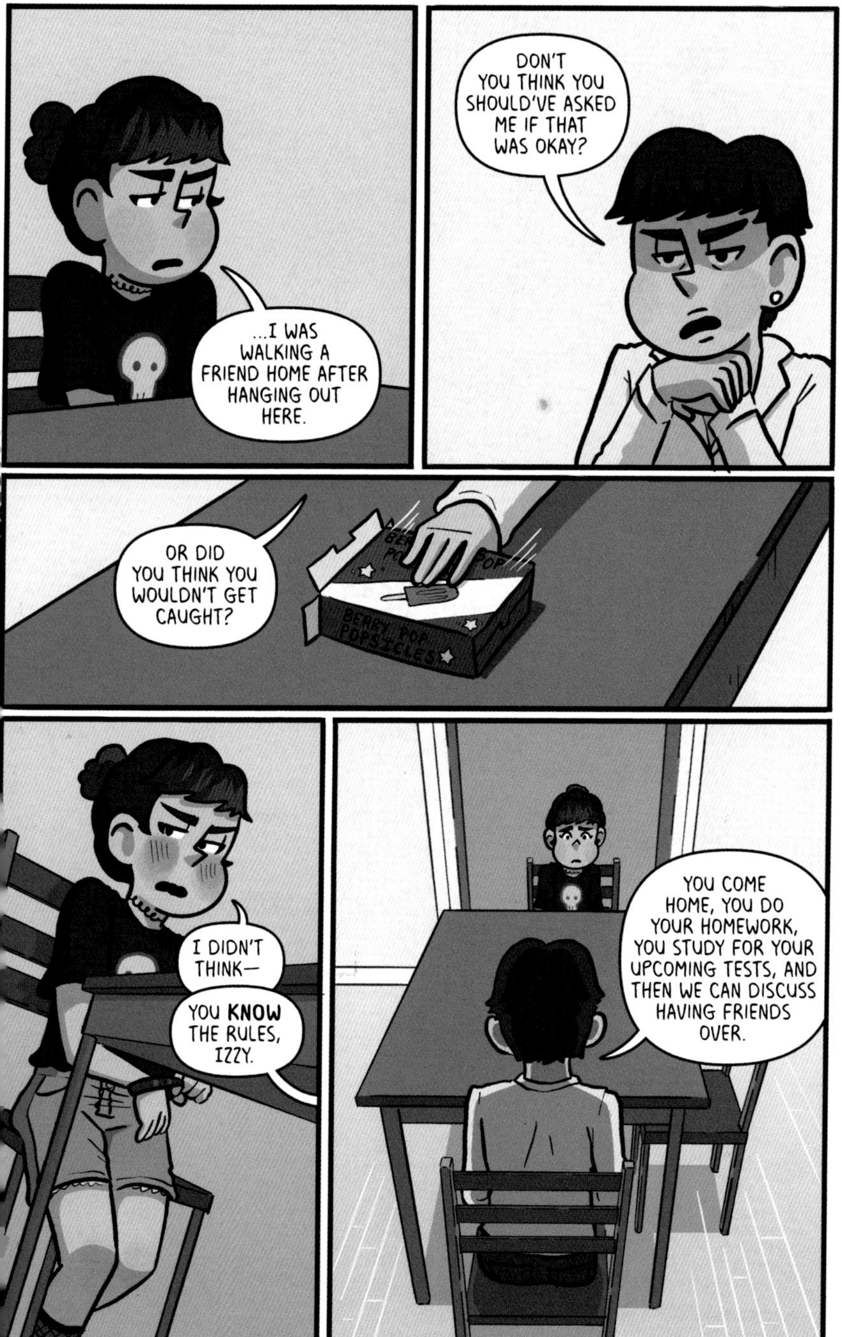
...I WAS WALKING A FRIEND HOME AFTER HANGING OUT HERE.
DON'T YOU THINK YOU SHOULD'VE ASKED ME IF THAT WAS OKAY?
OR DID YOU THINK YOU WOULDN'T GET CAUGHT?
BERRY POP POPSICLES
I DIDN'T THINK—
YOU **KNOW** THE RULES, IZZY.
YOU COME HOME, YOU DO YOUR HOMEWORK, YOU STUDY FOR YOUR UPCOMING TESTS, AND THEN WE CAN DISCUSS HAVING FRIENDS OVER.

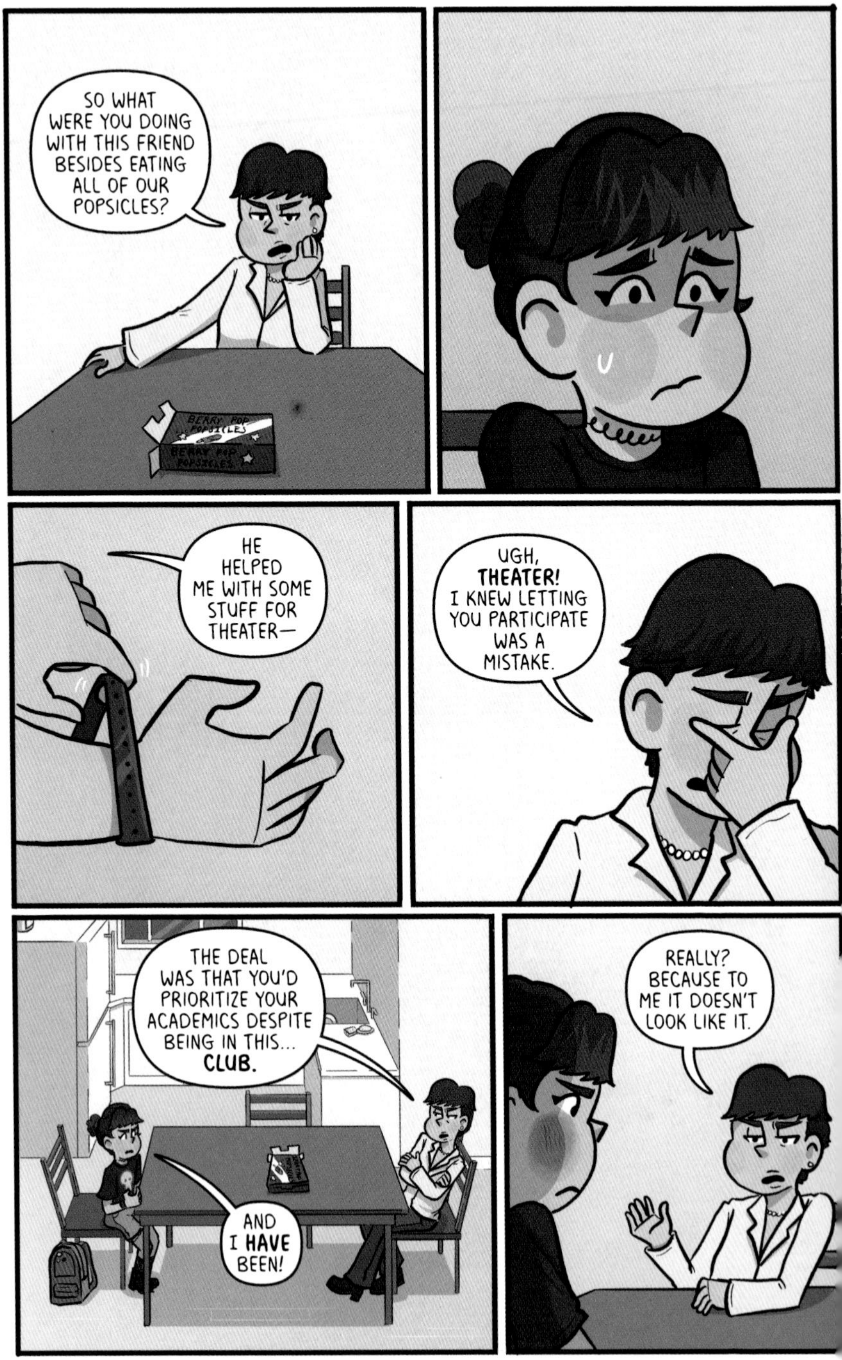
SO WHAT WERE YOU DOING WITH THIS FRIEND BESIDES EATING ALL OF OUR POPSICLES?
BERRY POP POPSICLES
HE HELPED ME WITH SOME STUFF FOR THEATER—
UGH, **THEATER!** I KNEW LETTING YOU PARTICIPATE WAS A MISTAKE.
THE DEAL WAS THAT YOU'D PRIORITIZE YOUR ACADEMICS DESPITE BEING IN THIS... **CLUB.**
AND I **HAVE** BEEN!
REALLY? BECAUSE TO ME IT DOESN'T LOOK LIKE IT.

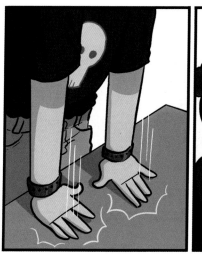

I'M **TRYING** MY **BEST!**

...GO TO YOUR ROOM.

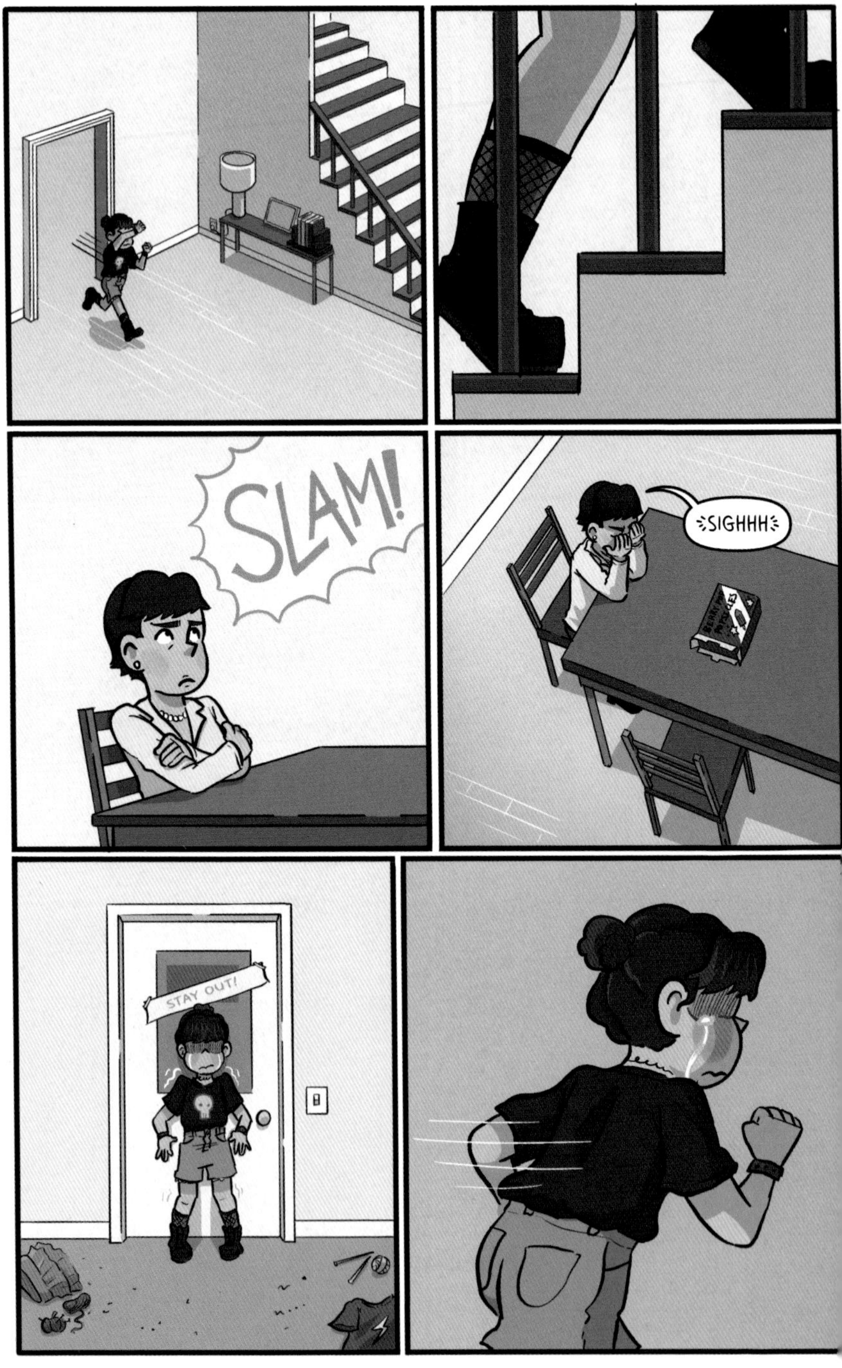
SLAM!
SIGHHH
STAY OUT!

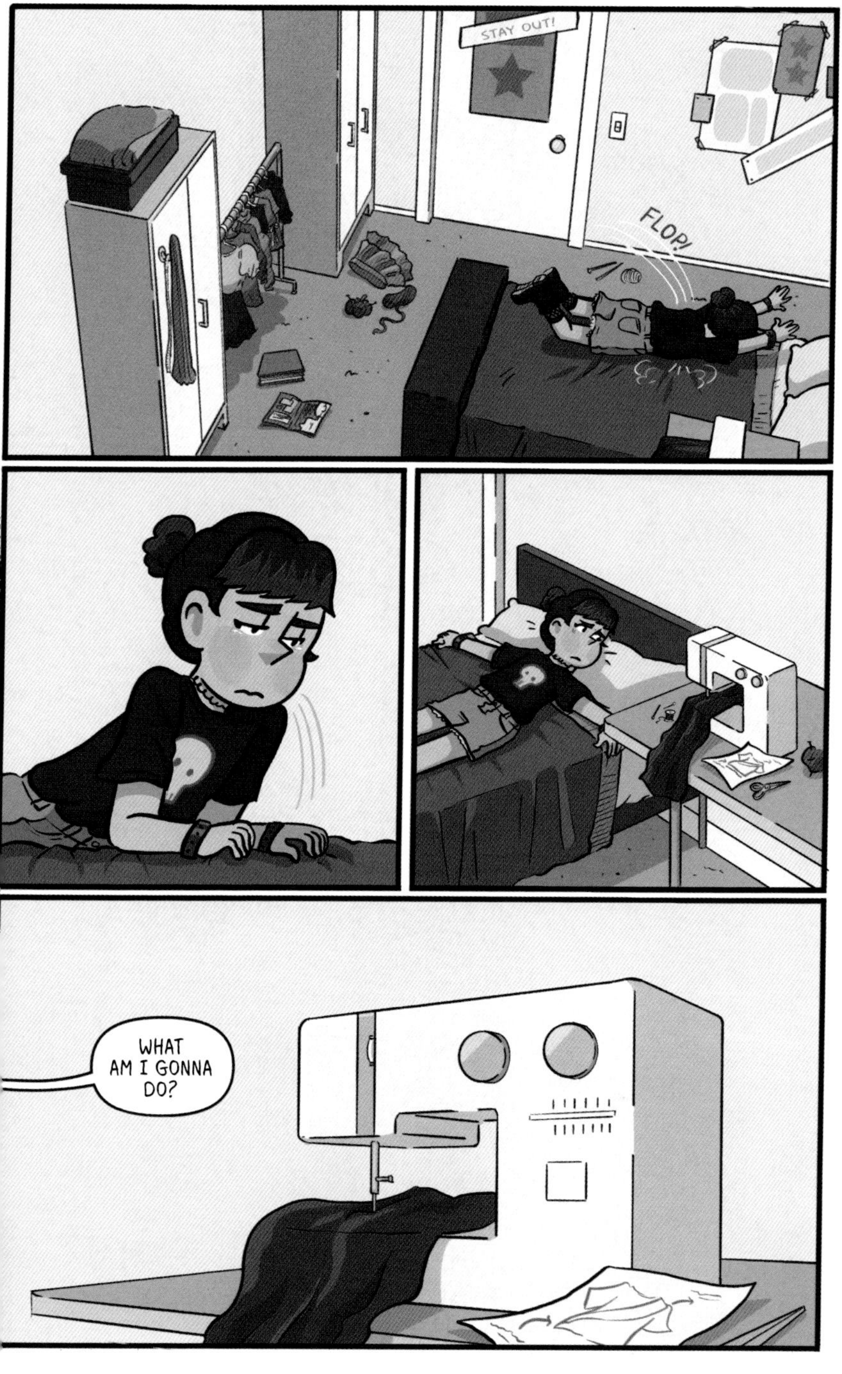
STAY OUT!
FLOP!
WHAT AM I GONNA DO?

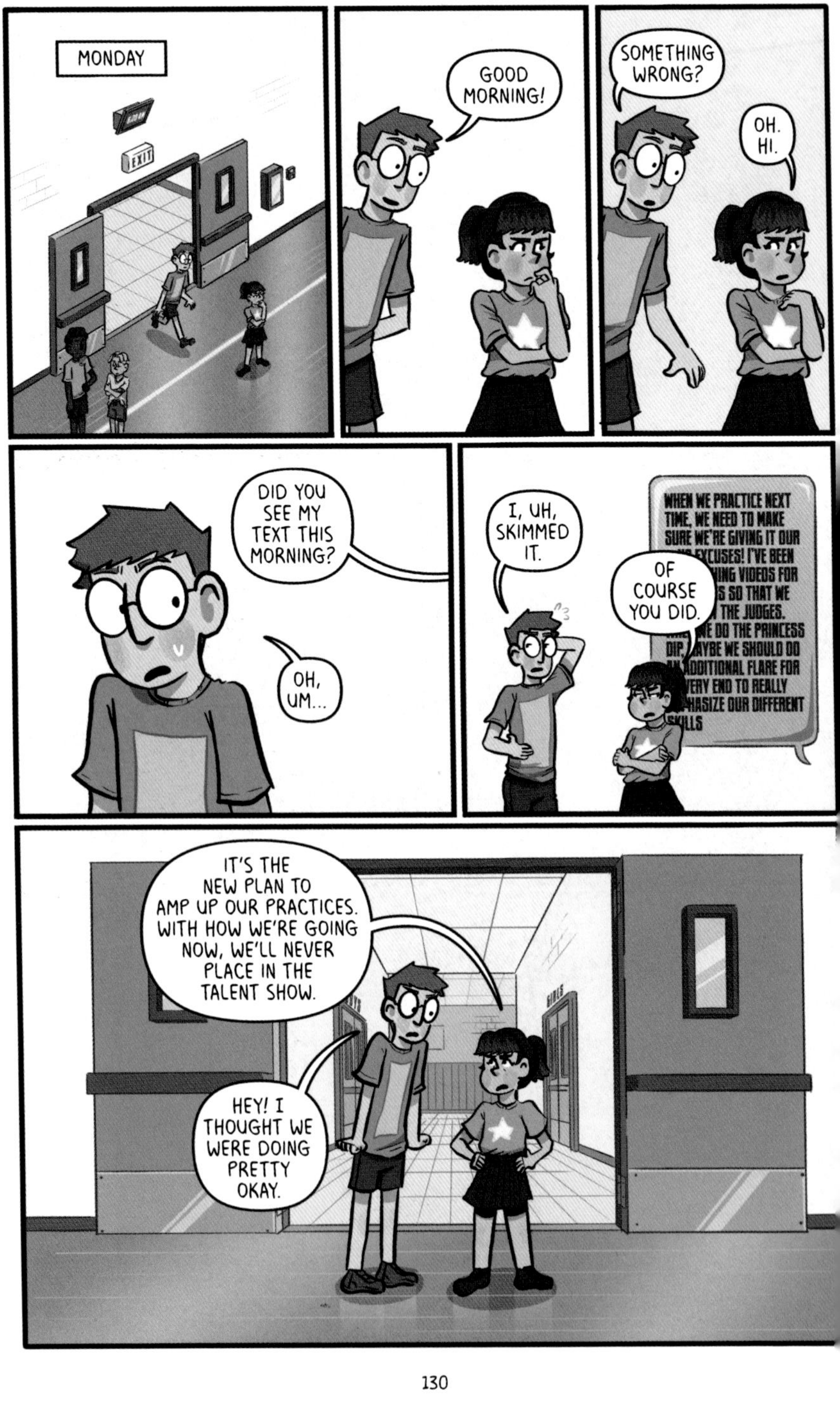
MONDAY
GOOD MORNING!
SOMETHING WRONG?
OH. HI.
DID YOU SEE MY TEXT THIS MORNING?
OH, UM...
I, UH, SKIMMED IT.
WHEN WE PRACTICE NEXT TIME, WE NEED TO MAKE SURE WE'RE GIVING IT OUR
EXCUSES! I'VE BEEN
VIDEOS FOR
S SO THAT WE
THE JUDGES.
E DO THE PRINCESS
DIP,
AYBE WE SHOULD DO
DDITIONAL FLARE FOR
VERY END TO REALLY
HASIZE OUR DIFFERENT
SKILLS
OF COURSE YOU DID.
IT'S THE NEW PLAN TO AMP UP OUR PRACTICES. WITH HOW WE'RE GOING NOW, WE'LL NEVER PLACE IN THE TALENT SHOW.
HEY! I THOUGHT WE WERE DOING PRETTY OKAY.

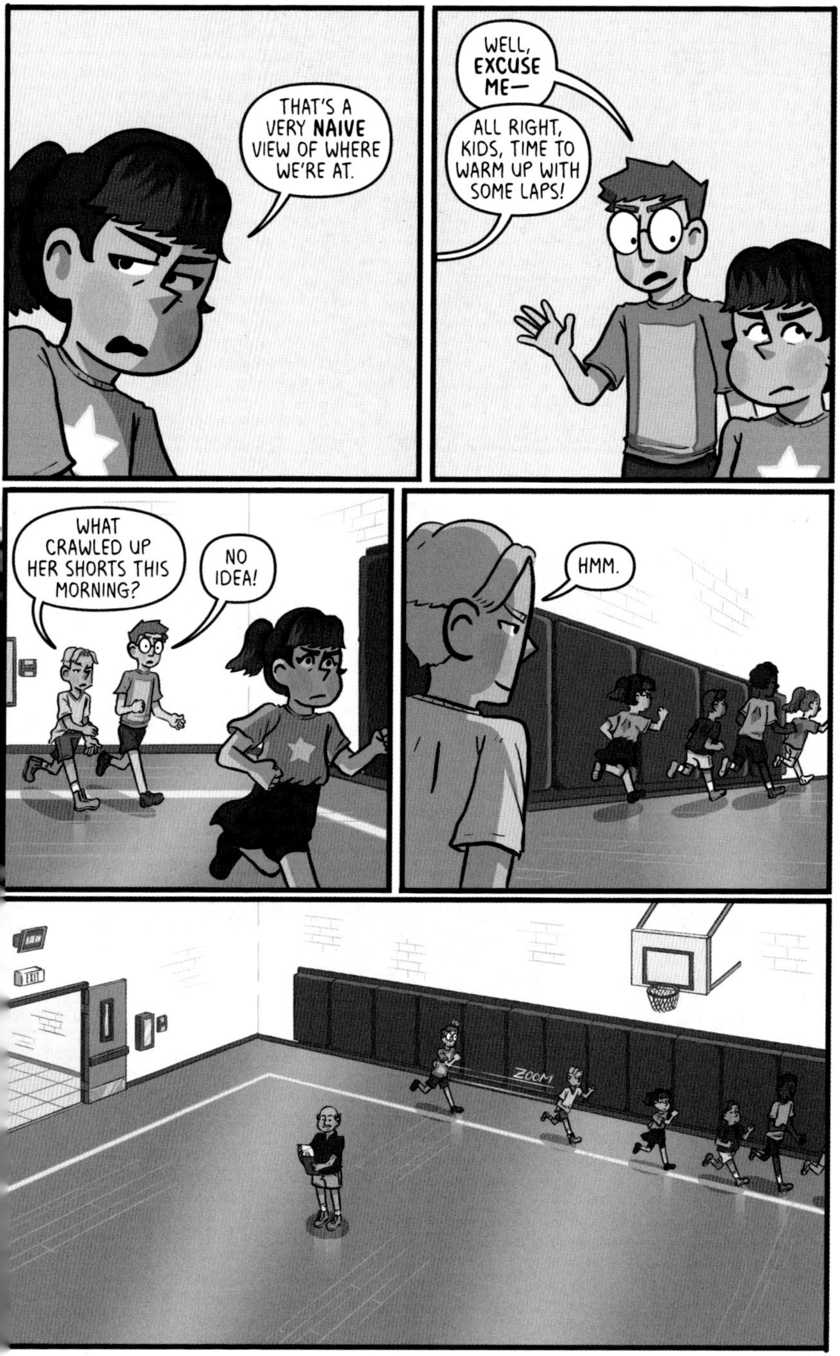
THAT'S A VERY NAIVE VIEW OF WHERE WE'RE AT.
WELL, EXCUSE ME—
ALL RIGHT, KIDS, TIME TO WARM UP WITH SOME LAPS!
WHAT CRAWLED UP HER SHORTS THIS MORNING?
NO IDEA!
HMM.
EXIT
ZOOM

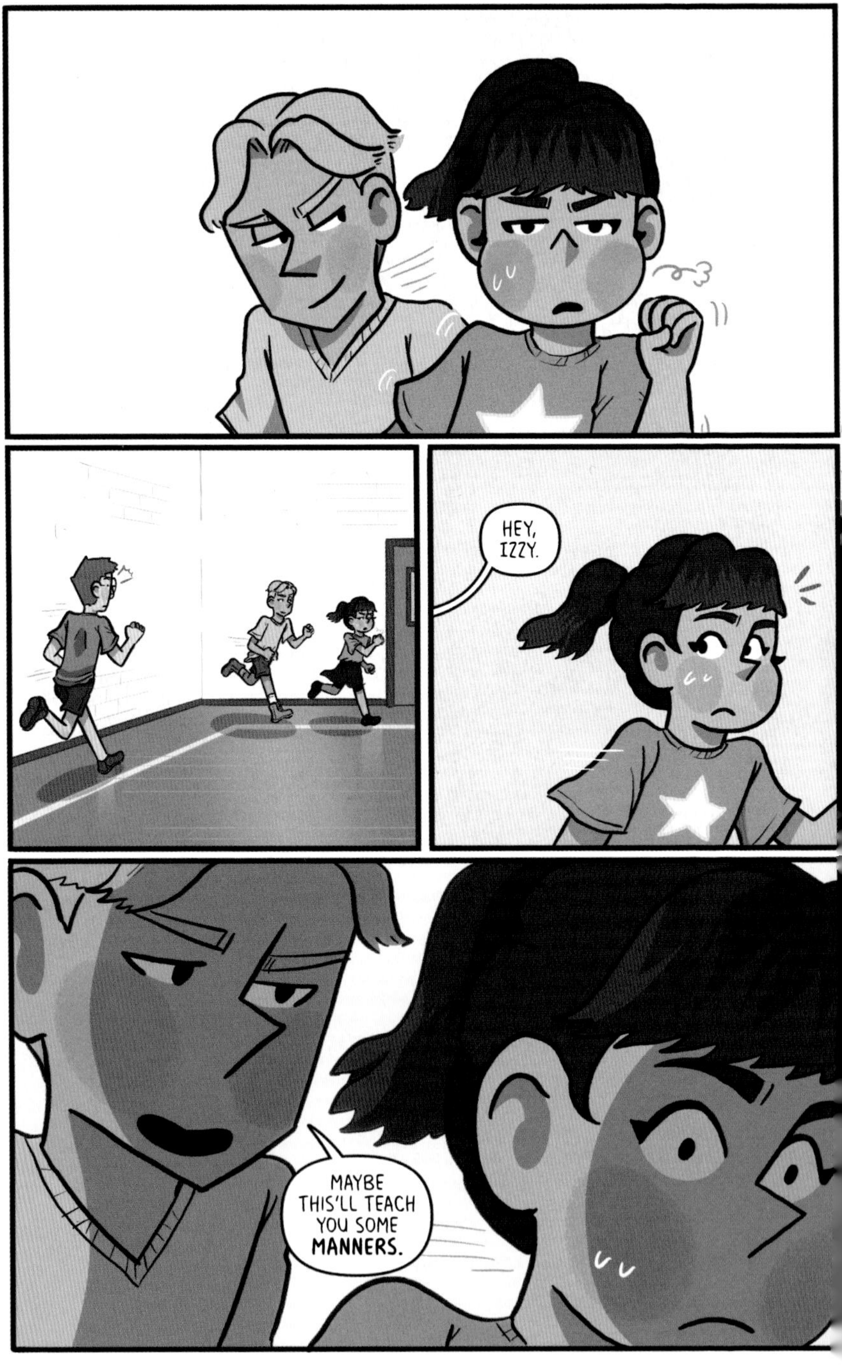
HEY, IZZY.
MAYBE THIS'LL TEACH YOU SOME **MANNERS.**

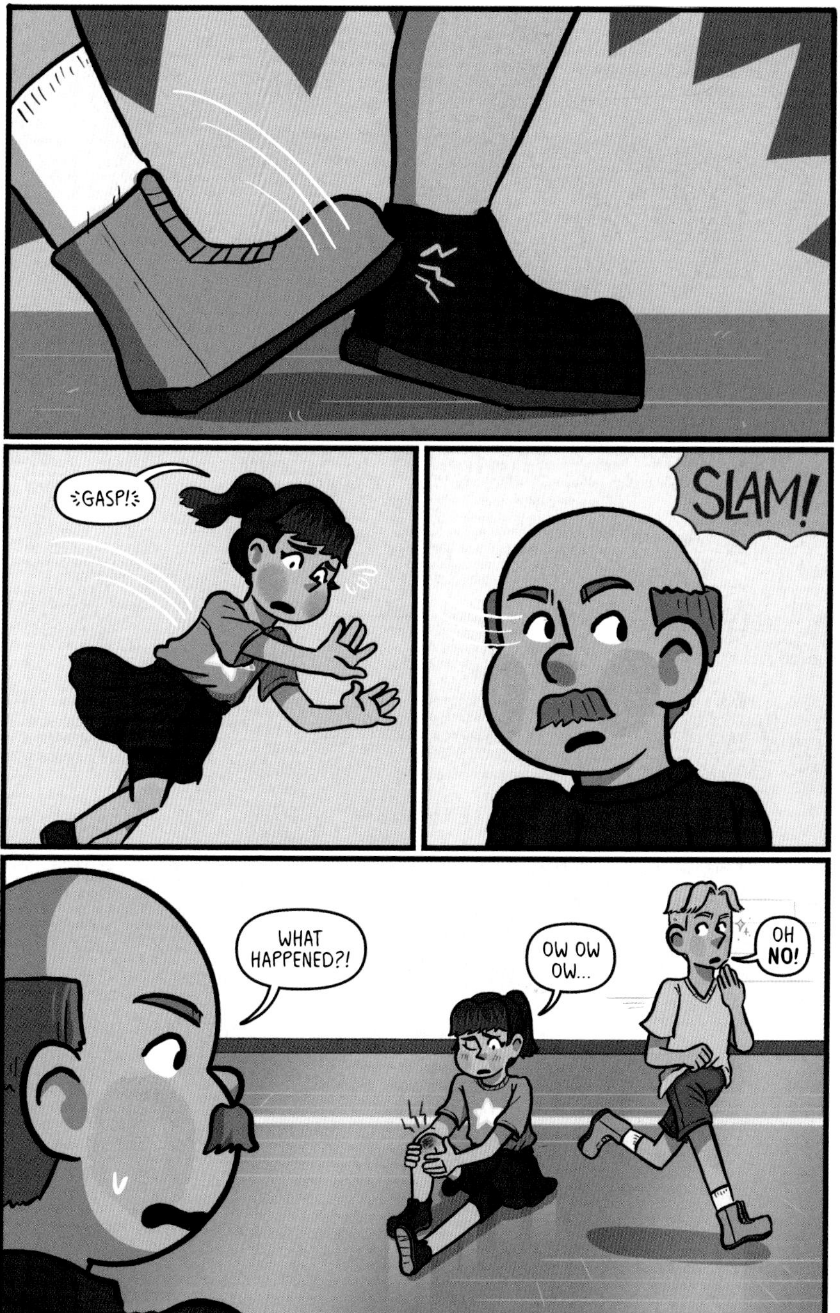

GASP!
SLAM!
WHAT HAPPENED?!
OW OW OW...
OH NO!

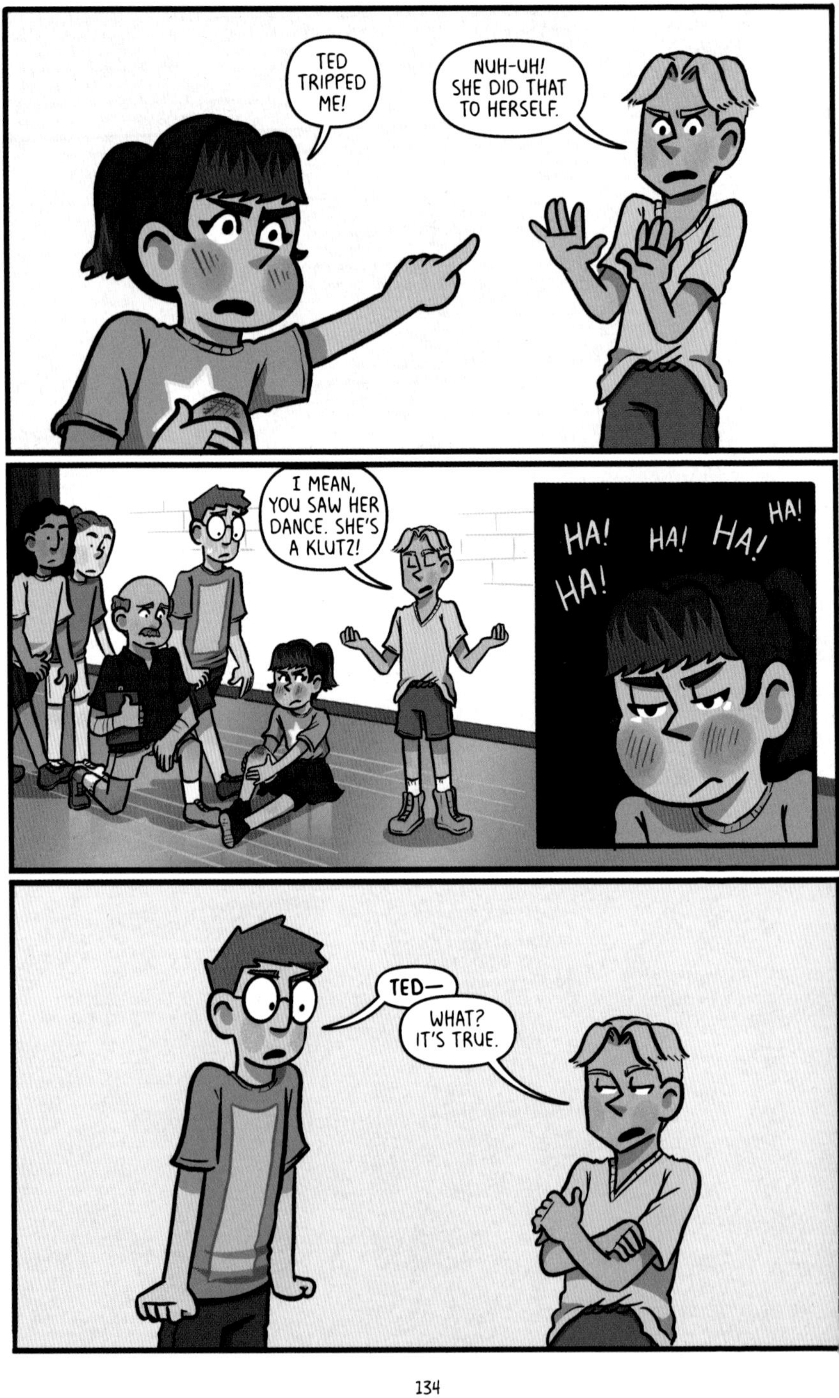
TED TRIPPED ME!
NUH-UH! SHE DID THAT TO HERSELF.
I MEAN, YOU SAW HER DANCE. SHE'S A KLUTZ!
HA! HA! HA! HA! HA!
TED—
WHAT? IT'S TRUE.

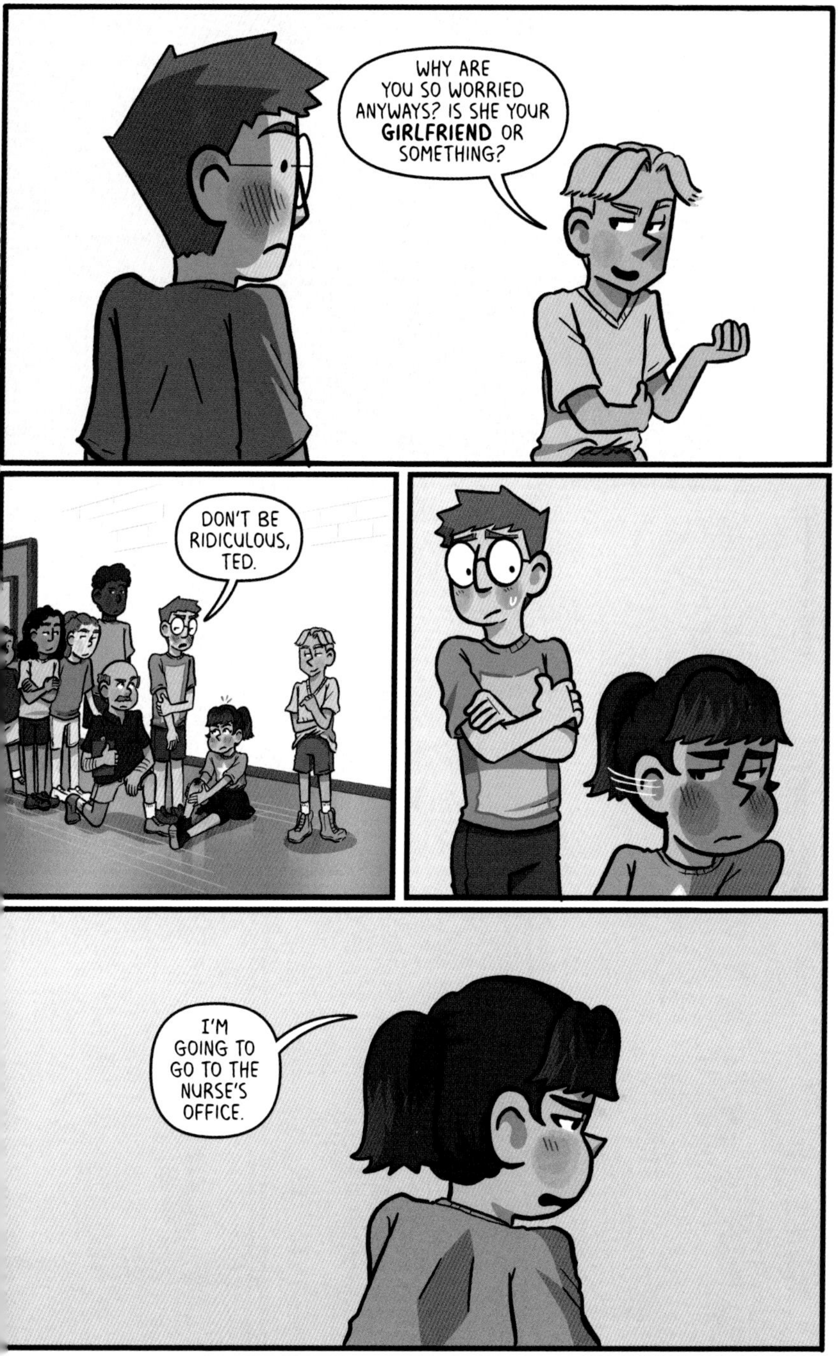
WHY ARE YOU SO WORRIED ANYWAYS? IS SHE YOUR **GIRLFRIEND** OR SOMETHING?
DON'T BE RIDICULOUS, TED.
I'M GOING TO GO TO THE NURSE'S OFFICE.

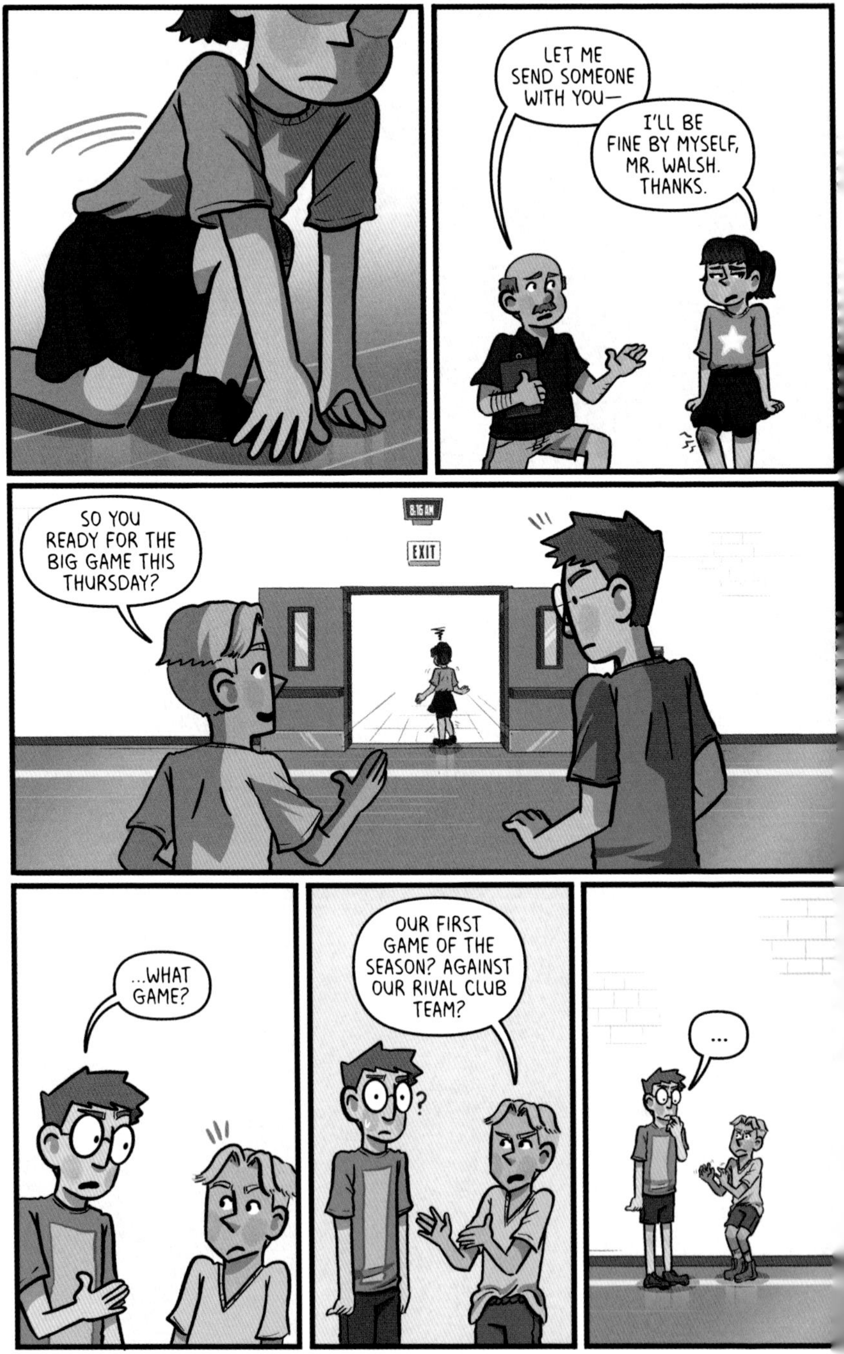
LET ME SEND SOMEONE WITH YOU—
I'LL BE FINE BY MYSELF, MR. WALSH. THANKS.
8:16 AM
EXIT
SO YOU READY FOR THE BIG GAME THIS THURSDAY?
...WHAT GAME?
OUR FIRST GAME OF THE SEASON? AGAINST OUR RIVAL CLUB TEAM?
...

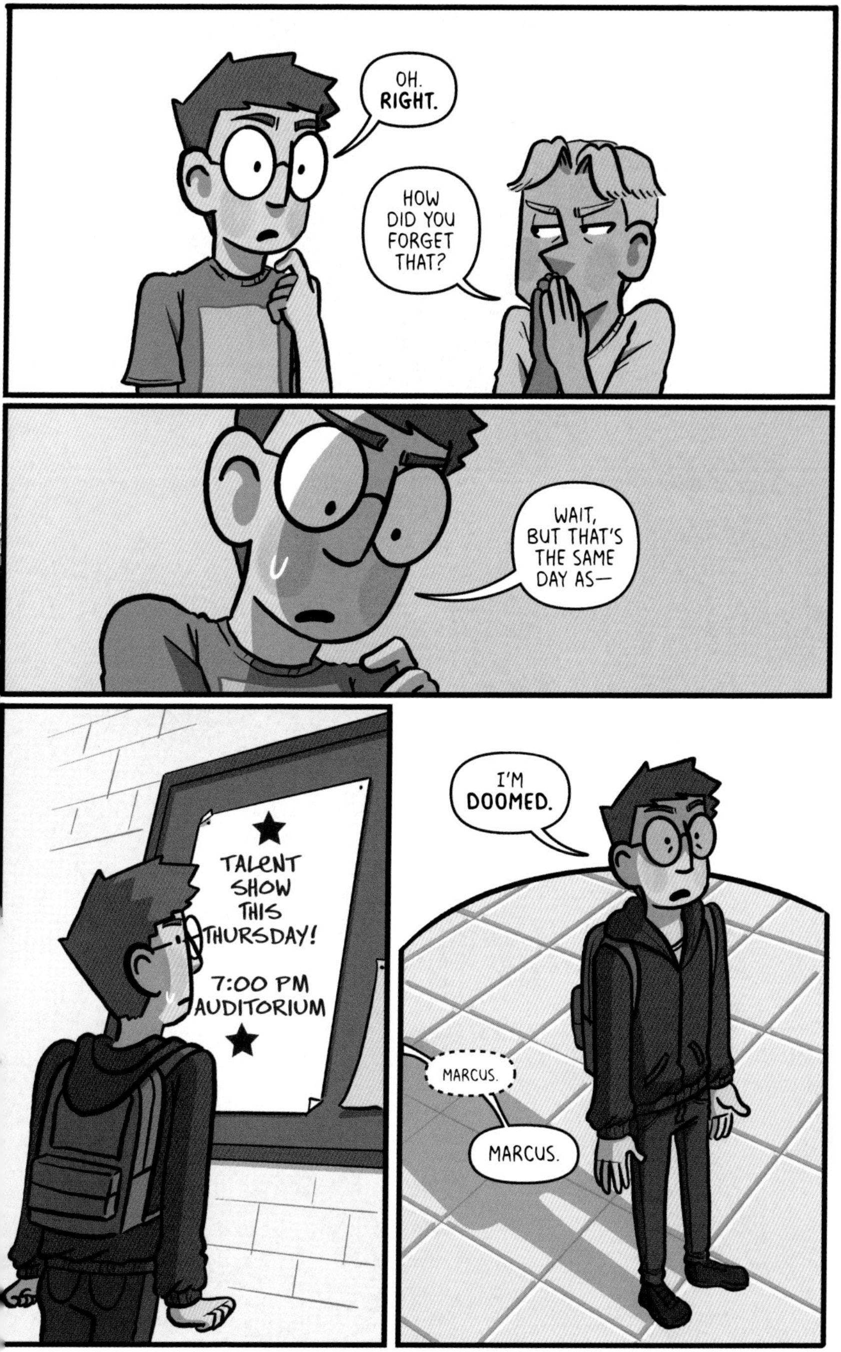
OH. **RIGHT.**
HOW DID YOU FORGET THAT?
WAIT, BUT THAT'S THE SAME DAY AS—
TALENT SHOW THIS THURSDAY!
7:00 PM AUDITORIUM
I'M **DOOMED.**
MARCUS.
MARCUS.

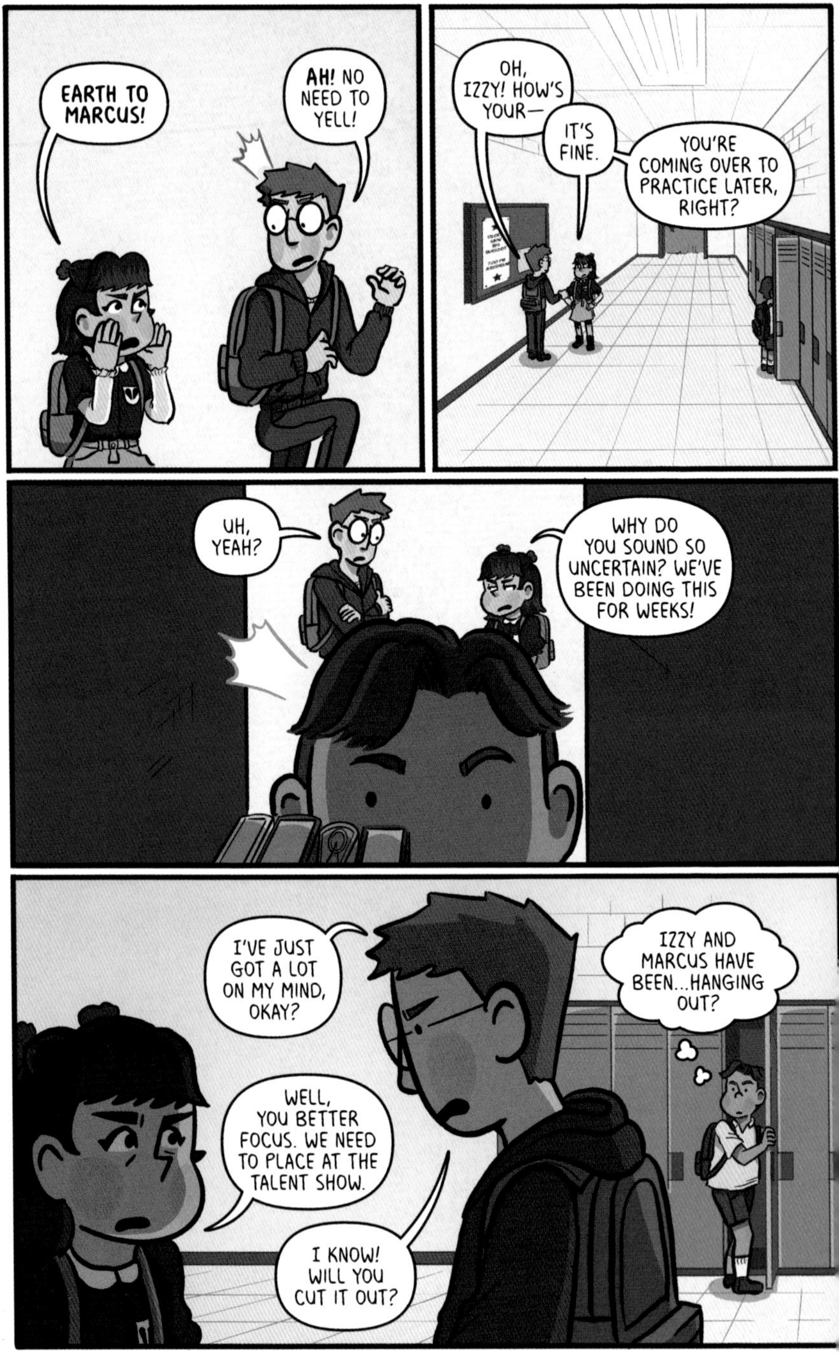
EARTH TO MARCUS!
AH! NO NEED TO YELL!
OH, IZZY! HOW'S YOUR—
IT'S FINE.
YOU'RE COMING OVER TO PRACTICE LATER, RIGHT?
UH, YEAH?
WHY DO YOU SOUND SO UNCERTAIN? WE'VE BEEN DOING THIS FOR WEEKS!
I'VE JUST GOT A LOT ON MY MIND, OKAY?
IZZY AND MARCUS HAVE BEEN...HANGING OUT?
WELL, YOU BETTER FOCUS. WE NEED TO PLACE AT THE TALENT SHOW.
I KNOW! WILL YOU CUT IT OUT?

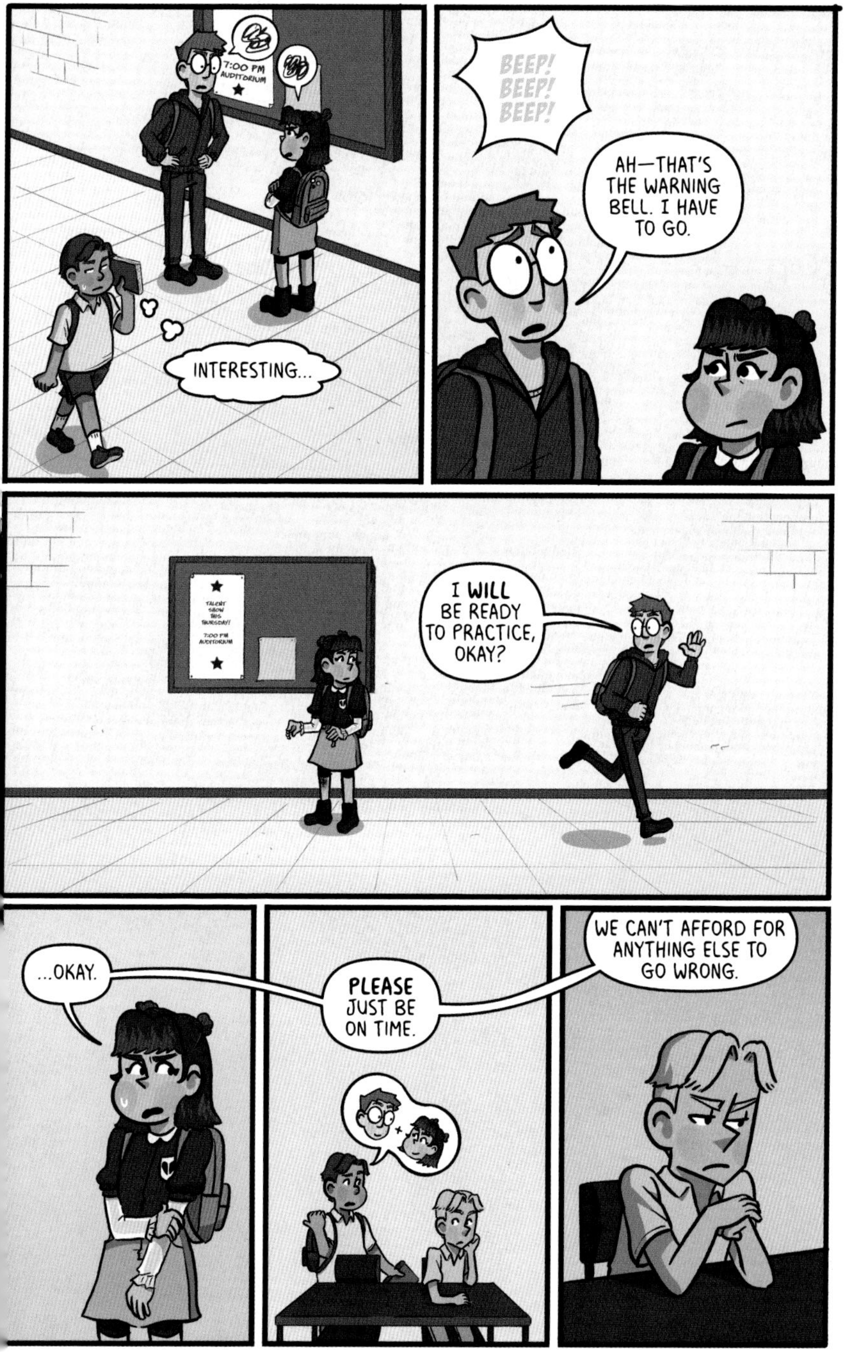
7:00 PM
AUDITORIUM
INTERESTING...
BEEP! BEEP! BEEP!
AH—THAT'S THE WARNING BELL. I HAVE TO GO.
TALENT SHOW THIS THURSDAY!
7:00 PM
AUDITORIUM
I **WILL** BE READY TO PRACTICE, OKAY?
...OKAY.
PLEASE JUST BE ON TIME.
WE CAN'T AFFORD FOR ANYTHING ELSE TO GO WRONG.

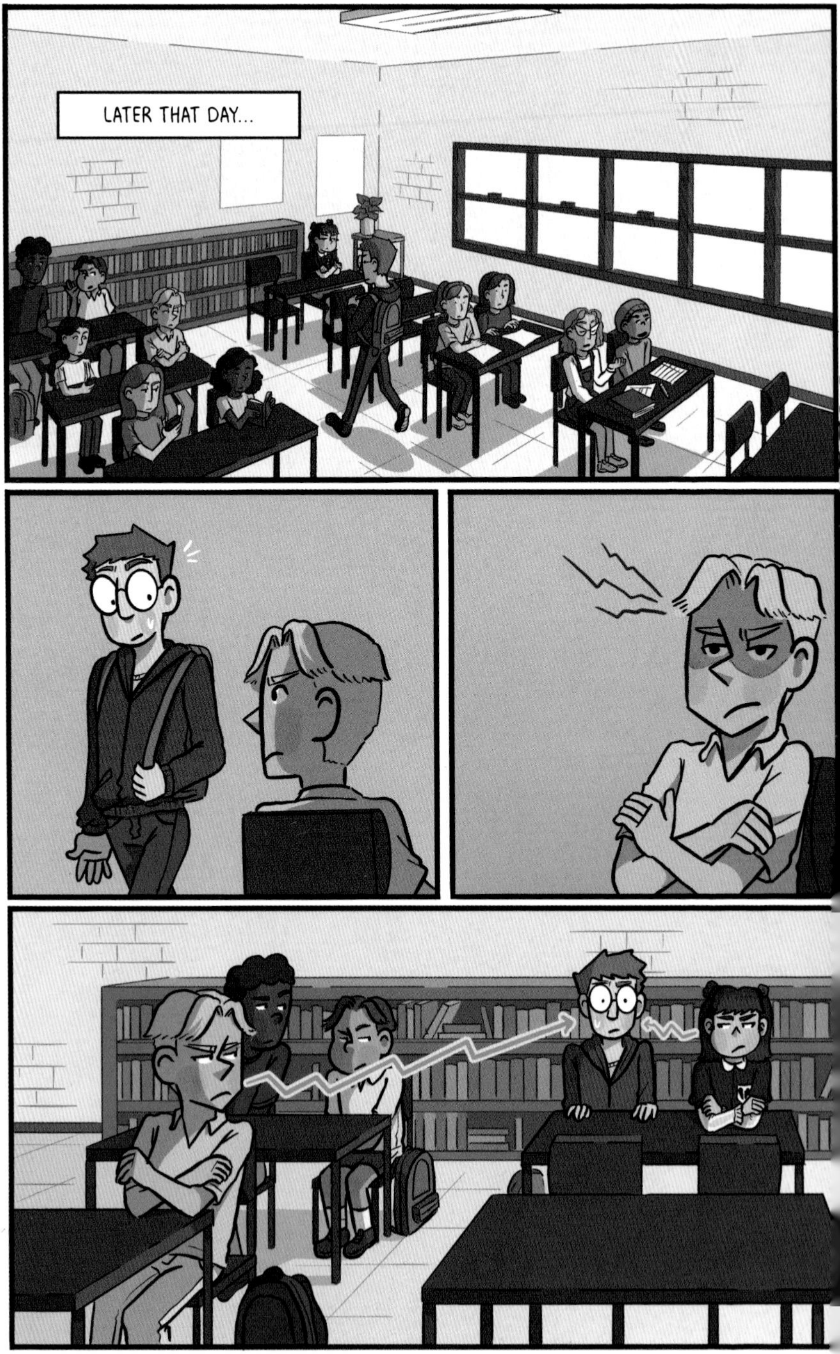
LATER THAT DAY...

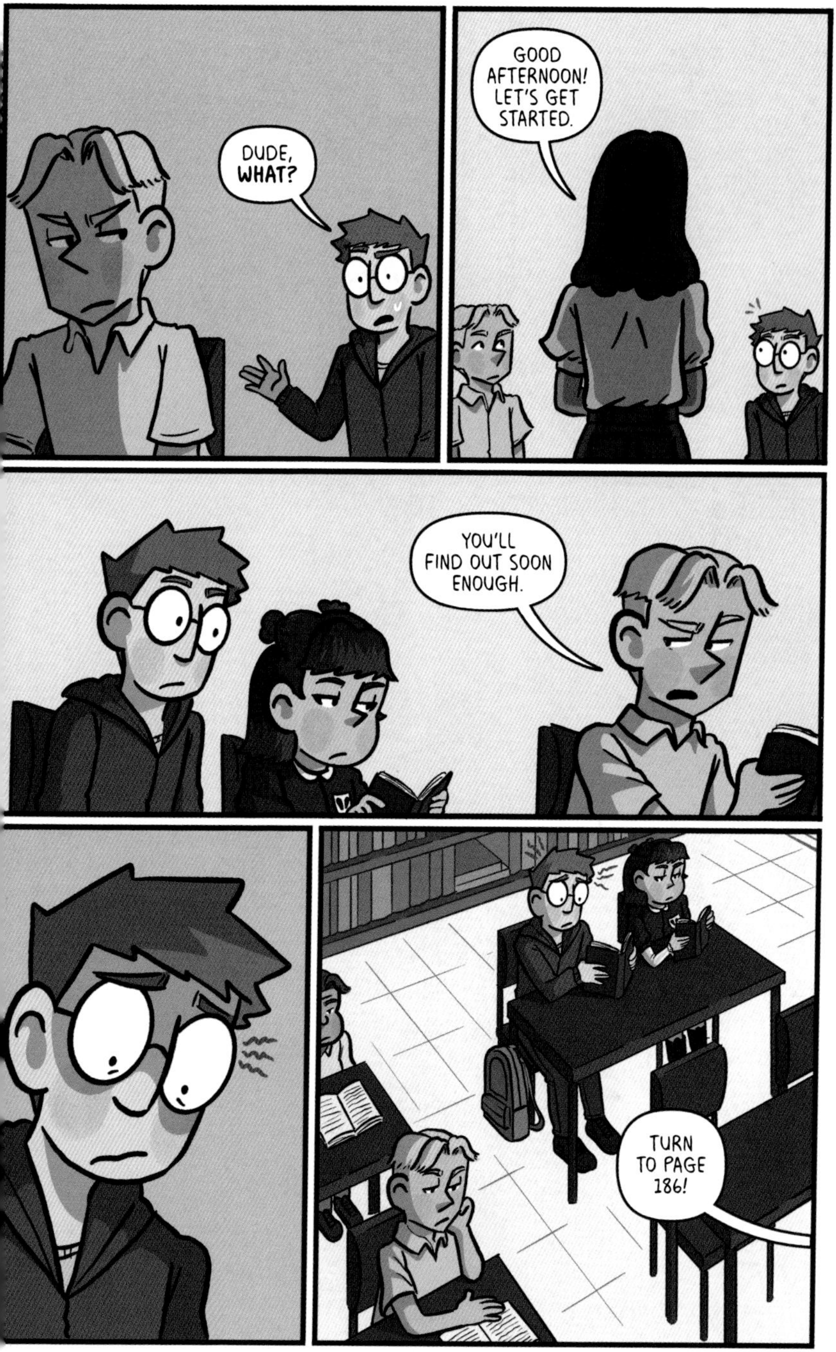
DUDE, **WHAT?**
GOOD AFTERNOON! LET'S GET STARTED.
YOU'LL FIND OUT SOON ENOUGH.
TURN TO PAGE 186!

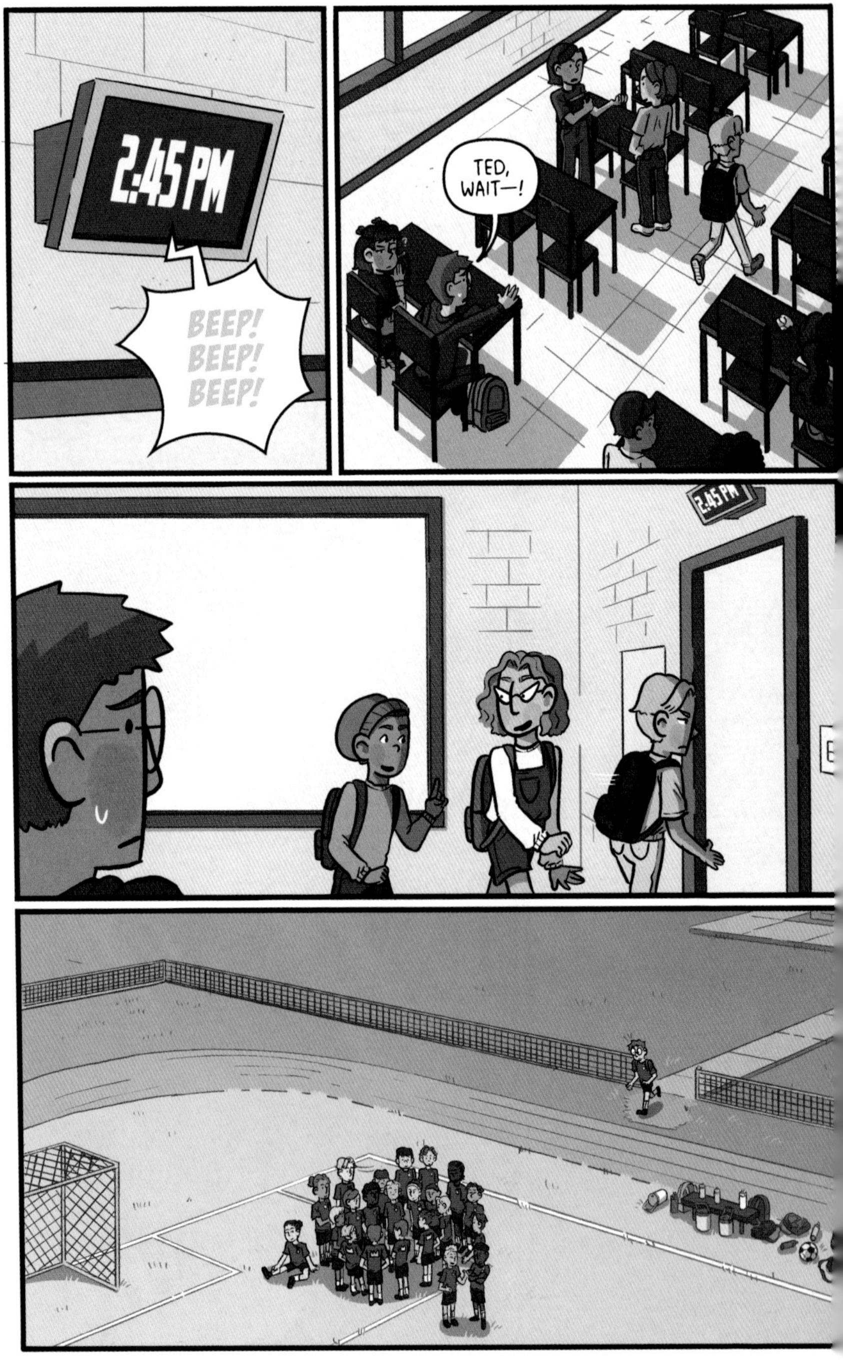
2:45 PM
BEEP! BEEP! BEEP!
TED, WAIT—!
2:45 PM

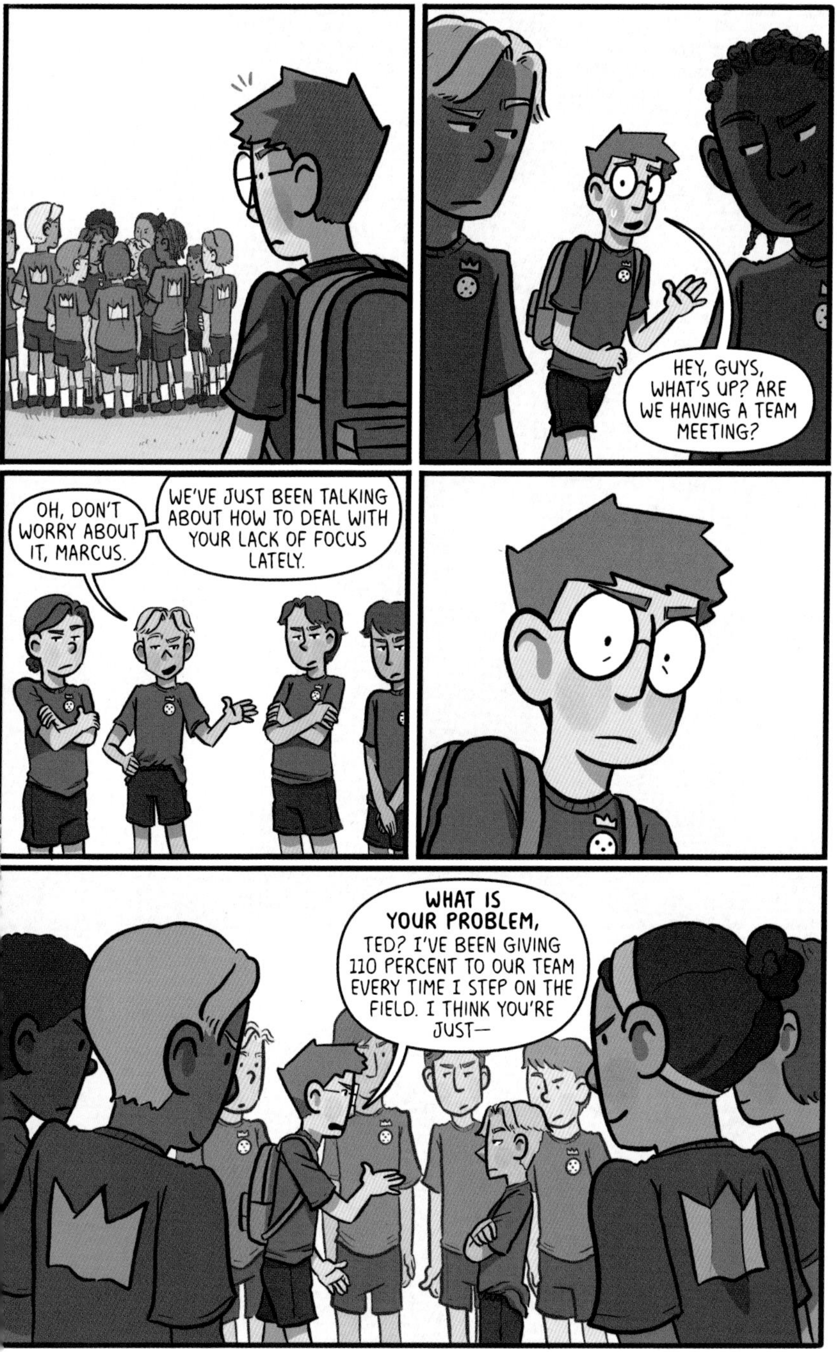
HEY, GUYS, WHAT'S UP? ARE WE HAVING A TEAM MEETING?
OH, DON'T WORRY ABOUT IT, MARCUS.
WE'VE JUST BEEN TALKING ABOUT HOW TO DEAL WITH YOUR LACK OF FOCUS LATELY.
WHAT IS YOUR PROBLEM, TED? I'VE BEEN GIVING 110 PERCENT TO OUR TEAM EVERY TIME I STEP ON THE FIELD. I THINK YOU'RE JUST—

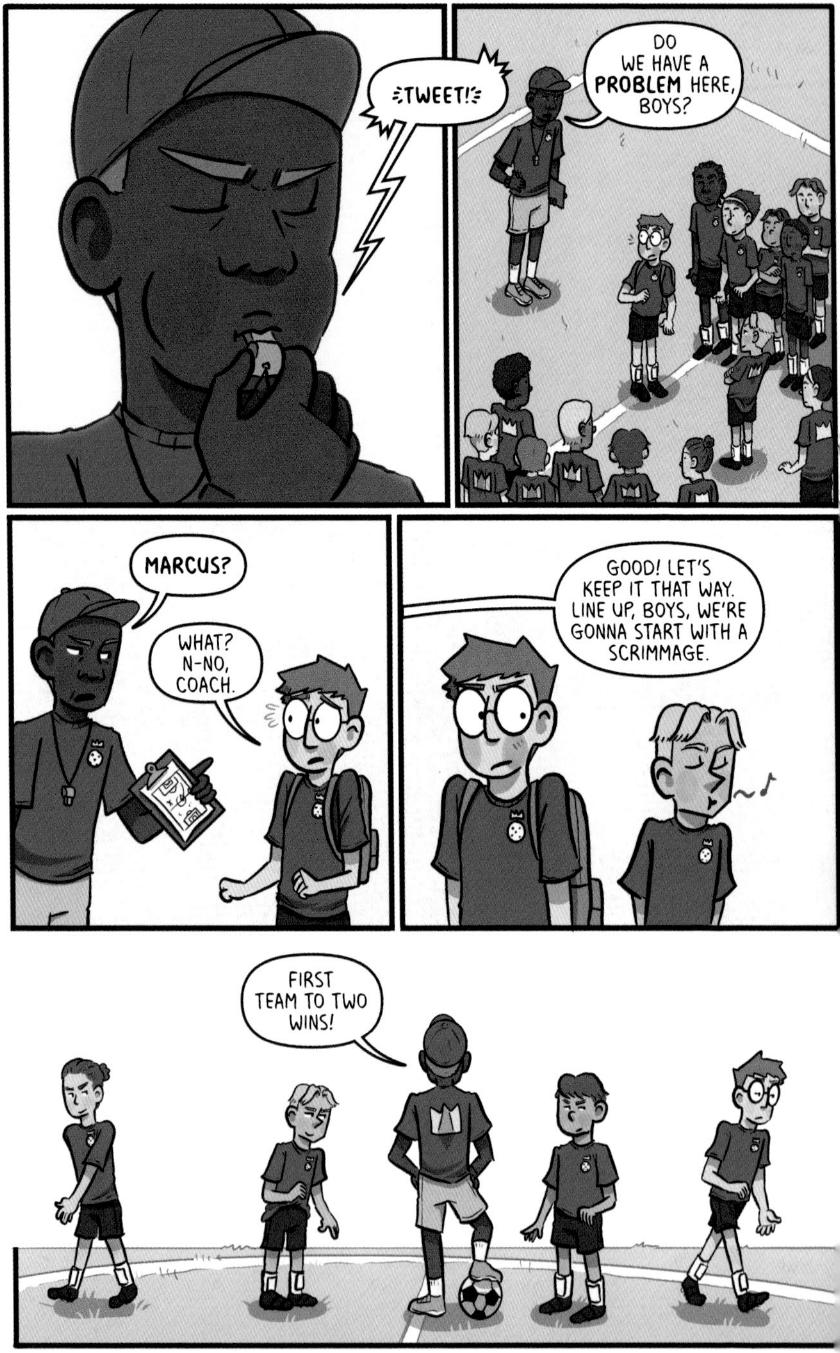
TWEET!
DO WE HAVE A PROBLEM HERE, BOYS?
MARCUS?
WHAT? N-NO, COACH.
GOOD! LET'S KEEP IT THAT WAY. LINE UP, BOYS, WE'RE GONNA START WITH A SCRIMMAGE.
FIRST TEAM TO TWO WINS!

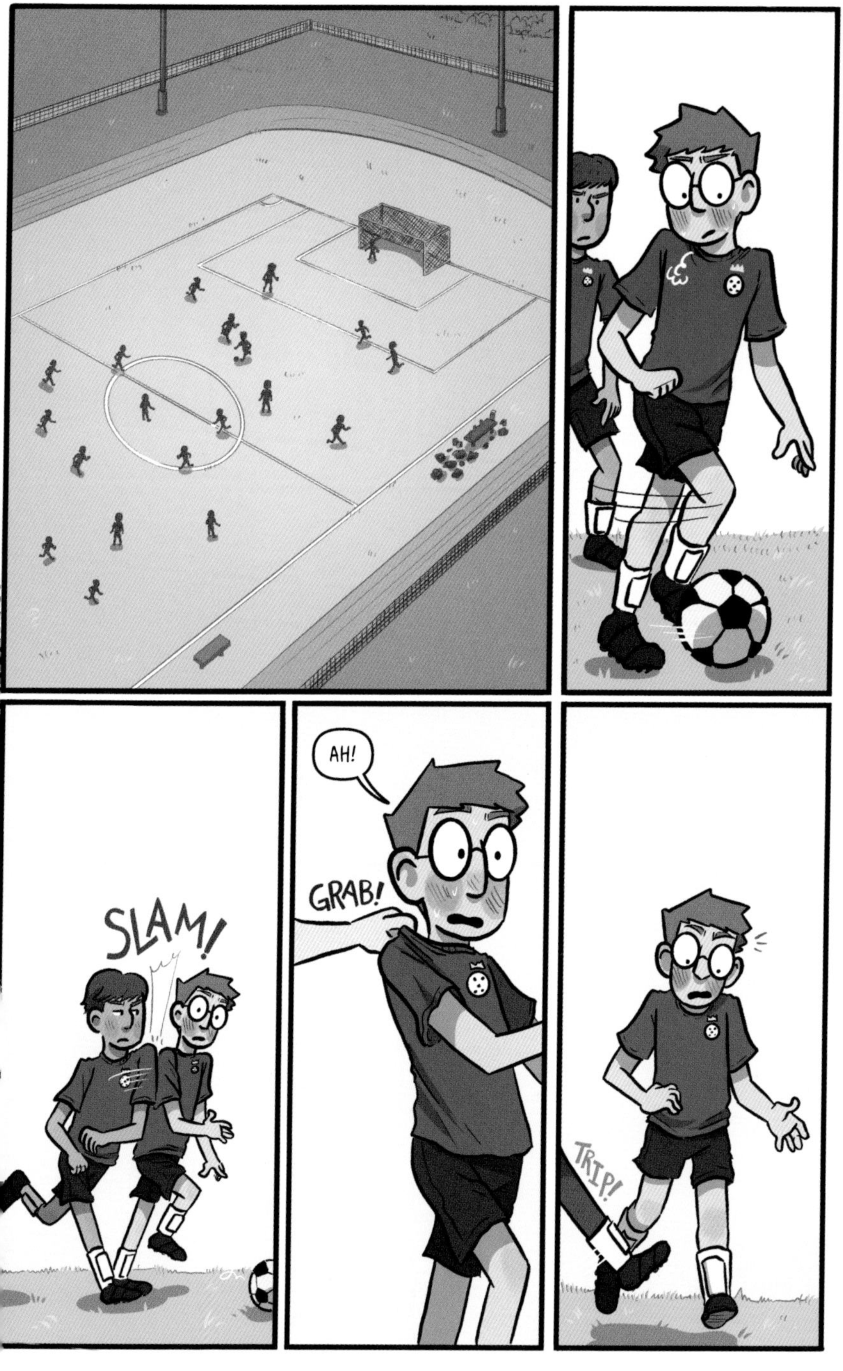
SLAM!
AH!
GRAB!
TRIP!

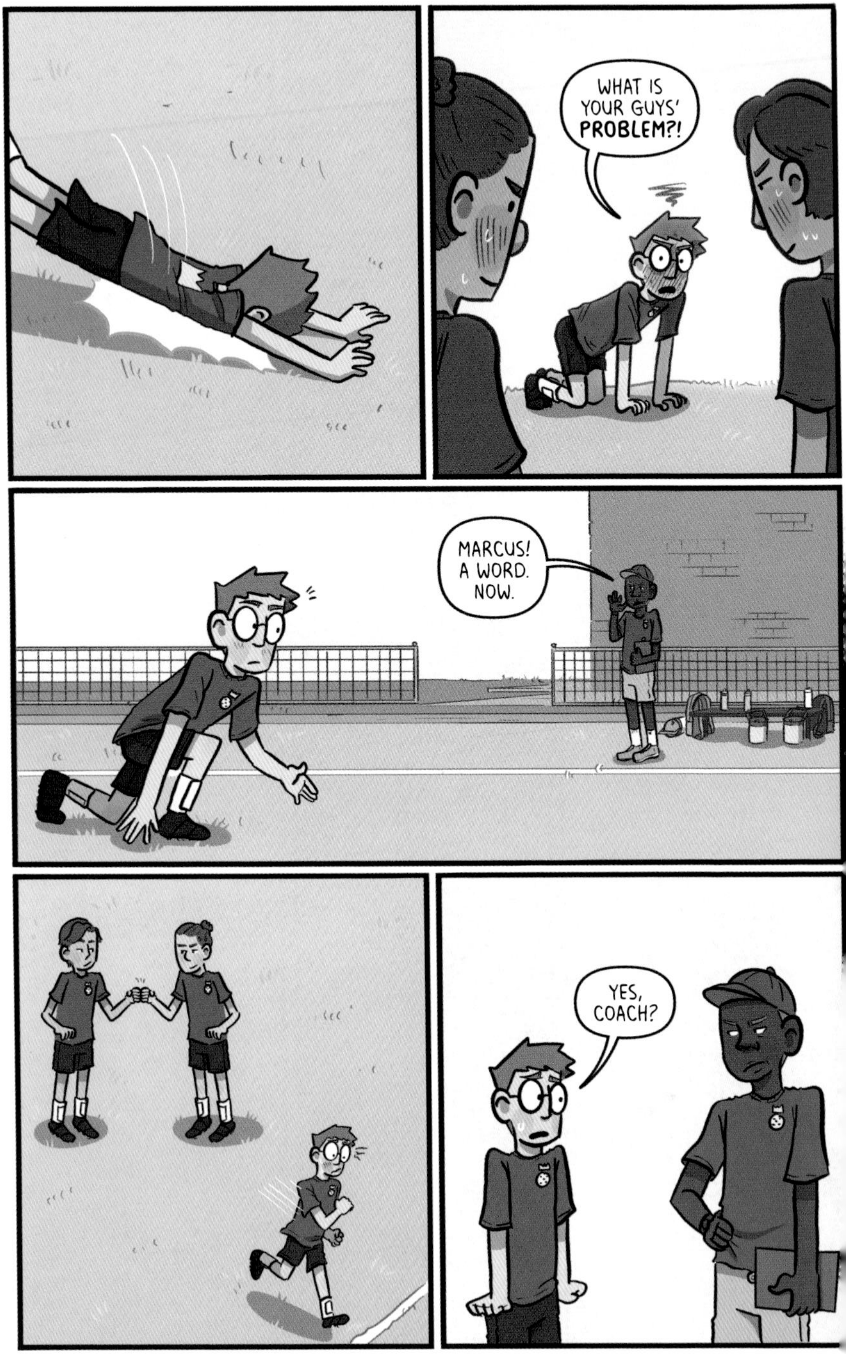
WHAT IS YOUR GUYS' **PROBLEM?!**
MARCUS! A WORD. NOW.
YES, COACH?

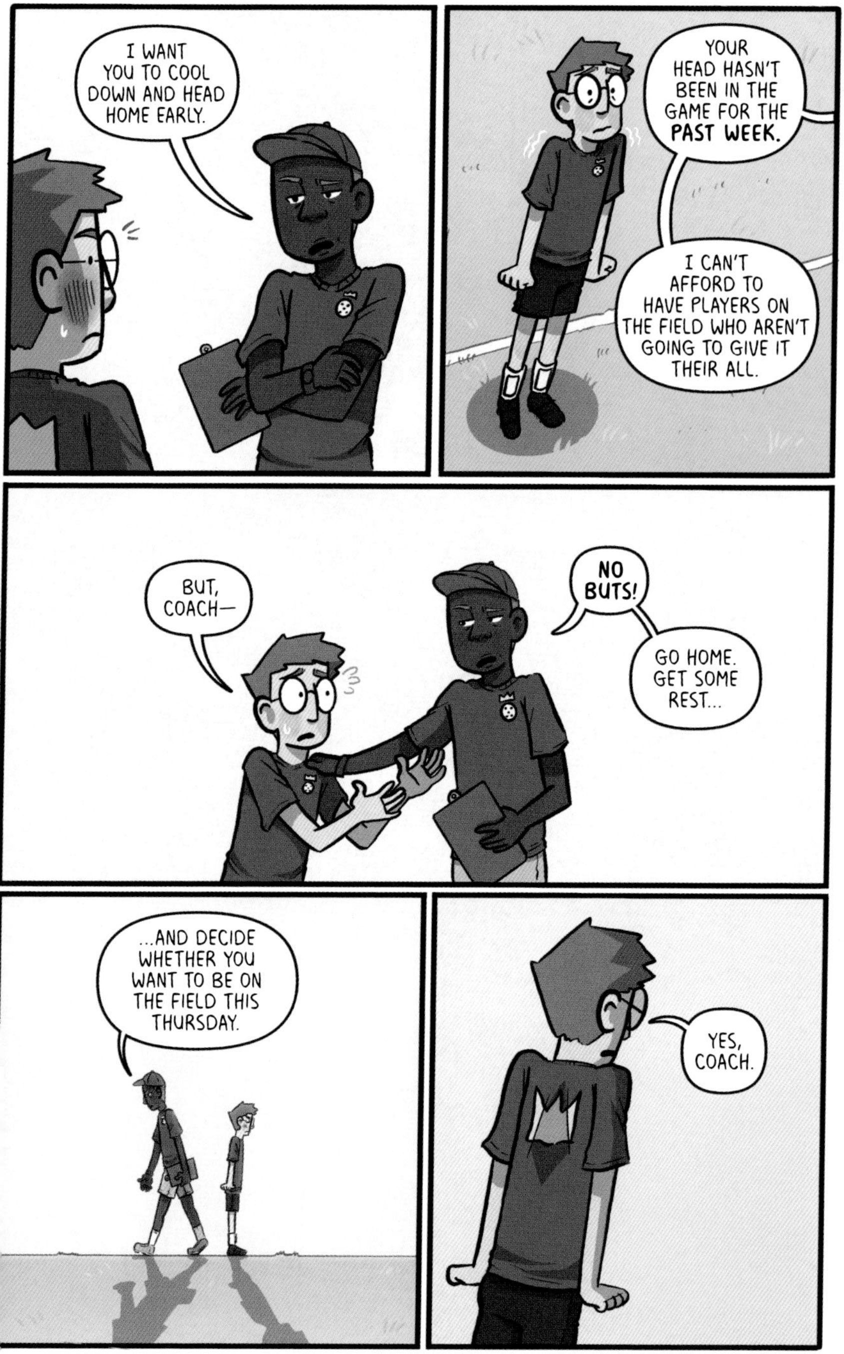
I WANT YOU TO COOL DOWN AND HEAD HOME EARLY.
YOUR HEAD HASN'T BEEN IN THE GAME FOR THE **PAST WEEK.**
I CAN'T AFFORD TO HAVE PLAYERS ON THE FIELD WHO AREN'T GOING TO GIVE IT THEIR ALL.
BUT, COACH—
NO BUTS!
GO HOME. GET SOME REST...
...AND DECIDE WHETHER YOU WANT TO BE ON THE FIELD THIS THURSDAY.
YES, COACH.

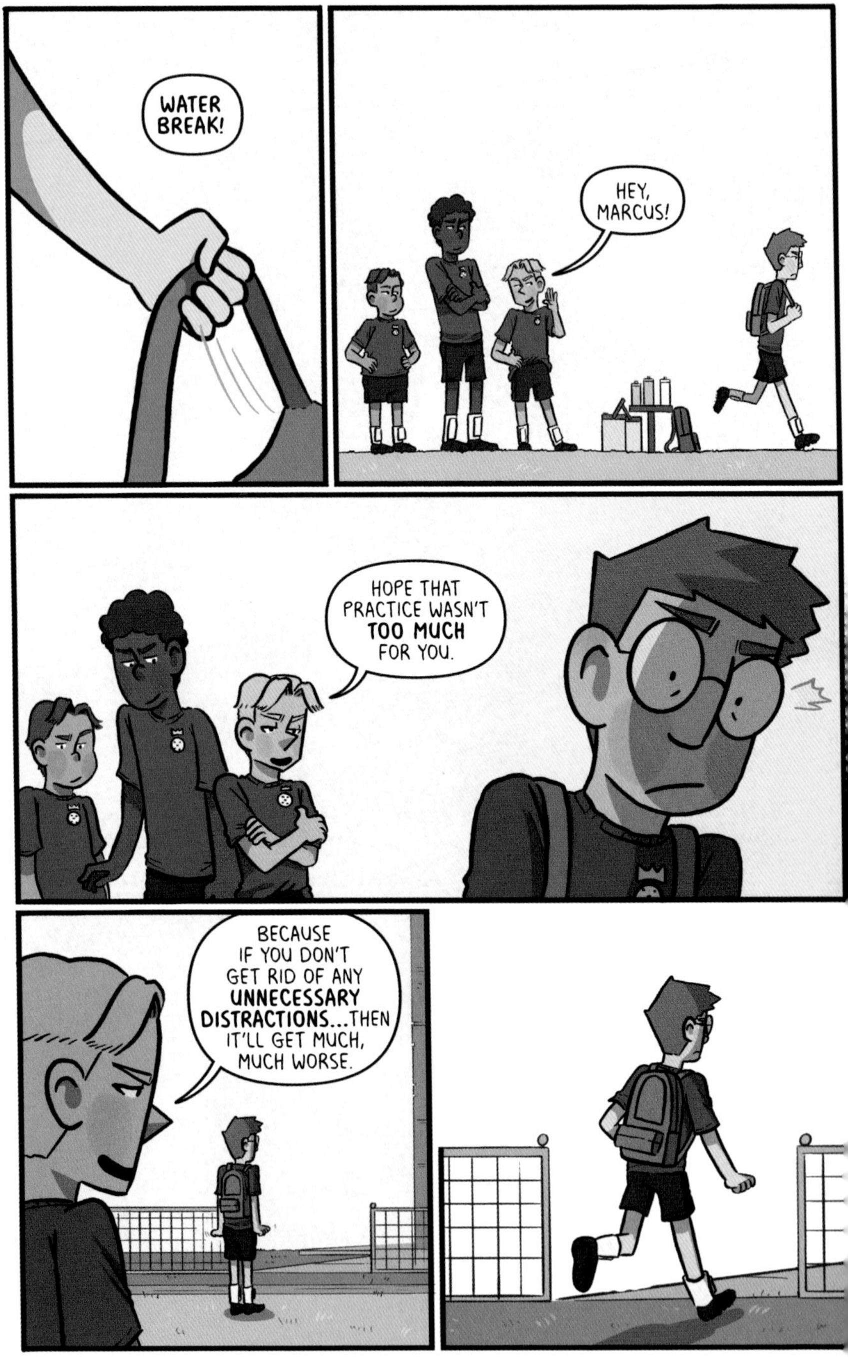
WATER BREAK!
HEY, MARCUS!
HOPE THAT PRACTICE WASN'T **TOO MUCH** FOR YOU.
BECAUSE IF YOU DON'T GET RID OF ANY **UNNECESSARY DISTRACTIONS...** THEN IT'LL GET MUCH, MUCH WORSE.

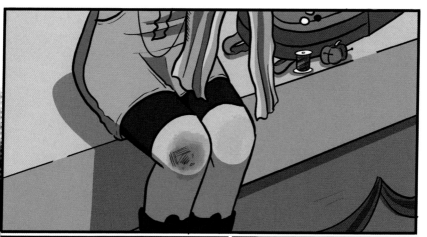

OUCH!

ARE YOU SURE YOUR KNEE IS OKAY? THAT BRUISE LOOKS PRETTY BAD.

I PROMISE, I'M FINE.

FINISHING UP THE UNIFORMS IS MY NUMBER ONE PRIORITY.

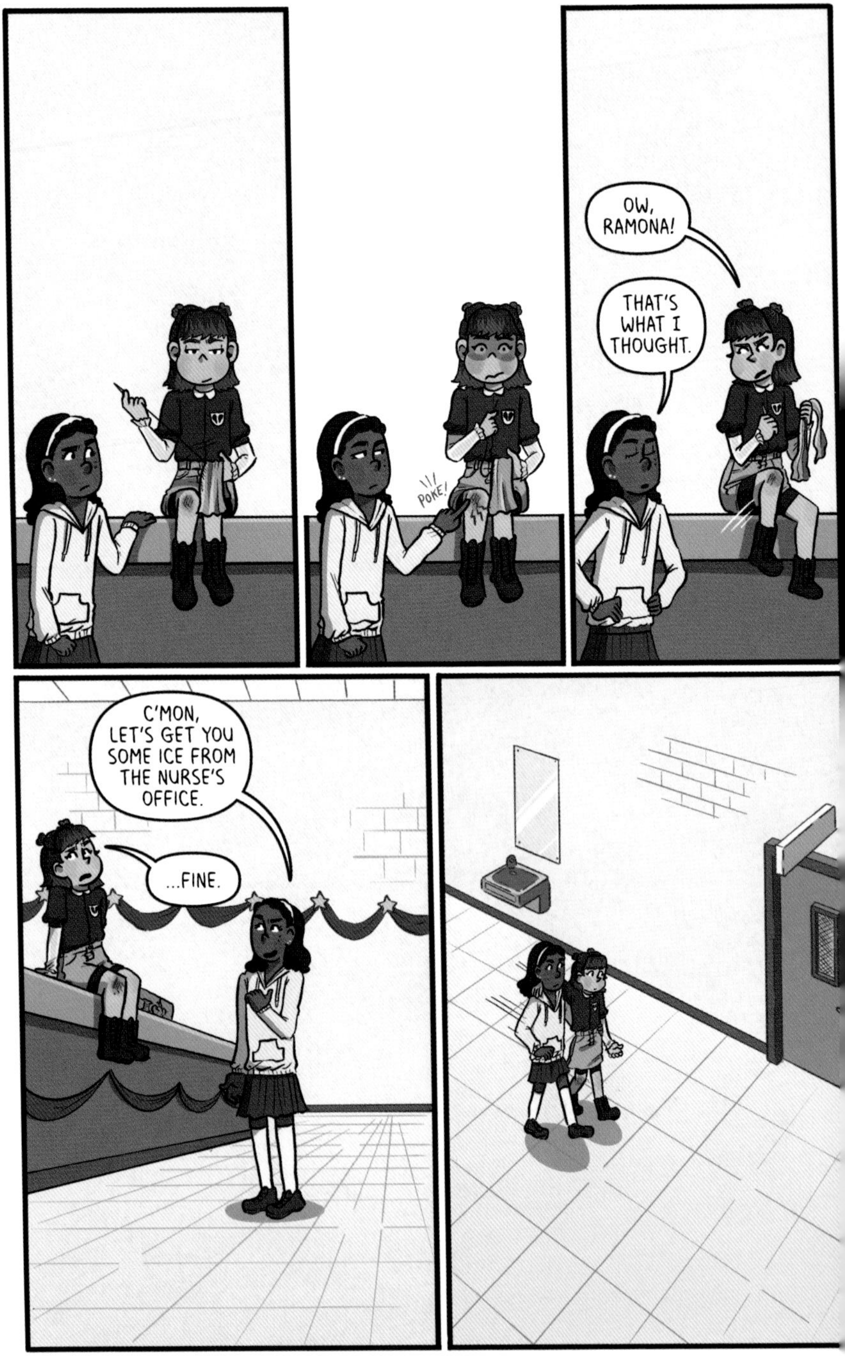
POKE!
OW, RAMONA!
THAT'S WHAT I THOUGHT.
C'MON, LET'S GET YOU SOME ICE FROM THE NURSE'S OFFICE.
...FINE.

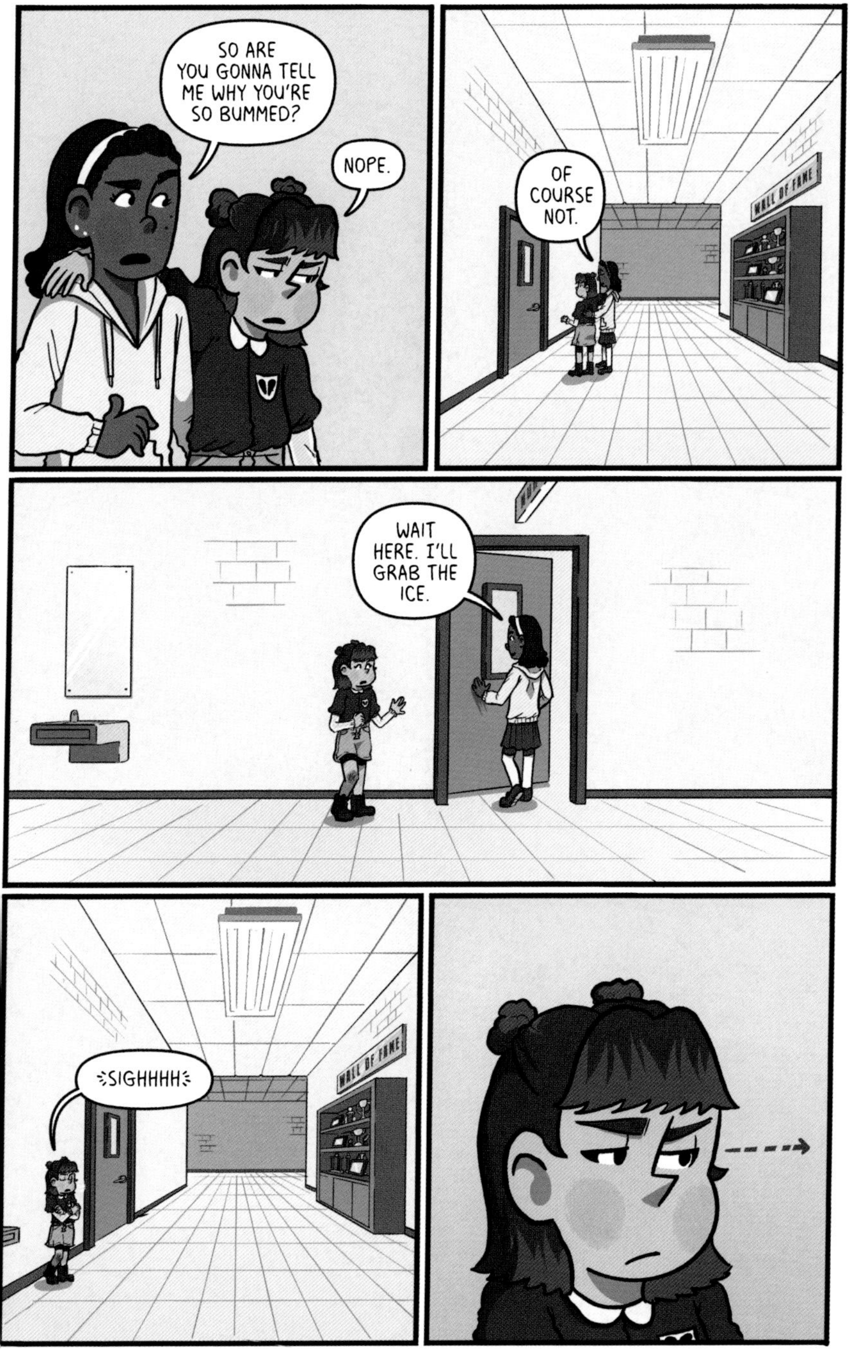
SO ARE YOU GONNA TELL ME WHY YOU'RE SO BUMMED?
NOPE.
OF COURSE NOT.
WALL OF FAME
WAIT HERE. I'LL GRAB THE ICE.
WALL OF FAME
SIGHHHH

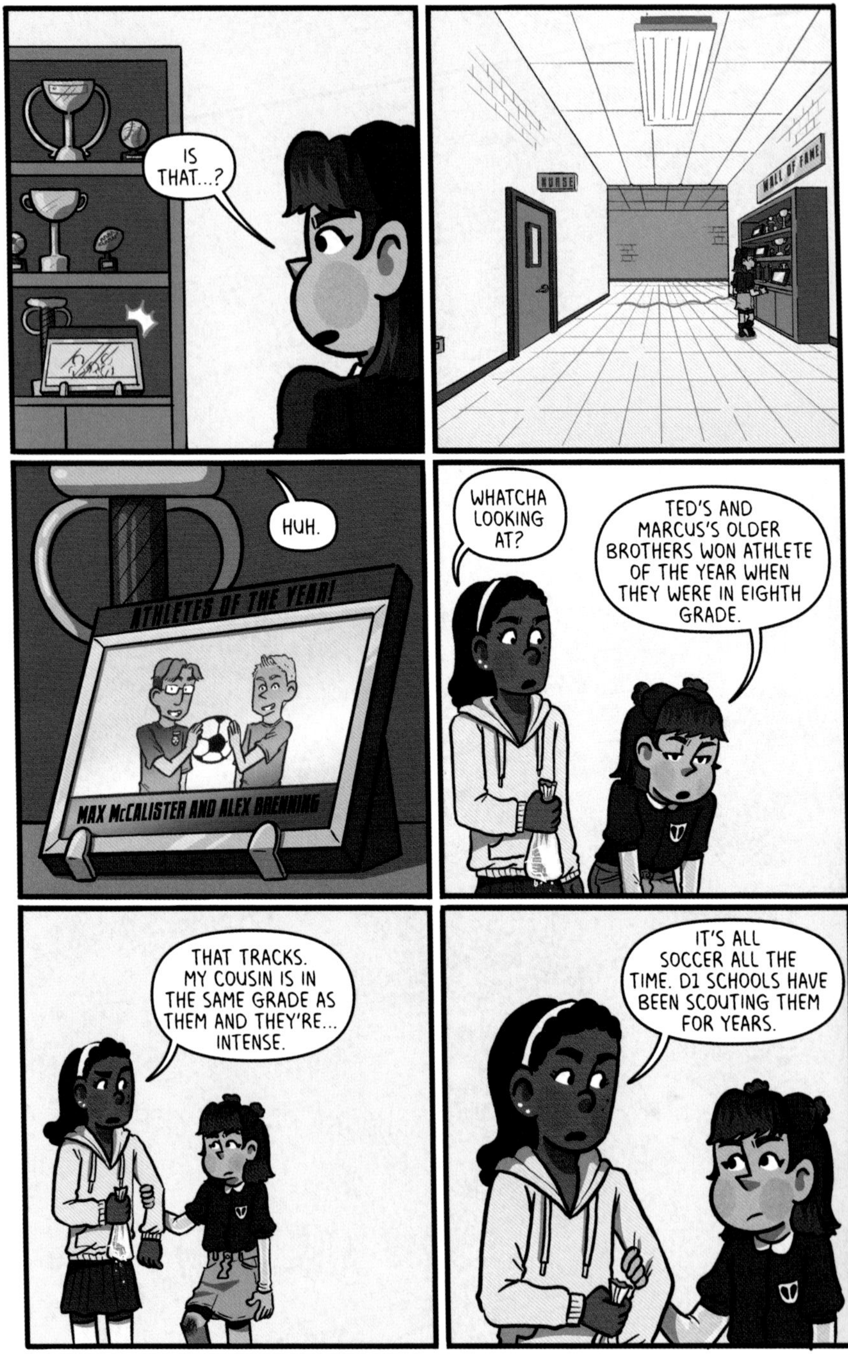
IS THAT...?
NURSE
WALL OF FAME
HUH.
ATHLETES OF THE YEAR!
MAX McCALISTER AND ALEX BRENNING
WHATCHA LOOKING AT?
TED'S AND MARCUS'S OLDER BROTHERS WON ATHLETE OF THE YEAR WHEN THEY WERE IN EIGHTH GRADE.
THAT TRACKS. MY COUSIN IS IN THE SAME GRADE AS THEM AND THEY'RE... INTENSE.
IT'S ALL SOCCER ALL THE TIME. D1 SCHOOLS HAVE BEEN SCOUTING THEM FOR YEARS.

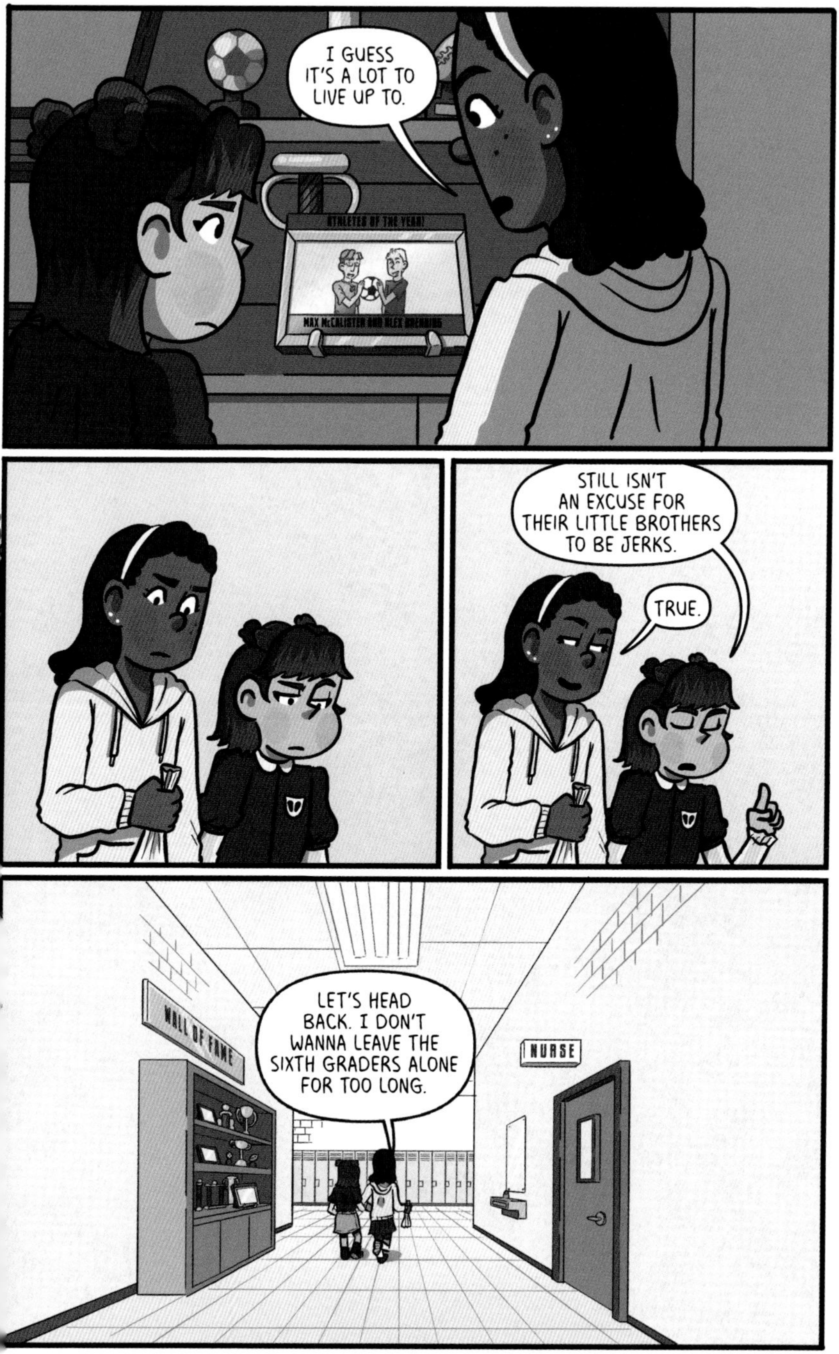
I GUESS IT'S A LOT TO LIVE UP TO.
ATHLETES OF THE YEAR!
STILL ISN'T AN EXCUSE FOR THEIR LITTLE BROTHERS TO BE JERKS.
TRUE.
WALL OF FAME
NURSE
LET'S HEAD BACK. I DON'T WANNA LEAVE THE SIXTH GRADERS ALONE FOR TOO LONG.

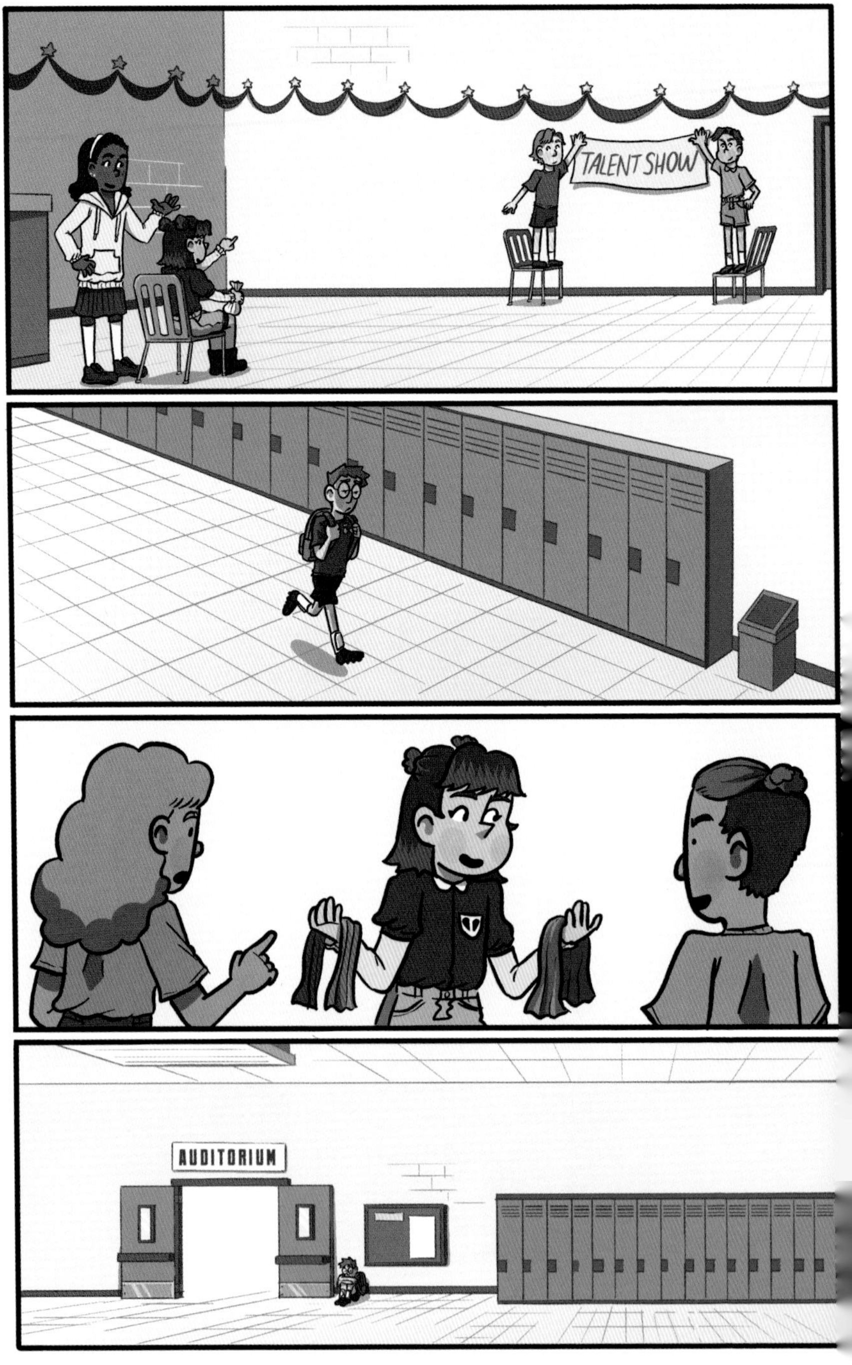
TALENT SHOW
AUDITORIUM

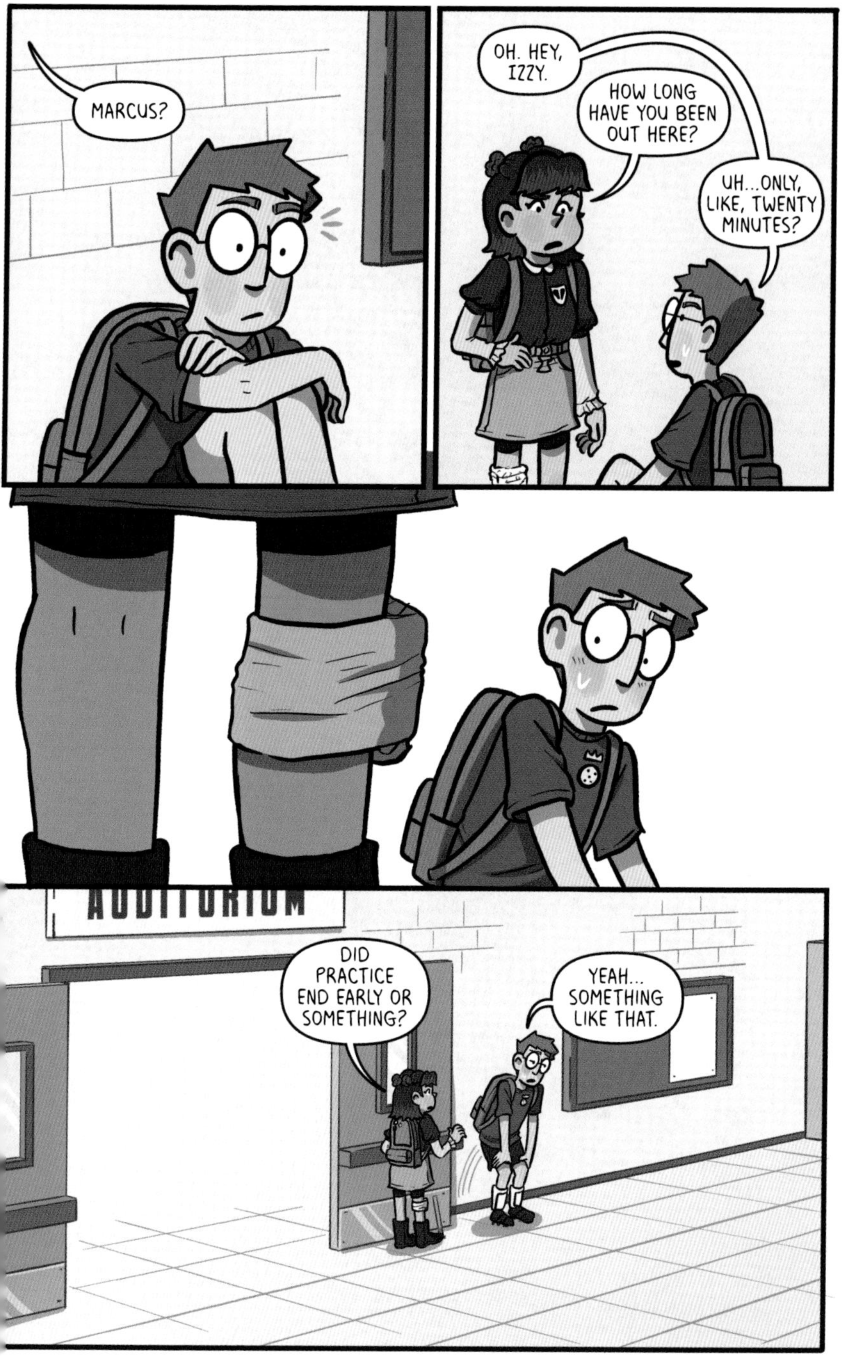
MARCUS?
OH. HEY, IZZY.
HOW LONG HAVE YOU BEEN OUT HERE?
UH...ONLY, LIKE, TWENTY MINUTES?
AUDITORIUM
DID PRACTICE END EARLY OR SOMETHING?
YEAH... SOMETHING LIKE THAT.

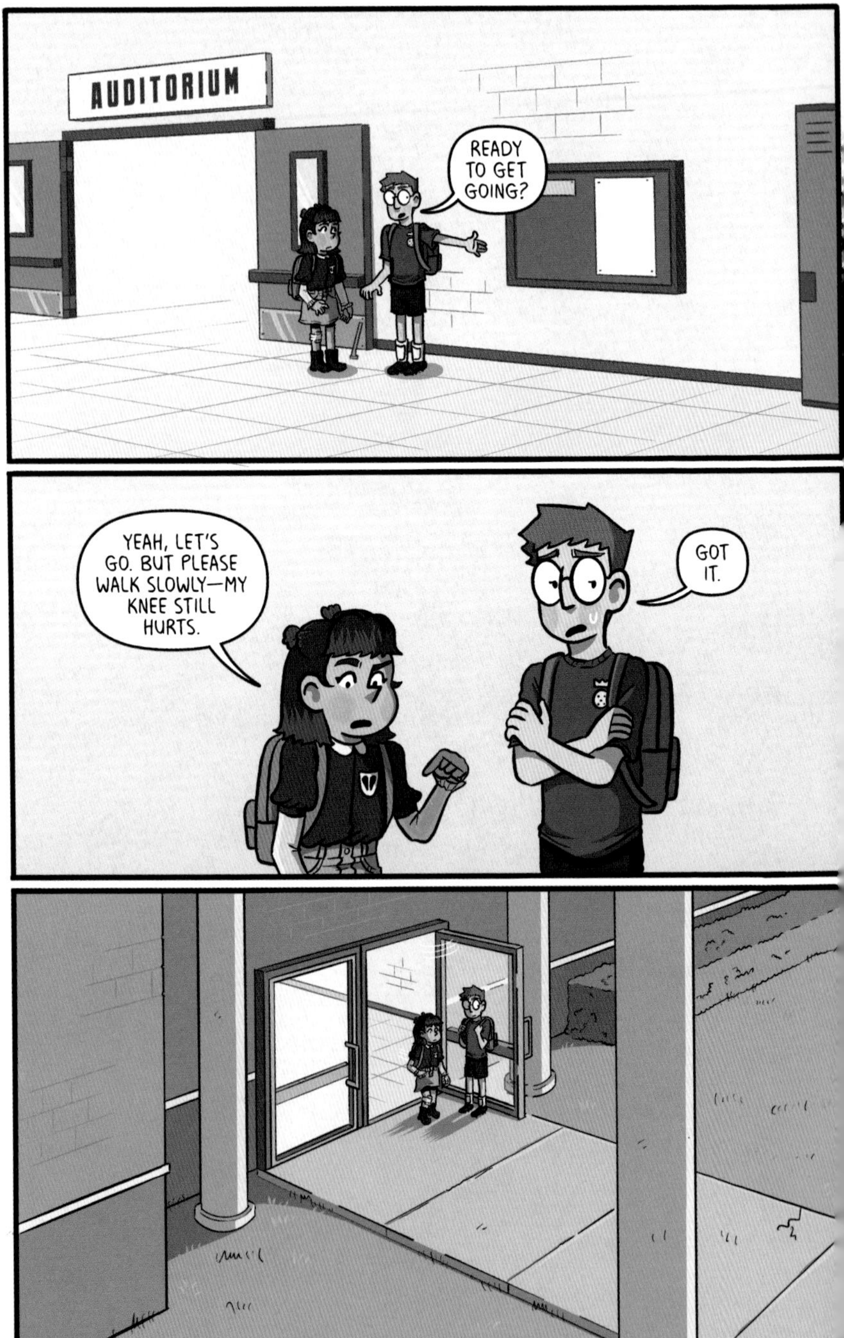
AUDITORIUM
READY TO GET GOING?
YEAH, LET'S GO. BUT PLEASE WALK SLOWLY—MY KNEE STILL HURTS.
GOT IT.

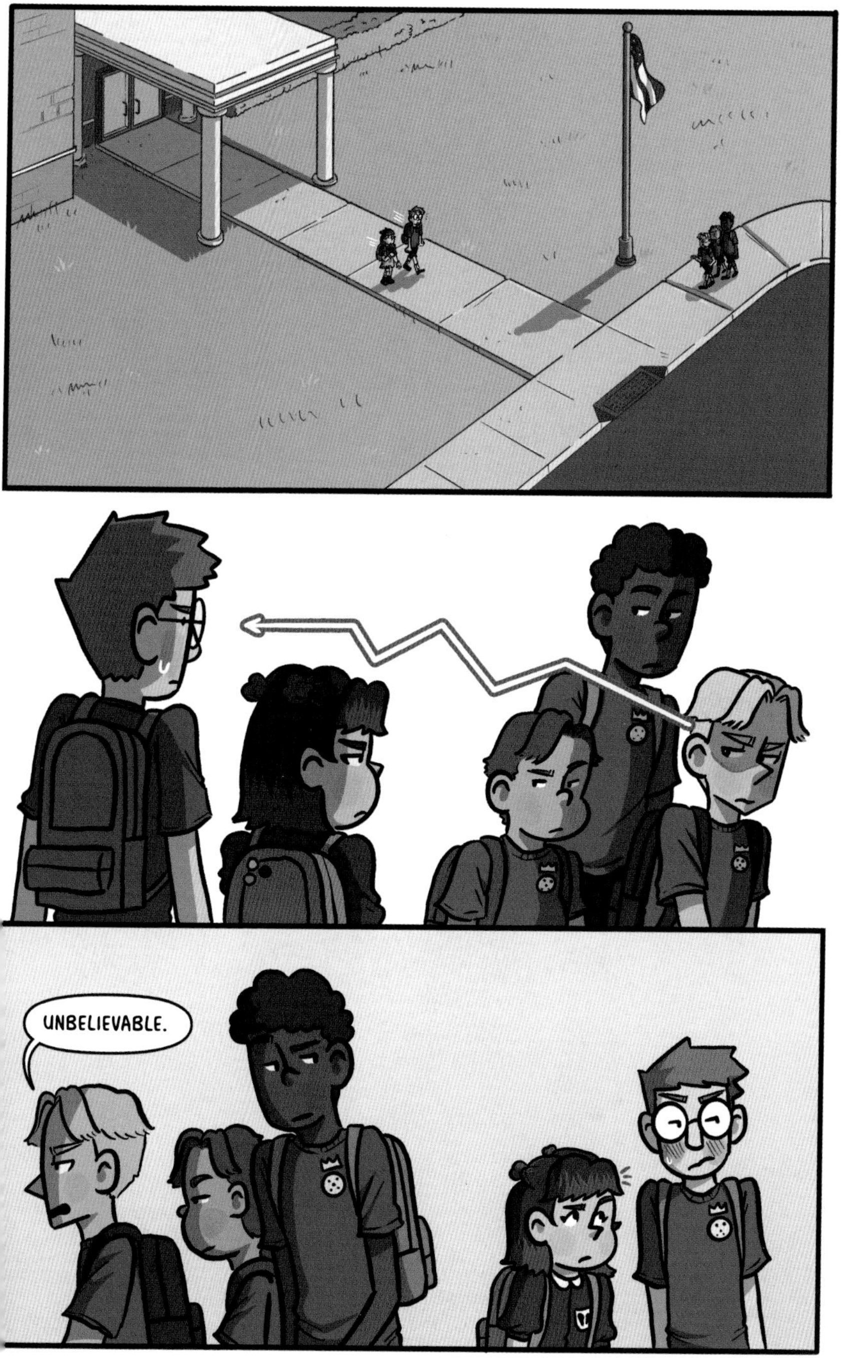
UNBELIEVABLE.

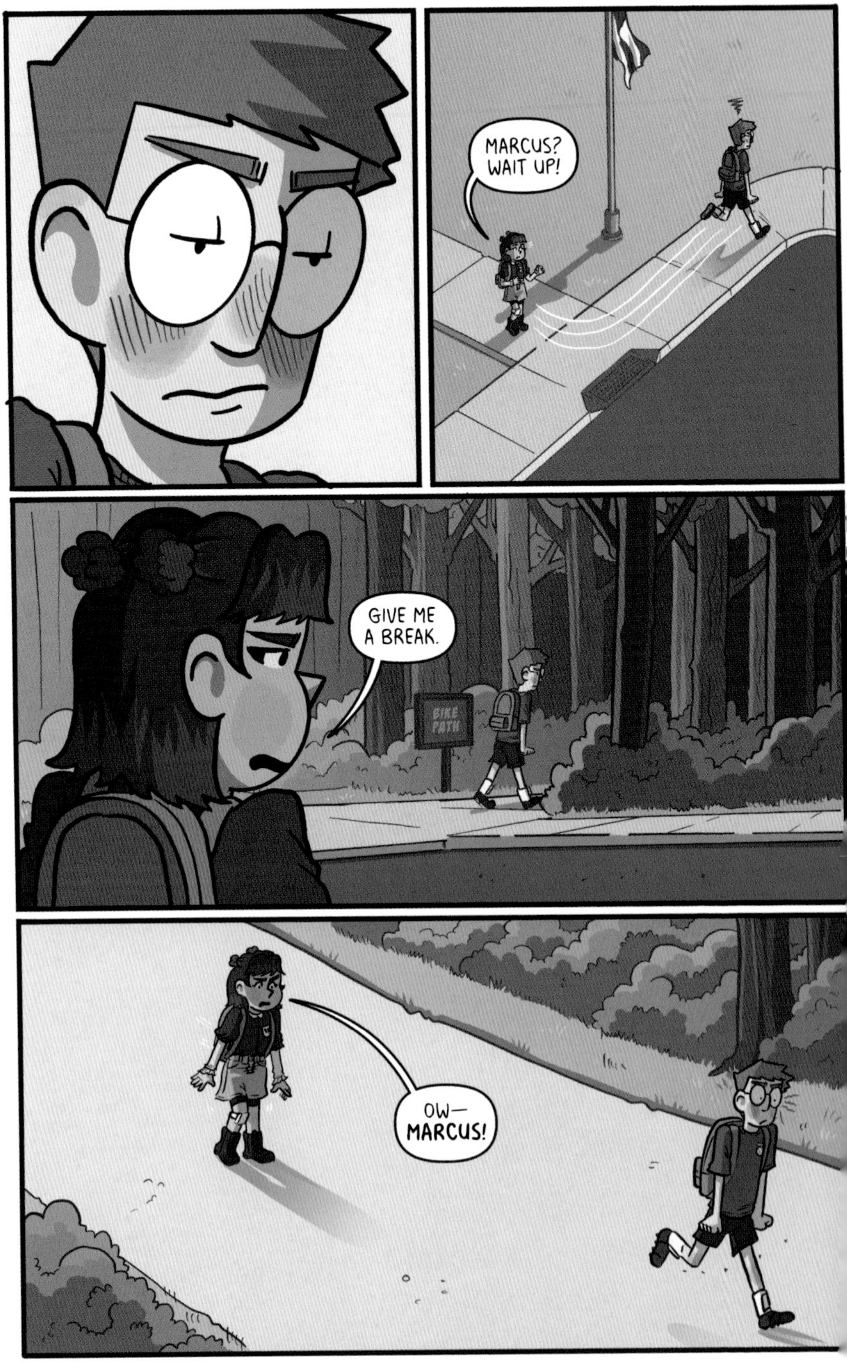
MARCUS?
WAIT UP!
GIVE ME
A BREAK.
BIKE
PATH
OW—
MARCUS!

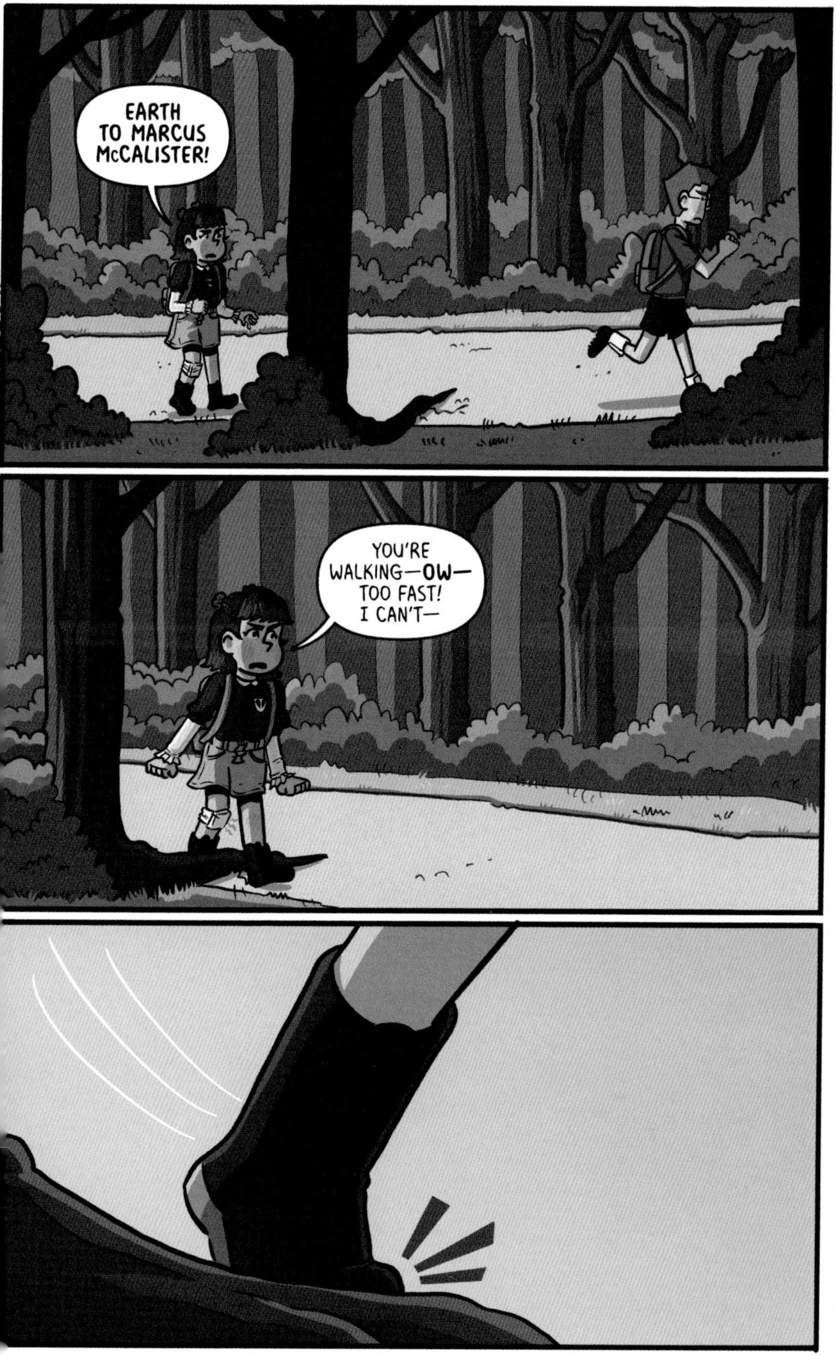
EARTH TO MARCUS McCALISTER!
YOU'RE WALKING—**OW**—TOO FAST! I CAN'T—

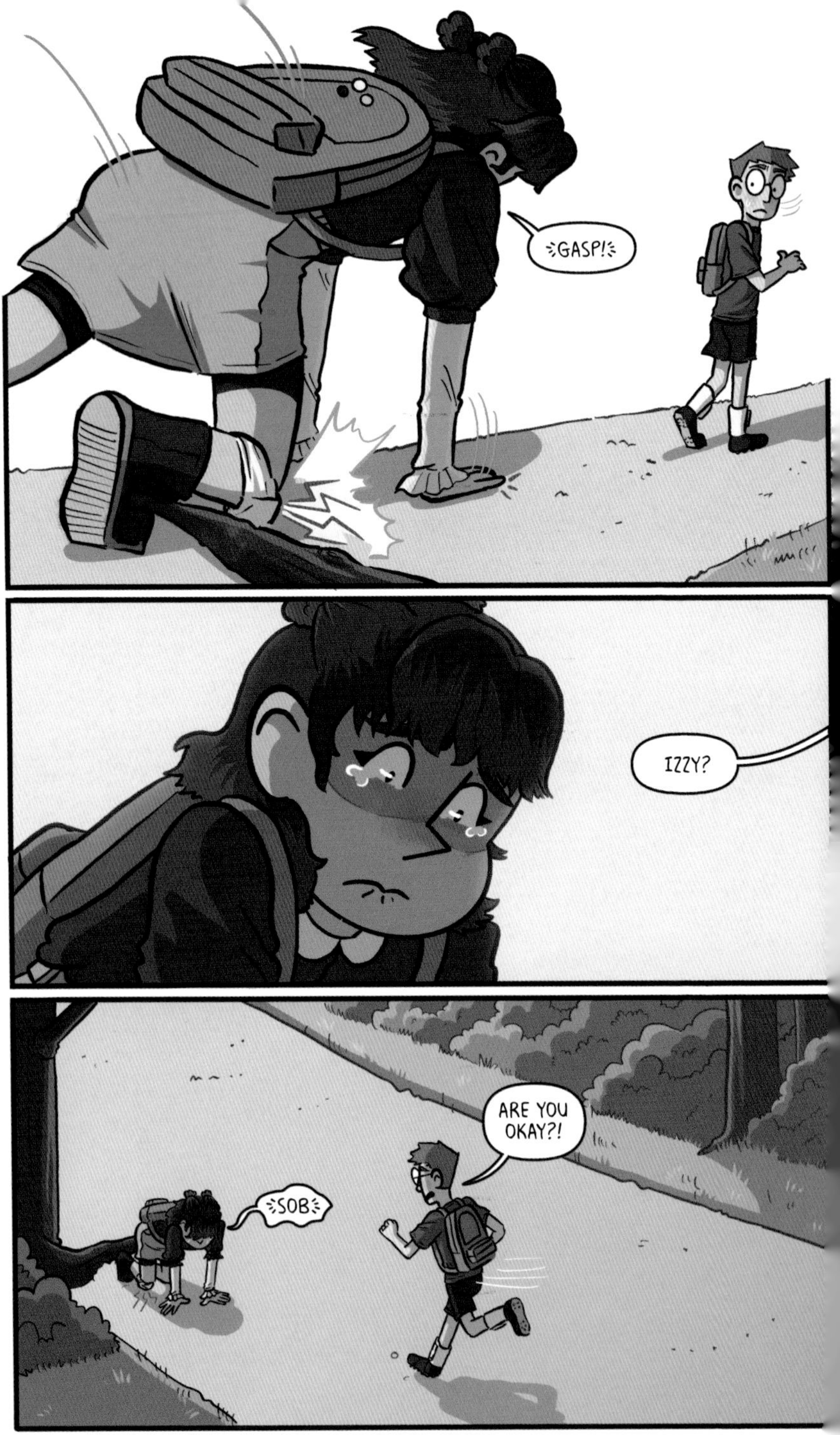
GASP!
IZZY?
ARE YOU OKAY?!
SOB

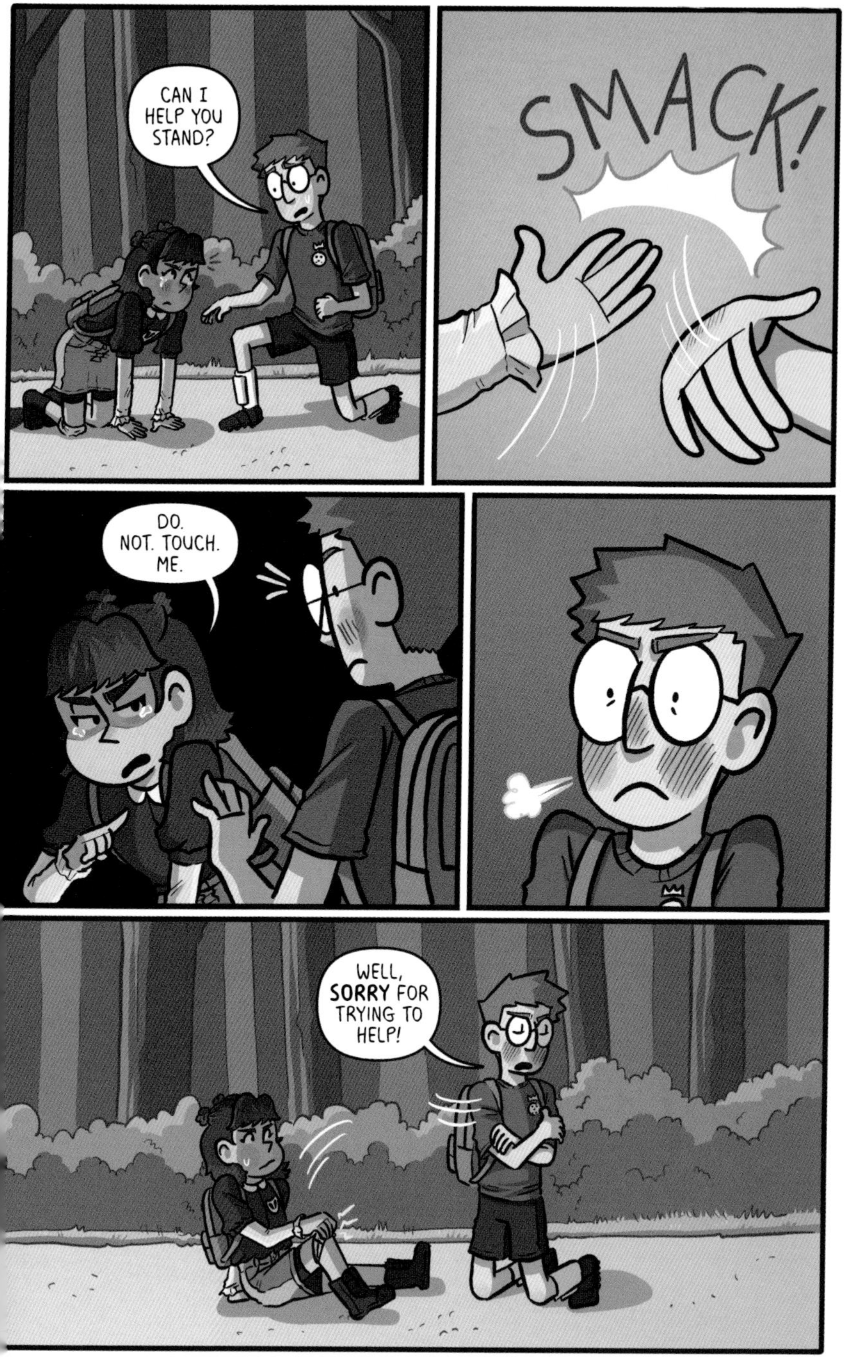
CAN I HELP YOU STAND?
SMACK!
DO. NOT. TOUCH. ME.
WELL, SORRY FOR TRYING TO HELP!

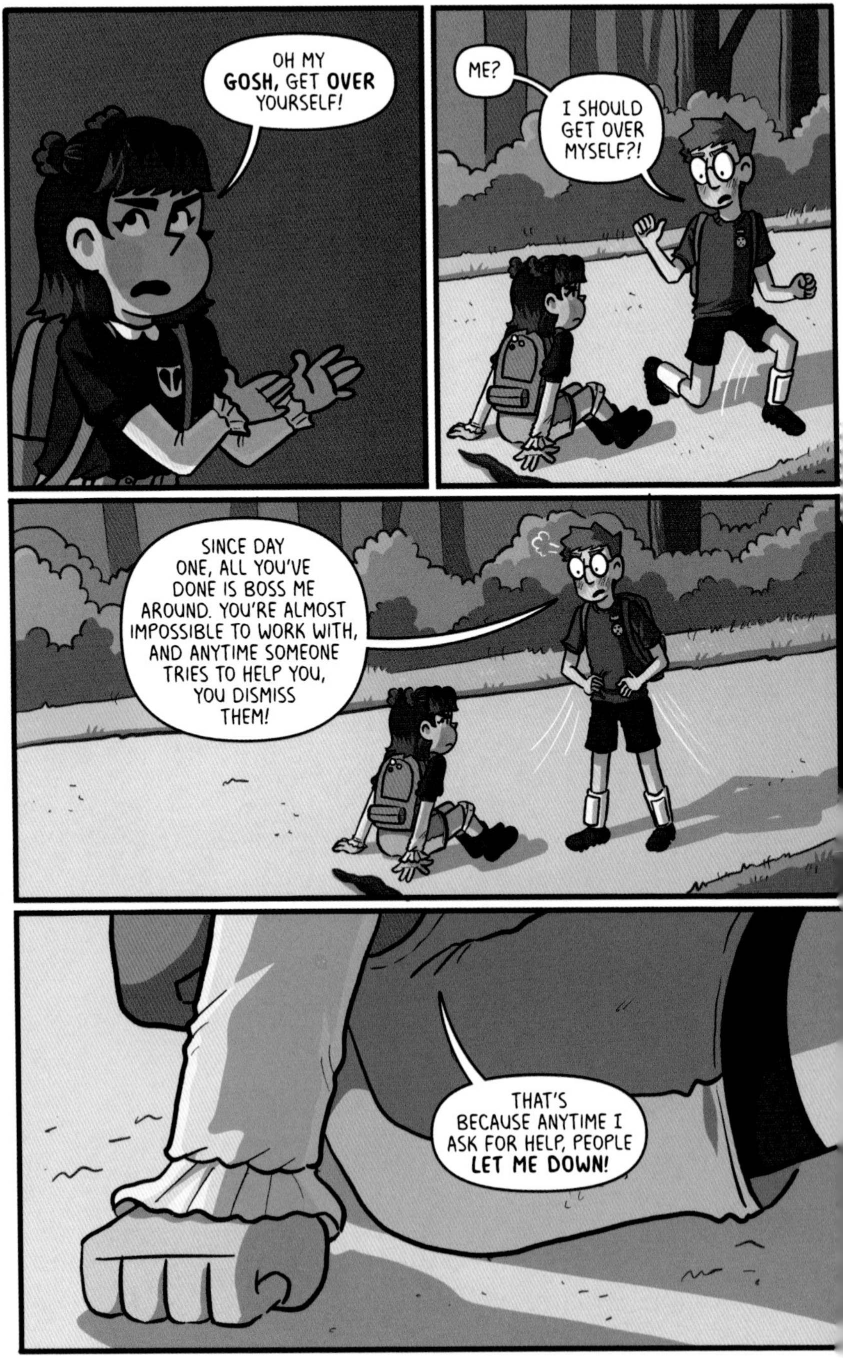
OH MY **GOSH,** GET **OVER** YOURSELF!
ME?
I SHOULD GET OVER MYSELF?!
SINCE DAY ONE, ALL YOU'VE DONE IS BOSS ME AROUND. YOU'RE ALMOST IMPOSSIBLE TO WORK WITH, AND ANYTIME SOMEONE TRIES TO HELP YOU, YOU DISMISS THEM!
THAT'S BECAUSE ANYTIME I ASK FOR HELP, PEOPLE **LET ME DOWN!**

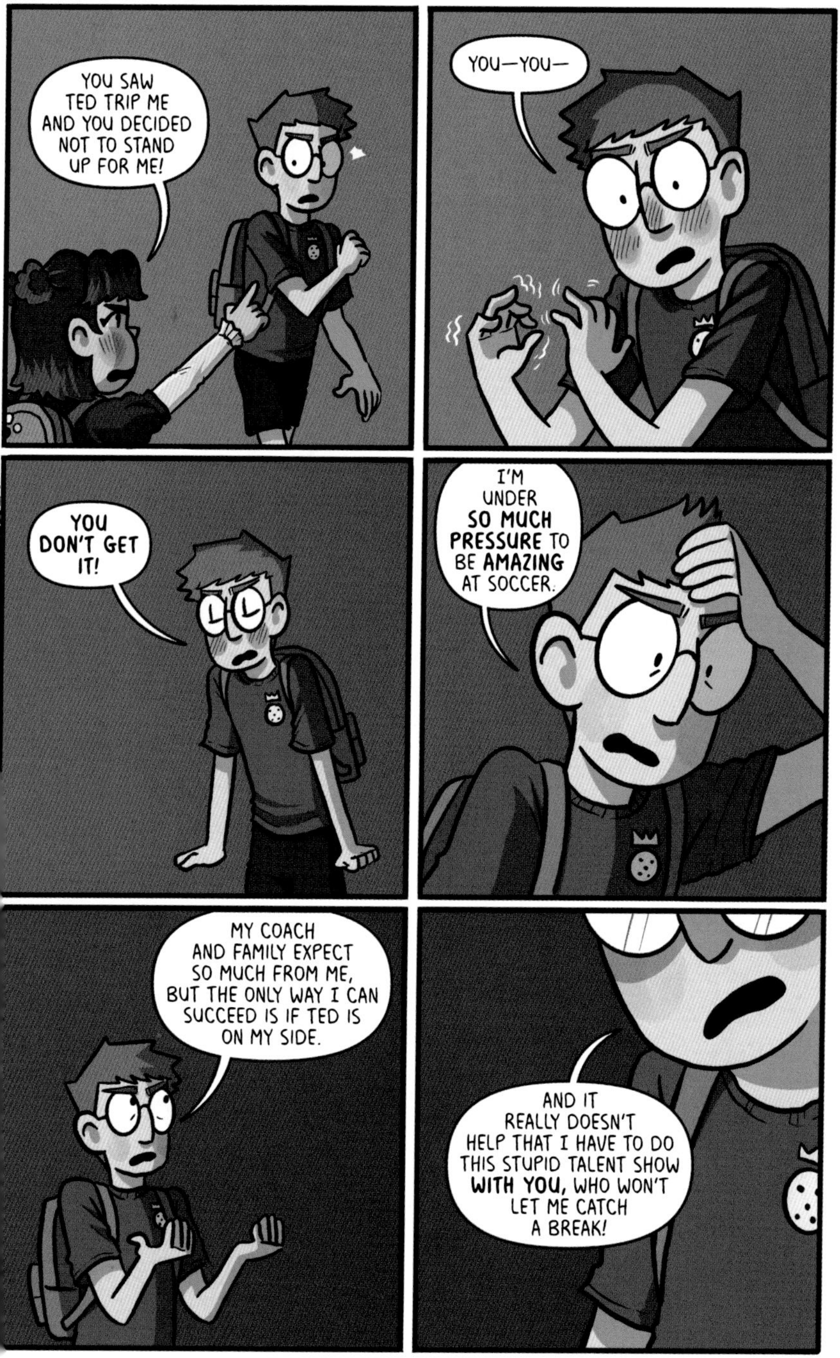
YOU SAW TED TRIP ME AND YOU DECIDED NOT TO STAND UP FOR ME!
YOU—YOU—
YOU DON'T GET IT!
I'M UNDER SO MUCH PRESSURE TO BE AMAZING AT SOCCER.
MY COACH AND FAMILY EXPECT SO MUCH FROM ME, BUT THE ONLY WAY I CAN SUCCEED IS IF TED IS ON MY SIDE.
AND IT REALLY DOESN'T HELP THAT I HAVE TO DO THIS STUPID TALENT SHOW WITH YOU, WHO WON'T LET ME CATCH A BREAK!

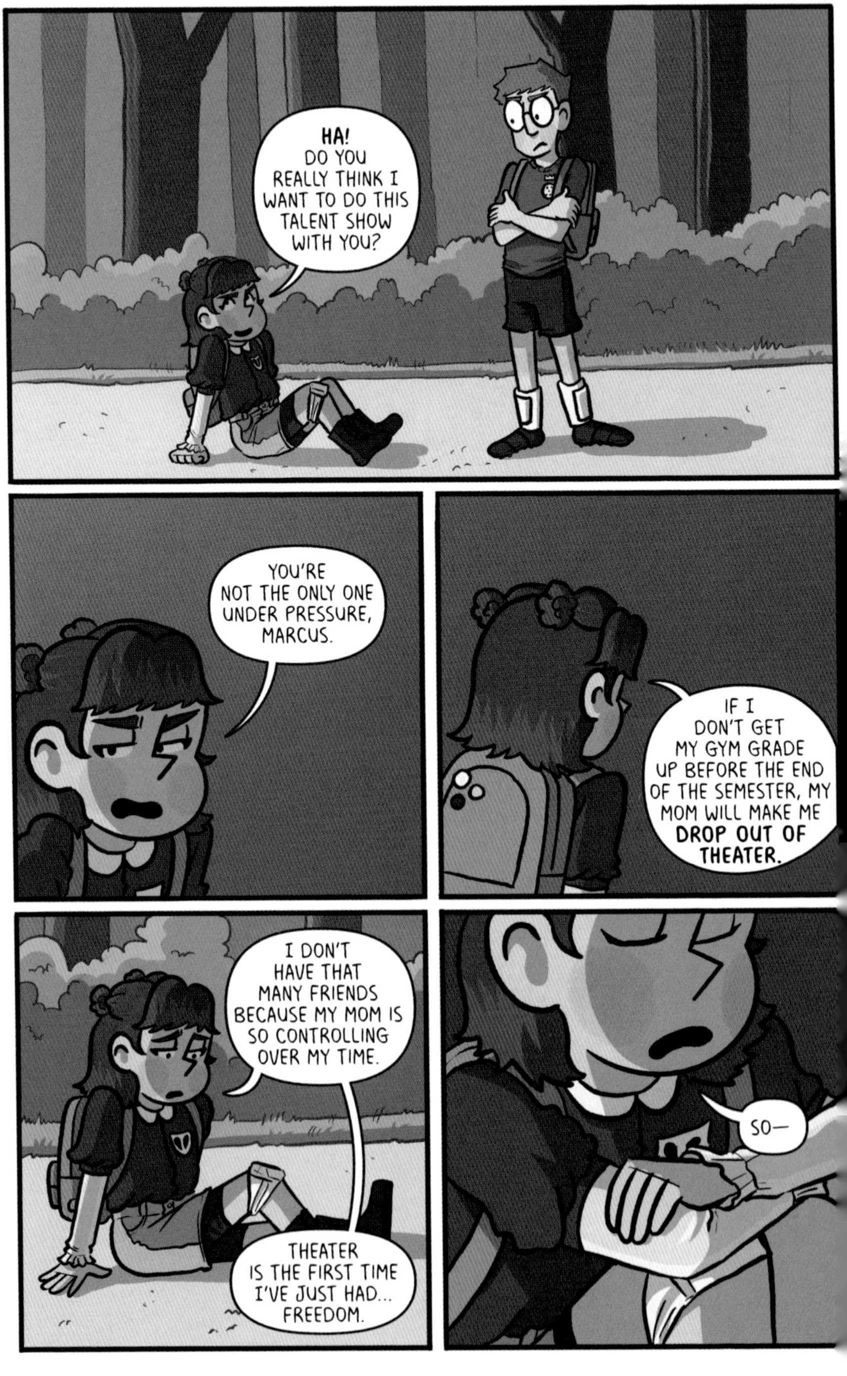
HA! DO YOU REALLY THINK I WANT TO DO THIS TALENT SHOW WITH YOU?
YOU'RE NOT THE ONLY ONE UNDER PRESSURE, MARCUS.
IF I DON'T GET MY GYM GRADE UP BEFORE THE END OF THE SEMESTER, MY MOM WILL MAKE ME **DROP OUT OF THEATER.**
I DON'T HAVE THAT MANY FRIENDS BECAUSE MY MOM IS SO CONTROLLING OVER MY TIME.
THEATER IS THE FIRST TIME I'VE JUST HAD... FREEDOM.
SO—

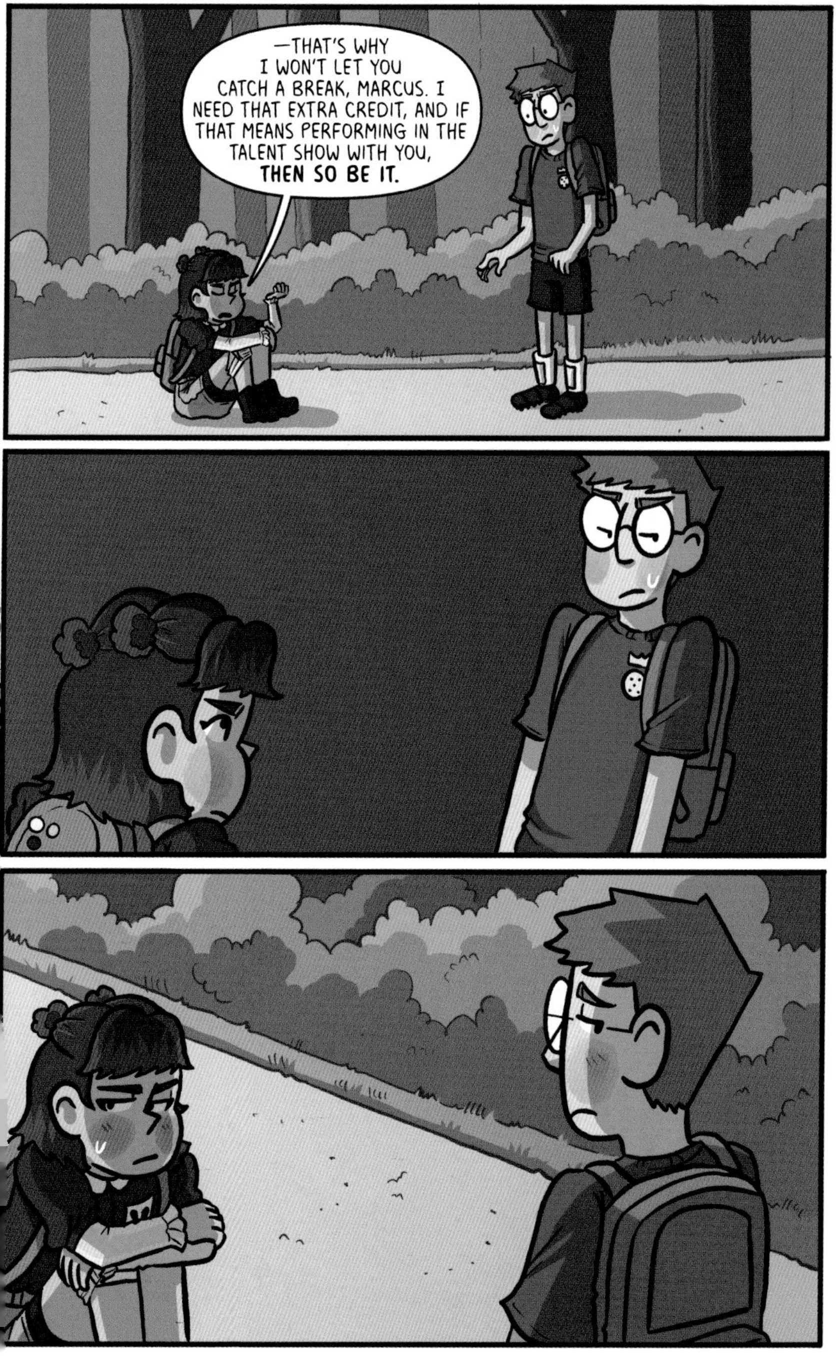
—THAT'S WHY I WON'T LET YOU CATCH A BREAK, MARCUS. I NEED THAT EXTRA CREDIT, AND IF THAT MEANS PERFORMING IN THE TALENT SHOW WITH YOU, **THEN SO BE IT.**

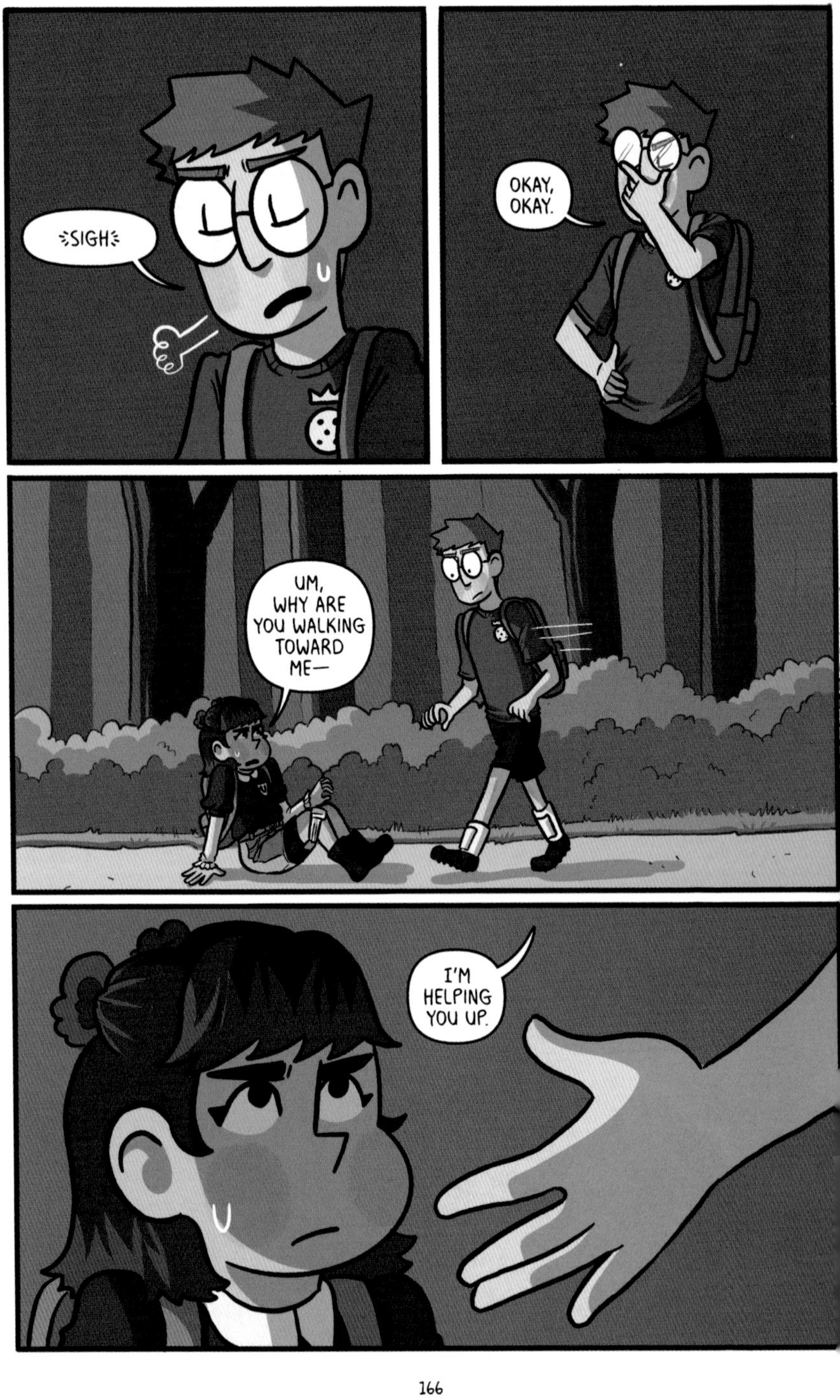

SIGH
OKAY, OKAY.
UM, WHY ARE YOU WALKING TOWARD ME—
I'M HELPING YOU UP.

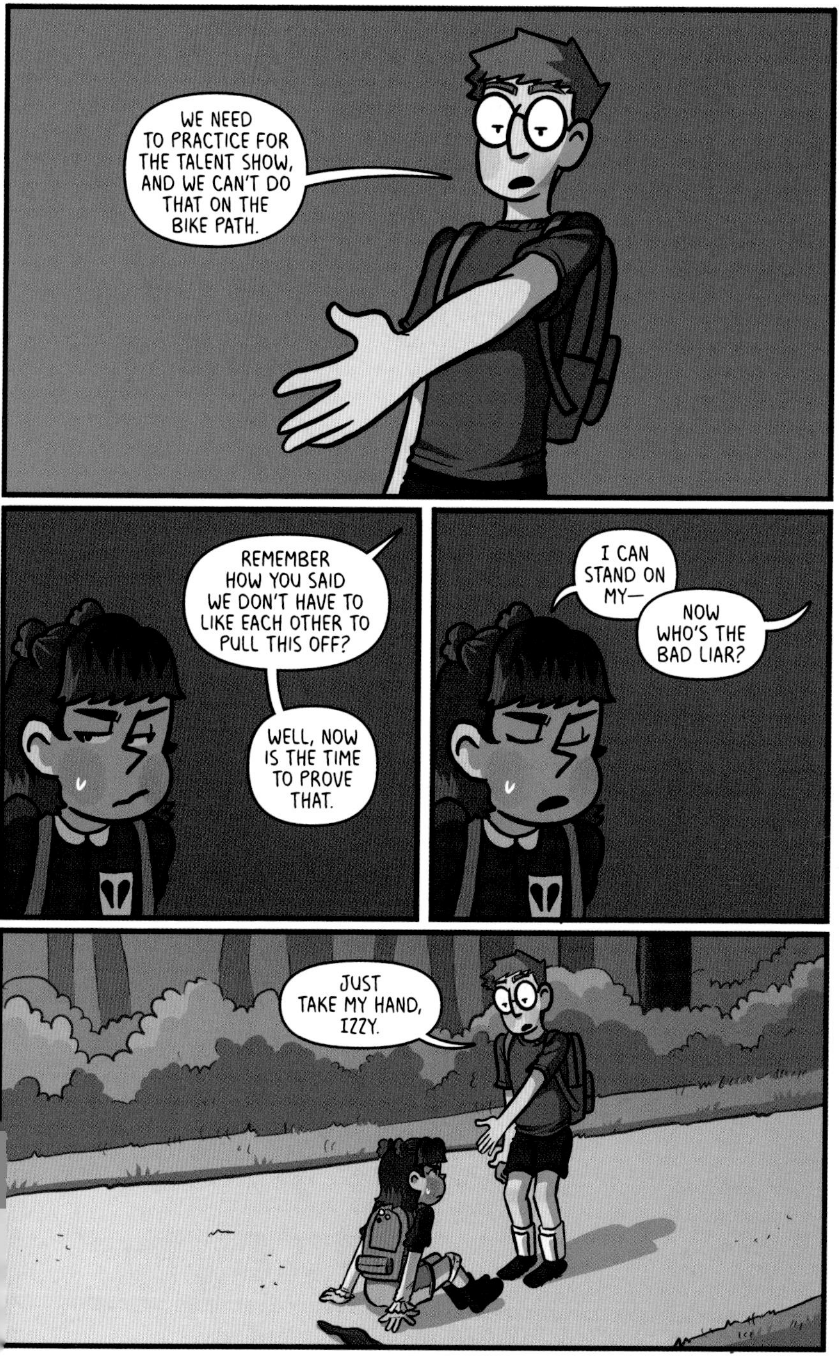
WE NEED TO PRACTICE FOR THE TALENT SHOW, AND WE CAN'T DO THAT ON THE BIKE PATH.
REMEMBER HOW YOU SAID WE DON'T HAVE TO LIKE EACH OTHER TO PULL THIS OFF?
WELL, NOW IS THE TIME TO PROVE THAT.
I CAN STAND ON MY—
NOW WHO'S THE BAD LIAR?
JUST TAKE MY HAND, IZZY.

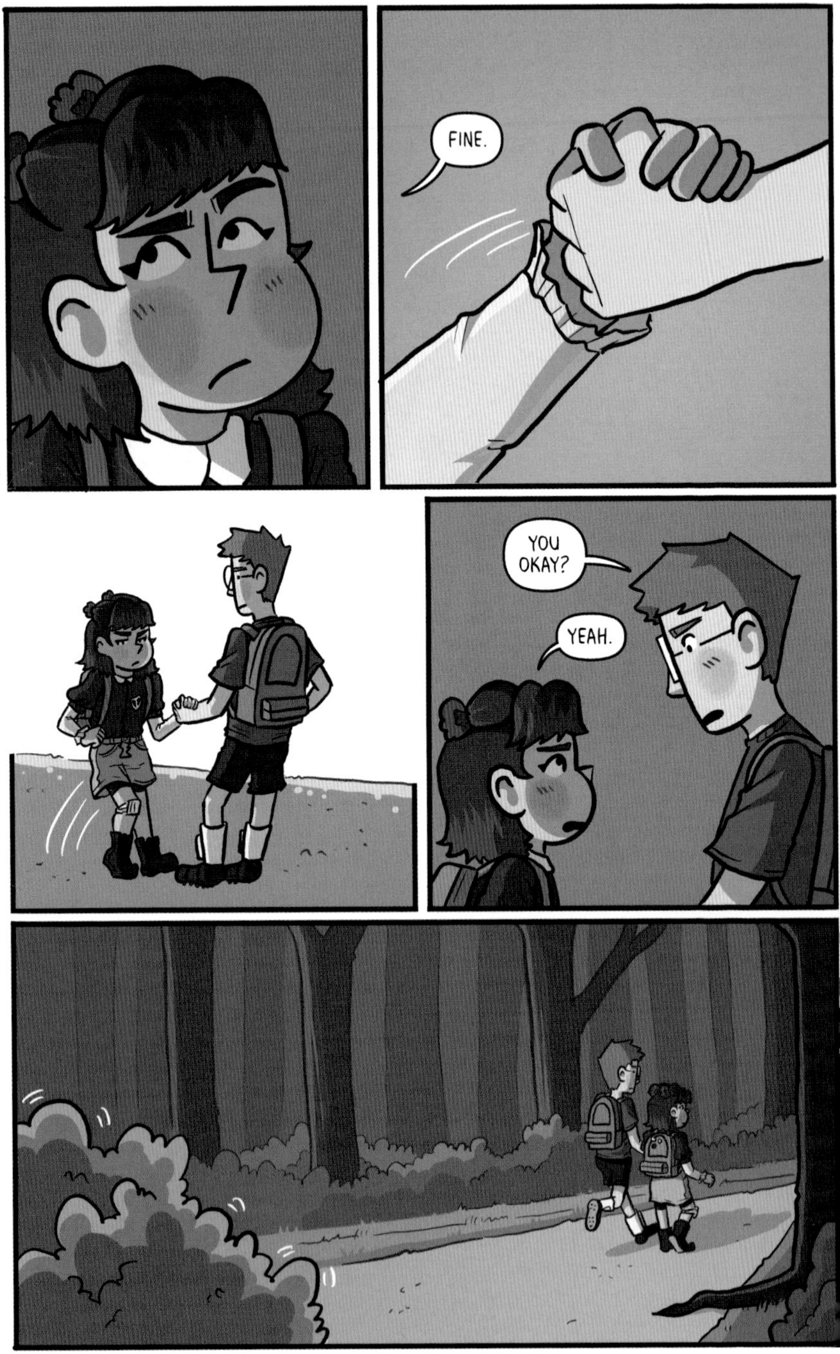
FINE.
YOU OKAY?
YEAH.

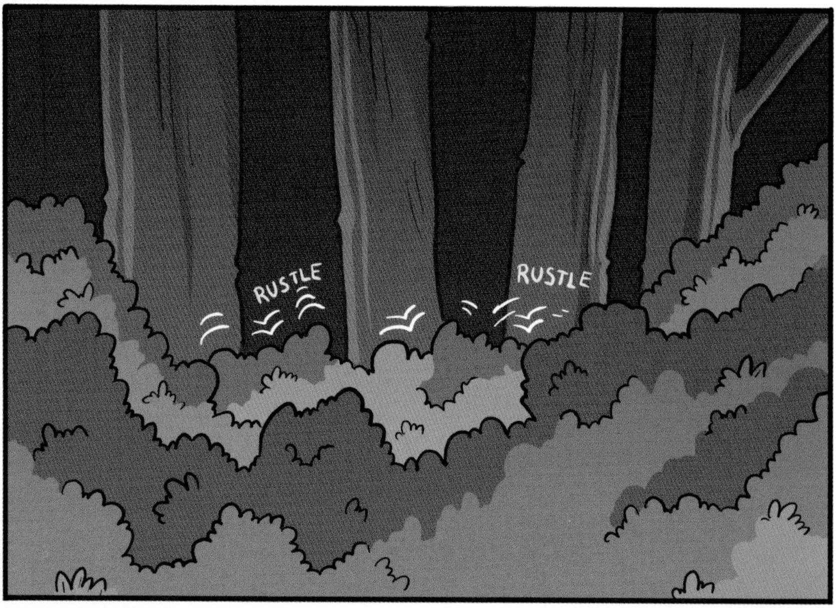
RUSTLE
RUSTLE

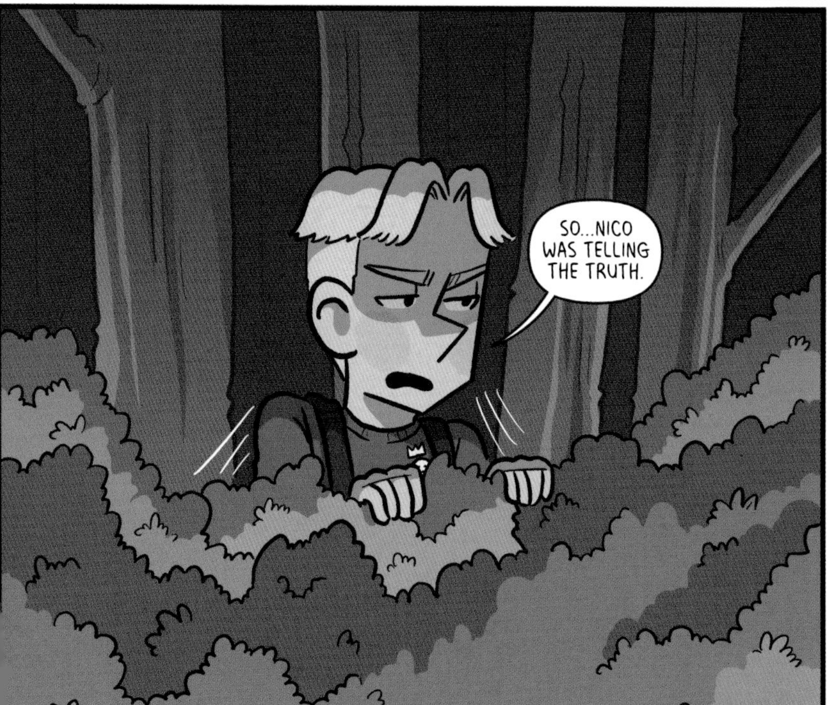
SO...NICO WAS TELLING THE TRUTH.

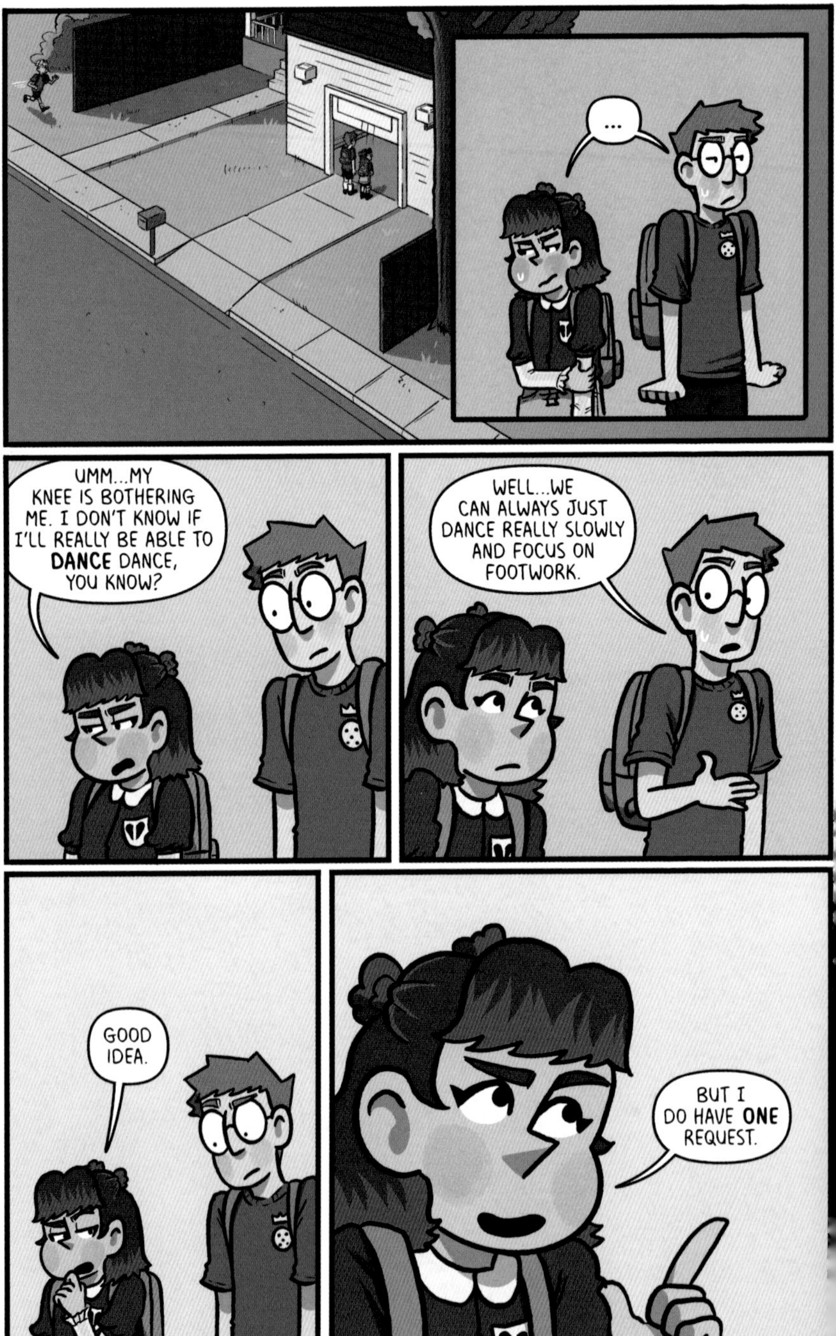
...
UMM...MY KNEE IS BOTHERING ME. I DON'T KNOW IF I'LL REALLY BE ABLE TO **DANCE** DANCE, YOU KNOW?
WELL...WE CAN ALWAYS JUST DANCE REALLY SLOWLY AND FOCUS ON FOOTWORK.
GOOD IDEA.
BUT I DO HAVE **ONE** REQUEST.

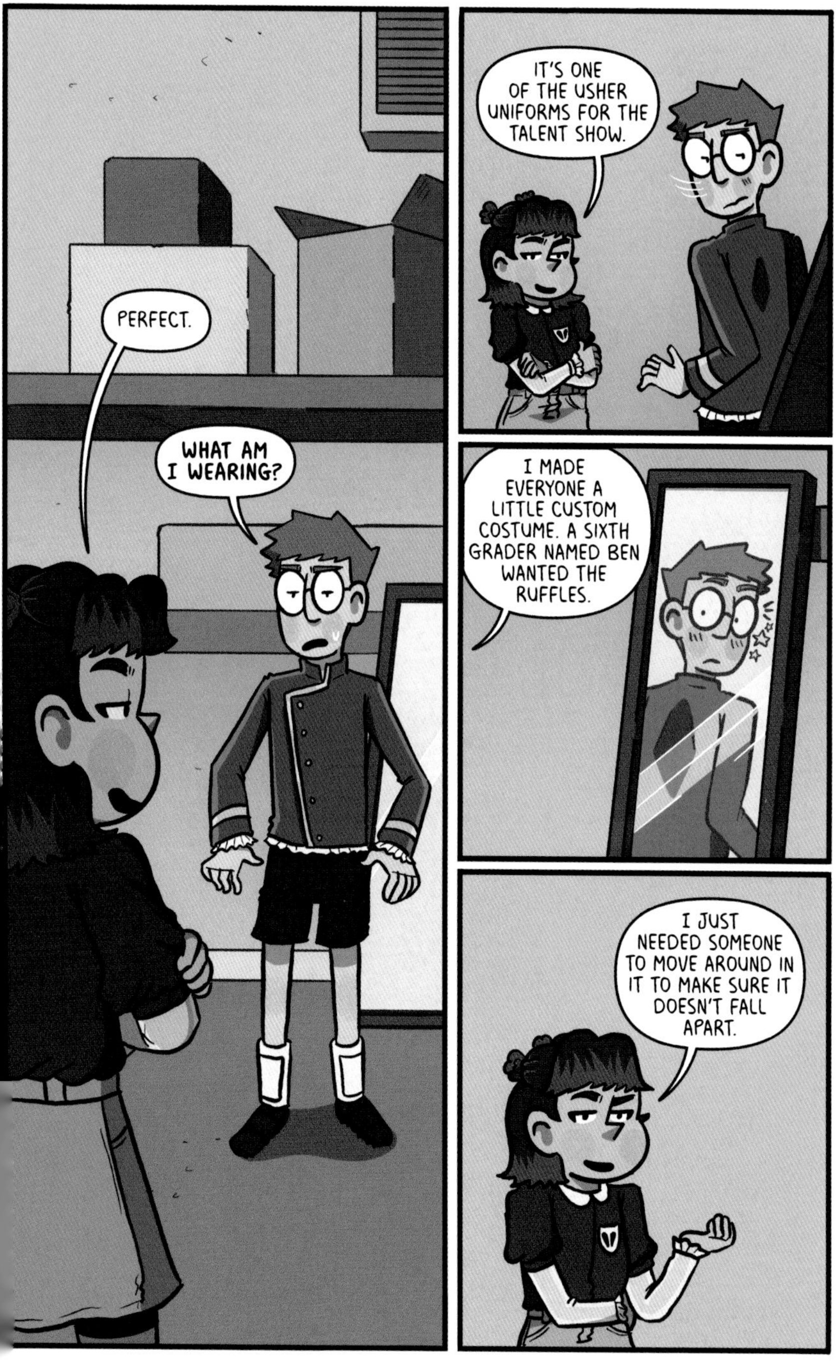
PERFECT.
WHAT AM I WEARING?
IT'S ONE OF THE USHER UNIFORMS FOR THE TALENT SHOW.
I MADE EVERYONE A LITTLE CUSTOM COSTUME. A SIXTH GRADER NAMED BEN WANTED THE RUFFLES.
I JUST NEEDED SOMEONE TO MOVE AROUND IN IT TO MAKE SURE IT DOESN'T FALL APART.

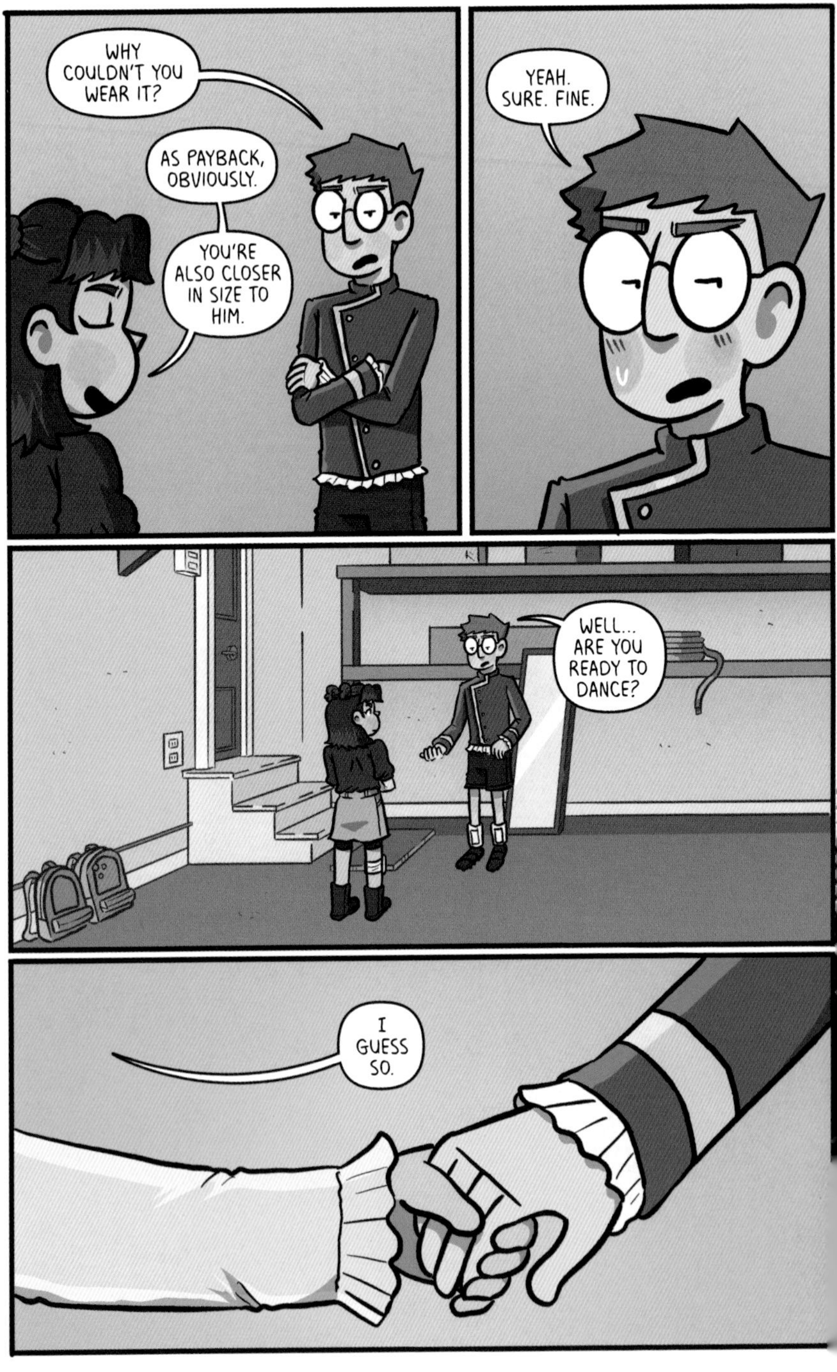
WHY COULDN'T YOU WEAR IT?
AS PAYBACK, OBVIOUSLY.
YOU'RE ALSO CLOSER IN SIZE TO HIM.
YEAH. SURE. FINE.
WELL... ARE YOU READY TO DANCE?
I GUESS SO.

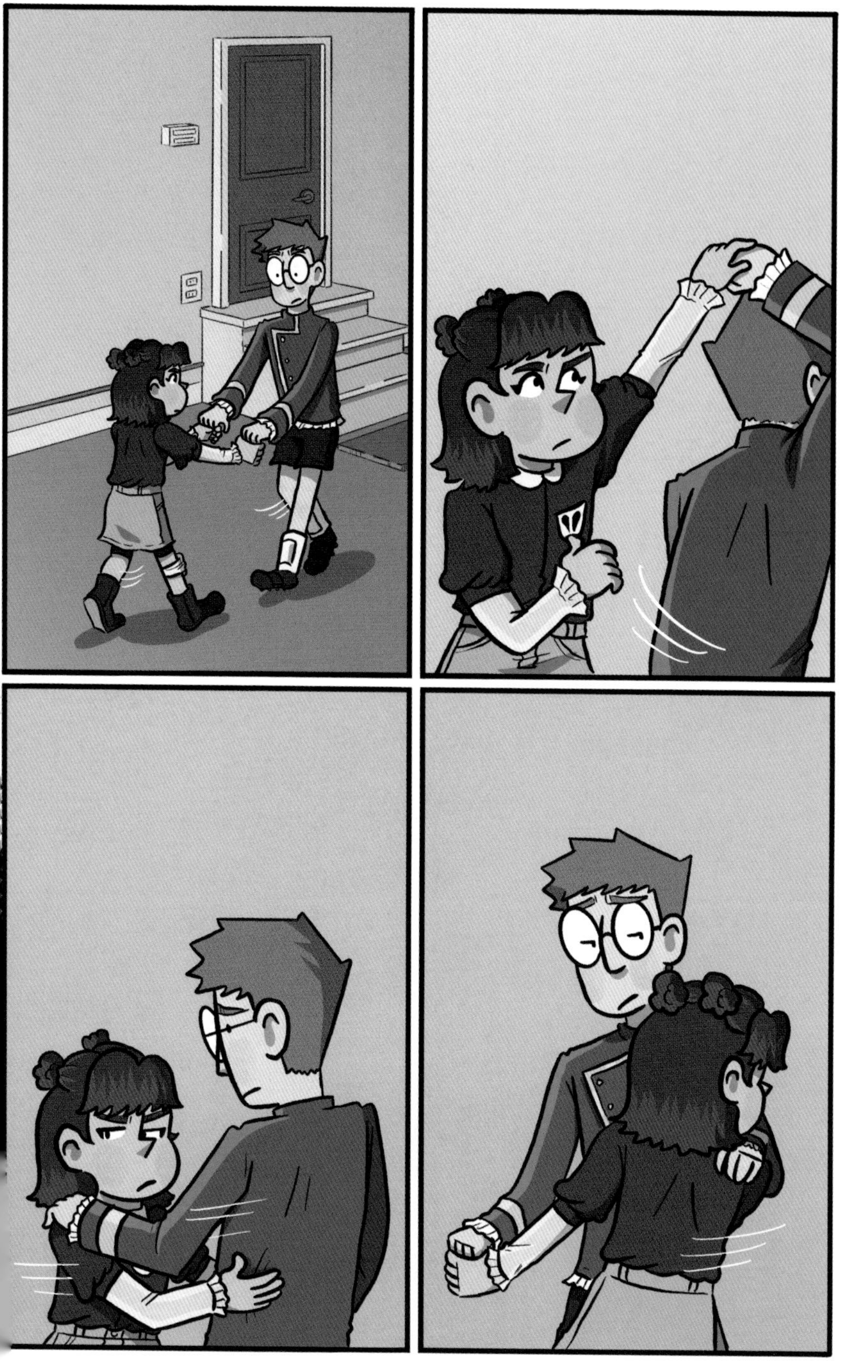

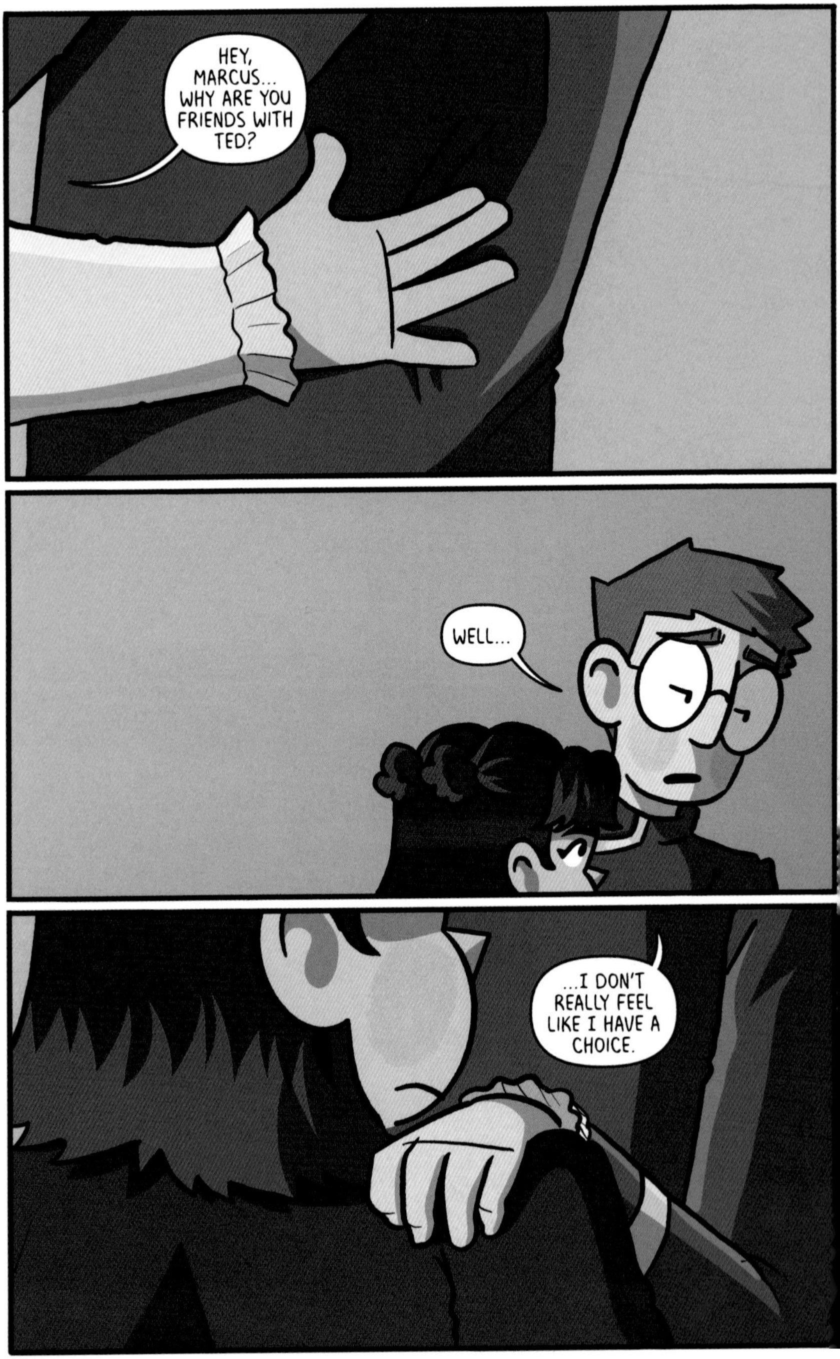
HEY, MARCUS... WHY ARE YOU FRIENDS WITH TED?
WELL...
...I DON'T REALLY FEEL LIKE I HAVE A CHOICE.

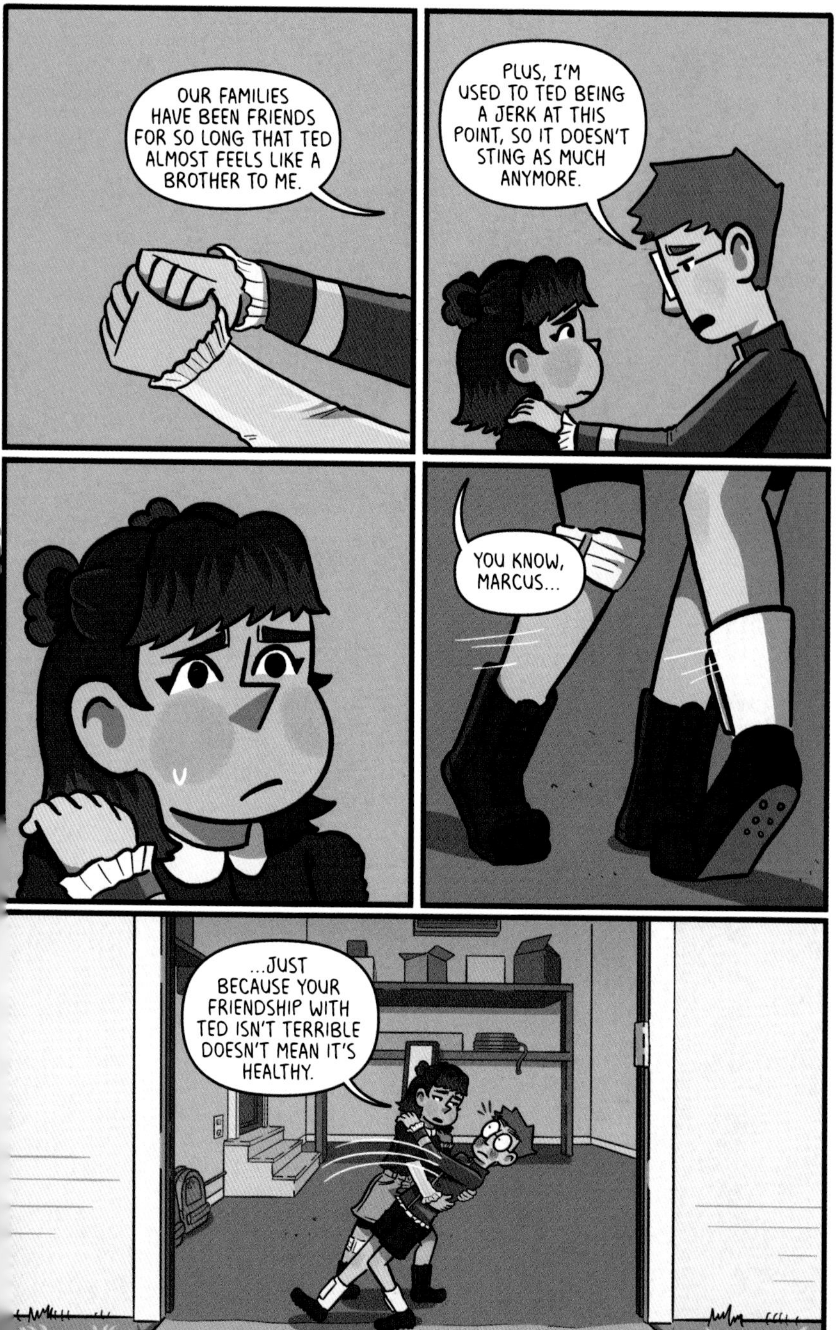
OUR FAMILIES HAVE BEEN FRIENDS FOR SO LONG THAT TED ALMOST FEELS LIKE A BROTHER TO ME.
PLUS, I'M USED TO TED BEING A JERK AT THIS POINT, SO IT DOESN'T STING AS MUCH ANYMORE.
YOU KNOW, MARCUS...
...JUST BECAUSE YOUR FRIENDSHIP WITH TED ISN'T TERRIBLE DOESN'T MEAN IT'S HEALTHY.

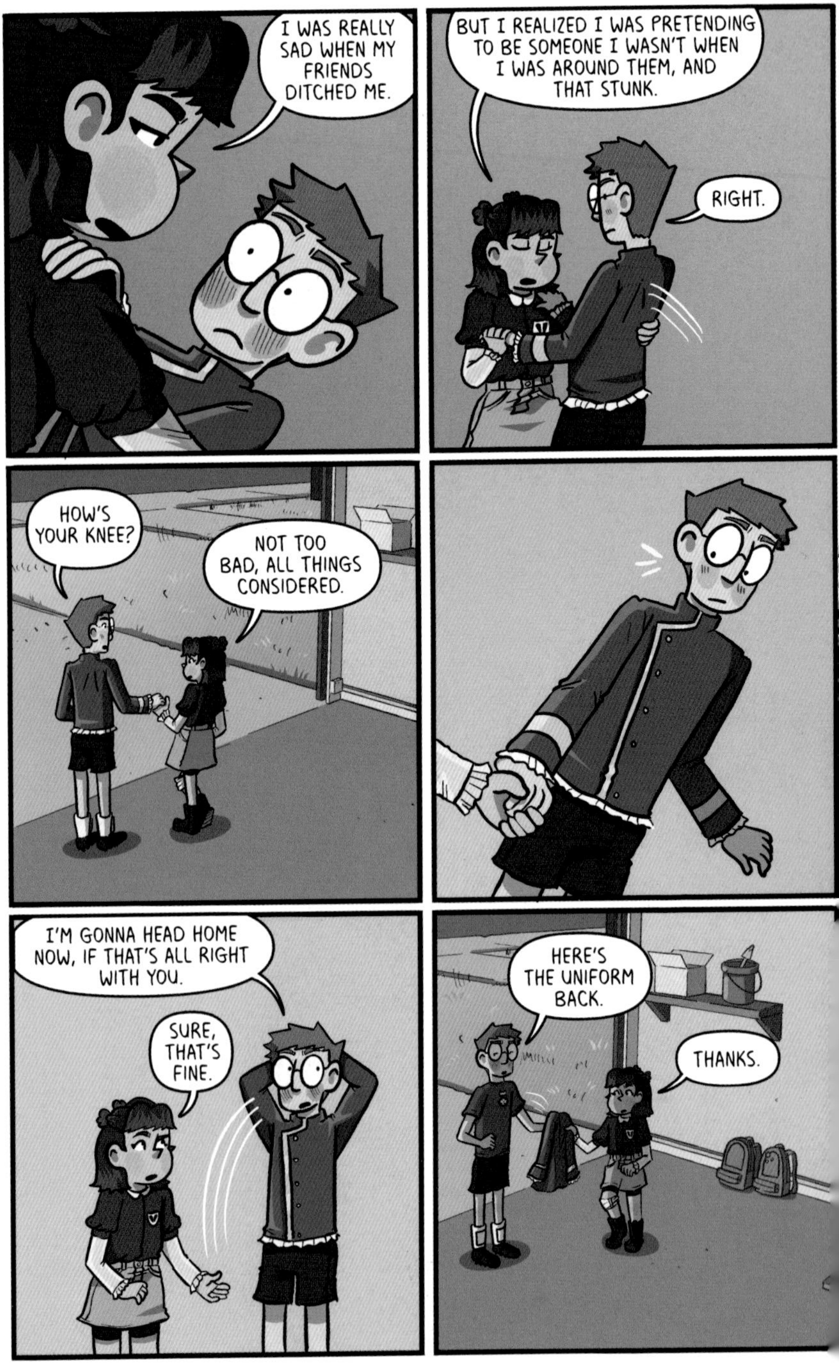

I WAS REALLY SAD WHEN MY FRIENDS DITCHED ME.
BUT I REALIZED I WAS PRETENDING TO BE SOMEONE I WASN'T WHEN I WAS AROUND THEM, AND THAT STUNK.
RIGHT.
HOW'S YOUR KNEE?
NOT TOO BAD, ALL THINGS CONSIDERED.
I'M GONNA HEAD HOME NOW, IF THAT'S ALL RIGHT WITH YOU.
SURE, THAT'S FINE.
HERE'S THE UNIFORM BACK.
THANKS.

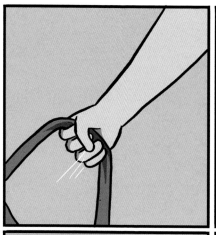

MARCUS!

IF WE MAKE IT THROUGH THE TALENT SHOW...

...WE SHOULD GET POPSICLES TO CELEBRATE!

SOUNDS LIKE A PLAN!

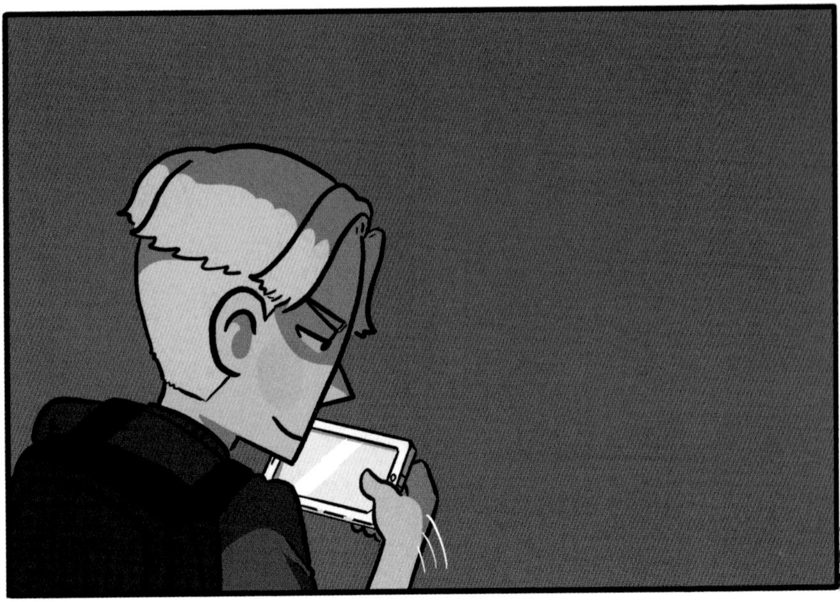

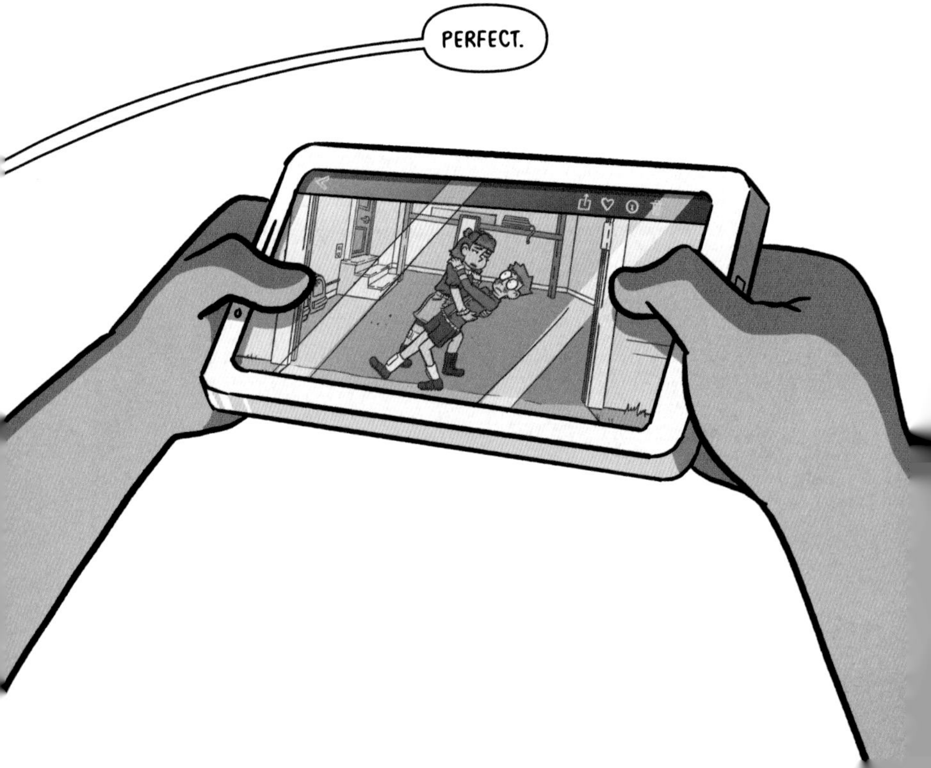
PERFECT.

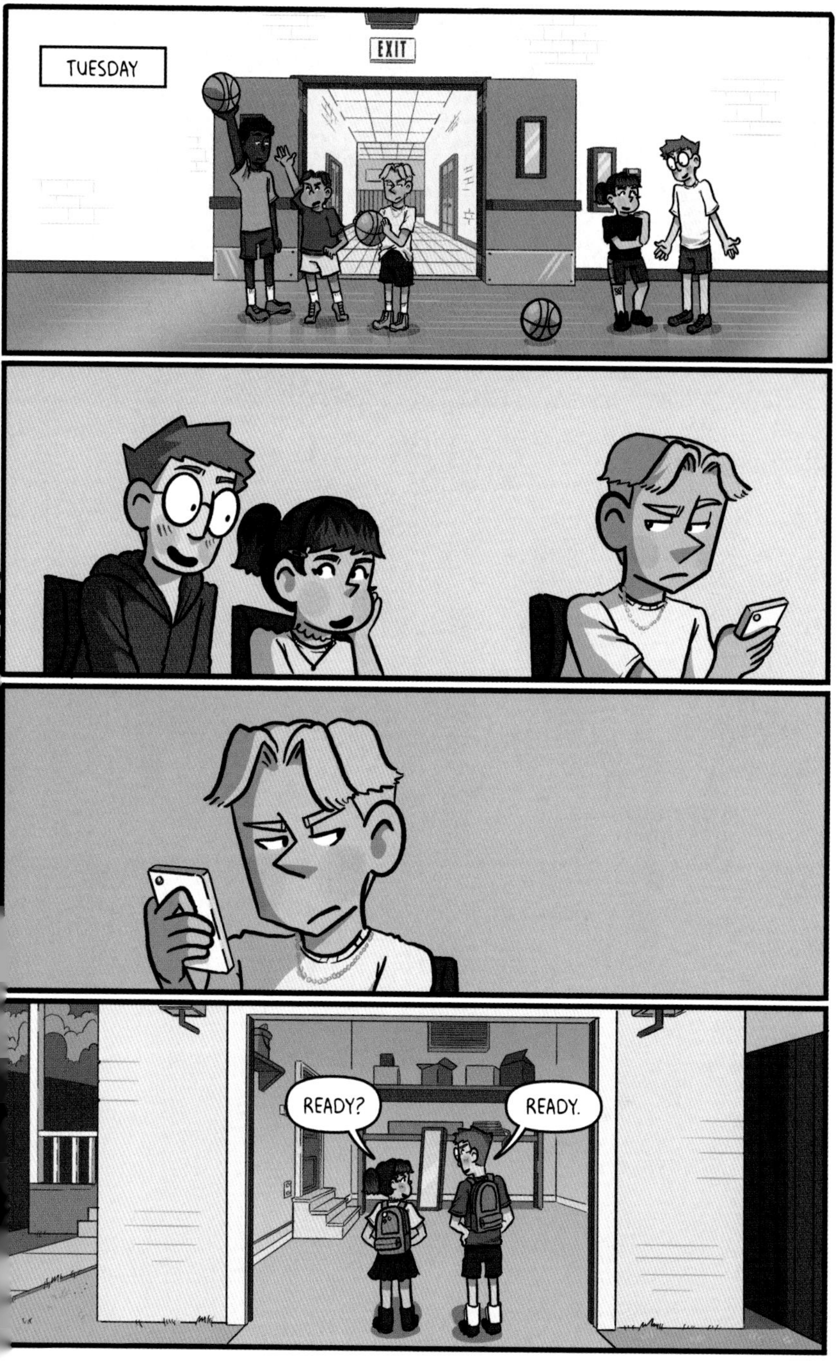
TUESDAY
EXIT
READY?
READY.

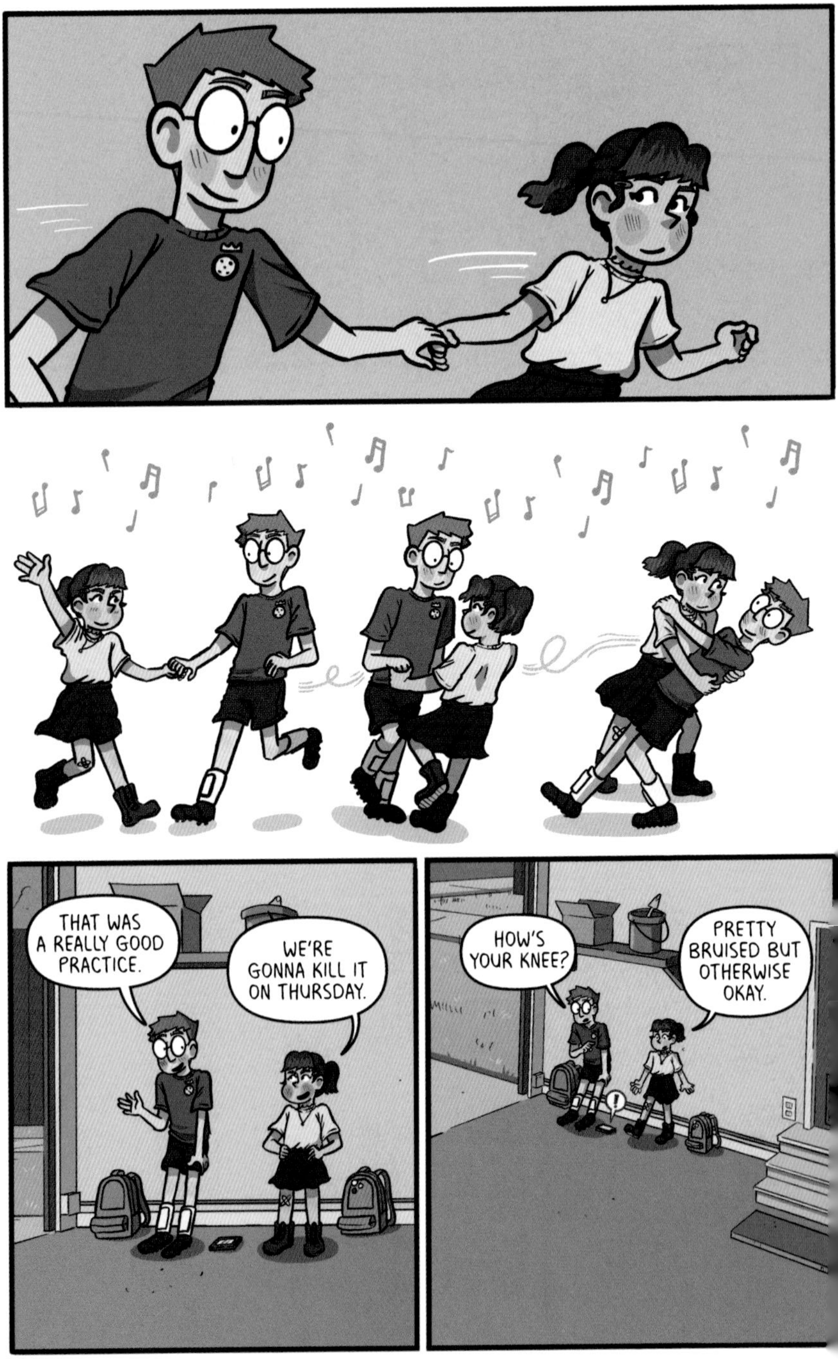
THAT WAS A REALLY GOOD PRACTICE.
WE'RE GONNA KILL IT ON THURSDAY.
HOW'S YOUR KNEE?
PRETTY BRUISED BUT OTHERWISE OKAY.

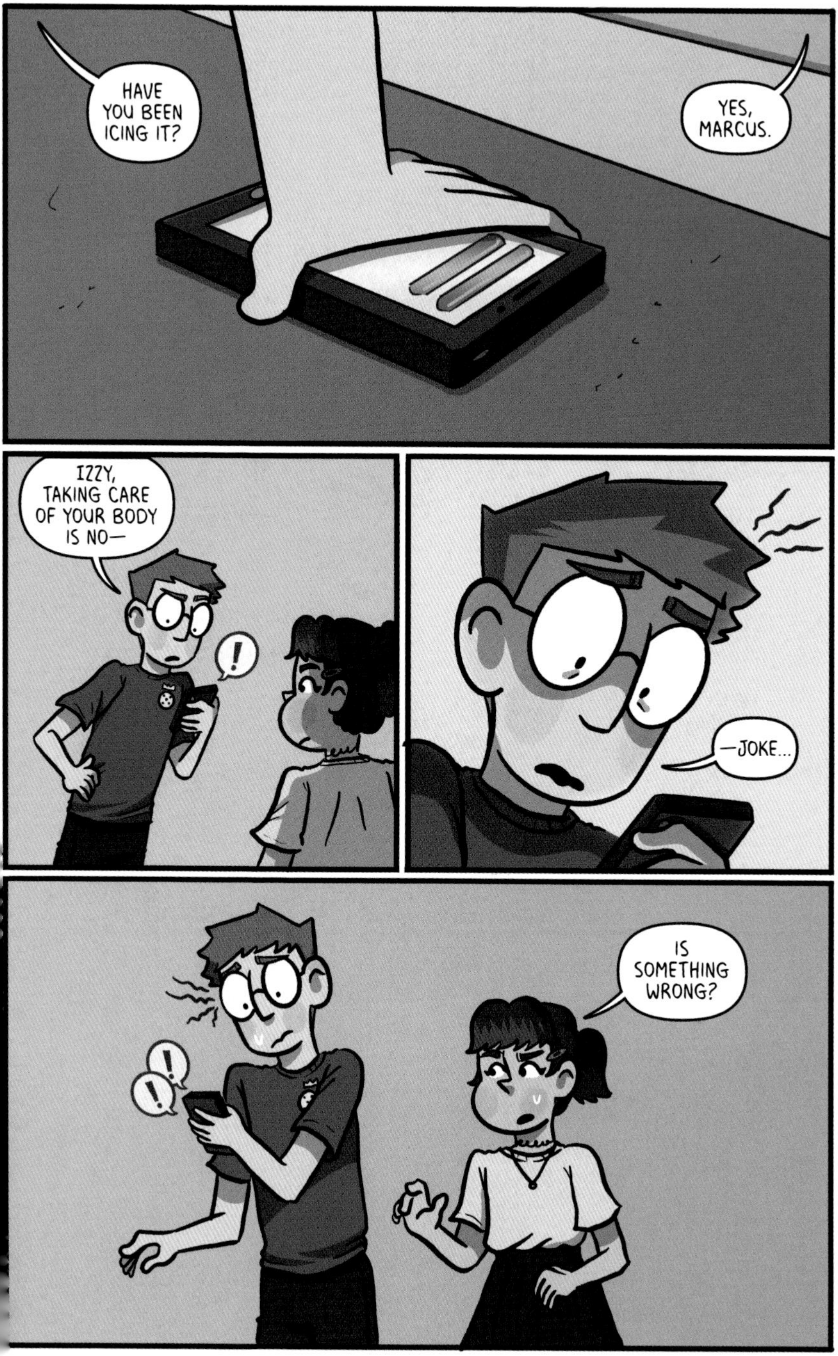
HAVE YOU BEEN ICING IT?
YES, MARCUS.
IZZY, TAKING CARE OF YOUR BODY IS NO—
!
—JOKE...
!
!
IS SOMETHING WRONG?

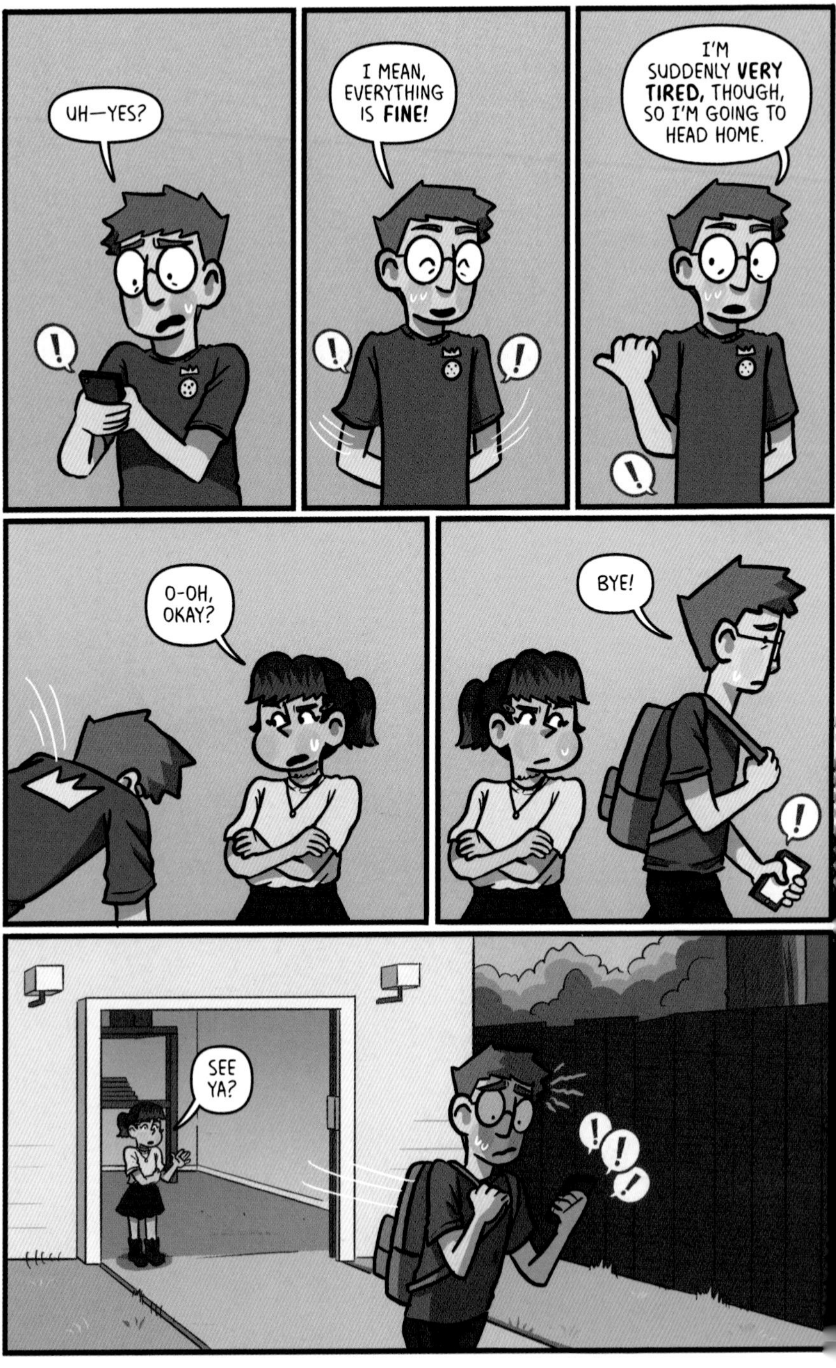
UH—YES?
I MEAN, EVERYTHING IS **FINE!**
I'M SUDDENLY **VERY TIRED,** THOUGH, SO I'M GOING TO HEAD HOME.
O-OH, OKAY?
BYE!
SEE YA?

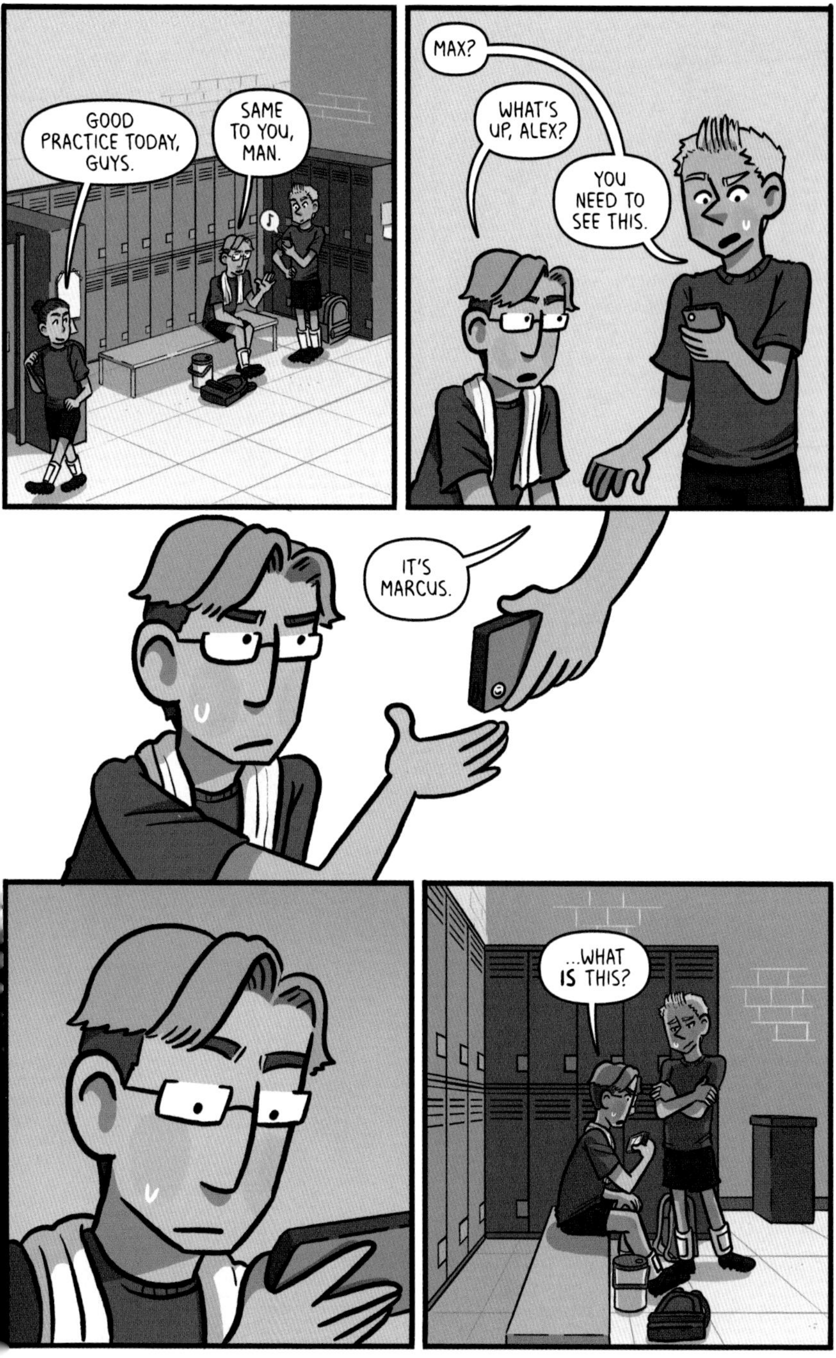

GOOD PRACTICE TODAY, GUYS.
SAME TO YOU, MAN.
MAX?
WHAT'S UP, ALEX?
YOU NEED TO SEE THIS.
IT'S MARCUS.
...WHAT **IS** THIS?

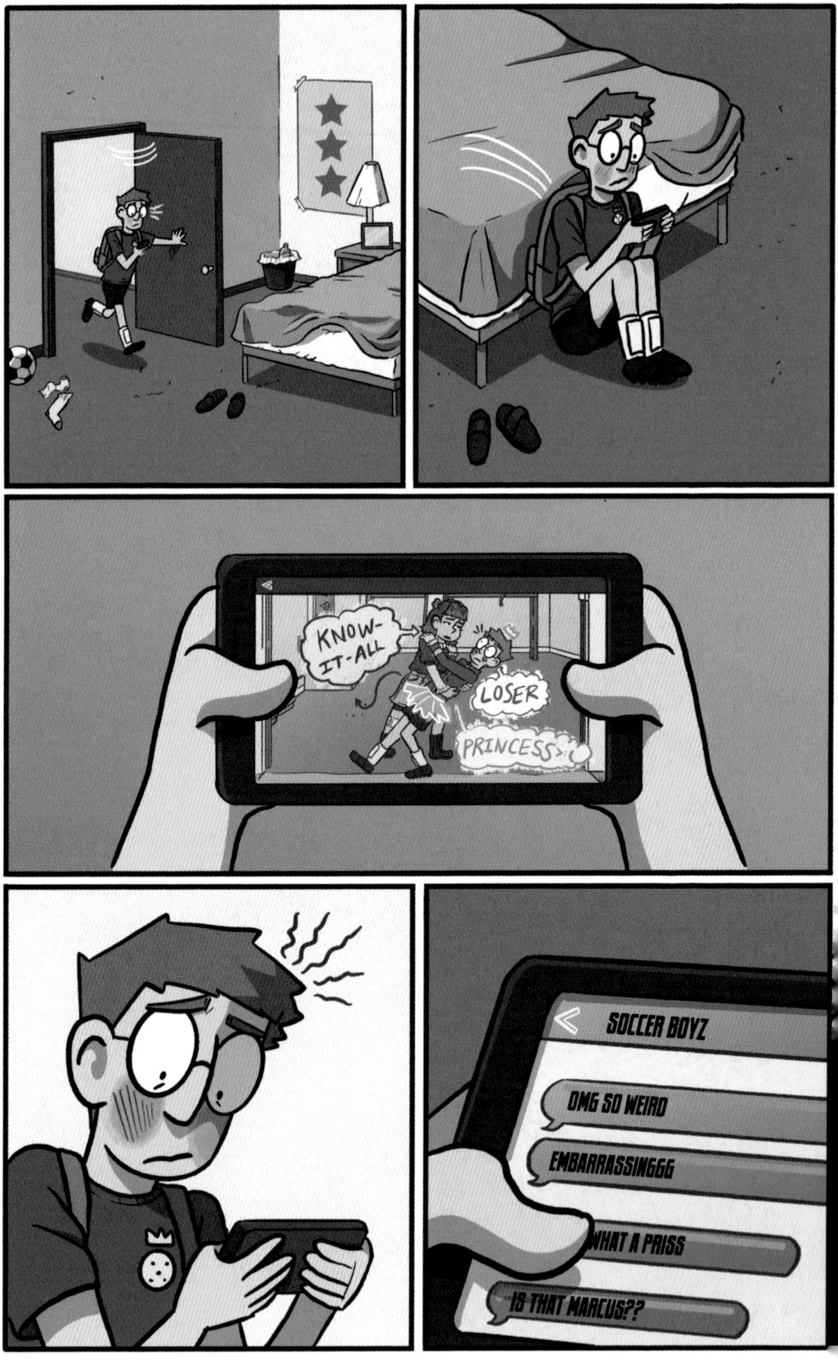
KNOW-IT-ALL
LOSER
PRINCESS
SOCCER BOYZ
OMG SO WEIRD
EMBARRASSINGGG
WHAT A PRISS
IS THAT MARCUS??

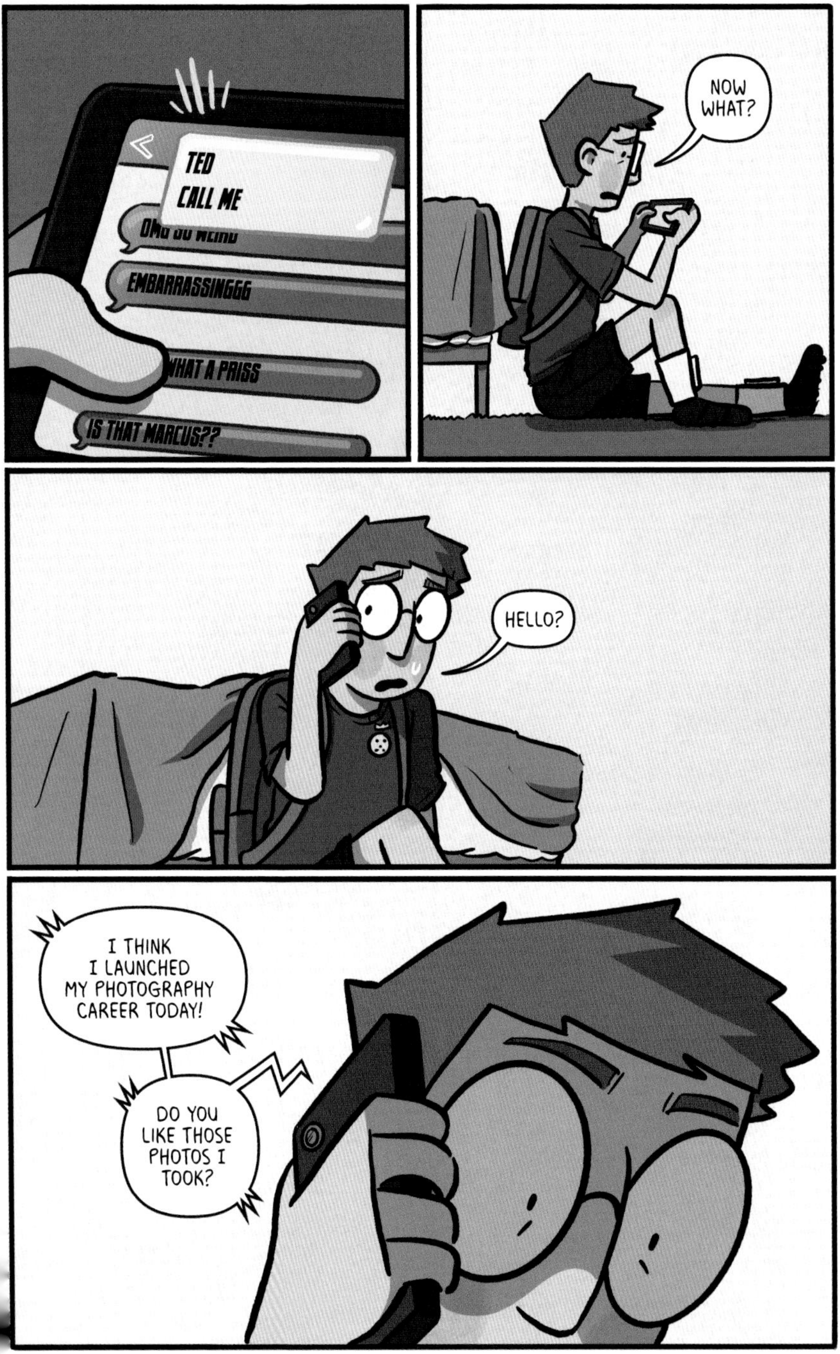
TED
CALL ME
EMBARRASSINGGG
WHAT A PRISS
IS THAT MARCUS??
NOW WHAT?
HELLO?
I THINK I LAUNCHED MY PHOTOGRAPHY CAREER TODAY!
DO YOU LIKE THOSE PHOTOS I TOOK?

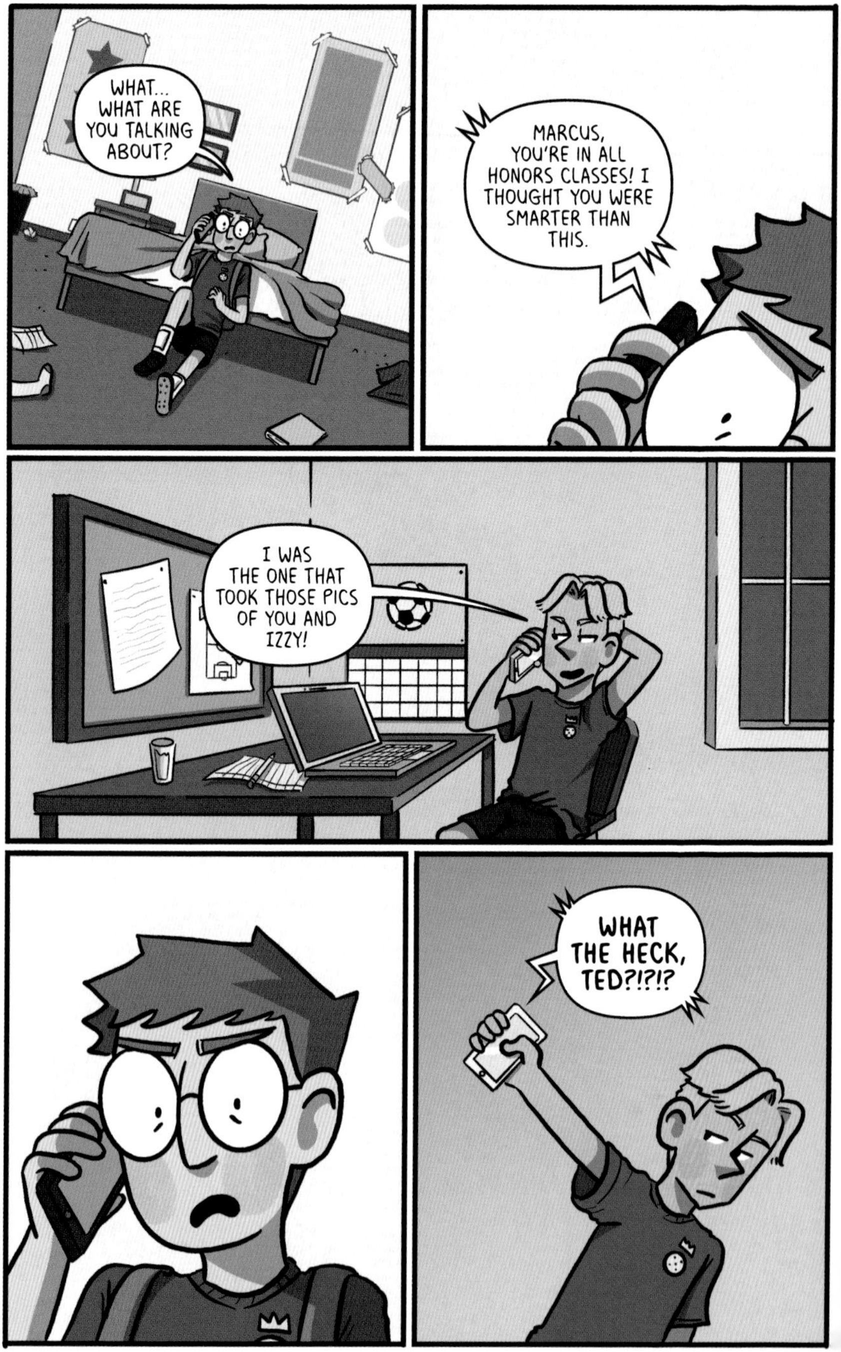
WHAT... WHAT ARE YOU TALKING ABOUT?
MARCUS, YOU'RE IN ALL HONORS CLASSES! I THOUGHT YOU WERE SMARTER THAN THIS.
I WAS THE ONE THAT TOOK THOSE PICS OF YOU AND IZZY!
WHAT THE HECK, TED?!?!?

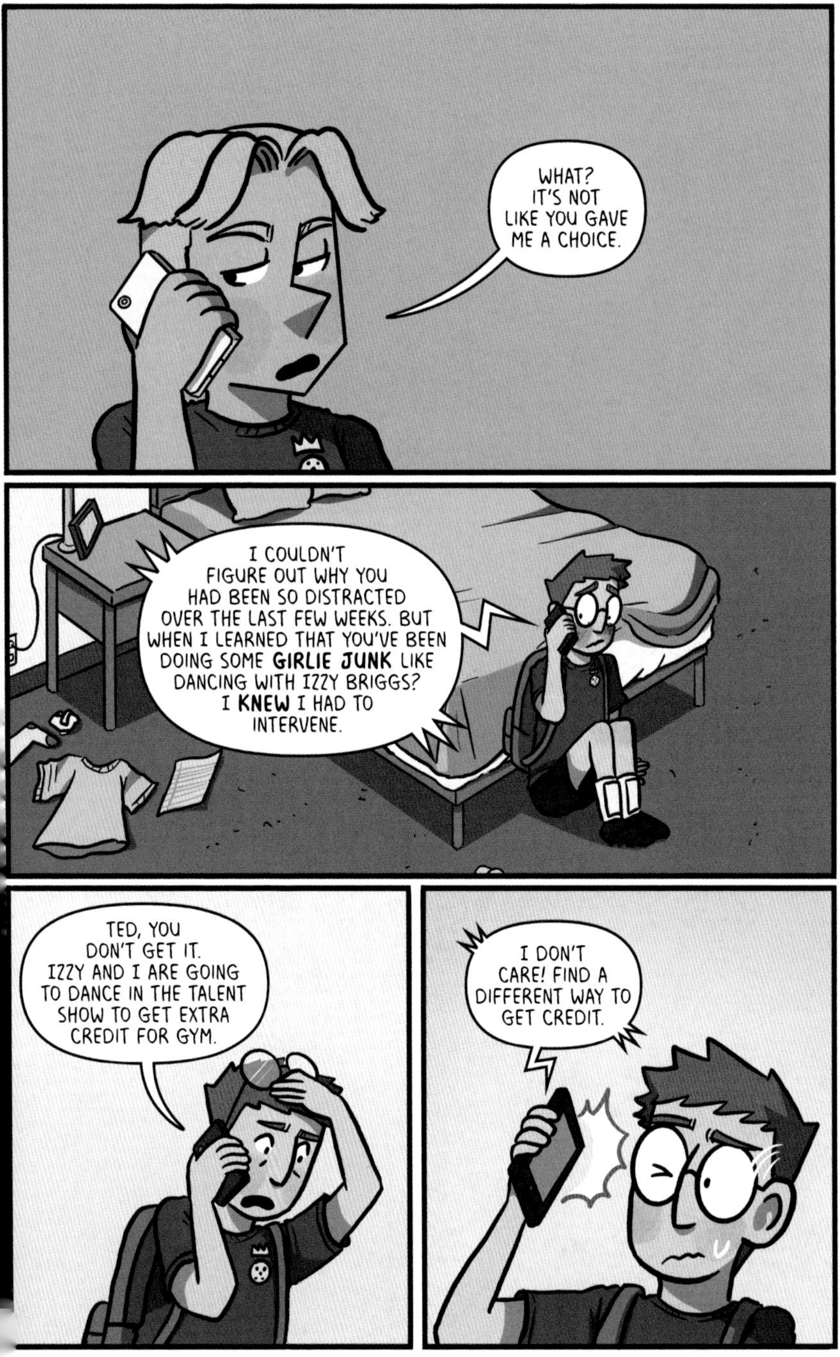
WHAT? IT'S NOT LIKE YOU GAVE ME A CHOICE.
I COULDN'T FIGURE OUT WHY YOU HAD BEEN SO DISTRACTED OVER THE LAST FEW WEEKS. BUT WHEN I LEARNED THAT YOU'VE BEEN DOING SOME **GIRLIE JUNK** LIKE DANCING WITH IZZY BRIGGS? I **KNEW** I HAD TO INTERVENE.
TED, YOU DON'T GET IT. IZZY AND I ARE GOING TO DANCE IN THE TALENT SHOW TO GET EXTRA CREDIT FOR GYM.
I DON'T CARE! FIND A DIFFERENT WAY TO GET CREDIT.

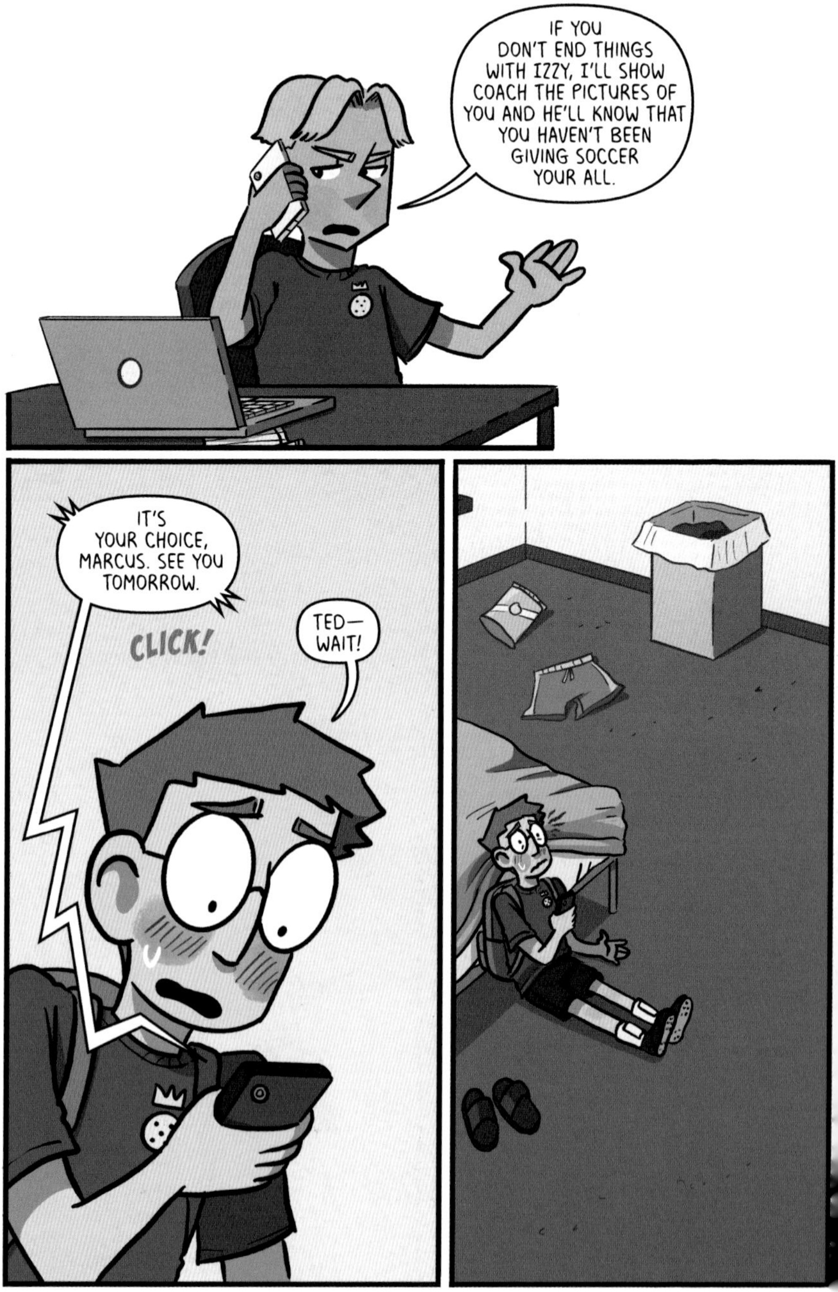
IF YOU DON'T END THINGS WITH IZZY, I'LL SHOW COACH THE PICTURES OF YOU AND HE'LL KNOW THAT YOU HAVEN'T BEEN GIVING SOCCER YOUR ALL.
IT'S YOUR CHOICE, MARCUS. SEE YOU TOMORROW.
CLICK!
TED— WAIT!

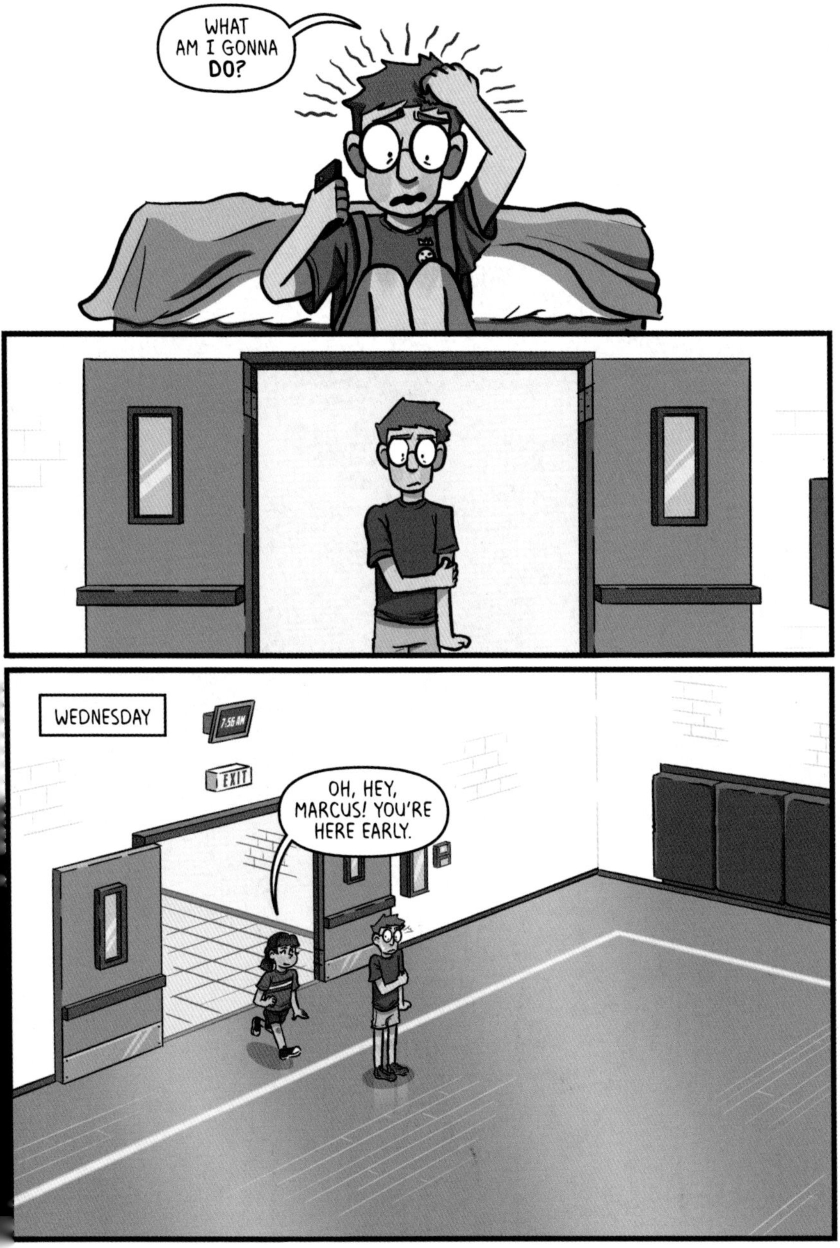
WHAT AM I GONNA DO?
WEDNESDAY
7:56 AM
EXIT
OH, HEY, MARCUS! YOU'RE HERE EARLY.

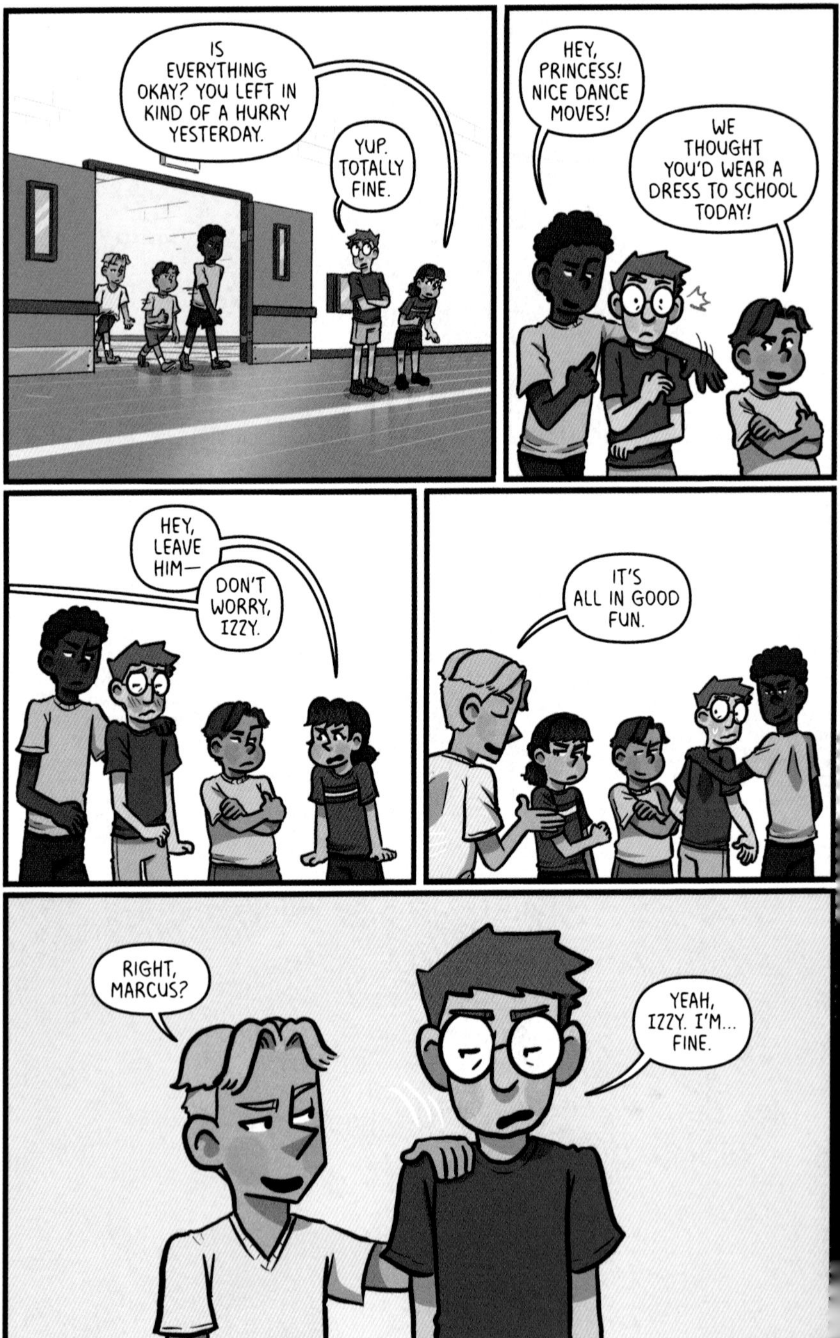
IS EVERYTHING OKAY? YOU LEFT IN KIND OF A HURRY YESTERDAY.
YUP. TOTALLY FINE.
HEY, PRINCESS! NICE DANCE MOVES!
WE THOUGHT YOU'D WEAR A DRESS TO SCHOOL TODAY!
HEY, LEAVE HIM—
DON'T WORRY, IZZY.
IT'S ALL IN GOOD FUN.
RIGHT, MARCUS?
YEAH, IZZY. I'M... FINE.

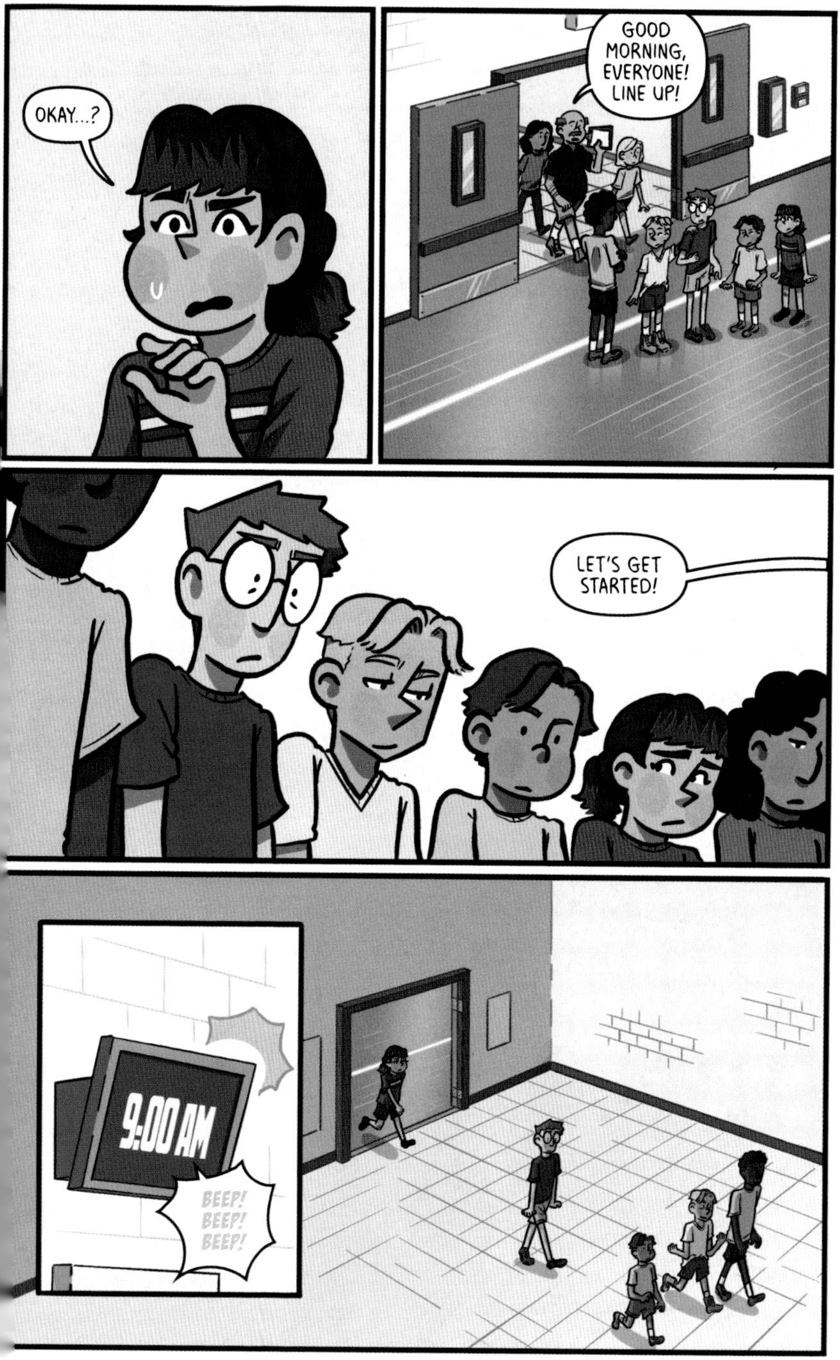
OKAY...?
GOOD MORNING, EVERYONE! LINE UP!
LET'S GET STARTED!
9:00 AM
BEEP! BEEP! BEEP!

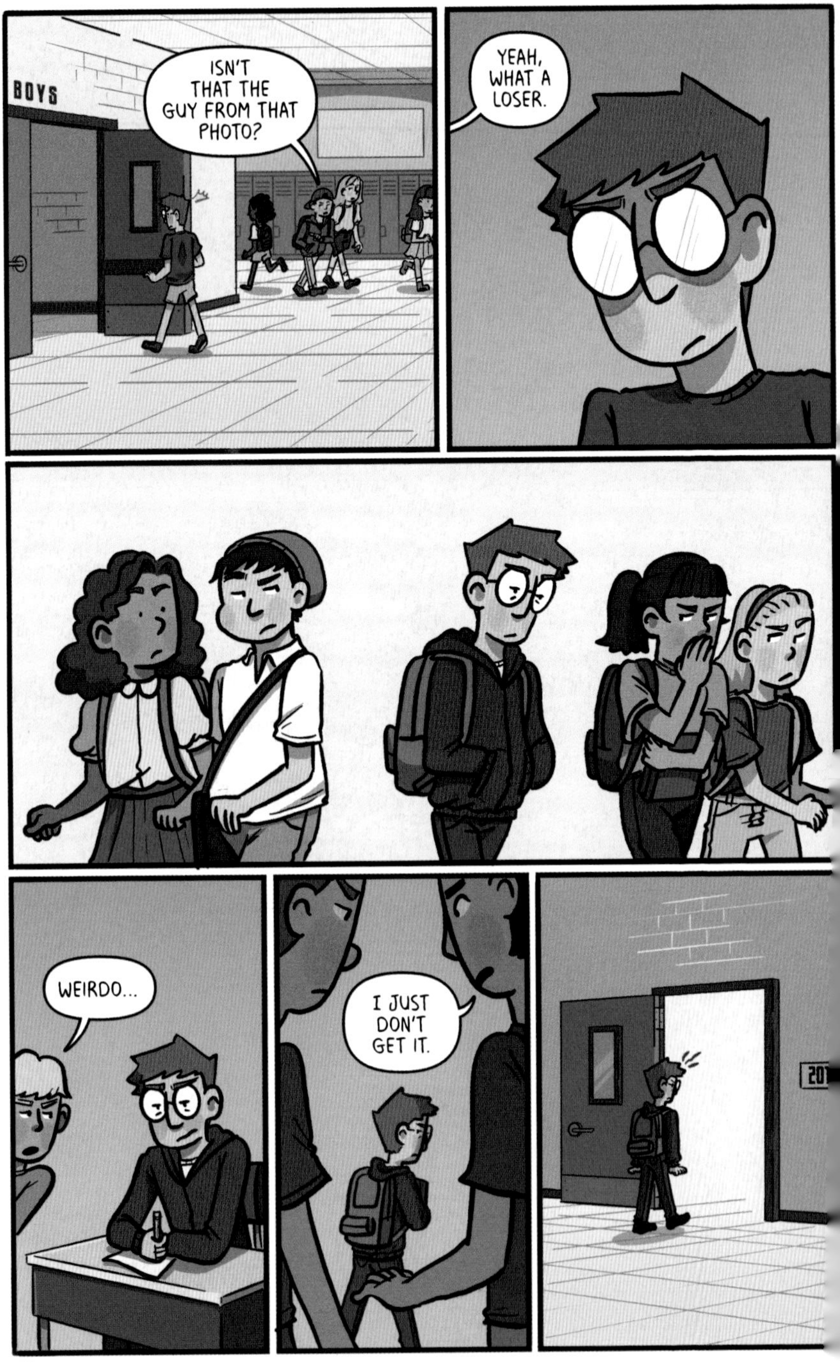
BOYS
ISN'T THAT THE GUY FROM THAT PHOTO?
YEAH, WHAT A LOSER.
WEIRDO...
I JUST DON'T GET IT.

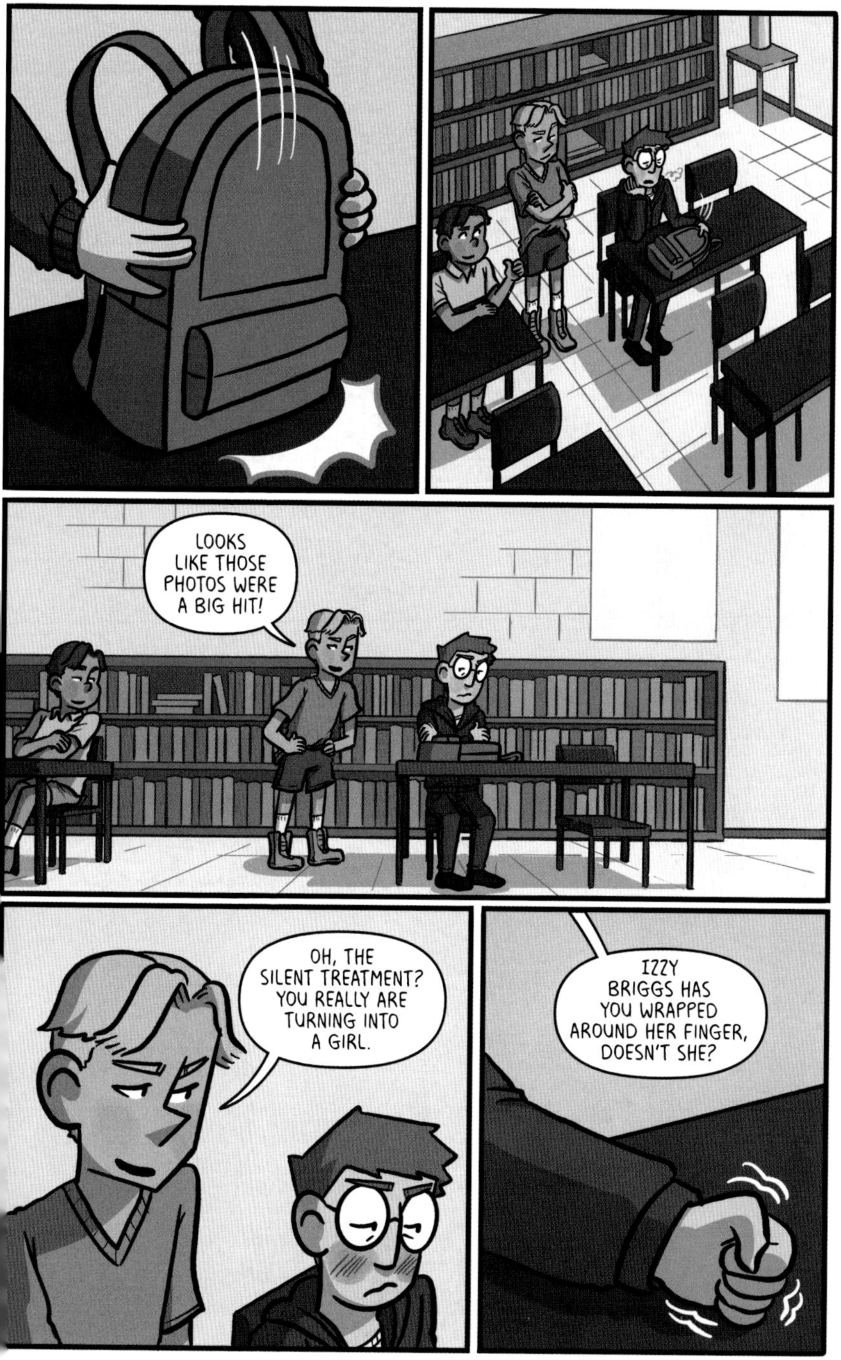
LOOKS LIKE THOSE PHOTOS WERE A BIG HIT!
OH, THE SILENT TREATMENT? YOU REALLY ARE TURNING INTO A GIRL.
IZZY BRIGGS HAS YOU WRAPPED AROUND HER FINGER, DOESN'T SHE?

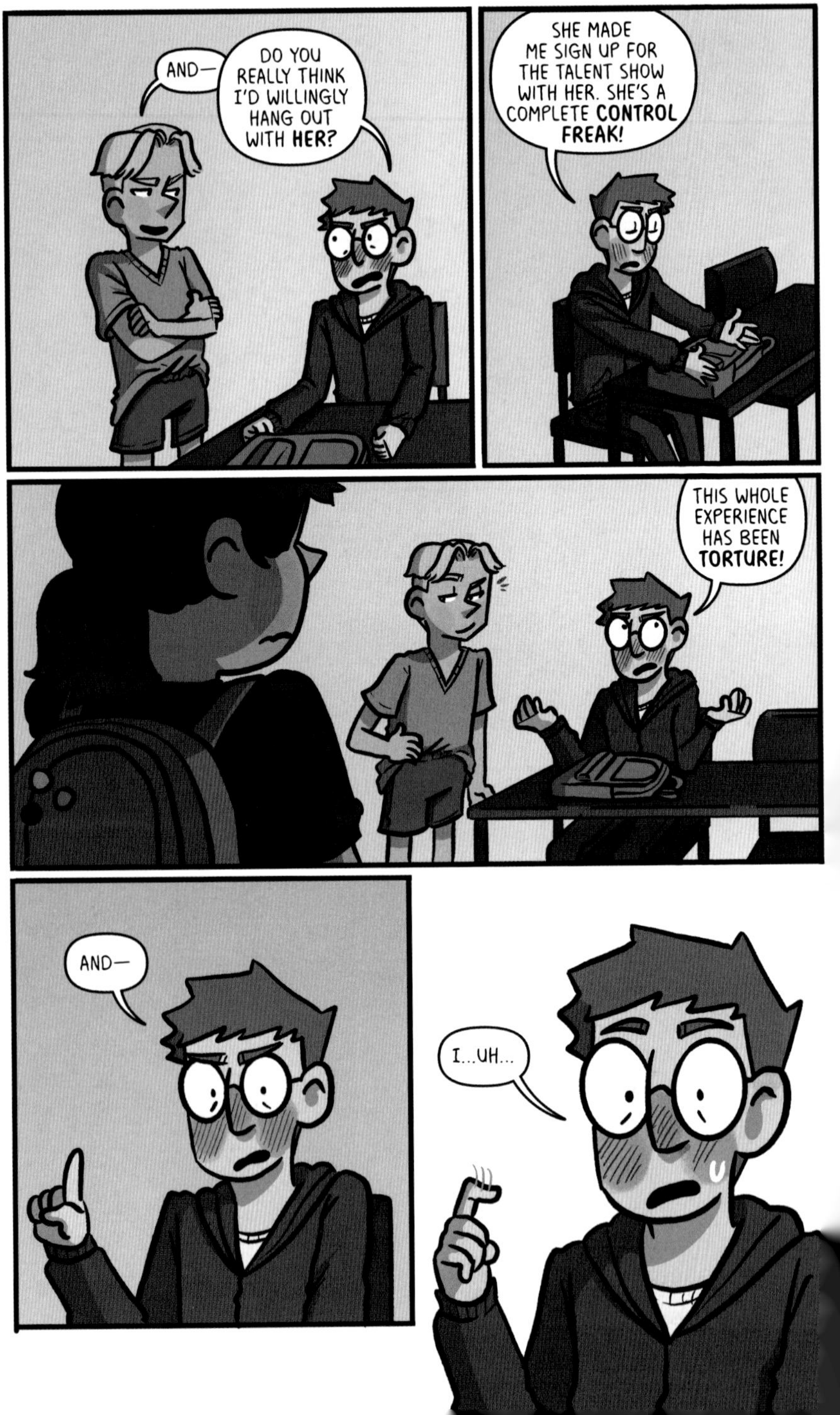
AND—
DO YOU REALLY THINK I'D WILLINGLY HANG OUT WITH **HER**?
SHE MADE ME SIGN UP FOR THE TALENT SHOW WITH HER. SHE'S A COMPLETE **CONTROL FREAK!**
THIS WHOLE EXPERIENCE HAS BEEN **TORTURE!**
AND—
I...UH...

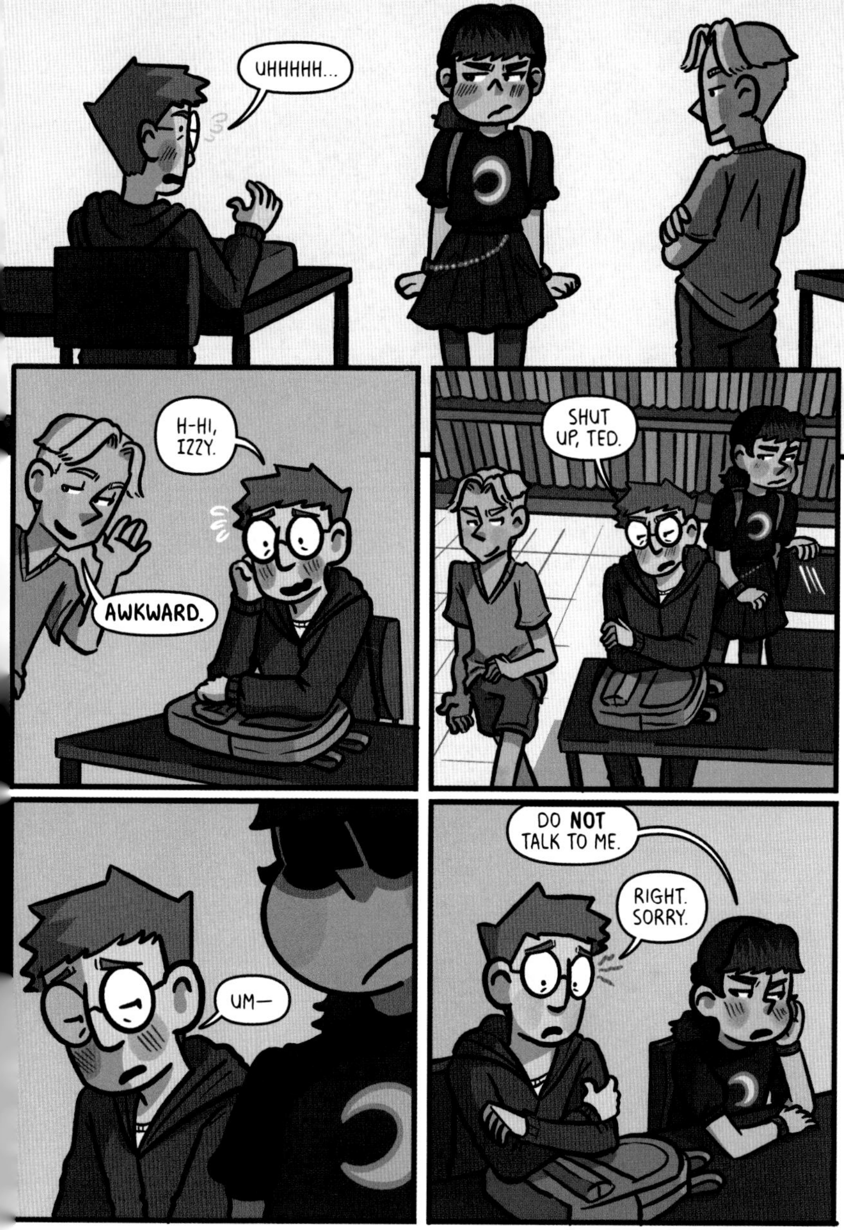
UHHHHH...
H-HI, IZZY.
AWKWARD.
SHUT UP, TED.
UM—
DO **NOT** TALK TO ME.
RIGHT. SORRY.

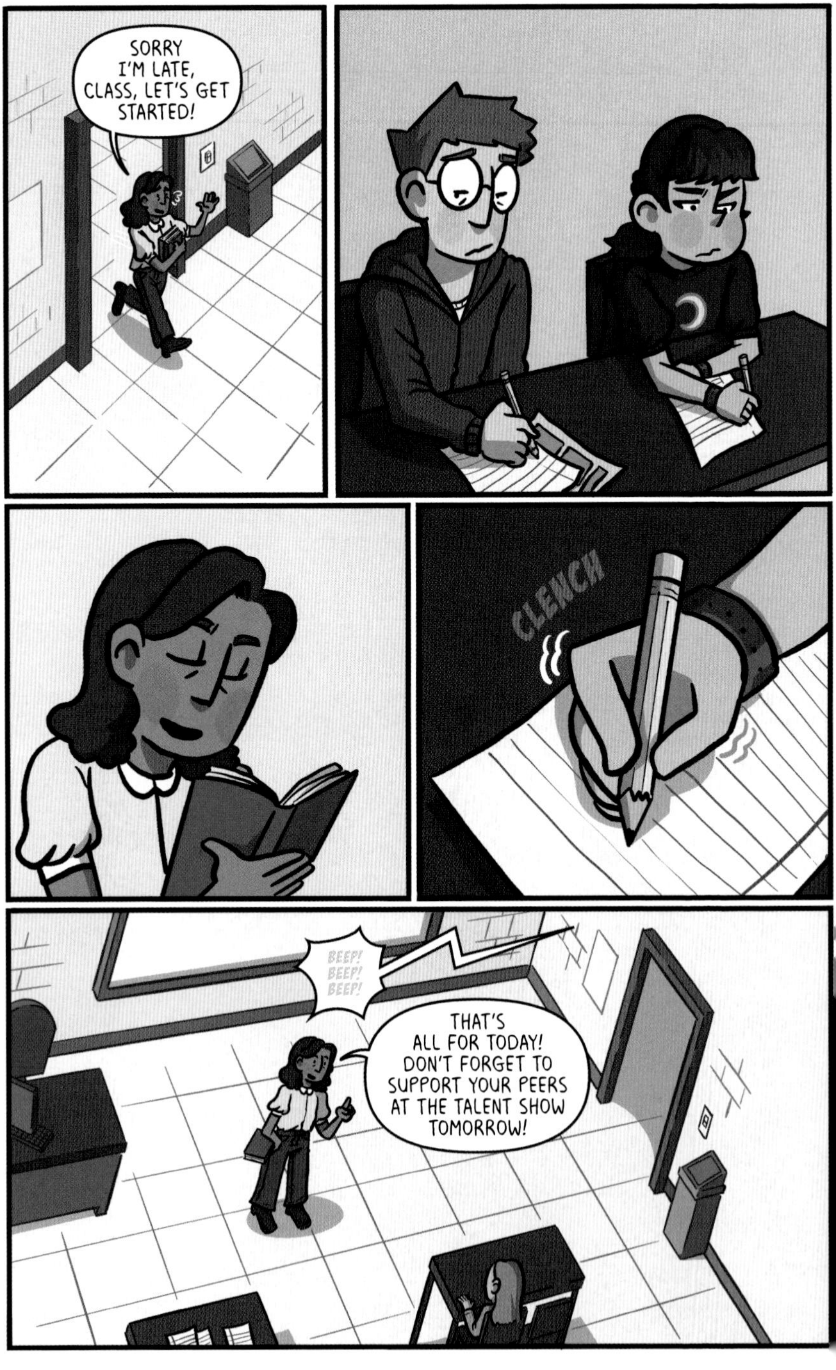
SORRY I'M LATE, CLASS, LET'S GET STARTED!
CLENCH
BEEP! BEEP! BEEP!
THAT'S ALL FOR TODAY! DON'T FORGET TO SUPPORT YOUR PEERS AT THE TALENT SHOW TOMORROW!

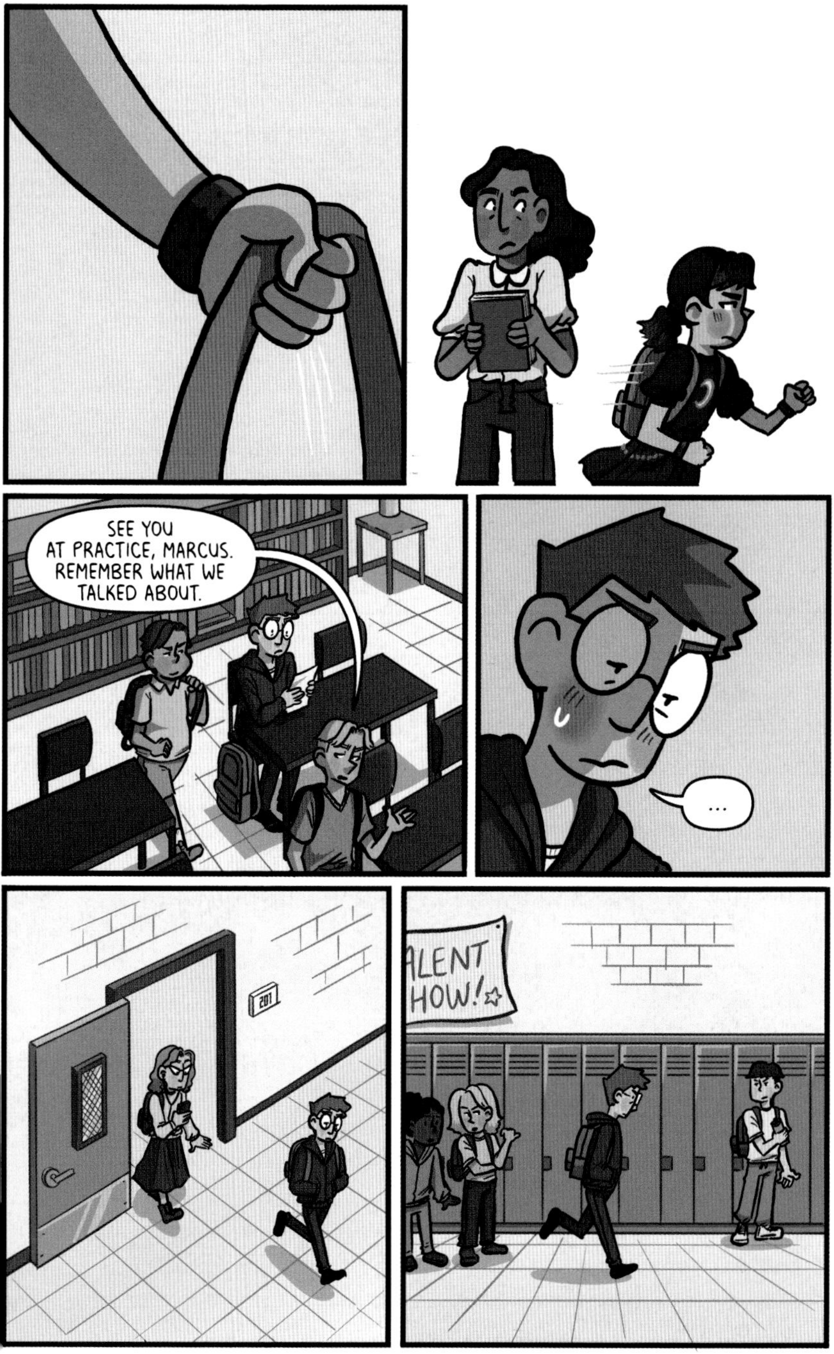
SEE YOU AT PRACTICE, MARCUS. REMEMBER WHAT WE TALKED ABOUT.
...
201
ALENT
HOW!

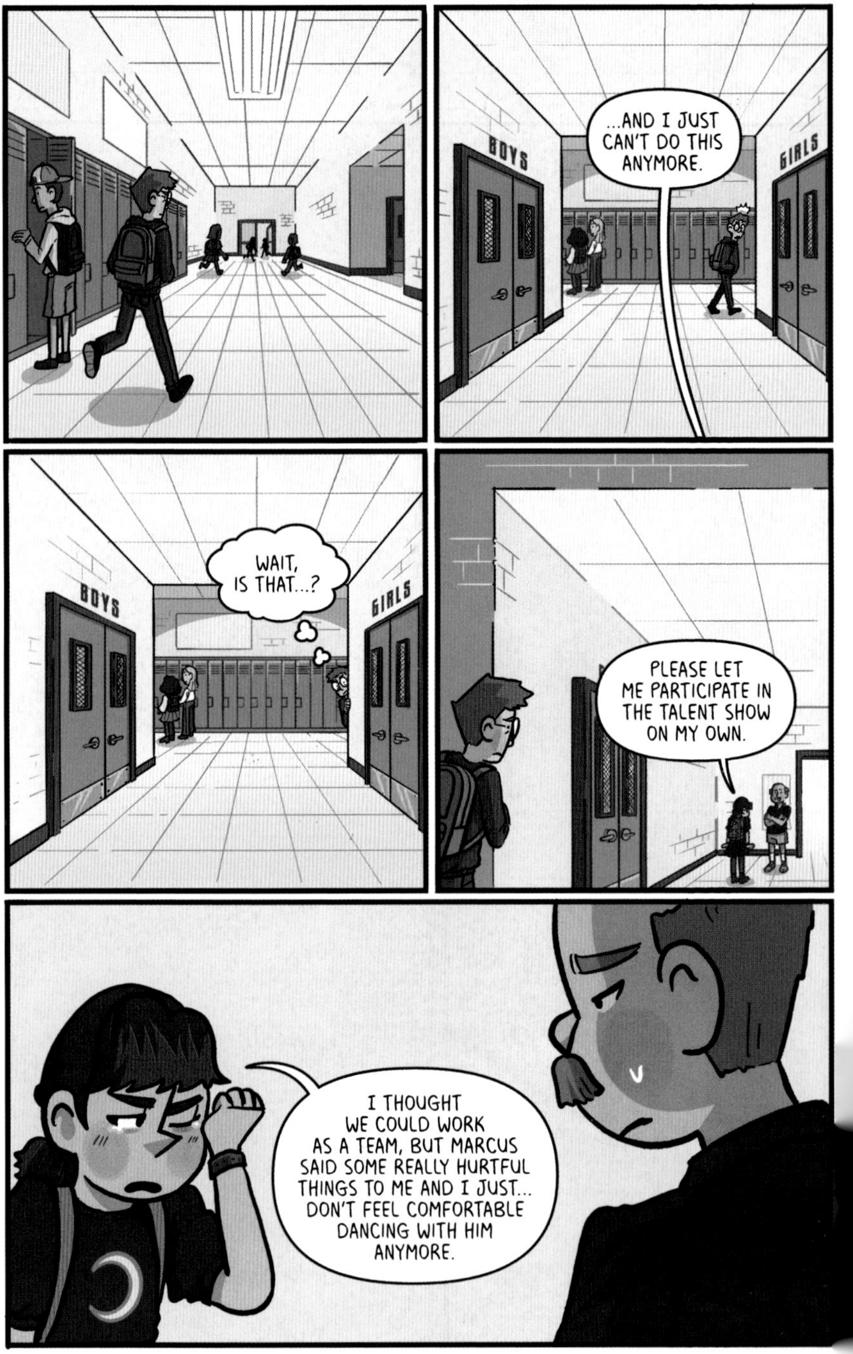
BOYS
GIRLS
...AND I JUST CAN'T DO THIS ANYMORE.
BOYS
GIRLS
WAIT, IS THAT...?
PLEASE LET ME PARTICIPATE IN THE TALENT SHOW ON MY OWN.
I THOUGHT WE COULD WORK AS A TEAM, BUT MARCUS SAID SOME REALLY HURTFUL THINGS TO ME AND I JUST... DON'T FEEL COMFORTABLE DANCING WITH HIM ANYMORE.

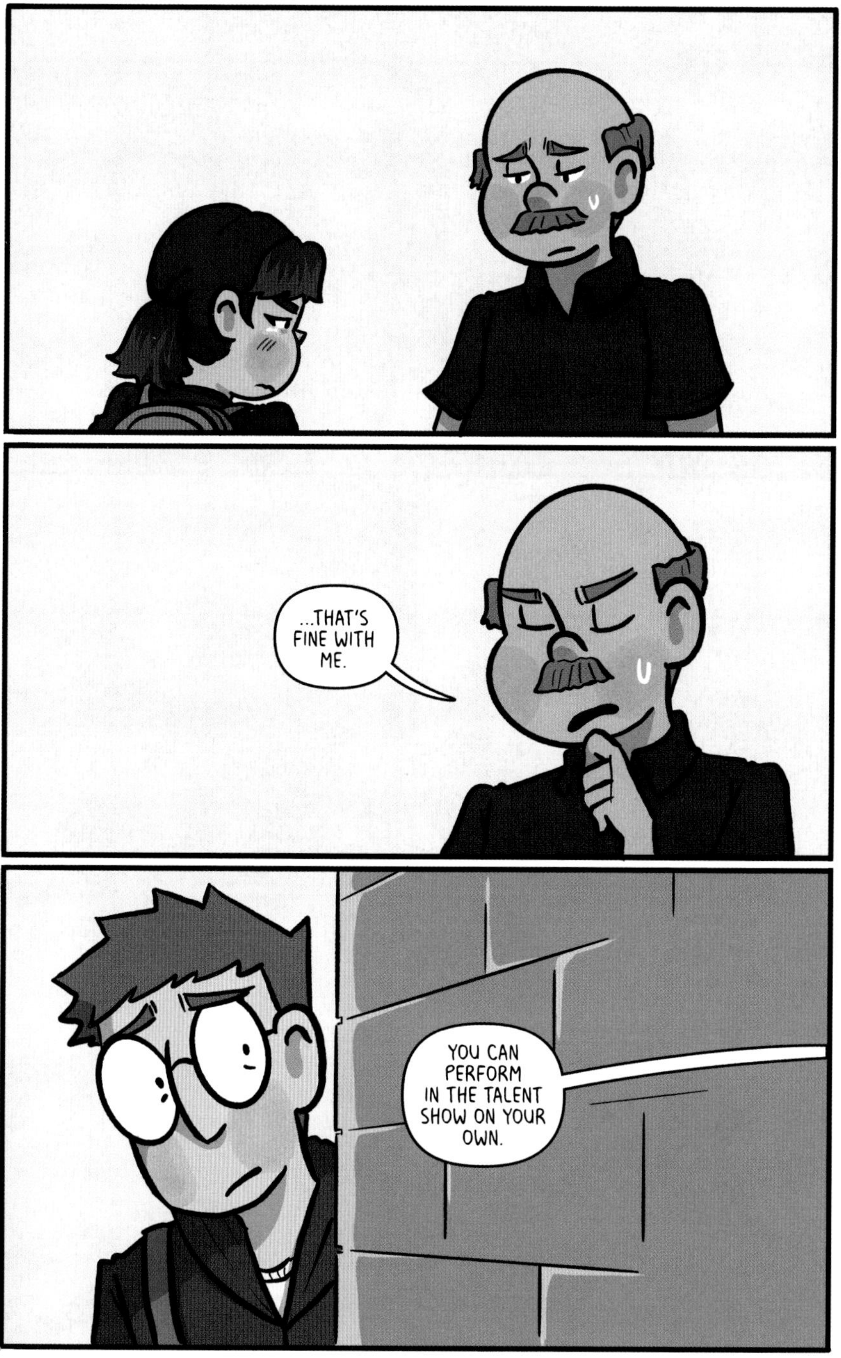
...THAT'S FINE WITH ME.
YOU CAN PERFORM IN THE TALENT SHOW ON YOUR OWN.

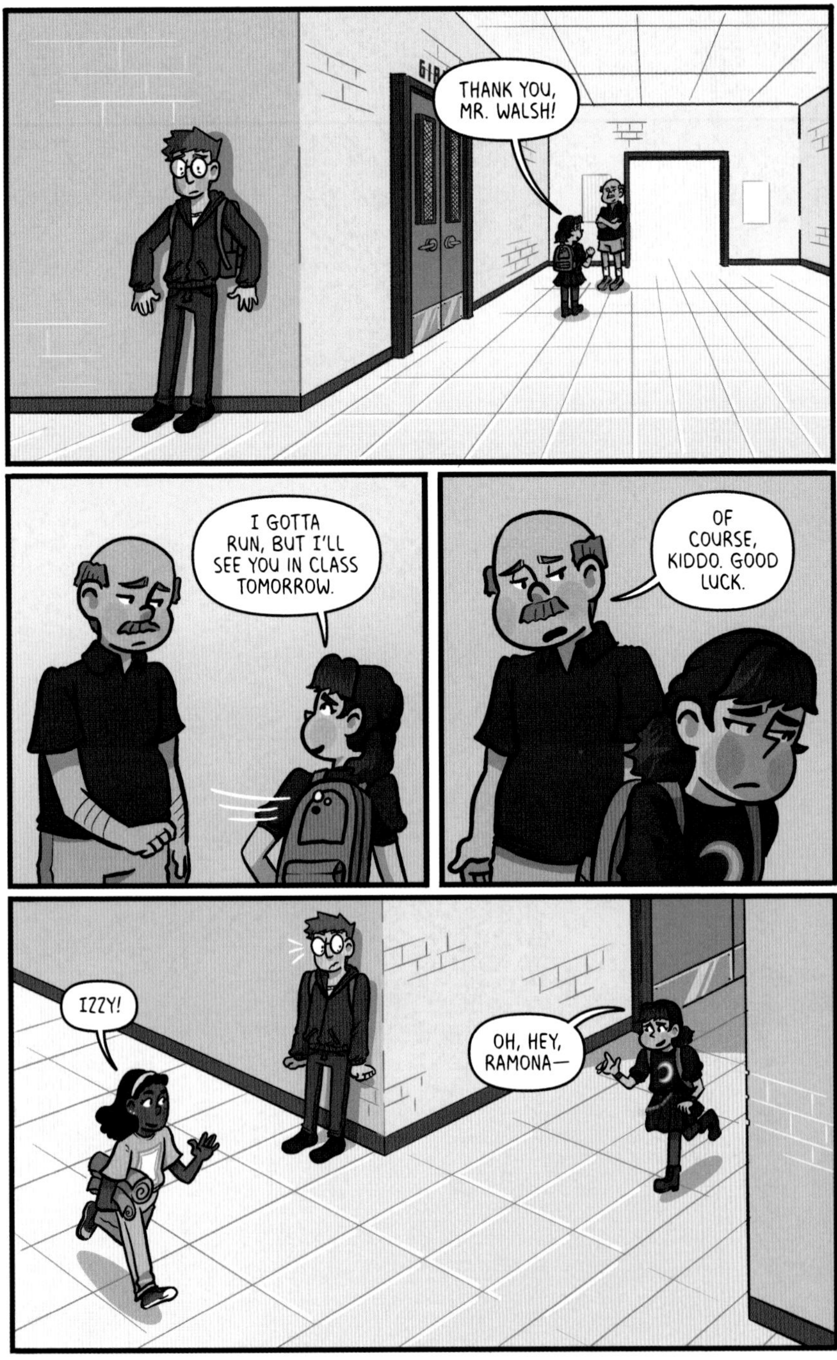
THANK YOU, MR. WALSH!
I GOTTA RUN, BUT I'LL SEE YOU IN CLASS TOMORROW.
OF COURSE, KIDDO. GOOD LUCK.
IZZY!
OH, HEY, RAMONA—

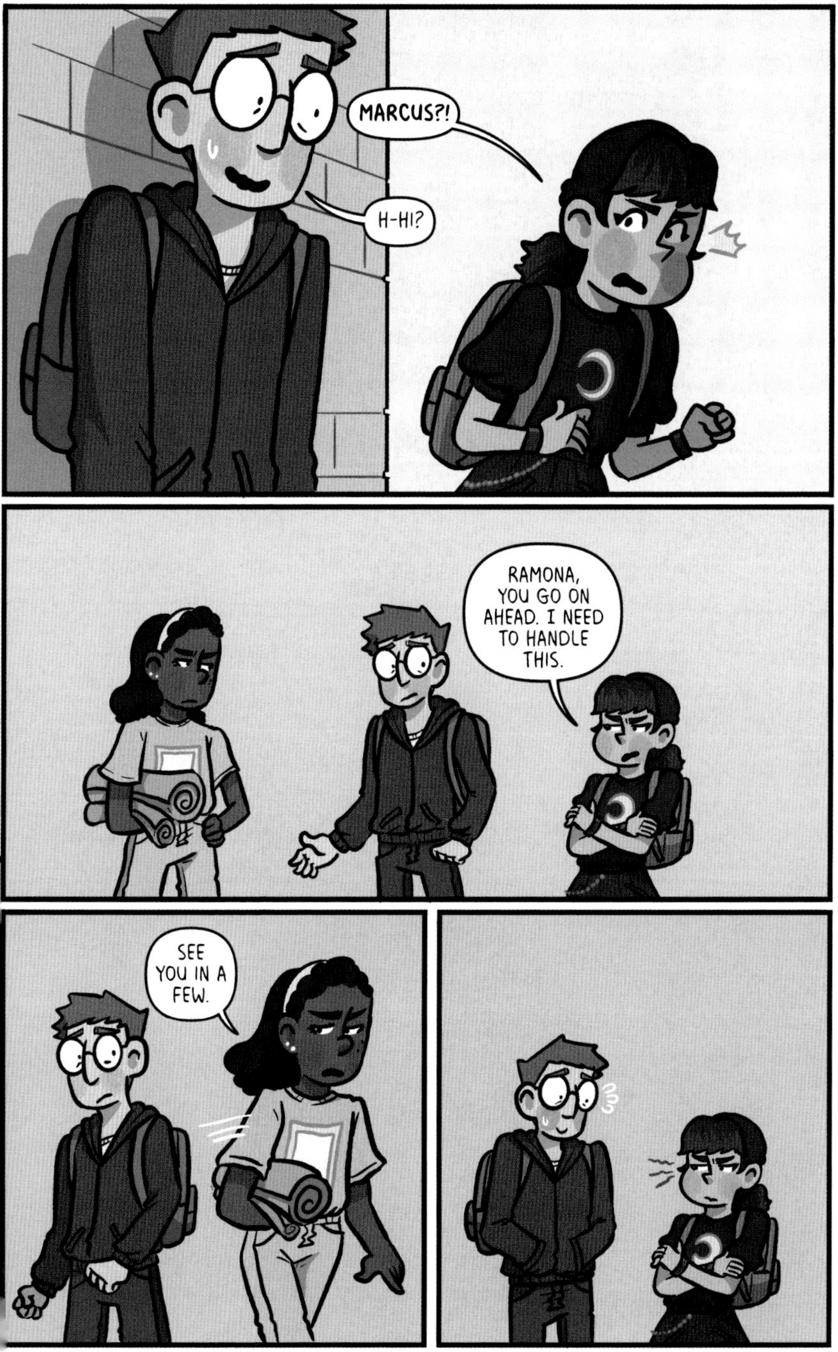
MARCUS?!
H-HI?
RAMONA, YOU GO ON AHEAD. I NEED TO HANDLE THIS.
SEE YOU IN A FEW.

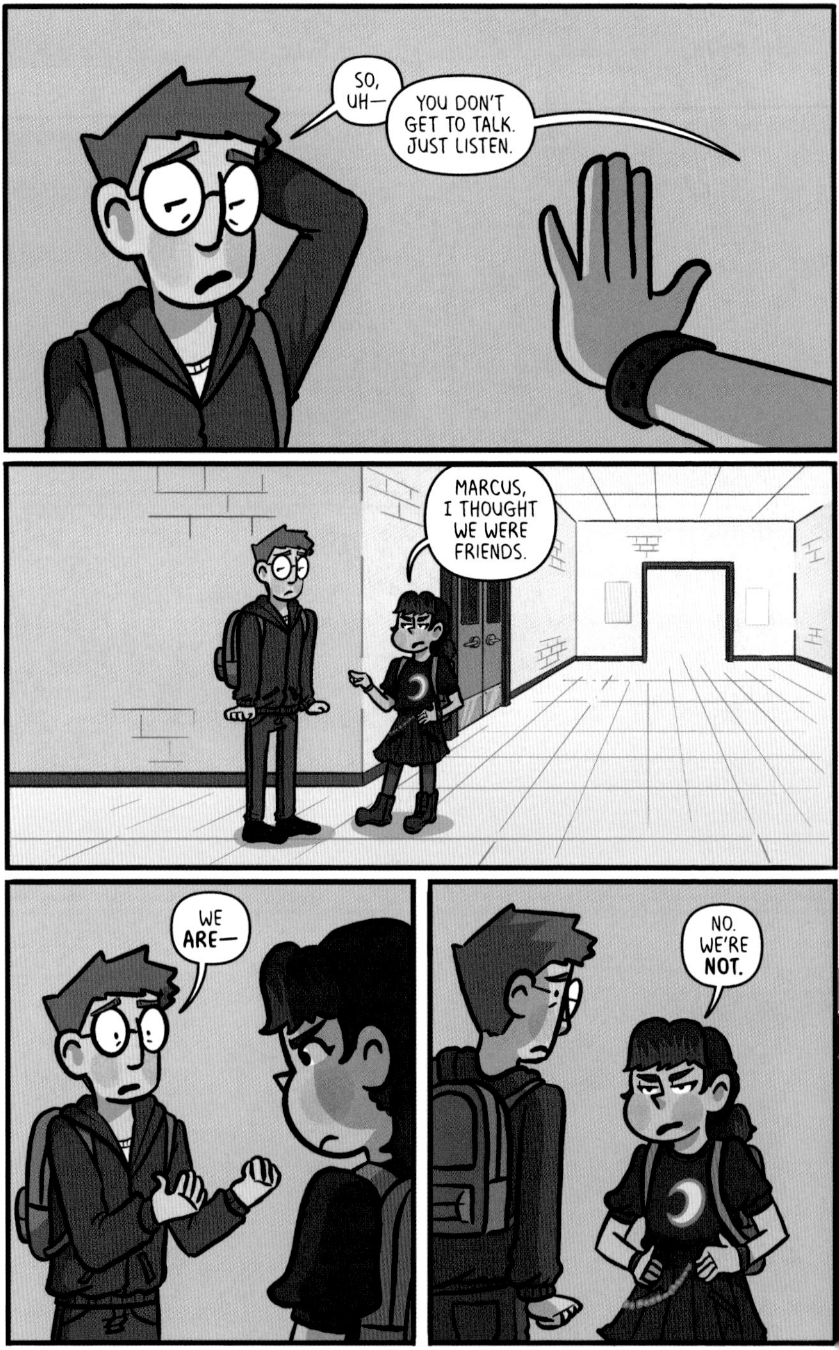
SO, UH—
YOU DON'T GET TO TALK. JUST LISTEN.
MARCUS, I THOUGHT WE WERE FRIENDS.
WE **ARE**—
NO. WE'RE **NOT.**

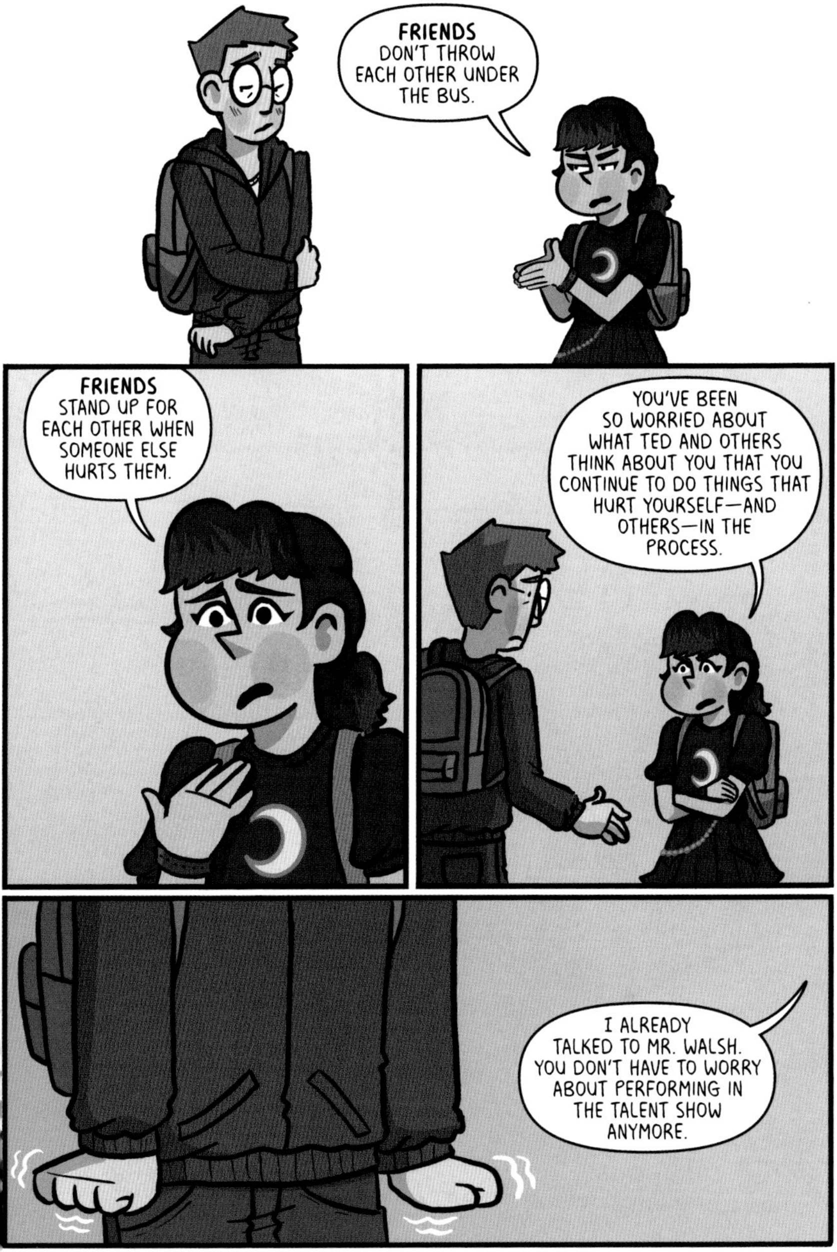
FRIENDS DON'T THROW EACH OTHER UNDER THE BUS.
FRIENDS STAND UP FOR EACH OTHER WHEN SOMEONE ELSE HURTS THEM.
YOU'VE BEEN SO WORRIED ABOUT WHAT TED AND OTHERS THINK ABOUT YOU THAT YOU CONTINUE TO DO THINGS THAT HURT YOURSELF—AND OTHERS—IN THE PROCESS.
I ALREADY TALKED TO MR. WALSH. YOU DON'T HAVE TO WORRY ABOUT PERFORMING IN THE TALENT SHOW ANYMORE.

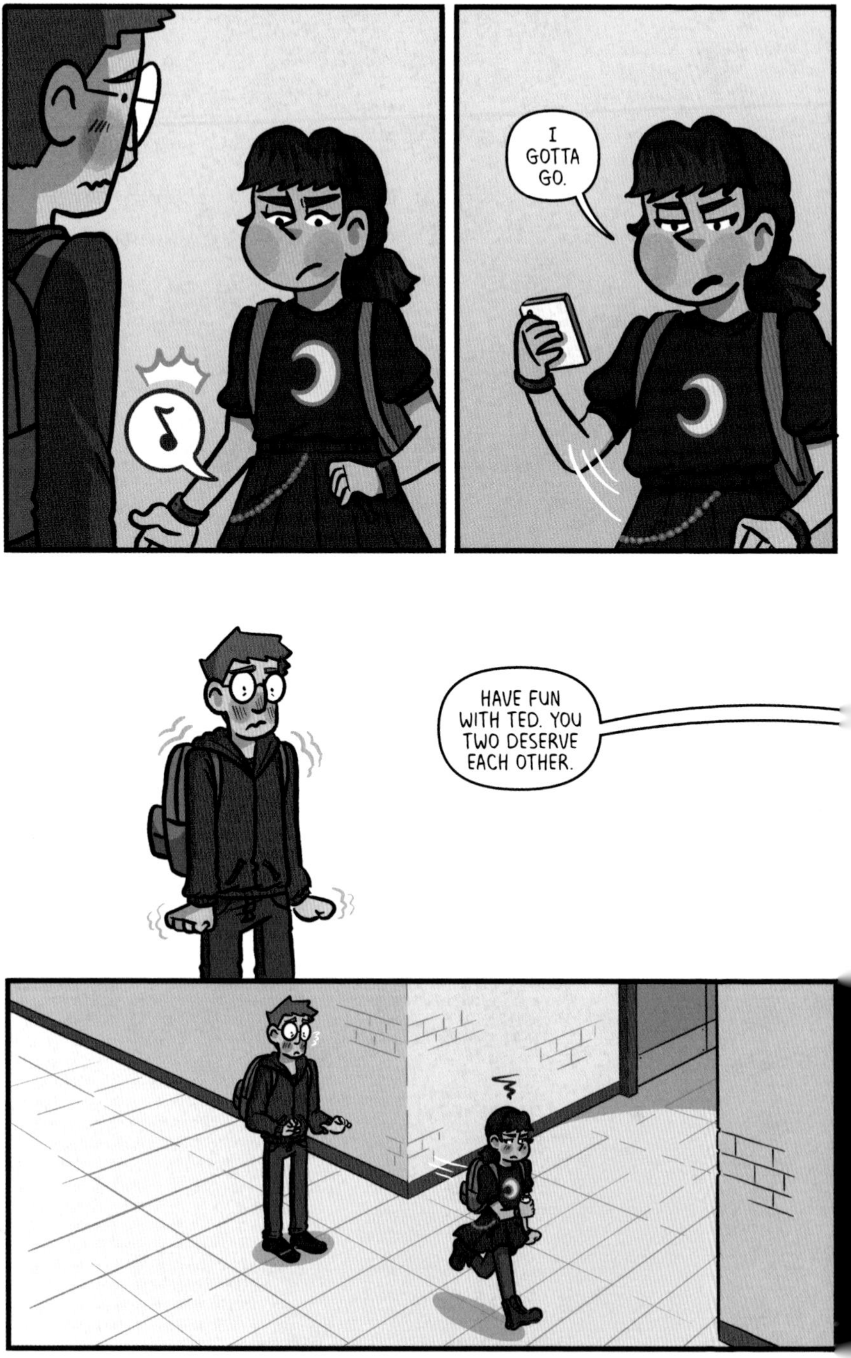
I GOTTA GO.
HAVE FUN WITH TED. YOU TWO DESERVE EACH OTHER.

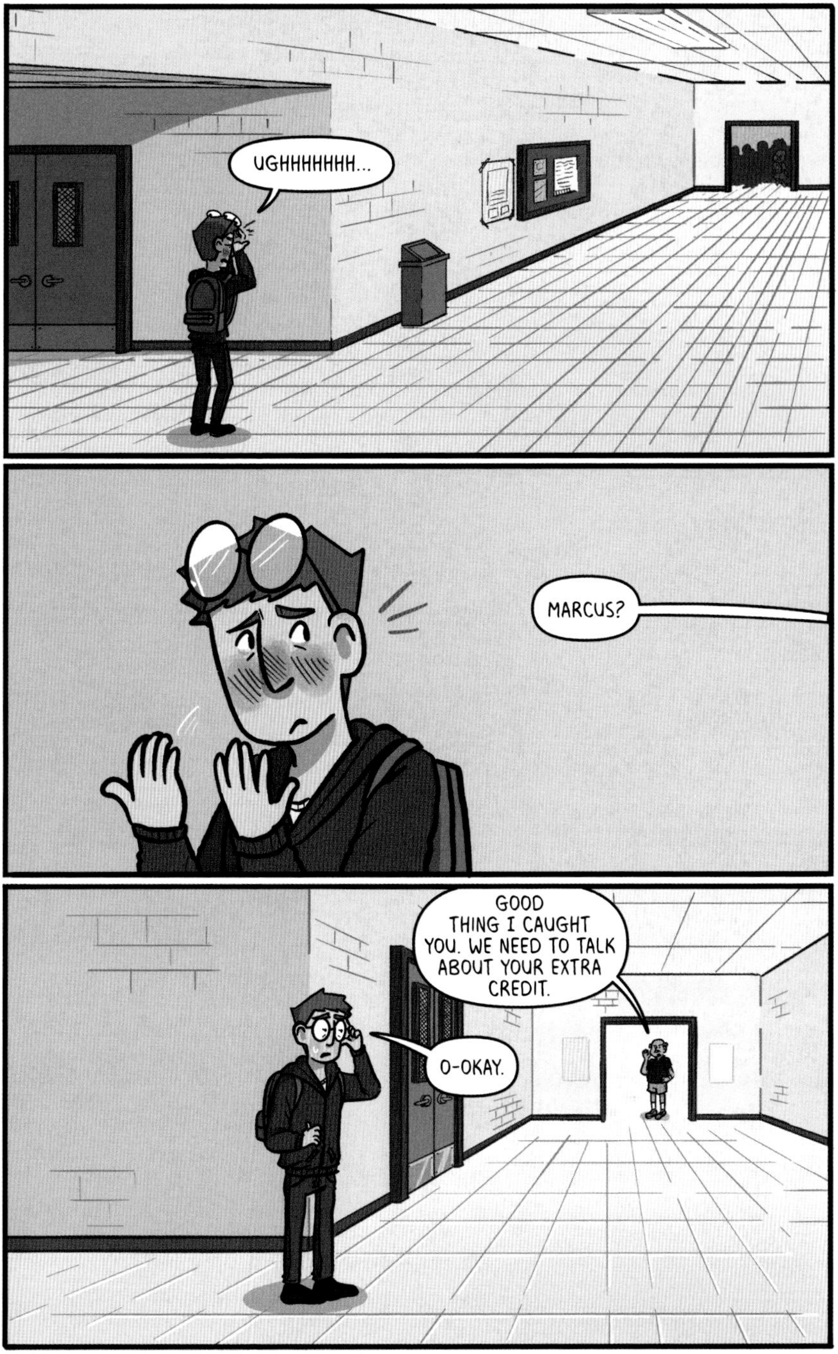
UGHHHHHHH...
MARCUS?
GOOD THING I CAUGHT YOU. WE NEED TO TALK ABOUT YOUR EXTRA CREDIT.
O-OKAY.

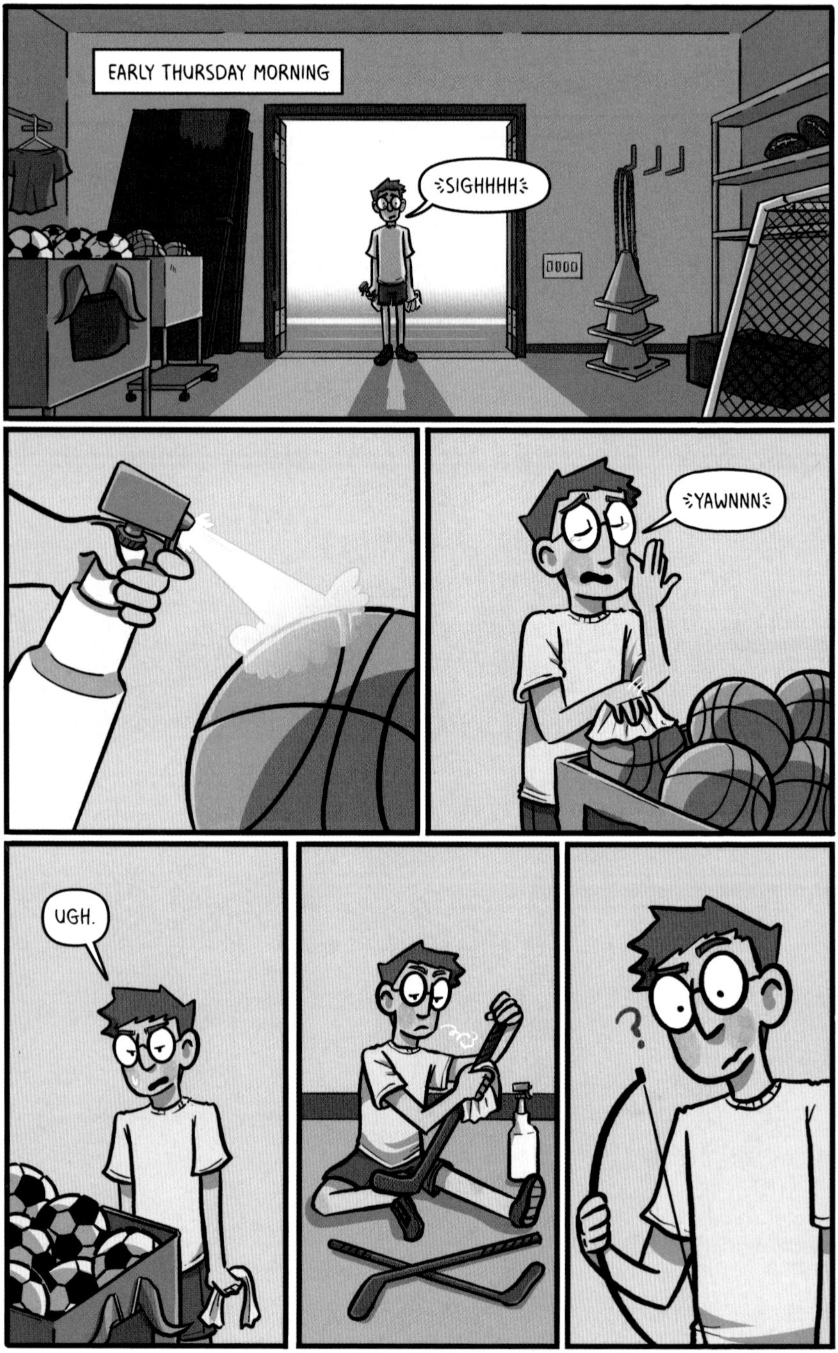
EARLY THURSDAY MORNING
SIGHHHH
YAWNNN
UGH.
?

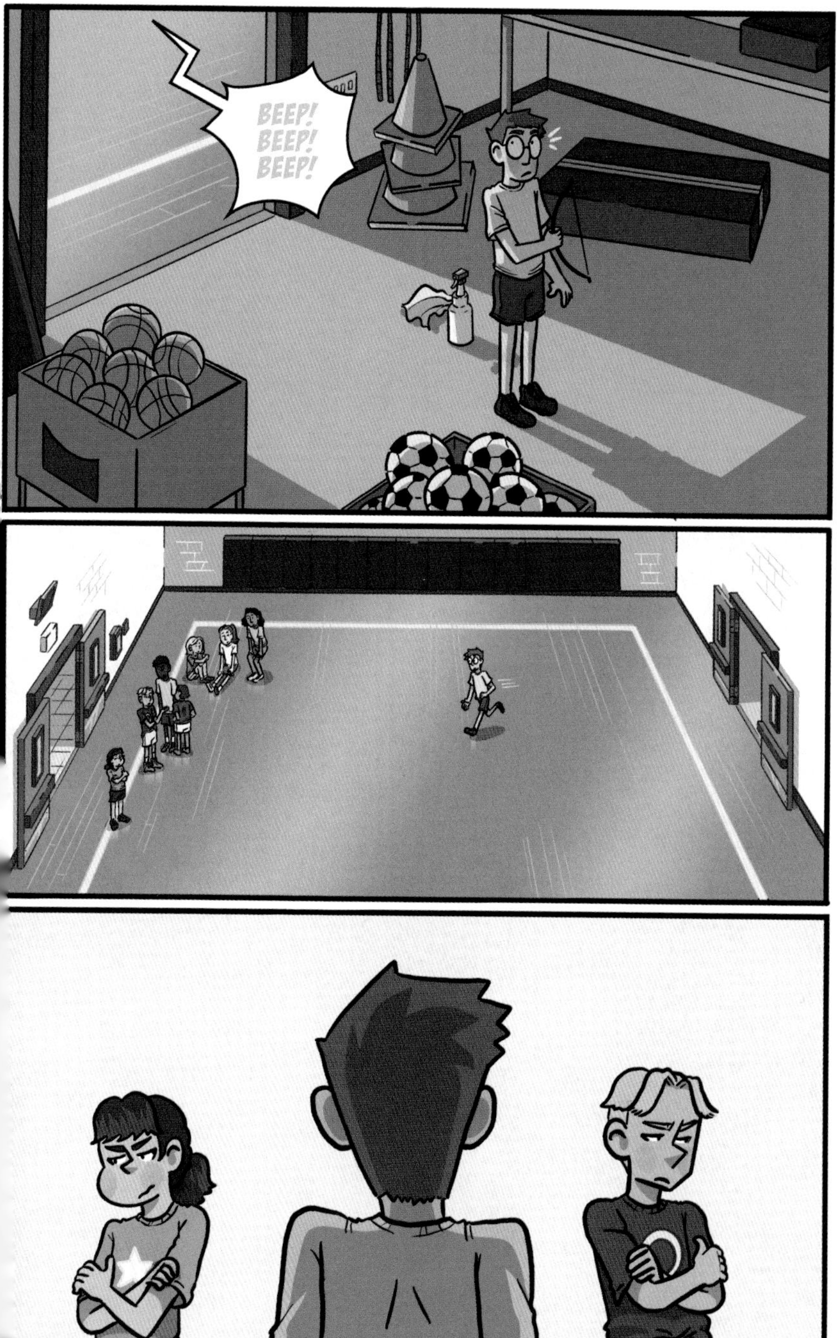
BEEP! BEEP! BEEP!

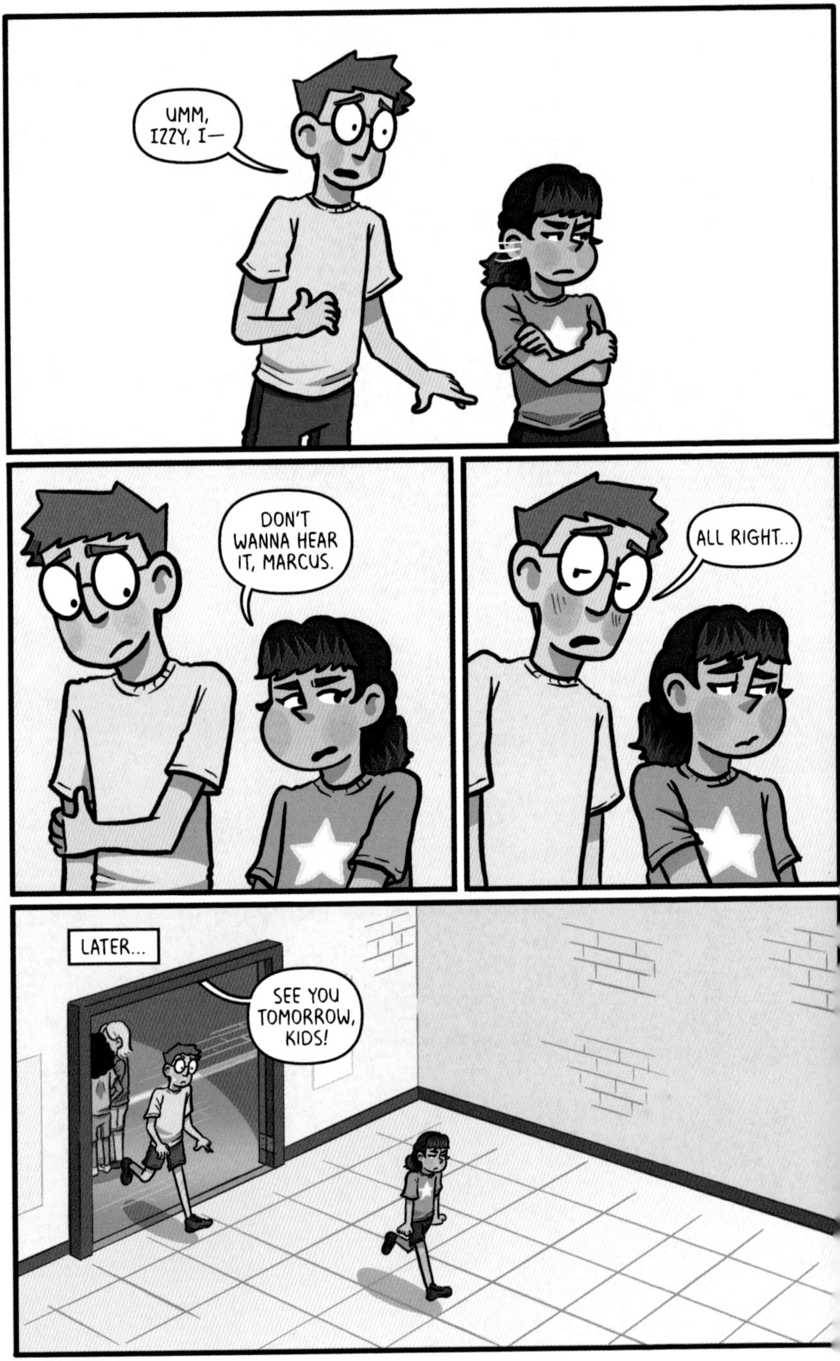
UMM, IZZY, I—
DON'T WANNA HEAR IT, MARCUS.
ALL RIGHT...
LATER...
SEE YOU TOMORROW, KIDS!

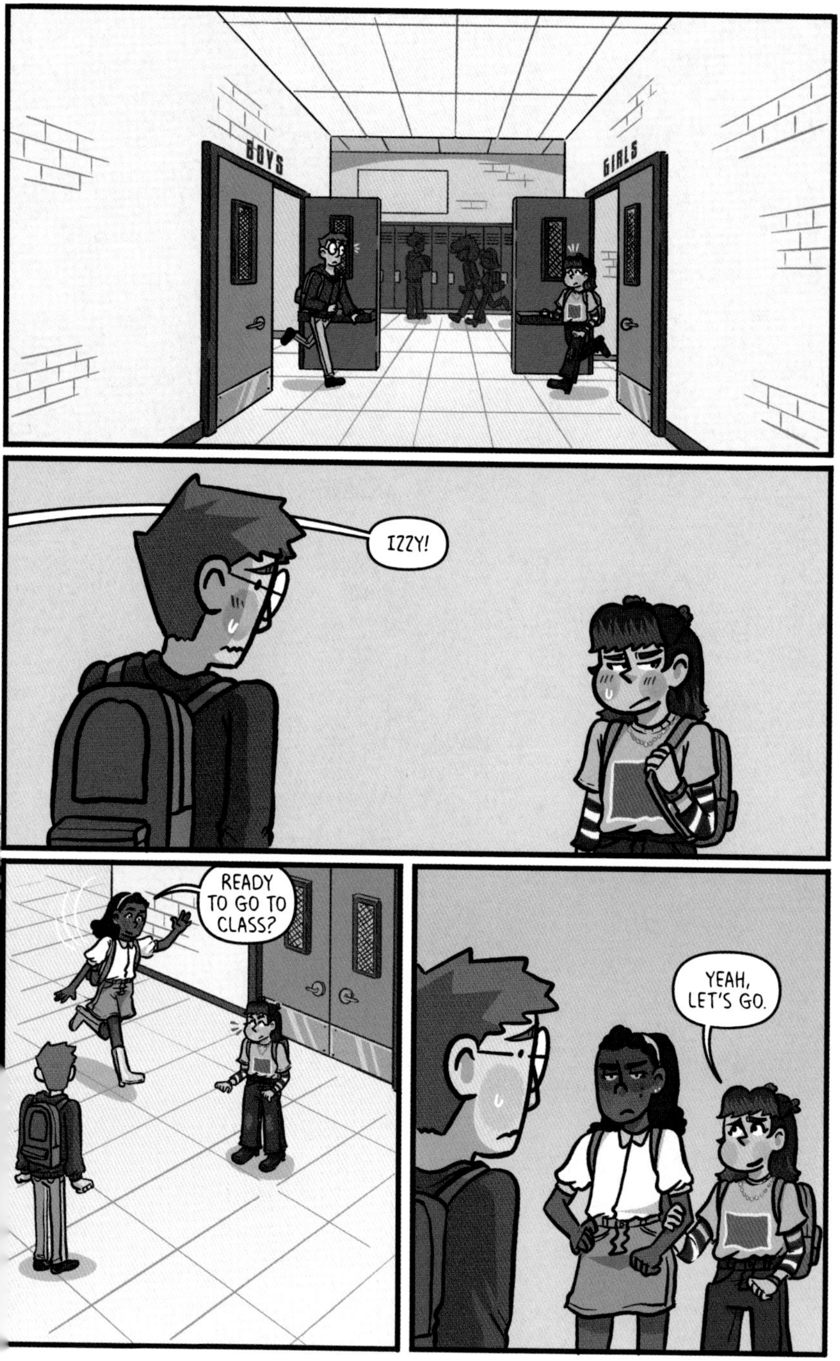
BOYS
GIRLS
IZZY!
READY TO GO TO CLASS?
YEAH, LET'S GO.

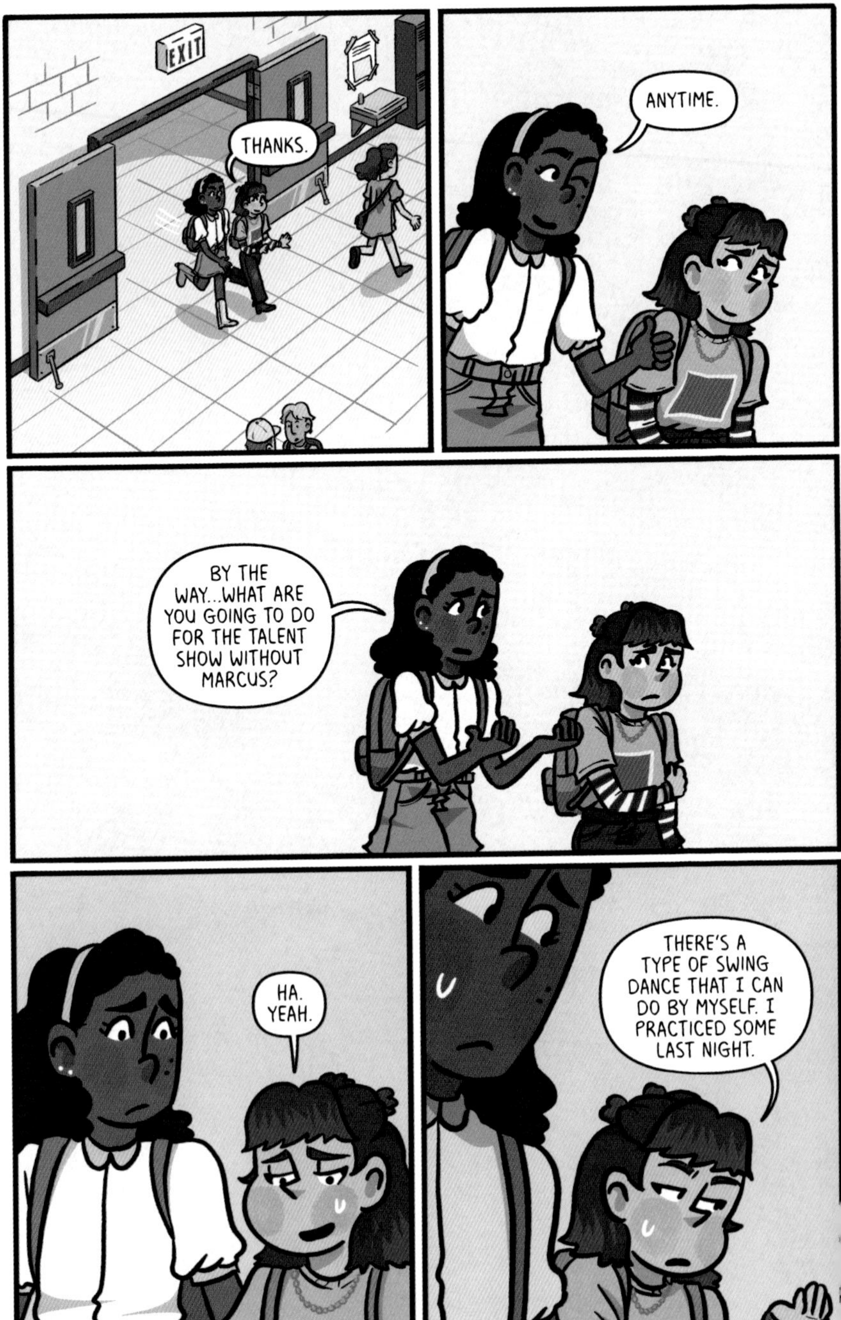
EXIT
THANKS.
ANYTIME.
BY THE WAY...WHAT ARE YOU GOING TO DO FOR THE TALENT SHOW WITHOUT MARCUS?
HA. YEAH.
THERE'S A TYPE OF SWING DANCE THAT I CAN DO BY MYSELF. I PRACTICED SOME LAST NIGHT.

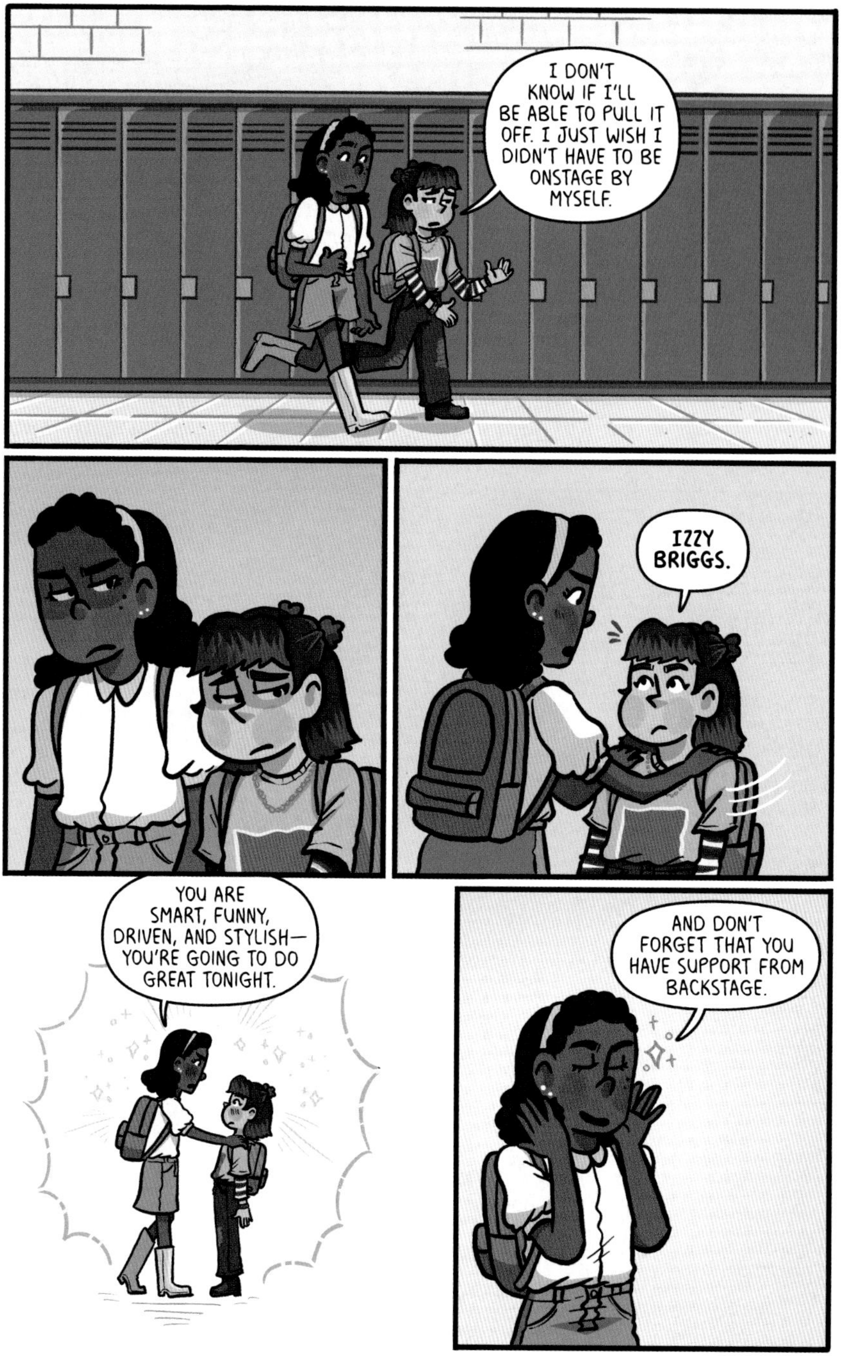
I DON'T KNOW IF I'LL BE ABLE TO PULL IT OFF. I JUST WISH I DIDN'T HAVE TO BE ONSTAGE BY MYSELF.
IZZY BRIGGS.
YOU ARE SMART, FUNNY, DRIVEN, AND STYLISH—YOU'RE GOING TO DO GREAT TONIGHT.
AND DON'T FORGET THAT YOU HAVE SUPPORT FROM BACKSTAGE.

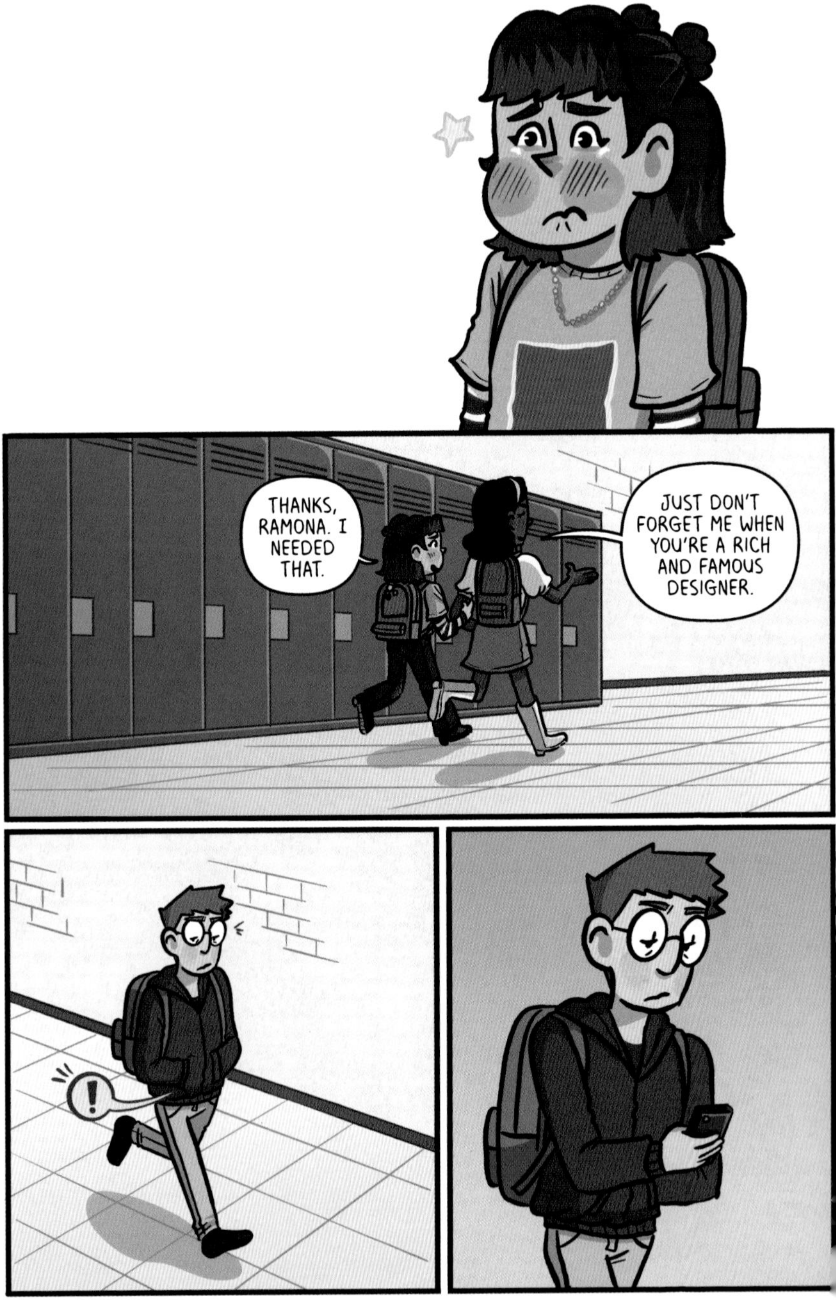
THANKS, RAMONA. I NEEDED THAT.
JUST DON'T FORGET ME WHEN YOU'RE A RICH AND FAMOUS DESIGNER.
!

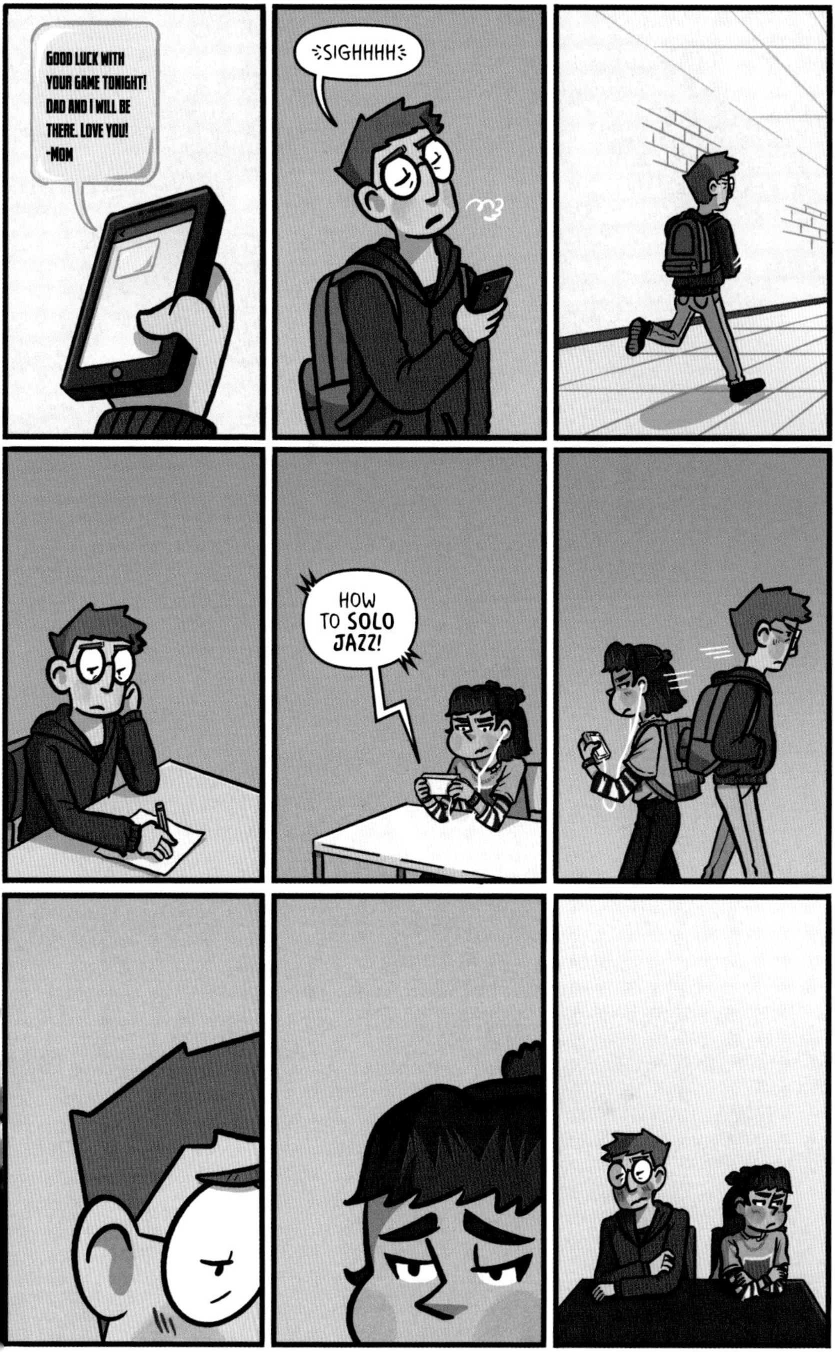
GOOD LUCK WITH YOUR GAME TONIGHT! DAD AND I WILL BE THERE. LOVE YOU! -MOM
SIGHHHH
HOW TO SOLO JAZZ!

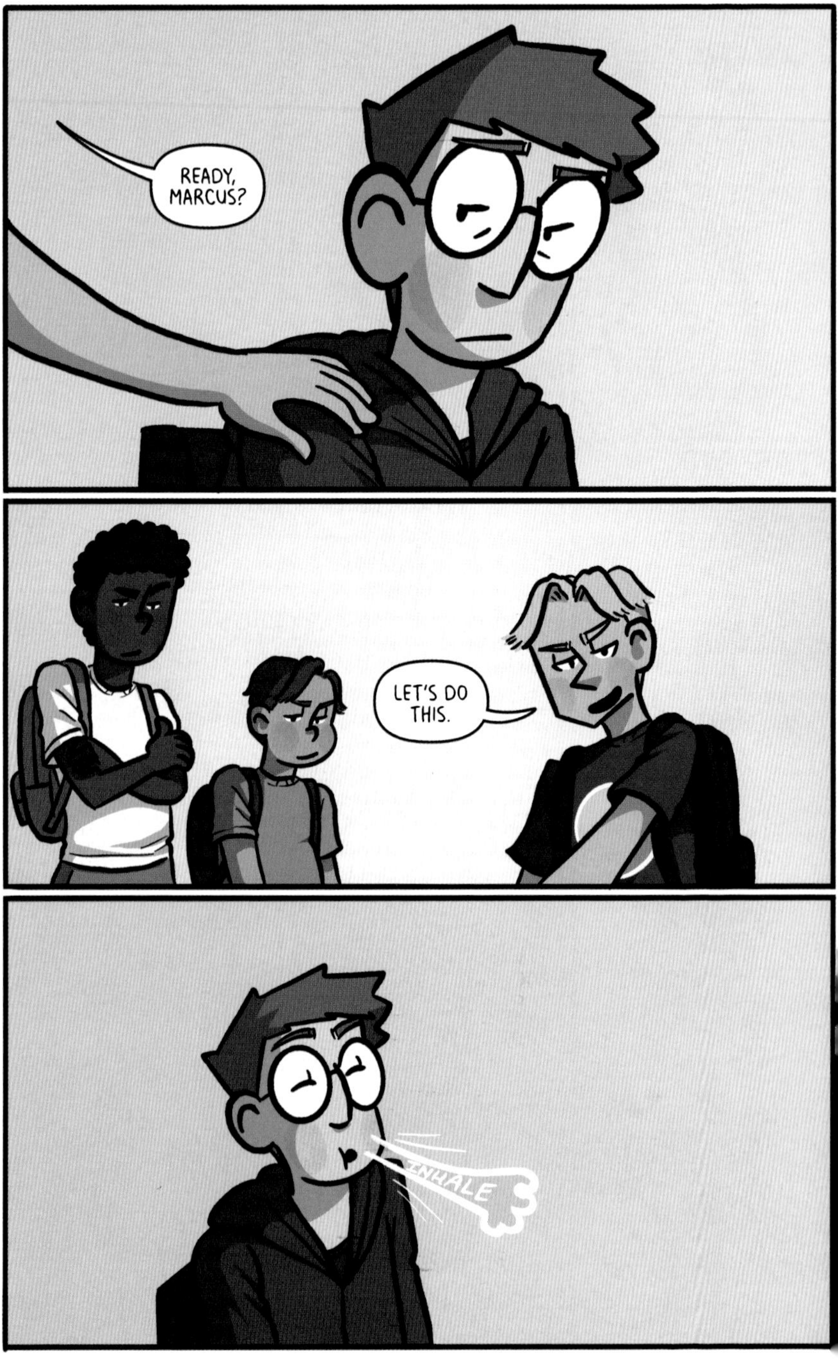
READY, MARCUS?
LET'S DO THIS.
INHALE

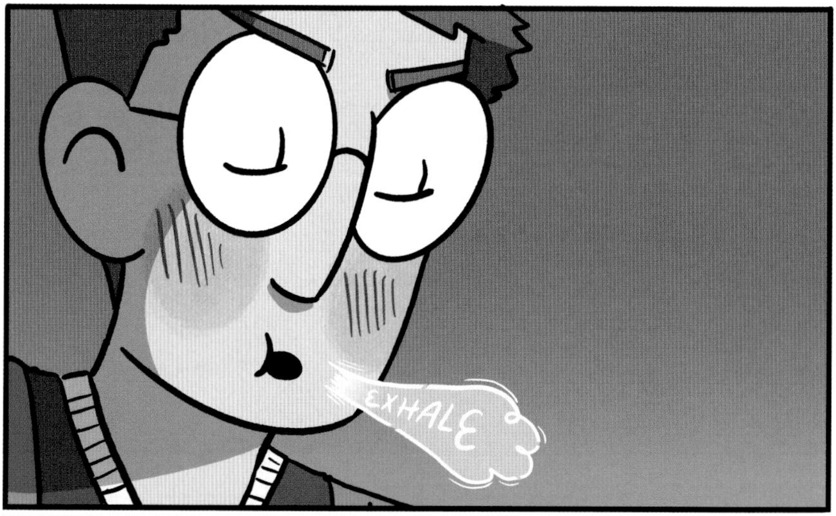
EXHALE

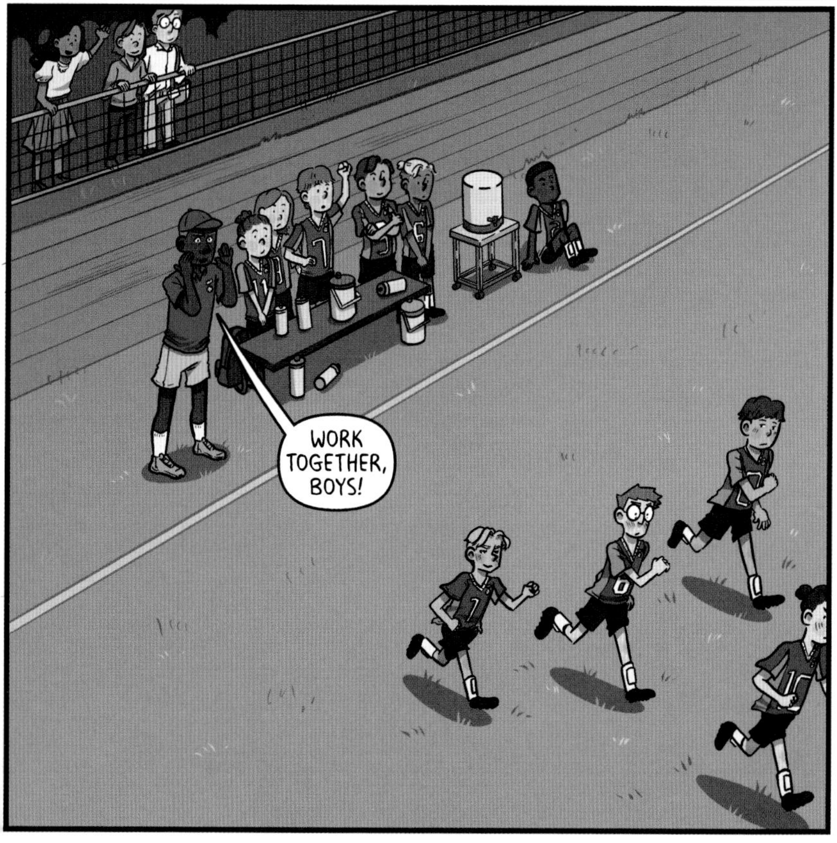
WORK TOGETHER, BOYS!

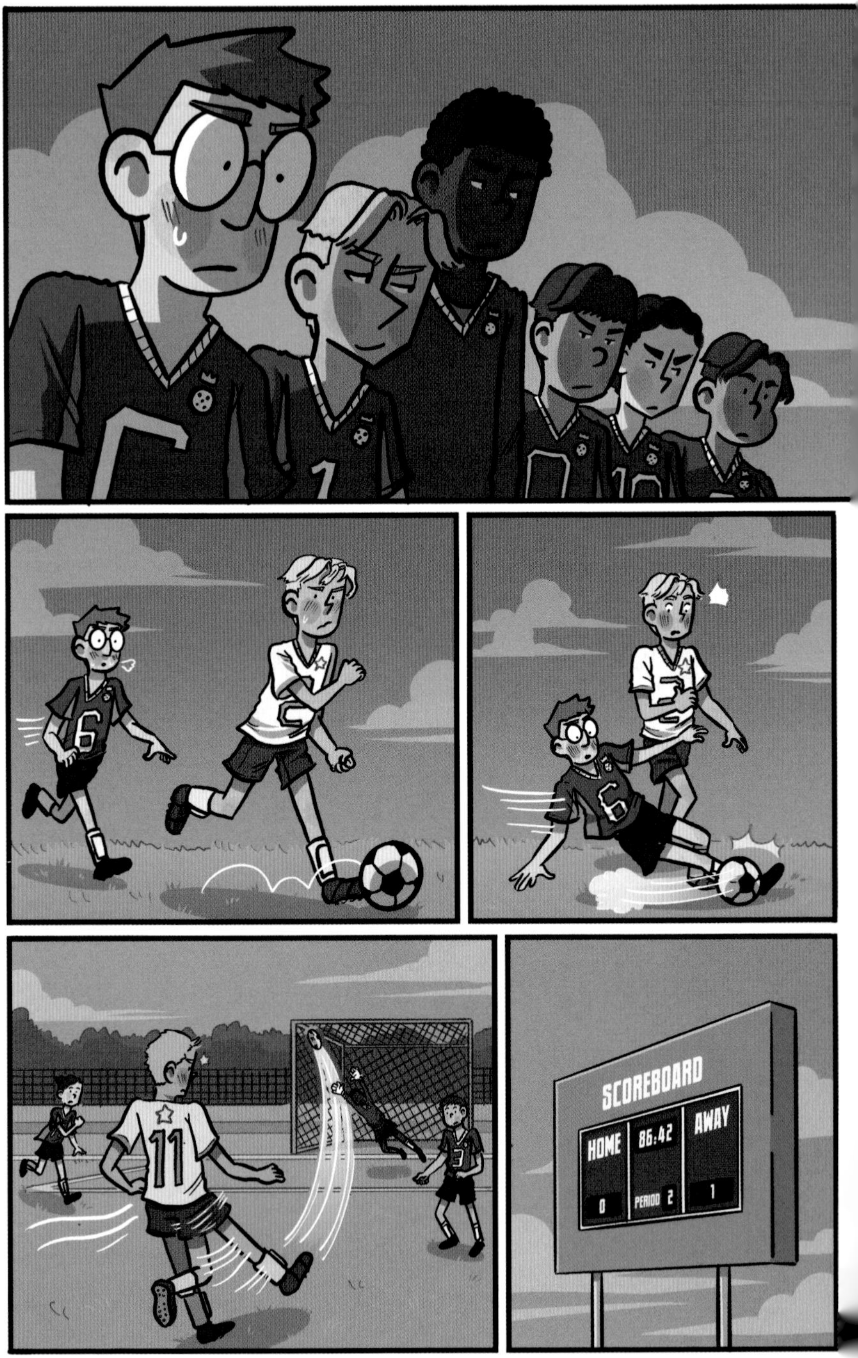
SCOREBOARD
HOME
86:42
AWAY
0
PERIOD 2
1

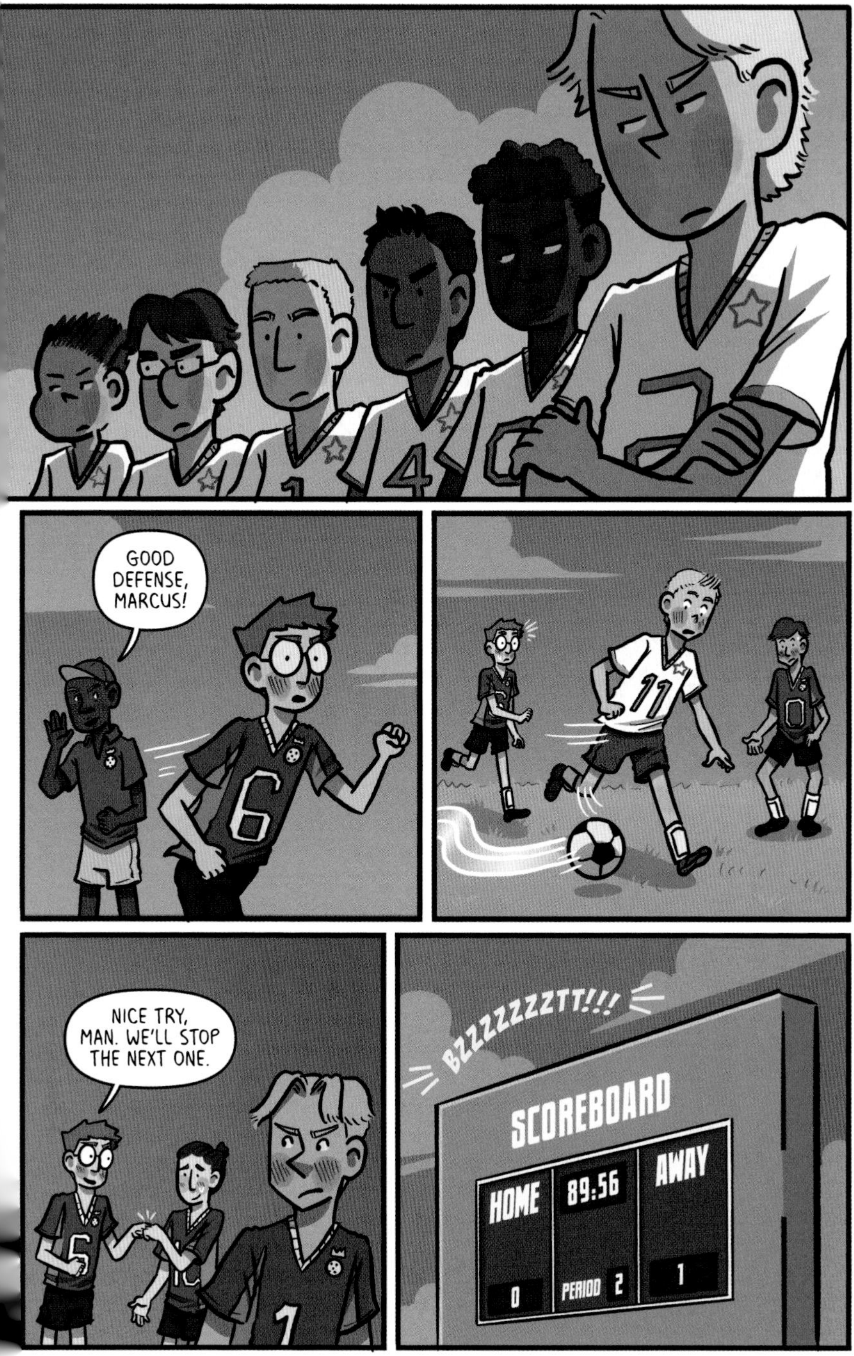
GOOD DEFENSE, MARCUS!
NICE TRY, MAN. WE'LL STOP THE NEXT ONE.
BZZZZZZZTT!!!
SCOREBOARD
HOME
89:56
AWAY
0
PERIOD 2
1

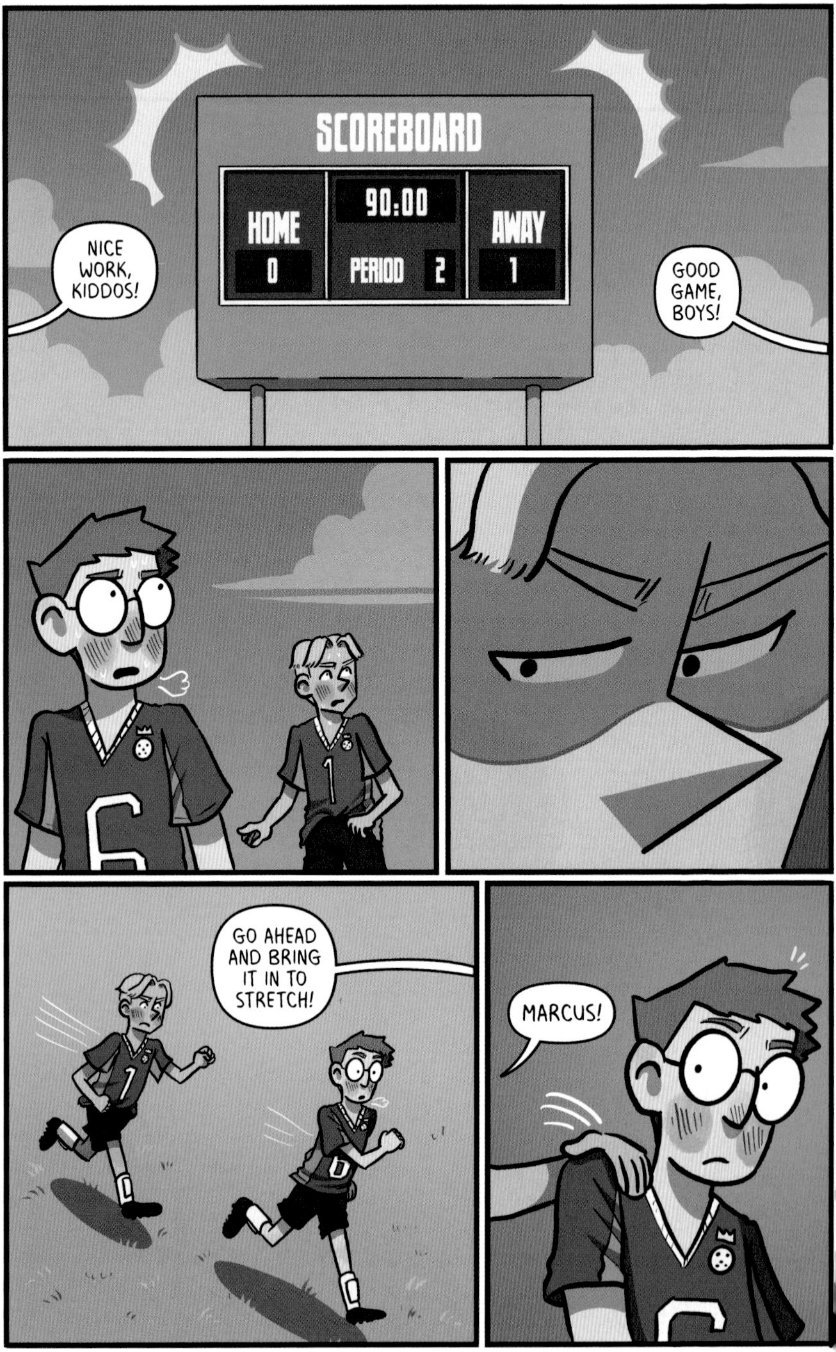
SCOREBOARD
HOME 0
90:00
PERIOD 2
AWAY 1
NICE WORK, KIDDOS!
GOOD GAME, BOYS!
GO AHEAD AND BRING IT IN TO STRETCH!
MARCUS!

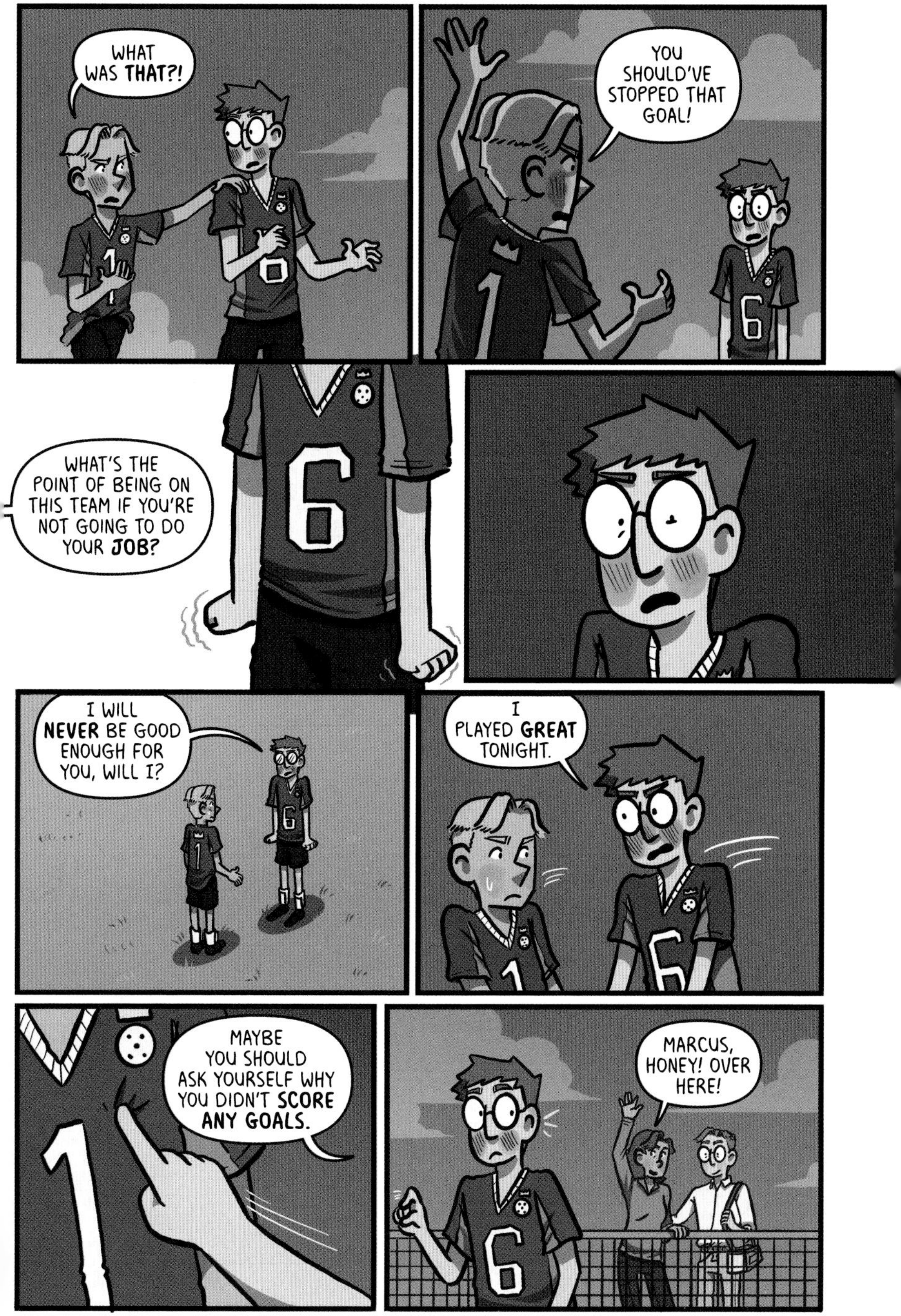
WHAT WAS THAT?!
YOU SHOULD'VE STOPPED THAT GOAL!
WHAT'S THE POINT OF BEING ON THIS TEAM IF YOU'RE NOT GOING TO DO YOUR JOB?
I WILL NEVER BE GOOD ENOUGH FOR YOU, WILL I?
I PLAYED GREAT TONIGHT.
MAYBE YOU SHOULD ASK YOURSELF WHY YOU DIDN'T SCORE ANY GOALS.
MARCUS, HONEY! OVER HERE!

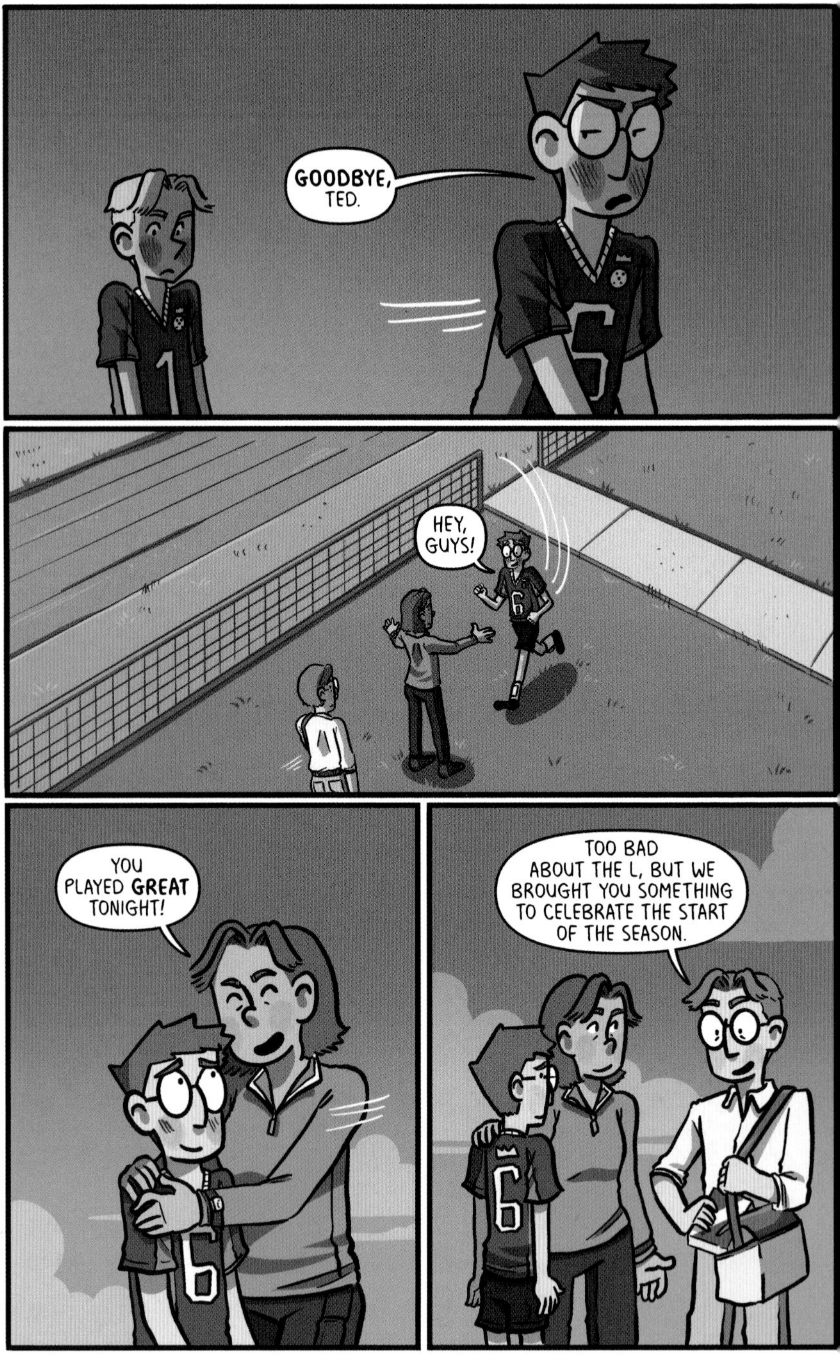
GOODBYE, TED.
HEY, GUYS!
YOU PLAYED **GREAT** TONIGHT!
TOO BAD ABOUT THE L, BUT WE BROUGHT YOU SOMETHING TO CELEBRATE THE START OF THE SEASON.

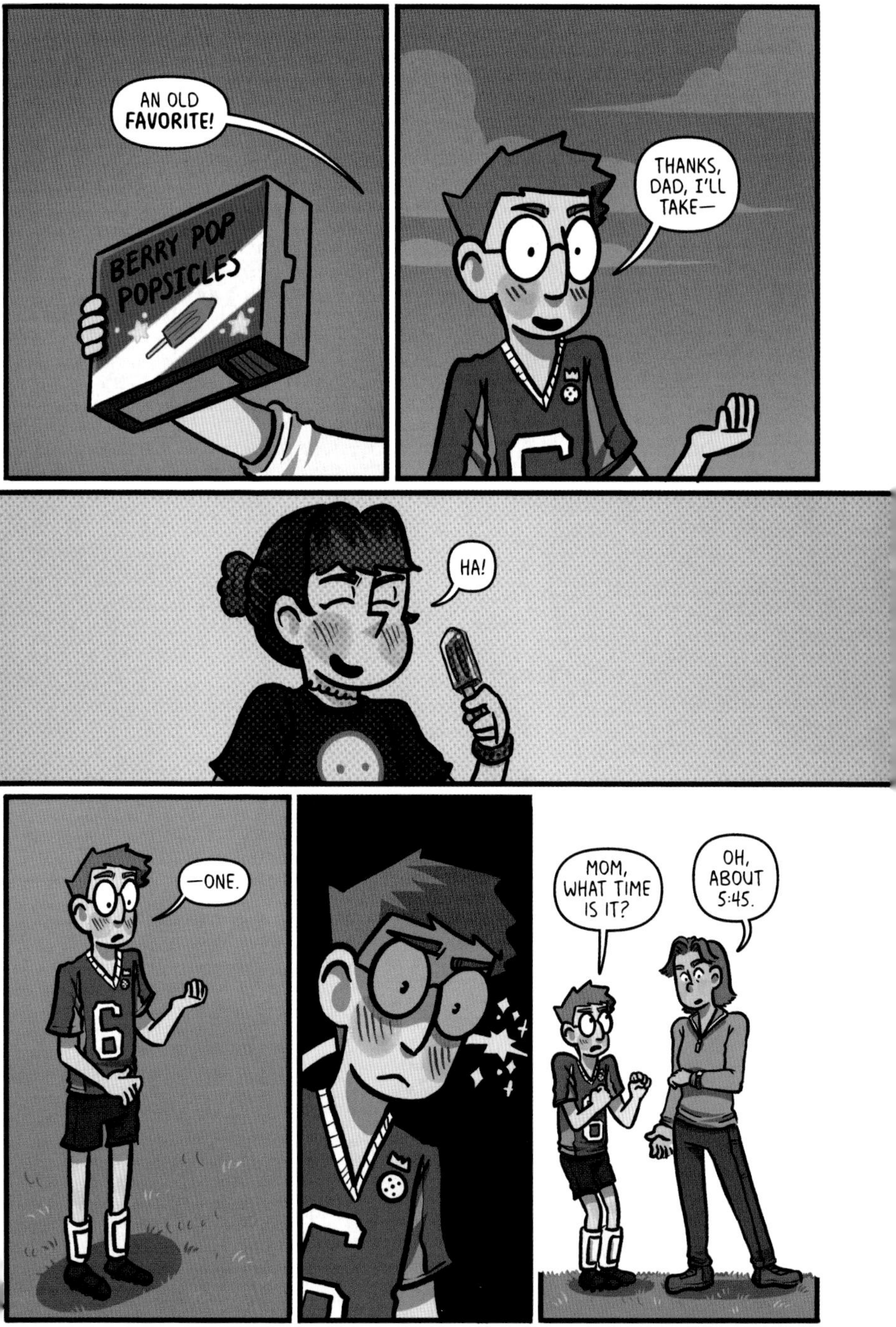
AN OLD FAVORITE!
BERRY POP POPSICLES
THANKS, DAD, I'LL TAKE—
HA!
—ONE.
MOM, WHAT TIME IS IT?
OH, ABOUT 5:45.

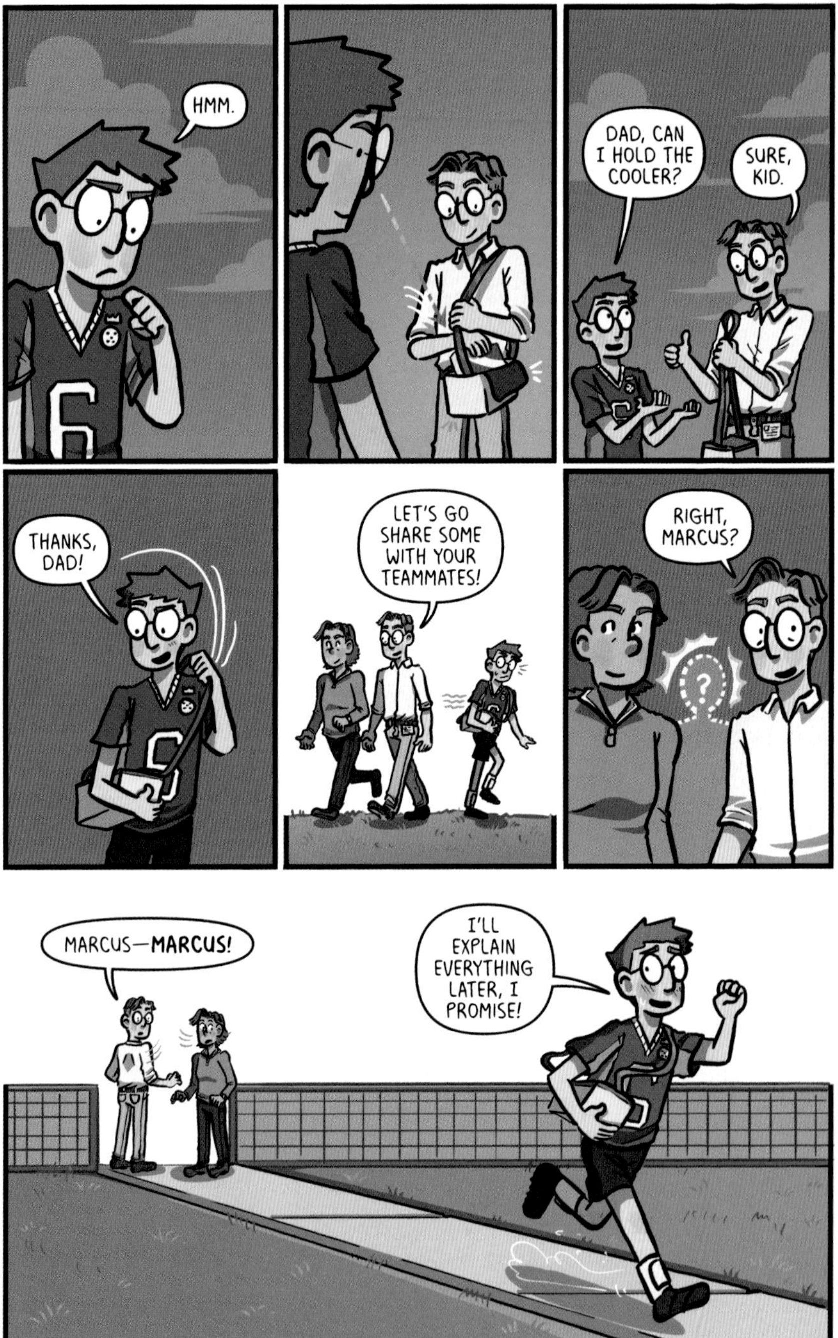
HMM.
DAD, CAN I HOLD THE COOLER?
SURE, KID.
THANKS, DAD!
LET'S GO SHARE SOME WITH YOUR TEAMMATES!
RIGHT, MARCUS?
MARCUS—**MARCUS!**
I'LL EXPLAIN EVERYTHING LATER, I PROMISE!

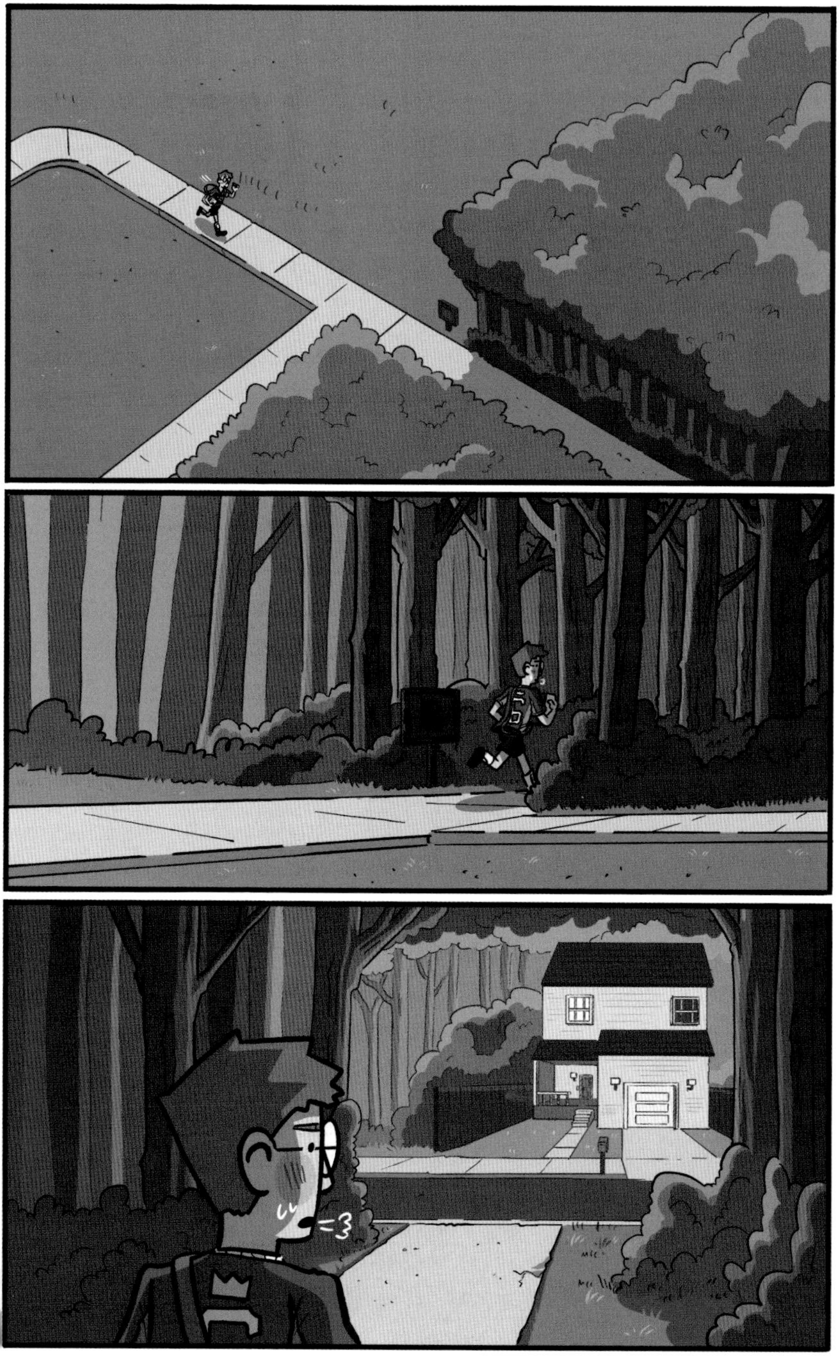

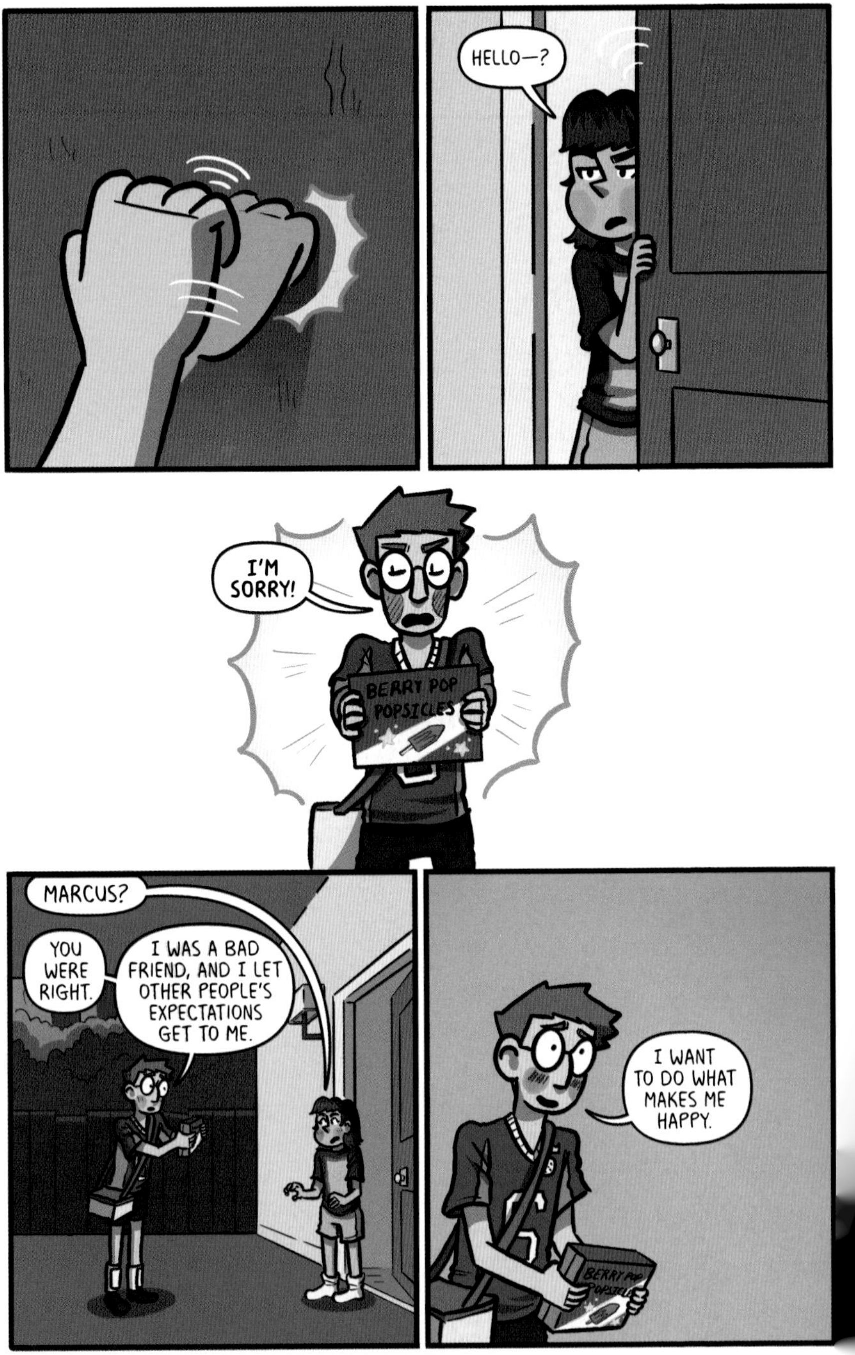
HELLO—?
I'M SORRY!
BERRY POP POPSICLES
MARCUS?
YOU WERE RIGHT.
I WAS A BAD FRIEND, AND I LET OTHER PEOPLE'S EXPECTATIONS GET TO ME.
I WANT TO DO WHAT MAKES ME HAPPY.

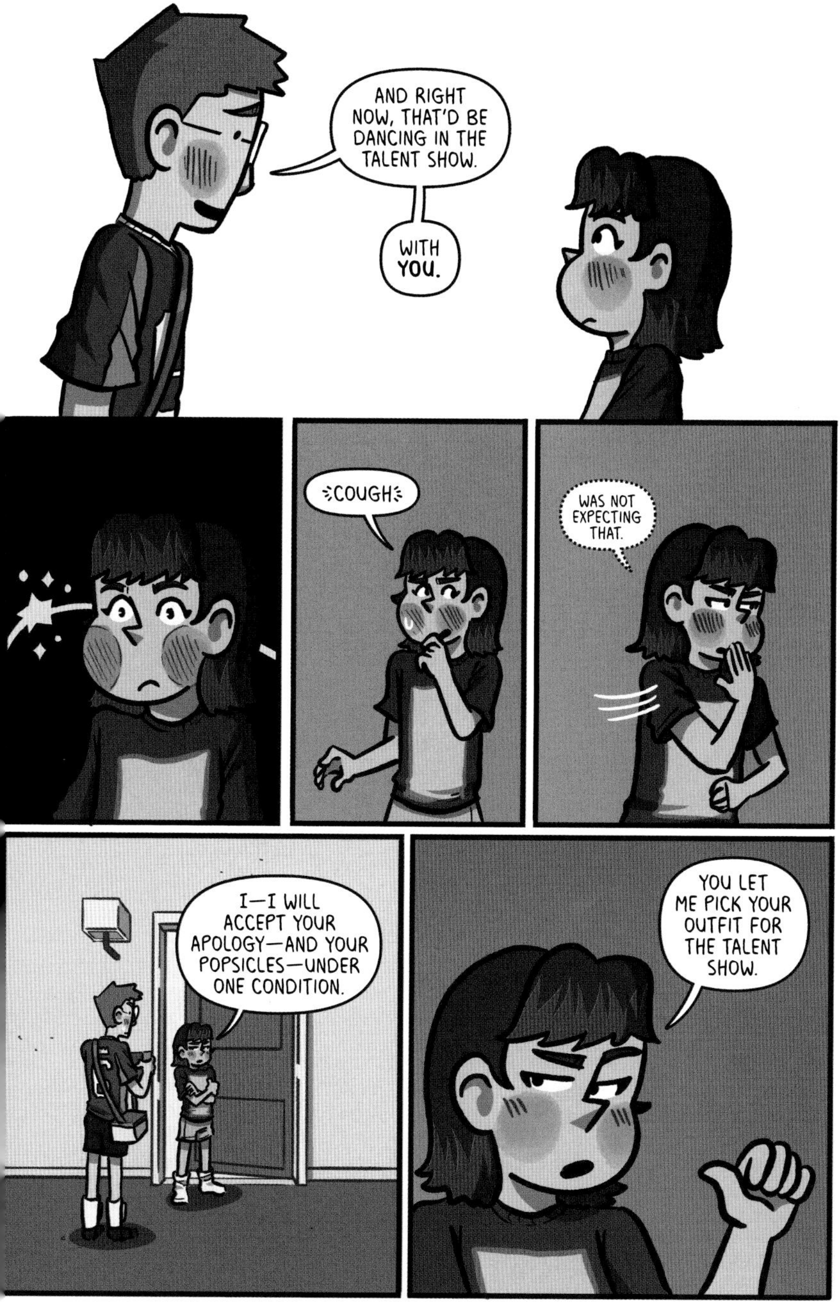
AND RIGHT NOW, THAT'D BE DANCING IN THE TALENT SHOW.
WITH YOU.
COUGH
WAS NOT EXPECTING THAT.
I—I WILL ACCEPT YOUR APOLOGY—AND YOUR POPSICLES—UNDER ONE CONDITION.
YOU LET ME PICK YOUR OUTFIT FOR THE TALENT SHOW.

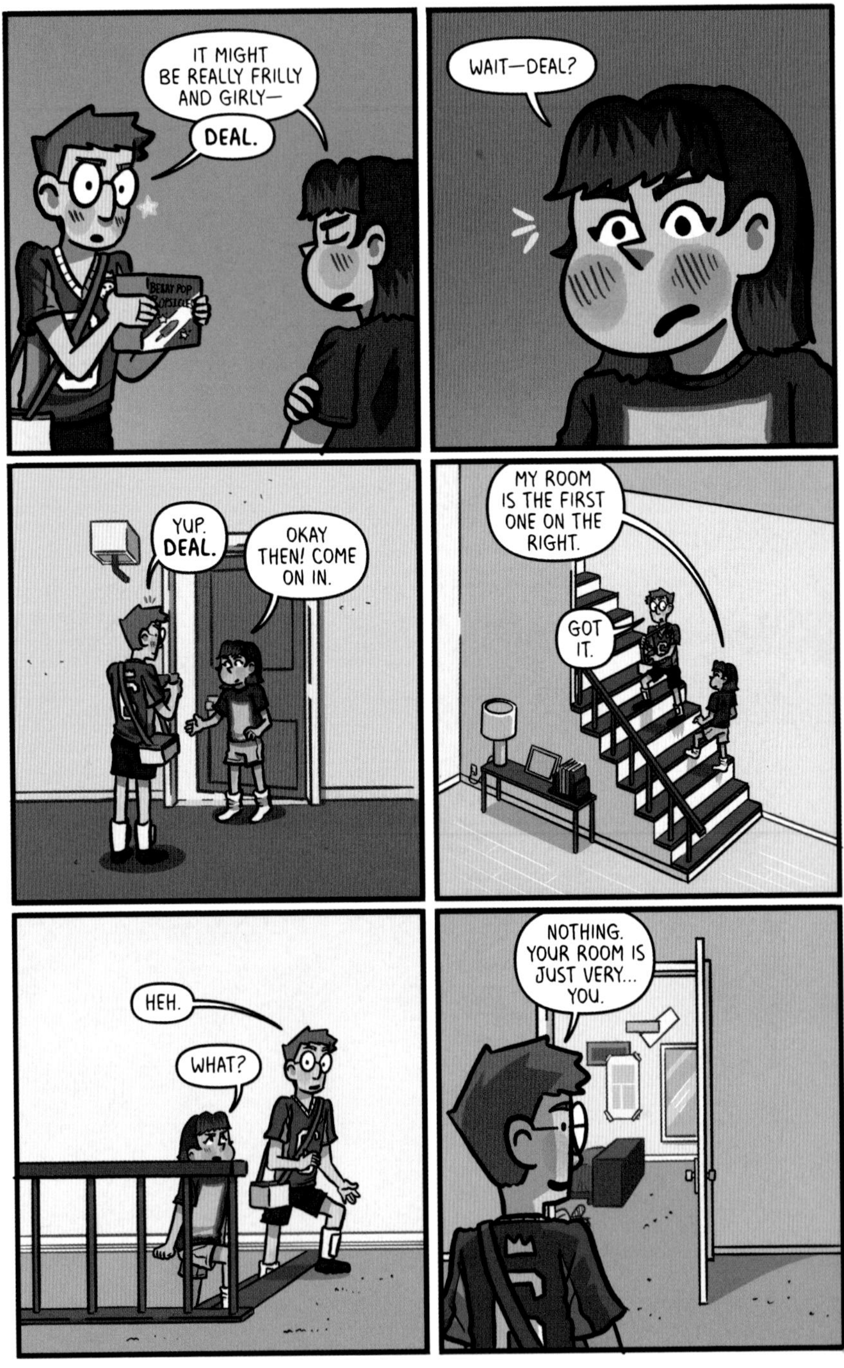
IT MIGHT BE REALLY FRILLY AND GIRLY—
DEAL.
BERRY POP POPSICLES
WAIT—DEAL?
YUP. DEAL.
OKAY THEN! COME ON IN.
MY ROOM IS THE FIRST ONE ON THE RIGHT.
GOT IT.
HEH.
WHAT?
NOTHING. YOUR ROOM IS JUST VERY... YOU.

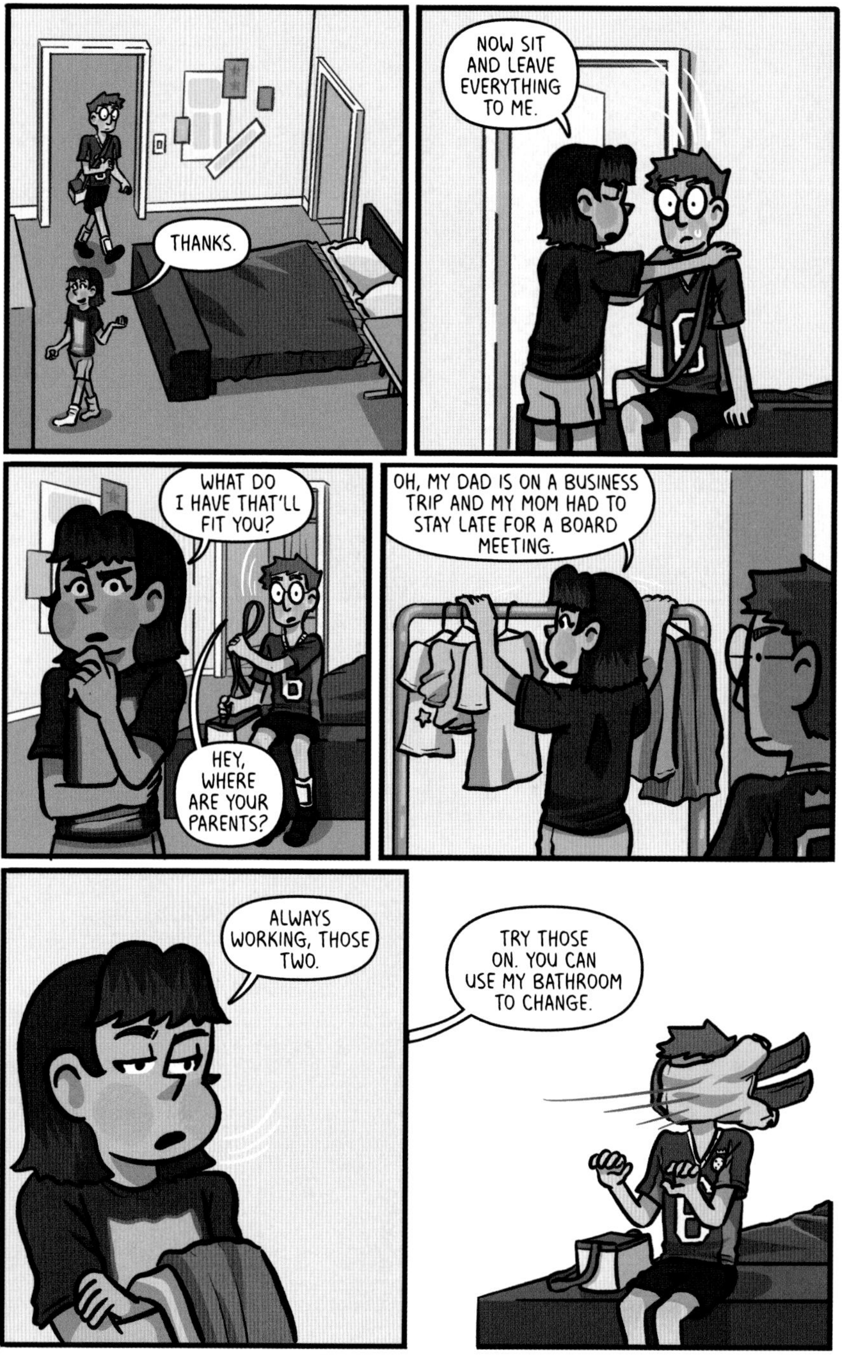
THANKS.
NOW SIT AND LEAVE EVERYTHING TO ME.
WHAT DO I HAVE THAT'LL FIT YOU?
HEY, WHERE ARE YOUR PARENTS?
OH, MY DAD IS ON A BUSINESS TRIP AND MY MOM HAD TO STAY LATE FOR A BOARD MEETING.
ALWAYS WORKING, THOSE TWO.
TRY THOSE ON. YOU CAN USE MY BATHROOM TO CHANGE.

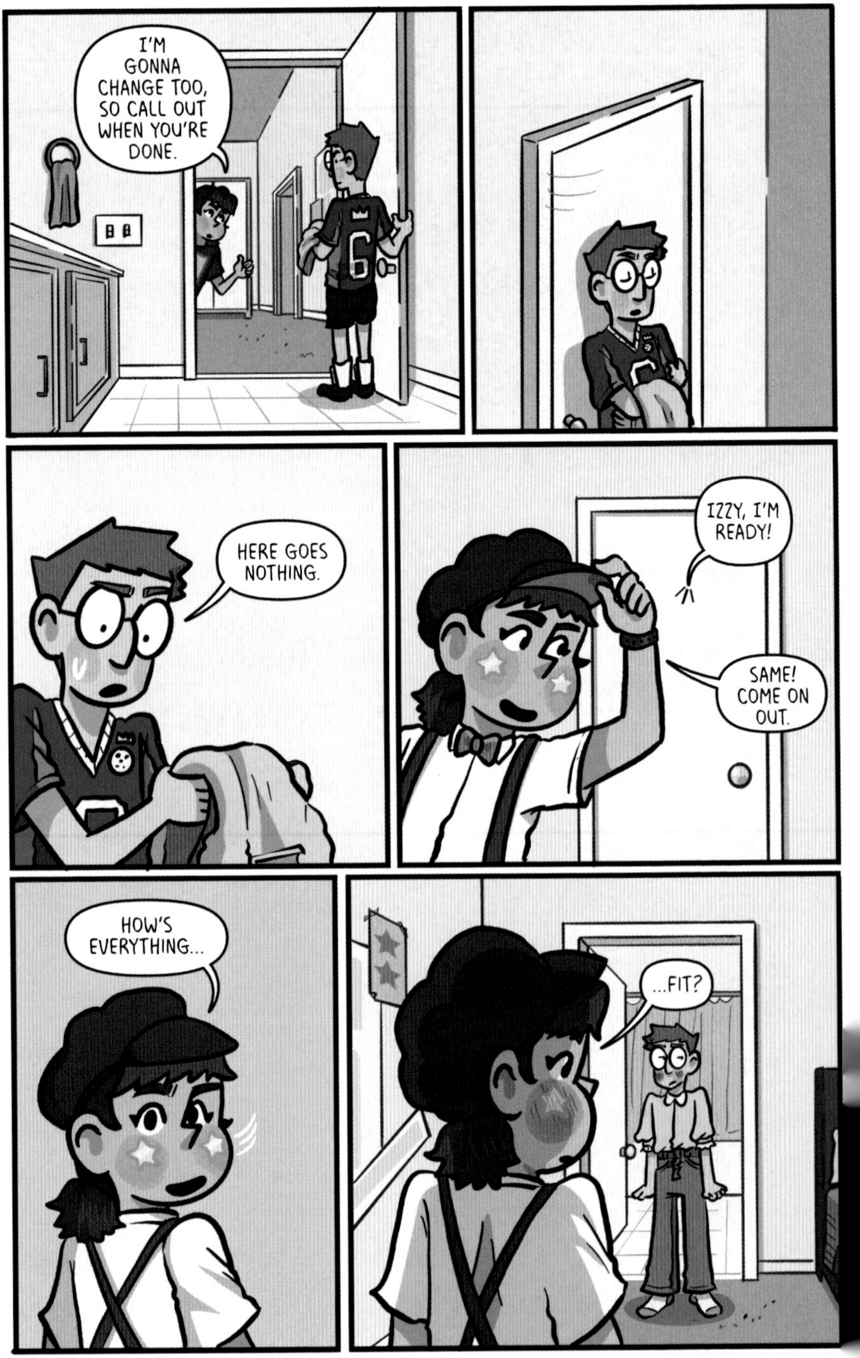
I'M GONNA CHANGE TOO, SO CALL OUT WHEN YOU'RE DONE.
HERE GOES NOTHING.
IZZY, I'M READY!
SAME! COME ON OUT.
HOW'S EVERYTHING...
...FIT?

THE PANTS ARE A LITTLE TIGHT, BUT EVERYTHING SEEMS OKAY TO DANCE IN.

I HAVEN'T LOOKED THAT CLOSELY YET, THOUGH.

PERFECT.

YOU LOOK NICE!

THANKS!

NOW, BEFORE YOU REALLY LOOK AT YOURSELF...

...LET'S DO SOME MAKEUP!

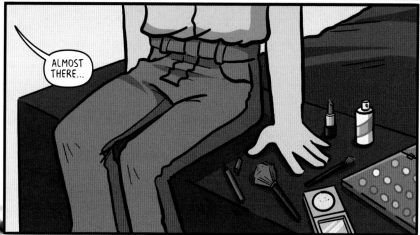

ALMOST THERE...

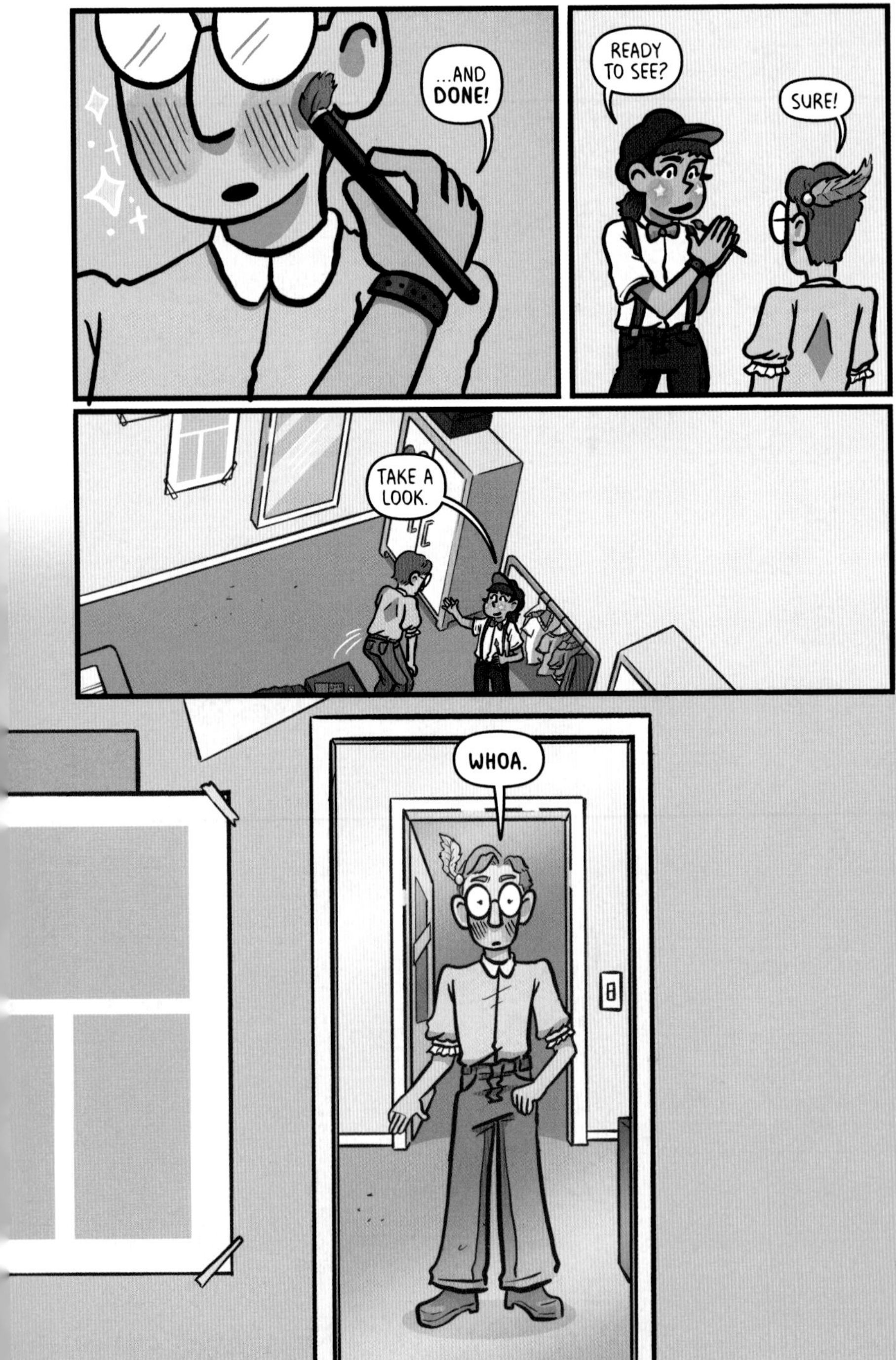
...AND DONE!
READY TO SEE?
SURE!
TAKE A LOOK.
WHOA.

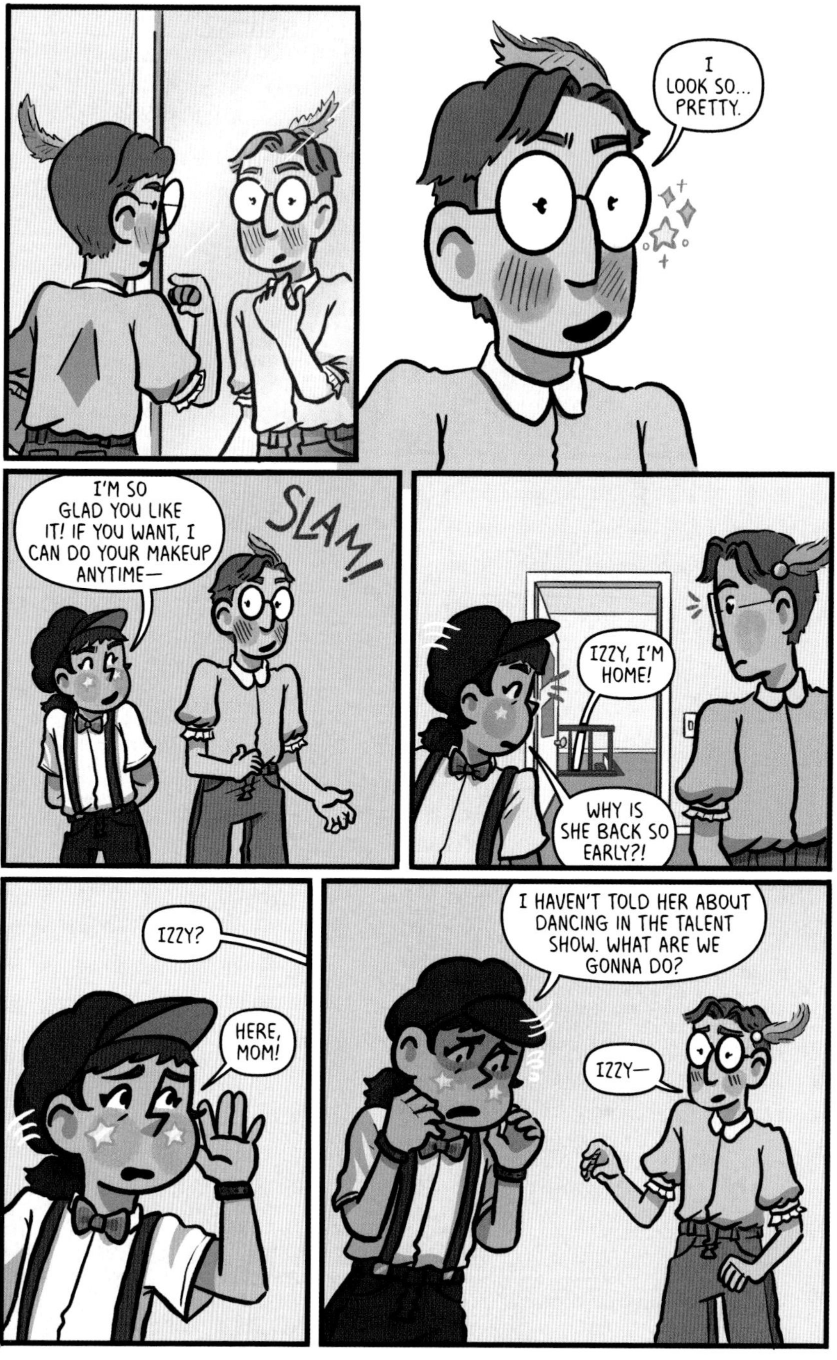
I LOOK SO... PRETTY.
I'M SO GLAD YOU LIKE IT! IF YOU WANT, I CAN DO YOUR MAKEUP ANYTIME—
SLAM!
IZZY, I'M HOME!
WHY IS SHE BACK SO EARLY?!
IZZY?
HERE, MOM!
I HAVEN'T TOLD HER ABOUT DANCING IN THE TALENT SHOW. WHAT ARE WE GONNA DO?
IZZY—

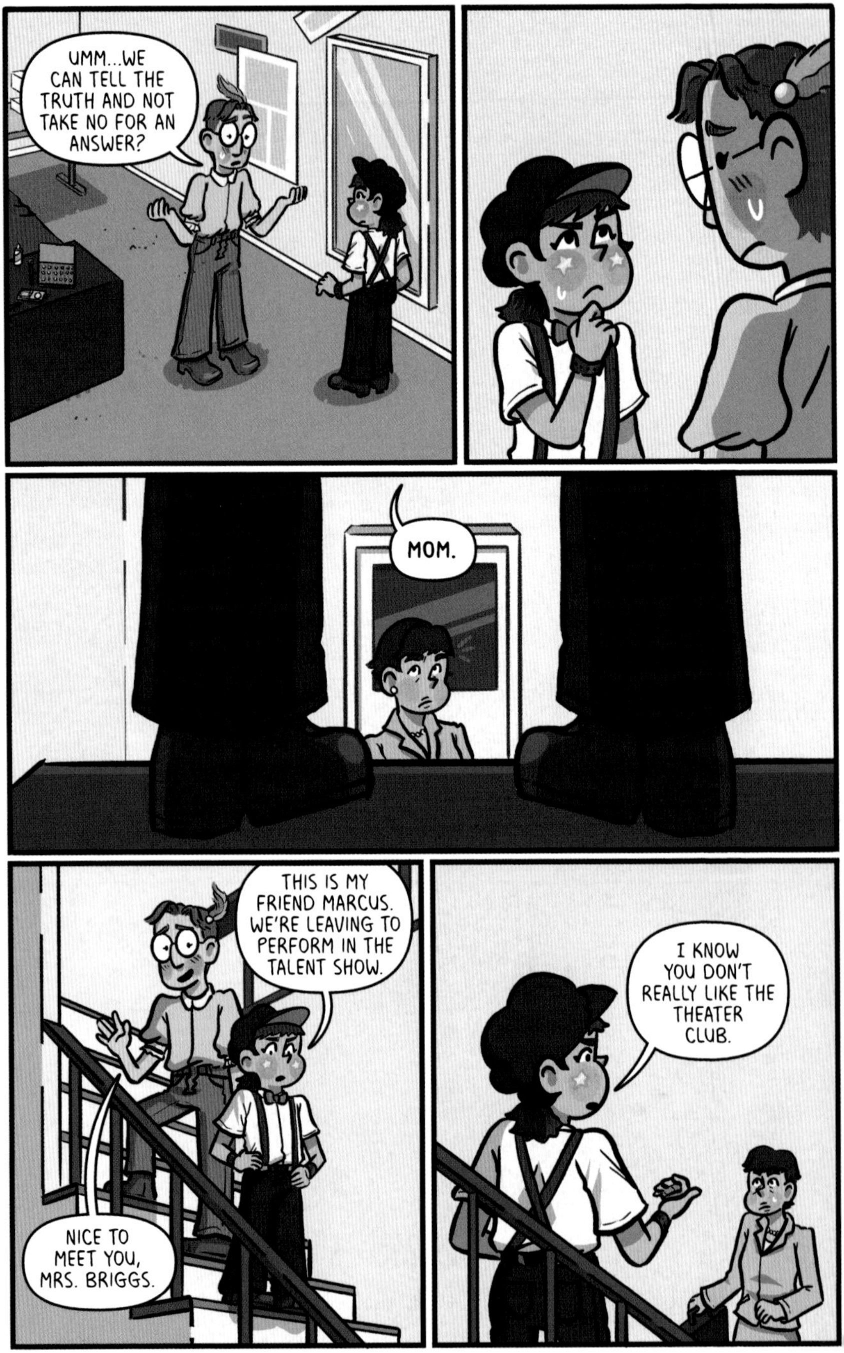
UMM...WE CAN TELL THE TRUTH AND NOT TAKE NO FOR AN ANSWER?
MOM.
THIS IS MY FRIEND MARCUS. WE'RE LEAVING TO PERFORM IN THE TALENT SHOW.
NICE TO MEET YOU, MRS. BRIGGS.
I KNOW YOU DON'T REALLY LIKE THE THEATER CLUB.

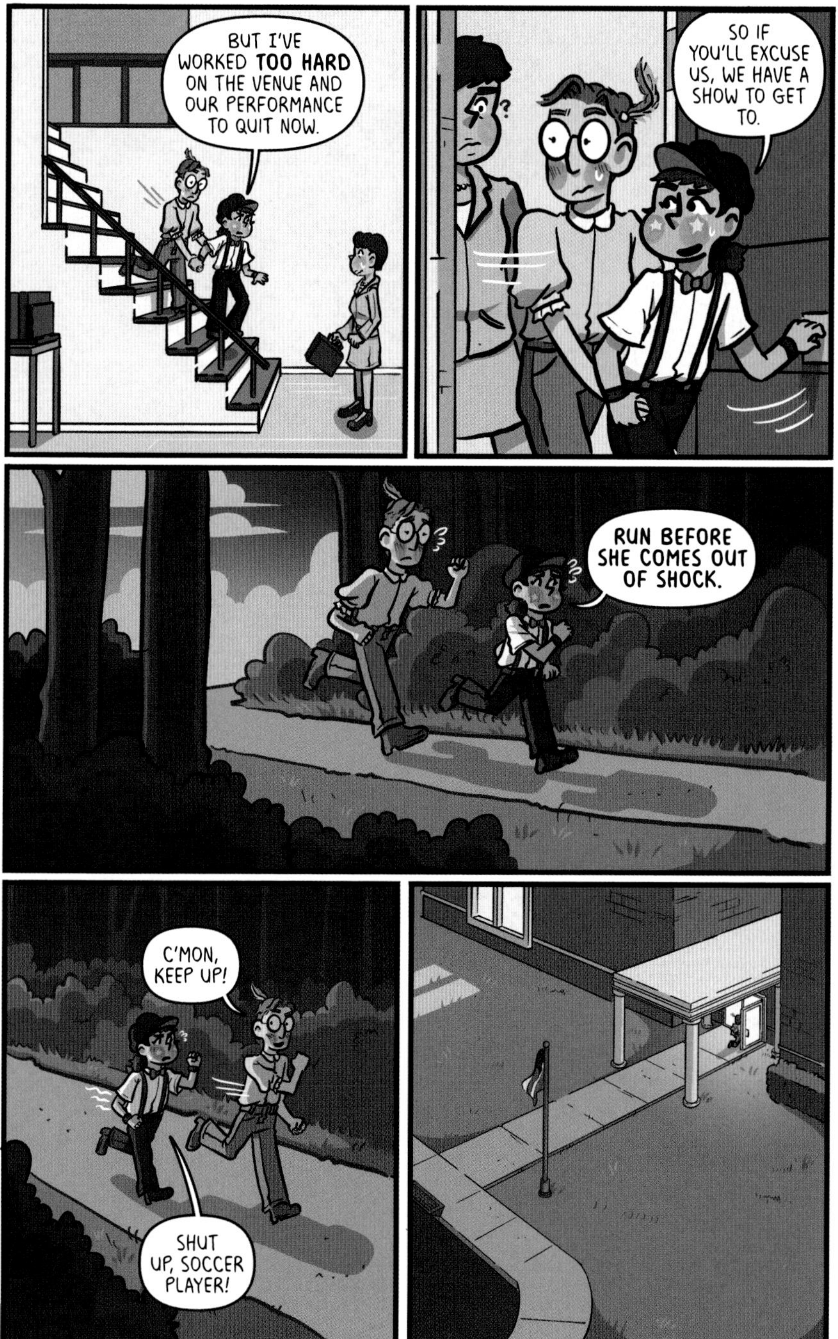
BUT I'VE WORKED TOO HARD ON THE VENUE AND OUR PERFORMANCE TO QUIT NOW.
SO IF YOU'LL EXCUSE US, WE HAVE A SHOW TO GET TO.
RUN BEFORE SHE COMES OUT OF SHOCK.
C'MON, KEEP UP!
SHUT UP, SOCCER PLAYER!

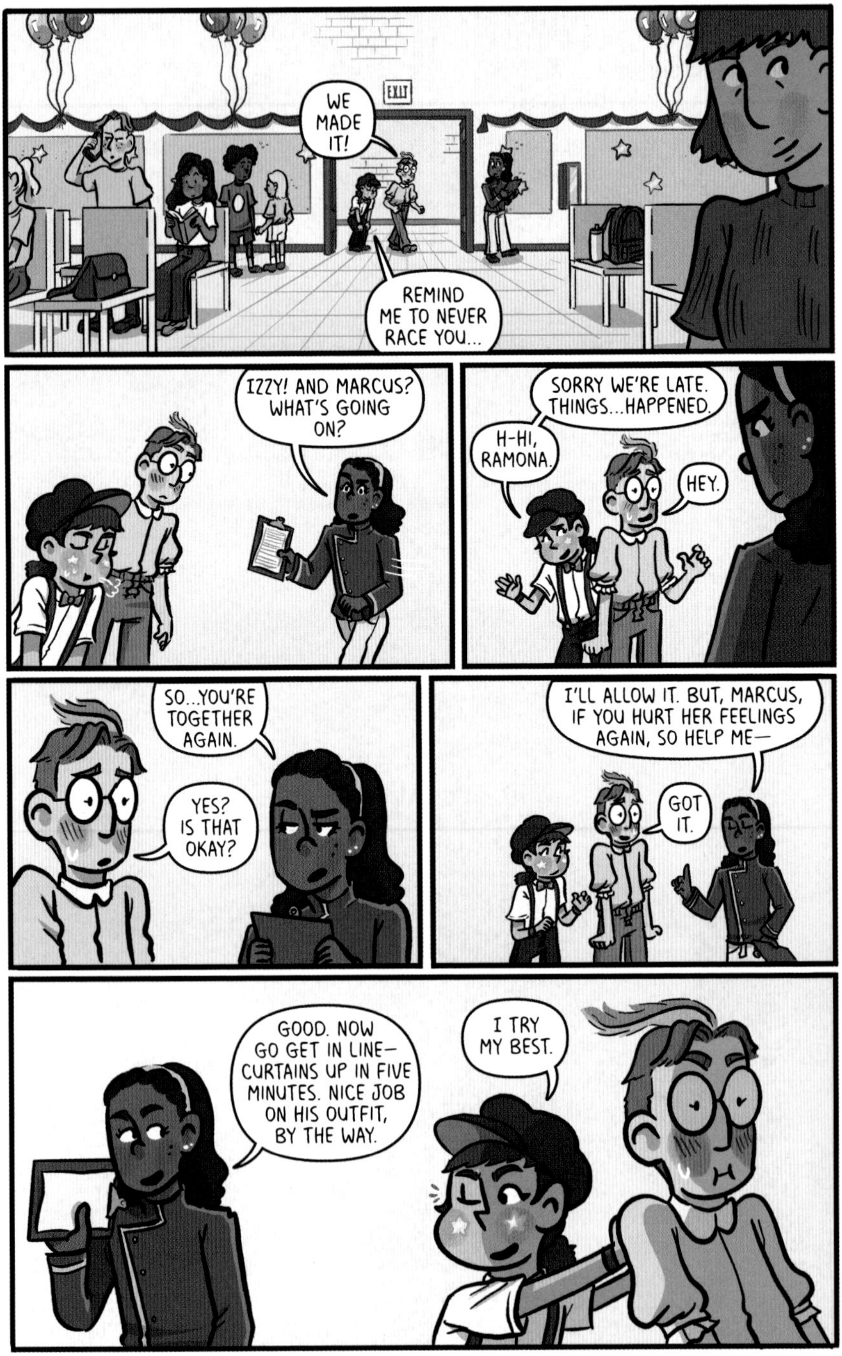
EXIT
WE MADE IT!
REMIND ME TO NEVER RACE YOU...
IZZY! AND MARCUS? WHAT'S GOING ON?
SORRY WE'RE LATE. THINGS...HAPPENED.
H-HI, RAMONA.
HEY.
SO...YOU'RE TOGETHER AGAIN.
YES? IS THAT OKAY?
I'LL ALLOW IT. BUT, MARCUS, IF YOU HURT HER FEELINGS AGAIN, SO HELP ME—
GOT IT.
GOOD. NOW GO GET IN LINE—CURTAINS UP IN FIVE MINUTES. NICE JOB ON HIS OUTFIT, BY THE WAY.
I TRY MY BEST.

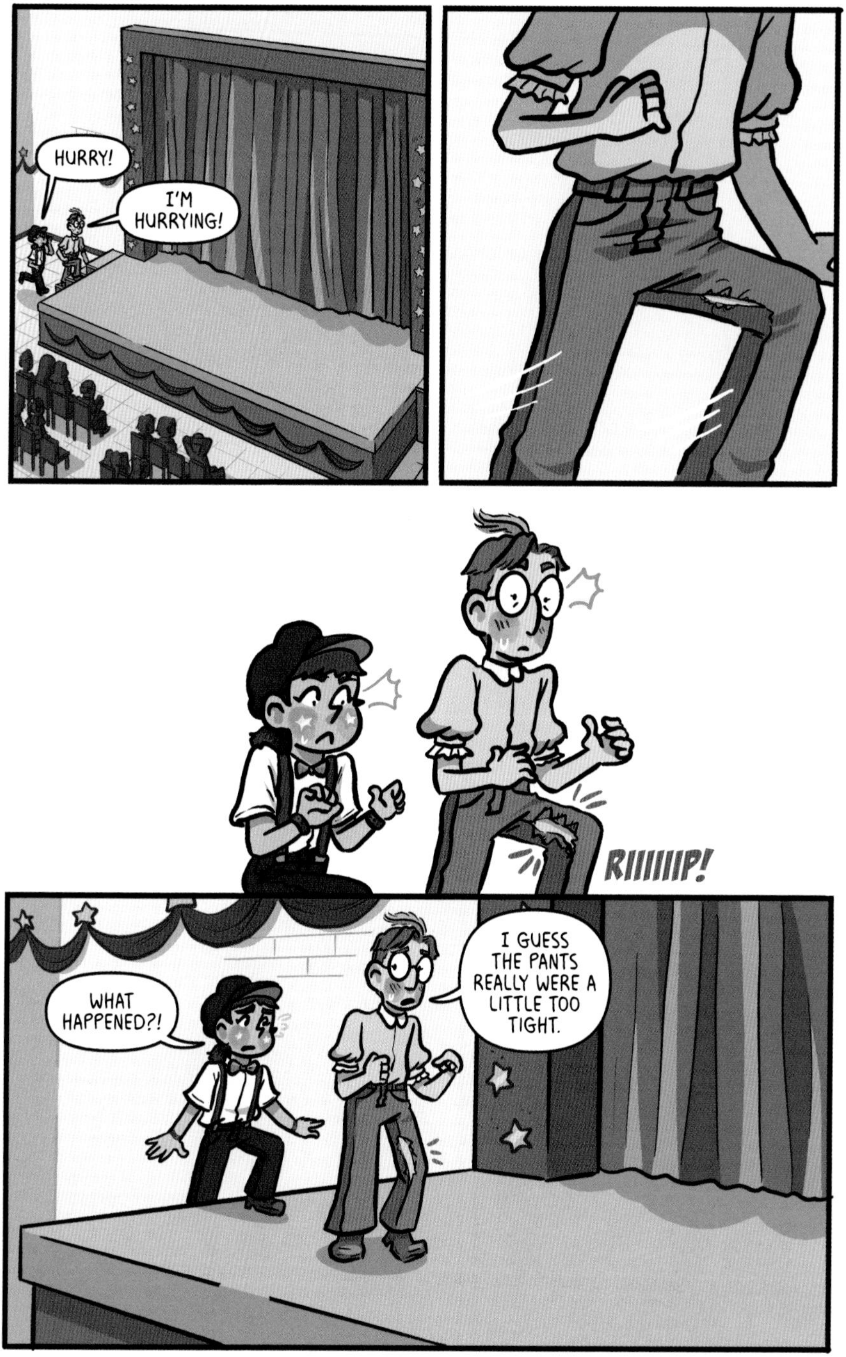
HURRY!
I'M HURRYING!
RIIIIIIP!
WHAT HAPPENED?!
I GUESS THE PANTS REALLY WERE A LITTLE TOO TIGHT.

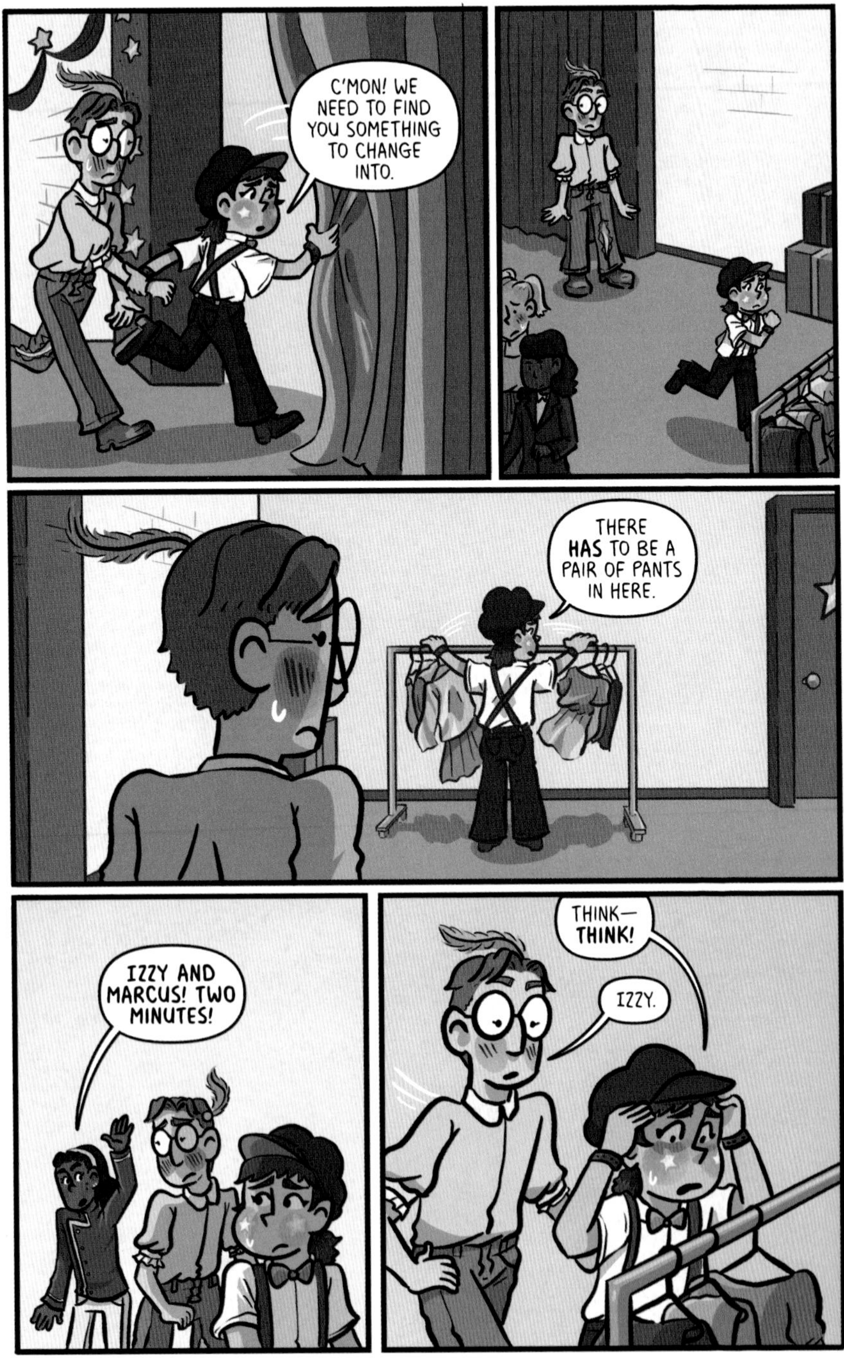
C'MON! WE NEED TO FIND YOU SOMETHING TO CHANGE INTO.
THERE **HAS** TO BE A PAIR OF PANTS IN HERE.
IZZY AND MARCUS! TWO MINUTES!
THINK—**THINK!**
IZZY.

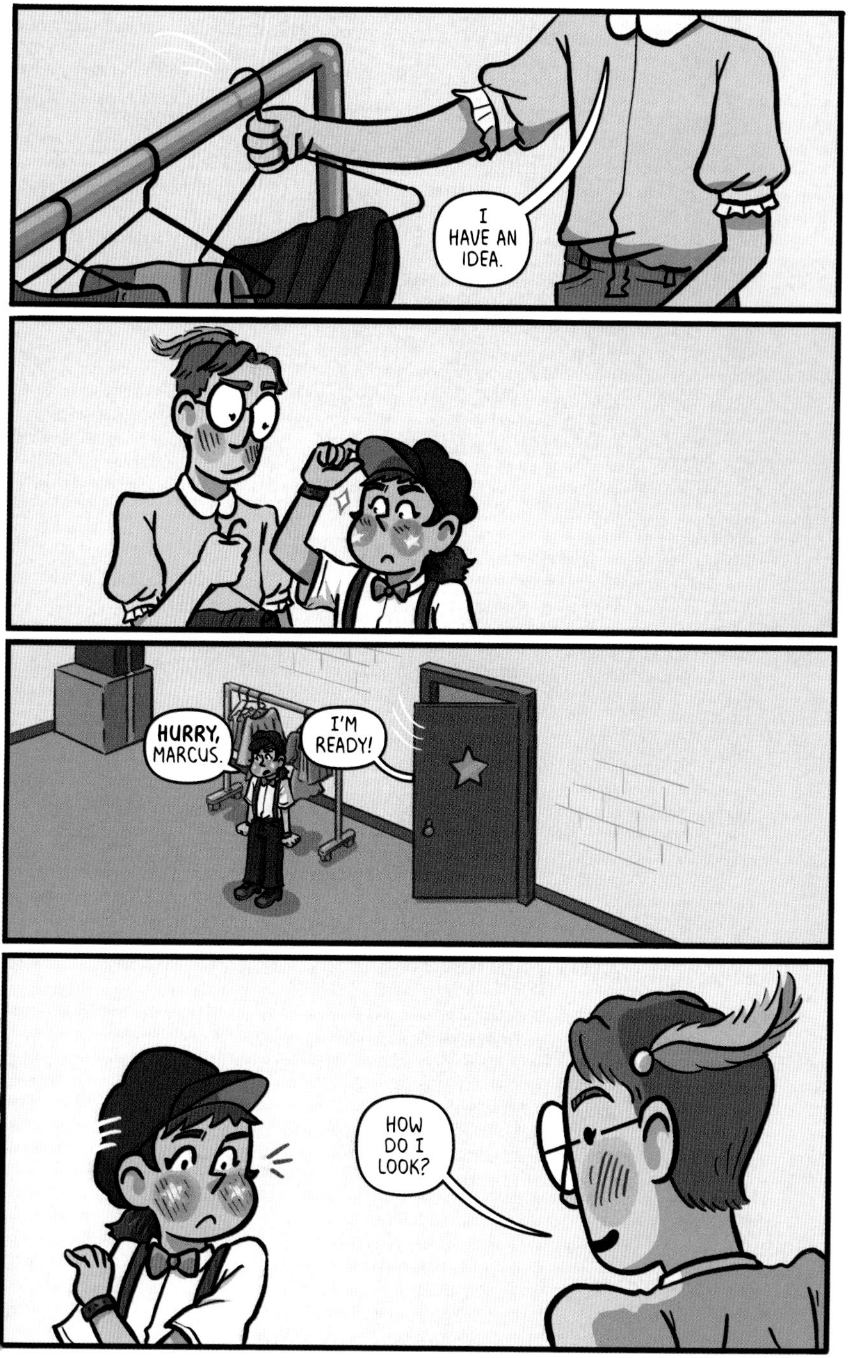
I HAVE AN IDEA.
HURRY, MARCUS.
I'M READY!
HOW DO I LOOK?

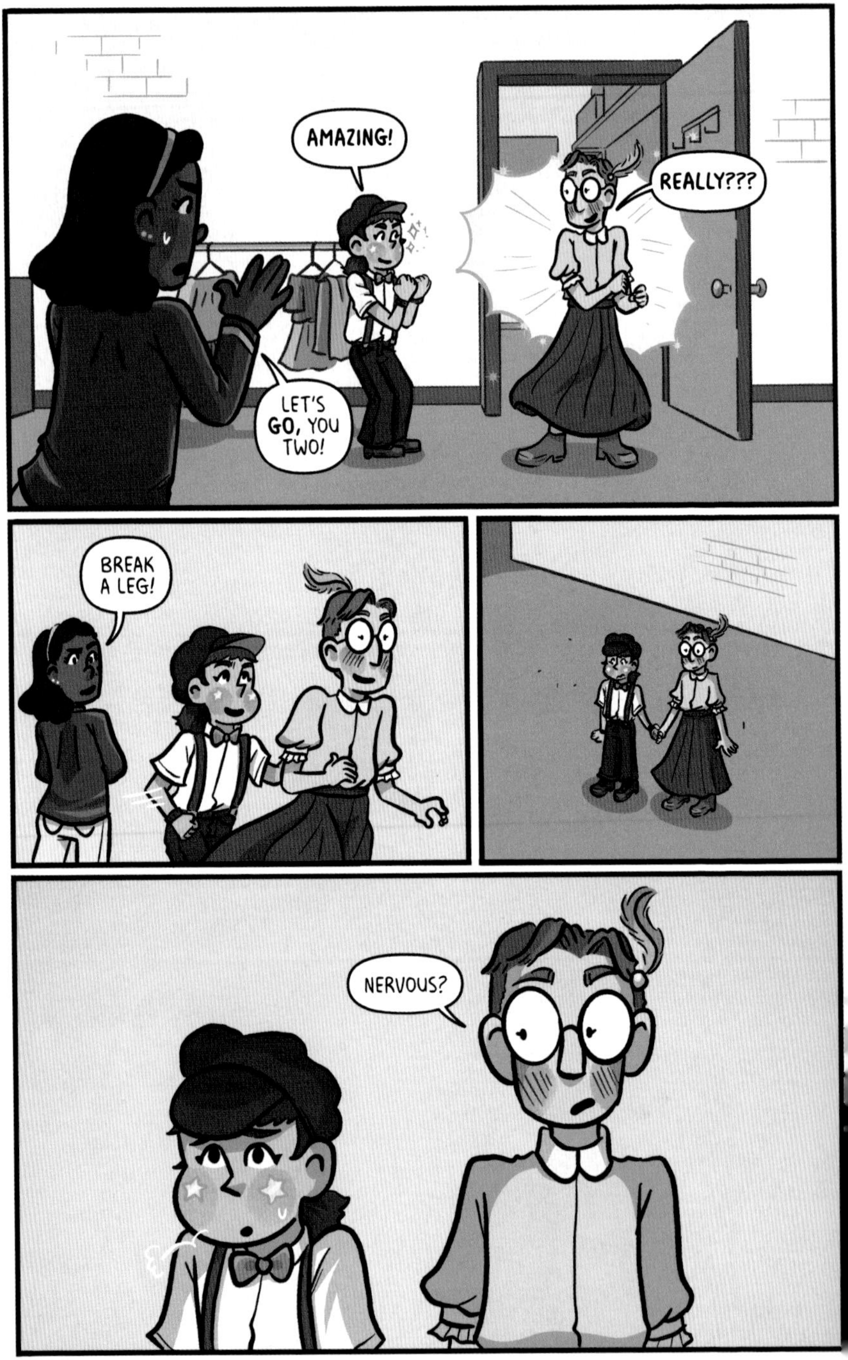
AMAZING!
REALLY???
LET'S **GO,** YOU TWO!
BREAK A LEG!
NERVOUS?

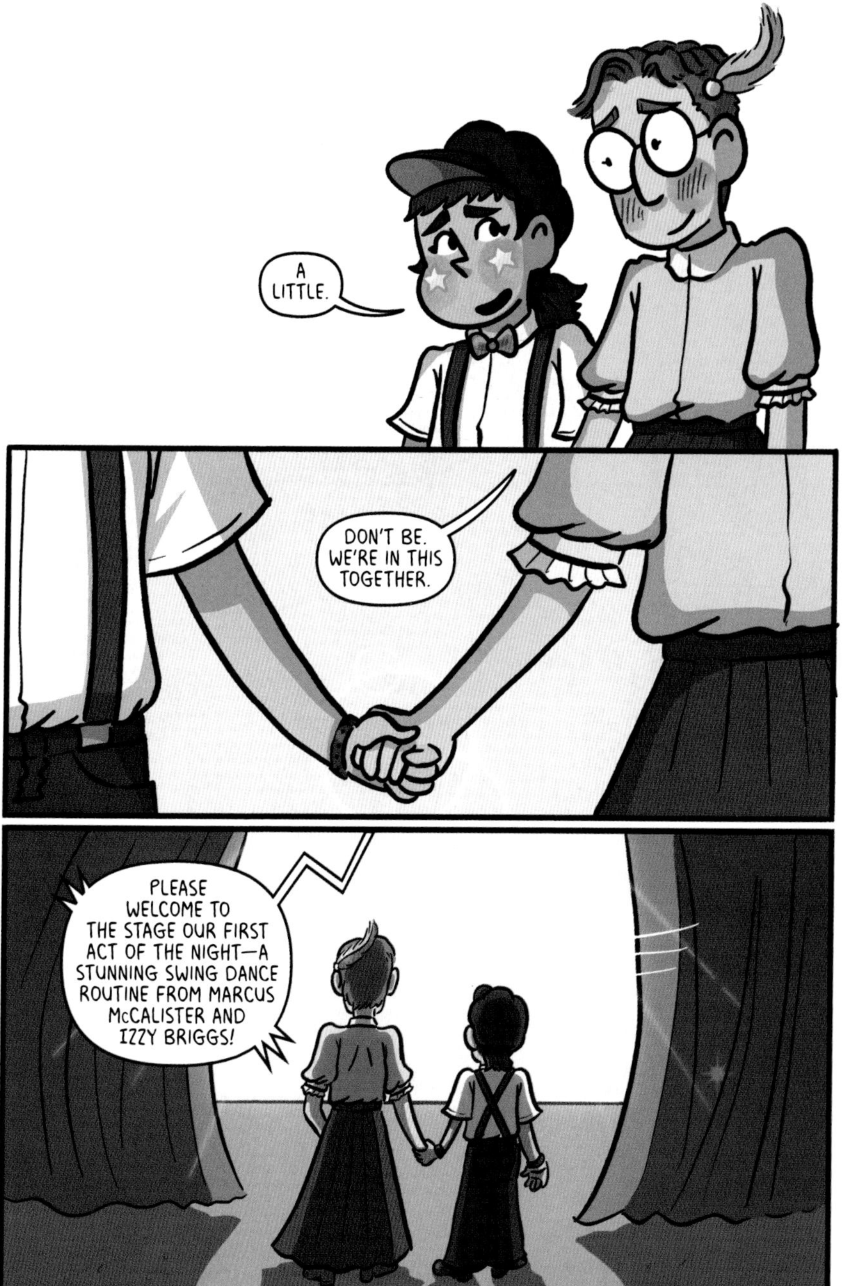
A LITTLE.
DON'T BE. WE'RE IN THIS TOGETHER.
PLEASE WELCOME TO THE STAGE OUR FIRST ACT OF THE NIGHT—A STUNNING SWING DANCE ROUTINE FROM MARCUS McCALISTER AND IZZY BRIGGS!

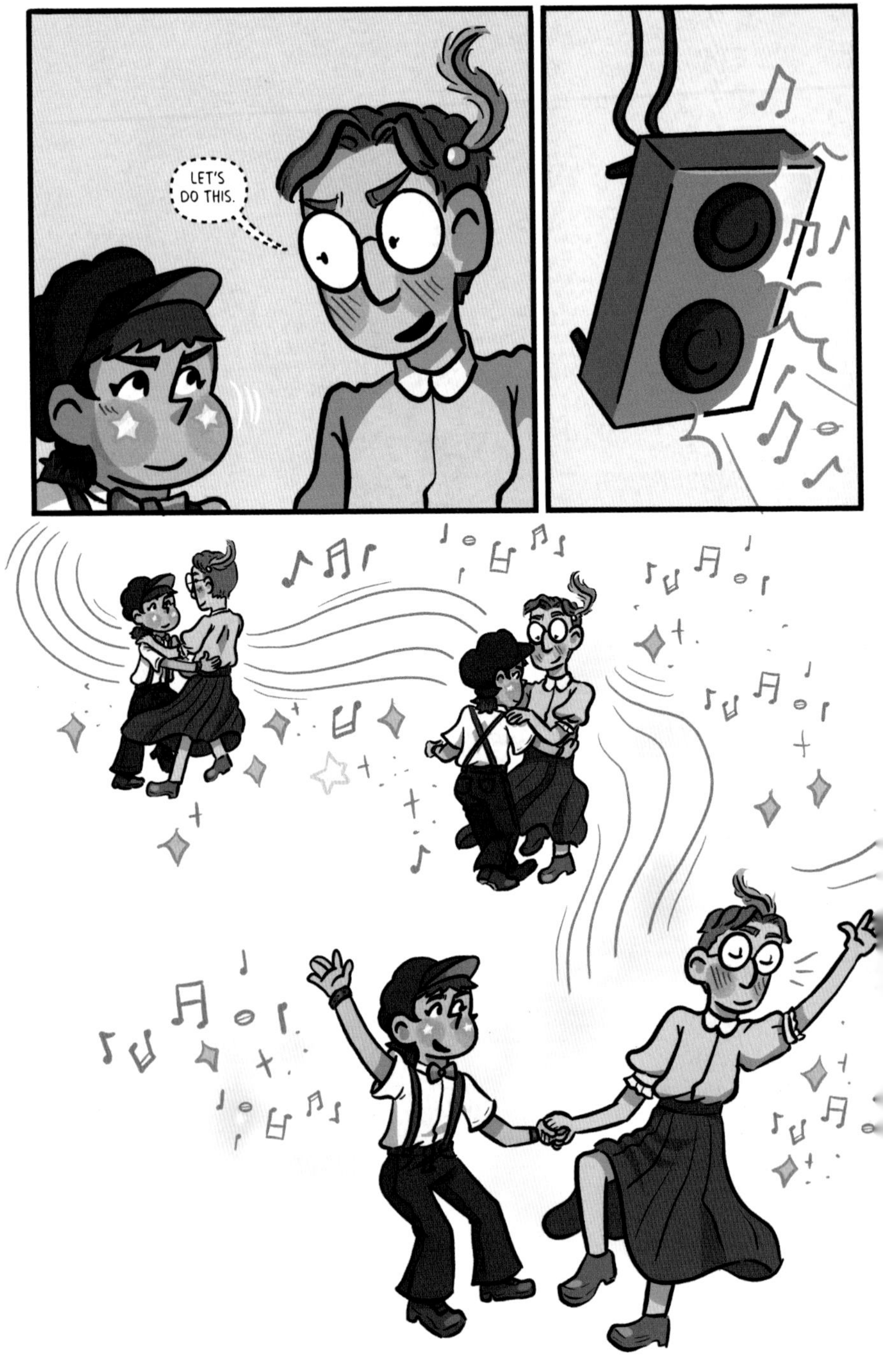
LET'S DO THIS.

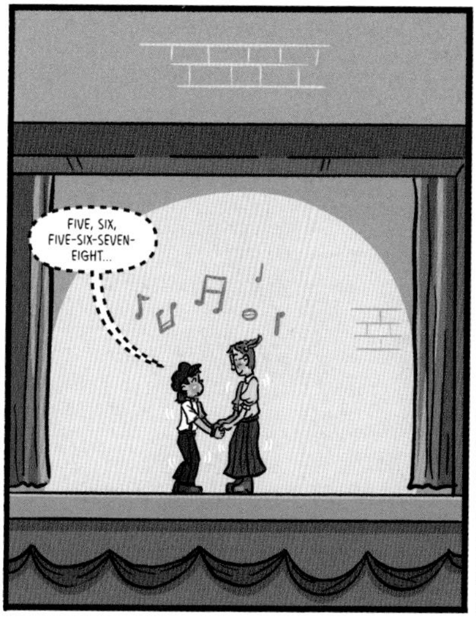
FIVE, SIX,
FIVE-SIX-SEVEN-
EIGHT...

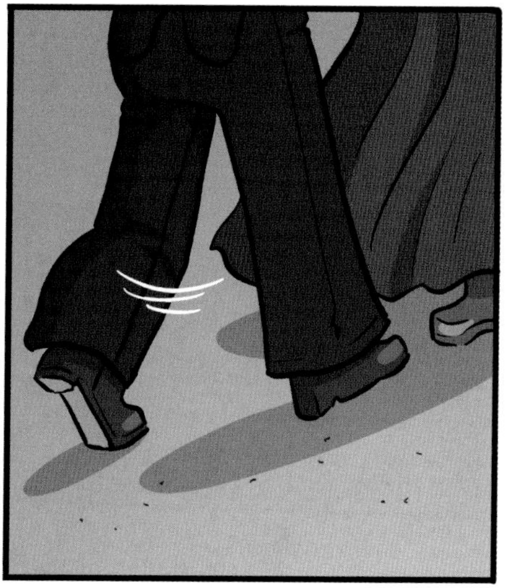

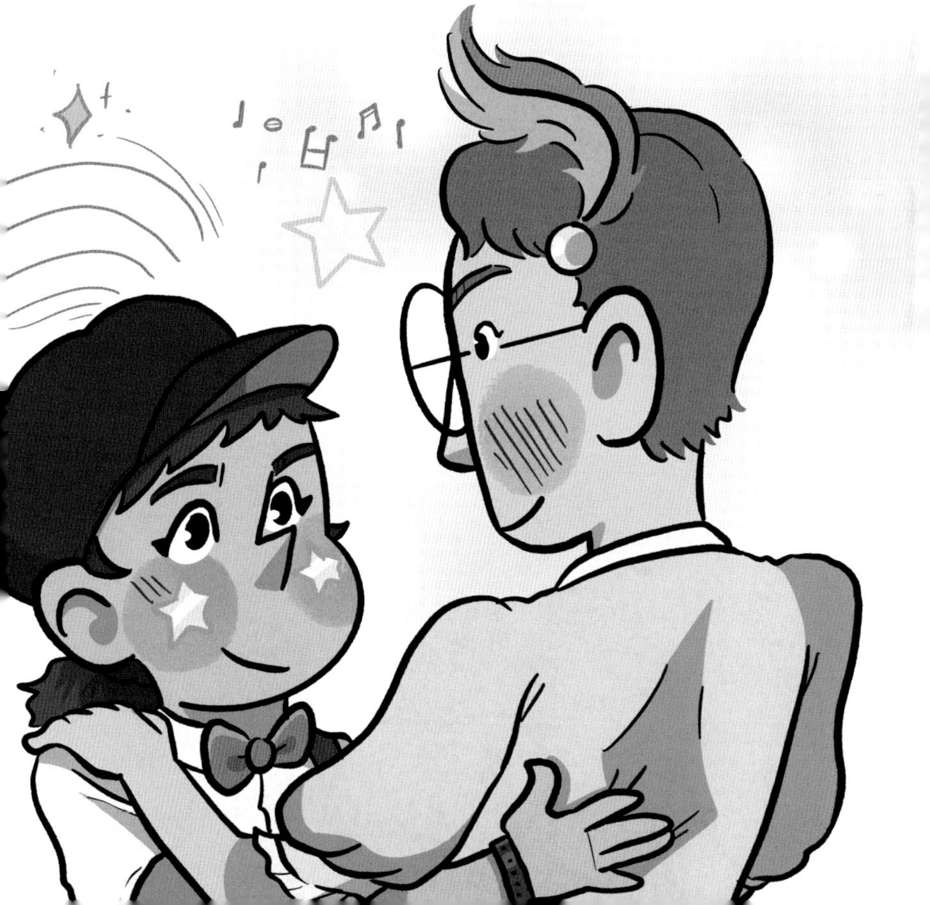

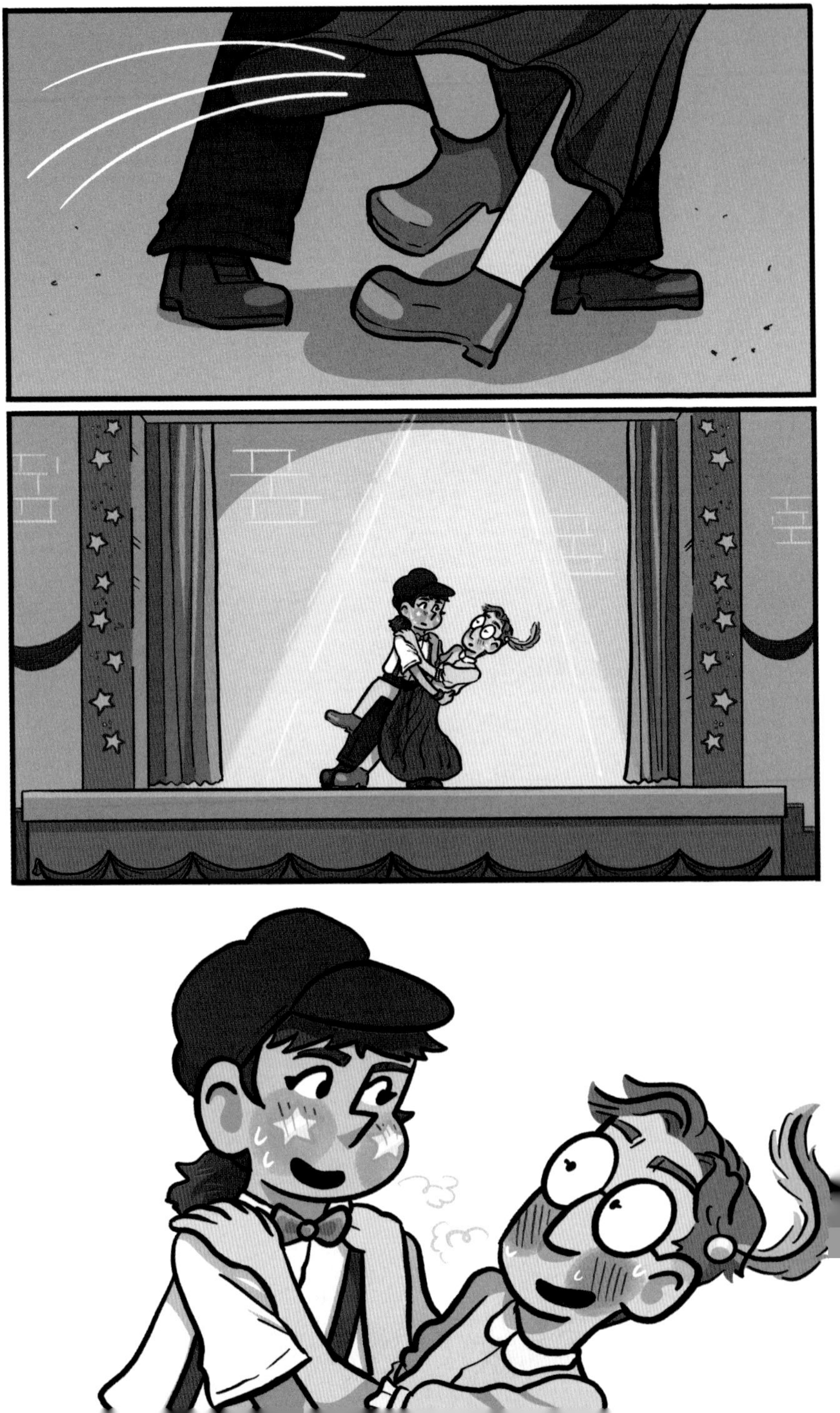

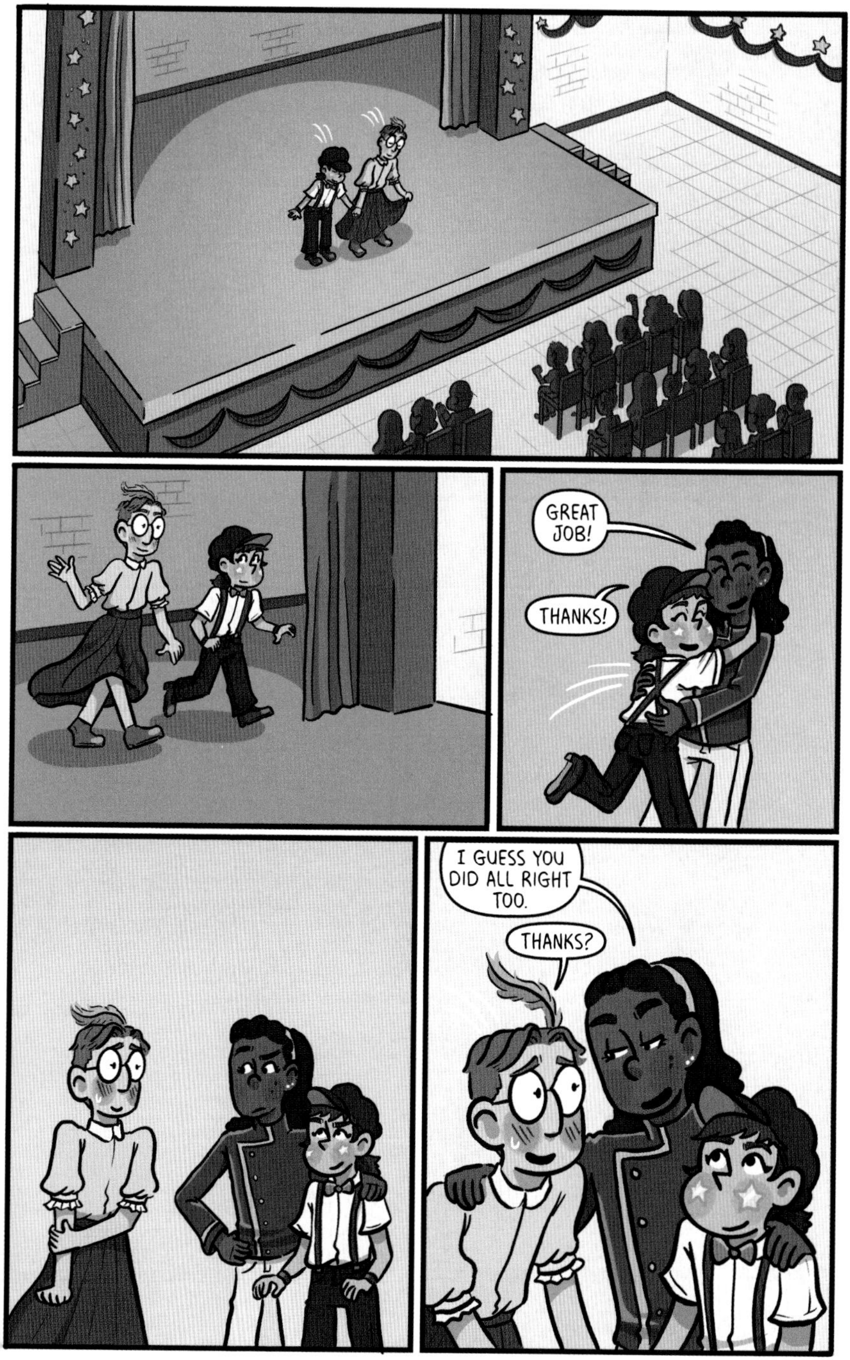
GREAT JOB!
THANKS!
I GUESS YOU DID ALL RIGHT TOO.
THANKS?

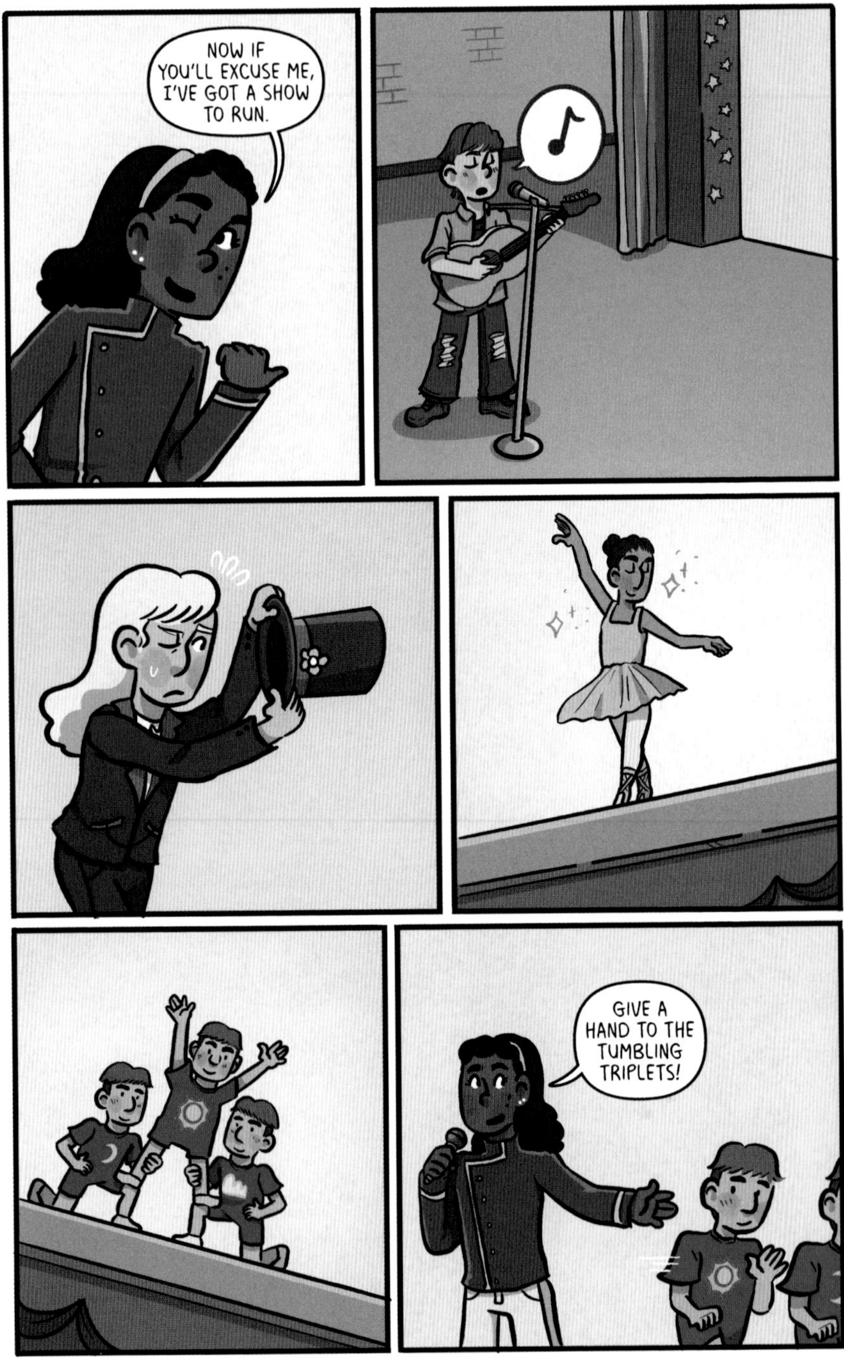
NOW IF YOU'LL EXCUSE ME, I'VE GOT A SHOW TO RUN.
GIVE A HAND TO THE TUMBLING TRIPLETS!

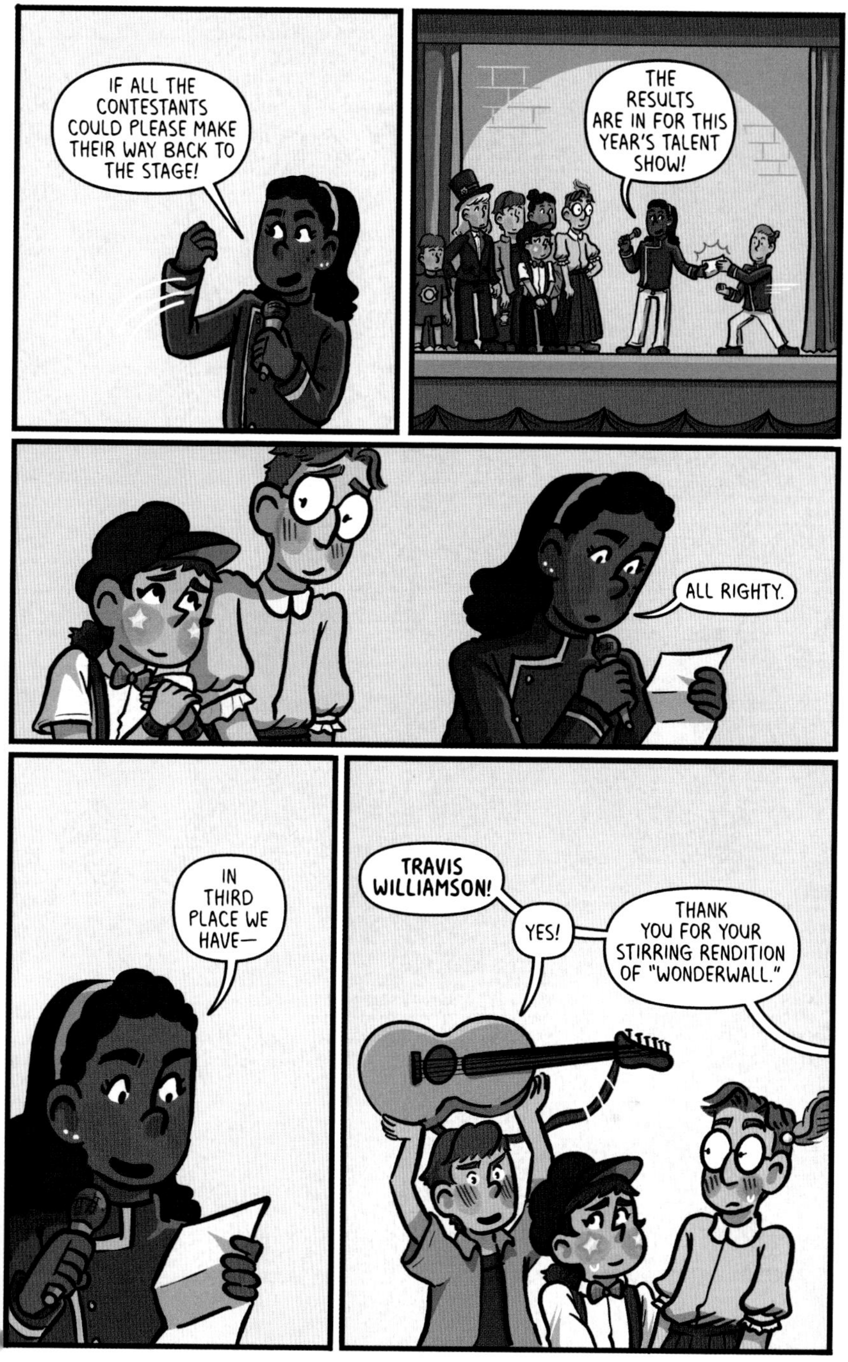
IF ALL THE CONTESTANTS COULD PLEASE MAKE THEIR WAY BACK TO THE STAGE!
THE RESULTS ARE IN FOR THIS YEAR'S TALENT SHOW!
ALL RIGHTY.
IN THIRD PLACE WE HAVE—
TRAVIS WILLIAMSON!
YES!
THANK YOU FOR YOUR STIRRING RENDITION OF "WONDERWALL."

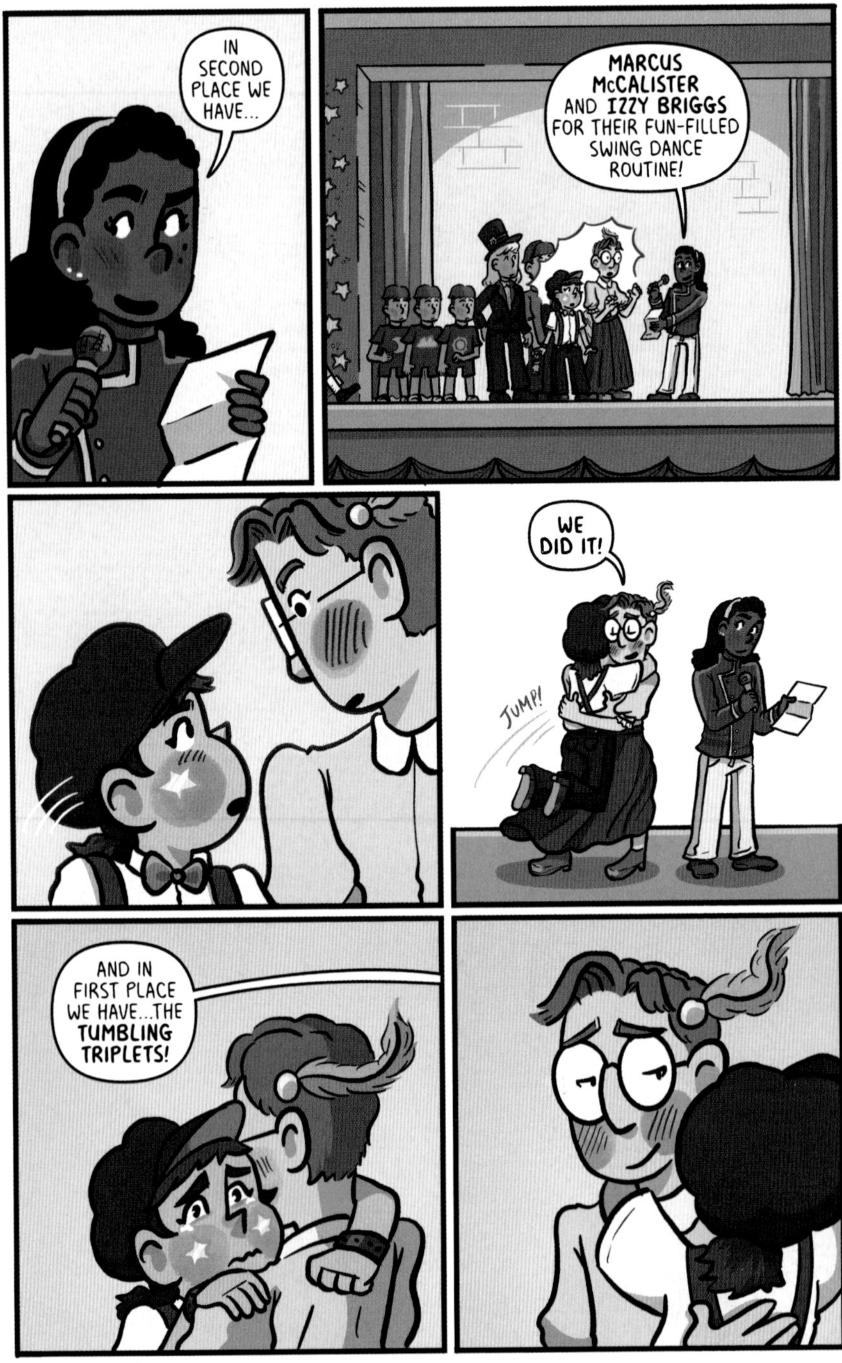
IN SECOND PLACE WE HAVE...
MARCUS McCALISTER AND IZZY BRIGGS FOR THEIR FUN-FILLED SWING DANCE ROUTINE!
WE DID IT!
JUMP!
AND IN FIRST PLACE WE HAVE...THE TUMBLING TRIPLETS!

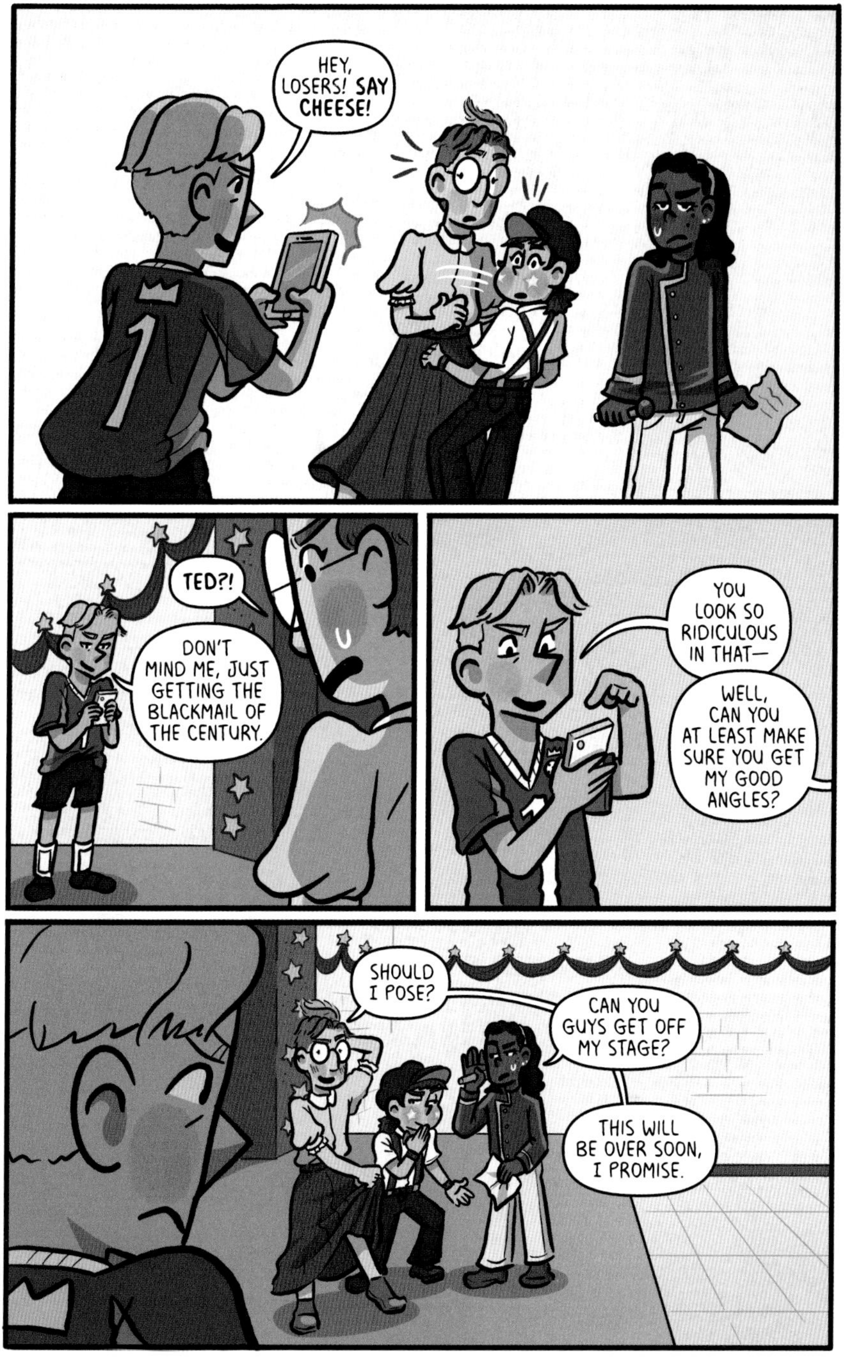
HEY, LOSERS! **SAY CHEESE!**
TED?!
DON'T MIND ME, JUST GETTING THE BLACKMAIL OF THE CENTURY.
YOU LOOK SO RIDICULOUS IN THAT—
WELL, CAN YOU AT LEAST MAKE SURE YOU GET MY GOOD ANGLES?
SHOULD I POSE?
CAN YOU GUYS GET OFF MY STAGE?
THIS WILL BE OVER SOON, I PROMISE.

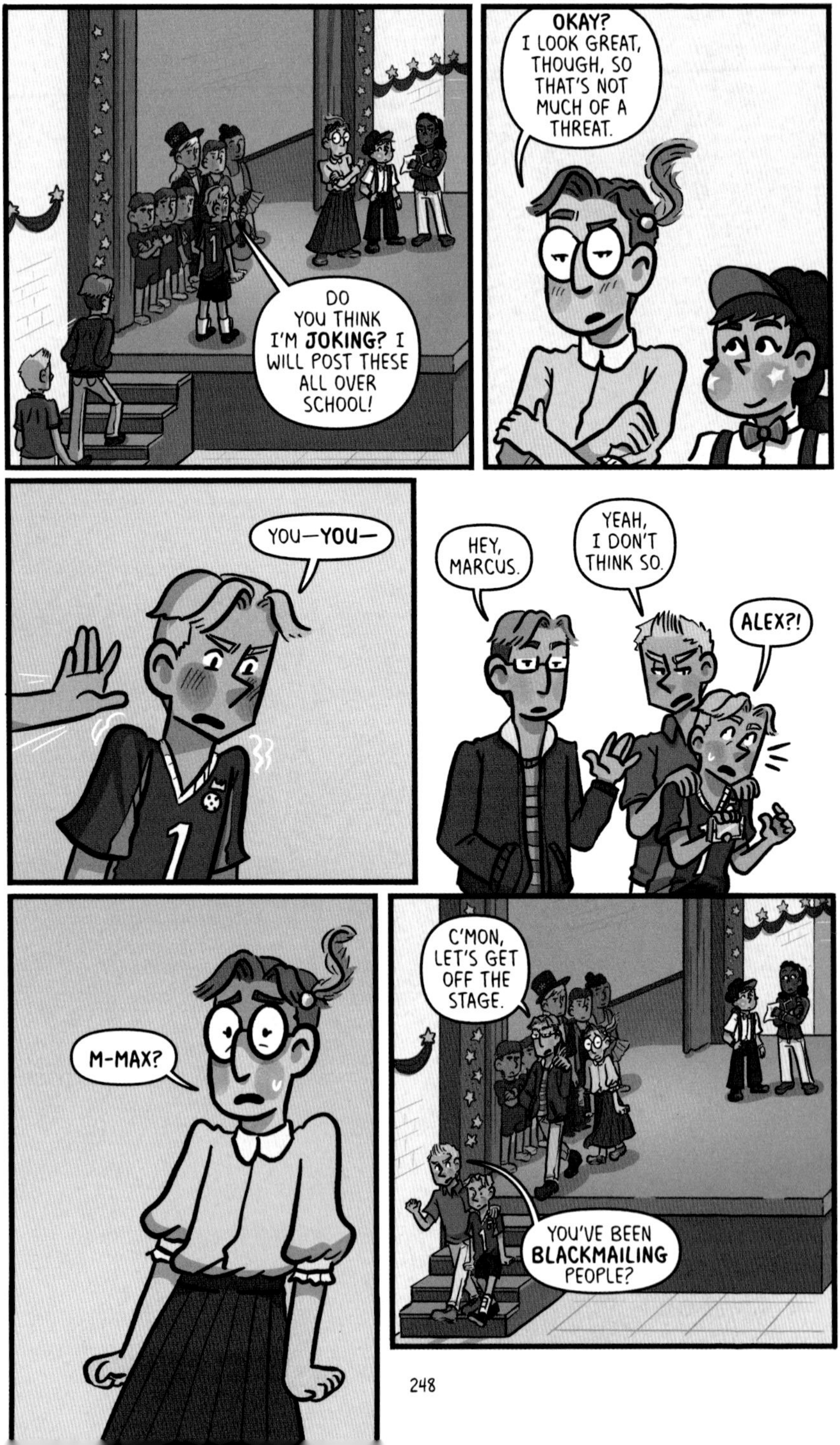
DO YOU THINK I'M **JOKING?** I WILL POST THESE ALL OVER SCHOOL!
OKAY? I LOOK GREAT, THOUGH, SO THAT'S NOT MUCH OF A THREAT.
YOU—**YOU**—
HEY, MARCUS.
YEAH, I DON'T THINK SO.
ALEX?!
M-MAX?
C'MON, LET'S GET OFF THE STAGE.
YOU'VE BEEN **BLACKMAILING** PEOPLE?

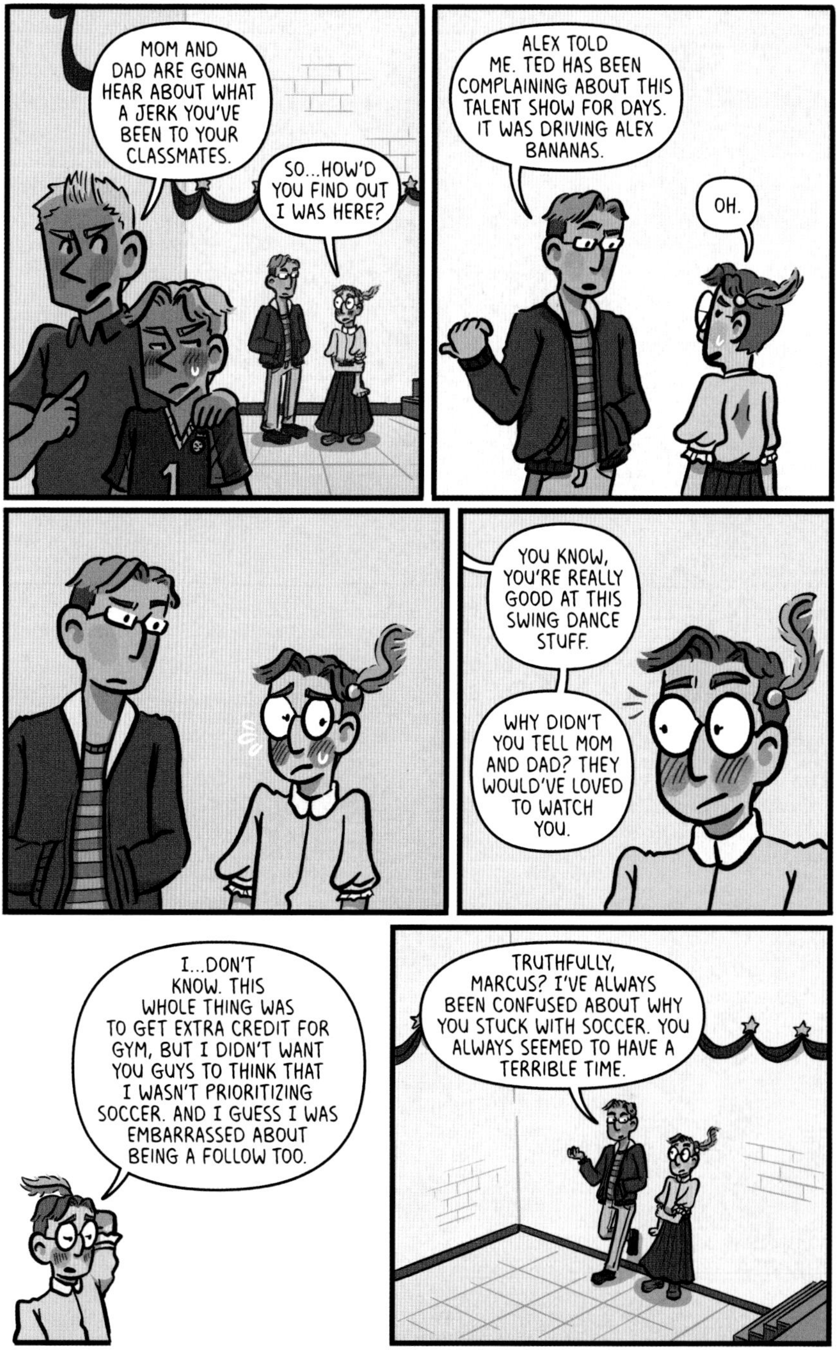
MOM AND DAD ARE GONNA HEAR ABOUT WHAT A JERK YOU'VE BEEN TO YOUR CLASSMATES.
SO...HOW'D YOU FIND OUT I WAS HERE?
ALEX TOLD ME. TED HAS BEEN COMPLAINING ABOUT THIS TALENT SHOW FOR DAYS. IT WAS DRIVING ALEX BANANAS.
OH.
YOU KNOW, YOU'RE REALLY GOOD AT THIS SWING DANCE STUFF.
WHY DIDN'T YOU TELL MOM AND DAD? THEY WOULD'VE LOVED TO WATCH YOU.
I...DON'T KNOW. THIS WHOLE THING WAS TO GET EXTRA CREDIT FOR GYM, BUT I DIDN'T WANT YOU GUYS TO THINK THAT I WASN'T PRIORITIZING SOCCER. AND I GUESS I WAS EMBARRASSED ABOUT BEING A FOLLOW TOO.
TRUTHFULLY, MARCUS? I'VE ALWAYS BEEN CONFUSED ABOUT WHY YOU STUCK WITH SOCCER. YOU ALWAYS SEEMED TO HAVE A TERRIBLE TIME.

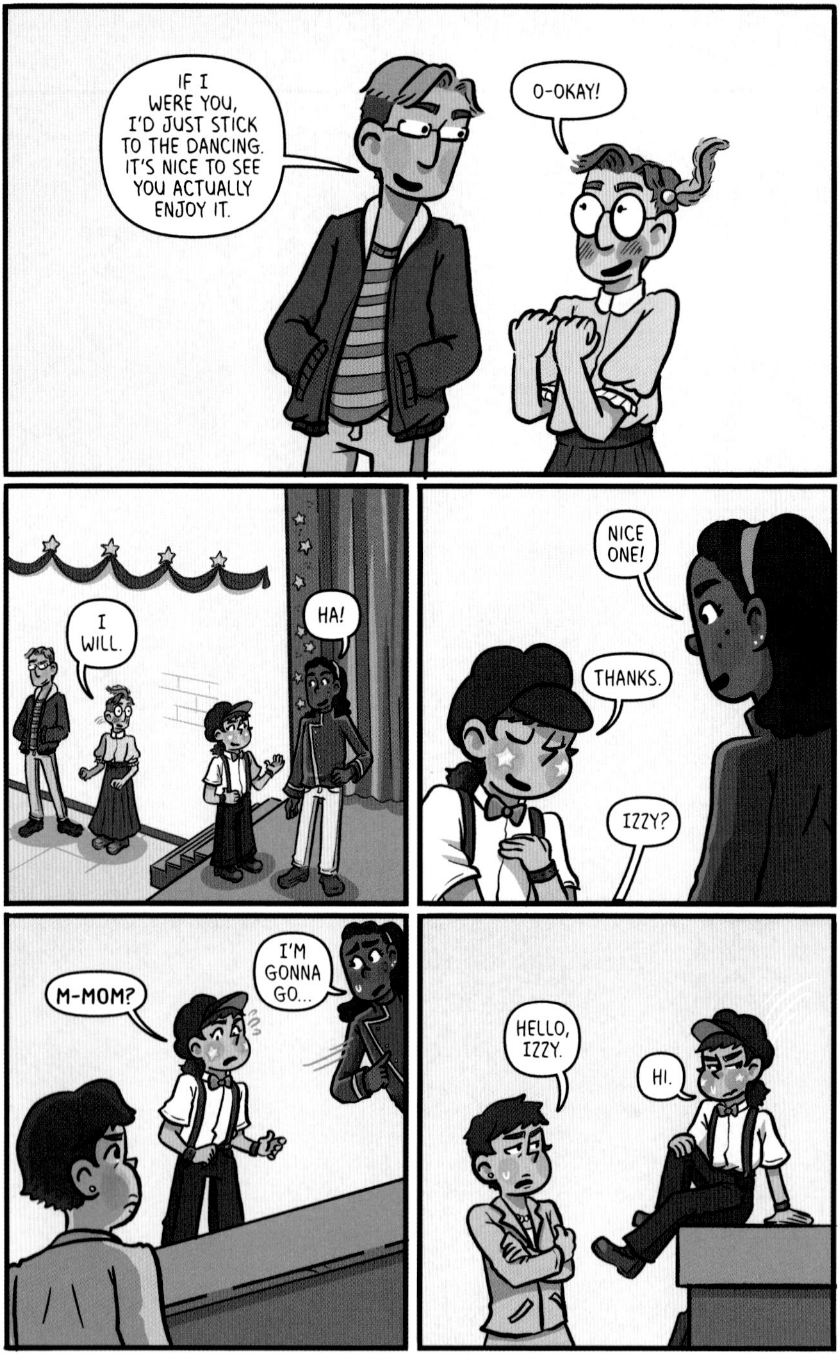
IF I WERE YOU, I'D JUST STICK TO THE DANCING. IT'S NICE TO SEE YOU ACTUALLY ENJOY IT.
O-OKAY!
I WILL.
HA!
NICE ONE!
THANKS.
IZZY?
M-MOM?
I'M GONNA GO...
HELLO, IZZY.
HI.

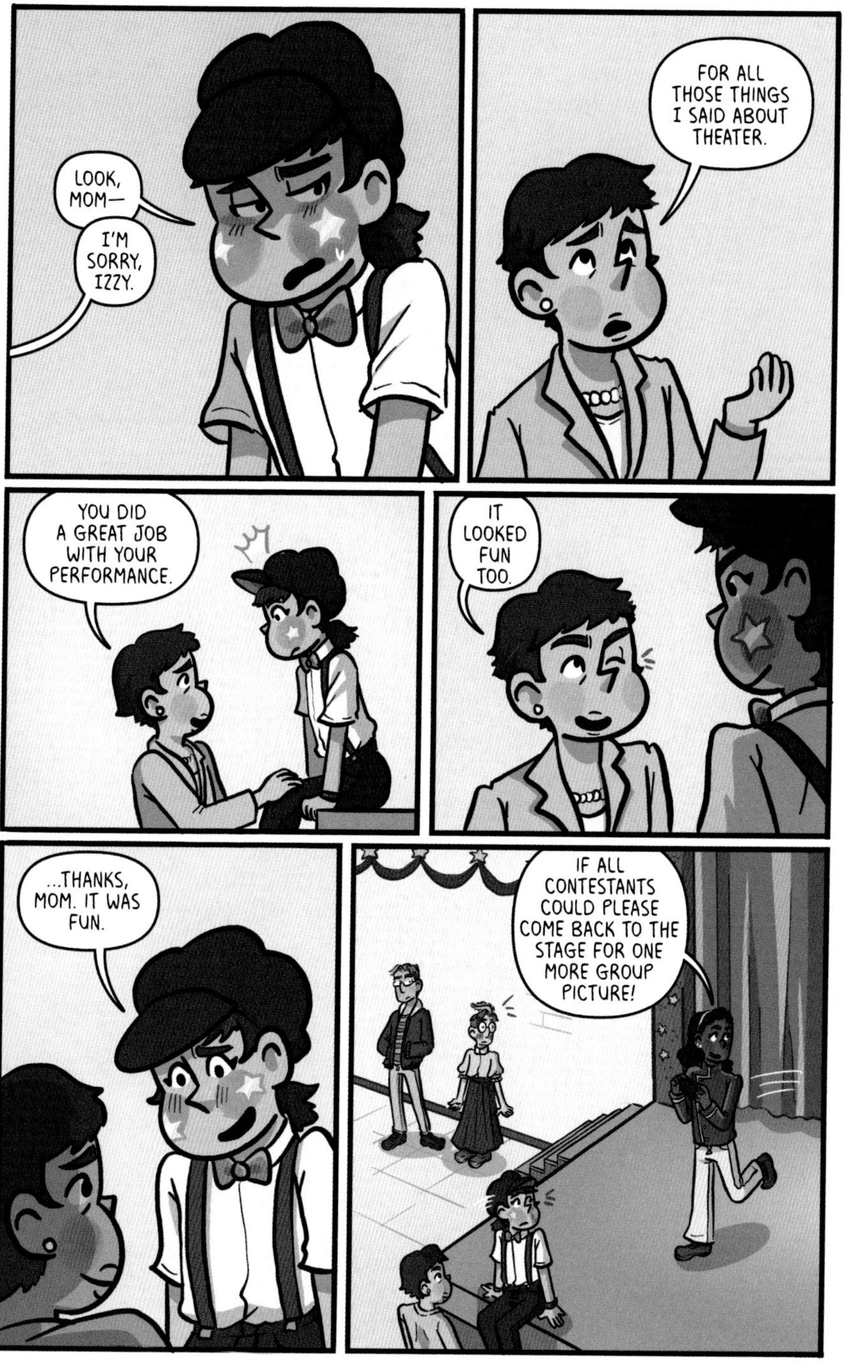
LOOK, MOM—
I'M SORRY, IZZY.
FOR ALL THOSE THINGS I SAID ABOUT THEATER.
YOU DID A GREAT JOB WITH YOUR PERFORMANCE.
IT LOOKED FUN TOO.
...THANKS, MOM. IT WAS FUN.
IF ALL CONTESTANTS COULD PLEASE COME BACK TO THE STAGE FOR ONE MORE GROUP PICTURE!

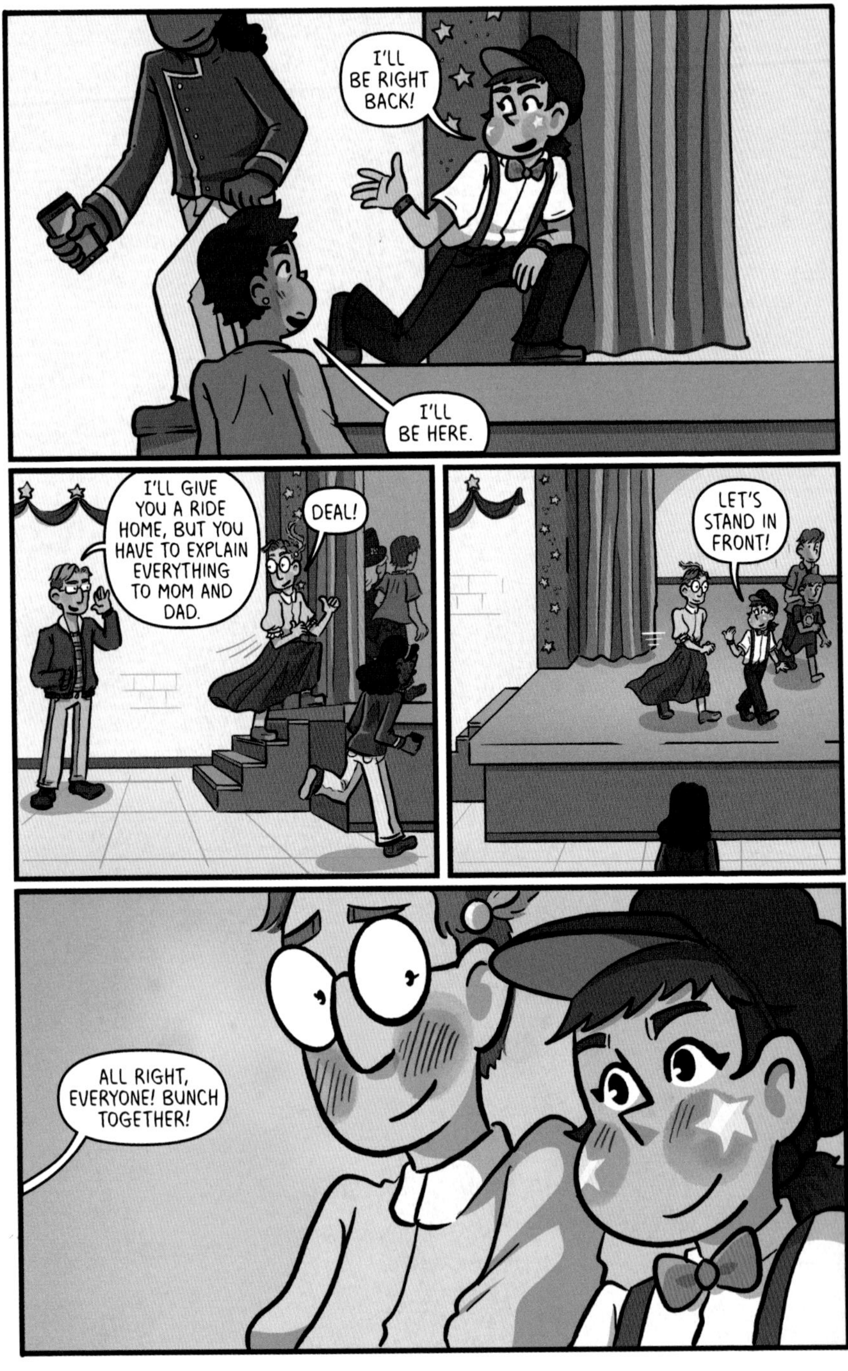
I'LL BE RIGHT BACK!
I'LL BE HERE.
I'LL GIVE YOU A RIDE HOME, BUT YOU HAVE TO EXPLAIN EVERYTHING TO MOM AND DAD.
DEAL!
LET'S STAND IN FRONT!
ALL RIGHT, EVERYONE! BUNCH TOGETHER!

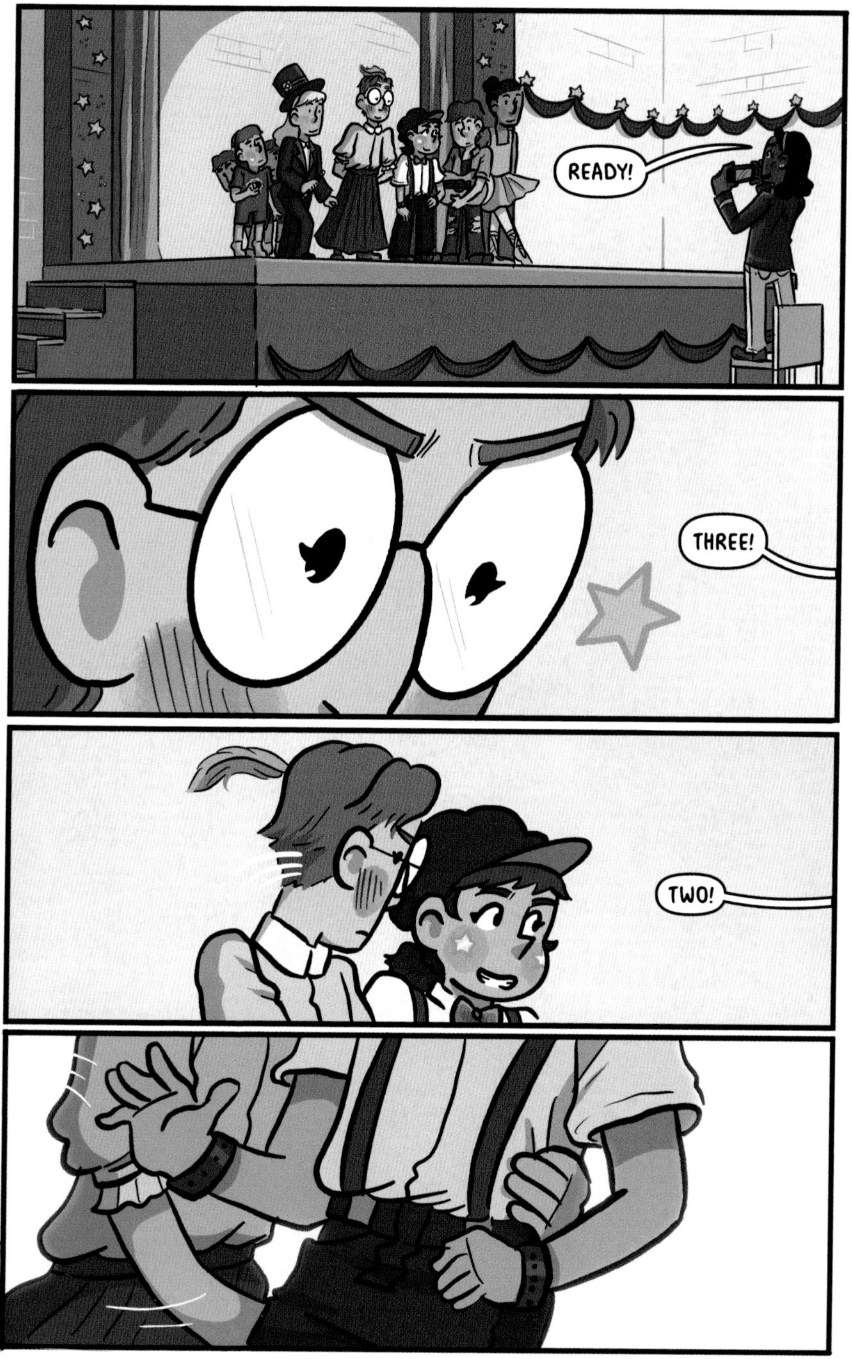
READY!
THREE!
TWO!

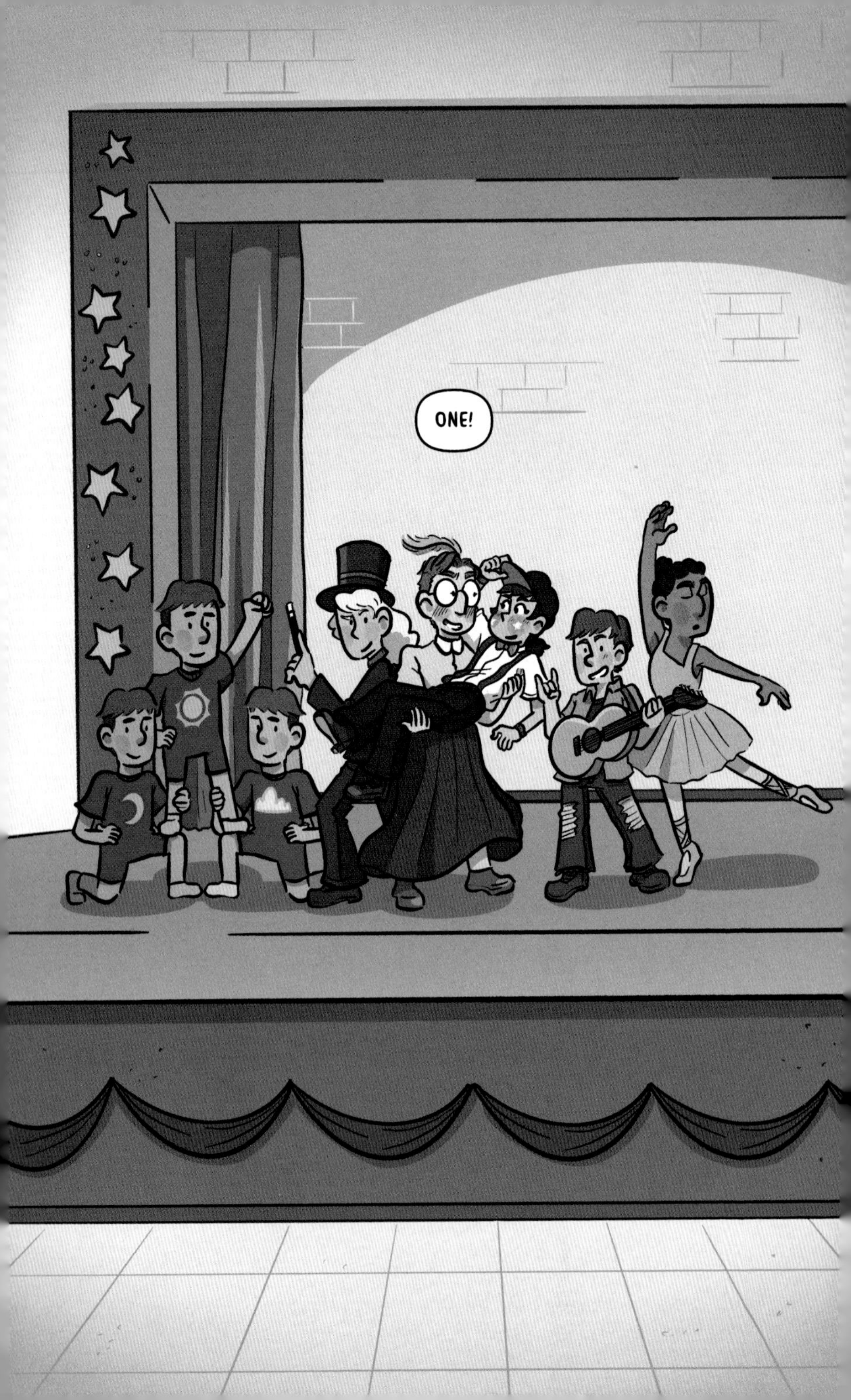
ONE!